The Dry Bones Society

The Complete Series

DAN SOFER

Complete series omnibus edition: June 2020

ISBN-13: 978-0-9863932-9-7 (Paperback)
ISBN-13: 978-1-950139-03-3 (Hardcover)

FIC026000 FICTION/Religious
FIC042080 FICTION/Christian/Fantasy
FIC060000 FICTION/Humorous/Black Humor
FIC009100 FICTION/Fantasy/Action & Adventure

dansofer.com

Cover images by Damonza

Readers' Favorite 2017
Silver Medal Winner

An Unexpected Afterlife

The Dry Bones Society
Book I

DAN SOFER

CHAPTER 1

Moshe Karlin emerged from a deep and dreamless sleep with a premonition of impending doom. The world seemed out of place. The dawn chorus of summer birds filled his ears, but louder than usual, as though an entire flock had perched on the windowsill above his bed. The mattress pressed against his back, hard and coarse. A chill breeze tickled the hair on his bare chest.

Bare chest?

His eyelids snapped open. The endless blue velvet canopy of heaven stretched overhead, and as he gazed, a star winked out. His heart thumped in his rib cage. He was not in his bed. Or his bedroom. Or even his house.

He craned his neck forward. He lay on his back in a stony field, as naked as the day he was born.

His head slumped to the ground.

Moshe Karlin, you are in deep trouble.

Galit would kill him when he got home. That is, if she ever found out.

As his bold plan for sneaking home unnoticed grew flesh and sinew, the crackle of a loudspeaker jarred his thoughts, and a nasal voice boomed: *Allahu akba-a-ar! Allahu akba-a-ar!*

Moshe heard the East Jerusalem *muezzin* most mornings but always from a safe distance. This morning, however, the

7

blaring call to morning prayers seemed to issue from only a stone's throw away.

Correction. You are in very *deep trouble.*

He rolled onto his side and scrambled to his feet, covering his privates with his hands. The field was perched on a hilltop. In the valley below, streetlights still burned and the Dome of the Rock glowed golden behind the ancient walls of Jerusalem's Old City.

A low rock wall snaked along the edge of the field and around the gnarled trunk of a large olive tree. Above the wall, rows of rounded headstones poked at the sky like accusatory fingers.

Moshe knew the cemetery well. His parents' twin graves lay a short walk away. He hadn't visited them lately but he was in no state to do so now.

How in God's name had he spent the night—naked—in the Mount of Olives Cemetery?

Hayya alas sala-a-ah! Hayya alal fala-a-ah!

A ball of searing pain burst behind his right eyeball. He fell to one knee and released a hand from modesty duty to massage his temple.

Of course! His birthday party last night. He had sipped a glass of Recanati Merlot as he discussed his business plans with Galit's grandmother. He had looked about for Galit and then... a black interplanetary void. He had never drunk to blackout before, not even in his single days, but that would explain the headache. It might also help explain his current predicament.

The *muezzin* call ended.

He glanced at his wrist and swore under his breath. His watch—his dear father's Rolex, the heirloom from his grandfather—was gone. Moshe took it off only to shower. One person alone would dare take his watch. One person alone would abandon him overnight and buck naked in an East Jerusalem graveyard. Moshe would deal with him later. For now, he had to get home.

He hobbled in the twilight toward the access road—rough

and lacking shoulders—that bordered the field. Sharp stones bit into the tender soles of his feet. The headache spread to his left eye and throbbed with his every step.

With luck, he'd avoid early-bird terrorists. With more luck, he'd slip under the covers before Galit got up to dress Talya for kindergarten.

He quickened his pace. A truck whooshed along a hidden street far below. Thankfully, the access road had no streetlights. As the road fell, walls of stone rose on either side.

Through a breach in the wall, he spied a yard with a clothesline. He reached through the hole and, with some effort, snagged the edge of a bedsheet. After brushing dirt and leaves from his goosefleshed body, he fashioned the sheet into a crude toga. His new attire would still draw stares but the sheet was dry and covered the important bits. He lacked only a laurel wreath to complete his Roman emperor costume. Pity it wasn't Purim today. He would have blended right in.

The road meandered around stone houses with dark windows and emptied into a two-lane thoroughfare. Sidewalks. Streetlamps. Civilization. He flagged down a white taxi and climbed into the back seat.

"Shimshon five," he said.

The driver, a young Israeli in a leather jacket, started the meter, and the car pulled off.

Moshe inhaled the sweet scent of new leather. He had worked with taxis all his life but he had not hired one in years. The upholstery felt soft and smooth through the thin sheet.

Eyes watched him in the rearview mirror and they crinkled at the edges. "Wild party, huh?"

Details of the previous night surfaced in Moshe's bruised brain. "My fortieth birthday," he said. "My wife threw a party at the Botanical Gardens."

He regretted the words the moment they left his mouth. Karlin & Son ran the largest taxi dispatch service in Jerusalem and he did not need this story circulating among the city's cabbies.

The driver, however, did not seem to recognize his voice. Newbie. Of course—who else drew the graveyard shift?

The eyes in the mirror narrowed. "Botanical Gardens?" he said. "That's the other side of town."

Newbie or not, he knew the lay of the land. The Italian restaurant at the Botanical Gardens overlooked a large pond in western Jerusalem. Moshe had sipped his merlot and told Savta Sarah of his plans to extend Karlin & Son from Jerusalem to Tel Aviv. They already controlled the shuttle routes to Ben Gurion Airport. He had looked around for Galit. He had wanted to raise a toast in her honor. They had hardly spoken with each other all day and, with his recent work schedule, they had spent little quality time together. He had wanted to tell her how much she meant to him. Where was she? And then… another gaping abyss in his memory.

"Avi," he said. He spat the word like a curse.

"Who?"

"My friend." The word "friend" dripped with sarcasm. "He's always trying to drag me to nightclubs like the old days. Last night, I guess he succeeded."

Moshe massaged his temples with his fingers. He needed an Acamol.

The driver laughed. "With a friend like that, who needs enemies, right?"

After a short, annoyed pause, Moshe laughed as well. In the safety and comfort of the backseat, on his way to his warm home, the stunt seemed harmless enough. Hilarious. A juicy story for the grandkids. *Did I tell you the one about my fortieth birthday? Now that was a bash to remember. Or not!*

The road rounded the high crenellated walls of the Old City, hugged Mount Zion, and dipped through the Hinnom Valley.

Avi, you crazy bastard. They say you can choose your friends—but that wasn't always true. Moshe could never shake off Avi, practical jokes and all. Too much history. And Moshe had given him a job at Karlin & Son. They ran the business together.

You overaged rascal. The time had come for the eternal bachelor to settle down. A wife. Kids. He'd have a word with him later in the office, if he even showed up after last night. He was probably hung over too. Ha!

The trickle of cars thickened on the triple lanes of Hebron Road. God turned His great dimmer switch in the sky and the heavens brightened.

Forty years old. How time flew by! He didn't feel forty. The Israel Defense Forces had released him from reserve duty, all the same. He had many reasons to be grateful: a loving—if stormy—wife; a delightful little girl; a booming business and a beautiful house; and a best friend who moved mountains to create an unforgettable fortieth birthday surprise. Perhaps *unforgettable* was not quite the right word.

The cab turned into the suburbia of the German Colony, past the sleepy storefronts, apartment buildings, and houses in white Jerusalem stone.

He'd sneak another hour of sleep before heading to the office. He'd drive to Tel Aviv and nudge his list of cab operators and independent drivers to sign on the dotted line. *First, we take Jerusalem,* he thought, channeling Leonard Cohen's baritone, *then, we take Tel Aviv.*

An invisible hand moved him, pushing him harder and farther. After Tel Aviv, he'd spread north to Haifa, and south to Beersheba. Within a few years, he would conquer the entire country, one cab at a time.

A dark cloud settled over his mind. What then? Was that to be his sole "dent in the universe"?

He yawned and shook the dreary thought from his head. The hangover—or an on-schedule midlife crisis—had hijacked his brain. A national dispatch network would be a fine achievement. His father, of blessed memory, would be proud.

The car pulled up beside Moshe's duplex on Shimshon Street. The driver stopped the meter and printed a receipt.

Moshe reached for the wallet in his back pocket and got a handful of buttocks. No wallet. No underwear either. He decided to keep that information to himself.

"Wait here a moment," he said. "I left my wallet at home."

He skipped up three steps of cold stone and slid the spare key from beneath a potted plant. A row of purple cyclamens caught his eye. When did Galit get those? Takeaways from the Botanical Gardens?

He unlocked the door, tiptoed inside, and padded down the hall. In a drawer of the telephone table, he found a fifty-shekel note among the memo pads, pens, and car keys. He handed the driver the money through the open car window, told him to keep the change, and hurried back indoors. All he needed was an insomniac neighbor to spot him wearing a borrowed sheet. People loved to talk.

He closed the door behind him with a soft click. Silence in the dim entrance hall. *So far, so good.* He climbed the staircase tile by chilly marble tile, then eased down the handle of their bedroom door and slipped inside.

Shutters down and door closed, the room sank in Egyptian darkness. He inched over the cool parquet toward the sound of soft breathing until his leg touched the hard edge of the bed frame.

He let the sheet slip from his shoulders to the floor and kicked the pile under the bed. Never mind pajamas—the creak of a closet door might wake her. He lowered his rump to the soft bedsheets, transferring his weight ounce by ounce. Not a single spring squeaked. The mattress upgrade had proved to be a good investment.

He leaned back, slipped his legs beneath the covers, and rested his head on the pillow.

Mission accomplished!

He exhaled a lungful of pent, anxious breath and shifted further onto the bed. The surface of the mattress sank. Galit must have rolled onto his half of the bed. He turned toward her. The warmth of her body radiated through her pajama shirt. He pressed his shins against her hairy legs.

Hairy legs?

A reflex fired in his brain stem. With a primordial cry—

wooo-aa-ahh!—a mixture of terror and revulsion, as though he had snuggled up to a large cockroach, he sprang out of bed.

CHAPTER 2

Moshe stood barefoot in the darkness of his bedroom. His entire body quaked.

"What's that noise?" said Galit's voice, thick with sleep.

Before Moshe could answer, a man said, "Who's there?"

There was a loud click. Yellow light flooded the room and seared a horrifying image in his brain. Two figures lay in his bed: Galit and another man.

Moshe froze, his eyelids shuttering in the bright light. The two sleepers gawked at him. Their eyes moved from his face to his nether regions. Moshe didn't care about that—he had other things on his mind right now.

The man brushed a fringe of oily hair from his face.

"Avi?" Moshe said. Shock gave way to disbelief. Then rage shoved them both aside. He stood over them, a lone accusatory presence. "What the hell are you doing here?" he roared, as though he hadn't figured it out for himself.

His ex–best friend blinked at him as though Moshe had just stepped off the ramp of a steaming spaceship. He didn't grab his clothes and flee out the window. He didn't beg for his life or claim that this was "not what you think." Instead, he slunk out of bed and reached a quivering hand toward him. When his fingers touched Moshe's forearm, he recoiled. "Dear Lord!" he gasped.

Moshe turned to his cheating wife. "Galit, how could you?"

She sat in bed, silky black hair falling over her shoulder, her eyes large and white, her mouth open. She didn't cry. She didn't beg for forgiveness.

That deep, dark pit opened beneath Moshe's feet again. Something was wrong with the scene. Something *besides* the fact that he had caught his best friend in bed with his wife—in *his* bed and on the day after his birthday. The entire scene felt wrong, like an Escher sketch where the floor had become the ceiling and he could not tell which way was up. Why did he, the only non-adulterer in the room, feel out of place?

He did not ponder the situation for long. Galit screamed—a loud, high-pitched banshee shriek—and the two men cringed. When her lungs emptied, she sucked in air and screamed again.

Avi rose to his full height, a full head shorter than Moshe. "Get out!" he shouted.

"What? Me?" The bastard sure had *chutzpah*! "*You* get out!"

Galit bounced on the bed, screaming her head off. She wore the Minnie Mouse pajama shirt he had bought her for her birthday. She ran to the far corner of the room and clawed at the walls, like a hamster trying to escape her cage.

Avi swiped at him with a black shoe. "Get out! Get out!"

Moshe almost fell over backwards. Avi charged forward, opened the door, and herded him out of the room and down the corridor.

Moshe glanced around for a suitable weapon and found none. The heel of the shoe pummeled his head and arms. "Hey! Stop that!"

Avi halted the barrage to put a finger on his lips. "Keep it down, or you'll wake Talya."

"What?" Waking Talya was the least of their problems.

Avi came at him again with the shoe, and Moshe retreated down the stairs. "Out! Out!"

"This is my house! *You* get out!"

Avi grunted as he thrust and swiped. "Get out now or I call the cops."

"Call the cops!" Moshe staggered into the entrance hall. "This is *my* house, and that is *my* wife." Did he even recognize him? "It's me, Avi. Moshe Karlin."

Avi paused to catch his breath. He shook his head. He stared at Moshe with wild eyes. "That's impossible."

"Oh yeah? Why?"

"Because Moshe Karlin is dead."

"Excuse me?" He might as well have slapped Moshe. That had to be the lamest excuse in the history of cheating friends.

"Dead and buried. Two years ago."

"*What?*"

Avi swung the shoe again.

It was the shock of those words. Or the conviction with which Avi delivered them. Either way, Moshe found himself outside his front door. He slipped on the steps and sprawled on the cold hard stone.

"Wait!" he cried. But the door slammed shut and bolts shifted into place.

CHAPTER 3

For the second time that morning, Moshe stood alone and naked in a public space. He banged on the front door with his fist. "Hey!" He banged some more. He pressed the buzzer. He pressed it again. A car engine started nearby. Soon, the neighbors would pass by on their way to work.

Overhead, a window slid open. Avi poked his head out, a portable phone in his hand. "Go away," he hissed, "or I'll call the cops."

"Some clothes would be nice."

The face disappeared. Then a pair of jeans and a T-shirt rained from the sky, and the window slid shut. Moshe pulled them on. Avi's jeans barely closed over his waist and the hem of the legs reached his shins. No underwear. No shoes or socks. He shook his fist at the window.

Seeing Galit and Avi in his bed had been traumatic enough, but to be thrown out of his own home! He charged at the door and bruised his shoulder. He kicked it and stubbed a toe. He pressed the buzzer again.

He paced the welcome mat. *Call the cops. See if I care. Dead, my foot!* Dead people didn't come knocking on a person's front door. *Moshe Karlin is alive and well, thank you very much.*

He sat down on the top step.

And then he understood.

The bedroom scene, like the cemetery, was part of one big, extended joke. A very bad joke. Not funny at all. Avi was always pressing people's buttons, and a fortieth birthday had provided him with an irresistible opportunity to push all of Moshe's buttons and then some.

How had he convinced Galit to play along? Phenomenal job, he had to admit. He had fallen for it. Freaked out. The cemetery routine was probably her idea. Maybe now he'd agree to see that darned cardiologist.

Moshe drew a long, deep breath and stretched his neck. Soon they'd open the door and bring out a cake to the tune of "Happy Birthday." No rush. He'd wait outside until they decided he had suffered enough.

A bearded man in a black suit jacket and fedora hastened along the street—Rabbi Yosef Lev, his phylactery bag under his arm, on his way to morning prayers.

Perfect.

Moshe had last seen the rabbi at the synagogue down the street on the Day of Atonement. This morning, he was muttering a prayer as he walked. He glanced at Moshe, nodded a greeting, and continued on his way. Moshe had managed to dress with only seconds to spare.

Suddenly, the rabbi stopped in his tracks. He turned slowly and peered at Moshe. His mouth dropped open. His face turned deathly white.

"Morning, Rabbi." Moshe chuckled and pointed at the door. "Locked out. Silly me. Nothing to worry about. All under control."

"Moshe?" the rabbi muttered. He seemed to be thinking aloud, not speaking to an actual person. He grabbed his thigh with his free hand and gave it a hard squeeze. Then he slapped his face and rubbed his eyes. "Moshe *Karlin?* God save us."

"Rabbi, are you OK?"

The rabbi cackled, a man teetering at the edge of sanity. "Sure," he said. "Besides for seeing ghosts. Otherwise, thank God, I'm fine." He gave another nervous laugh.

Moshe rolled his eyes. Not the rabbi as well. "OK," he said, loud enough for Galit and Avi to hear through the upper window. "The joke is over. It wasn't funny anyway. As you can see, Rabbi, I am not dead."

"You certainly are. I officiated at your funeral. I visited the house of mourning."

Moshe got up, walked over to the wide-eyed rabbi, grasped his bony shoulder, and shook his cold, limp hand. "See? When was the last time you shook hands with a ghost?"

The rabbi swallowed hard, and for a moment, Moshe thought he was going to collapse. Then an expression of wonder animated his face and understanding blossomed in his eyes. "Ribono Shel Olam!" Master of the World! "You're alive!"

Moshe's weird sensors fired again. A shiver slithered down his back like a snake over a fresh grave.

The rabbi's face fell from joy into sudden doubt. "Or am I hallucinating? Come with me. Please. I must show you to Rocheleh."

So that's the plan, is it? The party had moved to the rabbi's house. He had to hand it to Avi—Moshe would never have expected that. Galit and Avi must have ducked out the back door and beat him to the rabbi's house. Moshe looked up and down the street and sighed. "OK."

He followed the frantic rabbi, who turned back every few steps to make sure his guest had not evaporated into thin air. Moshe winced as his tender feet stepped on stray stones and cracks on the sidewalk.

A small single-level house of old stone sat at the end of the street near the grassy tracks of a defunct railway line. The rabbi knocked on the door, jiggled a key in the lock, and stepped inside.

Moshe had never visited the rabbi's home. Pictures of bearded rabbis hung on the walls of a small, tidy living room. There were no balloons. No birthday cake. No signs of people hiding behind the worn couches, or the bookcase—its shelves droopy with holy books—or beneath the dinner table of scratched, dark wood.

At a counter bordering the kitchen, a woman looked up from her newspaper and coffee. She wore a stern expression.

"What have you forgotten now?"

Moshe had never met the rabbi's wife. The kerchief on her head covered every strand of hair.

"Rocheleh, do you remember Moshe Karlin?"

The rabbanit sniffed at her husband's guest and his bare feet, unimpressed.

"Hi," Moshe said. He pointed in the general direction of his house. "I got locked out."

"Isn't he dead?"

Here we go again.

The rabbi smiled. "So he's not in my imagination! It's a miracle!"

Moshe felt his patience run out. "Rabbi, I think I would know if I had died."

The rabbanit put down her mug and ignored him. "If you're home, you can get the boys ready for school."

The demand seemed to jog the rabbi's memory. "I have to open the shul." He turned to Moshe. "I'll be right back. Please wait here. Make yourself at home. Help yourself to some coffee. Breakfast. Is there anything you need?"

Moshe clenched his fists. He wanted to shout "I am not dead!" but he held back for the sake of the rabbi and his wife. He didn't have time for this. He needed his car keys and his own clothes to get to work, but he could not get into his house. He resigned himself to a late start. He might as well accept the rabbi's offer. He said, "I could do with a shower."

Rabbi Yosef led him down a corridor, through a main bedroom with two single beds and peeling wallpaper, and into a pokey bathroom. He handed him an old but clean towel and a new bar of soap, and hurried off.

The bathroom sink and counter were a mess of creams and makeup, hairbrushes and dental equipment. The wall tiles had chipped and the scent of damp rot hung in the air. But a shower was a shower.

Moshe locked the door, stripped, and stepped into the shower closet. Pipes groaned in the walls and then a jet of hot water burst from the showerhead. He massaged his scalp, shoulders, and back. *That's better.* He worked up a lather with the soap and wiped the patina of dirt from his feet and legs.

How long would the prank go on? Rest assured, Moshe would return the favor in double measure. Avi's birthday fell in December. Plenty of time to prepare. An alien landing, a terrorist kidnapping. Leave him outside and naked overnight. In winter. That would cure him of practical jokes.

Moshe soaped his arms and chest, and his hands worked their way down his body.

When his fingers slid over his belly, he screamed.

CHAPTER 4

The Prophet sat at a small, round table outside Café Aroma. He typed away on his laptop and ignored the stares of the waitress.

He enjoyed his daily coffee on Emek Refaim. The outing allowed him to get some work done and mingle among the common people without attracting too much attention. He savored the colors and whispers of their clothing, the scent of food and perfume, the snatches of conversation in a hodge-podge of languages and accents, as tourists and locals drank their coffee and bustled along the strip of trendy stores and restaurants. He had to keep up with the changing times, and in the last few centuries, the times had changed at a break-neck pace.

Women were one of few constants, their unwanted atten-tions an occupational hazard. The present hazard—a waitress with a blond ponytail and intelligent green eyes—leaned against the wall at the edge of his peripheral vision and watched him like a hawk as he emptied the small silver pot of hot milk into his cup. Waitresses left their telephone numbers on his receipts and napkins. The bolder ones sat down at his table and struck up conversation. When that happened, he moved on.

What drew them to him? The shock of untamed black

hair? The persecuted expression? Or his refusal to make eye contact? Humanity desired what it could not have. Experience had taught him that only too well.

This waitress rocked on the balls of her feet. Was she a scribbler or a sitter? She launched from her perch and tended to an elderly couple that had settled at another table.

He lifted the empty silver pot. Waving the waitress over for a refill would only invite conversation, so he took the easy way out. He tilted the pot and flexed the muscle in the center of his brain. Hot milk poured into the cup. He tilted the pot a second time and espresso flowed. He sipped his coffee. *Perfect.*

The scent of fruity perfume reached him before she did.

"How on earth did you do that?" asked the waitress, sitting down across from him. A broad, incredulous smile split her face and revealed perfect white teeth. Her large green eyes threatened to swallow him whole.

Pity. He had liked the coffee and the view. Jerusalem had only so many coffee shops at a convenient distance from his apartment.

"Do what?"

"That trick with the milk pot."

Busted. He kept a straight face. "What trick?"

She rolled her eyes. "I've been watching you. Sometimes milk comes out, sometimes coffee. Always steaming hot."

Time for a change of subject. He said, "Like those bottles of black and white liqueur?"

Her eyes narrowed and confusion wrinkled her pretty brow. "Sheridan's?" She glanced over her shoulder. "Am I on candid camera?" She seemed delighted at the prospect.

"Yes." He closed the laptop. "You're on candid camera."

He shoved the laptop into his shoulder bag and applied his charming smile. "Do you like magic tricks? Why don't you leave me your number, and we can talk at leisure?" He winked and dropped a fifty-shekel note on the table.

A flush washed over her face. "I'll get your bill." She got up and rushed indoors to the cash register.

He slung his bag on his shoulder and walked off. Let her believe in magic tricks. In her memory, he'd be the cute big tipper who got away. Humanity believed what it wanted to believe. Never the truth.

As he crossed the road, he felt a familiar tingle in his core. A breeze ruffled his hair and the world froze. Café patrons paused mid-bite. Shoppers and dog-walkers struck stiff poses like wax models. An Egged bus halted in mute mid-motion. The wind swirled and rose, became a turbulent storm cloud that wrapped around him, and then fell silent. And in the silence, the Thin Voice spoke. Without words. Without language. With absolute clarity.

In an instant, the Prophet knew what he must do. The where, the how, the why. He would obey. He always obeyed. Against his better judgment.

Then the world thawed. Mouths chewed, legs walked, and vehicles zoomed, none the wiser.

He reached the curb and sped off on foot. The Day had arrived. He had better move fast.

CHAPTER 5

"Heart attack?" The question burst from Moshe's mouth like an accusation. He sat on the low couch in the rabbi's living room, his arms folded over his chest, his feet in velvet slippers one size too small.

Rabbi Yosef nodded and lowered his eyes. He sat on an old wooden chair from the dining table set. He reminded Moshe of the visitors at the house of mourning after his father had passed and, years later, his mother.

At this *shiva* house, however, Moshe filled the roles of both bereaved and deceased.

The rabbi nodded. "You collapsed at the Botanical Gardens. The paramedics were unable to revive you."

Moshe had suspected that much. Heart attack. Without warning. Like his father and grandfather. He should have seen that coming, but he'd been too busy to bother with doctors.

After his shower, he had drifted through the house, alone with his thoughts. The rabbanit had taken the boys to school and continued to her own teaching job. He paced the living room like an angry tiger, from the overloaded bookcase to the sagging couches to the kitchen counter and back. The framed rabbis on the walls watched him without expression as the ball of hot magma grew in his chest.

He could try to explain away the morning's events, but he could not account for the signs on his body or the date of the newspaper on the kitchen counter. Just over two years had passed with Moshe dead to the world.

When God's representative returned home from morning prayers, the volcano erupted.

"It's not fair!" Tears flooded his eyes and seeped into his nasal cavity.

Rabbi Yosef handed him a tissue and studied the floor.

Moshe blew his nose. "Dead at forty. No sons to say *Kaddish* or carry on the family name." He shuddered. What would his father have thought of that? "We moved into our house only a year ago. I was about to expand my business. I left so much undone."

The rabbi nodded, then brightened. "But you're alive now. You can pick up where you left off."

Moshe emitted a short, bitter laugh. "Tell that to my wife. You should have seen her face this morning." A sudden doubt drained his sense of humor. "We're still married, aren't we?"

The rabbi shifted on his seat. "Marriage ends with divorce or death, so the moment you died…" He let Moshe draw the conclusion. "But," he added, "you can remarry."

Moshe spared the rabbi the gory details of finding Avi and Galit in his bed. That ship had sailed. Of all the men in the world, why Avi? Had she not married Moshe first, he would have seriously doubted her taste in men.

"Galit inherited everything?"

Another nod. Moshe constructed a mental syllogism. His worldly possessions now belonged to Galit; Galit belonged to Avi. That bastard had taken over his life. The joke was on Moshe, all right, and it ran far deeper and darker than he had thought.

"Moshe?"

"Yes?"

"If you don't mind me asking…"

"Go ahead, Rabbi."

"What was it like?"

Moshe gave him a confused look.

The rabbi said, "The World of Souls."

"World of Souls?"

The rabbi's cheeks reddened above his beard. "You know—after the tunnel and bright light."

Moshe racked his memory. He had been talking to Savta Sarah at the Botanical Gardens, wineglass in hand. He had looked about for Galit. And then... he had woken up on the Mount of Olives to the sound of the *muezzin*.

He shook his head. "I don't remember anything. No tunnels or lights either."

"Did you meet God?"

"Not that I can recall."

"Deceased relatives?"

"Nope."

"Angels? Cherubs?"

"None."

The rabbi seemed disappointed. Moshe had died and lost everything, including any memory of the Hereafter. And yet, here he sat, alive again, in the rabbi's living room. "Rabbi," he said. "How can this be?"

The rabbi rediscovered his enthusiasm. "It's a miracle!"

"Yes, you said that. But how? Has this happened before?"

"Not in three thousand years."

Now the rabbi had his attention. "So people *have* come back from the dead?" That did not sound like a very Jewish idea.

The rabbi walked over to the shelf and returned with a small, thick, and well-thumbed volume. He opened the Hebrew Bible halfway and flipped the pages. "Elijah the Prophet revived the son of a widow in Zarephath. His successor, Elisha, resurrected the son of a rich benefactor in Shunem." He read from the book: "'Elisha lay on top of the boy, placed his mouth on his, his eyes on his eyes, his hands on his hands, and the boy's body became warm.'"

"I don't know," said Moshe. The passage sounded suspiciously like CPR, but he kept his doubts about the Biblical story to himself. "I was dead for two years. There wasn't much left to resuscitate."

"Unless," the rabbi said, "you didn't decompose! There are stories about saintly rabbis—"

Moshe raised his hand, cutting the rabbi's argument short. "Then how do you explain this?" He lifted his shirt.

The rabbi's eyes narrowed with alarm and then widened with surprise. He squinted at Moshe's exposed belly. "*Ribono Shel Olam!* You have no navel." The rabbi jabbed a finger at the spot. "But that means…"

"Exactly. I wasn't revived. My body was… regenerated."

The rabbi's face lit up with that now familiar ecstatic expression. "I've got it!"

"Don't tell me," Moshe said. "It's a miracle."

"Better than that!"

"What could be better than a miracle?"

"A prophecy!" He fanned the pages of the Bible again, bouncing on the couch in excitement. "Isaiah, chapter twenty-six: 'Your dead will live, their corpses rise. Awake and sing praise, you that dwell in the dust, for your dew is the dew of light…'"

A shudder ran down Moshe's spine. The verse described a zombie apocalypse. Was he in the lead role? He had no desire to eat brains. He couldn't even stomach a Jerusalem mixed grill.

The rabbi turned more pages. "Ezekiel thirty-seven. The prophet had a vision—a valley full of dry bones. Human bones. The Spirit of God assembled the bones into skeletons, wrapped them in sinew, flesh, and skin, and breathed life into them."

That was more like it. "What happened to them?"

"There are two opinions in the Talmud. They either lived forever or died of natural causes."

Moshe preferred the first option. "You mean the rabbis don't know?"

Rabbi Yosef shrugged. The unresolved debate over that

critical detail didn't seem to bother him.

"But if they lived regular lives, what was the point?"

"You could ask the same question," the rabbi said, stroking his beard, "about life in general."

Moshe waited for Rabbi Yosef to answer the question of questions, but he didn't. "The vision of dry bones," he continued, "was a symbolic message for Ezekiel's generation, the Jewish exiles in Babylon: don't lose hope; soon you will return to the land of Israel and revive your independent state, just as God revived the dry bones. But on another level the prophecy predicts an actual resurrection of the dead."

The rabbi found a passage toward the end of the tome. "Daniel, chapter twelve. 'And many of those that sleep in the dirt will wake, some for eternal life, others for eternal shame.'" More turning of pages. "'And you, find your end and rest; but you will rise for your destiny at the End of Days.'" He closed the book.

"The End of Days?" Moshe asked. It sounded like a Hollywood blockbuster, not an event in the here-and-now.

The rabbi's smile widened. "The Messianic Era. We believe that the End of Days will see the Resurrection of the Dead, the return of Elijah the Prophet, and the revelation of the Messiah-King, son of David. The Messiah will gather the exiles from the Diaspora and rebuild the Temple in Jerusalem. He'll restore the Kingdom of Israel to its former glory and bring peace and justice to the land."

"Peace?" Moshe asked. "In the Middle East? Good luck to him."

The rabbi was undeterred. "The order of the events is unclear. The Ingathering has begun already. Jews have poured into the State of Israel from across the globe: holocaust survivors from Europe; entire communities fleeing persecution in Arab countries; airlifts of Jews from Morocco and Ethiopia. Every day planeloads of Jews from around the world land at Ben Gurion Airport." The rabbi sighed at the thrill of it all. "When these signs come to pass, the Messiah will usher in the World to Come."

"Wait a moment," Moshe said. "I thought that the World to Come is the Afterlife, the—what did you call it—the World of Souls?"

The rabbi produced a sheepish grin. "The rabbis argue that one too." Moshe should have guessed. "Maimonides says you're right—the World to Come is the Spirit World after death. But according to Nachmanides, the World to Come refers to life after the dead have risen in the Messianic Era, when the world will reach perfection."

Moshe's head spun with resurrections, messiahs, and Worlds-to-Come. His credulity choked on the cocktail of conflicting beliefs. The rabbis really needed to get their act together. None of it made any sense, and none of it was helping him get his life back.

The volcano of bile erupted again in his gut. He hated Avi. He hated ancient prophecies and the valley of dry bones. And he sure as hell hated the Resurrection.

He jumped to his feet and threw his hands in the air. "I don't get it," he said, louder than he had intended. He stomped around the room again. "I've lost everything. God could have saved my life if He had wanted to. Why bring me back now—just to satisfy some stupid old prophecy?"

Rabbi Yosef stared at the floor and said nothing.

Red-hot lava bubbled in Moshe's belly. "No, sir," he said, to Rabbi Yosef or God, he couldn't say. "I'll have none of this."

He leaned against the wall and sucked in long drafts of air.

"Rabbi," he said, when his voice had calmed. "May I use your phone?"

CHAPTER 6

Moshe dialed his home phone number by heart and paced the rabbi's living room as he waited for the call to connect.

Galit had quit her receptionist job to stay home with the baby. When Talya started kindergarten, they had forgone the meager second salary. On a Tuesday morning, Galit should be at home.

The phone rang twice. Galit answered. "Alo?"

He fought the urge to talk to her, to beg her to kick Avi out and take him back. Instead, he hung up. She was home, that was all he needed to know. On the phone, she could easily cut short the conversation; he stood the best chance of tugging at her heartstrings face-to-face. He would need all the help he could get. He'd be asking a lot of her—he'd be asking her to turn back time.

The rabbi's living room lacked mirrors, so Moshe patted the hair of his reflection in the tin Blessing for the Home hung on the wall beside the framed pictures of bearded rabbis. Still wearing the velvet slippers, he made for the door.

"Shall I come with?" said Rabbi Yosef.

Moshe considered the earnest rabbi. A familiar religious figure at his side might help convince Galit that he was not a ghost.

"Yes. Thank you, Rabbi."

The trees along Shimshon Street murmured in the breeze and made the morning sunbeams dance over the cracks in the sidewalk. The cars that usually choked the street had moved to the parking garages of office buildings across the city. An alley cat sunbathed on the green lid of a municipal garbage bin and watched them pass.

Every human being is a network of desires and fears. This was a truth that Moshe knew well, and he had plugged into those wants and needs to clinch deals with new customers. To independent cabbies—hard-working men with mortgages and mouths to feed—he sold a steady stream of patrons; to the managers of taxi fleets he peddled the freedom to focus on growing their business. Nothing beat the rush of a hand-shake at the end of a long negotiation. This was how Karlin & Son had conquered Jerusalem and this was how Moshe would reclaim his old life.

A white Kia Sportage lazed at the curb outside number five. "That's her car," Moshe told the rabbi. "Bought it for her last year—no, make that three years ago."

The venetian blinds blocked his view, but he knew every detail of what lay beyond the windows. He and Galit had selected everything together at factory outlets in the Talpiot industrial zone, deliberating over floor tiles and faucets, and taking turns to run after Talya when she climbed into a bath-tub or danced on a plate of Italian marble tiling.

He remembered the day that Talya had burst into the world. At 3 AM, he had sped down Herzog Boulevard to rush Galit to the labor ward at the Shaare Zedek Medical Center. That experience, like the night they had first met— now there was a story!—bound Moshe and Galit forever. Even death could not part them, he felt it deep inside.

Moshe and the rabbi climbed the three steps to the front door of the house. Moshe's house. Their house.

He'd break the ice with two choice words, the very first words he had spoken to her.

If romantic nostalgia didn't melt her defenses, he'd drop the gloves and use guilt. Every little girl needed her father—

her real father. Galit could not deny Talya that.

With a plan and a backup, Moshe rubbed his palms together and pressed the buzzer with a trembling finger. He needed this too much. He had to gain some mental distance. He was just a salesman; his product—a family healed after being torn by tragedy. He only hoped that she had calmed down since the morning. Hell hath no fury like Galit in a sour mood. Worst case scenario, he could take cover behind the rabbi.

He listened for her footfalls. He waited for the light in the peephole to darken.

He envisioned success. Galit would rush into his arms. She'd welcome him back into her home and her life. In fact, he convinced himself, it was her overpowering love for Moshe that had driven her to marry his best friend—that even made sense! But loyal consumers always prefer the original brand to cheap imitations.

Still no movement in the house.

Until today, Moshe had encountered religion mostly at major life-cycle events: circumcision; bar mitzvah; marriage; death. He visited the neighborhood synagogue once a year, on the Day of Atonement. He had never given much thought to God's existence. If he had harbored doubts before, now he had none. God alone was responsible for Moshe's new lease on life. He worked in mysterious ways—even the rabbis had no clue—but He was no figment of the imagination. And now, for the first time in both his lives, Moshe mouthed a silent prayer.

Oh, God. Please help me. Make things the way they were before.

He made a mental list of the good deeds he would do in return. He'd join the rabbi at synagogue every morning and strap on phylacteries. He'd write fat checks to the city's soup kitchens. And, for Heaven's sake, he'd see a cardiologist.

Moshe had learned his lesson. He had internalized the moral of the story. God had given him a second chance and this time he would do better.

If You can resurrect the dead, surely You can do this?

He pressed the buzzer again.

Come on, Galit. Give me a break.

The handle rattled.

Thank you, God!

The door opened but a security chain held fast. Through the crack, a little girl peered up at him, her dark eyes framed by thick black glasses.

It took him a moment to make the connection. "Talya?"

His precious four-year-old with the bushy crown of black curls had transformed into a young lady with satin locks that fell over her shoulders. He wanted to kneel on the floor and hug her.

Her solemn expression and tight mouth told him not to dare. "*Ima* says she's not home."

Moshe beamed at the adorable little girl. His girl.

"Talya, it's me. Your *aba*." Did she remember him? Galit had taken her to kindergarten each morning, and she was usually asleep by the time he got home from work.

Talya bit her lip. "*Aba*'s at work," she said.

The thought of Avi as her father winded him. *She doesn't know me. My little Talya doesn't know me.*

Her eyes flitted to the rabbi and her mouth twitched. "I have to go now."

Moshe put his foot forward and the closing door bit through the slipper and into his foot. "Ow!"

Talya's eyes widened and her hands shot to her mouth. *Great. Now you've frightened her.* "It's OK," he said. *Stay calm. Don't panic.* "I know *Ima* is home," he whispered. "I really need to speak to her. Please. It's super important."

Talya's lips squirmed while she mulled it over. She glanced over her shoulder. "*Ima* doesn't want to speak to you," she whispered. "You have to go away."

He removed his bruised foot from the door as a gesture of good will. They were on the same side now.

"You can open the door. It's OK. Please. I'll give you candy."

Her eyes sparkled.

Bingo! He had said the magic word.

"What candy?"

Galit's voice carried from upstairs. "Talya, close the door and come here."

He was close. So close. Choose the right words and he'd mend his broken world.

"What candy do you like?"

The sparkle in her eye vanished. Her real *aba* would have known the answer.

"I have to go now," his daughter said, as she shut the door. "I'm not supposed to talk to strangers."

CHAPTER 7

Moshe woke in the dark with a start. In his nightmare, he had died and lost everything he held dear. *Just a dream, a horrible, unbearable dream.* What a relief. Anxiety drained away from his chest and he breathed at ease.

He sat up and banged his forehead. Something very hard had impeded his movement and forced him down onto the stiff pillow. He caressed the fresh bruise on his head. His eyes adjusted to the dark. He lay on the lower level of a bunk bed. Wooden boards pressed against his back through the thin mattress. His legs stretched beyond the bed frame and his bare feet hovered in the air. The bed smelled of grimy feet and pee. On the pillow case, Superman punched a fist in the air.

Oh, no.

He lingered in limbo, unable to move after his nap. This was no dream. He had nothing, was nothing. God had not answered his prayers. Why on Earth had Galit shut him out? They had been a team. Together they were going to conquer the world. Didn't she at least want to see him again?

The door creaked open and sent a shard of yellow light into the room. The silhouette of a little boy peered around the door. A large skullcap sat on a thick tangle of hair.

"Hey," Moshe said and raised a forearm. The feat spent

his energy.

"Are you dead?" the boy asked.

Moshe wished he were. He said, "What do you think?"

The boy mulled the question over. "Do dead people talk?"

"Probably not."

That seemed to satisfy the boy, and he walked off. "*Aba*," he said, from the corridor, "the dead man woke up."

Rabbi Yosef appeared at the door. "Sorry about that. You OK?"

Moshe pondered the question. Was he OK? He was lucky to be alive, but he felt anything but lucky.

"Hungry?" the rabbi said. "Dinner is served."

Moshe said nothing. He had lived the modern suburban dream: the ideal family; the ideal career; the ideal home. That perfect life floated in his mind. Magical. Complete. And unobtainable.

He stared at the beams of the upper bunk bed. Dark swirls in the grain of the wood eyed him in the gloom, unseeing. The rings testified to long years of sun and wind. Good years, as a living tree. Now, only hardened struts remained. Dead wood.

"You can stay with us as long as you want."

The offer touched the tiny corner of Moshe's heart that could still feel anything. The rabbi had a small house and many mouths to feed without Moshe's dead weight. But he could not muster the strength to accept. He did not belong in the rabbi's home. He didn't belong anywhere. In the cosmic game of musical chairs, Moshe remained without a seat.

"I'm better off dead."

Rabbi Yosef sat down on the edge of the bed and placed a warm hand on his shoulder. "Don't say that."

"My parents are gone. I'm an only child. My daughter thinks I'm a stranger. My wife won't even talk to me."

"People react differently to death," the rabbi said. "And to life. She might be angry at you."

"Angry? I didn't choose to die."

"Emotions don't always make sense. You left her and that

hurt. She had to move on, and now the sight of you brings it all back."

Moshe had not looked at his death that way. He could see Galit getting angry at that. She owned the quickest temper in the Middle East. And she had moved on. Avi was the man in her life now, and Talya's new father. The eternal bachelor had finally settled down—into Moshe's shoes. There was no room left for him.

"Besides," the rabbi continued, "the sight of you must have scared her half to death. I almost had a heart attack when I bumped into you."

The rabbi had finally succeeded in making him laugh.

"Give her time," he said. "Where there is life, there is hope."

"Rabbi, I'm beyond hope."

"I wouldn't be so sure of that," he said. "I know something that can help. We'll do that tomorrow morning. But tonight," he added, "you must eat."

CHAPTER 8

The Prophet heaved two bulging plastic bags onto the marble countertop in his kitchen that afternoon. He untied one bag, widened the opening, and a mound of glistening green olives stared back at him. His order of five kilos of Nabali had elicited a double take from the stall owner at the Machaneh Yehuda market, but he had shoveled the choice fruit from a large vat all the same.

The Prophet sat on a designer stool beside the kitchen island, and dropped a well-formed and unblemished specimen into the funnel of the specialized stainless steel press he had rigged to the countertop. He turned the long arm of the crank, and a single drop of buttery liquid dripped into a glass beaker. He released the crank, extracted the bruised olive, and repeated the process with the next.

By the time daylight faded through the large windows, an inch of golden-green virgin oil had settled at the bottom of the beaker.

Why do I bother? A bottle of extra-virgin from the corner mini-market would suit his purposes too. But tradition was tradition, and the rich, bitter juice of the local species reminded him of the sacred oils of his youth.

Battered olives littered the island countertop. The sight would have appalled his interior decorator, who had decked the kitchen in dark panels of wenge, chrome, and the best marble money could buy. He had settled into the penthouse only a few months ago. Soon he'd have to leave it all behind.

He extracted the beaker from the press and poured the contents into a small glass vial, which he sealed with a cork, wrapped in a thick cloth, and slipped into his shoulder bag alongside the hollowed-out ram's horn that he had set aside for the occasion.

He dismantled the press, cleared the discarded olives into a large garbage bag, and wiped the counter. His work done, he retired to the adjacent living room with a tall glass of Shiraz.

He stood at the large French windows and sipped the fruity wine. The setting sun painted the Jerusalem skyline orange. Below, cars and buses crawled along Jaffa Road like scarab beetles, their engines and horns a soft murmur. The city appeared calm, blissfully unaware that tomorrow the world it knew would end.

If everything went according to plan. In his experience, nothing to do with humanity ever did. In all likelihood, the oil would remain in the vial, the *shofar* would never touch his lips, and his toil would be in vain. *Again.*

For all their industry and technology, humankind remained a horde of shortsighted brutes. They erred; they paid the price. Every time. Without fail.

But the Boss was a romantic, and He called the shots.

Darkness settled over the city. "Here's to tomorrow," he said, and drained the glass. Tomorrow, humanity would get another chance.

CHAPTER 9

The rabbi's old Subaru had seen kinder days. The door creaked when Moshe, wearing the same ill-fitting jeans and T-shirt as the day before, yanked it open Wednesday morning. Springs in the passenger seat groaned under his weight. The interior smelled of dust. He fastened the seat belt and fed the strap back into the retractor hole. The mouth of a cassette player gaped on the dashboard. Moshe had not seen one of those in decades. The jalopy was an accident waiting to happen.

His palms left wet patches on the armrest. He prayed that the car would fail to start. An earthquake or tidal wave would do nicely too. Anything to force the rabbi to cancel the excursion. Their destination was the one place on the planet Moshe wanted to avoid at all costs.

Rabbi Yosef turned to him and held out a thin roll of bank notes.

"I can't."

"Please," the rabbi said, and dropped the money on Moshe's lap. "You'll need some money to get back on your feet."

The rabbi was right. Moshe examined the worn bills. Two hundred shekels: a lot of money for the rabbi. He had probably not consulted with the rabbanit before parting with their grocery money.

Back on your feet. The smiling rabbi made it sound possible.

"I'll pay you back," he said.

Rabbi Yosef turned the key. The engine turned over, coughed twice, and started. God had sided with the rabbi.

The cassette player kicked into action as they pulled off. To Moshe's surprise, he recognized the song. He had expected the wail of violin and clarinet—the traditional klezmer music of Eastern European Jewry—or the festive Chasidic wedding ditties he stumbled upon when scanning through radio frequencies. Instead, the air filled with synthesizers and an '80s dance beat that shouted teenage rebellion. A girl sang.

"'Girls Just Want to Have Fun'?" Moshe said. "You listen to Cyndi Lauper?"

The rabbi's cheeks turned pink. "Cyndi is the best," he said. "A great soul."

There was more to Rabbi Yosef than Moshe had imagined.

The rabbi seemed to feel obliged to explain. "I wasn't always religious," he said.

Moshe found it hard to imagine the bearded rabbi with the constant smile and unbeatable optimism as a secular Israeli, but he didn't press him for details. He didn't have to.

"I spent a year in India after the army. I suppose I was searching even then. At university, I lost my way. Cigarettes. Alcohol. Girls. You name it." The rabbi's cheeks went from pink to tomato red. "One day, the campus rabbi invited me to a Shabbat meal at his home, and the rest, as they say, is history."

The sun climbed in the sky. The morning traffic choked the back roads of Baka but eased up as they turned onto Hebron Road toward the Old City. Throughout the country, millions of people rushed about their daily lives and worried about their everyday concerns. Moshe envied them.

They passed the Old City and his stomach knotted. *Are you ready for this?* That morning, his body had answered a loud and unequivocal "no," but the rabbi had been adamant.

The road dipped into a valley, and then they climbed the winding access road that Moshe had descended, on foot and naked, exactly one day ago—the narrow, walled road to the Mount of Olives Cemetery.

The rabbi parked in the small lot of gravel at the top and they got out. The car hissed. Unseen parts creaked as they cooled beneath the hood.

Moshe pointed to the empty field, walled on three sides. "That's where I woke up yesterday."

The rabbi studied the lot in solemn silence, then said, "You ready?"

Moshe swallowed hard. The rabbi patted his shoulder and led the way, past the field and along a path of long, flat stones.

"This is Jerusalem's oldest cemetery," he said. He seemed to be talking for Moshe's benefit, to distract him from what lay ahead. "Jews have buried their dead here for three thousand years, since the time of King David."

With every step, Moshe's feet grew heavier. He had followed that path many times before. The rabbi walked down the aisle between the long rows of tombstones. Crumbled edges and cracks. The ravages of time and vandals. Tufts of wild grass rose between the stepping-stones and wavered in the mountain breeze. In daylight, above the silent rise and fall of the Jerusalem hills, the graveyard radiated serenity.

Rabbi Yosef pointed. "Nachmanides is buried down there. Bartenura, too. And a host of other famous rabbis."

He turned left and stepped between the graves. He halted before a line of gray headstones in polished granite. The etched names and dates stood out in white lettering beneath a patina of dust and the occasional spatter of bird droppings. Moshe passed the graves of his grandfather and his grandmother, then his father and mother, of blessed memory. His mother's stone was shinier and cleaner than the others. He placed a white pebble on each grave.

Moshe had not visited enough. Did the dead care? Did they even know when a relative paid their respects? Moshe had no recollection, and yet there he stood, living proof that the spirit survived death.

"It is a great merit to be buried here," the rabbi said. "They ran out of space years ago."

"My great-grandfather bought plots in bulk and divided them up between his children. Turned out to be a good investment."

He remembered his father's funeral in every detail. The sight of the body on the stretcher, wrapped in a white shroud, had startled him even as a young man.

"Only soldiers are buried in coffins," the officiating rabbi had explained.

The somber bearded men of the *Chevra Kaddisha* lowered the body into the gaping hole. They sealed the space with rough slabs of concrete, climbed out, and took turns shoveling dirt.

Why had God resurrected him and not his dear mother or his father, or any of the thousands of righteous men and women around them?

Rabbi Yosef touched his shoulder again, not to comfort him for his parents, but to give him courage for the next and final stop, and stepped aside.

Moshe stood before the next grave in the row.

Moshe Karlin. Mourned by his wife and daughter. May his soul be bound in the Bundle of Life.

A pile of white pebbles lay at the corner of the slab. The wind whispered in his ear and caressed his face.

One step forward, and six below, lay his corpse. What remained of a man after two years in the earth? Or twenty? Or two hundred?

A tremor spread from his legs through his body. He sank to his knees at the foot of his grave.

"I'm dead." There—he had said the words. His breath came in halting gasps. Then he broke down and bawled into his hands.

Moshe Karlin had died. Nothing would change that fact. But if Moshe Karlin was dead and buried, who was he?

He stared at his tombstone, tears trickling down his cheeks.

A tissue materialized in front of his face. He thanked the rabbi and blew his nose. He drew three long, deep breaths. He leaned back, his hands in the dirt, and stretched his legs at the foot of his grave. He looked up at the rabbi. "Yet, I'm alive," he said, in wonder.

He held out his hand and the rabbi helped him to his feet. He brushed the dirt from his jeans. His vision cleared. "Look." He pointed at the horizontal slab. "Over there."

A small, round hole lay opened in the earth at the corner of the grave, like the mouth of a mole tunnel.

They stepped forward to get a better look, when the crunch of gravel behind them cut their investigation short. They spun around. A pale figure flitted between the graves and cowered behind a tombstone. A woman. She reminded him of the fairies in storybooks for young girls: large eyes, a hint of a nose, and a head of short matted hair so blond it seemed white. She lacked only a pair of fairy wings. And clothes.

She peered at them over the headstone, her eyes flitting between the bearded rabbi and his teary companion, her brow a battleground of need and confusion.

"Please," she said in Hebrew, her accent heavy with Russian. "Help me!"

Moshe and Rabbi Yosef exchanged a meaningful glance. He too had noticed the key detail, and drawn the same conclusion.

During her split-second dash between the grave markers, Moshe had glimpsed milky skin dusted with flecks of dirt. One arm pressed over her breasts, the other thrust over her lap, and, between the two, a clear patch of milky skin. No dirt. No freckles. Not even a belly button.

CHAPTER 10

In a parking garage beneath Jaffa Road, the Prophet pulled on a black leather jacket and a pair of matching riding gloves. The winged Harley Davidson emblem gleamed in the cool fluorescent light on the matte black chassis of the Sportster Iron 883.

He kicked his leg over the decal of a fiery chariot on the rear fender and settled on the leather seat. He squeezed the clutch, lifted the shift lever to neutral with his boot, and thumbed the starter. The V-twin engine growled to life.

He clicked the remote, and the gate of the private parking bay rolled upward. He eased back on the throttle and launched up the ramp and onto the street.

Air blew through his hair. He didn't bother with a helmet. He never stopped or slowed—the traffic lights of downtown Jerusalem knew better than to get in his way—and soon he tore along open road toward East Jerusalem.

Jonah, man, I feel your pain. He would have preferred to stay in bed. The Redemption had loomed so many times that he had lost count. Why would today be any different?

And yet...

And yet a small thrill of anticipation quickened in his chest.

He reached the Mount of Olives and gunned along the

walled access road like a bullet through the barrel of a rifle. An old white car hugged the perimeter wall at the top of the hill. Two men emerged from the cemetery: a brown-bearded man in a hat and shirtsleeves, and a clean-shaven companion in jeans and a T-shirt. They glanced toward the Harley's rumble. *There you are. Right on schedule.*

A third figure appeared behind them. The woman wore a man's suit jacket over her shoulders and, it seemed, nothing else. The bearded man held the car door open for her. *Hello? What do we have here?* The Thin Voice had not mentioned the girl.

He pulled back on the throttle and the bike hurtled forward. He would career around, spinning the wheels and spraying pebbles, and stop at their feet. Humanity loved dramatic entrances.

As he crested the hill, however, a horn blared—very loud and very close. Too close. The world became the flat metal front of a large truck, and the driver opened his mouth to scream.

Bam! He flew forward. His head connected with the windshield. Bones crunched. Glass shattered. He floated in the air, an astronaut in zero gravity. Then planet Earth rose up and slammed into his back.

Pale blue sky filled his world. He tried to think. He tried to move.

A face replaced the sky. The bearded mouth moved but the words fluttered away. He felt a wetness at his back. His backpack. *Oh, no, the oil!* Clean-Shaven joined Brown Beard, his face as pale as a ghost.

He tried to move his lips. Say the words. Deliver his message. He must!

Brown Beard spoke into a mobile phone and the men moved out of his field of vision.

Far above, a cloud hovered in the blue morning sky, a hand with one long accusatory finger aimed at him.

His head tingled. Weariness washed over him. He closed his eyes and knew no more.

CHAPTER 11

The fairy-woman nursed a cup of steaming tea on the couch in the rabbi's living room. She had borrowed a potato-sack gown from the rabbanit's wardrobe and her hair stuck to her forehead in damp, blond leaves.

Twenty-four hours ago, Moshe had sat on the same spot on the couch. The young woman was coping well—her hands didn't even shake—despite the two extra complications. The first had involved a motor accident.

The leather-jacketed biker had passed out while they waited for an ambulance. The truck driver, an old Sephardic man, emerged from the truck without a scratch on his body, but a large gash in his conscience. He wrung his hands and muttered prayers as the paramedics shifted the biker onto a stretcher and into the ambulance.

When Moshe and Rabbi Yosef finally came around to questioning the fairy-woman, after providing her with two Acamol tablets for her head along with a shower and fresh clothing, they discovered the second complication.

"Let's try again," Rabbi Yosef said. He sat opposite on a wooden chair and clasped his hands. "What is your name?"

Her large eyes searched the bookcase at the end of the living room for answers. She shook her head.

"Where do you live?"

Another shake.

"Do you remember anyone? Anything?"

They had hoped that a hot shower and drink would jog her memory. The poor thing had started life over in every way: no clothes; no memory; not even a name. One creature walked the earth more miserable than Moshe, but the discovery gave him no comfort.

The woman on the couch sipped her tea and glanced from Rabbi Yosef to Moshe and back, with surprising calm and detached curiosity.

She doesn't even know she's been dead! With no memory, how could she?

Moshe and the rabbi exchanged an uneasy glance. *Do we tell her?* The rabbi frowned and gave his head a mild shake. He was right: rather let her figure it out herself.

Moshe had experience with lost people, usually in the form of customers who needed a taxi but had no clue where they were. "Do you remember any landmarks?" he said. "Street names?"

Another shake of the head. She sat there, erect and proud, and took another long sip.

"You can stay here while we figure it out," the rabbi said.

"And I'll help too," Moshe said. "Many thousands of Russian Jews moved to Israel after the iron curtain fell. That trail should lead to who you are, or at least to some people who know you."

"Thank you," she said.

"Until then what should we call you?"

"*Chava?*" the rabbi suggested. Chava was the Hebrew name for Eve.

"Hmm," said Moshe, his voice a moan of uncertainty. "A bit old-fashioned. How about Eva?" That sounded more Russian.

Her big blue eyes searched the walls. Then her face beamed.

"Or Irina," she said. "Yes. I like Irina."

The rabbi grinned. "Irina it is." He glanced at his wristwatch. "I have to teach a class now. I'll be back in a few hours. Moshe, can you help her with lunch?"

"Sure."

Moshe had learned the ropes. The Lev family divided their kitchen into meat and dairy halves, each with separate sets of plates, cutlery, cooking ware, and even a separate sink. He chopped tomatoes, cucumbers, and red peppers, and served the salad with slices of toast, a block of white salted butter, and a tub of five percent cottage cheese. He scrambled the three remaining eggs in the box, thus exhausting his entire cooking repertoire.

Moshe and Irina munched away at their Israeli brunch. She polished off her fifth slice of toast and cheese, and then stared at the fridge, her eyes distant.

"I'm dead, aren't I?" she said.

Moshe almost choked on a cucumber.

She tapped her slim stomach. "I'm pretty sure I should have a belly button. And if some mad scientist had cloned me, I would have woken up in a laboratory, not a graveyard." She was no dumb blond. She gazed at him with defiance, daring him to deny the evidence. There was no point.

"We thought you had enough to deal with already," he said, by way of apology. "Yes, you died. But you're very much alive now." Her shoulders relaxed and she let out a deep breath. Her speculations were over, no matter how bizarre the conclusion.

"We're the same, you and I," he continued. At least she would not feel alone. "I woke up in the cemetery yesterday. I died two years ago."

"So you remember your life?"

"I don't remember dying or anything in between, but yes, I remember my life before. I had a hard time accepting that I had died."

She let the idea sink in. "How did this happen?"

Moshe washed down his scrambled eggs with a tumbler of tap water. "Rabbi Yosef thinks it's the fulfillment of a prophecy. The Resurrection of the Dead." He decided to skip the

Valley of Dry Bones, the Messianic Era, and the World-to-Come. Too much information. Had she been religious in her former life? She looked at home in the rabbanit's gown even without the head covering.

"So no one is looking for me?" She studied his eyes.

He shook his head. "Don't worry. We'll figure it out." She had the kind of face he'd expect to see on billboards for Fox Clothing, although she sure didn't eat like a supermodel.

"How do you know that?"

"Sooner or later your memory will return. And if it doesn't, someone is bound to remember you. You're not easy to forget."

She smiled and avoided his eyes. An awkward moment passed in silence.

"Were you born here?"

"Born and bred. Seventeen generations in Jerusalem, on my great-grandmother's side."

"So you must have a lot of family here." He knew what she was thinking: you, at least, have a place to go.

"Yes and no. None of them are on speaking terms. Some old feud. Nobody even remembers how it started."

"Oh." Another silence. "Do you have a family of your own?"

"A wife and a little girl."

She smiled. "You're lucky."

"I don't know about that. My wife locked me out and my daughter doesn't remember me. You have a clean slate," he told her, his inner salesman taking over. "A fresh start. All I can think about is what I lost."

Irina considered his words. "If you know what you lost," she said, "you can get it back."

Moshe laughed. "Easier said than done."

"Why?"

"My best friend took over my life: my wife, my business."

"A best friend might understand."

"Not Avi. He's a real ugly Israeli."

Her eyebrows arched. The Russian immigrant had not encountered the term. *Lucky you, Irina.*

How could he explain without causing the new immigrant to lose faith in society?

"Most Israelis are decent and caring people," he said, transforming at once into a spokesperson for the Jewish Agency. "Hard workers with family values who help old ladies cross the street." He cleared his throat. "There is, however, a small but loud group of people that gives the rest a bad name. They push in line. Run you off the road. Trash their hotel rooms and steal anything not nailed to the floor. Real scumbags."

Irina did not seem too bothered. "There are scumbags all over the world," she said.

"True," he conceded. "But Avi won't give a centimeter without a fight." He threw up his hands in preemptive surrender.

She nodded in sympathy but didn't cut him any slack. "Some things," she said, "are worth fighting for."

CHAPTER 12

Gastric juices sloshed in Moshe's stomach as he boarded Egged bus number seven on Emek Refaim.

The driver took his twenty-shekel note and handed back thirteen in coins. Ticket prices had risen in the decade since Moshe had used public transportation last. He'd have to do more walking to stretch his budget.

The commuters didn't give the man in jeans and slippers a second look as he found a seat next to an old lady with pale round cheeks and a halo of white hair. The bus rose and fell, roared and sighed, as gears changed and they charged along King George Street.

By his count, he had been away only two days, but he missed Karlin & Son already—the frantic buzz of telephones, the brusque exchanges on CB radio, the large mounted television screen with the numbers of waiting calls and routed customers.

He missed his team: Arkadi and his crude Russian jokes; Sivan's no-nonsense practicality and feminine touch; mild-mannered Pini with his large white *kippah*, kosher sandwiches, and the unintelligible Moroccan Arabic he had suckled at his mother's breast. And, of course, Mathew's Wisconsin accent and frequent tantrums.

They were more than employees; they were friends.

Among the four of them, they spoke five languages—Pini could get by in French too. Mathew and Moshe handled the English speakers. Sivan understood crap in any language and answered in kind.

The bus turned left and climbed Jaffa Road.

Soon he'd arrive at his destination. How would the team react to his return? His plan: get inside and spark a rebellion. None of them liked Avi much, especially Mathew, and Sivan swatted Avi's constant advances and innuendos like flies. Galit had inherited the ship, but Moshe was still the only rightful navigator. A mutiny would force her to parley with the pirate captain.

A sudden doubt stirred the acidic juices in his belly. In two years, the workload must have skyrocketed, the headcount doubled to keep up with demand in Tel Aviv. He'd need a majority of the team on board if he was to challenge Avi. If they had pushed northward to Haifa as well...

"Don't worry," said the devil on his shoulder. "Avi won't even let you through the door, never mind start a mutiny."

Moshe thumbed the button on the handrail and got off at the next stop.

Clal Center loomed on Jaffa Road, a hulking gray ghost. In the seventies, shoppers had flocked to the tiered corridors of Jerusalem's first indoor shopping center and filled the consumer stores.

By the turn of the millennium, most businesses had migrated to shinier office buildings far from the crammed city center, and foot traffic along the tired corridors petered out.

Moshe walked through the open door of the defunct shopping center and passed an abandoned security desk. Not even terrorists bothered with the faded building. The jingle of the coins in his pocket echoed off the blackened windows of stores, many of which served as storage warehouses for stalls at the nearby Machaneh Yehuda street market. Everything changes, and faster than one expects.

Moshe had renewed the rental contract every three years, for the low price and the sense of continuity. His father had inaugurated the offices, and many of his happiest childhood memories haunted the corridors.

The elevator—graffiti etched in the panels, the last working fluorescent flickering—groaned all the way to the third floor.

Moshe walked down the corridor to the door of frosted glass. He touched the proud silver lettering: Karlin & Son. His first love. His firstborn.

His finger hovered over the buzzer. The ominous silence behind the door unnerved him. Did Avi know he was on his way? Had he preempted the visit and cleared the place?

He pressed the buzzer.

He shifted on his feet. His heart thumped in his chest. His mouth went dry.

He buzzed again.

Still no movement behind the glass.

Moshe slapped his forehead. *Of course!* Karlin & Son must have relocated. By now, the call center would fill an entire floor in the Malcha Technology Park. Avi had lobbied for fancier premises even before their expansion. He must have pushed ahead as soon as the cash had started flowing.

Moshe needed a computer and an Internet connection. He'd settle for a telephone book, if Bezeq still printed them. He made for the elevator, when a door handle squeaked.

He turned around. Avi stood in the doorway. Moshe's chest tightened at the sight of him. His muscles braced for fight or flight.

Avi brushed his long, greasy fringe from his eyes. "Moshe," he said, spreading his arms wide. He stepped forward and wrapped Moshe a tight hug.

The warm welcome dumbfounded Moshe. Avi held him out at arms' length and looked him over. "I missed you, pal. C'mon in."

Moshe followed him inside. The cubicles stood empty, the headsets on the keyboards, the screens dark. *Where is everyone?*

"Coffee?" Avi said. "One sugar and a splash of three percent, right?"

"Sure. Thanks."

Moshe breathed in the familiar scent of the carpet while ceramic jars of coffee and sugar tinkled in the kitchenette.

The mounted LCD television was a silent black square between framed black-and-white photographs. A man wearing an impeccable suit and tie stood outside the stenciled door of Karlin & Son. A square watch glinted on his wrist. His hands rested on the shoulders of a young boy with combed hair. In the next photo, the man sat at a desk and held a bulky radio receiver to his ear.

Hot water poured from the water fountain, or "the bubbler" as Mathew used to say.

The imposing façade of a house in Jerusalem stone filled the third photograph. Two men stood on the street corner. The bearded man in the shiny dark suit and top hat stuck his chest out, the tail of his coat brushing the cobblestones. An Arab in a baggy gown and white headdress touched his arm and grinned beneath the bushy mustache and bulbous nose.

The ghostly quiet of the cubicles gnawed on his nerves.

Avi emerged from the kitchenette. "Here you go."

Moshe accepted the mug of coffee. "Thanks." He sipped it. If Avi was trying to kill him, he had used a tasteless and odorless poison. "You kept the photos."

"Are you kidding me, my brother?" Avi said. He called everyone his brother or his uncle, a habit that now annoyed Moshe. "What is Karlin & Son without the Karlins?" He pointed to the first photo. "That's you with your dad at the opening of the office, right?"

"Uh-huh."

"And there he is again with the first two-way radiotelephone system. Hard to believe we used to route cabs without computers, hey brother?"

Avi had been present at neither of those events. What he knew, he had learned from Moshe. He had called him "brother" twice in as many minutes. What was he plotting?

"What's with the Arab dude?"

"The man in coattails is my grandfather, also Moshe

Karlin. That was his house in the Old City."

"Pssh. You have a home in the Old City? Must be worth a fortune."

"It would be if we still had it. His parents—my great-grandparents—had to flee that home in 'twenty-nine. They returned when the violence settled, but lost it again in 'forty-eight." Moshe didn't have to explain the dates. As every Israeli knew, Arab mobs massacred Jews throughout the country in 1929, and in 1948 Arab armies invaded the nascent Jewish State. They expelled Jews from the Old City of Jerusalem and blew up synagogues.

"Our old neighborhood," Moshe continued, "is now in the Arab Quarter. The guy in the *kaffiyeh* was my grandfather's neighbor."

Avi, invader of Moshe's life, shook his head at the invaders of the past. "Let's have a seat."

They settled at the kitchen counter. A veil of steam rose between them. Moshe felt like a stranger in his own office. Which of them was the trespasser?

Avi said, "You scared the crap out of me yesterday."

"I was pretty surprised myself."

Avi studied Moshe's eyes. "You don't remember, do you?"

"Remember what?"

"Dying."

"I remember the party. Then I woke up on the Mount of Olives."

Avi leaned back on the kitchen chair. "So why did you come back? To haunt me?" He gave a nervous laugh. "Ghosts don't drink coffee, do they?"

Moshe put himself in Avi's shoes. How would he react if a dead friend showed up on his doorstep? He shrugged. "I'm alive. That's all I know."

"So you didn't see Heaven or whatever?"

"Nothing."

"God?"

"Nope."

Moshe sipped his coffee. He was getting used to this sort

of conversation. Whatever he had expected of his confrontation with Avi, it had not involved chitchat over coffee like old
friends.

He could hold out no longer. "Where is everyone?"

Avi put his coffee down on the counter. "I let them go."

Had his ears heard correctly? "You did what? Why?"

"Business has gone downhill. Fast."

"But we were about to expand."

Avi placed his iPhone on the counter. "And then this
came along. Some kid made an app for ordering taxis and our
drivers jumped ship. *We don't need you and your monthly
fees. Customers go direct.*"

Coffee spilled over Moshe's fingers. "Ow!" He put the
cup down.

"How many did we lose?"

"A trickle at first. Then the dam wall burst."

"But they still need the radios, don't they?" Karlin & Son
provided custom dual-frequency handsets and CB radios to
drivers free of charge. It was a major selling point.

"Obsolete," Avi said. "Now all a cabbie needs is a
smartphone and a data plan."

Moshe thought of the cab he had flagged down that first
morning at the Mount of Olives. The young driver had not
recognized his voice. He had probably never heard of Karlin
& Son.

"There's cash for a few more months," Avi continued,
"but without a miracle, I'll have to close the doors for good."

Avi might as well have floored him with a five-kilo sledge-
hammer. Moshe had died all over again. Karlin & Son—his
purpose in life, not to mention the decades of devotion—
poof! The flame of three generations sputtered out. On his
shift. Or right after. He had known that technology would be
the next step, but this—he had not seen this coming. He had
not evolved Karlin & Son in time. He had failed.

Or had he?

"Did you reach out to this—what is the company called?"

"Ridez. With a zee."

Moshe groaned. A company with a typo for a name had torpedoed Karlin & Son. "Have you reached out to them?"

"Why would I do that?"

Moshe wanted to cry. "To make a deal! They want to grow fast; we have the clientele. We can partner up."

Avi's face went pale. The strategy, apparently, had never occurred to him. His jaw clenched. "It's too late for that. They don't need us."

A dozen different pitches for cooperative ventures flashed in Moshe's mind, but during the last two critical years, he had not stood at the helm. Avi had.

Avi pulled a bunch of paper towels from the dispenser and dumped them on the spilled coffee. His face twisted with sudden rage. "They've always hated us," he said.

"Who has?"

"The drivers. They were dying to give us the finger. All but a few loyals and not enough to pay the rent."

Moshe stared at the mess of coffee and soaked paper towels on the counter. He had failed his father and his grandfather.

Avi's rage passed as quickly as it had arisen. He patted Moshe on the shoulder. "I'm sorry," he said. "Never thought you'd live to see the end of Karlin & Son, hey, brother, never mind to rise from the dead?"

Moshe gaped like a fish, unable to speak.

Avi got to his feet. "I've got something for you that will cheer you up." He strode to the corner office—Moshe's old office.

What could possibly cheer him up? A note from Galit? Or better yet—his wife and daughter in person. Were they waiting for him in the office?

Avi returned with a white plastic bag. He pulled out a folded beige sheet. "This must be yours."

Another parting prank from Avi? Galit had laundered the sheet. Moshe made a mental note to return it to the clothesline on the Mount of Olives.

"I thought you'd want this too." Avi handed him a square

silver rectangle on a black strap of battered leather. "It was your father's, right?"

Moshe caressed the heavy angled frame and weathered strap of the Rolex. He never thought he would see it again. "My grandfather's. Made in 'forty-eight."

"So it's real?" Avi seemed surprised. Would he have parted with it had he known it was valuable?

Moshe strapped his family heirloom to his wrist before Avi could change his mind. "This watch," Moshe explained, "was the last purchase he made before the war took everything. He once said that he would never sell the watch. It was a reminder that..." He trailed off.

He remembered that day in every detail. The thick square of silver had felt unbearably heavy in the hands of the young Moshe, but sunlight had glinted off the glass face like fairy dust, and he had accepted the challenge. Now, the added weight of the timepiece made his arm feel whole again.

A Karlin never quits. His father's words rang in his ears and a chill spread down his spine.

"Reminder of what?" Avi said.

"Of the life he wanted to regain." His vision blurred and he blinked back the tears. "Thank you."

"And then there's this." Avi held out a blue identity book. Moshe opened it. The card within displayed Moshe's mug shot and official details. Across the card and in large black letters, a rubber stamp had printed the word "deceased."

The surreal sensation Moshe had experienced at his own grave swept over him again. He pocketed the booklet.

Avi watched him closely. The watch was a peace offering, the identity card a veiled threat: *Moshe Karlin is dead. Move along, pal.*

Moshe held his gaze. He wanted more than his father's watch. Much more. How much was Avi willing to give? If the tables had turned, if Avi had come knocking on his door, would he have stepped aside?

Moshe folded his arms over his chest. "So," he said, addressing the elephant in the room, "how is Galit?"

Avi stretched his arms and inflated his chest. "You know Galit. A new malady every day. Every sore throat is strep. Every mosquito bite a cancer. No shortage of drama." He chuckled. "Last week she threw a plate at my head, shattered all over the kitchen floor."

"She can do that." Moshe laughed. Another tear crept into the corner of his eye. He missed her tantrums.

"Piece of work, isn't she? Tell me, my brother, how did you ever get her to calm down?"

Moshe adjusted the strap on his wrist. The drama had never bothered him much. In a perverse way, he had enjoyed the challenge. "Humor," he said. "Make her laugh."

Avi nodded. They were old friends joking around about shared experiences, only this shared experience happened to be Moshe's wife.

"Avi, I just—"

Avi raised his hands as if to deflect a blow. "Listen," he said. "This has been *very* difficult for us all. Especially Galit. And I understand you wanting to jump back into her life, really I do. I'm your best friend, remember? I miss you too. You think I want to keep little Talya from her dad?"

Moshe's lips parted. Avi had opened a door. He had argued Moshe's side. "If I could just speak to her for a few minutes—"

Avi shook his head and hugged his chest. "Do you have any idea what this has done to her? Seeing you, out of the blue, after two years in the ground? Give her time. A month, at least. Let her get used to the idea that you're alive, and then, slowly, we'll work something out."

The display of maturity and compassion humbled Moshe into silence. He wanted to hug Avi. He had misjudged his old friend, slandered him to Irina. Avi, the eternal playboy and ugly Israeli, had changed. Moshe owed him an apology. Tears welled up in his eyes again. "I don't know what to say."

"Don't mention it." Avi stood. Their meeting was over. He put an arm around Moshe's shoulders and escorted him to the door.

"Call me in two months?"

"You said one month."

Avi pointed a finger pistol at Moshe and winked. "One month it is," he said, and he shut the door.

CHAPTER 13

By the time Moshe reached the rabbi's home, the sunlight was fading fast. He had danced along the back alleys and streets of Jerusalem on his way back and taken far more time than necessary.

Irina answered the door in her potato sack of a gown. "I was worried about you," she said. "Are you OK?"

"More than OK. I'm getting my life back!"

Her face glowed. "That's wonderful!"

"Where's the rabbi?"

"They're bathing the kids. Might take a while."

"Let's go."

She gave a cautious smile, as though suspecting that he had lost his mind. "Go where?"

"Out for dinner. We're celebrating."

He led her across the defunct train tracks, overgrown with grass, toward Emek Refaim and told her about his visit to Karlin & Son. The girl in the formless gown and the man in the house slippers won amused glances from passersby, freshly showered and dressed for dinner dates. Moshe would have to speak with Rabbi Yosef about expanding their wardrobe.

They stopped at Pizza Sababa on Emek Refaim, ordered slices, and sat at one of two wobbly square tables. Not a fancy

meal, but within budget, and it felt good to get out of the
rabbanit's hair—and fridge—for a change.

In a month, he'd be back in Galit's life.

He asked Irina how her day had gone. She had spent the
morning at the Mount of Olives Cemetery with Rabbi Yosef,
searching for another disturbed grave and hoping that the
names on the tombstones would jolt her memory, to no avail.

Irina gobbled a strand of melted cheese that dangled from
her slice of mushroom pizza. "How did you and Galit meet?"

Moshe took a sip from his bottle of Coke. "Avi dragged
me to Hangar 17, a nightclub in Talpiot. I remember that
night as if it was yesterday. Fake smoke. Disco ball suspended
from the rafters. Seventies music. They played that Bee Gees
song from Saturday Night Fever. 'Somebody help me. I'm
going nowhere.'"

"'Staying Alive'!" Irina said.

"Yes! Wait a minute—how do you know that?"

Irina seemed just as surprised and delighted as he was. Her
fairy eyes widened like those of a little girl. "I don't know. I
know all sorts of useless things, just nothing about me. Go
on, maybe I'll remember more."

"I saw her from across the room," he said. The moment
had frozen in time: the shiny jeans that hugged her hips; the
frills on her shirt that drew his eye from her neckline to the
generous orbs below; her long, dark hair that fell over her
shoulders; large eyes; red lips. "When our eyes met and she
smiled I felt an electric current rip through my body."

"Like a fairy tale," Irina said, enthralled.

Moshe continued, "I walked up to her, through the crowd.
A dozen pickup lines came to mind but I felt as though we
already knew each other, so I just said, 'You're late.'"

Irina's mouth dropped open. "You didn't."

"Crazy, right? She didn't bat an eyelid. She said, 'I got here
as fast as I could.'"

Irina giggled. "Are you making this up?"

"Then Avi arrived with our beers. I swept them from his
hands with a 'thanks' and gave one to Galit. I found us a nice,

quiet spot and we talked. We danced. We went for a stroll and landed up at the Tayelet." Irina shook her head, so he explained. "The Haas Promenade. South of the Old City. Great view. We sat on the wall of the promenade, side by side, our feet dangling over the edge. We stared at the huge walls of the Old City as they glowed in golden spotlight, and we talked until morning. 'So what do you want out of life, Moshe Karlin?' she asked me. 'To conquer the world,' I said. She just laughed. 'And how are you going to do that?' 'One day at a time,' I said. 'One day at a time.' It became a running joke. 'Time to conquer the world,' we'd say after breakfast and head out to work."

Moshe took another bite of pizza. That last morning, the day of his birthday party and the day he had died, there had been no playful banter at the breakfast table. He had dined alone and hurried off to the office. He had not made much of that then but now that solitary last breakfast seemed like a sign. An omen.

"That's very special," Irina said. Her eyes glazed over. "I hope I find a love like that."

"Maybe you already have," he said. "And he's waiting for you to come home."

They chewed their pizza in silence. He had tried to encourage her but his words had only made her sad.

A month. Thirty days seemed unbearably long. And what exactly had Avi promised him after that month? Galit had moved on. Would she turn back the clock two years, or would he remain a ghostly spectator at the sidelines of her life forever?

Avi had been right about one thing: Moshe had never thought he'd live to see the end of Karlin & Son. It still seemed unreal. Had he lived, he probably would have been powerless to stop that. The rosy image of his perfect former life lost its shine.

Even if, by some miracle, Avi stepped aside, how would Moshe provide for his wife and daughter? Like his grandfather, he'd have to start over from nothing. He had never prepared for that possibility. His urge to celebrate now seemed grossly premature if not outright delusional.

"Are you OK?" Irina asked.

"It's not going to be easy," Moshe confessed. "Karlin & Son was the only job I've ever known. I didn't go to university. Why bother? A thriving family business waited for me. Now that's gone. I don't know how I'll survive."

"Don't worry," she said. "I'll help you."

Moshe had to laugh. She didn't even know who she was, but she was ready to solve all his problems. Memory loss had its perks.

"What?" Her lower eyelids twitched. Was he making fun of her?

"Nothing." He raised his bottle of Coke. "To friends."

The brave fairy-woman answered his toast and their bottles met in mid-air with an optimistic clink. "To friends."

Moshe would need all the friends he could get.

Then, as he swallowed the last of his drink, he remembered. He had a friend. An old friend. A friend with unrestricted access to Galit. How had he not thought of her before?

CHAPTER 14

Irina had never seen the inside of a police station. Not as far as she could remember. In other words, not in the past twenty-four hours.

She could count the clues to her former life on the fingers of one hand: late twenties; Russian; speaks Hebrew; and no sign of childbirth. The last fact meant nothing—her brand new body provided little evidence. Cancer and Car Accident topped her list of probable causes of death, but she preferred not to think about her demise.

Instead, she filled the blank pages of her past with fantasies. As a wealthy heiress—a modern-day princess—she flitted across the globe to exotic getaways and dodged the advances of celebrities and moguls. Then she fell into the powerful embrace of her tall husband and doted on her brood of laughing children. The contradictions in her alternate pasts didn't bother her in the least; she got to live the best of all possible worlds.

As she followed Moshe, however, into the low building of Jerusalem stone and beneath the legend that read "Israel Police," other possible worlds loomed in her mind and her stomach tightened. Did she have a criminal record? Would the officers arrest her on sight and lock her away for crimes she didn't remember? Would she even know whether she was guilty? Her fate lay at the mercy of other people's memories. She was glad to have Moshe at her side.

A police officer at the entrance waved a metal detector baton over their clothes. Her jeans had frayed at the hems and the T-shirt showed bleach stains from too many laundry cycles, but they beat the rabbanit's shapeless gowns. That morning, Rabbi Yosef had escorted them to Tal Chaim, where she and Moshe selected old clothes from cardboard donation boxes and clothes hangers in a basement. The rabbi paid a few shekels for each item and they promised to pay him back as soon as they could. Then Rabbi Yosef hurried off to work and they set out for the station.

Irina studied the eyes of passersby for a glimmer of recognition: commuters on the bus; old ladies towing wheeled trolleys; loiterers dragging on cigarettes. Did they know her? Would they open a window on her former life? Most women ignored her. Not the men. One middle-aged man locked eyes with her so long that she stopped to ask him whether he knew her. "No, honey," he said and winked. "But I'd like to." Moshe had placed a protective hand on her shoulder and they moved on. Men stared. She'd have to get used to that.

The police officer waved them in. Two women with blue uniforms and dark ponytails sat behind an information counter. They looked like identical twins. Twins with very different temperaments. One sat upright and typed away at a hidden computer terminal. The other glanced at them, her eyelids droopy with boredom. "Yes?"

"My friend has lost her memory," Moshe said. "We were hoping you could help us find out who she is."

My friend. His voice was clear and confident, his words polite. Even with the bus driver.

"Lost person inquiries are down the hall, room 113 or on the telephone service."

Moshe glanced at Irina. "I'm not sure that will help. We don't think she's missing."

The other policewoman stopped typing and perked up. "If you don't know who she is, how do you know she's not missing, ah?"

Moshe did not say, "Because until yesterday she was dead." That would earn them a referral to a psychiatric ward.

Bored Cop turned to Irina. "Identity card?"

"She doesn't have one."

"*Your* identity card?" she countered.

No Nobel Prize for Bored Cop this year but she got points for determination. Moshe produced the card jacket of blue plastic. Bored Cop studied the contents.

A barrel-chested policeman with coffee-colored skin strutted behind the counter. His eyes lingered on Irina for a split second and her stomach clenched again. He continued down the corridor. The tension dissipated. *Was that disappointment or relief?*

Bored Cop elbowed Perky Cop. "Says here that he's dead." She handed the blue card jacket to her colleague. Perky studied the document and then Moshe.

"That's a mistake," Moshe said, with a good-natured chuckle. "Obviously."

Perky tapped at a hidden keyboard and stared at the hidden screen.

"Moshe Karlin?"

"Yes."

"Moshe Karlin died two years ago. So how can this be your ID, ah?"

Their search for Irina's identity had turned them into identity theft suspects.

"I told you, there was a mistake. Can I have that back?"

"Everything in order?" Barrel-Chested Cop leaned a large, hairy hand on the counter. A handgun poked out of the holster on his belt. His mouth drew a tight, short line. His skin reddened about his cheeks. Irina's stomach tightened again.

"My friend has lost her memory," Moshe repeated.

Perky handed Barrel-Chest the ID and pointed. "And he's dead." The silver plate above the badge on his chest read "Golan."

"I'll take it from here," he said. "This way."

Irina and Moshe exchanged a nervous look. Were they in trouble or was this a lucky break? They followed Golan down the corridor of closed doors. He opened one and stepped into an office. The sign at the door read *Detective Alon Golan. Homicide.*

Irina felt her throat dry.

A desk dominated the room. He pointed to two empty chairs, then closed the door and perched on the edge of the desk.

"Memory loss?" he said.

Irina nodded.

He clasped his fingers and turned to Moshe. "How do you know each other?"

"We met yesterday. I'm just trying to help."

Golan studied them, his eyes large, dark, and expressionless. "Are you sure you don't remember anything? People? Places?"

Irina shook her head.

Golan nodded. "I'll see what I can do."

"Thank you," she said. He stepped behind the desk and poked thick fingers at a keyboard.

She breathed, finally at ease. Moshe gave her a reassuring smile. *Lucky break, it is.*

Thick fingers drummed the desk as Golan waited.

Irina held her breath. This is it. Princess or pauper. Mother or maid. Which will it be? Her hand reached for Moshe's and he gave hers a squeeze.

Golan leaned toward the screen. "There are no missing person reports for your description."

Irina felt her shoulders slump.

He clasped his hands over the desk. "We can test your fingerprints. Not all citizens are in the database but it's worth a shot. Is that OK?"

"Yes, of course."

"Follow me."

He led them to another room, where a policewoman with

half-moon spectacles and a mane of thinning red hair asked Irina to press the thumb and four fingers of each hand onto an electronic pad. The woman clicked a mouse and glanced at a screen. Officer Golan leaned against the wall and folded his arms.

Irina tried to keep her breath even. Convicts had fingerprints on file for sure. If they found a match, would that make her a criminal?

The policewoman tutted, peering at Golan over her glasses. "She's not in the system."

Irina released pent-up air from her lungs. Back to square one.

Golan thanked the policewoman and led them out. In the corridor, he took a photo of Moshe's identity card on his mobile phone and returned the blue book. "I'll be in touch if anything comes up," Golan said. "Contact me if you need anything." He handed them each a business card.

They thanked him and left the station, down the steps to street level in the Talpiot industrial zone.

"Disappointed?" Moshe asked.

"I suppose. For a moment there, I almost wished I were a felon. Any identity is better than none."

He laughed. "We can put your photo on fliers and pin them up around the city."

She remembered the leers of the men on the street. "Maybe later," she said. "If nothing else comes up."

Moshe nodded. He understood. Her new friend glanced down the street and a sadness fell over his features.

"She'll come around," Irina said. He looked up, surprised that she had read his thoughts. "If she has a brain in her skull, she'll beg you to come home." That made him grin.

Home. A short word. Simple. Warm. And yet so elusive. Home was all she wanted.

He gave her a quizzical look. "Do you mind if we make a detour on the way back?"

"Not at all. My busy schedule just freed up." Moshe had given her a few hours of his time; she'd be happy to return the favor.

He asked, "Are you hungry?"

"Very." She had started the day with a single bowl of Telma cornflakes in the rabbi's kitchen.

"Good," he said. "You'll need a healthy appetite."

CHAPTER 15

"Today," Rabbi Yosef said, "we will learn something new."

Excited noises rippled down the neat rows of desks, and smiles bubbled on the expectant faces of twenty boys. The second graders loved the spice he sprinkled into his classes: stories of villagers in India who carried pails of water from the communal hand pump; the laws of physics that keep airplanes afloat in thin air.

The enrollment requirements at Daas Torah Primary excluded children who had a television at home, and although their parents instructed their children in matters of Jewish custom, they offered little insight into the mundane world beyond the four cubits of *Halakha*. And what normal young boy wouldn't welcome a break from the intricate laws of the blessings recited before consuming food and drink.

Rabbi Yosef stood before the class, his back to the whiteboard. Once he opened the can, the worms of curiosity would not return without a struggle. But how could he remain silent? First Moshe, then Irina. An isolated incident had developed into a pattern. At night, awake in his bed, he could think of little else.

Before class that morning, he had driven to the Mount of Olives and stalked between the rows of the dead. The heavy slabs over the graves, once the final seals of fate, were actually revolving doors. He peered behind headstones and the trunks of the olive trees. His failure to discover new arrivals did not dampen his spirits. Both Moshe and Irina had awoken from death in the early morning. The miracle obeyed rules, as did Nature, and the mounting discoveries bounced inside him like bubbles in a well-shaken bottle of champagne. If he didn't share the good tidings soon, he'd explode.

The expectant smiles widened with anticipation. A new healing sun rose on the horizon. Warm rays of change sped toward them. Today, a pair of protective glasses would serve his students better than a debate entitled, "Bananas, fruit or vegetable?"

"Who knows the song *'Ani Maamin'*?"

The first two words of the familiar song got the boys singing.

"I believe with perfect faith in the coming of the Messiah. And even though he may tarry, nonetheless, I wait every day for his coming."

"Very good. That is number twelve of Maimonides' thirteen principles of faith. The last principle is this." He read from a prayer book. "'I believe with perfect faith that there will be a revival of the dead at the time willed by the Creator, blessed be His name and exalted be His mention for eternity.'"

The boys stared in silence. Talk of the Resurrection required wrapping their minds around death, a concept far removed from their youthful world.

"In other words," he continued, "at some time in the future, God will give life to people who have died."

He swapped the prayer book for a Bible, but before he could turn to Ezekiel's Valley of Dry Bones, a little hand shot into the air.

"Yes, Menachem?"

"Will Grandpa Isaac come back to life too?"

"I'm sure he will."

A smile washed over Menachem's face. He'd see his grandpa again. Then he looked concerned. "Will he be back today?"

"Probably not today. God alone knows when. But," he added, "it might be sooner than we think."

"But," the boy said, his concern deepening, "my sisters have already moved into his room."

He had a good point. The resurrected would need a place to stay. Rabbi Yosef would not be able to host them all. Clothing too. The basement outlet for secondhand clothing at Tal Chaim would not meet future demand.

Rabbi Yosef improvised, "We'll all help him as best we can."

Menachem raised his hand again. "Will Grandpa still have his wheelchair?"

Rabbi Yosef had scoured the volumes of Talmud and Midrash in his library for details on the awaited resurrection, following cross-references, and hunting down more obscure sources on the Internet. "No," he said. "He will rise in full health. Although, according to one opinion, the blind and lame will rise with their disability so that the Messiah can heal them."

The little boy's smile threatened to split his face.

Another hand waved in the air. "Will Tuli come back too?"

A murmur of muffled laughter.

"Who is Tuli?" The rabbi had met Yankel's father at the parent-teacher evening, but he was sure that neither his mother nor his siblings went by that name.

"I found him on the street and gave him milk but Ima said he's dirty and that cats belong outside. The next day, Ima said he died."

"Oh." The seven-year-olds revealed far more about home life than any parent imagined. "Sorry," he said, with a sympathetic frown. "The resurrection is only for people."

Another hand. Then three more. Class had become a news conference. He pointed to a questioner.

"And the goyim? Will they come back as well?"

Yosef had hoped to avoid that one. "Only Jews," he said. "And only in Israel," he added, preempting the follow-on.

"According to some Midrashic sources," he added to appease his conscience. Few details of the End were unanimous.

"My *zeidi* is buried in America," said a distraught little Yankel. "Won't he come back to life?"

"Don't worry," Yosef said. He was *really* hoping to avoid that one. "God will provide tunnels." He swallowed hard. "The dead will roll through the tunnels to the Land of Israel and then come back to life. Next question!"

Another hand. "Uncle Dudi married Auntie Avigayil after Auntie Ora died. If Auntie Ora comes back, will Uncle Dudi have two wives?"

The kids giggled. For every answer, three more hands rose. No hope of squeezing the worms back in the can now. He did his best to answer or parry the rest before the bell chimed.

"We will have a lot of questions in those days," he said. "But Elijah the Prophet will return in time to answer them all."

Thankfully, the second graders had not raised the topic of reincarnation—whether a soul would be resurrected in a separate body for each previous incarnation—or class would never have ended.

In the staff room, he ate his packed lunch: a tuna sandwich and an apple. He could do with Elijah's wisdom now. The Resurrection weighed large and heavy on the shoulders of a simple schoolteacher with modest beginnings. The World to Come called for the Messiah, for rabbis of the greatest stature and purest lineage.

He paused mid-bite. *You silly man. What did you think you were trying to do?* He abandoned his sandwich and reached for his phone. He searched for the number—the number he dialed in his darkest moments, the number he had not used in over four years. He reached the end of his contacts list and tuna churned in his stomach. Had he erased the number by accident? Had he failed to transfer the details from his old phone?

Then the precious ten digits displayed on the screen and

Yosef breathed again. God had sent Moshe and Irina his way for a reason. Even a humble teacher could serve as a stepping-stone on the path to the Final Redemption. For he, unworthy Yosef, knew just the man to usher in the Messianic Era.

CHAPTER 16

Noga stared at the mystery patient in room 419C of the Shaare Zedek Medical Center. Slings hung from the ceiling and suspended the plastic casts on his left arm and right leg. A tuft of thick, jet-black hair fell over the white bandage that wrapped his forehead. Stubble peppered the solid jawline above the spongy neck brace. The name on the clipboard at the foot of the bed read *Ploni Almoni*. John Doe. Under the covers he slept, his handsome face a picture of serenity.

She shouldn't stare. She shouldn't even be in his room. Noga had wandered the wards, as she did, wearing a white cloak—although, being neither doctor nor nurse, she had no right to either activity—when she noticed the leg cast on the bed through the open door. On a hunch, she ventured inside and now her eyes would not budge from him.

"Cute, isn't he?" said a voice behind her. She spun around. Eliana smirked. The Russian senior nurse with the beefy forearms and dirty mind moved about the ward with surprising stealth.

"I was just..." Noga began in her defense. What exactly was she doing?

"Feast your eyes. He won't mind." Eliana stripped the sheets from the bed on the other side of the partition curtain.

"What happened?"

"Motorcycle accident. Out cold since he arrived yesterday morning. Dr. Stern operated on him most of the day."

A biker. Noga's interest surged.

"Will he be OK?"

Eliana bobbed her head from side to side. "Time will tell."

Noga looked him over. The nurse was right: he was cute.

"I wouldn't get my hopes up if I were you," said Eliana, reading her mind.

"Why not?" Eliana had tried and failed to set her up with any number of doctors. Why stop now?

Eliana placed her hands on her hips, the stance of a protective mother. "If by some miracle he survives, he'll probably have brain damage. Which might actually be an improvement," she added with a sour grin. "The fool wasn't even wearing a helmet."

"Oh."

Eliana bustled out of the room to her next task.

That explained a lot. Noga had terrible luck with men. Scumbags flew to her like fruit bats to overripe mangos. Her extreme bashfulness around men did not help. The result: still single at twenty-eight.

An ECG blipped on a stand. She moved to the head of the bed and placed her transparent folder of forms on the bedside table. She stood over him. His breath came deep and even. *What a waste.*

He lay there. Nameless. Helpless. Alone in the world. Like her.

She put out her hand and—fingers trembling—she touched his shoulder. His skin felt warm through the hospital gown. *What am I doing?* She moved her hand to his forehead and stroked the shock of black hair.

There was a sudden movement, and she gasped. Fingers tightened around her wrist. He stared up at her, an urgent plea in his dark brown eyes. And a fire.

He spoke, the words flowing with a mad intensity. Noga didn't wait for him to finish. She wrenched her arm free and fled the room.

CHAPTER 17

Moshe knocked on the door of the second-floor apartment. The sound bounced off the lumpy wall plaster in the dingy stairwell. Was he doing the right thing?

The visit could be dangerous. Not for him or Irina, but for their hostess. The surprise that waited outside her front door might succeed where Hitler had failed.

The apartment building in Jerusalem's Katamon neighborhood had no elevator. The hall light flickered out, so he pressed the light button again.

In the 1950s, the State of Israel had built the long, unimaginative apartment blocks to house the waves of Jews who had fled Arab countries in North Africa and the Middle East with little more than the clothes on their backs. These *shikunim* returned maximum living units for minimum investment. At the time, the refugees must have felt lucky to trade their shanties in the absorption towns for a solid roof over their heads. Two generations later, however, the cement monstrosities still marred large swaths of prime Jerusalem property, even as realty prices skyrocketed.

He used the buzzer. He shifted on his feet, which itched inside the scuffed sneakers from the Tal Chaim secondhand store.

Behind the door came the sound of shuffling feet. The

lock rattled and a hunched old woman stared up at Moshe. Her eyes filled the thick lenses of her glasses. She froze. Had an aneurysm paralyzed her? The visit was a terrible mistake.

Then Savta Sarah reached out both arms. "Moshe!" she gushed. An ecstatic smile split her wrinkled face from ear to ear. She pulled his head down, kissed both his cheeks in Hungarian fashion, and beckoned him inside.

Had she forgotten that he was dead? He returned Irina's surprised glance and shrugged. The familiar homey scents of carpet, wood polish, and old lady hung in the air of the square living room. He closed the door behind them.

"This is for you." He held out his offering: a small plastic doll in a ballroom gown.

The old woman's eyes lit up like those of a little girl. She turned the doll over and played with the limbs. "Beautiful!" She shuffled to the vitrine of shiny wood that covered one wall of the pokey room and contained books and ceramic dishes, and she positioned the doll on a shelf beside a dozen other dolls. "Thank you, Moshe. You always thought of me."

Thought. Her use of the past tense jarred him. She had not forgotten his passing, and the idea of a ghostly visitation didn't seem to bother her.

"Sit! Sit!" she implored.

She waved them to a small square table of worn plywood. The hard surfaces of the steel-framed chairs pressed against his back and bottom. Savta Sarah set two large and flowery dinner plates before them, and disappeared into the kitchen.

They sat at the table. A clock ticked over the background music of busy kitchen sounds.

A large black-and-white family portrait dominated the adjacent wall. Six children orbited two seated parents. Pins held the mother's hair in a tight bun. The frilled edges of a laced bodice peeked out the neck of her coat. The husband looked respectable with his trimmed beard and heavy frock coat. Four daughters—with prim white dresses and braided hair—stood behind their parents, and two little boys—trousers, wooly coats, and red cheeks—stood at attention on either side.

Irina followed his gaze. "Is that her family?"

"Savta Sarah is second from the right. Dark curls."

"All in Jerusalem?"

"All dead. Murdered in the Holocaust. Only Savta Sarah survived. When the Russians liberated Auschwitz, she moved to Palestine. Married. Gave birth to Galit's mom and uncle. That's them as kids." He pointed to the framed photo of a little boy and girl on a cracked sidewalk, one of many smaller color photographs that surrounded the portrait. "The rest are grandchildren and great-grandchildren." He did the math. "Four grandchildren. A bunch of great-grandchildren too."

The photos of her descendants circled the black-and-white portrait with defiance. *Take that, Hitler.*

"Wow," Irina said. "What a large family."

"We didn't see them much. Galit's uncle moved to America after the Six Day War. Her parents followed soon after we got married."

"Why?"

"They were convinced that, any day, our Arab neighbors would wipe Israel off the map. You can liberate Jews from a concentration camp, but a little shard of Auschwitz still lodges in their heart. The hearts of their children and grandchildren too."

Irina didn't probe further. Instead, she pointed at another framed photograph. "There you are," she said. She had found the close-up from the wedding. Galit leaned her head on his chest. White dress. Big smiles. Love sparkling in their eyes.

Savta Sarah reappeared and unloaded a stack of tinfoil trays onto the table. She shoveled mounds of food onto their plates: steaming white rice; meatballs in tomato gravy; sticky triangles of baked chicken with potato and sweet potato. The savory smells made his stomach growl. Their octogenarian hostess returned to the kitchen.

"Wow," Irina said, her mouth full. "This is delicious!"

"Pace yourself," he said. "She's only getting started."

On cue, Savta reappeared bearing fresh trays: cabbage

stuffed with minced meat and rice; ox tongue boiled soft as butter; beef goulash; *nokedli*, the Hungarian dumplings of oddly shaped egg noodle; and wobbly squares of beef jelly. Hungarians, it seems, had never heard of cholesterol.

"How did she know we were on our way?"

Moshe chewed a juicy meatball. "She didn't. She used to run a catering business and never learned to cook for less than a hundred people. She didn't stop when she retired. The cooking keeps her going."

Savta Sarah pulled up a chair and watched them eat. "Have some more stuffed cabbage, Moshe. It's your favorite. You've hardly eaten a thing. Is it any good?"

"Excellent!" Moshe and Irina said as one.

Savta Sarah didn't seem to hear them. "The meat didn't come out well today." She clucked. "The chicken burned on the stove."

"Not at all," Irina said. "Aren't you going to eat?"

"I ate earlier."

Moshe had never seen Savta Sarah eat. A sad, distant look clouded her eyes. *Here we go.*

"We had a lovely home," she said. "In Poton," she added for Irina's sake, "a village near Dunaszerdahely in Hungary. Or Czechoslovakia. We moved countries every other year without even moving house." The bags under her eyes seemed to sag lower. "One day, the Germans took my father. We never saw him again. There was no money. I was fourteen. What could I do? I went to the city and bought fabric to sell at home. That was how we survived. Then the Germans came for us too."

She shook her head at bygone years. "I was the worst of the children. The troublemaker. My sisters were angels. Why did God take them and leave me?"

Moshe had heard the stories countless times and for once he understood how she felt. He wiped his mouth on a paper napkin. "Savta, you do know that I died, don't you?"

"Of course." She leaned forward, conspiratorial. "And now you're back! Edith told me." Savta had named her daughter after her dear mother. Galit had told her mother, who, in turn, had told her mother, Savta Sarah. The news of his return had crossed the Atlantic twice. He interpreted that as a good omen.

"I told her to go back to you," Savta continued. She reached over and pinched his cheek. "Moshe is like me," she told Irina. "*Businessman.*" She had used the one and only English word she seemed to know. "I was so glad when Galit married you." Her face darkened. "And so sad when you passed."

"Galit won't speak to me," he said.

"You must make her listen," Sarah said. "Before she marries that no-good friend of yours."

His mind did a double take. "Before she... what?"

"You don't know? The wedding is in two weeks."

He steadied himself on the table. "They're not married?"

"No." She tutted. "He moved into her home without even a ring."

Moshe reeled with the sudden discovery: Galit and Avi were not married. Moshe had assumed too much. He didn't know whether to jump for joy or to punch the wall. *Avi, you lying bastard!*

"I have to speak to Galit."

"Not dressed like that, you won't." Savta eyed his worn shoes under the table.

"I have no choice. She inherited everything. I have only a hundred shekels to my name."

Savta got to her feet. "That will do," she said. "I'll show you."

CHAPTER 18

Yosef waited in the foyer of Frumin House in downtown Jerusalem and hoped that he would not sound crazy.

The stately block of rounded Jerusalem stone stood three stories tall over King George Street in the center of town. Once home to the Knesset—the legislative branch of the Israeli government—the structure now housed the Rabbinical Court.

Beyond the security fences and guards, the foyer teemed with rabbis and their clients, who awaited hearings on matters of marriage, divorce, and religious conversion. Yosef felt out of place among the sure-footed, bustling masses. When the great doors of the main courtroom swung open, he glimpsed rows of wooden seats and white pillars, and heard snatches of arguments and pronouncements.

The doors swung open again and a tall, straight-backed rabbi in a black bowler and impeccable suit emerged between the doors, a briefcase of black leather in his hand. He scanned the rushing crowd and, when his eyes fell on Yosef, he smiled.

"Reb Yosef," he said, gripping Yosef's hand, his perfect ivory teeth gleaming. "Good to see you again, my friend."

Although Rabbi Emden soared leagues above the poor teacher and neighborhood rabbi, he always addressed his former student as a colleague. "Coffee?"

Rabbi Emden treated him to a Nescafe from a vending machine. The rabbi placed his briefcase on a vacant bench and they sat side by side.

After an exchange of pleasantries, Yosef got to the point.

"A man in my congregation passed away two years ago," he said. "A few days ago I bumped into him on our street, alive and well."

The older rabbi studied Yosef for a while. Would he dismiss the story out of hand? Did he think his old pupil had lost his mind?

"Are you sure of this?"

"I officiated at the funeral. I saw the body. It's him. He's been staying at our house since I found him. He eats and sleeps. Remembers nothing since he died. And one more thing." Yosef leaned in close and whispered. "He has no navel."

Rabbi Emden seemed to understand immediately. "The grave?"

"I checked the next day. Undisturbed, except for a small hole in the ground at the corner of the cover stone. And we found a woman."

"Also resurrected?"

"Yes, and with severe memory loss."

Rabbi Emden's eyes moved as he processed the data and matched the facts with the sea of Jewish learning stored in his great mind. A high-profile rabbi would have to think twice before diving into speculations of the Resurrection.

"This is big," he said eventually. "Very big."

Yosef sucked in air. He had known that his mentor would not let him down.

"We need to tell the world," Yosef said. "To announce the miracle. What a Sanctification of God's Name this will be! We must prepare for the others that will come."

Rabbi Emden rested a reasonable hand on his shoulder. "Slow down, Yosef. Two resurrected Jews do not the Resurrection make. Now, start again. From the beginning. Tell me all you have learned. We must prepare our case."

"Our case?"

"Yes, my friend." His wise eyes glittered. "We must present your findings to the Great Council."

CHAPTER 19

The Prophet opened his eyes. He lay on a bed in a strange room. Clear liquid dripped into a thin plastic tube from a pouch on a metal stand above him. Electric sockets and mounted equipment lined the headboard behind. A framed print of Van Gogh's *Sunflowers* hung on the shiny green wall.

A machine emitted rhythmic beeps. Outside the room, busy feet hurried and voices spoke in hushed tones. A telephone rang.

He knew about hospitals from TV, but had never had cause to visit one. How had he gotten there? Images flashed before his eyes. The rock walls of the Mount of Olives. Two men and a white car. The blare of a truck horn. Glass shattering. Bones crunching. *His* bones.

That's impossible!

He turned his head. Blue sky filled an open window of steamed glass.

He must get out. He must complete his mission. He moved, and pain flared in his head. His left arm and right leg swayed heavily in slings. The thick casts locked his joints in position.

"Good morning," said a man's voice. The man at the foot of the bed wore a white cloak and gave him an appraising glance. "Or rather," he added, "good afternoon." The doctor drew near and flashed a light in his eyes. He asked him to watch his finger as he moved it back and forth. Patches of gray hair covered his temples and worry lines furrowed his cheeks. The identification card clipped to the pocket of the gown read Dr. Yariv Stern. He pocketed the flashlight and trained his grim, penetrating stare on his patient.

How much does he know? The Prophet swallowed hard. "How long have I been here?"

"A day."

"When can I go home?"

Dr. Stern gave a short laugh. "Your skull is fractured. Your leg is broken in two places. You have a shattered left arm and three broken ribs. You're lucky to be alive. We weren't sure you'd wake up. You'll be here for some time." He drew a breath. "Now tell me: What's your name?"

Panic seized the Prophet. He racked his memory. Who was he? What year was this? *Remember!*

"Eli," he said. "Eli Katz." *Yes, that was it!* Relief washed over him.

Dr. Stern repeated the name. He mulled over the information like a wine connoisseur swishing a new vintage in his mouth. Pale blue eyes searched his face. "Are you sure?" he said.

The dread returned. *Does he know?* Eli managed a slight nod of his head.

"That's strange. Earlier you claimed to be Elijah the Prophet from the village of Tishbe in Gilad."

Oh, God, no! He feigned surprise. "Did I?"

"Yes indeed. You were quite adamant."

Eli managed a nervous laugh. "Must have been a fever dream."

"You also said that the End of Days is nigh and that you had an urgent mission to fulfill. A mission from God."

Oh, crap! Never tell anyone. The Golden Rule. The only thing standing between him and the stake or, these days, the insane asylum. He had broken the Golden Rule for the first time in two millennia. *Quick! Think of something!* He said, "Could it be the drugs?"

The doctor pursed his lips. "You're not on painkillers, if that's what you mean. You were comatose. I can prescribe some if you like."

"Yes, please." He had never taken medication, not even vitamins. He had never had the need, but now he was eager to start. By the time the pills arrived, he would be gone, but the request would get the doctor out of the room. A few seconds alone. That was all he needed.

The doctor walked to the foot of the bed, picked up a clipboard, and scribbled with a pen. "Your medical aid?"

"Don't have any. I'll pay direct."

The doctor's eyebrows lifted. "That'll be very expensive."

"I'll take care of it."

"Would you like me to contact anyone? Relatives? Friends?"

"No." Then he added, "Maybe later," to allay suspicion.

The doctor put down the clipboard. "I'll stop by later," he said. "Mr. Eli Katz."

When his footfalls faded, Eli closed his eyes. "God, please. Heal me, please." He flexed the muscle in the center of his brain. He pictured the bones mending, torn flesh and sinew regenerating throughout his battered body.

He held his breath. *Sit up!* He willed his limbs to move, his neck to lift from the pillow. The suspended leg trembled. *That's it!*

Pain burst in his skull and tore along his spine like a bolt of lightning. His head slumped back on the pillow. He breathed in short, fast spurts. The beep of the heart monitor accelerated. The room began to spin and fade to white. Sweat trickled down his brow and stung his eye. He blinked back the pain.

This can't be happening!

Tak-tak-tak.

The sound of tapping on glass came from the end of the room. He turned his head. A large black bird hopped on the windowsill. The bird tossed its head from side to side and studied him with bulging black eyes. A strip of torn meat dangled from the sharp beak.

A crow. A cruel bird. And an old friend. The Boss had a flair for poetic justice.

The bird gulped down the morsel. *Caw! Caw!*

Eli groaned. "OK," he said aloud. "I get the message. Now, please, get me out of here."

The bird shook its head, and, with a final, loud caw, flew off.

CHAPTER 20

A bell jingled as Moshe and Irina left the throng of pedestrians on Jaffa Street and followed Savta Sarah into the shop.

The old lady made a beeline for the till. She had dressed in a beige blouse and skirt for the occasion and donned a matching round hat with faux flowers.

Moshe fell back. He folded his arms over his chest. "This will be embarrassing," he whispered.

Irina scanned the display shelves of men's shoes. "Why?"

"You'll see."

Savta Sarah adjusted the strap of her handbag on her shoulder and placed a hand on the counter, which came to her chin. "Good afternoon, sir," she said with the well-oiled voice of an attendant to the Queen of England. "My grandson-in-law requires a pair of your finest shoes."

The man behind the counter looked as though he had just rolled out of bed. He pulled at his crumpled T-shirt and straightened his toupee. He peered at the little old lady, and a cunning smile cracked his pockmarked face, the smile of a Tyrannosaurus rex scenting a wounded herbivore. "Today is my lucky day," the smile seemed to say. Unbeknownst to him, a grandmother-sized asteroid hurtled toward the planet at dinosaur-extinction speed.

With a generous sweep of a hairy arm, he indicated the

display shelves and haphazard piles of shoeboxes. "Madam, we have the widest selection of the best quality footwear in the country. What type of shoe does your grandson desire?" He had adopted the old lady's genteel speech in a display of showmanship that jarred with his shabby outer appearance. The street show had begun.

All eyes turned to Moshe and so he pointed to a pair of brown loafers.

"An excellent choice," he said, in his Savile Row voice, and he hurried to the storage room behind the counter.

Moshe sat down on the low padded shoe bench and liberated his sore feet from the worn sneakers.

Two weeks. Avi had always had an eye for Galit—who didn't?—but he had been his best friend. Friends didn't deceive friends. They didn't steal their wives. The treachery made Moshe's blood boil.

"You're in luck," said the shoe salesman.

He carried a shoebox in two hands as though presenting the Crown Jewels. He pulled the new shoes from their wrapping of crinkly paper and applied them to his customer's limp feet, giving Moshe an unparalleled view of the misaligned toupee.

Galit's refusal to speak to him now made perfect sense. Avi had deceived Moshe with his one-month waiting period, and he had probably deceived her as well. Moshe had been a bad dream, a ghost, a hallucination, or—better yet—an undead zombie from a cheap horror flick. It was a wonder she hadn't fled the continent.

Moshe felt a tap on his shoulder. "If Sir will stand up and take a few steps?" The salesman's glance said: be a good boy and please the old lady.

Moshe clambered to his feet. He paced the shop under Savta's eagle eye. "They fit well," he said.

The salesman beamed. "First time! Madam, you came to the right establishment. Shall I dispose of the old shoes?" He lifted the grimy sneakers by the laces like a dead rat.

Moshe nodded. He slumped back on the bench. A pair of

new shoes would not shatter Avi's lies, nor would they grant him an audience with Galit.

Irina sat down beside him. "Are you OK?"

His shoulders rose and fell with despair. "Avi loved to tell me about his nightclubs and one-night stands. 'You married too soon. You're missing out.' Now he's stolen my wife. I thought he was my friend. The lowlife."

Irina nodded. "There's something I don't understand," she said. "How did someone like Avi become your best friend?"

Moshe took that as a compliment. "That's simple," he said. "Years ago, he saved my life."

Savta Sarah plopped her handbag on the counter and fished out her wallet.

Moshe said, "Here it comes."

The salesman pecked at the cash register. "That will be six hundred shekels," he said. "Credit card or cash?"

Savta Sarah threw a single bank note onto the counter. "Fifty shekels!" she declared.

The man's mouth fell open. "Lady," he said, the polish slipping from his voice. "These are imported shoes. Real leather. And this is the start of the season. You know what? You're a fine, respectable woman. I'll give them to you for five hundred."

Savta folded her arms over her bosom and lifted her nose in the air. "Fifty!"

"You have got to be kidding me." The polish evaporated. "Four hundred," he said. "You won't get that price anywhere. Believe me."

"Fifty!"

"Lady, this isn't the Machaneh Yehuda market." The man looked to Moshe for help. Moshe shrugged. "Three hundred. Final offer. That's the rock-bottom discount we offer at the end of the season but I'll give it to you now."

Savta Sarah slapped the counter. "Fifty shekels!"

The man turned purple. Veins pulsated at his temple. "Where are you from, lady?" he yelled. "The jungle?"

"Yes!" she cried. "The jungle!"

His mouth opened and closed like a fish. Moshe knew what he was thinking: women liked to talk, especially about bad shopping experiences, and this nice old lady probably knew many, many potential customers. "Great God! Two hundred and fifty."

Savta Sarah mulled over the offer. She threw another note on the table. "Seventy shekels."

"Are you trying to starve me? I won't make a profit. Fine! Two hundred shekels. Just get out of my store."

"Seventy!"

The man pulled at his hair and the toupee came away in his hand. He didn't seem to notice.

Moshe hid his face in his hands. He couldn't bear to watch. Poor guy. And poor Savta Sarah. She had learned to survive on a prayer and sheer force of will. Old habits die hard. He could learn from her tenacity; maybe then he'd win back Galit.

Two hours and four stores later, they sat at a bus stop. Moshe wore his new shoes, beige trousers, and a designer collared shirt. Irina looked beautiful in her new summer dress and fashionable pumps. Savta Sarah had parted with five hundred shekels in total. The storeowners had probably taken the rest of the day off.

"Thank you, Savta," Moshe said. Irina thanked her too. Savta Sarah had refused to take his hundred shekels.

"I could have got him down further," she said, wistfully, of the last salesman. "But I felt sorry for him."

The sun crept toward the horizon. In a few hours, working men and women would crowd the streets on their way home. Moshe had woken up that morning hoping to build a bridge to his estranged wife. By lunchtime, he had lost a best friend, but gained two weeks in which to win back his wife. The stakes had soared while the odds of success plummeted.

Once, when he had forgotten their anniversary, Galit had thrown kitchen plates at his head. He longed for her to hurl plates at him now. He could work with an angry Galit, a Galit who still cared, but not with this brick wall. A new set of clothes would not make a dent.

Savta said, "At least now you'll be dressed properly when you see Galit."

"But Savta, she won't speak to me. She wouldn't even come to the door. And if Avi answers—"

Savta Sarah patted his arm. "Don't worry, Moshe," she said. "Tomorrow is Friday and I happen to know exactly where she'll be and when. I can promise you this: you will speak to her and Avi won't be able to stop you."

"You're the greatest!" He lifted her hat and planted a kiss on her forehead. A private meeting with Galit—an open miracle!

"And this time," she added, and her red lipsticked lips curled into a devilish grin, "she will not get away."

CHAPTER 21

"Hey. It's me."

"I told you never to call me on this number."

"We need to speak. It's urgent."

"I'm ending the call."

"I saw the girl. Hello? You there?"

"What girl?"

"The girl."

"You're mistaken."

"It's her, all right. She says she lost her memory. Doesn't remember a thing. Not even her name. She goes by Irina. She showed up with a man, a Moshe Karlin. And get this: his ID says he's supposed to be dead. Hello? Hello?"

"It's not her. Forget about them."

"But if she talks, we're screwed. I thought you said you'd taken care of her. What if—"

"Calm down. Stop worrying and keep your mouth shut. It's not her."

"How can you be so sure?"

"Trust me. I know."

CHAPTER 22

Friday morning, Moshe walked down Emek Refaim, his heart galloping in his chest. The huge bouquet of roses on his arm won smiles from the women who bustled along the sidewalk with fresh *challah* loaves and other Shabbat groceries.

Thorns pricked his palms through the cellophane and made him loosen his grip on the flower stems. The roses had gobbled what remained of his cash and although Moshe was not a gambling man, today he had gone all in.

He paused outside a storefront of tall glass windows. Two large words hung above the store: Zohar Raphael. Moshe had heard the name but he had never met the legend. He peered at the long row of women seated inside. The whir of a blow dryer resonated on the street. No sign of Galit. Had Savta Sarah miscalculated?

Moshe rehearsed his two-pronged plan, patted his hair in the reflection, drew a deep breath, and pushed the glass door inward.

The pungent smells of dye and singed hair assaulted his nostrils, the thunder of the blow dryer his ears. A line of women faced the wall mirrors, their heads buried in round plastic orbs, their hair wrapped in foil, like abducted humans in an alien laboratory. A longer line of women sat reading Cosmopolitan and Oprah magazines on the chairs and couches along the opposite wall. Between the rows of women, a skeletal girl with rings under her eyes swept severed hairs around the floor with a broom.

The blow dryer fell silent.

"Ooh," crooned the man who held the blower. "Some lucky girl is in for a big surprise." Zohar seemed to slouch even while standing. A strip of skin peeked from between the low waistline of his tight jeans and the hem of the faded T-shirt.

He looked Moshe up and down and smirked. "Can I help you, honey?"

No one had ever sized up Moshe that way—or called him "honey" for that matter—and he was not enjoying the experience. The woman in the seat before Zohar stared at her reflection like a well-trained poodle with long blond curls. She didn't seem to mind the interruption.

Moshe scanned the rows of women. "I'm looking for…"

Before he could complete the sentence, a slender form strolled toward him down the aisle of the salon. A towel wrapped her hair like a pink turban. Her shapely hips gyrated to a familiar rhythm, but when she caught sight of Moshe, she froze. Her eyes narrowed and flitted to the exit, as though she wanted to sprint past him and escape. After a moment's hesitation, her mouth tightened. She plopped onto one of the padded hairdressing chairs and trained her eyes on the mirror.

Savta Sarah, you are a genius! Galit was not prepared to lose her appointment, even if it meant facing Moshe's ghost.

Moshe made for her chair and stared at her in the mirror. As beautiful as ever, turban and all. Words lodged in his throat. Her reflection stared at her feet.

"Looks like our Galit has an admirer," said Zohar. "Shiri, get a vase for those heavenly flowers."

The skeletal assistant dropped the broom and took the roses from Moshe. He had hoped for a moment of privacy but that was not going to happen. *Remember the plan. Right!*

He said, "You're late." With those two words, the first he had ever spoken to her, he hoped to conjure their fondest shared memories.

"Oh, no," said a meek voice behind him, an old lady in the waiting line. "She was here before I got here, oh, two hours ago."

"Two hours?" Moshe could not hide his disbelief. He had never waited more than ten minutes for a haircut.

The blond poodle spoke up. "I waited three." She nodded with pride. "Last week I waited four hours." A murmur of commiseration ran along the line of waiting women.

Zohar raked her hair with his fingers. "That's the price of art, honey," he said.

Of all the women in the salon, only Galit seemed not to have heard him. This was not going the way he had planned. "Galit," he said. "It's me, Moshe."

"Well, well, well," Zohar said. "If it isn't Mr. Karlin, back from the grave." He rolled his eyes.

Moshe didn't know what surprised him more: Zohar's knowledge of his return or the sarcasm in his voice. He ignored both.

"Hangar 17?" he said. "The night we first met?"

Had she made the connection?

Zohar snorted. "Might as well give up now. You won't get a word out of her."

Moshe gave him a warning look that said, "Stay out of this."

Zohar didn't take the hint. "And I don't blame her," he added. He shot an imaginary bullet at Moshe with the blow dryer, and blew smoke from the barrel.

What was he on about? *Stay focused.*

"Galit," he said, desperation crawling into his voice. "We've been through so much together. Aren't you glad to see me again?"

Her head stayed down; her mouth tightened further.

Zohar snorted again. "Typical," he said. "Men think they can run off and have fun, and when they come home everything will be just fine."

Moshe could ignore him no longer. "What are you talking

about?"

Zohar hooted. "I know all about you, Moshe Karlin. I know your type. The girls keep no secrets from me, right, girls?" The rows of women sang a chorus of agreement.

Zohar removed the plastic gown from the blond with a flourish. "See you next week, dear. Regards to that no-good husband of yours. And do me a favor—throw out that blouse. You look a hundred years older in that *shmata*. Excuse me." He bumped Moshe aside with his hips, pulled the towel from Galit's head, and placed his hands on her damp hair like a mind reader.

"Look at those ends! You need a cut, darling. And highlights. Shiri, get the color ready."

Galit seethed on her seat. She had eyes only for the hairdresser. Moshe could use that to his advantage.

"What did she tell you?"

Zohar combed a length of her hair and chopped at the ends with a pair of scissors.

"You're like poor Etti's husband." He tutted. "Business trips to America for weeks at a time. Years on end. As it turns out, he was very busy indeed. Married another girl. Had children with her too! Etti was devastated when she found out."

Moshe could not believe his ears. "But that's not me! I didn't run off. I died!"

Zohar rolled his eyes again. "Oh, please! Have you no shame? To fake your own death—funeral and all!"

"What? No! I didn't fake anything. That's ridiculous."

"Less ridiculous than rising from the dead? Did you honestly expect her to believe that?" Zohar threw up his hands and tossed the implements onto the wheeled trolley of rollers and hairpins. "This is too much for me! I need a smoke." He sashayed out the door.

Moshe looked around at the flock of cowed women. "He hasn't finished her hair." On the sidewalk, Zohar lit a cigarette and stared at the sky.

"Oh, he does that all the time," said the meek old lady in

waiting. "He can go off like that for a half hour."

"He's an artist," said another. Heads nodded in awe.

Moshe sighed. Some things he would never understand.

Galit sat in the chair, her hands clenching the armrests. A trapped animal.

"I didn't leave you, Galit. I died. I know this is hard to believe—I don't understand it either—but I've been given a second chance. *We've* been given a second chance." He had to prove it to her. "I have to show you something," he said. He lifted his shirt. Behind him, voices gasped. "See. No belly button. This is a new body."

Her eyes flitted to his stomach. Her mouth twitched. Her barriers were crumbling.

The door whooshed open. "You still here?" said Zohar, trailing a cloud of smoke.

"Please," Moshe said. His time was running out. "Things will be just the way they were before."

"Ha!" said Zohar. "And things weren't exactly wonderful then."

"Yes, they were!" Moshe fought the urge to throttle the hairdresser right in front of his worshippers.

"OK, Mr. Right. When was the last time you brought her flowers?"

The question caught him unprepared. He had not been big on flowers. The stores only opened after he set out for work, and closed before he left the office. Galit had never seemed to mind.

"Um," he said.

"Exactly," said the hairdresser. "Avi buys her flowers every week."

Moshe disliked Zohar more with each passing second.

"And," the hairdresser continued, "he's better in bed."

Giggles behind him. Moshe did not need to hear that. The very thought of Avi in bed with Galit made him want to puke.

Zohar waved the scissors in the air and resumed chopping at her hair. "Living with you wasn't easy, you know. Working late every night. Never paying attention. It's a wonder she didn't throw you out sooner."

Was it true? Was life with him so bad?

"I'll do better," he said. "I'll change."

"Ha! How many times have you heard that, girls?"

The women in waiting muttered their agreement. Zohar was their God; his every word, their Holy Scripture.

Time for Plan B.

Moshe said, "What about Talya? She needs a father in her life—her real father."

Zohar stopped chopping. "Look what you've done. You've made her cry."

He gripped Moshe by the shoulders, scissors still in hand, and shoved him toward the door.

"Please," Moshe said. "Give us a chance. Don't marry him!"

Zohar pushed him onto the sidewalk and closed the door behind him. "You're not welcome here," he said. "If you care about her at all, you'll leave her alone."

CHAPTER 23

Sunbeams poured through the leaves above and warmed the patches of dirt and wild grass in the courtyard. Birds squawked in the trees. The sounds and smells of Rocheleh's Shabbat cooking drifted through an open window.

Yosef sat in the center of the yard on a low stool of hard plastic designed for a child. He dipped the horsehair brush in the circular tin of polish and spread thick black paste along the side of a leather Sabbath shoe.

He loved Friday mornings. After dropping the boys at school and shopping for groceries at the store, he continued his preparations at leisure. The air tingled with an almost palpable tranquility streaked with eager anticipation. Each passing second brought the Sabbath sanctity closer.

This particular Friday morning, his anticipation skyrocketed, as he sensed the approach not only of the weekly Sabbath, but the final and long-awaited Day of Complete Sabbath. The Messianic Age.

He tilted his hand inside the shoe and polished the other side.

And yet...

After morning prayers, he had stopped by the Mount of Olives. Again, he patrolled the rows of tombstones. Again, he searched the perimeter of trees and bushes. Again, he found nothing.

Two resurrected Jews do not the Resurrection make.

Rabbi Emden's words echoed in his ears and unsettled his Shabbat eve peace of mind. Two days had passed since the discovery of Irina, yet the count of resurrected Jews remained the same.

Have faith, Yosef.

God worked at His own pace and by His own rules. Human impatience would not dictate the course of history. The world had waited two thousand years. The world could wait a little longer. One thing was clear—the Final Redemption had begun. He found no other way to read the facts.

He placed the blackened shoe on the square of old newspaper, then replaced the lid of the tin with a loud click.

A sudden thought vaulted Yosef to his feet, and he rushed indoors to his bedroom. He opened the closet door and ran his fingers over the nylon plastic cover among the suspended shirts and dresses.

The Redemption could arrive any day and without warning, the Sages of Blessed Memory taught, and one should forever be ready to greet the Messiah at a moment's notice. And so, the day after his wedding, Yosef had dry-cleaned his suit and hung it in his closet, awaiting the call of the ram's horn over the hills of Jerusalem. Four children and two homes later, the suit remained in the plastic cover.

Yosef lifted the suit from the rack and slipped the trousers from the hanger. He kicked off his shoes and wriggled out of his weekday slacks. The suit trousers rose over his shins and thighs, but the metal clasps refused to meet over his waist. Yosef shook his head at his own stupidity. He'd need to visit the tailor on Sunday morning. A small delay in the Redemption would not be a bad thing, after all.

"Yossi," said Rocheleh. She stood in the open doorway, a stained apron over her house gown. She had caught him, literally, with his trousers down. "What are you doing?"

"Just trying on my old suit."

She shook her head at his silly antics and got to business.

"It's been four days, Yossi. We have four children to feed. Five, counting you. And now your two houseguests too. We can't go on like this."

"You're right," he said. Their teaching salaries barely covered their own basic needs, and the added load in cooking and laundry fell to her. Good thing he had not discovered more resurrected Jews!

His poor Rocheleh. Born and raised in the ultra-Orthodox community, she had never dreamed that she would marry the once-secular Yosef. The real catches—the Torah prodigies and sons of the Charedi aristocracy—had married her girlfriends whose families had deeper pockets. Rocheleh, however, had collected dust on the shelf until her age had convinced her to settle for a lesser man. Her fortune was about to change.

"Rabbi Emden called this morning," he said. "We're going to meet the Great Council on Sunday evening."

"*The* Great Council?" Her eyebrows lifted on a gust of awe mixed with suspicion.

"Yes! When they find out about Moshe and Irina, they'll want to visit them in person."

Rocheleh brushed a rogue strand of hair beneath her kerchief. "Here, in our house?" The corners of her lips curled into a smile. Her eyes explored the wall, already preparing a menu of delicacies to serve the leading rabbis of the generation—and their wives—in her home.

"Yes! What great merit we have had to have discovered and honored them first in our home."

The smile dropped. He had overdone it. "Sunday they'll be gone?"

"Add a few days to make arrangements. Tuesday, tops."

Rocheleh grunted, cast a parting contemptuous glance at his bare legs, and returned to her pre-Sabbath tasks.

Yosef dressed and returned the suit to the closet.

In every generation, the Sages taught, a Messiah is born. He waits in anonymity and longs for the Redemption, when the time will come for him to reveal his true nature. Coming to think of it, the Messiah must surely be one of the great Torah authorities of the Great Council.

Oh, no!

Yosef grabbed the suit and ran to Emek Refaim. If he hurried, he'd reach the tailor before closing time. If he begged, his suit might be ready on Sunday. If Yosef had the merit to greet the Messiah, he would not do so shabbily dressed.

CHAPTER 24

Noga hesitated outside room 419C in the Shaare Zedek Medical Center.

You have nothing to fear. According to Eliana, the cute mystery patient had woken from his coma. He had a name, and his behavior was as sane as that of the other patients. But Noga remembered the crazy dark eyes and the pink lines his fingers had left on her wrist, and her pulse raced as though she was about to enter a lion's cage.

She should probably stay away, but she could not resist the call. The attraction went beyond his looks or even curiosity about his sudden recovery. He had a name but no family or friends. No visitors. He remained a lonely island in a sea of indifference. *We have a lot in common.* She wasn't exactly hitting on him, either. She was just doing her job.

She drew a deep breath, clutched the transparent folder of papers to her breast like a shield, and stepped over the threshold.

The leg in the cast hung from the sling, the other lay beneath the blanket. As she rounded the divider curtain, more of his body came into view. *Be asleep!* But the fairy godmothers ignored her wish. Mr. Eli Katz lay in bed, his eyes fixed on the blank television screen in the corner.

She cleared her throat. "How are you feeling today, Mr.

Katz?"

His head rolled on the pillow. The mop of jet-black hair fell over the bandage on his forehead. His dark eyes considered her. Then the head returned to the blank screen. If he remembered her from yesterday, he hid it well.

"Trapped," he said.

Not a man of words. She would have to do the talking. She didn't do small talk, although her job forced her to speak with strangers of all sorts. For some causes—and some people—she was willing to make the effort.

She got to the point. "I'm conducting a study," she said. "Genetic research. We're—"

"I'm not good with blood," he said, interrupting her without even making eye contact.

A full sentence. Progress. She rushed ahead with the good news. "No need for that," she said. "The lab already has samples."

That got his attention. "The lab has *what?*"

She felt her cheeks redden under the gaze of those deep, dark eyes. "Samples. Of your blood. When you arrived, they had to run tests before surgery. It's standard."

He ran his uninjured hand through his hair as though she had just informed him that his mother had died. What was his problem?

She took advantage of the silence to plow on with her sales pitch. "We're tracing a particular gene—"

He raised his hand for her to stop. "I'm not interested. Just… just leave me alone, OK?"

Her cheeks burned again but with an entirely different emotion. "As you wish," she snapped. She had liked him better comatose.

She turned to leave, but stopped at the curtain to deliver a parting shot. "You're going to be here a long time, Mr. Katz," she said. "You might want to make some friends."

CHAPTER 25

Moshe and Irina followed Rabbi Yosef down Shimshon Street. The setting sun bathed the low stone buildings and leafy trees of Baka in gold. The rabbi's sons ran ahead in black trousers and white collared shirts, their curled side locks swinging at their ears. Their footfalls reverberated off the homes and apartment buildings of the quiet suburban street. In a window, twin Shabbat candles burned on silver candlesticks. The smells of freshly baked bread and chicken soup wafted in the gentle breeze. Cars straddled the sidewalk as their owners relaxed at home after a tiring week.

Moshe and Irina fell a little behind.

"How did it go?" she asked. She looked particularly fairylike in the green dress from Tal Chaim and the rabbanit's makeup—a fairy on her way to a palatial ball. In the rush of Shabbat preparations, he had not had time to update her.

"Good, at first," he said. The hot shower and fresh clothes had raised his spirits. Then details of the encounter rose in his memory. "Terrible, actually," he added.

Irina chuckled. "Good and terrible?"

"I finally got to see her and speak to her," he explained. "But she didn't say a word. She's furious. She thinks that I faked my death and that I've been leading a double life. Oh, and that I was a terrible husband."

He had reeled from the revelation for a full hour after Zohar Raphael had thrown him out of the hair salon.

"I find that hard to believe," she said.

"Which part—the double life or the bad husband?" At least he still had his sense of humor.

"Either."

They passed his old home. The blinds remained down, the door shut. Slivers of light at the edges hinted at the warmth of his old life, the warmth he would probably never know again.

"I thought we were doing well," he said. "We were a team. We were going to conquer the world together. But toward the end, I suppose I ran too far ahead. I didn't even notice that she had fallen behind."

Irina said, "But you've stopped running now. Maybe she just needs time to catch up. Don't give up, Moshe."

He smiled. "'A Karlin never quits,'" he said. "That's what my father used to say."

"Those are good words to live by."

They strolled along in silence. It felt good to have her support—a pair of objective eyes to keep him sane. And thank God for Shabbat. He sorely needed a break from the strain of his new life.

They turned a corner. Rabbi Yosef held open the metal gate of a low-walled courtyard and ushered them inside.

The Emek Refaim Synagogue on Yael Street—a humble oblong of rough stone blocks—reminded Moshe of the Western Wall in the heart of Jerusalem's Old City.

In the late 1800s, German Templers journeyed to the Holy Land to promote the rebuilding of the Temple and to await the Second Coming. The former Protestants bought large swaths of land in Haifa, Jaffa, and Jerusalem's Refaim Valley, where they tilled the holy soil and invented the Jaffa orange.

New suburbs mushroomed around their German Colony in Jerusalem—Katamon, Talbieh, and Baka—and housed wealthy Arabs.

During World War II, however, the British deported the

German settlers. Only their cemeteries and the stone home-steads with arched doorways and metal shutters remained as reminders of their presence.

Then, in 1949, Jewish immigrants established the Emek Refaim synagogue in one of the old stone structures of Baka, abandoned during the War of Independence. And so, by yet another ironic twist of history, the pious Germans had helped build not a Temple for a resurrected Jesus Christ but a syna-gogue for holocaust survivors—and now, two newly resurrected Jews.

The rabbi directed Irina to the door of the women's sec-tion. Inside the synagogue, he handed Moshe a velvet *kippah* and a prayer book, and seated him at a pew of dark, carved wood and navy blue velvet upholstery.

The rabbi took his seat at the front, facing the congrega-tion, and recited the Song of Songs, in a traditional singsong.

Never in his life had Moshe been the first to arrive at syn-agogue. Old men wearing their Sabbath finery trickled inside and filled the pews. Moshe caught snatches of conversations in German, Hungarian, French, Persian, and English.

According to a bronze plaque on the wall, the furnishings had once belonged to a synagogue in the small town of Busseto in northern Italy. Moshe studied the elaborate carv-ings of the Holy Ark, the banisters of the raised dais, and the pews.

In this renovated Jerusalem ruin, beneath a canopy of Arabian arches, European Jewish refugees rested on furniture rescued from an extinct Italian Jewish community.

Emek Refaim—*the Valley of Giants*. Or *Valley of Ghosts*—for what was this nation if not a heap of disenfranchised souls, a valley of dry bones drawn together from the four corners of the Earth, after enduring every catastrophe, and surviving every prophecy of doom? In the middle sat Moshe, the biggest ghost of all.

The singsong ended. Rabbi Yosef nodded at a bony old man in a blue suit, who hobbled to the central podium, wrapped a fringed *talit* over his shoulders, and led the afternoon prayers.

The congregation rose for the silent Standing Prayer. Moshe placed his prayer book on the stand and turned the pages. The first of nineteen blessings invoked the patriarchs: Abraham, Isaac, and Jacob. The second made the hair on the back of his neck stand on end.

You are eternally powerful, Lord; You are the Resurrector of the Dead, and redeem abundantly.

You sustain life with loving kindness, revive the dead with great mercy; you support the fallen, heal the sick, release the fettered, and are steadfast to those that sleep in the dust.

Who is like You, Master of Powers, and who even resembles You? The King Who kills and revives, and nurtures redemption.

And dependable You are to give life to the dead.

Blessed are You, Resurrector of the Dead.

Moshe had read the blessing countless times, but he did not recall the focus on resurrection. The living pay little attention to the dead.

Jews uttered this prayer three times a day as their ancestors had over the centuries. As a vulnerable minority, and the target of entrenched prejudice and blind hatred in many countries, the specter of sudden death haunted their every step. The return to Jerusalem and a national homeland on their holy ground must have seemed as impossible and incredible as Ezekiel's dry old bones standing up and breathing again. And yet it was that unreasonable hope that had kept them going.

His thoughts drifted to the words of the Israeli anthem.

Od lo avda tikvatenu / Our hope is not yet lost
Hatikva bat shnot alpayim / The hope of two thousand years
Lihyot am chofshi be'artzenu / To be a free nation in our land.

The synagogue windows darkened. The congregation welcomed the Sabbath Bride with song. Their voices rose and fell, then rose again. On the Sabbath day, Jews in synagogues around the world sang these same words and notes. Moshe hummed along and found a measure of comfort.

He too hoped to revive the past. That past, however, had

lost its rosy hue. He had spent little time with his daughter. He had steered Karlin & Son toward the sharp rocks of disaster. He had neglected his wife. Did that old life deserve revival?

His wrist itched beneath the heavy watch.

Now that he knew his shortcomings, he knew what to fix. To win back Galit, he would need to change. Spend more time with her. Work less. That part shouldn't be a problem. With Karlin & Son diving toward bankruptcy, he'd soon have plenty of free time.

You have two weeks.

Two weeks until the wedding. Two weeks to reinvent himself. To prove to her that he deserved a second chance.

The prayers concluded. Rabbi Yosef approached the podium and announced the prayer times for the next day. The congregants poured out the doors and into the courtyard.

Irina emerged from the women's entrance, green sleeves reaching beyond her elbows. She and Moshe exchanged Sabbath greetings in the yellow streetlight. The sweet scent of the rabbanit's deodorant clung to her.

They waited for the rabbi, who shook hands with the line of exiting congregants, some of whom gave Moshe strange looks and whispered to each other. The rabbi's children dived between the men and women, darted out of the courtyard, and down the street like a flock of young sparrows.

Irina looked at home in the modest garb, and again he wondered whether religion had played a role in her forgotten former life. She looked equally comfortable in jeans and T-shirts. Without memory, we could be anyone. Without memory, we are all the same.

There was a movement in the corner of his eye. He turned, but not fast enough. A freight train slammed into his jaw and threw him off his feet. He sprawled on the dusty cobblestones. Women cried out. Shoes shuffled behind him. He rolled over. A man lunged at him, held back only by the rabbi, who stood between them with outstretched hands.

Avi straightened his shirt. A fire glowed in his eyes.

"Come near her again," he said, "and you'll regret it."

Irina crouched over Moshe and touched his shoulder. The few remaining congregants watched from a safe distance.

Moshe tasted blood in his mouth and touched his bruised lip. "She's still my wife," he said.

"No she isn't. You died, remember? Now it's my turn."

"*Your turn*. What is she—the village bicycle? You're a thief."

Avi jabbed a finger at him in the air. "Just stay away from her, unless you think you'll come back from the dead twice." He nodded at the rabbi and skulked away.

Moshe knew a threat when he heard one. "So now you're a thief *and* a murderer?"

"Murderer?" Avi said and laughed as he disappeared into the night. "Can't murder a dead man."

CHAPTER 26

Moshe washed dust from his hands and blood from his face in the rabbi's bathroom. His hands trembled. Avi had a point. In the eyes of the State, Moshe Karlin no longer existed. What charges would a prosecutor file against his murderer—desecration of a corpse? Would the police even make an arrest? The law provided no protection for the deceased Moshe Karlin.

He added Death Threat to his growing list of challenges and returned to the living room. Uriel, the rabbi's oldest son, read a book on the sofa. Simcha and Ari played with soccer cards on the carpet. Little Yehuda pushed a toy car along the edge of a shelf and made it fly in the air.

"Boys," Rabbi Yosef said. "Let's start."

His children dropped what they were doing and took their seats at the dinner table. Moshe had never encountered such obedient kids. They had helped with the Sabbath preparations without complaint. They had dusted the furniture, washed the floors, set the dinner table with a white tablecloth and white faux china.

The rabbi and his wife sat at either end of the dinner table. Moshe made for the empty chair between the rabbi and Irina. Uriel, Yehuda, and Simcha eyed him from across the table and over the two polished candlesticks that held burning tea lights.

Rabbi Yosef led the singing of two songs. The first welcomed the Sabbath angels, and the second praised the industrious mother of the household. The rabbi stood and called on each of his sons to approach him for a whispered blessing sealed with a kiss on the forehead.

Friday nights in the Karlin residence had involved TV dinners and weekend newspapers. In the rabbi's home, however, time seemed to have stopped, and an otherworldly calm replaced the flurry of pre-Shabbat activity.

A warm glow spread over Irina's face. She must have been thinking the same thing.

Blessings completed, Rabbi Yosef raised a silver goblet that brimmed with red wine and he recited the Sabbath *Kiddush* prayer. He poured the wine into plastic shot glasses and passed them down the table. Moshe downed his in one gulp. *Grape juice.* He could do with something stronger.

They filed into the kitchen to wash their hands using a double-handled jug. A tall tin urn hissed on the counter. On a hot tray perched over the gas stove, a large pot of soup and a pile of tinfoil trays bubbled. The rabbi had set timers in wall sockets around the house to turn lights and fans on and off as desired, for the *Shabbat* rules prohibited the use of electric switches on the holy day.

They returned to their seats at the table. Rabbi Yosef removed the velvet cover from the twin plaited loaves of bread, recited the blessing—*Who brings forth bread from the earth*—and broke off clumps of bread, dipped them in salt, and tossed them across the table to his guests and family.

"Welcome," he said as he sliced the rest of the loaf with a silver bread knife. "It's not every week we have such honored guests."

A chair leg creaked as the rabbanit stood and made for the kitchen.

"Thank you for taking us in," Irina said. "This"—she indicated the Sabbath table—"is lovely."

Moshe agreed. The bread was warm and sweet. A spirit of

contentment filled the home. Even the rabbi's wife seemed to have softened.

The rabbi leaned back, a king on his throne. "Shabbat," he said. "Me'en Olam Habah." A taste of the World to Come. The rabbi must have been referring to the World of Souls, for Moshe's bodily afterlife had been anything but relaxing.

The rabbanit placed steaming bowls of watery chicken soup before them.

Yehuda, the boy who had asked him whether he was dead that first day, ogled him as he ate. "What happened to your mouth?"

"Yehuda!" the rabbanit chided.

"It's OK," Moshe said. The soup tasted heavenly but the salt stung his torn lip. "A man hit me outside synagogue."

The boy's eyes widened. "Did you hit him back?"

"No."

"Oh." He seemed disappointed.

Not now, Moshe thought. *And not with fists in the street.*

Rabbi Yosef cleared his throat. "Moshe, Irina. I almost forgot. I have good news. Rabbi Emden, a close friend and a great man, has arranged for us to meet with the Great Council on Sunday night."

Irina looked to Moshe for an explanation but he had none. "The Great Council?"

"The Council of Great Torah Sages. The leading Torah authorities of our generation. Rabbi Alter. Rabbi Teitelbaum. Rabbi Auerbach."

"I have Rabbi Auerbach!" cried Simcha. He pulled a wad of crumpled soccer cards from his trouser pocket and fanned through them. He held up a card. Instead of a soccer superstar, the laminated surface framed the stern face of a bearded rabbi.

"Hey, give that back," Ari said from between Irina and the rabbanit.

"No, I won it fair and square!"

"Enough!" said the rabbanit. She had seated Ari and Simcha across the table from each other for a reason.

Irina glanced at Moshe, her eyes conveying a mix of delight and concern. "Should I go as well?" she asked the rabbi.

The beard twitched. Heavy-duty rabbis avoided interacting with women, but Rabbi Yosef had enough tact not to say so. "Just Moshe for now."

"And these rabbis," Irina asked, "they'll be able to explain what happened to us?"

"Yes, and more. The sages of the Great Council head famous yeshivas. They have connections to charitable institutions..."

The rabbi faltered and lowered his eyes to his bowl of soup.

"In other words," the rabbanit said, "they will find you a new home."

They slurped their soup in silence. Her last sentence had killed the conversation.

Moshe didn't blame her. Moshe and Irina could not sponge off them forever. But he had hoped to stay close to Galit a little longer, long enough that he would not need another home.

The bookish Uriel interpreted the lull in conversation as an invitation to ask questions.

"Moshe, what do you do?"

Moshe's soup spoon hovered in the air. He had no answer for that most trivial of questions for an able-bodied adult man. Karlin & Son was not just a job—he *was* Karlin & Son. At forty-two, Moshe found himself penniless, jobless, and in the throes of an identity crisis.

He felt his brow moisten with sweat. "I'm still figuring that out," he said.

Confusion dumbfounded the boys as they struggled with a new mental box: a grown man with no profession.

Rabbi Yosef came to his rescue. "Life is a journey," he said. "We might start out in one direction, and later try another until we find our true path."

Moshe would settle for a regular paycheck.

The rabbi turned to his guests. "Rabbi Nachman of

Breslov said that the entire world is a very narrow bridge. And what is the main thing?" His voice rose in a school-teacher tone of expectation.

"Have no fear at all!" the boys responded, like good students. The rabbi winked at Moshe and then he and his sons broke into song.

Kol ha'olam kooloh / The whole world is
Gesher tzar me'od / A very narrow bridge.

They accompanied the slow, calming melody with well-rehearsed hand gestures. The pace picked up for the chorus.

Ve'ha'ikar / And the main thing
Lo le'fached klal / Is to have no fear at all.

By the end of the song, youthful smiles had returned to the table. The rabbanit placed tinfoil trays of browned chicken, potatoes, and steaming white rice on the table.

"Rabbi Nachman lived two centuries ago," Rabbi Yosef said. "He taught that we are forbidden to lose hope. No matter what we did in the past, today—every day—we start our lives anew."

Moshe piled food onto his plate. The chicken drumstick fell apart under his knife. *Start our lives anew.* Again, the rabbi made it sound easy, as easy as putting one foot ahead of the other and not looking down.

There came a loud knocking at the door.

Moshe's heart skipped a beat. He pictured Avi outside the door with a large club. Irina gripped his arm.

Rabbi Yosef stood and approached the door. He peered through the peephole. Moshe held his breath. *Don't open it, Rabbi. Don't do it.*

The rabbi, however, did not obey Moshe's thoughts. He turned a baffled expression to the table, and pulled the handle.

A woman stood on the doorstep. Short. Olive skin. Young. Her dress dusted the ground. The shawl on her head covered most of her mousy brown hair. She scanned the room behind the rabbi with the large dark eyes of a frightened deer.

"Rabbi Yosef?" she said. Her Hebrew had a guttural edge, the unmistakable accent of a tongue more at home in Arabic. "I'm sorry to disturb you." She looked over her shoulder at the dark street. "Please. May I come in?" she said. "I need your help."

CHAPTER 27

From his bed, Eli heard the chant of a man's voice down the hall. The Friday night *Kiddush* blessing. The nurse had dimmed the lights in his room. The weekday hospital sounds in the hallways had subsided as staff and visitors returned home for the holy day.

That morning, the Russian nurse had detached the sensors of the heart monitor from his chest but he remained immobile and helpless. The Thin Voice, silent. His powers, fled. He was starting to miss the crows.

A terrifying thought whispered in his ear. *You will never heal. Your fate is that of the mortals now.*

The chant ended and a motley chorus answered *Amen*. Eli added a prayer of his own. *Don't abandon me! Don't deny me your Holy Spirit!* Somewhere in the hospital, vials of his blood awaited the scrutiny of modern medicine. The results would raise questions. Questions would lead to further tests and yet more questions. He had to get out now, while he still could.

He inhaled three deep breaths and closed his eyes. He focused on the muscle in his head. *Flex!* A tingling sensation crept down his spine and along his limbs.

Yes!

He commanded his shattered leg to heal.

He wriggled his toes. He lifted his leg from the sling.

Yes! Yes!

Now, to the side—

Pain erupted in his bones. The leg fell limp and swung in the sling.

This can't be. Tears welled in his eyes. He had a job to do. The destiny of the entire world weighed on his shoulders. After waiting long centuries, to be trapped just when—

Something moved. At the edge of the divider curtain, a hand floated in thin air. A white-gloved hand, palm out.

Eli blinked. *Have I gone mad?* The glove hovered like the Divine hand at Belshazzar's feast. This hand, however, did not write riddles on the wall. Instead, it extended into the room and grew a forearm—a naked, hairy forearm. A second hand joined the first. The two gloved hands shifted sideways, one by one, feeling their way along an invisible wall. A head appeared above the hands. Wild orange hair. Large white frown painted over the mouth. Large red ball of a nose.

The clown jumped into Eli's private space with a flourish and a bow.

"Get lost," Eli said.

The clown waggled a finger at him and placed his hands on his hips.

"Scat!"

The clown seemed to consider his advice, then thumbed his nose, stuck out his tongue, and pranced back to the safety of the curtain.

"And don't come back."

He waited for the fool to return. He didn't. *Good!* He hated clowns. He hated humanity. He hated hospitals.

He sighed. Hate would not free him. The girl in the white cloak was right. He needed friends. How did one make friends? He was out of practice.

The large Russian nurse charged into the room and glanced at the clipboard that dangled at the foot of his bed.

"Shabbat shalom, Mr. Katz. Would you like to hear *Kiddush*?"

"Did you see... a clown?"

She gave him a quizzical look. "A clown? Afraid not." She placed his nightly painkillers and a plastic cup of water on the bedside stand, and she replaced the drainage container at the end of the catheter.

Had he dreamed the mime act? This was no time to lose his mind. He needed all his wits about him.

A plan condensed in his mind. The plan involved risk and deception, and a small sacrifice, but what was the alternative?

"Drink up," said the nurse. She towered over him, hands akimbo.

He read the name on her tag. "Eliana," he said. "Can you do me a favor?"

CHAPTER 28

Yosef held the door open for the Arab girl. He had a bad feeling about this. The sleeves of the dress fell past her hands. He studied her body for signs of a machete or an explosive belt. Arabs worked at the shops on Bethlehem Road and Emek Refaim but they did not wander around his neighborhood at night, certainly not a young, lone woman.

She stepped inside, barefoot.

"The woman at Tal Chaim said that you help people like me," she said.

People like me. His intestines tied in a knot. *She couldn't possibly mean... No, that was impossible.*

Her eyes moved to the hot food on the table. The aromas filled his nostrils as they surely did hers. His heart went out to her.

"Please," he said. He indicated the chair of his youngest son. "Sit there. Yehuda, move over and sit with me." Yehuda jumped off the chair and made for the head of the table.

"Rocheleh," he added, "please fetch a bowl of soup for our guest." She glared at him for a second, then did as he asked.

Abraham, the first Jew, had welcomed desert wanderers and idol worshippers into his tent. His wife, Sarah, prepared the delicacies and Abraham served the guests himself. Should

Yosef Lev do any less? Was this not an opportunity to teach his children the *mitzvah* of hospitality?

The girl took her place at the table and thanked Rocheleh for the bowl of soup.

Yosef returned to his seat and placed Yehuda on his lap. The uneasy sense of déjà vu returned and unsettled his Sabbath peace. He had seen this film before. Twice. But this third showing made no sense!

The girl mopped up the remnant of her soup with a slice of challah bread and wolfed it down.

"What is your name?"

She looked at her host, and the hunted look returned to her eyes. "Samira," she said in a low voice, as though the mention of her name might bring misfortune.

"Are you in trouble?"

She lowered her eyes to the table and nodded. She closed her eyes as though the memory was too difficult to bear. "They might be looking for me."

"Who?"

She shook her head.

"Who, Samira? Who is looking for you?"

She opened her eyes and stared, unseeing.

"My father. Or my brother."

"No one knows you are here, Samira. It's OK." His words seemed to comfort the girl.

He relaxed on his chair too. The girl had run away from home. An ordinary domestic dispute. He would hand her over to social services as soon as Shabbat ended. She was not a resurrectee. Of course not. A resurrected Arab? That was impossible.

"They must not find me," she said.

"Your family?"

"My father."

What could make her shudder so at the mention of her father? "Why not, Samira?"

"Because," she said, choking on the words, "the last time we met, he killed me."

CHAPTER 29

Saturday night, Moshe plunged his hands into the soapy water of the kitchen sink. He pulled a plate from the pile of meat dishes and scoured the surface with a sponge. Irina worked beside him at the dairy sink.

It felt good to be busy after the long summer day of rest. Moshe had never kept the Sabbath in all its restrictions—he had not even known how extensive they were. No computer. No phones. No cars. No cooking. No preparations for after the Sabbath day.

He had slept on the couch Friday night as Irina and Samira had taken over the boys' room. When he awoke Saturday morning, the rabbi had already left for synagogue. After Avi's attack the previous night, Moshe had preferred not to stroll past his old house alone.

He spent the morning lounging in the living room. He studied the rabbis on the wall. Maimonides struck a regal pose in his turban and clerical gown, his tidy beard and mustache. The Chofetz Chayim gazed through shuttered eyelids beneath a simple Polish cap, his prolific white beard tucked into a heavy black coat.

Moshe perused the rabbi's library. He read from the Bible for the first time since childhood. Abraham's journey to the Promised Land. Isaac's devotion to the land despite conflict and famine. Jacob's return after a forced exile. Joshua's conquest of Canaan. David's united kingdom. Solomon's golden temple in Jerusalem.

The calamitous destruction. The exile to Babylon.

During two thousand years of national dormancy, like disembodied souls, the Israelite nation turned inward. The exiles found comfort in their Torah and its prophecies of dry bones.

"Son of Man," God asked Ezekiel. "Can these bones live?" Moshe felt as though God was speaking to him as well. "They say 'Our bones have dried, our hope is lost; we are done for.'" But God had not lost hope. "I will raise you from your graves, My nation, and I will bring you to the Land of Israel."

Among the many religious works on the shelves, Moshe found a biography of the early Prime Ministers of the State of Israel. Ben Gurion. Levi Eshkol. Menachem Begin. They invoked the heroes of the Bible as they burst back onto the pages of history. The returning Jews no longer resembled the shepherd prophets and glorious monarchs of the past, but the same ancient spirit animated their new collective body.

Moshe placed a clean dish on the drying rack and scrubbed the next. Down the corridor, bathwater splashed and little feet pounded on the floors, as the rabbi and his wife prepared the boys for bed. Occasionally, the rabbanit raised her voice at the rabbi. Moshe could not hear her words but he guessed their meaning.

"We need to find a new place to stay," he said. "I'm not sure we'll like the accommodations the Great Council will provide, if they do."

Irina squirted dish soap on a blue sponge. "Where can we go?"

By "we," she meant the three of them. A Russian, an Israeli, and an Arab—it sounded like the start of a bad joke, but circumstances had bound their fates together. With Irina's forgotten life and Samira's murderous family, the task of finding a new home would fall to Moshe.

"I'll call in a few favors."

He cleaned out the sink and dried his hands. The rabbi marched into the living room and pulled a book from the shelves.

"Rabbi, may I use your phone?"

The rabbi turned and smiled. "Sure."

The title on the spine of the book read Deeds of Our Sages. Bedtime stories about righteous rabbis. Rabbi Yosef deserved to feature there too.

"And the laptop?"

"Of course, I'll get it right away."

Moshe opened the computer—a bulky ASUS with duct tape holding the disc drive in place—on the dinner table and jotted down telephone numbers from the Bezeq online telephone directory. He dialed the first number into the rabbi's home telephone and pressed the receiver to his ear.

He had interviewed many prospective employees over the years but he had never sat on the other side of the table. He was not enjoying the experience.

The number rang, then switched to an answering service.

"Sivan," Moshe said, after the tone, "it's Moshe Karlin. I've got a lot of explaining to do." He left the rabbi's home phone as his contact number.

One down, two to go. Arkadi was not listed. That left Mathew and Pini. If his former employees had a spare bedroom, he was sure they'd help him. He would have done the same for them in an instant. Pini had a large family of his own to feed, so Moshe tried Mathew next.

After two rings, he picked up.

"Holy crapola!" Mathew said in English. Moshe breathed a sigh of relief. Finally, a figure from his old life who was willing to speak to him. "I heard rumors but I didn't believe them. You've got to come by my place."

The walk to the end of Palmach Street took ten minutes. Moshe and Irina stared at an old soot-stained apartment block. Samira, who had spent most of the day cowering in her room, had opted for an early night. Moshe had dropped

Mathew home after many a long shift at Karlin & Son, but he had never ventured inside. They climbed the three flights to apartment number six.

The door opened before he could knock. Mathew slouched on the threshold wearing shorts and a T-shirt. Stubble on his chin. Lanky hair. Unemployment had taken its toll.

"Moshe Karlin," he said. "Back from the dead." His mouth hung open, and he nodded his head. He was always nodding his head. He wrapped Moshe in a bony hug. He glanced at Irina. "Who's your friend?"

Moshe made the introductions.

"Come on in. Soda or beer?"

He made for the refrigerator in the corner of the living room. No, not the living room. The entire apartment. An unmade bed lined one wall beneath the window and faced a lopsided closet, a mounted flat-screen television, and a framed print of a castle atop an immense rock that floated in thin air above the crashing waves of a seashore. A white plastic chair and a wheeled coffee table filled the little living space that remained.

There was no spare couch for Moshe in the American immigrant's studio apartment, never mind Irina and Samira. With no family in Israel, and no safety net, Mathew was as alone and defenseless as they. Without his job at Karlin & Son, how far was he from landing on the street?

Mathew handed out Carlsbergs in green bottles of frosted glass. He spread the sheet over the bed, indicated for them to sit, and pulled up the white plastic chair. He asked the usual questions about Moshe's death, return, and Heaven. The answers rolled off Moshe's tongue.

Moshe said, "I'm sorry about your job."

"Don't be. Getting fired was the best thing that could have happened to me."

"It was?" Moshe sipped his beer to hide his disappointment.

"Avi is an asshole. He didn't come up to your ankles, man,

and I'm not just saying that." He gave a bitter laugh. "That jerk got under my skin from day one, even before he became the big boss." He took a swig of beer. "But besides that, getting fired opened my mind. I signed up for unemployment and took a course in technical writing. I start my first job next week. I'll earn double what I used to and work fixed office hours."

"That's great," Moshe said. "Good for you."

"You should try it."

"Try what?" Moshe's English was workable but not on a level for technical writing.

"Unemployment." Mathew nodded his head with enthusiasm. "Go to the Ministry of Employment. Fill out a form. Check in once a week. You don't even have to look a human being in the eye—just use the self-service terminal. You worked hard all those years, right? Might as well get something back. Until you find your feet."

Unemployment benefits. The thought had never occurred to Moshe. Mathew had a valid point. Irina nodded her support for the motion too. Moshe had kept careful books. He had paid his social security levies to Bituach Leumi every month. The Ministry might even find him a job. He had never spent so long without the buzz of an all-consuming project, and the days of inactivity gnawed on his nerves. Why not?

"Thanks, Mathew," he said. "I'll try that."

"You're welcome." He nodded his head some more. The immigrant had lived in a large box for years, lost his job—but not his optimism—and still came out smiling. Life in Wisconsin must be pretty tough.

"Mathew," he said, curiosity bubbling up through the beer, "do you ever regret moving to Israel?"

Mathew blinked at him and then searched for his answer on the blank wall.

"Nope," he said. He took another long gulp of beer. "But sometimes," he added, "I regret that some of the other people moved here."

CHAPTER 30

Avi ducked as a dinner plate hurtled overhead and shattered against the wall of the living room. Shards of china and plaster rained on his head.

Galit reached for another plate. "You lied to me!"

He spread his hands like a lion-tamer in the corner of a cage. "Calm down. Please."

She had spent the day crying in their bedroom. When she emerged Saturday night, Avi thought that she had settled down. He was wrong.

"You said he faked his death," she said.

Avi dodged another plate and stepped closer. Eventually she'd run out of ammunition. He hoped to reach her before then. They had no money for a new dinner service, but now was probably not the best time to tell her about the financial crisis at Karlin & Son.

This was Moshe's fault. Everything was Moshe's fault. Not for the first time, Avi wished that he had never met Moshe Karlin. He sure as hell wished he had never saved his neck. Moshe had stolen Galit from him once before—he was not going to steal her again.

"I was wrong," he lied. "I made a mistake. What made more sense—that he came back from the grave?"

Moshe's death had been a windfall. Finally, Avi had gotten

the girl and inherited a business—the head start that life had never offered him.

But Moshe couldn't let him enjoy it, could he? He had to return from the dead and ruin his life. Again.

Another plate spun through the air. This time, he ducked too late. The plate glanced off his temple and crashed on the marble tiles. He touched his wound and his fingers returned red and wet.

Humor, Moshe had said. *Make her laugh.* Avi saw nothing to laugh about, so he said, "Just listen to me for a second, will you?"

Galit allowed the ceasefire, her chest heaving. He didn't blame her for freaking out. The sight of Moshe in their bedroom had made him almost pee his pajamas. But the apparition had neither torn him limb from limb, nor cursed him for his sins. The ghost had not remembered dying. He didn't even know that he was supposed to be dead.

When Moshe moved to throw him out, Avi chose fight over flight. This time he would not step aside.

"You're right," he said. "He died. But that doesn't change who he is. It doesn't change what he did to you."

Galit loosened her grip on the plate. Avi stepped closer. He understood how she felt. He felt it too. The terror. The anger. The fear. *Aim those emotions at Moshe.*

"Can't you see what he's doing?" he said. "He's trying to confuse you. To make you forget."

One more step forward and he wrapped his arms around her. She shuddered in his embrace as she sobbed. "It's him. It's really him."

"I know," he said. "But I won't let him hurt you again."

Avi's knuckles were still raw from decking Moshe the previous night. In two weeks, Avi would marry Galit and—dead or alive—Moshe wouldn't matter anymore. Two weeks was a long time to keep Moshe at bay.

"But God brought him back..." she said.

"Shh." He rocked her in his arms. She was asking questions again. He feared those questions the most. He had to act fast—fast and smart—to remove Moshe from the scene for good.

And now he knew how.

"He won't bother you again," he said. He kissed her head and smiled. Moshe would never see it coming.

CHAPTER 31

Noga curled up on an oversized beanbag and tried to get the dark eyes of Eli Katz out of her head.

The television stood blank and silent in the living room of her rental off Ussishkin Street in Nachlaot. She took a sip from her mug of coffee.

Why can't I meet a normal guy?

When she was eighteen years old, her body had shed the extra pounds of adolescence. Her podgy face and bloated limbs became slim and slender, and all of a sudden, the cocky boys who had ignored her for years vied for her attention. She saw right through them and she despised their advances. Then loathing had turned to fear: that one day an exceptionally sly brute would penetrate her defenses, conquer her heart, and make her his trophy wife. Would he care about the girl behind the pretty face?

She built walls of suspicion around her, relying on well-meaning friends and coworkers at the hospital for a supply of random single men.

The term "blind dates" did not do them justice. She preferred to think of them as "blind, deaf, and dumb dates" as the slew of doctors, computer geeks, and academics fell into three classes: men who saw only themselves; men who didn't listen to a word she said; and men blessed with the conversation skills of a dead fish.

Noga preferred the company of her library. Books provided hours of entertainment. You could shut them if they bored
you. And you never had to wait for them to call.

As she approached thirty, fewer invitations came her way.
Which did she prefer—the torrent of disappointments or the
deathly silence?

The click-clack of high heels on hard floor tiles announced
that Sharona had entered the living room. The young student's denim skirt barely covered her behind and the neckline
of her Guess tank top dipped toward her navel. New Yorkers
had different ideas about fashion.

"Going out with girlfriends," she announced in English.
"See you later!" Noga had asked her flatmate always to let her
know where she was going in case she went missing. Yes, she
had turned into a crazy old aunt.

Noticing Noga sprawled on the beanbag, Sharona gave her
a sad, puppy-dog face. "Aw. Do you wanna come along?"

*Poor old maid mopes at home alone on a Saturday night. Let me
save her.*

"Thanks, but I've got work to do," Noga lied.

Sharona's eyes brightened. "I can help with your makeup."

She was always offering Noga a makeover. "With the right
clothes and hair," she had once told her, "you'll be stunning."

Thanks a lot.

Sharona wasn't the brightest crystal in the chandelier. She
studied International Relations at Hebrew U and her field-
work seemed to involve visiting every mall and coffee shop in
the capital. She took pride in the fact that her parents had
named her after a pop song in the late seventies.

At the end of the year, Sharona would pack her bags and
return home to Manhattan, and Noga would find a replacement, as she did every year.

"You have a good time," Noga said. Sharona didn't need
her aging Israeli flatmate to spoil her night on the town.

Sharona gave her one last pained look and marched out
the door in a cloud of powdery perfume.

Her young flatmate meant no harm. She might even be right. *Crawl out of your shell. Maybe then you'll meet a normal guy.*

Like Eli Katz.

She almost sprayed Nescafe over her legs as she laughed. What a waste of time that had been. Her curiosity about the mystery patient had grown into sympathy for a lonely and tormented invalid. When he grabbed her arm, however, a dormant emotion stirred inside her. The sensation went beyond his magnetic gaze, boyish locks, or manly jaw, although she could not deny those. She had felt a sense of belonging—that he had claimed her, that she had come home.

She had been willing to write off the delusional outburst to brain trauma and drugs. Yesterday, however, the illusion had shattered into tiny jagged shards: Eli Katz was a first-rate jerk. *Then why am I still thinking about him?*

Noga's phone jingled.

"Hi, Sarit."

"We're going out tonight."

"No, thank you."

"I'm not accepting 'no' for an answer."

Sarit, her old classmate from Hebrew U, never ran out of bubbly optimism. It drove Noga insane.

"What are we doing this time?"

"Folk dancing at Binyanei Ha'uma."

"Folk dancing? What are we—seventy years old?"

"Hey, be grateful. The other option was a sing-along. I'm sure there'll be lots of single guys there tonight."

"Yeah. Seventy-year-old singles. Who like folk dancing. Besides, I just met someone at work."

"Really? A doctor?"

Noga had planted the half-truth to avoid death by folk dancing, but she regretted her words already.

"No, a patient."

"Is he married?"

"No, he's not married."

"I thought you worked with couples from IVF."

"Mostly. This guy is in a different ward."

"Which ward?"

"Neurology. Motorbike accident."

"So he's brain dead? Sounds like a match made in heaven."

"Very funny. He's mentally sound, I'll have you know, except..." She trailed off.

"Except what?"

Noga had already said more than she had planned to, but the rest was too good to omit. "Well, sometimes he thinks he's Elijah the Prophet."

Laughter on the line. "Shut! Up!"

"No kidding."

"Well, at least you actually spoke to him. That's a step forward for you. Now, about tonight—"

"I told you, I'm not interested."

"Forget about yourself for a minute. *I* need you, remember? You're the bait."

"What am I—a worm?"

"A diamond. You attract the big fish. I reel them in. We're a team."

"You're crazier than the guy at the hospital."

"Fine, stay home and be miserable."

"I will. Warm regards to the granddads."

"Yeah, same to Elijah. Who knows, maybe he's legit."

Noga ended the call. At least Sarit made her smile, even if it was at her own expense.

She drained her coffee and got up. She stepped under a hot shower and combed the knots from her hair. Then she poured herself a tall glass of Shiraz, turned on her Logitech UE Boom wireless speaker, and returned to the living room. She hit play on her phone and leaned back on the beanbag.

The lazy jazz musings of a piano and bass guitar mellowed the atmosphere, and the soothing, husky voice of Norah Jones sang "The Nearness of You." Noga swirled the red wine in the glass, breathed in the fruity scent, and took a sip. The dark eyes of Eli Katz bored into her. His fingers tightened on her skin.

She opened her laptop on the coffee table and searched the Internet. According to Wikipedia, the biblical Elijah—zealous prophet and miracle-worker—had championed the cause of God in the northern kingdom of Israel and fought against the worship of Baal. He poured oil from empty vessels, called down fire from the heavens, and even raised the dead, until a whirlwind had whisked him away to heaven on a chariot of fire.

As such, he never died, and he continued to pop up throughout Jewish history: he rebuked the sages of the Talmud, imparted esoteric wisdom to saintly rabbis in the Middle Ages, and—to this day—paid surreptitious visits to Passover meals and circumcision ceremonies around the globe. Elijah was a busy man.

Two details stood out. Legend identified Elijah with the biblical Phineas—grandson of Aaron, the brother of Moses and the first High Priest. This factoid crowned Elijah as both prophet and priest, and dovetailed nicely with her own research project.

Secondly, Jewish tradition tapped Elijah the Prophet as harbinger of the Messiah, and predicted his return to the stage of history ahead of the "great and terrible Day of the Lord." At that time, Elijah would create peace within families and restore the Ten Lost Tribes of Israel.

She remembered Eli Katz's deranged speech about the End of Days. He had spoken with such urgency and conviction. Her anger at his rudeness evaporated, leaving a silt of pity. Poor creature. Confined to a hospital room. Broken. Depressed. Alone. Once again, she found her own face reflected in his dark eyes.

She closed her laptop and took another long sip.

Too bad, she thought. Time to move on.

CHAPTER 32

Eight o'clock Sunday morning, Irina and Moshe walked through Safra Square, an expansive plaza of checkered gray stone in downtown Jerusalem. The large government buildings on every side made Irina feel very small.

Samira had remained at the rabbi's house, fearful of bumping into family members who worked at the government institutions. What had the Arab girl done to enrage her family so? Irina had not dared to ask. She could not hide at the rabbi's home much longer. None of them could. Tonight, Moshe and the rabbi were to appear before the Great Council, which would probably split them up. This might be her last day with Moshe.

Moshe greeted the guard at the door of the Ministry of Employment. The elderly man raised his fluffy eyebrows and returned the greeting. Moshe always had a kind word for waiters, janitors, and security guards—the invisible people that others ignored. Irina noticed that. Moshe was a gentleman.

He plucked a ticker tape number from a dispenser at the entrance to a large waiting hall and found two empty bucket seats of hard plastic. They watched a digital display. Each time the number changed, a computerized voice instructed the bearer to approach a numbered counter. Twenty turns to go. Irina didn't mind. She savored her last hours with Moshe, one of her few friends in her new life and the one she trusted most.

A dark cloud hovered over him this morning. His wife had refused his advances and flowers. Her loss. If she didn't recognize a good man when she saw one, then she didn't deserve him. In addition, his treasured family business had failed—the main reason for their excursion to the Ministry of Employment. She wished she could ease his pain.

"You never told me the rest of the story," she said. This might be her last chance to find out.

Moshe looked up. "Which story?"

"How Avi saved your life."

"Oh." He folded his arms over his chest. "We were on reserve duty together in the South Hebron Mountains. Eight-hour shifts securing the roads between Jewish villages. There were four of us in the pillbox—that's a cement watchtower surrounded by concrete blocks and barbed wire—in the cold."

Irina pictured him in an olive uniform, a rifle slung over his shoulder like the soldiers she saw on the streets and buses.

"Avi had something to say about everyone," he continued. "Especially Nimrod, a rich kid from North Tel Aviv. Nimrod said his wife complained all the time, so Avi said..." Moshe trailed off.

"Said what?"

His cheeks reddened. "Well, he said: 'Women always moan; you get to choose the reason,' implying that Nimrod didn't, well, you know…"

"I get it," she said. This Avi was not a gentleman.

"Avi loved to get under his skin. One afternoon, Nimrod came down to the yard and handed out cigarettes. His wife was pregnant. 'Boy or girl?' Avi asked. When Nimrod said 'girl,' Avi laughed. 'The Arabs have a saying,' he said: 'What you put in is what you get out.'"

Irina took a few seconds to figure out that one. "Oh, my."

Moshe continued. "Yep. Nimrod didn't let that one go.

He lunged at Avi and I had to keep them apart. Then Avi tackled me to the ground, and the world exploded. Machine gun fire. The ricochet of bullets. A terrorist had walked right in. Avi rolled over and returned fire. The terrorist got away. Nimrod wasn't so lucky. He never saw his daughter. If Avi hadn't pulled me down, I would have joined him."

"Wow." She had assumed that Moshe had served in the Israel Defense Forces, but never imagined what he had gone through in uniform.

A loud noise startled her, and she grabbed Moshe's arm.

He looked over his shoulder. "It's OK," he said. "Someone dropped a book. Half the room had a heart attack."

Irina released his arm. "I'm sorry."

"Don't be," he said. "Anyway," he continued his story, "Avi was out of work, so I offered him a job. And so our lives became entwined."

The automated voice announced their number and directed them to counter number four, where they found a desk and another two bucket chairs.

"ID?" their attendant asked without looking up from the screen. The well-preserved woman had dyed her long hair black. She squinted at a computer monitor over reading glasses that clung to the tip of her nose. Her nametag read Dafna Siman-Tov.

Moshe recited his nine-digit identification number, and the lady pecked at the keyboard with two fingers.

She clucked and shook her head.

"Stupid computer. They put in a new system yesterday. Rinat?" she called. A younger woman in a white blouse arrived and peered over her shoulder.

"Says here he's dead."

Rinat pointed at the screen with long, pink manicured nails. "Click Override. I'll approve it. Must be another glitch."

Irina and Moshe exchanged glances and hid their smiles. They might actually make progress here.

Dafna moved the mouse, gave it a click, and her face brightened.

"Right, Moshe Karlin." She glanced at him now that he officially existed in the system. "How long have you been unemployed?"

"A week."

"First time here?"

"Yes."

"Last job?"

"I ran my own business."

"We're fresh out of CEO positions, sweetie. You'll have to fill in the survey." She squinted at the screen and jabbed at the keyboard. "Do you have any degrees?"

"I didn't go to university."

Click. Click. "Skills?"

"Uh, management?"

She shook her head. "No Management here. Typing?"

"No."

"Brick laying?"

"Nope."

"Agricultural work?"

"Never got around to it."

"Sanitation?"

"Not if I can help it."

Poor Moshe. His humor plastered over his embarrassment. Work meant so much to a man's ego.

Click. Click. Dafna frowned. "Nothing," she said.

"Nothing?"

"There's telemarketing and call center work, but you need to be a student. Oh, wait, what's this?" She squinted at the screen again.

Irina held her breath. *Give him something. Anything.*

"Public office."

"Pardon?"

Dafna turned the screen around. "See for yourself. Mayor. Member of Parliament. Prime Minister."

Irina laughed. Was this a joke?

Moshe laughed too. "Prime Minister?"

"That's what it says. They're the only jobs that don't require skills or education."

Irina read the screen. Dafna wasn't joking.

"So do I just sign up?"

"No, it's a self-employment recommendation. You have to join a party, or create one. Politicians do it all the time. Hard to keep track. Next elections are in three months, so you better get started. Your unemployment payments start in a few days. Check in every week at the self-service computers on the first floor."

"Every week?"

"If you're still unemployed. I'll need your bank details and pay slips for the last six months."

"I... I don't have them with me."

The clerk's shoulders sagged. *Silly man*, they seemed to say. *Didn't do your homework, did you?* She folded her hands on the desk. "Then you'll have to come back and reregister. What about your wife?"

"Oh no," Irina said. "We're not married."

"She's a friend," Moshe said.

"Just friends," Irina added. Her cheeks felt hot.

"Are you unemployed too?"

"Yes."

"ID?"

"I don't remember. I don't have my identity book."

"Name?"

Moshe said, "We'll come back another time."

They crossed Safra Square toward Jaffa Street and a line of tall palm trees. The late morning sun reflected white off the public buildings of Jerusalem stone. People flowed around them. People with skills and jobs. Hawkers offered them hot bagels and bottled water. Moshe's shoulders slumped as he walked.

"I'm sorry," Irina said.

"It's OK. We had little chance of getting anywhere."

"What do we do now?"

"Odd jobs, I suppose. Wait tables." Moshe stared at something behind her.

She turned around. A man stood in the middle of the square, an island in the stream of pedestrians. A sign with large black letters hung from straps on his shoulders: "Honest Work. Honest Pay."

"Jobs!" the man cried, first in Hebrew, then Russian. "Money! No documents required."

A passerby took a slip of paper from his hands. Moshe and Irina walked over and took one too. No company name or logo. No marketing copy. Just an address in Talpiot.

"What is this?" he asked.

"Shto?" the man said. What?

Irina took over in Russian. "What jobs?"

He shrugged. "I just hand out the fliers, miss."

She translated for Moshe, who was still staring at the address.

"Sounds good," he said.

"Yes. Too good."

Moshe shrugged. "What do we have to lose?"

CHAPTER 33

Yosef stared at his sandwich on the staff room table. He had not touched his lunch. In a few hours, he would stand before the Great Council of Torah Sages bearing the best possible tidings, but a drop of doubt muddied his excitement.

In his mind's eye, Samira stood on his doorstep in a makeshift hijab, desperation in her eyes. None of the ancient sources had mentioned resurrected gentiles; some had explicitly limited the miracle to Jews. How was this possible?

He glanced at his wristwatch. Half an hour until his next class. He had debated whether to call Rabbi Emden Saturday night, and decided not to bother the busy rabbi. Yosef must have misread the sources. As the meeting drew closer, however, he changed his mind. Best to update the good rabbi before they stood before the leading sages of the generation. No surprises.

He dialed the number on his phone. The call cut to an answering service. He didn't leave a message. *Stop worrying, Yosef.* The Great Council would know what to do, no matter what.

"May I have a word with you, Rabbi Yosef?" said a calm, crisp voice.

Yosef looked up. Rabbanit Leah Schiff, the principal of Daas Torah Primary, stood over him. He pocketed the phone with a sudden sense of guilt, as though she had caught him cheating. Rabbanit Schiff had that effect on him.

"Of course." He followed his employer to her office. He did not close the door. Jewish law forbade seclusion with a married woman.

Rabbanit Schiff sat down behind her desk, her back ramrod-straight. Her fingertips formed a steeple as she considered Rabbi Yosef with unblinking eyes. With her symmetrical *sheitel* of short, dark hair, she reminded him of the humanoid robots from the science fiction movies of his youth. The rabbanit ran a tight ship and always smiled. On occasion, the smile had moved unfortunate teachers to tears. Today she aimed her smile at Yosef.

"Rabbi Yosef," she said, choosing each word with care. "Do you know why parents choose our school?"

Yosef knew better than to reply.

"Purity," she said. "Parents entrust their children's pure minds to our pure environment where we teach them pure Torah." She let the weight of her words sink in. Her gaze dropped to the edge of the table. "I have ignored your little adventures beyond the approved syllabus in the past. Harmless tidbits for a child's wandering mind. But now we have received complaints."

"Complaints?" Yosef squeezed the seat of his chair.

The unblinking eyes trained on his. "Last week, children in your class returned home with questions about their dead grandparents. Disturbing questions. Our job is to fill their minds with knowledge, not questions."

"But the Talmud is filled with questions."

"Yes, Rabbi Yosef. Questions that arrive with ready answers. The questions you have raised only lead to more questions. They are... dangerous." She straightened the row of pens on her desk. "There are enough distractions in the outside world. We don't want to unsettle their pure minds. Do you understand?"

Yosef blinked. He needed the job. If one school blacklisted him, word would spread, and he would need a new career.

"Yes," he said. "Of course. No more talk of the Resurrection. My apologies."

Her smile widened. "Thank you, Rabbi Lev. That will be all."

He got to his feet and left the office. Never mind. Tonight the sages of the Great Council would hear all and, within minutes, the religious world would know the joyous truth: the long-awaited Redemption had begun! Then the Resurrection would be on everyone's lips.

CHAPTER 34

The sudden screech of tires on asphalt made Irina grab Moshe's arm again. All eyes turned to the white car that had halted before the bus shelter on Jaffa Street where they sat. The man in the passenger seat lurched forward and whipped back in his seat. The smell of burning rubber wafted in the air. On the roof of the car, the word "taxi" was displayed in a yellow half-moon.

Hearing no crunch of fenders, the startled pedestrians continued on their way, but Irina's relief was short-lived. The driver's door opened, and a short, dark-skinned man of middle age walked around the car and marched toward her.

Moshe stood and the man stopped inches from him. "Moshe Karlin," he said, "is that you?" His voice had a rough, raspy edge.

The old man didn't wait for an answer. He threw his arms around Moshe and hugged his chest. Moshe gave Irina a helpless, bemused look.

The driver held Moshe at arms' length and inspected him like a long-lost lover. "Great God! Moshe Karlin. I thought you were dead."

"Hey! Driver!" the passenger yelled out the window. "The meter is running."

The cabbie didn't seem to hear. "I heard rumors but I

didn't dare believe them. How can this be?"

"God alone knows," Moshe said.

"Fantastic! Wonderful news!"

He seemed to notice Irina for the first time.

"This is Irina. Irina, meet Rafi. A very dear friend."

"A friend?" Rafi seemed insulted. "More like family. I've known Moshe since he was in his mother's womb."

The passenger got out of the cab, slammed the door, and flagged down another taxi.

Rafi wiped a tear from his crinkly eye. "I didn't hear you on the radio. Are you back at work?"

Moshe's smile faded at the mention of his company. "It's complicated."

"Of course," Rafi said, as though not keen to pry. "And Galit? She must be overjoyed to see you."

"I'm afraid that's complicated as well."

"I see." Rafi seemed genuinely distressed at his friend's plight. "I can imagine. After, what, two years? Where are you heading? Let me give you a ride. Let's talk in the air conditioning."

They got inside and the taxi pulled off.

Irina had the back seat to herself. The soft upholstery was a welcome change after the hard plastic chairs of the Ministry of Employment.

Rafi caught her eye in the rearview mirror. "Let me tell you about the Karlins," he said with pride. "Moshe's father, David, got me into this business. I was a young soldier when the Yom Kippur War hit. The Egyptians crossed the Suez Canal and marched across Sinai. Syrian tanks rolled through the Golan. Iraq and Jordan joined the assault. Their leaders talked of driving us into the sea. In Tel Aviv, the government dug mass graves. This was the end of us." His face sobered in the mirror.

"My battalion charged the Golan Heights. Brothers-in-arms died around me. Of my whole platoon, only I lived to tell the tale." He drew a labored breath at the memory. "We survived the war but the country was a mess. Hard to believe that now. My head was a mess. I wanted to get as far away as possible. I bought a ticket for Argentina. My mom told his dad"—he nodded at Moshe—"and the night before my flight, he came over to our house. 'Work with me,' he said. He helped me finance a taxi. Made sure I had enough clients to cover the payments and then some. A year later, I bought two more cars and hired drivers. I owe it all to David Karlin."

"Wow," Irina said. "That's quite a story."

The motor purred as they meandered through the city center. A woman in sunglasses bustled along with oversized shopping bags on her arm. A man wearing a large black skullcap bit into a slice of pizza as he stared at his phone.

Moshe asked, "Is your Mercedes in the shop?"

"Sold it."

"For a Seat?"

"Nothing beats a Mercedes, I know. But the services! And the gas! This car is not as comfortable, but that's cash in the bank. Times are not what they used to be, Moshe." Rafi sighed. Gloom settled over the eyes in the mirror. "These youngsters and their fancy mobile apps." He shook his head at the corruption of the youth. "Soon after you died, the dispatch calls dried up. I had to rely on street pickups and long-haul routes, but even those became rare. I had to let go of my drivers and sell the cars."

Moshe seemed shocked. "How many?"

"All of them. Twenty in total. Some days I get a call, some days none. But I cut my expenses. I get by. Sold the house too, moved to a two-room apartment. The boys are in the army now and the house was getting too large for Rivka anyway. She... she hasn't been very well." His eyes darkened in the mirror.

"I'm very sorry to hear that," Moshe said, but he didn't press him for details. Then, he said, "I don't understand. What about that mobile app?"

Rafi's voice filled with fire. "And turn my back on Karlin & Son? Never! I told those toddler techies to shove their stupid app you-know-where."

Moshe ran his hand through his hair and Irina understood his anguish. A good man had thrown away his business to keep faith with the dead.

"Rafi," Moshe said in a kind voice, "Karlin & Son had a good run, but times have changed."

Rafi was not convinced. "Those little squirts have no respect."

"My father wouldn't want you to suffer in his name," Moshe said. "And I sure don't want you to lose out. You've paid back our family ten times over with your loyalty. So please, my friend. Move on. For my sake. For my father."

Rafi said nothing for the rest of the trip, but in the rearview mirror, the eyes blinked back tears.

The cab stopped at a run-down backstreet. Rafi refused to let them pay for the ride. He handed Moshe a business card through the window. "If you need anything, just call," Rafi said. "Anything." Moshe shook his hand, and the cab pulled off in search of better days.

Irina scanned the deserted street corner. Large silent buildings lined the street in varying degrees of decay. "There's nothing here."

Moshe rechecked the flier. "This is the address."

Cracked planks boarded the doors and windows of an old store. The name stenciled on the wall had faded beyond recognition.

"These guys have a very bad sense of humor."

The sound of footfalls made them turn. A man in a tweed suit jogged toward them. His hair was a mop of gray, as was his thick mustache.

"Can I help you?" Another thick Russian accent.

Moshe handed him the flier.

The man pocketed the paper without reading it. He sized them up with small, beady eyes. Irina gave him a polite smile and straightened her shoulders, as if to say, *I'm as good as any man, buster!* It seemed to work.

"This way," he said, and he trotted down the street.

They followed.

He turned a corner, then another, and waited for them outside a warehouse of corrugated fiberglass. He opened a sliding door and closed it behind them. They stood in a large airy hangar. Plastic curtains divided the grounds into cubicles that contained low steel-framed cots.

The man climbed a metal stairwell and the clank of their shoes on the steps echoed off the fiberglass walls. A narrow walkway led to a square office with large windows.

He unlocked the door and waved them inside. "Coffee? Tea?"

They declined the offer.

He took his seat behind a cheap desk and waved them to two rickety chairs. A laptop and filing cabinet lent the room an air of businesslike respectability. He leaned back in his chair and smiled.

"My name is Boris," he said. "Many people want to work but don't have the right papers. The State doesn't make life easy. Foreign workers, they call them. Infiltrators. They hunt them down. We can help."

"What kind of work?" Moshe asked.

"This and that. Manual labor. Training on the job. The pay is modest but you get two solid meals a day, and an apartment downstairs."

Irina would not have called the refugee camp of changing booths below "apartments" but she could excuse the exaggerated marketing language for a roof over her head and food in her belly, all earned by her own labor.

"Two apartments," Moshe said.

Irina nodded.

Boris made a show of deliberation. "Two apartments, then. No extra charge. Agreed?" They nodded. "First, a few technicalities." He turned to Irina. "Raise your chin." He pointed to a small mounted camera behind him. He clicked a button on his laptop. Irina and Moshe swapped seats, and he repeated the procedure. A few more clicks and a printer came to life and pushed out two sheets of paper.

The paperwork reassured her. For all its shabbiness and

dodgy advertising, Boris ran a bona fide operation.

The manager slid the pages of fine print toward them, along with two ballpoint pens. "Sign at the bottom," he said. "Good." He reclaimed the sheets and tucked them in a folder. "You start tomorrow at six AM."

Six AM! Irina had missed that in her very cursory review of the contract, but she would do whatever the job required. Moshe glanced at her, a question in his eye. Irina nodded. They had learned to read each other's thoughts.

He said, "A friend of ours needs a job too. She can stay with Irina."

Boris shrugged. "Bring her along and I'll make the arrangements. If you'll excuse me, I have other work to attend to."

He escorted them out and slid the doors of the hangar shut.

"That was simple enough," Moshe said. "Things are looking up."

"Yes," Irina said. No matter what the rabbis of the Great Council decided that night, she would stay by Moshe's side for the near future. That alone was worth the early mornings.

CHAPTER 35

Eli felt his pulse quicken in his neck when the girl appeared at the foot of his bed.

She folded her arms over her chest. "The nurse said you wanted to speak with me," she said, apprehension in her eyes and her mouth shut tight. After their last encounter, he didn't blame her. But why had his own mouth dried up?

His free arm twitched. "Yes," he said. "Eliana. Your name is Noga, right?"

She nodded. She had tied her hair up, exposing a creamy neck and her large intelligent eyes. Had the sudden vision of beauty triggered his involuntary responses, or his unease with what he was about to do? He had always kept interactions with humanity to a minimum and for good reason, but now he needed this girl.

"I owe you an apology," he said. "I had no right to talk to you like that." That much was true. The large eyes fixed on him, so he continued. "This has been very difficult for me." Another truth. "I was... not my usual self." Not strictly accurate but the words had the desired effect. Her shoulders relaxed, as did the corners of her mouth. She was starting to thaw.

"You mentioned that you were heading a research project. Could you tell me more?"

The arms loosened over her chest. "Sure," she said.

Bingo! I'm not as rusty as I thought. "Please," he said and indicated the empty visitor's chair. "Sit with me."

She did. He lifted his bandaged leg from the sling and orchestrated a soft landing on the bedsheet. Then he pressed his palms to the mattress, pushed back, and raised his body to a sitting position. He had practiced the procedure all of Saturday. The pain had subsided a little each time.

"What?" he said. She was gawking at him.

"Nothing. Just… Are you supposed to be doing that already? I thought you'd be immobile for weeks."

He shrugged. "I'm on the fast track. Now tell me about your study."

"I'm measuring gene markers across demographic groups."

"So you're a gene detective?"

She smiled. "More like a gene archaeologist. Genes mutate over time, but most pass unchanged from generation to generation. We can trace the spread of genetic markers from one ethnic group to another as populations mingled and interbred. That's how we discovered that all humans are descended from a single female."

"I could have told you that without drawing blood."

"Well, now we have scientific proof."

Scientific proof. A rationalist.

"And what genes are you tracing now?"

"The Cohen Gene."

"The Cohen Gene—as in Jews of priestly descent?" This would be easier than he thought.

"Exactly!" She leaned forward. "Priests claim to descend from one man, Aaron, brother of Moses and the first priest. If that is true, there should be genetic markers unique to priests."

"And do such markers exist?"

"We've identified a number of candidates. We call them the Cohen Modal Haplotype, a pattern of six Y-STR markers—or short tandem repeats—on the male-only Y chromosome." She paused. "Sorry, I'm boring you with the details."

"No, not at all." He suppressed a yawn. "Please go on."

"Historically, the Jewish community has been genetically aloof," she continued, her eyes flashing and her smile widening, "only marrying within the faith, and so the gene signatures are quite homogenous. That breeds genetic diseases like Tay-Sachs, but it also allows us to follow the path of specific genes, like the Cohen Gene."

Aloof. Signatures. Homogenous. Does she always hide behind long words?

"So our genes tell a story, is that it?"

"Exactly! Even if the memory of your past is forgotten, your story is embedded in your genes." She halted and her eyes glazed over, as though she had revealed too much.

What is your story, Noga? The geneticist had become more interesting by the minute.

Eliana swept into the room and they fell into an awkward silence. The nurse made a show of checking his clipboard, then winked at Noga and bustled out. Checking up on her little girl.

Time to take their relationship to the next level. "We have a lot in common," he said.

Noga flushed. "What do you mean?"

"I also find genealogy fascinating."

She raised a doubtful eyebrow. "Do you now?"

Eli had never shared this with a soul, but the circumstances warranted sacrifice. If the Day of the Lord arrived soon, as seemed likely, this revelation wouldn't matter anyway.

"In fact," he said, "I run a genealogy website."

"Really? Which one?"

"Have you heard of OpenGen?"

She cocked her head and raised both eyebrows. "You're OpenGen?"

"Not a big deal. Runs itself mostly but pays the bills. Don't worry, I won't go digging around your family tree."

She looked away and her cheeks reddened again. His attempt at humor had touched another sensitive topic. Invasive parents? Genetic deformities? He made a mental note to steer clear of her family tree in conversation.

"I'll do it," he said.

"Do what?"

"Take part in your study. Where do I sign?"

She brushed a stray lock of hair from her face, pulled a sheet from her plastic folder, and handed him a pen.

He read the printed text of the agreement. "It's anonymous?"

"Yes. We have no way of connecting individuals to their results."

"Even if the results are off the charts?"

"Mm-hmm. And our statistical analysis will ignore the outliers anyway."

Eli signed on the dotted line. A vial of his blood donated to an anonymous research project was a vial not undergoing invasive testing at the hospital. How many vials were there?

He handed her the form and pen. "There's only one problem," he said, and he produced his charming smile. "I'll need to find another excuse to see you again."

Another blush. She stood and brushed off her jeans. "I'm sure you'll think of something." She left with a satisfied smile on her lips.

He shifted his body down the mattress, returned his damaged leg to the sling, and lay flat on his back.

He needed to conserve energy. He might be home sooner than he thought.

CHAPTER 36

Sunday night, Moshe looked out the passenger window of Rabbi Yosef's Subaru and his mouth dropped open.

The giant cube of the Belz Great Synagogue blazed golden in powerful spotlights and hung over the old apartment buildings in north Jerusalem like a spaceship landing in a murky forest.

Seven narrow windows ran the length of the facade, beneath a crown of pointed merlons. The design conjured thoughts both of Herod's ancient Temple—as a boy, Moshe had viewed a model of the structure at the Holy Land museum—and, strangely, the Knesset building of the Israeli government.

"Is that it?" he asked.

The rabbi nodded. He wore a fresh black suit. He had turned off the Cyndi Lauper cassette and spoken little during the short drive. When Moshe told him about their new jobs, the rabbi had avoided his eyes and offered to drive them early the next day to their new lodgings. Did he feel guilty about their departure or was the rabbi merely nervous ahead of their meeting with the Great Council?

They plowed into the thicket of Kiryat Belz and the golden synagogue disappeared behind the bland apartment buildings. The rabbi maneuvered the car through the narrow streets, climbing upward toward the holy sanctuary. They dodged green garbage bins, men in coats and hats, and kerchief-headed women pushing strollers.

They rounded a corner and the Belz Synagogue burst overhead, a silent beacon in the night. Rabbi Yosef parked his car in the empty lot beside the synagogue. The sound of their closing car doors bounced off the walls.

Moshe placed a white velvet skullcap on his head. The great twin doors of the synagogue rose to triple his height. The ultra-Orthodox, known for their abject poverty and devotion to Torah study, must have paid a king's ransom for the extravagant synagogue. Just the monthly electricity bills must cost a small fortune. Some of the devout, apparently, had very deep pockets.

The rabbi touched the large golden knob but stopped short of opening.

"Everything all right?"

Rabbi Yosef turned to him. He seemed to wake from a trance. "I've never addressed such a gathering of great rabbis."

"You've never met them before?"

"This is the Great Council of Torah Sages. The leaders of the generation. They assemble only to discuss matters of great communal importance."

"Good thing we're on time."

The rabbi grinned. He pushed, and the door swung inward. They stood in the dim light of a wood-paneled corridor. A tall man with a long, tidy beard turned to them and smiled.

"Yosef, my friend." The rabbi, who wore a silken suit and fine black bowler, embraced Rabbi Yosef. He extended his hand to Moshe. "You must be Mr. Karlin. Pleased to meet you."

Rabbi Yosef introduced Rabbi Emden.

"Follow me, my friends," he said. "The Great Council awaits."

They followed Rabbi Emden down the corridor. The furnishers had spared no expense on the interior either. They passed carved benches and miniature crystal chandeliers but not a living soul. The synagogue must be off limits during sessions of the Great Council. A security arrangement? Moshe imagined a row of consulate-grade SUVs with tinted windows parked in a VIP garage beneath the synagogue.

Rabbi Emden halted outside another set of tall wooden double doors in a spacious foyer.

"The sages have other matters to discuss this evening," Rabbi Emden explained. "Their attendants will call when they are ready to receive us. How have you been adjusting to your new life, Moshe?"

The question caught him off guard. He had not expected small talk with a friendly, stately rabbi. "It's been challenging."

The tall rabbi gave him a good-natured smile. Moshe had not encountered a rabbi like Emden before, so suave, well groomed, and polite. Moshe had dispatched Charedi commuters for years but never chatted with any at length. Rabbi Emden was no street Charedi but a diplomat who would feel equally at home rubbing elbows in cabinet meetings as he would in the study hall.

"Oh," he said, as though just remembering an important detail. "The discussions are in Yiddish, so I'll translate where possible."

Moshe had forgotten that some people still spoke Yiddish. Although the language mixed Hebrew and German, he'd probably understand only a few scattered words.

"Rabbi Emden," Rabbi Yosef said. He shifted on his feet as though desperate for the men's room. "I tried to reach you earlier. A third survivor joined us on Friday."

"A third?" Rabbi Emden displayed rows of perfect square ivories and his eyes sparkled in the dim light. "Excellent."

"Yes, but—"

Yellow light poured from between the double doors of the main synagogue. A young bearded man in a gown of black silk and long black stockings stood in the opening and murmured a few words to Rabbi Emden.

"Our turn has arrived," said the elder rabbi. He adjusted his hat and followed the messenger inside with Rabbi Yosef and Moshe at his heels.

Moshe's heart jumped from his chest into his throat. He had never experienced a hall so enormous or so full of light. They stood at one extremity of the rectangular room. The Holy Ark towered above them, ten meters of finely sculpted wood. Nine immense chandeliers of brilliant crystal hung high overhead like funnel-shaped spaceships. The messenger moved fast, and they marched down a long aisle between rows of wooden pews, away from the Holy Ark and toward a central clearing dominated by an imposing raised platform of the same carved wood.

Bearded men in black gowns and white collared shirts filled a large block of pews beyond the platform—a few hundred men at least, but not a word between them. Some eyed the four approaching men with inquisitive expressions, but most trained their attention on the base of the platform, still hidden from view.

Moshe had entered a surreal and alien world where the laws and norms of the outside world held no sway, and he, in his new trousers, white shirtsleeves, and glossy white *kippah*, felt very out of place.

They rounded the platform. A long conference table of polished wood extended along the base, and a row of wizened old men in immaculate black attire and impressive white beards peered over the table at the seated masses.

The attendant led them to the no-man's-land between the pews and the conference table, and the three visitors faced the Great Council of Torah Sages, their backs to the many rows of silent students.

The seven sages sized them up with intelligent old eyes like judges inspecting defendants. Moshe recognized the generous white beard of Rabbi Auerbach from Simcha's soccer card.

"Reb Emden," said the sage in the center of the council.

He spoke a few more words in Yiddish. His eyes sparkled with warmth and kindness, but whether he extended those sentiments to all three of the visitors, Moshe could not tell. Rabbi Emden replied at length in Yiddish.

"Who is that?" Moshe whispered to Rabbi Yosef.

"Rabbi Alter," Rabbi Yosef whispered back, without taking his eyes from the formidable sages. "The Rebbe of Belz Chasidism. On his left is Rabbi Auerbach; Rabbi Teitelbaum on his right. Heads of Chasidic lines and leading *poskim*— authorities on Jewish law."

The Chasidic world, it seemed, had its own aristocracy, and Moshe stood before the kings of this parallel universe.

A gasp washed over the seated multitude behind them. Some of the rabbis of the council stirred as well, but not the three central figures. Emden must have gotten to the crux of their story.

Rabbi Emden concluded his address. Rabbi Alter raised his hand, and the murmurs fell silent. He turned his warm, kind eyes to Moshe and spoke in Hebrew. "Mr. Karlin," he said. "Please show us the sign."

Moshe felt all eyes train on him, and his cheeks warmed. "The sign?" He looked to Rabbi Emden for an explanation.

"Your shirt," Rabbi Emden said, with an encouraging smile. "Go on."

Moshe was not in the habit of exposing himself in synagogue, but he overcame his inhibitions. He pulled the edge of his shirt from his jeans and lifted the hem above his belly. The sages leaned forward and squinted. Eyes widened behind thick glasses.

The rabbis whispered quiet consultation, and Moshe tucked in his shirt.

Rabbi Alter raised his hand again for silence and the hall obeyed as one. He fired off a series of short questions and Rabbi Emden replied. Then Rabbi Alter spoke at length. The warmth faded from his eyes, and his tone hardened.

For the first time in his life, Moshe wished he understood Yiddish. "Is everything OK?" he whispered. Rabbi Yosef gave his shoulders a helpless shrug.

"Mr. Karlin." Rabbi Alter had switched back to Hebrew and turned his icy gaze on Moshe. "We of the Great Council long for the Redemption and the Messiah, son of David. But false hopes and deceivers litter our history. We see before us neither the mass resurrection of Ezekiel nor the return of the prophet Elijah. The Third Temple has not descended from on high with fire and wonders." The sage paused. Not a peep from the crowd.

"And yet," he continued, "here you are. A dead man walking among us. A secular Jew, who remembers nothing of the World of Souls. The sacred responsibility of this council is to safeguard the tradition of Sinai, as handed down through the ages. It is clear to us, Mr. Karlin, that you seek to undermine that tradition, to plant seeds of doubt, and to challenge our holy Torah."

A scandalized murmur rose in the ranks behind them. Moshe opened his mouth to object that he wasn't *seeking* anything, only survival, when Rabbi Alter raised his hand again for order.

"This council has reached its decision. We can find only one explanation." He spoke the next sentence in Yiddish, and banged his fist on the polished table like a judge sealing his verdict with the slam of a gavel. The murmur rose again and filled the hall. Not surprise, this time—but indignation. The murmur surged into an agitated roar. Hinges squealed behind them as seats pivoted and a hundred men got to their feet.

The robed attendant appeared beside them. "Leave," he said in Hebrew. "Now!" He waved his arm. "Out! Out!"

Rabbi Emden pointed to the door at the end of the synagogue. "Go! Go!" he said.

Moshe wasted no time. If he didn't escape now, the mob might rip him limb from limb. Rabbi Yosef seemed to fear the same outcome. At first, they walked—around the platform and down the endless aisle toward the Holy Ark. Then they ran, the footfalls of the angry mob in their ears. The roar coalesced into a chant of two strange words, over and over, the same two words Rabbi Alter had used at the end of his verdict.

"What are they saying?" Moshe asked as they rounded a block of pews and high-tailed it toward the large twin doors of the exit.

"*Sitra Achra*," Rabbi Yosef said, his voice a gasp as he sprinted. It sounded like the end of the world. "*Sitra Achra!*"

CHAPTER 37

Early Monday morning, on a derelict street in the Talpiot industrial zone, Moshe climbed out of Rabbi Yosef's white Subaru for the last time. He held his worldly possessions in one plastic grocery bag. Irina and Samira waited on the cracked sidewalk.

Moshe leaned on the open window of the passenger door. "Thank you for all you've done, Rabbi. We appreciate it."

Rabbi Yosef looked forlorn. "I'm sorry," he said, the first words he had spoken during the short journey.

"It's OK. There's nothing you can do." After the Great Council's verdict, they were lucky the rabbi had let them stay the night.

His words did not seem to console the kind-hearted rabbi. "Good luck," he said, and he drove off.

Sitra Achra. In hushed tones the previous night, the rabbi had explained the expression. The concept seemed bizarre to Moshe, but all the same, the result was "goodbye." They had found new accommodations just in time.

Moshe glanced at the gray corrugated wall of the nondescript warehouse. *Home sweet home*. He pulled at the metal handle and the corrugated wall slid sideways on a track.

They stepped inside. Nothing had prepared Moshe for the sights, sounds, and smells that greeted them. The warehouse floor teemed with men and women under the harsh white light of fluorescents that dangled in the air. Tall Nigerians in grimy overalls. Scruffy Europeans in sweat-stained undershirts. Workers of every size and shape sat on cots and peered at them with suspicious eyes. A fat bald man ladled lumpy porridge into tin cups.

A lanky Ethiopian sauntered in their direction. He looked them up and down. "Moshe and Irina?"

"Yes," Moshe said. "And this is Samira." He reached out his hand.

The Ethiopian stretched his shoulder. "Call me Damas. You work with me. Put your things in twenty-three and twenty-four, and get in line if you want to eat. We leave in ten minutes. You"—he indicated Samira with a nod of the head—"go upstairs and sign. Don't be late."

He padded off.

"He's a bundle of joy," Moshe said.

Irina forced a brave smile. Samira clambered up the metal stairwell toward the supervisor's office, and Moshe caught sight of Boris, the Russian with the bushy gray mustache, through the glass window.

The apartment was a two-meter square of tarpaulin. A tin mug. Dusty sleeping bag. Thin mattress. Rusty spring cot. Moshe kicked his plastic bag under the bed and closed the door flap.

He surveyed the hive of activity in the warehouse. Moshe had heard about the Sudanese refugees and fortune seekers who infiltrated the borders and occupied Southern Tel Aviv, but he had never given much thought to how they made their way through the country without papers or money. He was finding out firsthand. He slipped his watch into his pocket. No need to advertise his good fortune.

Irina emerged from her tent.

"Hungry?"

"Not anymore," he said.

"Yeah, I think I'll skip the line too." Good thing they had gobbled a slice of toast in the rabbi's kitchen before they left.

A loud whistle drew their attention. Damas waved at them to approach the entrance, and herded them into a white minivan that idled outside, the morning air filling with diesel fumes. A balding middle-aged man sat in the back. Moshe and Irina took the middle row. A minute later, Samira emerged from the warehouse and climbed into the van. She seemed relieved to see them and sat in the row in front.

Damas slid the door shut, climbed into the seat beside the driver, and the van pulled off.

"Thank you," Samira said, with an eager smile. "This is my first job."

"You've never had a job?"

"My husband wouldn't let me work outside the home. He made me stop going to school. I couldn't leave the house alone." Her husband. Samira still spoke of the man as though she was still under his thumb. The improvised hijab made her look far older than her twenty-one years.

"Don't thank us yet," Moshe said. "Let's see how the day goes."

"Did the rabbis of the Great Council arrange the jobs?"

"Not exactly. They said we're the *Sitra Achra*."

"The what?"

"It's Aramaic for 'the Other Side.'"

"Other side of what?"

Irina spoke up. "Demons, Samira." Irina had a way of cutting to the chase.

"Oh." Samira's smile disappeared. "Are we? I mean we were dead."

"Do you think you're a demon?"

She shook her head.

"There's your answer. But let me know if you grow horns."

Samira patted her hijab, then smiled at her own foolishness. "So that's why the rabbi...?" She trailed off, either failing to find the Hebrew words or uncomfortable about speaking against their former host.

"Threw us out? Yes."

The man in the seat behind them coughed.

"I'm sure everything will be OK," Moshe said. He should be careful about what he shared with whom.

Damas rested his arm on the backrest of the front seat and tapped the upholstery with his hand. The hand had a thumb and two fingers. The other two digits ended at the first joint.

A shiver traced his spine. Very careful indeed.

CHAPTER 38

Noga sat at the desk of the interview room at the hospital. She ran her fingers through her hair. After a half hour of fussing at the bathroom mirror that morning, she had decided to wear her hair down. She had even allowed Sharona to comb her lashes with mascara and dust her cheeks with blush.

In an hour, she would take the lift to the fourth floor and wheel Eli Katz to his first physiotherapy session. An hour seemed like an eternity. *You've fallen for him.* She giggled. The thought didn't alarm her.

Eli Katz had gone from zero to hero in a single meeting. He had apologized and volunteered to help with her research. He even shared her interest in genealogy. More importantly, he had listened attentively as she ranted about genes and haplotypes. His dark, magnetic eyes and stubbly cheek floated in her mind whenever she closed her eyes.

"Excuse me, miss," said the man across the desk. The young Arab gazed at her with concern. "You were saying?" He wore jeans and a T-shirt; his wife, a brown burka from head to toe.

Noga sat up. "I'm sorry," she said. "The study is anonymous." She recited her sales pitch by heart. Every couple undergoing genetic counseling—a euphemism for fertility treatment—passed through her interview room, regardless of

170

their ethnicity. Most signed the consent forms. Did they really care about science or did they hope that a random act of kindness would increase their chances of success?

After a short hushed deliberation, the couple signed on the dotted line and Noga thanked them for their cooperation. She had recruited Christians, Bahai, Ethiopians, and even Swedish medical tourists in addition to the expected mass of Ashkenazi Jewish hopeful parents. She was glad that this couple had consented. She needed more Arabs to round out the control group.

She escorted the couple to the corridor, wished them luck, and made for the bathroom. Five minutes until her next interview. She washed her hands and inspected her makeup in the mirror. She rubbed her lips together to spread the fading lipstick.

Does this count as a first date? If so, her physio session with Eli would be the only date she had looked forward to in years.

She threw a paper towel in the bin and charged down the corridor. A voice called her name.

"Dr. Stern." She paused. "Is everything OK?"

The head of neurology had a distant look in his pale blue eyes. "Noga," he said. "May I consult with you?"

Consult with me? "Of course."

"The patient in room 419C," he said. "Mr. Katz. You're familiar with him, I understand?"

Rumors spread faster than viruses along the hospital corridors. "What about him?"

"He's recovering fast, wouldn't you say?" The speedy recovery seemed to worry him.

"He's making good progress, yes."

"*Very* good progress. His fractures have healed in record time. I think his case could be of great scientific interest. Now, there was a mix-up with his blood work, and, as I just discovered, the last remaining sample is marked for genetic research."

"Yes. He signed the forms." She clenched her jaw. She

was not about to give up her prized sample, or give it away without Eli's approval. Suddenly, she didn't like the idea of other doctors poking around his DNA. He belonged to her.

She said, "Have you tried obtaining another sample?" Fat chance that Eli would agree to another test. Bad with blood, he had said.

Dr. Stern frowned. "I was hoping to avoid that. He's been through enough already, don't you think? Especially after that nasty incident last week."

She could see where he was going with this.

"He's been clear since then. All the nurses agree."

"So they say." He studied her over his glasses. "But delusions are a tricky phenomenon. I think we might have to ship him off to Kfar Shaul for observation."

A hint of coercion had slithered between his words. Relocation to the Kfar Shaul Mental Health Center would mean the end of her visits with Eli and the end of his freedom for the near future. Although her gut resisted the manipulation, the fear of losing Eli won out.

She swallowed. "I'll speak with the lab," she said. "I'm sure we can split the sample."

Dr. Stern inclined his head. "Thank you."

She turned to go, eager to put a healthy distance between her and the doctor.

"And, Noga, dear," he called after her. "Take care. Delusionals can be very convincing."

CHAPTER 39

Moshe peered out the window of the van. They sped south on Hebron Road, toward Baka. Turn right and they'd land up near his old home. Near Galit and Talya.

The night they had moved into Shimshon Street, Galit had jumped for joy in the entrance hall like a little girl and wrapped him in a tight hug. She might be quick to anger but she also radiated warmth and affection. He thrived on her love. With Galit at his side, he could conquer the world.

His new job had distanced him from her.

If Galit came knocking on the rabbi's front door, she'd find an empty house. But as the van sped toward Baka, it seemed that his new job might be returning him home after all.

The van, however, gunned down Hebron Road without slowing. Soon they would cross the 1967 armistice lines and enter Arab Bethlehem. He straightened on his seat. Was Damas shuttling them into stone-throwing territory in a vehicle without shatterproof windows?

He worried in vain. The van veered right at the last moment and climbed into Gilo, Jerusalem's southernmost suburb. The van pulled up next to a new apartment block of white Jerusalem stone.

Damas turned to face his crew. "New people, listen up.

Don't speak to the customers. Not a word. Speak only to me. Understand?"

They nodded.

"Now, get out."

At the back of the van they collected tins of paint, overalls, and a wooden ladder—all streaked with white—and carried them up two flights of stairs to an empty apartment. Damas mixed cement with water in a bucket and showed them how to fill holes in the wall. While the plaster dried, they poured paint into plastic trays and whitewashed the walls with long strokes of roller brushes. Damas came in and out, leaving them to their tasks for hours at a time.

During one of those stretches, the middle-aged man rested his roller brush in the tray.

"I couldn't help overhearing," he said. He patted strands of hair over his balding pate and hope glimmered in his tired eyes.

"Overhear what?" Moshe said.

"About your new lives."

Irina looked down from the ladder. Samira stiffened. This was just the sort of attention they had hoped to avoid. This information could complicate matters with their new employers.

The man raised a conciliatory hand. "I won't cause any trouble," he said. "My name is Shmuel. I'm like you." He unbuttoned his overall and lifted his T-shirt. Shmuel was indeed like them. Moshe returned the favor. Exposing his belly in public had become a habit.

All of a sudden, Shmuel shuddered. He sank onto a closed tin of paint and bawled into his hands. "I thought I was alone," he said.

Moshe touched the older man's shoulder. "When did you return?"

"A few days ago. Woke up in the cemetery, managed to get home." He shivered at the memory. "My son has moved into my house. Wouldn't believe it's really me. The greedy little runt kicked me out."

"Welcome to the club," Moshe said.

"Yes," said Samira, her voice devoid of sarcasm. "Welcome to the afterlife." Her role of afterlife hostess gave her new confidence.

Moshe said, "Not what you expected, right?"

Shmuel gave a gruff laugh. "I wasn't expecting anything."

Moshe made the introductions.

"Tell me," Shmuel said. A sense of urgency crept into his voice. "How long do I have?"

Good question. Were they newborns or had God pre-aged their new bodies? "I don't know," Moshe admitted. "We'll have to figure things out as we go."

Shmuel's joy of discovery ebbed. He lowered his voice. "Be careful what you say here. Our employers aren't exactly philanthropists."

As if on cue, Damas sauntered into the room and scowled at them. "What is this? A summer camp? Eat your lunch." He tossed a plastic bag onto the floor. "Don't screw around. You have an hour to finish. We have another job waiting."

"What's his problem?" Moshe asked when their taskmaster had left.

Shmuel opened the plastic bag and handed out the sandwiches. "He's always like that. Do your work and keep your mouth shut and you'll be OK."

Moshe decided not to ask what would happen if he were to ignore that advice. The answer would probably not involve severance pay and no hard feelings.

His sandwich consisted of two stiff slices of white bread held together by a brown smear of chocolate spread. They munched their meal without complaint, and washed the stale bread down with tap water cupped in their hands under a kitchen faucet. Their employers did not splurge on creature comforts.

What was the company's name? The warehouse had no markings. He had not retained a copy of the contract. He had been elated to find a place to work and sleep.

They completed the paint job and boarded the minivan for

their next task: weeding the large yard of a house in Beit Zait on the wooded outskirts of West Jerusalem. Moshe and Shmuel traded afterlife stories. Shmuel, a retired journalist, had died four years ago. When Moshe asked how he had passed, however, the older man had clenched up. "Too soon," he said. Moshe didn't press the matter.

Moshe hacked at a patch of weeds with a garden hoe. He had passed the entire day in hard labor and was no closer to his family. He thought of little Talya with her bushy black curls and her mother's eyes, and acid burned in his gut.

"You OK?" Shmuel asked. He rested on his shovel. Moshe had taken out his frustrations on the undergrowth with more violence than necessary.

Moshe straightened and drew a long breath. "My daughter," he said. "She's growing up so fast and I won't see it. I'm not there for her." He listened to his own words and gave a short, ironic laugh. "I suppose nothing much has changed. When I was alive, I wasn't around much either. I spent all my time at the office."

He pulled a large wild plant from the ground and shook dirt from the roots. He had lost two years of his life and now he would miss his chance to get to know his daughter.

"You should speak with her," Shmuel said. He was still watching him.

"I tried that. She doesn't even remember me."

"When is her birthday?"

Moshe massaged the pain in his back. Black grit filled the lines of his fingers. "In a month."

"Surprise her with an early birthday present. She'll warm to you. And your wife will be more responsive if your daughter is on your side."

That was good advice. Avi's threat to his life had revolved around Galit, but not little Talya. Gifts, however, required money, and his first payday was a month away—and two weeks after the wedding date. But the idea hogged his thoughts until the sun dipped toward the horizon and the minivan drove them back to Talpiot, drained and caked in sweat.

The smells of cooking and soiled clothing filled the warehouse. Laborers limped about in small packs of Africans and Romanians. Some kept to their tents and hung damp clothing on the partition walls. A line led to the bald cook who ladled soup into tin cups. Another line led to field showers, judging by the scant dress and towels.

They waited for their soup. Moshe's stomach growled. A fight broke out further up the line. A Nigerian shoved a Romanian. Shoves turned to blows, but not for long. A giant in a gray suit marched across the warehouse floor. He swatted the brawlers to the ground with hands like boulders and dragged them away, a human King Kong, without breaking a sweat.

The line re-formed. The soup was thick with barley and beans, and after they ate, they prepared to shower.

"Go ahead," Moshe told the others. "I need to have a word with the boss."

He climbed the stairwell, crossed the metal bridge, and knocked on the door of the corner office. Hearing nothing, he tried the handle.

Boris shoved a thick wad of shekel notes in a drawer and looked up at him. King Kong stood behind his boss, his back to the wall, his arms and neck as thick as tree trunks.

"Do you have a minute?"

Boris waved him to an empty chair.

"My daughter has a birthday soon."

"Mazel tov." The lids beneath the bushy eyebrows drooped with boredom.

"I'd like to get her a gift. I was wondering: can you advance me my salary for this month? Or part of it?"

Moshe had never had to beg in his life. He felt two inches tall. He'd have to get used to that. The gray mustache wriggled like a ferret. Did Boris have children? Would he understand?

His boss drew a deep breath. "I don't do this, usually," he said. Moshe's heart did a double flip. He had expected a flat no, but Boris opened the drawer, reached in, and threw a two-hundred-shekel note on the desk.

Moshe picked up the crumpled note. He held ten percent of his monthly salary—far below minimum wage—but enough for a Barbie doll and a small cake. "Thank you."

"Don't thank me. It's your time."

"My time?"

"It'll take longer to pay back your debt."

"What debt?"

The mustache tilted. "The apartment. The food. Someone has to pay for those."

"I don't understand."

"You signed the contract. Board and lodging: eighteen hundred per month. Paid up front. Interest at ten percent."

"I didn't agree to that."

"Yes you did." Boris pushed a document on the desk toward Moshe. He had signed the same form the day before. "From the moment you signed on the dotted line, you owe us."

Moshe had not read the fine print. He didn't need to. "That's not legal."

Boris laughed. "What are you going to do?"

King Kong cracked his knuckles. Moshe was not about to make threats, but Boris read his mind. "The police don't bother us here."

"I want out."

Boris shrugged. "Walk out the door anytime you like. A few have tried. They always come back. Our associates are very persuasive. Ask Damas about that."

King Kong grinned. Moshe thought of the angry Ethiopian and his two missing fingers.

"And if you cause more trouble than you're worth, we'll call the police ourselves and give them this." His reached into the drawer and laid a card on the table like a gambler revealing the winning ace. The identity card contained Arabic writing and a photo of Moshe's face.

"Musa Ibrahim," Boris explained. "An Egyptian citizen

and an illegal alien in this country. He looks rather like you, don't you think?"

Moshe shot to his feet. The chair crashed behind him. "You can't do that!"

King Kong took a heavy step forward.

Boris kept his eyes on Moshe. "Work hard. Keep your mouth shut. If you're smart, you'll buy your way out."

"How can I buy out at ten percent?"

"There are ways. You could climb the ranks. We have other, more profitable jobs for men with the right skills and inclination."

"What skills?"

The gray mustache tilted again. "I'm glad you asked."

CHAPTER 40

That night, Moshe dreamed of his father and grandfather. He had never seen the two men together in life, but there they stood, shoulder to shoulder, in a misty twilight, on a grassy bank at the end of a long suspension bridge. Moshe shifted his feet over the rotted planks. He clutched the frayed handrails. The old ropes groaned and rocked in the chill wind over a black abyss. His forebears watched him, their faces inscrutable.

Moshe struggled to keep his balance. *Don't look down!* He urged his stiff limbs to advance. *A Karlin never quits.* But with each brave foot forward, the security of the grassy bank drifted further away.

He awoke in a dew of sweat. He felt his wrist for his watch—he had strapped it on before zipping up his sleeping bag—and relaxed when his fingers found the familiar square of cool metal.

Above his cot, black wires and rusty metal struts crisscrossed the void beneath the roof of the warehouse. The stale air smelled of dust and damp clothes. A hundred manual laborers snored in the night, like frogs trapped in a muddy swamp.

He squinted at the watch face. 4:35 AM. He reviewed his plan in his mind. All the other options he had considered would have put his friends and family in harm's way. He had no choice. He had one hope of escape, and the thought made his heart pound.

Last night, he had learned that Boris had expanded his dodgy operation beyond forced labor.

"What skills?" Moshe had asked. He should have kept his mouth shut and gone to bed, but the shock and anger over his servitude had mobilized his tongue.

Boris smiled. "Persuasion. Stores all over the city pay hard cash for our protection. Some need a little convincing from time to time."

"That's extortion," Moshe had said.

The word did not seem to bother Boris. "Racketeering, technically." He leaned forward on the desk. "You'll make an excellent salesman. I have an eye for this sort of thing. I've even selected your first customer."

Moshe tossed and turned on his cot. Springs creaked as workers shifted in their sleep and dreamed of brighter tomorrows.

At five-thirty, he rolled off his bed and dressed. He made for the bathroom, splashed cold water on his face, and peered at his unshaven visage in the cracked mirror. If his father and grandfather could see him now—a penniless, homeless slave. A dismal end to their legacy. But he could descend further still into dishonor. By the end of the day, he would hit rock bottom.

He knocked on the flap of Irina's cubicle. She pulled the curtain aside. Her platinum blond hair pushed in all directions. The fairy had just awoken, but this was no fairy tale. Samira lay on her cot, bundled in her sleeping bag.

Irina watched him with concern. "You OK?"

Moshe nodded. He had to do it. He had no choice. "I have to go somewhere this morning," he said.

Her eyes widened. "I'll come with."

"No," he said. "I have to go alone." If he told her, she might talk him out of it.

Her cheek twitched. He had told her about his conversation with Boris the previous night, and she knew the consequences of not showing up for work. He imagined the questions that flooded her mind. Where? What? Why? Thankfully, she asked none.

"Be careful," she said.

He turned away from her before he could change his mind.

He pulled the warehouse door open on the tracks and slipped out into the early morning gloom. He hurried along the dank alleys of the industrial zone. He looked over his shoulder every few steps, expecting to find King Kong or another faceless thug at his heels, but he had escaped unnoticed.

Beep-beep-beep! The high-pitched alarm of a reversing delivery van made him jump as it backed up. He hurried through the gap between the van and a loading platform, and marched on.

Sunlight spilled over Pierre Koenig Street, the two-lane backbone of Talpiot, and glinted off the trickle of commuter cars. He slackened his pace. A few blocks down, he found an empty bench, and sat like a traitor awaiting execution.

An Egged bus hissed to a stop, and a herd of cashiers and garage workers disembarked and hurried to their jobs. Did they have any idea about the forced labor camp a few streets away? Did any of them care?

Soon Damas and his minivan would set out without him. He had missed his shift. His taskmasters would deduct the workday from his salary and sink him deeper into debt. If he failed to return by lights out, their goons would seek him out. They would find him. They would make him go back. Moshe was not going back. Not as a slave.

Exhaust fumes carried in the air. His stomach groaned, but he had no desire to eat. He would not be able to keep the food down.

Across the street stood his target, a small store squeezed between a haberdashery and a hole-in-the-wall selling cheap household plastics. Moshe had driven by a thousand times and never imagined that, one day, fate would lead him to that particular store.

Soon, the store would open. He had a few minutes to contemplate what he was about to do—his last moments of innocence before he sold his soul.

CHAPTER 41

Irina boarded the minivan and sat in the middle row—the seat she had shared with Moshe the day before. Her arms hugged her chest. The idling engine made the seats vibrate and her body seemed to shiver in the morning twilight. She had never spent a day apart from Moshe, and she felt vulnerable in his absence.

Last night, Moshe had told them about his meeting with Boris.

"So we're slaves?" Shmuel cried out.

Moshe asked him to keep his voice down but said no more. He had not told them all he knew. Had he been trying to protect them?

Samira climbed into the van and claimed the seat beside her. The Arab girl turned her wide, innocent eyes on her. "Has he left us?" she whispered.

"No, of course not. Moshe would never do that." But the girl had voiced Irina's own deepest fear.

"How do you know?" The question came from Shmuel on the seat behind her.

"I know."

Their Ethiopian taskmaster leapt into the front cabin. He turned and counted them like sheep. He scowled at Irina. "Where's your friend?"

She shrugged.

"Gone fishing?" His sense of humor lasted all of one second before he slammed his fist on the backrest. "You're mine, you understand? You do as I say. Nobody runs off. OK?" Then he smiled. It was an ugly smile. "You know why they don't lock the door at night?" He let their imaginations run wild. "That's right: they don't need to. Every once in a while, a genius tries to run away. We have ways of finding lost property. We always get our property back." He held up his hand.

Samira gasped and Irina looked away. Two of his fingers ended in short stumps.

He laughed again, turned around, and tapped the driver.

As the van set out, he spoke into his mobile phone, loud and clear, for their benefit. "Boris, yes. Moshe Karlin didn't show up for work today. Good." He put away the phone.

"The dogs are out, boys and girls. Once they get a scent, nothing can stop them. Your friend will be back soon, one way or another." He glanced at the driver and they laughed.

The van accelerated toward their next job.

Shmuel leaned forward and whispered in Irina's ear. "I hope Moshe knows what he's doing."

Irina hoped so too.

CHAPTER 42

Moshe watched the store across Pierre Koenig Street. An old man wearing a flat cap rolled up the security gate and unlocked the door.

Moshe waited ten minutes. Then he crossed the street at the light. He paused outside the dusty display window. A chair of carved oak with an embroidered seat. A stuffed owl. A brass trumpet. Plates and figurines of painted China.

Bells jingled as he entered. The old man looked up from his coffee and newspaper on the glass counter. A large wisp of white hair like cotton candy had replaced the hat. He gave his customer the once-over with hungry vulture eyes.

"Let me guess," he said. "The wife's jewelry?"

Moshe had encountered yet another creature that enjoyed feasting on the unfortunate. He disliked the man already. That would make his task easier.

He drew a deep breath and unstrapped the watch on his wrist. The word "Rolex" glittered in gold leaf. He ran his fingers over the shiny silver frame for the last time, then he placed the last vestige of his family's former greatness on the counter, and imagined his forebears turning in their graves.

The vulture eyes ogled the timepiece with restrained, calculating greed. The old man snatched up the watch. He lodged a long monocle in his eye and examined the face. He turned the metal casing over and tested the black leather straps with gnarled, spotty fingers. Desire flashed in the pawnbroker's eyes.

Then he returned the watch to the glass counter, as though he had handled a dead lizard.

Moshe's heart sank. The old man had rejected his most prized possession.

"I'll give you five," he said.

Moshe's relief at the offer soon evaporated.

"Five what?"

"Five magic beans. What do you think? Five hundred shekels."

"Five hundred? You must be joking. For a Rolex Bubbleback 1948 Limited Edition? My grandfather paid a king's ransom for that watch and it has only appreciated since."

The old man shuttered his eyelids. "For all I know it was made in China."

His blood boiled. "That is no imitation. My grandfather bought it firsthand. Three generations in the family. It's worth at least forty thousand."

The old pawn dealer made a dry sound that was either a cough or a laugh. "For forty thousand I'll sell you the shop. I don't even know if I'll be able to move this trinket, never mind turn a profit."

The old man was a wily one; he had to be for his store to survive. Moshe needed to survive too. He would have to find another dealer.

Moshe made to collect the watch.

"Five thousand." The words pinned Moshe's hand like an arrow. "Five thousand. Not an *agorah* more."

Hello! The old man's bluff shattered on the dusty floor, but Moshe needed more than five thousand. Aim too high and he'd miss the deal. He needed a deal and the old man held all the cards.

"Twenty."

The old man locked his eyes on Moshe, who made a mental note never to play poker with the old vulture.

"Ten thousand. Cash."

Moshe had no bank account. No ID for cashing checks. The old man seemed to know that. Ten thousand might just be enough.

"Fifteen," he said.

A clock ticked out five seconds and then the old man nodded his head. Moshe released a sigh from deep within his chest. The pawnbroker scurried about the store, opening drawers, extracting wads of hundred-shekel notes from shoeboxes and crannies. He counted the bills on the glass counter in crumpled piles. Moshe shoved the cash into his pockets and, casting one final glance at the watch, he left the store.

Cars whizzed by on Pierre Koenig.

Phase One complete. He had the money. Phase Two also involved no small amount of risk, but he was sure Phase Two would be easier. He was wrong.

Moshe took two steps down the sidewalk and froze. A large man in a gray suit stood thirty feet away and stared at him. King Kong looked no less intimidating in public.

The towering thug stalked toward him, the threat of violence in his every step.

Moshe opened his mouth to explain, but swallowed his words. Negotiations with this Russian would be short and painful.

So he turned and ran.

CHAPTER 43

"Stand aside," Eli said. "I want to show you something."

Noga released the rubber handles of his wheelchair and stood beside the wall of the corridor.

His stamina was returning. Even after the physio session, he had strength enough to show off. He gripped the metal push rings inside the wheels, pushed with his arms, and the chair inched forward. His right leg jutted out on the footrest like a cannon. He shifted his hands back on the rim and pushed again. The chair rolled forward.

Push, roll. Push, roll.

He picked up momentum.

"Hey," she called behind him. "Wait up!"

He didn't. He careened down the hallway. A nurse entered the corridor and jumped out of his way. The wheels spun so fast, he could no longer grip the rubber tire. He pressed the plaster cast on his arm against the left wheel to adjust his course and avoid a row of chairs, and then he slammed on the brake lever. The chair stopped inches from the potted plant at the end of the corridor.

Noga reached him, panting and laughing. "Since when can you do *that?*"

"Since this morning."

"And you still let me wheel you to physio and back."

Eli winked at her. "I was enjoying your company too much."

She had no answer to that. Her flushed cheeks said it all. She said, "I'll take you back." She stepped behind the chair. "You should be more careful. Your bones still need to mend."

"Casts are coming off next week," he said.

"Next week? Are you sure?"

"Got a CT scan to prove it."

"That's... that's great."

She fell silent. He couldn't see her face. Was she impressed with his speedy recovery, or sad at the prospect of losing him?

Lose him she would, and sooner than he had thought. His body was healing and his mind would not be far behind. Once the casts came off, he would be able to complete his mission. Yet, for the first time since his arrival at Shaare Zedek, he wasn't in a mad rush to leave.

They passed a doorway and he clamped his hands on the wheels. Something had caught his eye.

Down a corridor, a man juggled colored balls. He had fuzzy orange hair.

"So there *is* a clown."

A child's voice squealed with delight and a little boy stepped into view. He reached for the flying balls. He wore a hospital gown. His head was as smooth and hairless as the plastic balls.

"That's Moti," Noga said. "The therapeutic clown. He spends most of his time in oncology."

The balls rained down on the clown's head and he fell to the floor with dramatic flair. The little boy convulsed with laughter. He coughed. He clutched his chest and doubled over. A nurse drew near and held his shoulders.

"Poor kid," said Noga.

"Yeah," Eli said. "Poor kid."

The clown inflated a blue balloon with much huffing and puffing and handed it to the boy. He pretended to fall over again and the young patient ran at him and hugged him for all he was worth.

Eli stared at the little boy and his moment of joy. The clown turned his head. He looked straight at Eli with his sad eyes and white frown.

"Let's go," Noga whispered.

They continued down the linoleum hallway. The little boy stuck in Eli's mind. Mortality sucked. How did humanity bear it? One week in the hospital had been more than enough for him.

They took the elevator to the fourth floor. Noga said hello to the nurse on duty, Nadir, a quiet Arab woman with a white headscarf that made her look like a well-tanned nun. Noga seemed to know all the doctors and nurses, and they always greeted her with smiles.

She wheeled him to his bed and supported his good arm as he rose with great effort and shifted his rear onto the edge of the bed. He stared at the small pearl buttons of her blouse. He inhaled her flowery deodorant. Her hands lingered on his arms a moment longer than was necessary. She lowered her head and took a step back.

"See you later?" she said.

He nodded and she left. He stretched out on the bed, alone with his thoughts and his racing pulse.

"*Love is in the air*," sang a man's raspy voice in English. "*Everywhere I look around.*" An old man lay in the next bed.

Eli scowled at him.

The old man didn't take the hint. He smiled and his loose jowls flapped. "Oren is the name. Checked in an hour ago."

Oren had a receding hairline. He spoke with a breathy tone and effeminate lisp. "Nothing serious," he said and he threw up his hands. "My doctor thinks it's a sinus inflammation, but he sent me here just to be safe. Are you also with Dr. Mohammed?"

Eli groaned. His new roommate loved to talk, and Eli now had yet another reason to escape the hospital pronto. He decided to kill the conversation with a curt reply.

"No," he said. "Dr. Stern."

Oren frowned. "Never heard of him. I like your girlfriend, by the way. Lucky guy."

It took Eli a full three seconds to realize about whom Oren was talking. A motormouth *and* a busybody. "She's not my girlfriend."

"I don't know," Oren said in an annoying singsong. "Body language doesn't lie."

"Whatever."

"Oh, I get it!" said Oren, as though he had just discovered America. "You're married."

Eli shook his head.

Oren clung on like a bulldog. "A girlfriend? A guy friend?"

"Cut it out, OK?"

"I'd snap her up if I were you. Take some advice from an old man. Don't delay. Life is too short."

Eli gave a short sarcastic laugh.

"What?" Then Oren gasped. "Brain tumor!" He slapped his forehead. "I should have known. I am *so* sorry."

"No, nothing like that. It's just... complicated." *Why am I talking with this stranger?*

"Then what are you waiting for? She likes you. I'll tell you that for nothing."

"Just forget about her, please."

Silence settled over the room. Golden, glorious silence. He didn't have feelings for her. He was playing a part. Soon he'd flit away in a storm and a chariot of fire.

"Love is in the air!"

The silence had lasted five seconds. Eli wrapped his pillow over his ears. Some miracles were beyond even his powers.

Love? Please! He had moved beyond those mortal emotions long ago. What, then, was the flicker in his gut whenever he thought of the girl in the white cloak?

The sudden realization hit him harder than the truck on the Mount of Olives. Of course! The accident, the hospital—in one Divine flash, the pieces of the puzzle slid into place.

How had he not seen this before? The fracture in his skull

was probably to blame. His mind, however, was healing, and his sixth sense had transformed, a vague intuition taking the place of the Thin Voice. A new prophecy for a new era. Once he had learned to see, the message appeared crisp and clear before his inner eye. The future rolled on before him, and he knew which path he must take.

CHAPTER 44

Moshe turned a corner and sprinted down an alley in the Talpiot industrial zone. He stuffed his hands in his pockets to prevent the wads of hundred-shekel notes from fluttering to the sidewalk.

He hazarded a glance over his shoulder. King Kong lumbered after him, his face tight with concentration. Moshe, lighter and faster, might actually escape the henchman, so long as he didn't trip or wander into a dead end. He needed to put a few more feet between them before he changed direction for his next destination. King Kong would never think to look for him there.

Moshe ducked into an auto garage, running down a line of cars suspended on forklifts. Moshe had dispatched taxis to customers on every street corner in Talpiot, but he knew little of the yards and footpaths that connected them. He pushed past two greasy mechanics and out a door into a large dirt lot. Plenty of cars. A passerby or two. None would save him from the tree-trunk arms of King Kong.

He dashed to the end of the lot and took cover behind a dented fence of corrugated iron sheeting. Air burned in his throat and lungs. His heart galloped in his chest. He peeked over the fence. No sign of his pursuer.

He scampered along the fence, crouching to avoid detection. When he ran out of fence, he made sure the coast was clear and sprinted off.

Lost him. That had gone easier than he had expected. Not bad on an empty stomach. He doubled back, checking behind him every few steps and peering around each corner.

Boris was right. He could not run forever. He might escape King Kong today, but the goon would catch up with him tomorrow. Or the next day. When he least expected it. A life on the run was no life at all. Play his cards right, and Moshe would never need to run again.

He turned into a tired street dotted with litter. The slave warehouse stood across the road in dilapidated silence. Moshe scanned his surroundings a second and third time for signs of hulking thugs. He crossed the street and slid the door aside.

He had barely closed the door of the empty warehouse behind him when a brick wall crashed into him and flung him to the ground. He sprawled on the cement floor, pain throbbing in his shoulder and down his arm. King Kong stood over him. He stared down at his prey, then stepped up to finish the job.

Moshe's shoes slipped and scraped as he launched to his feet. Not fast enough. Large blunt fingers grazed his neck and clamped onto his shirt. Moshe strained against the iron grip for all he was worth. The nape pressed into his throat and threatened to choke him. He threw up his arms and slid downward, slipping out of his shirt and landing on his behind. He scrambled to his feet and ran for all he was worth.

He leaped onto the metal staircase, which trembled and twanged as King Kong followed at his heels. Moshe pulled at the handrail and bounded up the steps, three at a time. *Not far now.*

A large hand closed over his foot. Moshe kicked and wriggled until the shoe came loose and he shot upward.

He sprinted across the metal walkway and dived toward the door of the corner office. *Please be there! Please open!*

The door swung inward and Moshe fell into the room. He

thrust his hands into his pockets and dumped the stash of bills onto the desk.

King Kong filled the doorway, panting and scowling. Boris gave his head a slight shake and the thug stood down.

Boris stared at the heap of money and raised his bushy eyebrows.

"That's very generous of you."

"Not just me. My friends too: Irina, Samira, and Shmuel. Three grand each. Fifty percent more than we owe."

Boris fingered the bills.

The moment of truth. Their future lay in the slaver's hands. Moshe could only hope that self-interest would beat out spite.

His boss wiggled his mustache. "A deal is a deal," he said.

Moshe breathed again.

Boris raked in the money like a winner at a casino table. "And you," he spoke to King Kong. "You owe me a hundred shekels." The thug groaned, and Boris chuckled. "Don't be a sore loser."

Moshe waited on the street corner beside his plastic grocery bag of possessions. The sun warmed his face.

He breathed in the free air. A giddy sense of release washed over his mind. Only a slave understood the sweet thrill of freedom.

The minivan returned a few hours later. Damas jumped out and scowled at him as he charged into the warehouse.

Irina ran to him. Shmuel said, "Moshe, what's going on?"

He greeted his friends with a wide smile. "We're free to go." His eyes met Shmuel's. "You too."

Irina jumped on him. Shmuel hugged him. Samira bowed and blew kisses.

He explained, and then they collected their things and regrouped on the street.

"For a moment there," Shmuel said, "I thought you'd run off without us."

"I'm sure you would have done the same for me."

They looked to him, tears glistening in their eyes. They

would follow him anywhere. For a fleeting moment, he had returned to the helm of Karlin & Son. The feeling energized him. He wished he had more hope to dispense. A plan. A future. A promised land. He had nothing.

"Never again," Moshe said. "We must make sure this never happens again." They nodded as one, knowing that they had no power to enforce the words.

"Let's go," he said. "Before Boris changes his mind."

"Where to?" Shmuel asked.

Moshe drew a deep breath. Of their few options, only one felt right. Only one rekindled the hope for a return to his former life.

He said, "The only place we can."

CHAPTER 45

Rage drove Damas up the metal stairs inside the warehouse.

Few had left the Pit and none escaped without scars. A boiling pot of injustice brewed inside him as he launched across the walkway to the corner office. He pushed open the door without knocking.

Boris looked up. He sat at the desk, the phone to his ear, and mumbled in Russian. The Rottweiler stood at the wall and folded his thick arms. Damas didn't know his name. There was a lot he didn't know about his employers. Boris told him only what he wanted him to know. He had not even consulted with him before setting free his entire team.

Boris put the phone down and watched Damas through droopy eyelids, his face expressionless. "Have a seat."

Damas stood tall in the middle of the room. He scuffed the floor with his feet like an edgy stallion. "Why did you let them go?"

Boris considered his words, as though deciding whether to answer. He slouched back in the chair. "We made a deal. He kept his part. This is a business, Damas. The deal closed our gap for the quarter. We must keep the Big Boss happy."

"You shouldn't have let them go. It sets a bad example."

The Rottweiler took a step forward but Boris raised his hand.

"Forget about them, Damas. You'll get a new team."

Damas was not going to stand down. Moshe Karlin and his friends were laughing at him right now. Let them laugh. He would laugh last.

"We must bring them back," he said.

"Must we now?" His tone indicated that he was losing his patience. He was not used to receiving orders from a worker. Damas didn't care. For once, Damas knew something that Boris didn't, and he had saved his secret weapon for a moment like this.

"Yes," he said. "They are not ordinary people."

Boris raised a bushy gray eyebrow.

He told his boss what he had overheard and what he had seen. Every word. Every detail.

Boris stared at him for half a minute. "So these dead people just wake up in the cemetery?"

"Yes."

"Have you lost your mind?"

In his anger, Damas had not paused to think how the story would sound to a man who had not heard and seen for himself. "It's true," he said. "I swear to it by my other fingers." He held up his maimed hand for display.

Boris ground his teeth. "One good thing about dead people," he said, "is that they do not come back. They do not talk." His boss had understood right away how the discovery could complicate business.

Adrenaline burst into his arteries. "Hunt them down," he said. "Interrogate them. Tear out their secrets."

Boris put his hands together and touched them to his lips while he thought. Damas had presented his case, but would the judge rule in his favor?

"You have made a very bold claim, Damas," he said. Damas swallowed hard. His phantom fingers itched, and he hid his hands behind his back. "But a claim we can easily verify. And if you're right, this could be very profitable."

Profitable? What did he mean? He had expected fear and action, but instead, Boris smiled. Why was he smiling? When the Russian chuckled, Damas could stand the tension no longer. "I don't understand," he said.

"Soon you will." His boss leaned forward and rested his elbows on the desk. "Forget about Moshe Karlin for now. Think about the possibilities. Their lives," he added, "are our opportunity."

CHAPTER 46

Rabbi Yosef closed the Laws of Blessings on his podium at the front of the class. Five minutes until the chime of the schoolyard bell. Time enough to atone for his sins.

"Boys," he said, "I want to discuss another topic."

Menachem raised his hand. "Rabbi," the boy said, "is it about the Resurrection?"

"No!" Yosef said, with more force than he had intended. "Something even more important."

He had their undivided attention. What could be more important than the dead rising for Judgment Day and the Final Redemption? He picked up a black marker and scrawled two words on the whiteboard.

"*Emunas Chakhomim*," he read aloud. Faith in the Sages. "Who can tell me what that means?"

Menachem's hand shot up again, but Yosef called on Dudi. "Our rabbis are always right."

"Close," Yosef said. "God gave us two things to guide our actions. He gave us our intellect"—Yosef tapped his forehead—"and He gave us the Torah. But how are we to know whether we have understood the Torah correctly?"

Menachem waved his hand so hard that Yosef feared he might dislocate his shoulder. "The rabbis tell us how to understand the Torah."

"Very good. But surely the Sages of Blessed Memory also make mistakes?"

Twenty pairs of fearful eyes stared at him. "That is *Emunas Chakhomim*. We trust that God guides the leading rabbis of the generation to the correct interpretation. The Torah tells us, 'Do not turn from what they instruct you neither to the right nor to the left.' The Midrash comments, 'Even if they seem to tell you that left is right and that right is left, obey them.' Trust their judgment, even above your own."

The bell rang. The boys collected their study materials and prepared to go home.

Yosef leaned against the wall of the empty classroom. During the meeting of the Great Council two days ago, something inside him had broken.

Sitra Achra. He shuddered. He had invited them into his home. Exposed his family. How had he not realized that his undead visitors were the agents of the unholy *Other Side*? Two secular Jews. If that had not set off alarm bells, the Arab girl certainly should have!

And yet, neither Moshe nor Irina had struck him as evil. Not even Samira. They were people struggling to survive. They were victims, not demons. They needed his help. How could that be wrong? Had his moral compass lost its bearings?

Yosef collected his bag and left the low school building. Shards of orange sunlight slipped between the apartment complexes of Jerusalem stone in Sanhedria. As Yosef climbed into his battered white Subaru, two teenagers in black hats and suits passed by, holy books in hand.

Black and white. The uniform of the *frum* world. Life was easier in black and white. Right and wrong. Nothing in between. That required faith. *Emunas Chakhomim.* To surrender his intellect and heart to the guidance of God's true representatives. *Have faith, Yosef.*

He turned the key and, defying the odds of probability, the engine started.

He negotiated the curves of the suburban streets, slowing

as hats and gowns crossed on foot. He bypassed the crowded hive of Meah Shearim, the heart of ultra-Orthodox life, and turned south onto Route 60. Traffic choked the highway, as workers returned home after a long day.

Yosef rested his elbow on the door. The world crawled on, tired and colorless. Empty. Purged of the intoxicating scent of the Redemption. Once you had a whiff, sobriety became intolerable. Yosef knew that only too well. False hope was worse than no hope at all.

Twenty minutes later, he parked on Shimshon Street. His boys had beaten him home. The scent of barley soup wafted from the kitchen, to his surprise. Rocheleh never cooked dinner on a weekday. Since Yosef had removed their unholy guests, however, she had made an extra effort. She even smiled at him.

He had not mentioned the verdict of the Great Council, and she had not asked. Best not to disturb the purity of his home with talk of the *Sitra Achra*.

Life had returned to normal. Better than normal. He poured a cup of coffee and settled at the dinner table with Uriel, his eldest, for their weekly study session.

Last time, they had completed the Chapters of the Fathers, the ethical teachings of the Mishna. Tonight they started the Eight Chapters, the introduction to those teachings penned by Maimonides. After a feverish week of Resurrection speculations, Yosef welcomed the return to timeless first principles—character building and human decency—the bread and butter of religious life.

Uriel read the text; Yosef corrected and commented as necessary. The famed philosopher kicked off with an analogy. Doctors need to understand the human body to heal illness. Similarly, we need to understand our mental faculties to correct our faulty character traits.

Yosef listened to the sound of his own breathing, the rustle of the page beneath his son's hand. In the kitchen behind them, a pot hissed on the stove. Compared to the tumult of their strange guests, the house felt empty. In time, he would forget them. *All that the Merciful One does is for the best.*

Uriel giggled.

"What?" Yosef had drifted off.

"Look, Aba." His finger marked the passage.

Yosef read the words. "'Things that make no sense or that are inconceivable.'" Nothing humorous there. He scanned the next paragraph. "The faculty of imagination," he said. "What's funny about that?"

"Aba!" Uriel said in the exasperated tone of a teenager. "Read on."

He did. "'For example, a metal boat flying in the air—'" His son giggled again. "What?"

Uriel rolled his eyes. A teenager, indeed. "A metal ship," he said. "Flying. What about airplanes?"

"Ha. You're right." Yosef had missed the glaring error.

"Aba, didn't he know about airplanes?"

"Maimonides lived a very long time ago," he explained. "In the twelfth century, a flying boat was unimaginable. But today…"

He gazed at the turbaned rabbi in the framed picture. Maimonides had erred—black on white. Not by any fault of his own. According to the physics of his day, a flying metal ship was, indeed, inconceivable. But still, the passage gave him pause.

For three seconds.

There came a knocking at the door.

"Expecting anyone?"

Uriel shrugged. Yosef rose to his feet and crossed the living room. He opened the front door.

Moshe Karlin stood on his doorstep. Behind him stood Irina, Samira, and an older stranger. "Sorry, Rabbi," Moshe said. He gave him an apologetic smile. "We had nowhere else to go."

CHAPTER 47

Irina awoke Wednesday morning to the sound of angry voices. The rabbi and his wife were arguing again, or, more precisely, she was shouting and he was emitting meek consoling noises.

Irina lifted her head from the armrest of the couch and rubbed the pain in her neck. How had Moshe slept there five nights in a row? Samira lay huddled in a blanket on the other couch. Moshe and Shmuel made the most of the living room carpet.

In the kitchen, spoons clinked in cereal bowls and mouths slurped chocolate milk.

The voices grew louder. She lowered her head and pretended to sleep.

"Boys," the rabbanit called with forced restraint. "Time to go. Wait for me outside. Now!"

Chair legs scraped the kitchen tiles and little feet pattered out the front door.

"Get rid of them today," she continued in the harsh tone she reserved for her husband, "or I will. Do you understand? Think of our children!"

The front door slammed shut.

Silence reigned for a few seconds.

Rabbi Yosef was a good man. A kind man. He didn't deserve this. None of them did. But what were they supposed to do?

The rabbi cleared his throat. "Moshe?" he whispered. Moshe raised his head from the floor. The rabbi stepped into view. "I have to go to work. Help yourself to food and drink—whatever you need."

Moshe nodded. "Thank you."

The rabbi gave him a brave smile and left the house.

Moshe sat up, rubbed his eyes, and yawned.

Irina said, "Sleep OK?" She had slept fitfully herself, waking at every creak of a door, gripped by the sudden fear that Boris and his henchmen had come to drag them back to slavery. *You don't have to worry about that anymore. You're free.*

Moshe smiled. "Better than last night. And probably better than I will tonight."

Humor, even in desperate situations. That was Moshe. His attitude made their predicament seem less hopeless.

She swung her legs off the couch. "I'll make breakfast."

She freshened up and got to work in the kitchen. They had raided the fridge the previous night, wolfing down frozen dinners as fast as the rabbi could heat them. Irina toasted the last four slices of bread and fried the last three eggs.

She served Moshe, Samira, and Shmuel at the kitchen table. They chewed their last foreseeable cooked meal.

"How many of us are out there?" Moshe asked.

"How many resurrected people?" Irina said.

He nodded

Shmuel said, "More than the four of us, that's for sure. And good luck finding them. I hadn't told a soul until you lot showed up."

They pondered the fate of their fellow resurrectees as they ate.

"What do we do now?" Samira asked.

Moshe washed down his egg with a glass of tap water. "I'll make some calls. Let's shoot in all directions: anyone who might take us in for a night."

He withdrew a wad of shekel notes from his pocket and

divided them into four equal mounds on the table. "We have seven hundred shekels each. That won't get us very far."

Irina stared at the money. The crumpled bills were all that remained of Moshe's treasured family heirloom. He had bought their freedom and now he was treating them to the rest of his cash. He did it without fanfare, as though it was the most natural thing to do. The others shared her sense of awe and gratitude. They would do anything for Moshe Karlin.

"I have a nephew in Hadera," Shmuel said. "It's a long shot but I'll see what he can do."

Irina had nobody to call. "I'll clean up," she said.

"And I'll wash their clothes," Samira added. "Maybe the rabbi's wife will grow to like us."

They laughed.

Irina got to work on the dishes. Galit Karlin was a very poor judge of character. She didn't know her husband at all. Over the past week, Moshe had passed up many opportunities to make advances on her. Lately, she had been inclined to accept. But Moshe still loved his wife. Were all good men stupid?

She hung the dishcloths to dry.

Moshe sat on the couch with a notepad in one hand and the house phone in the other. The rabbi's battered laptop lay open on the dining room table.

Irina sat at the computer and nudged it awake. She opened an Internet browser and searched for two words.

Moshe had sacrificed so much for her. She could at least return the favor. As a woman and an unknown, she could go where Moshe could not.

The results for "Galit Karlin" returned a Facebook profile—friends only—a genealogy site, and a Ynet listing. She clicked the link and arrived at the schedule for a club in Emek Refaim.

Well, well, well. Now who's been leading a double life?

Irina knew exactly when and where to find her. She would have to dress for the occasion.

"Galit Karlin," she whispered, "tonight is our first date."

CHAPTER 48

Wednesday noon, Rabbi Yosef returned home from school. He had made his decision and it tore him up inside.

When Moshe and his fellow resurrectees had shown up on his doorstep the previous night, he had acted on instinct. His visitors were no demons, just desperate people in dire need of help. How could he turn them away?

That morning, however, away from the eyes of his guests, Rocheleh's words had simmered in his mind. She was right. He could lose his job. His well-intentioned generosity might get his children expelled and ruin their marriage prospects. If he had told Rocheleh about the *Sitra Achra*, she would have thrown him out along with his evil guests.

"*Ve'chai bahem*," the Torah wrote. Live by these teachings. From this verse, the rabbis of the Talmud inferred that "your life takes priority over another's." Those who pity the cruel will, in the end, act with cruelty against those deserving of mercy. By pitying these strangers, he had endangered his innocent, young boys.

He piled on the quotations to strengthen his resolve, but the sharp talons of conscience still clawed at his heart.

He opened his front door quietly, like a thief. The living room had never looked tidier. Samira smiled at him from beneath her hijab. She folded a boy's T-shirt and placed it on a pile of freshly laundered clothes on the couch. Moshe and Irina emerged from the kitchen.

"Welcome home, Rabbi Yosef," Moshe said. Behind them, white grocery bags sat on the kitchen counter.

They were not making this easy for him. "My friends," he said. *Don't cry, Yosef. Hold it together.* "We need to talk." The smiles waned.

Shmuel entered from the corridor. "Come here, Rabbi, I want to show you something."

"Shmuel, I was just telling the others—"

"In a moment. Come on."

He gave in. He followed Shmuel down the corridor. The older man pushed open the glass-paned door that led to the yard. "What do you think?"

Yosef stepped into his yard. The weeds and wild grasses were gone. In their place, tidy rows of turned soil bordered the enclosure walls, with parallel lines of little circular ditches.

"Surprise!" said Irina.

"Gerberas on the sides," Shmuel explained. "Sunflowers in the middle. In a few weeks you'll have a lovely flower garden."

Yosef could hold back no longer. His shoulders trembled. He felt a gentle hand on his shoulder. "It's all right," Moshe said.

Yosef wiped his eyes. They stood before him, hands at their sides. Unarmed men and women facing the firing squad.

"You are good people," Yosef said. "I'm sure there's been a mistake and that, once they get to know you, the rabbis will change their minds. But you have to understand, I have a family. They need me and I need them. There's only so much I can do."

They listened in silence and studied the dirt. He had rehearsed the speech in the car on his way home. He had imagined a firm delivery and an amount of angry resistance. Reality had disappointed on both counts.

His next words would seal their fate. He had no choice. "And so," he said, "with much regret and a heavy heart—"

DAN SOFER

The doorbell rang. They looked at each other. Yosef was not expecting any visitors and Rocheleh had a key.

Oh, no! The boys had opened their mouths at school. Or messengers of the Great Council had arrived to ensure that he had complied with their decision.

"Wait here," he said. "Please." They nodded.

Yosef went indoors. "Just a moment," he called. He hurried down the corridor and brushed lint from his suit jacket. He peered through the peephole but saw neither Rabbanit Schiff nor men in Chasidic uniform.

He opened the door. A little old lady peered up at him. Her eyes filled her glasses. The aromas of tasty hot food rose from the tall stack of large tinfoil trays in her arms.

A middle-aged man with creased olive skin stood behind her. He carried a similar stack of trays, and yet more piles of trays waited on the backseat of the white taxicab that idled in the street.

"Rabbi Yosef?" the old lady said.

"Yes?"

"Here." She offloaded the trays onto his arms and stepped into the living room. "Where are the others?" she said. "It's time to eat."

CHAPTER 49

Noga strode into room 419C on a gust of anticipation, but when she rounded the divider curtain, she found Eli's bed empty.

The good feeling fled. They had arranged to meet that afternoon. Had he tried to walk and slipped? She had warned him not to push his luck. Or was he avoiding her? He had seemed edgy that morning. Had she crowded him?

"Oren," she said. "Where is he?"

The older man in the next bed peered over his *Yediot Acharonot* and shook his wobbly jowls. "Have a closer look." He nodded toward the empty bed and winked. "Romeo might have left you something."

She approached the bed and sure enough, a folded note of lined paper lay on the pillow. She read the spidery handwritten message and smiled. Every day she discovered a shiny new facet of Eli Katz.

She pocketed the note and marched down the corridor. She took the elevator to the first floor, walked past the Steimatzky bookstore and flower shop, and pushed through a glass door that led to a small green courtyard. She had pointed out the hidden garden to Eli on one of their wheelchair tours. He had remembered. What could Eli possibly want to say to her—or do with her—in the privacy of the courtyard?

Her cheeks warmed.

Eli had parked his chair beside the wooden bench. He had combed his hair and shaved. He hid his arms behind the chair. A gift? His lips trembled as he smiled. Eli Katz— nervous? She sat on the bench beside him.

"For you," he said. He revealed one arm. It held a single long-stemmed rose.

"Thank you." She accepted the flower, breathed in its scent, and savored its meaning. She was more than a friend. That explained the nerves.

"And there's this." He revealed his other hand. It held a small box in black velvet. Her heart skipped a beat. They had met barely a week ago. A rose was one thing, but a jewelry box…

Her concern must have displayed on her face. "Don't worry," he said. "It's not a ring."

She exhaled audibly, and he gave a short, nervous laugh. She placed the rose on the bench, accepted the box, and flipped the lid open. On a bed of black velvet sat a strip of white paper. He had printed four digits on the slip.

"I had to bribe a nurse to get the box," he said.

"I don't understand," she said.

"It's the code to my apartment. 103 Jaffa Road."

"Your apartment?" Was he asking her to move in with him? And what apartment had a code and not a key? None of this was making any sense. She would have preferred a ring.

He looked at the myrtle sapling in the corner. "I haven't been fully honest with you, Noga."

Her mouth went numb. She remembered the feverish intensity of his eyes when he had grabbed her arm that first time. *Oh, no, Eli. Please. Don't.*

"When we met," he continued, "I felt… a sudden connection. I had never experienced that before."

Her lungs inflated. This wasn't so bad. In fact, this was excellent. "Me too," she said, then she held back. *Don't be too eager.*

"What I'm going to tell you will seem absurd, even crazy."

Love at first sight, she thought, as crazy as it gets. *Spit it out already!*

"That's why I've given you the code. The proof is in my apartment. I wish I could show you some other way, but I can't... I can't..."

He seemed to teeter on the verge of tears. She reached out and touched his hand on the armrest of the wheelchair. "You don't have to prove anything," she said. "I feel the same way."

Finally. That intimate connection. The man she had longed for.

He shook his head. "Please," he said. "Promise you'll hear me out."

"Of course."

Then he spoke. As he spoke, the numbness returned to her face. His name was Elijah. He was three thousand years old. The Day of the Lord had arrived. And Noga had a special role to play in the unfolding Divine drama.

"That's why I had the accident," he said, his dark eyes flashing. "That's why I landed up here, in the hospital. To meet you!"

A breeze ruffled the leaves of the trees. The world shimmered around them.

She had said that she would hear him out. "So I'm part of this End of Days?"

"Yes!"

"What exactly is my role?" Her voice had an edge of impatience, sharpened on the rubble of her broken heart.

"I don't know yet," he said. "But we'll figure it out. Together."

Together. That would have sounded romantic—if he wasn't raving mad.

She hid her face in her hands. *You idiot. You simple, trusting fool.* Tears poured from her eyes. Dr. Stern had tried to warn her. Self-pity boiled over into rage. She shot to her feet. She wanted to slap him across his handsome face. Instead, she hurled the object in her hand. The jewelry box hit him right between the eyes and bounced on the dirt floor.

"Please, Noga. It's true."

She turned on her heels and stormed off, back to the hospital and out of his life.

CHAPTER 50

Moshe crammed trays of surplus food into the freezer. Rafi helped him rearrange the containers so the door would agree to close. Pity to waste good food. Their charm offensive had not changed reality and when the rabbanit arrived home, they'd be out on the street.

"Thanks," Moshe said to Rafi. "I really appreciate this."

"Anything for the Karlins."

And thank you, Dad. His father's kindness to a traumatized soldier forty years ago had returned to help Moshe in his time of need. Perhaps Rafi would let them crash on the floor of his apartment tonight. He hoped it wouldn't come to that. Moshe's loyal friend had lost enough in the name of the Karlins, and a band of homeless intruders would not help his wife's failing health either. Besides that, Moshe longed to stay on Shimshon Street.

"What's the matter?" Rafi asked.

"Nothing. Let's have lunch."

Trays of drool-worthy food covered every inch of the dining room table. Stuffed cabbage. Beef goulash. Baked chicken. Pullet on a bed of fried onion. Boiled ox tongue. White rice. *Nokedli.* Savta Sarah shoveled the steaming delicacies onto the plates. Moshe waited his turn and dug in.

The music of busy cutlery and contented eating filled the

air.

Savta sat back in her chair, her plate empty. A veil of melancholy fell over her features.

"The cattle train arrived at Auschwitz very early in the morning," she said.

Moshe knew the story by heart. At the death camp, SS men sorted the new arrivals: the able-bodied to the left, the young and old to the right. Sarah, her mother, and her younger siblings had stood in a long line that led to the showers.

"My baby sister cried for food," she continued, "so my mother asked me to run back for the bread in the bag we had left on the train."

The sounds of eating ceased.

"I ran back right away and grabbed the bag. But on the way back to my mother and the children, an SS officer stopped me. 'How old are you?' he said. I was fifteen. 'From now on, you are eighteen,' he said. 'Stay here.'"

Savta stared into thin air and shook her head. "I never saw them again. They were killed in the gas chambers that day."

Moshe glanced at Savta Sarah. She had prepared food all her life: wedding banquets and bar mitzvahs for Jerusalem's well-to-do, and pro-bono meals for the sick and needy. Generations of Jerusalem Jews had grown strong on her stuffed cabbage and meatballs. With each of those meals, a lost and lonely little girl tried to deliver a bag of bread to her beloved mother and siblings on a cold morning in Auschwitz.

A chill wave washed over Moshe. Was he any different? He had spent his new life paddling backward against the flow of time. Would he struggle forever? Or had the time come to raise his oars and follow the current of a new life?

Samira placed her fork on her plate. "My name is Samira," she said, and glanced at Rafi. Moshe had forgotten to make the introductions. Savta Sarah's confession seemed to have given her courage.

"I grew up in Deir Al Ghusun, near Tulkarem. I married when I was sixteen. At seventeen, I gave birth to a baby boy." She smiled at the memory. Then her beautiful smile faltered.

"My husband was a jealous man. He would lock me in the house when he went to work. He said he'd set me free and divorce me if I gave him full custody of our baby." Her lips trembled. Moshe thought she would cry but she steeled herself.

"He sent me back to my parents. He spread rumors that I had been unfaithful. He posted a petition on the doors of the mosques demanding that my father restore the honor of his family. Everyone signed it, even the elders and our cousins."

A lone tear rolled down her cheek. "My mother sent me to her sister in Ramallah for a few weeks, to wait until the pressure subsided. Then my parents brought me home. Everything would be all right, my mother told me. The next afternoon, however, my father came into my room. No one else was home. He had a cold look in his eyes. He hugged me, and I thought, 'At last the storm has passed.' Then he put his hand over my mouth and nose, and I couldn't breathe."

Irina touched her arm. Rabbi Yosef offered her a tissue and she wiped her eyes.

"I woke up in a garbage dump a few days ago, naked and alone. I don't think I even had a proper burial."

A reverent silence filled the room.

Moshe cleared his throat. Samira's intimate revelation demanded that he reciprocate. "I'm Moshe," he said, following her lead. "I don't remember dying but I did. I died." An unexpected knot of emotion lodged in his throat. Saying the words aloud in the company of friends had made his status more real and final. "I had a wife and daughter. A family business. But I think I've lost them all."

He paused. If he said another word, he'd collapse and weep.

Irina saved him. "Hi everyone," she said, upbeat. "I'm Irina. At least I think I am. I don't remember a thing about my life, so I'm done."

Chuckles all round. After three depressing life stories, they welcomed the comic relief.

"How about you, Shmuel?" Yosef asked.

The older man's eyes widened. He folded his arms. "I can't..." he said. "Not yet. And I don't want my old life back. I'm not wanted there."

"That's OK," Rabbi Yosef said.

A magical sense of unity, warmth, and acceptance hung in the air like pixie dust.

"This is wonderful," Moshe said. "We should do this again."

Rafi said, "Like a club?"

"Exactly. A weekly meeting. Like that group for people with drinking problems, what are they called?"

Rabbi Yosef coughed. "Alcoholics Anonymous?"

"That's it. There are bound to be more of us out there. Shmuel, you said as much last night. We can help each other. We should start an organization. A non-profit."

"We can't even work legal jobs," Shmuel said. "Now we're going to start a company? You need two signatories to start a non-profit."

Moshe felt his shoulders sag. "You're right. We'll need identity cards to do anything official." He was still dead in the eyes of the state bureaucracy. The trickle of inspiration dried up.

"I have an identity card," said Savta Sarah. "Will that help?"

"Me too," said Rafi. "Where do I sign?"

New life flowed in Moshe's veins. "Excellent!" he said. "We have our two signatories."

"We'll need five more," said Shmuel. His voice had softened as the idea gained support. "To get tax benefits." All eyes turned to him and he shrugged. "I was a journalist. You learn a thing or two over the years."

A plan grew flesh and bone in Moshe's head. "We can collect donations," he said, "and rent a place to live."

"What should we call ourselves?" asked Samira.

They shot down a flock of early suggestions: The Hope. Second Life. The Undead. The Living Dead. The Resurrection Club. They made good titles for zombie movies or computer games, but not a satisfying name for their fledgling social movement.

"Reborn?" said Shmuel.

"Too Christian," said Rabbi Yosef.

Inspiration flashed again. Moshe said, "The Dry Bones."

Rabbi Yosef smiled. Moshe knew the rabbi would like that one.

"Sounds like a comic strip," Shmuel said. "Or a rock band from the seventies."

"The Dry Bones *Society*," Rabbi Yosef said.

Heads nodded as they warmed to the idea.

Moshe said, "Let's vote on it. All those in favor raise your hand."

The front door opened behind him, and the enthusiasm drained from their faces. Moshe turned around. The rabbanit stared at the party in her living room, her mouth open. The four boys stood behind her like nervous ducklings.

Her face turned red and a vein throbbed on her forehead. "Yosef! What is going on here?"

Savta Sarah ambled up to her and offered her hand. "Rabbanit Lev?" she said, her voice radiating royal charm. "Sarah Weiss. Of Weiss Catering. How good it is to finally meet you!"

The rabbanit lowered her confused gaze to the friendly old lady. "Weiss Catering?" The name seemed to ring a bell. "*The* Weiss Catering?"

"The one and only. *Glatt* kosher. Strictly *glatt* kosher. Do I have a surprise for you!"

The aging chef snatched her hand and led her to the table. She introduced each dish as though announcing heads of state at a palatial ball. She sat the rabbanit at the table and the tasting began.

"This is *good*!" The rabbanit had tasted the ox tongue.

"There's more of everything in the freezer. You won't have to cook all week."

"How do you get the meat so soft?"

"The recipe is yours, my dear." Savta winked at Moshe.

"But not today. I'll be back tomorrow for a private demonstration. Moshe dear, please let me know how I can help with your promising new venture. Rafi, let's go. It's time for my nap."

The granny and her driver bid them farewell.

The rabbanit chewed another mouthful and closed her eyes. Then she opened her eyes and woke from Savta's trance. Annoyance and desire battled on her forehead. "One more night," she said to Yosef. "One more."

Shmuel punched the air. Samira jumped for joy.

One more day of borrowed time. They had better move fast. They cleaned the living room and kitchen, and huddled to assign tasks. Moshe would download the registration papers and coordinate with Savta and Rafi. Shmuel would contact a journalist friend to scrounge free publicity and search for a rental apartment. There were bank accounts to open and phones to order.

The rabbi helped his children with their homework and fed them an early dinner.

Moshe browsed government websites on the rabbi's laptop. He was speed-reading the legal requirements for non-profits when he noticed Irina slip out the front door.

Strange. She usually told him where she was going, so he wouldn't worry. They had no mobile phones yet.

"Samira," Moshe said. "Did Irina say where she was going?"

Samira folded a second load of washing on the couch. "No. Maybe she just needed some fresh air."

"Yeah," he said. "I suppose you're right."

CHAPTER 51

The skyscraper on Jaffa Road towered over Noga, blocking the late afternoon sun and casting a cool shadow over her. She had walked past the shiny new apartment building of polished white marble countless times but never considered that people actually lived there. Not anyone she knew firsthand. The tall glass façade of the lobby and the chrome banister whispered of private jets and luxury yachts, not of deranged invalids in the Shaare Zedek neurology ward.

That morning she had stormed down the hospital corridors, cursing Eli under her breath, and cursing herself for falling for him. Proof lay in his apartment, so he had claimed. Proof she would find, but not the kind he had intended. His fantasies would fade away in the harsh light of hard evidence for the existence of Eli Katz, mortal of flesh and blood.

She steeled herself before the tall doors of expensive tinted glass. She had never dared to enter the building, never mind sneak into one of the apartments. *Don't worry, Noga. You probably won't even need to.* His claim to an apartment at the exclusive location was most likely yet another delusion. This would be a very short visit.

She crossed the forecourt of white stone. The glass double doors snapped open with an audible whoosh and a blast of air-conditioning blew in her face. The expansive lobby stood two floors high. A security guard sat behind a long counter of black wood and studied a hidden book or screen. The doors snapped shut behind her. The rubber soles of her old walking shoes squeaked over the large slabs of white marble. The guard looked up, a question in his eyes.

"Mr. Eli Katz," she said.

His eyes moved from her old T-shirt to the frayed strap of her shoulder bag.

He did not throw her out, and the name Eli Katz did not seem to surprise him. "First time?" he said.

She nodded.

"The cleaning equipment is in the closet on the right as you walk in." Two degrees and a doctoral grant, and she still passed for the maid. The wonders of higher education.

"Which floor?" she asked.

"Penthouse."

She swallowed hard. "Thanks."

She made for the corridor of elevators at the far end. Eli Katz lived in the penthouse. What were the chances that another Eli Katz lived in the building? Or had he stolen the identity of a wealthy stranger? What did she know for sure about the mystery patient in room 419C?

A roman letter appeared above each elevator. Instead of the familiar round buttons for Up and Down, she found a golden keypad. She pressed the key for "Penthouse" and the letter A pulsated on a digital display. The doors of elevator A shot open with another elegant whoosh.

She stepped inside. Mirrors lined the walls. The letter P projected in black on the golden lintel, while another ephemeral digit climbed upward.

1. 2. 3.

P came after 21.

Time to see who you really are.

The doors whooshed open, and she almost walked into a mahogany door. Another golden keypad appeared above the handle. She punched in the four-digit code Eli had placed in the jewelry box and the door clicked open.

She entered a large dark expanse. She touched the wall and fumbled for a light switch, when hidden motors purred. Blinds swiveled and shifted along tracks, and sunlight flooded the room through large continuous windows. Her breath caught in her throat. A set of low couches in cream leather faced a one-hundred-eighty-degree view of the Jerusalem skyline. Eli had the entire top floor to himself!

She stepped onto the shiny marble tiles and avoided trampling the carpet of cream-colored fur with her street shoes—she could not afford that dry cleaning bill. She reached the French windows and her breath clouded the glass. A forest of downtown offices and hotels gleamed white in the afternoon sun. The city sprawl traced the hills and valleys that led to the thick ancient walls of the Old City, with its domes and minarets. Beyond the Old City rose the Mount of Olives, bristling with gravestones and tombs. It was like looking back over history.

As the awe of the view faded, she noticed the smell. The acrid stench of decomposition came from the open-plan kitchen in stylish chrome and dark wood paneling. She blocked her nose as she drew closer.

Leave now. Jump into that elevator and go! But—serial killer or sloppy housekeeper—she had to know. She pulled at the door of the closet beneath the sink and stepped back. No severed heads or limbs, only a pile of putrid olives.

Sloppy housekeeper. With a thing for olives.

She tied the strings of the garbage bag, pulled it out of the bin, and leaned the olive graveyard against the front door. She'd take the bag down on her way out. She had become his cleaner after all.

She washed her hands in the sink and dried them on a soft kitchen towel. *OK. So you're rich and you have a great interior decorator. That does not make you an immortal prophet.*

She ran her fingertips along the dining table—a thick glass plate on marble pillars—and leather, high-backed chairs.

A passageway opened onto a bedroom the size of her entire apartment in tasteful creams and dark paneling. She parted the blinds of another set of tall French windows. She sat down on the soft, unmade bed. The owner had woken up one morning and left in a hurry. He had not bothered to empty the trash. He had not expected to spend the next week in hospital.

No photos of family or friends. No mementos or collectibles. The man who lived here had loads of cash but no life.

A spacious walk-in closet. Piles of T-shirts, blue jeans, and a set of leather biker jackets. A spacious bathroom and Jacuzzi tub.

On the way back, she tried the door of a closet in the hall. Her fingers found a light switch on the wall and, with a satisfying click, she found herself in different world.

Five carpeted steps led downward, creating a square, sunken den in the center of the room. Objects hung on the outer walls. A shaggy fur cloak. A leather shield. A sword in a leather scabbard. A rounded clay urn. An oriental rug. A clunky pistol with a rounded handle. She had wandered into a private museum. Or a shrine. A shrine to what?

She scanned the walls, but touched nothing, sensing that her fingers would violate something very personal and secret. But Eli had sent her here.

She descended the steps into the central den. A padded bench lined the inner walls. A meditation chamber? A meditation chamber with bookshelves and a flat-screen television. She ran her fingers along the spines of the worn volumes. *The Jewish War* by Flavius Josephus. *The Innocents Abroad* by Mark Twain. A Hebrew Bible.

A universal remote lay on the padded bench. She sat down and pressed a button. The lights dimmed, and the television flickered to life.

Within minutes, everything made sense.

CHAPTER 52

As the shadows lengthened on Emek Refaim, Irina lurked beside a streetlight, wondering whether she had arrived at the wrong address. Pedestrians of all shapes and sizes flowed around her. They spoke English, French, and Hebrew and bustled toward coffee shops and boutique stores. Only a handful of the passersby, however, had entered the building across the street, all middle-aged women in ankle-length skirts and head coverings.

Irina assumed that Moshe's wife had not yet hit fifty.

The streetlight flickered on. *Time to go undercover.* Irina waited for a white taxi to pass and she crossed the street. At a thrift shop on the way, she had bought a pair of black leggings and a sports top, and the outfit had won her more glances than usual on the Jerusalem sidewalks.

She entered the office building and took the stairs to the second floor.

She assumed her role as a spy with ease. For all she knew, her current persona might be her true self. Or perhaps she had been a spy to begin with? She liked that idea best.

The pulse of club music carried down the stairwell. She entered a corridor on the second floor and stopped at the sign that read "Emek Refaim Fitness Club."

She opened a door and walked in. A dozen middle-aged

women in gym togs hopped on a wood-paneled floor, doing their best to mimic their instructor.

Her long ponytail of black hair swished as her body moved. Slim black leotard. Curves in all the right places. The face reflected in the mirror on the far wall had high cheekbones, large bright eyes, and full lips. Good skin, too. The girl from the wedding portrait on Savta Sarah's wall.

Irina's stomach tied in a knot. The thrill of espionage fled. *Am I jealous?* Her legs made to leave when Galit Karlin spun around, sent her a broad smile, and beckoned her to join in the fun. *No escape now.*

She dumped her plastic bag of clothes among the other gym bags in the corner and joined the back line. Hidden speakers blared an edgy pop tune worthy of a seedy dance club. A saxophone melody swirled as young women chanted, "I'm worth it," amid the grunts of a male rapper.

She did her best to match Galit's movements. She gyrated her hips and waggled her bum. She raised her arms above her head and shook her bust. Her thighs burned as she performed provocative squats.

The song segued to another fast-paced dance hit.

A competitive urge made her push her boundaries, but, according to the mirror, she had trouble keeping up even with the grannies. As they turned and contorted, she recognized the faces of the skirted and capped women she had observed on the street. In the safe and secluded environment of the studio, the religious wives and grandmothers pole danced like MTV pros to the chorus of "All the Single Ladies." Underneath their clothes, people were not very different after all.

The forty-minute class left her drenched in sweat and out of breath. She had cut corners toward the end, not bending as low or jumping as high when she thought no one was looking. The older women chattered and pulled skirts over their leggings and hats over their hair.

Galit Karlin walked up to Irina, radiant and energized, hands akimbo. "You're good," she said. "Have you danced

Zumba before?"

Irina understood how Moshe had fallen under the spell of those large, smiling eyes. "First time," she replied. "As far as I can remember."

Galit waved goodbye as the other dancers filed out the door. "How did you hear about us?"

"On the Internet."

Galit nodded.

The two women smiled at each other in silence. What had she planned to say to her? Had she wanted to bring them together or had she come here to check out the competition?

"Great workout, right?" Galit said to ease the silence that had grown between them.

"Yeah. You're in great shape."

Galit made a self-effacing grimace. "Thanks. I've been instructing for a year, so that helps."

Irina liked this Galit Karlin, despite herself. What had gone wrong between this lively, earthy woman and her kind-hearted husband?

For you, Moshe. As long as you want her, I'll do what I can.

She said, "Your husband is a lucky guy."

The smile dropped. The bright eyes narrowed with suspicion, then relaxed. "I knew you looked familiar," she said. "You're his new girl, aren't you?"

"His new girl? What's the matter with you?"

"I saw you walking together on our street. You have some nerve, you slut! Get out!"

"He doesn't have another girl. He loves you. Why won't you believe that?"

Galit picked up a gym bag and hugged it to her chest. She turned back, one foot out the door. "Ask his good friend Sivan," she said, her eyes dripping venom. "You'll have a lot to talk about."

CHAPTER 53

Ahmed opened his eyes.

Dark blue skies above. Raw earth below. A chill breeze. And a burst of intense heat as his body exploded.

He cried out and writhed in the dirt. Then he paused, panting hard. He patted his chest, his belly, his thighs. He was alive. Naked and filthy, but whole. The vision of fire was but a dream. No. Not a dream. A memory.

He rolled onto his side and looked about. An empty field. Leafy trees peered over a perimeter wall of rock. A mountain wind whistled through the cracks.

He laughed. He laughed long and hard, until tears collected in the corners of his eyes.

He had done it! He had fulfilled his mission, and now he had entered Paradise. Hasan had spoken the truth. *Eternal life. Eternal pleasure.*

The images of heat and flame flickered again in his mind. The sway of the bus as it pulled off. The wary eyes of the other passengers as he staggered down the aisle. The sting of sweat in his eyes. His final meal—a double Mac and fries, a poor choice on so many levels—threatened to surge up his throat. Cold electric wires snaked along the inner lining of his jacket sleeve and pressed against the flesh of his arm. His thumb hovered over the smooth curve of the detonator button. And then, that split-second of Hellfire and excruciating pain.

Hasan had been wrong about that—he had felt every nail and ball bearing as they ripped through his flesh.

He staggered to his feet. Pain flared in his head and he doubled over with a whimper. He caressed his temples. Hasan had not mentioned any headaches either.

In truth, to the last moment, he had not fully believed that he would wake from death. He had not wanted to press the button. He had not wanted to die or to drag tens of strangers with him.

Sons of pigs and monkeys, Hasan had said. *Killers of prophets*.

But the man at the back of bus number eighteen had reminded him of Yigal, his boss at the Rami Levi supermarket in Talpiot, where he unpacked crates, mopped floors, and laid out fresh vegetables for the Jewish customers to buy. Yigal had joked around with him in Arabic. He had asked after his family. He let him take Fridays off. How many Yigals had he killed that day?

He shivered. This was Hasan's doing. His cousin from Ramallah had visited for a few days. His mother had made Ahmed share his room with the guest. *He'll be a good influence, make a man of you*. She was always saying that, ever since his father had moved out with his new wife five years ago.

But Hasan had discovered the copies of Penthouse he had stashed inside his mattress. Ahmed had found the pile of shameful Israeli magazines in the supermarket's garbage enclosure and smuggled them home.

A disgrace, Hasan had said. To defile himself with infidel women. *Shame on his family name*. His father would hate him if he found out. There was only one way to cleanse the blemish on his family honor, only one way to purify his Jew-loving soul.

He stumbled forward, one hand at his head, the other over his privates.

Was his mother proud of her martyr son? Had the bulldozers destroyed their house? Perhaps now his father would think of him with pride. Perhaps now he would return home.

That's weird. The stony hillsides reminded him of East Jeru-salem. He hobbled toward a tarred road—were there cars in Paradise?—and a folding table. The white cloth billowed in the breeze. A man slouched on a chair behind the table. He wore a gray suit. He had the pale skin of a Westerner, fluffy gray hair, and a bushy mustache. He tinkered with his mobile phone but looked up as Ahmed approached, his hands cover-ing his privates.

The scene reminded Ahmed of the registration desk at the voting station. He had turned eighteen six months ago and exercised his right to vote only once.

"Welcome," the man said in Hebrew with a strong Rus-sian accent. He handed Ahmed a folded square of white fabric. A thin cloak.

Ahmed put it on and tied the paper-thin belt.

Roads. Phones. Hebrew. Not what he had expected of the Afterlife. The man did not even appear to be a Muslim. He offered Ahmed a plastic glass of water and two white pills.

"What is this?"

"Acamol," the man said. "For your head."

"Oh. Thanks." The man seemed to know how things worked. Ahmed washed the pills down with the water. At least the Afterlife was organized.

The Russian pulled a sheet of paper from a transparent folder. "Name?"

Ahmed told him.

He held out a ballpoint pen.

"Sign here."

"What's this?"

"A technicality. For your housing and food."

That's more like it. Infinite reward awaited martyrs. A palace. A seat at the Heavenly banquet. Despite his misgivings and half-hearted faith, Ahmed had done the deed. He had left his miserable, old life behind and stepped up for *istishhad.* As a *shaheed,* he would collect his due.

Ahmed signed on the line.

"Wait in the van."

He waved to a white minivan that idled down the road.

Ahmed hesitated. "About the girls…"

The man looked up from the paperwork and grinned a wide amused grin. "Your seventy virgins?" The man barked a laugh. He had fielded that question before.

Ahmed's spirits plummeted. "Sixty?"

The man coughed. "You'll find"—he read his name off the signed form—"Ahmed, that Heaven is a bit different from what you were promised."

Ahmed hid his disappointment. He could settle for fifty virgins. Or ten. Five would be sufficient. He would be happy with one pretty girl, if it came to that.

He limped down the road on bare feet and climbed into the white minivan. Strangers in the same flimsy cloaks filled two of the three rows of seats. They stared at him. Young and old. Dark-skinned and light. Some of their faces looked strangely familiar. An Ethiopian glared at him from his seat beside the driver.

Ahmed stared out the window as the engine purred and the seat quivered. His headache was subsiding. He hoped the Heavenly banquet would start soon. He had the mother of all appetites.

CHAPTER 54

Thursday afternoon, Eli lay on the hospital bed and stared out the window.

How could I have been so stupid?

The sunbeam had crept down the wall and slunk from the room. Half the day had passed and still no Noga.

He had opened his heart to her. She was the key to his mission, the reason for his injury and pain. The Boss had sent him to her. He had felt that in his bones. Together they would trigger the Final Redemption. He could not leave her in the dark.

"Aren't you going to eat your food?" said a soft, sympathetic voice.

Eli didn't shift his gaze from the window. His lunch tray sat on the side table, untouched. He was not in the mood for a chat with his nosy roommate. Every morning and evening, Oren's wife, children, and grandchildren filled their room with their chatter and the smells of their food and flowers. Their presence made him feel all the more alone. Why, after all these years, should that bother him?

"You can get her back," Oren said. He had put two and two together.

Eli turned his head. "What makes you say that?"

Oren smirked. "Experience."

Eli had to laugh. "You have no idea, Oren."

"You had a fight. You said something careless—it doesn't matter. Go get her back."

Eli closed his eyes and focused on the rise and fall of his chest. "She's gone. Trust me."

"Send her flowers. A card. Anything. But don't delay. Never delay. Or you *will* lose her."

"Thanks for the free advice."

"Well, what do you know," Oren said.

Eli opened his eyes. Noga stood at the foot of his bed. A T-shirt and jeans. No white cloak. Her mouth sealed tight. She wore her hair back, the way she had the first time they had met. He sat up on his elbows. Had she gone to his apartment? Did she believe him now?

Oren swung his legs over the side of the bed. "I'm going to go for a stroll," he said. He winked at Eli. "Stretch these old legs." He closed the door behind him. Eli was starting to like the old man.

Noga drew near, reached into her shoulder bag, and with the stiffness of a court messenger delivering a summons, she handed him a thick manila folder.

"What is this?"

"Facts," she said. "Newspaper articles. Official documents. All you'd ever want to know about Eli Katz."

"Where did you get this?"

"The Internet. The university library." She spoke with an even, restrained tone. "Your parents died in a car crash when you were sixteen months old. You attended the Miriam kindergarten in Katamon, then Chorev Primary. You enrolled for a first degree in Computer Science at the Open University then dropped out in your second year, the year you started OpenGen."

"Noga, wait—"

"You're a real person, Eli. You were born. You grew up. You had a life. And then, somewhere along the line, you became Elijah."

The girl was good. But not good enough. Eli accepted the

folder and placed it on top of his untouched meal. "I know all this," he said. "All the details. You know why?"

"Because they happened."

"Because I planted them."

"Give me a break! You can't plant public records."

"You can if you know how."

"And newspaper reports?"

"The parents died in a car crash. That much is true. Their little boy died later. But his identity number lives on."

Her chest heaved. "Like in the movie."

"What movie?"

She pulled a DVD jacket from her bag. A Scottish warrior in a sheepskin cloak stood on a hilltop, beneath stormy Highland skies. He leaned on the hilt of his Claymore.

He groaned. He knew how this must look. "That's just a movie."

She read the back copy. "'A group of immortals battling to the death....'"

"That's got nothing to do with it."

"I watched it," she said. "He leaves his wealth to a dead infant and takes over his identity. Sound familiar?" She had him on that. The screenwriters had copied a page out of his life.

"What about my collection?"

"Bought at antique stores. Or on eBay."

"But I know the story behind each piece. How do you explain that away?"

She looked both sad and frustrated. "False memories," she said. "The product of childhood trauma and movies like this." She eyed the manila folder. "There's a paper on reconstructive memory and confabulation in there too. You should read it."

She had him cornered. There wasn't an argument she couldn't cut down with that theory. It was like a self-reinforcing delusion. "No," he said. "That's not true."

"And then there's this." She held up another exhibit for the jury: a book. "101 Magic Tricks. I'm sure that came in handy for your 'miracles.'"

The Earth shuddered beneath him. Was she right? Was his entire life a comforting fiction for a lonely little orphan?

"No," he said. "That isn't true."

She reached for his shoulder, and he flinched. He had hurt her with the truth and she had avenged her pride with lies.

She sat down on the edge of the bed. "I never knew my parents either," she said. "My adoptive parents are good people, sure, but they weren't my real parents." She exhaled a long, deep breath. "They couldn't have just given me away, right? One day they'd sweep back into my life. I was so sure of it. They had made a mistake. They wanted me back."

She sniffed. "The years passed, and I grew up. No one came to claim me. My parents were stupid teenagers, or addicts. Who else abandons a newborn baby, right?"

She wiped her eyes with her fingers. "You were right. We have a lot in common. I guess that explains our interest in genealogy…" She gave a short ironic laugh and looked him in the eye. "There's no magic, Eli. No miracles."

Eli shook his head and avoided her eyes.

She gave him a long, hard stare. Then she stood up. "Keep that up and you'll never go home," she said. "Dr. Stern is itching to throw you in the madhouse."

He said nothing.

She exhaled another deep breath. She didn't seem angry anymore, only tired. "OK," she said, after another long silence. "I guess this is goodbye."

CHAPTER 55

Thursday morning passed in a flurry of activity.

First, Moshe printed the online forms he had completed on the Israeli Corporations Authority website. Rafi picked him up at 8 AM. They collected Savta Sarah and met with a lawyer friend of Rafi's at his downtown office on Shamai Street. In his presence, they signed a declaration that the non-profit did not involve any funny business. Then they rushed to the Corporation Authority offices to hand in the application and received an invoice to pay at the post office. After that, the waiting game began. Small wonder anyone accomplished anything in this country with so much red tape.

They raced Savta back to the rabbi's house, where the rabbanit awaited her first cooking lesson. Sitting in the passenger seat with the window open, a summer breeze in his hair, the white buildings ablaze with sunlight, Moshe felt alive for the first time in his second life.

The car jumped a speed bump and his stomach lurched.

"Sorry," Rafi said.

The vertigo transported Moshe to the rickety bridge over the black chasm. The dream had returned last night, except this time on the grassy bank stood Galit. Her hand rested on Talya's shoulder. He stepped onto the next cracked plank and shifted his weight forward. As before, with each step, the bank drifted further away. *No!* He called to them, but their stony faces disappeared in the misty gloom.

Afternoon sunlight warmed his arm on the windowsill of the passenger door. He should follow through on Shmuel's advice and buy that Barbie doll and cake. With one week until the wedding, he had no time to lose. But a numbing inertia had set in. Over the last few days, he had poured his energy into escaping slavery and finding shelter, leaving little bandwidth for Galit. All his attempts at reaching her had hit the same brick wall. Would today be any different? His thoughts drifted to the growing checklist of tasks for the new nonprofit.

They reached Shimshon Street at 1 PM. Moshe scarfed down his lunch of reheated Hungarian treats.

"How long can I keep up this diet," he said at the table, "before I have another heart attack?"

Rafi laughed. Rabbi Yosef smiled. Irina didn't respond. They hadn't spoken since she had skipped out of the house yesterday afternoon.

Before he could ask what was on her mind, the doorbell rang.

"I'll get it," he said.

He checked the peephole for angry best friends, murderous Arabs, and slave drivers. The stranger at the door belonged to none of the above.

"Moshe Karlin?" the old man asked when the door opened. He wore a pinstriped shirt, baggy gray trousers, thinning white hair, and a lost expression. He peered past Moshe and his face brightened. "Shmuel!" he exclaimed, and he hurried past Moshe.

Shmuel wiped his mouth and embraced the visitor.

"Back from the dead, you old bastard."

"Everyone," Shmuel announced. "This is Eran. A friend from the old days at Yediot."

"Channel Ten, now," Eran said. "Producer. Documentaries, mostly."

Moshe shook his hand. "Pull up a seat and have some

lunch."

"Don't mind if I do. Is that *nokedli*?"

Eran sat between Shmuel and Moshe and piled food on his plate. With Moshe's permission, he pressed Record on his iPhone. He asked questions between mouthfuls and listened while he chewed. Moshe described all that had happened since he had awoken last Tuesday morning on the Mount of Olives. Rabbi Yosef added the scriptural references and religious dogma.

"Incredible," the reporter said. He had wiped his plate clean. "This changes everything. Had I not known Shmuel here, I would never have believed it. Channel Ten hasn't had a groundbreaking report like this in… well, I don't think anything comes close. This is historic. Epic."

"When will the story air?"

"I'll need to come back with a camera crew. Interview a few more people. Dig around. You know—more perspectives to round the piece off. Then there's editing and scheduling. On the fast track, I'd say a week or two."

"Perfect." Moshe should have things ready by then. He pulled out the sheet of paper with his checklist.

Rafi leaned in to get a better look. "What's our next stop?"

"Bank account." Moshe glanced at his watch, then re-membered again that he had pawned the Rolex on Pierre Koenig Street. He found the time on Eran's iPhone. "Two PM. Banks are closing already. We'll continue tomorrow. Not bad for our first day."

Savta Sarah entered from the kitchen, undoing an apron and trailing a pensive rabbanit, with pen and notepad at the ready. "When it boils," Savta said, "put it on low and mix in salt, pepper, and paprika. Lots of paprika."

"How much?"

Savta shrugged. "As much as it needs. I never measure anything. Rafi, let's go. Time to rest. I'm not as young as I look."

She embraced Moshe. "I'll see you tomorrow." She sent a meaningful glance at the rabbanit, who tensed as she prepared to object, then relented. The list of recipes ran very long and Savta had started with the slow-cooking dishes. The rabbanit would require a long internship to learn Savta's culinary expertise. Moshe and his crew had won another night under the rabbi's roof.

Moshe escorted Savta and Rafi to the taxi and then cleaned up the dining room table. He stacked the dishes in the meat sink and soaped the sponge, his mind afloat with strategies for the week ahead. Their campaign should highlight their plight to create sympathy. They needed contacts in the Ministry of the Interior and National Health Insurance. Other resurrectees might have connections. How many wandered undiscovered on the streets? He stacked the last dish on the drying rack. They should buy the rabbi a dishwasher, too.

Irina huddled on the couch in the living room, her knees pressed to her chest.

"Where is everyone?"

She avoided his eyes. Was she crying?

He sat beside her. "What's going on?"

She wiped her eyes and forced a smile. "Who is Sivan?"

The name caught him off guard. "She works at Karlin & Son. Or used to. Why?"

Irina looked him in the eyes. "Did you sleep with her?"

"No. Of course not. She was my employee."

Irina emitted a nervous laugh. "I didn't think so. But Galit does."

"Galit?"

"I spoke with her last night. She teaches Zumba on Emek Refaim."

Zumba. Galit had signed up years ago but missed every class. Moshe had always returned home too late from work. With him out of the way, she had trained as an instructor. *Good for you, Galit.* He turned his attention from his past failings to the first part of Irina's revelation. *Sivan.*

"Dear God," he said. He leaned forward on the couch. The facts clicked together like falling dominoes. "She must have thought… Or Avi must have told her that…"

Zohar the Hairdresser's voice rang in his mind. *I know your type.*

The room pitched and tilted around him. Everything made sense. Galit's refusal to speak to him. Avi's threats. Even her choice of Avi.

"I have to tell Galit."

Irina sniffed. "She won't believe you. She even thinks that we're together now." Her red eyes held his, searching for an answer to her own silent questions.

"Then I'll have to convince her."

CHAPTER 56

Eli rolled down the polished corridor of the hospital. He slapped the wheels with unnecessary force. Tomorrow morning, come what may, he was out of here. He had mapped the route to the exit—fifty meters from his room to the elevator, seventy meters to the exit of Emergency Care on the first floor, and fifty more uphill to the taxi rank.

He had managed to go to the bathroom without assistance; they couldn't hold him against his will. He'd hire a private nurse if he had to. With Noga out of the picture, what was keeping him there?

Stupid, stupid, stupid. Stupid to open up to her. Stupid to think she would believe. They never believed. You could rain down fire from heaven, but the moment the embers cooled, their faith fled.

He pressed the button for the elevator. The doors of the large metal box opened at the speed of the continental drift. Eli rolled inside and parked beside a large wheeled bed and a male nurse in blue fatigues. He pressed the button for the fourth floor.

He had no time to twiddle his thumbs while his muscles strengthened. He had places to go, people to anoint. A Final Redemption to announce.

Or did he?

As the doors closed, one millimeter at a time, another explanation for his miserable situation rose in his mind, like a distant ripple on the ocean: The Boss had deemed this generation, like all earlier generations, unworthy. In the last minute, the balance of merit had shifted, and He had aborted the nascent redemption.

The Boss had pulled the plug before. King Hezekiah had come close. Bar Kokhba had crashed and burned. A handful of saintly souls throughout history had shown promise but fizzled out. But each time, the Thin Voice had whispered the verdict in Eli's third ear. Why the accident? Why the torment of human pain and helplessness?

If the Divine Will had postponed the End, surely Eli would have known?

A third explanation arose. This one accounted for all the facts. His accident. The lengthy recovery and missing powers. His wonky intuition.

This theory was no ripple on the horizon—it was a tidal wave! Ominous. Inescapable.

There would be no Redemption. Not today. Not ever. The Boss had heeded his advice, finally, and given up on humankind.

And with no hope of Redemption, there was no longer any need for a harbinger. The Boss had abandoned him to the whim of Nature. He would never regain his former strength and powers. He would remain trapped in this mortal coil to live out the rest of his, now numbered, days.

No. No!

The elevator doors opened on the fourth floor. Cold drops of sweat dripped down his forehead. The walls of the corridor swayed before his eyes.

He made for the kitchenette, pulled a plastic cup from the dispenser, and poured water from the cooler. He gulped the clear liquid and gasped for air. *Take it easy. Relax. That's it.* He poured another glass.

A familiar voice giggled in the corridor. One of the younger nurses. Liora.

Eli placed his cup between his legs and inched his wheelchair toward the doorway. Liora leaned against a wall, paper cup in hand. She smiled up at a man. Eli saw only the back of his head but knew him at once by his wild, carrot-colored hair and baggy, motley clothes.

The nurse giggled again.

Love is in the air. Oren had not been wrong about body language. He rolled to the edge of the doorway.

Liora sipped her drink and grew serious. "Don't you get depressed? All those poor kids?"

Moti the Clown gave his head a shake. "The kids are brave. Resilient. Distract them a little and they'll have fun like any healthy kid."

The bastard could speak after all. His voice was deeper than Eli had imagined.

"What really gets me down," the clown continued, "are the adults. They won't let go. Not for a second." He lowered his voice. "Like him." He nodded toward the end of the corridor.

"Who?"

"The nut case. The Messiah."

Liora tittered. "You mean Elijah the Prophet."

News traveled fast.

"Whatever. How do you help someone like that? He's trapped in his own world."

Eli rolled back an inch. So that's how they saw him. *Nut case. Trapped.* Let them jeer. They were the pitiful ones. Or were they?

A week in the hospital. A week as a cripple. A week without The Magic. Would he even recognize the Thin Voice if it spoke again? Had it ever truly spoken?

He waited for them to leave. He rolled down the corridor. Nadir glanced up from the nurses' desk as he passed. He avoided her eyes. Would he ever be able to look any of them in the eye again?

In his room, Eliana stripped the sheets off his neighbor's bed and made to leave.

Eli paused halfway to his bed. "Eliana," he said, "has he checked out already?"

She paused at the door. "Who?"

"You know. Oren. Older guy. Nosy. Many progeny. That was his bed." Oren would surely have said goodbye. Any excuse to talk.

Eliana straightened. "No one told you?"

"What?"

"He passed away. This morning, during surgery."

The world swayed again. Oren was dead.

Never delay, Oren had said. Wise words. They seemed all the wiser now that he was gone.

The touch of a hand on his arm jolted him from his reverie.

"I'm sorry," Eliana said. "Life is short." The beefy nurse gave him a long, compassionate glance and left.

He wheeled the chair around the empty bed, put his hands on the armrests, and heaved his body onto the edge of his own mattress. He lay down. He turned his head toward the naked, empty bed. Then he stared, long and hard, at the thick manila folder on the table.

CHAPTER 57

The hostess ushered Moshe and Irina to a corner table in Kaffit, a coffee shop on Emek Refaim. The pockets of teatime patrons didn't give them a second glance.

"Wouldn't it be easier to meet at the house?" Irina asked, when they settled at their table.

Moshe had wondered the same thing. "Maybe she's more comfortable meeting in a public place," he said. "Fair enough. Until a week ago, I was dead." Sivan had not sounded surprised to hear his voice on the phone, but had hesitated at his request for an urgent meeting.

A waiter in a black T-shirt and matching apron approached and Moshe ordered a jar of water while they waited. If Sivan stood him up, at least he wouldn't waste precious shekels.

Irina bit her nails and sent glances over her shoulder at the street traffic. She avoided his glance. A silent storm seemed to rage within her. Did she believe his innocence? Had he lost her trust? He didn't ask. Soon he'd clear his name—again—and open a back door to Galit.

Would his wife ever welcome him back? He had always thought his marriage strong and good. The past was not what it used to be. He had neglected her, pouring his energies into Karlin & Son, while the void he created at home had filled with suspicion and distrust. In the last few days, the void had widened. Was Zohar the Hairdresser right? Did she deserve better?

Moshe and Irina didn't wait long. Sivan walked in at a brisk pace, clutching a handbag. He almost didn't recognize her. The feisty young girl had traded her trademark torn jeans and T-shirt for a business suit and Louis Vuitton. She spotted their table. Her eyes flitted to Irina and her hand loosened on the bag.

Moshe stood. "Sivan, thanks for coming." His arm hesitated at his side. She didn't offer her hand either. A friendly kiss on the cheek would be a bad idea. Best not to feed the rumormongers.

The awkward moment passed. She sat in the empty chair and brushed a strand of blow-dried hair from her face. "I got your message Saturday night," she said. "I'm sorry I didn't return your call."

He had wondered about that, and now her apology gave him pause. Should he be offended? "Did you know—?" he began.

"Mathew told me," she said, interrupting him. "After all that had happened, I thought you hated me."

Moshe felt he had stepped into the middle of a conversation. "What do you mean? Why would I hate you?"

She looked him straight in the eyes. "After you passed, Avi called. He said you had wanted to fire me."

Just when Moshe thought he had a handle on things, everything he knew flew out the window. Avi had conspired to take over his life before his dead body had cooled. "I didn't know that," he said. "I thought you were laid off a few months ago, when the company ran out of money."

She studied the tabletop. "I was depressed for months. Then I pulled myself together. Got a job in customer service at a hi-tech company in Malcha. Got promoted a few times. Now I'm VP Marketing."

"No kidding? I mean, congratulations. That's fantastic." She smiled and flicked her hair behind a shoulder. *Don't lay it on too thick. But lay it on.* He was about to ask a lot of her.

"A VP in under two years," he added. Leaving Karlin & Son had been a wise career move for two of his employees. The fact made his ego twinge a little. "I didn't want to fire you at all," he continued. "And you're not the only one Avi lied to. I think he told Galit that we'd had an affair."

"You and me?" Her eyes widened.

He nodded. "He moved in with her—into my house. They're getting married next week."

"But now that you're back...?"

"She won't speak to me. I tried. Avi attacked me in the street and threatened my life. And on top of it all, we've both been struggling to survive with no home, no job, and no money."

Sivan looked to Irina. "So you're also... like Moshe?"

Irina nodded.

Moshe breathed in deep. "I'm really, really grateful that you came to see me today. We don't have many friends." His chest tightened. He'd been fighting every step of the way since the day he was resurrected. He'd been deceived and cheated and beaten up; slandered and enslaved. He could really do with a hand up.

Sivan glanced from Moshe to Irina and back. She said, "How can I help?"

CHAPTER 58

Dusk settled over the German Colony as Moshe, Irina, and Sivan walked down Emek Refaim. They crossed the defunct train tracks to Shimshon Street and paused a few houses down from the Karlin residence. The slatted shutters sealed the windows but Galit's white Kia Sportage hugged the curb outside.

"You should go alone," he told Sivan.

"What do I tell her?"

"The truth. There was nothing between us. Nothing romantic. If she responds well, I'll be right here."

She nodded and set out down the street, her heels echoing off the stone houses. Moshe's stomach churned. After all the failed attempts, he had almost despaired of ever breaking through the barriers to Galit's heart. Finally, he understood why she had locked him out. Finally, he held the key. But would the door open?

And if it did, would he come face-to-face with his deepest, darkest fear—that Galit simply did not want him back? He felt his cheeks drain of blood. In the next few seconds, one way or another, he'd find out.

Sivan climbed the three steps and knocked on the front door. She waited and cast a smile in Moshe's direction. After a few moments, she pressed the buzzer.

The shadows deepened as the light faded.

Any moment now, the door would open. Galit would appear at the threshold. From her reaction, Moshe would know his fate. Sivan shifted on her feet and jabbed the buzzer again.

She put her ear to the door. Then she turned and abandoned her post.

"Nobody's home."

"Her car's outside. It's seven o'clock."

Sivan shrugged. "Do you have her number?"

Moshe knew that one by heart. Sivan dialed the number on her phone. "Voicemail. Maybe they went out to eat?"

"And turned off her phone?"

That didn't make sense. Had Avi flown her overseas to escape his advances? A deep pit of dread opened at the base of his stomach. The ground had disappeared beneath his feet. Any moment, he'd fall.

Sivan scratched her neck. She had somewhere else to be. There was no sense in detaining her any longer. "I guess we'll call it a day," he said. "Thanks anyway."

She asked him to let her know if she could help further, and then walked away toward Emek Refaim.

Moshe and Irina made for the rabbi's house in gloomy silence. So close and yet so far. The darkest moment of night is right before the break of dawn. He had read that in one of the rabbi's books. They could try again tomorrow.

Rabbi Yosef answered the door to their knock. "Where have you been? Savta Sarah's called twenty times."

"What happened? Is she OK?"

"She didn't say."

Moshe dashed to the rabbi's phone and dialed Savta's number. Ambulances blared in his imagination. The four boys ate Savta's goulash at the dinner table and eyed him with concern. He gave them a brave grin. The number rang and rang. *Oh, no. Poor Savta.* He tried her mobile. This time, she answered.

"Moshe," Savta cried, breathless. "Where have you been?"

"Are you OK, Savta?"

"Get yourself over to Ramat Rachel now!"

"Ramat Rachel?" The neighborhood in South Jerusalem had a hotel and an event hall, but no hospitals.

"The wedding is starting."

"What wedding?" Again, the universe slipped from under his feet.

"Galit and Avi's. They brought it forward. They only told me half an hour ago. They must have figured out that we're in cahoots. I'm on my way in a cab. I'll see what I can do to hold things off."

Moshe put down the phone. Irina and Rabbi Yosef stared at him. He stared back at them, like a stunned fish.

"Rabbi Yosef," he said, his voice strangely calm. "Can you give me a ride?"

"Where to?"

"Ramat Rachel," he said. "I have to stop a wedding."

CHAPTER 59

Irina fastened her seatbelt. She watched, alone in the back seat, as events hurtled out of her control.

Rabbi Yosef started his car, and they pulled off into the night. Moshe sat in the passenger seat, silent and tense.

She should never have looked for Galit. Ever since their meeting last night, conflicting emotions had been colliding inside her. She had not believed the accusation of infidelity, not for a moment. She knew Moshe better than that. The one person she had not known well enough, though, was herself. The ticket to his reconciliation with Galit had dropped into her hands, and her first impulse had been to shred that ticket.

Fortunately—for Moshe, at least—she had been unable to keep the secret for long. She simply could not lie to him. Destroying his dream in order to fulfill her own—what would that make her? By the afternoon, she had confessed, and now she tagged along as Moshe tried to use that ticket to hurry back into his old life and out of hers forever. The wedding was her only hope.

"What are you going to do?" she asked. The engine gurgled and groaned as gears changed within the rusty beast.

"I don't know. Tell her the truth, I suppose, before it's too late."

Part of her cheered him on; the rest hoped that he would

fail.

"Ramat Rachel," Moshe said. "That's where we got married. That bastard Avi is trying to rewrite the past."

Irina and Avi shared an enemy: the past. The mound of memories that stood between her and Moshe.

Streetlights flew by. Rabbi Yosef changed lanes, weaving between cars, racing against time. Moshe turned the radio on and a cassette played. A soothing bassline of synthesizer chords. A drumbeat like a fast ticking clock. An electric guitar jangled to the rhythm of a young, breaking heart, and Cyndi Lauper sang of love, separation, and devotion.

The song seemed to speak for Irina. If Moshe fell, she'd catch him; she'd be waiting. Time after time.

Life had given her this tumultuous week with Moshe. Life might grant her more. Either way, Moshe would be a part of her forever.

The groaning of the engine had become a scream. Smoke billowed from the hood. "Oh, no!" Rabbi Yosef said, and he pulled over to the side of the busy two-lane boulevard.

They got out. Moshe walked around the ruined car. He tried to flag down a passing car or a taxi. None stopped.

"I'm sorry, Moshe," the rabbi said.

Moshe put his hands on his head. He had tried so hard. He didn't deserve this.

"How far is it?" Irina asked.

"Not far."

"Then run."

He stared at her. Hesitation flickered in his eyes. He didn't want to abandon them on the side of the road.

"Go on," she said. "We'll be fine. Go and get her."

He inclined his head in thanks. Then he sprinted down the street. He turned left and disappeared behind a wall.

"Good luck, my friend," she whispered. "And goodbye."

CHAPTER 60

The lab technician at Shaare Zedek had to work fast.

Her colleague was on maternity leave. A week of blood work had accumulated in the laboratory fridge and, in half an hour, she had to collect her daughter from ballet class.

She pulled a set of vials from the batch holder, scanned the bar codes, and slipped them into the microcentrifuge. Her fingernails clicked on the counter as the machine hummed and cells separated from the serum. She stopped the machine, added a drop of Laemmli buffer to each tube, and placed them in the slots of the heater. Then she pipetted the stained proteins into an acrylamide gel, which she placed in the electrophoresis apparatus. While the gels ran, she scanned the next batch of tubes and loaded them into the centrifuge.

Multitask or die—her motto at work and at home. In her kitchen on Friday mornings, a tray of chicken would brown in the oven while onions sautéed on the stove and schnitzels bubbled in a frying pan for her children's lunch. She used timers in both arenas to great effect. She could do with bar codes in the kitchen too.

She retrieved the gel sheets from the apparatus and moved them to the computer monitor. Each transparent strip displayed the characteristic blue smudges of protein electrophoresis that resembled a child's tie-dyeing experiment. She scanned a bar code and recorded the result on the keyboard of the lab computer.

Scan. Record. Click.

Scan. Record. Click.

Scan. Record. *Hello!*

The blue patterns on the sheet—the spread of proteins and enzymes—were unlike anything she had ever seen. She double-clicked for more details on the sample and found the referring doctor. She picked up the phone and dialed his number. Her fingernails clicked on the desk yet again as the phone rang on the other side.

Pick up, Dr. Stern. I don't have all day.

CHAPTER 61

Galit smoothed the fabric of the wedding dress over her hips in the mirror of the dressing room while her mother fussed with the lace of the veil.

She had worn the same dress at her first wedding. She had floated down the aisle on a cloud of joy to join Moshe under the *chuppah*. She had never imagined that, eight years later, she'd wear that dress again. This time around, a very different kind of butterfly upset her stomach.

Am I doing the right thing?

After tonight, there was no turning back.

"There," said her mother, her eyelids puffy from lack of sleep. "You're good to go."

"Thanks, *Ima*. Sorry about the short notice." Her parents had changed clothes on the eleven-hour flight from Newark and rushed straight from Ben Gurion Airport to the wedding hall in Ramat Rachel.

A crack appeared in her mother's smile. "I still think you should have waited for the appointed day. You've been dating for two years. What's another week?"

Her mother was right. Galit could have married Avi any day during those two years. Why had she held out? Avi loved her. He worshipped her. But he was no Moshe. Despite everything, a corner of her heart still belonged to Moshe.

When he had returned from the grave, those dormant emotions had erupted.

Avi had brought the wedding date forward. Had he sensed her doubts?

"It's complicated," she said. The sight of Moshe had raised her memories of the good times too. His dreams and drive had inspired her and given her hope. Together, they would conquer the world.

Her mother knew her only too well. "Who cares," she said, "if that cheating good-for-nothing is back? Who does he think he is?"

Right again. Galit detested liars and cheaters. When Avi had told her about Moshe and Sivan, her love had turned to hate. Moshe had betrayed their shared dream of conquering the world and turned to conquering other women. He would tread that path alone. God might have given him a second chance, but she would not. Cheaters didn't deserve second chances.

"I'm sorry," her mother said. She dabbed at Galit's eyes with a tissue.

"It's OK," she said.

Outside, a trumpet played a jaunty wedding song. Time to face the crowd. Time to put Moshe behind her. She sucked in a deep, brave breath.

"Let's go," she said. "I'm ready."

CHAPTER 62

As Moshe reached the hilly parking lot of the Ramat Rachel Hotel, he heard the festive sound of a trumpet and his heart fell. *Am I too late?* The hotel sprawled upward over the tiered hillside. He had no time to catch his breath from the climb; he pushed on.

He raced between rows of parked cars and launched up a stone staircase to the grassy knoll between the hotel building and the event hall. The *chuppah* stood at the edge of the green patch, overlooking the Judean hills, now shrouded in twilight. A white carpet ran between the rows of empty chairs dressed in white. White sheets and pastel nosegays adorned the wedding canopy. No sign of bride or groom. Had he missed the ceremony?

A wave of déjà vu disorientated him. Memories of his own wedding ceremony. Galit floated in his mind like a beautiful ghost in a white dress. Her ecstatic smile and adoring eyes through the diaphanous veil.

"It's a disgrace," said a voice. Moshe spun around. Savta Sarah wore a beige suit and matching hat covered in lace. She scowled through thick layers of makeup, like war paint. "No chopped liver," she said. "Or smoked salmon. And they call themselves caterers!"

"Where is Galit?"

Savta pointed to the tiered garden behind her. "Up there. The bridal chair."

Moshe sprinted along a path of irregular rock slabs. He dodged manicured bushes and colorful flowerbeds. A clarinet played "Pretty Woman."

He entered a green patch lined with food stations. He cut through the press of mingling guests in collared shirts and evening dresses. A woman with nebulous brown curls gasped and pointed at him—Galit's cousin. He dodged the waiters with their trays of Riesling and finger food.

No bridal chair. No Galit.

He continued up another set of steps to the next tier. A clump of women hovered around a wicker couch draped in white sheets and cushions. He parted the crowd of women and stopped dead. The bridal chair was empty.

He scanned his surroundings for a white dress and panted while the clarinet rose an octave for the chorus.

"The bride," Moshe asked the women. "Where is she?"

Blank stares and shaking heads. He had to find her!

"You!" said a familiar, whiny voice. Zohar Raphael sauntered over, a wineglass in hand. The celebrity hairdresser had not changed out of his low jeans and tank top. He jabbed a finger at Moshe. "What are you doing here?"

Moshe wished he'd keep his voice down. "Where is Galit?" he hissed.

"Come to cause trouble, have you?" The finger waved from side to side. "Oh, no you don't. Girls!" he yelled. "Meet Moshe, Galit's cheating ex-husband. He doesn't belong here."

A small army of petulant women mobilized behind their megalomaniac commander, brandishing miniature kebabs and heavy designer handbags and eying Moshe with extreme prejudice.

Moshe retreated to the reception tier, hoping to lose Zohar in the crowd. He ducked sideways and took cover behind a uniformed chef, slicing slivers of entrecote for a line of hungry guests. Moshe surveyed the enemy territory. Zohar led his platoon of angry women through the crowd to the other side.

The delicious scent of roast meat reached his nose, but he had no time for distractions.

His gaze shifted and his breath caught in his throat. Beyond the leaves of a shaggy bush, a man in a tuxedo engaged in a hushed conversation with a rabbi.

Moshe stepped through the foliage, squeezed between the bushes, trampled a patch of yellow gerberas, and emerged on the stone pathway. He marched over to the groom. "Where is she?"

Avi turned to him. His eyes widened, and his lips parted. His face drained of color. "Get away," he croaked. "Get out of here."

Moshe turned to the rabbi and offered his hand. "Moshe Karlin, Galit's husband. Yes—she's already married. You can't let this—"

"OK, OK," Avi said. He stepped between Moshe and the rabbi. "You win. I'll take you to her."

Avi led the way, leaving the befuddled rabbi on the rocky path. He stomped through the hotel lobby, the lapels of his tuxedo flapping. He opened a door labeled "Bridal Room" and closed it behind them. Gift-wrapped boxes, stacked chairs, and wheeled partitions littered the chamber.

"Where is she?"

Avi stuck out his chest. "Did you think you could just waltz in here and ruin my life?"

"You rotten liar. You told her I cheated with Sivan!"

Avi's face softened. He hadn't expected Moshe to know that.

"What if I did?"

"You knew that wasn't true. I love Galit. Always have, always will. You stole her from me."

"Can't steal from a thief."

The Hebrew proverb made no sense in the argument. "What are you talking about?"

"You're the thief," Avi yelled. "You stole her from me!"

"You've gone mad."

"Hangar 17. The night you met her. Newsflash—I spoke with her before you even laid eyes on her. The beers I bought—they weren't for you and me. You just took them from me, the way you took her too." His chest heaved.

The information threw Moshe off balance.

"All I could do was watch," Avi continued, his voice breaking, "while you charmed her and danced with her. At your wedding. Your daughter's birthday parties. I kept thinking, 'What if I hadn't saved his life? All this would be mine.'"

Moshe had not known about any of this suffering. But the call to pity would not make him give up all he held dear.

"You saw her first—is that what are you're saying? Are we in kindergarten?" Avi had no answer for that, so Moshe plunged on. "Stop feeling sorry for yourself. Stop blaming others. Get your own life. Stop turning Galit against me with your lies."

"I didn't have to turn her against you."

"What are you going on about now?" Moshe had no patience for another sob story.

"You turned her against yourself."

"Oh, please."

"You were never home. You worked late for months on end. You only cared about your precious company. You had no time for Galit. You were never around for Talya either."

The nerve! "Why do you think I worked so hard? It was all for them."

"No. Not for them. Face it, Moshe. You did it to prove yourself, to please those old photos on the wall. You cheated on her, all right. Just not with Sivan."

Moshe opened his mouth to speak but found no defense. Zohar had told the same story. Moshe the neglectful husband. Moshe the absentee father.

"She doesn't want you," Avi continued, smelling blood in the water. "She told me. I didn't think you needed to hear that, but you've given me no choice. Whatever love she felt for you died with you."

The words winded Moshe like a lightning punch to the solar plexus. His deepest, darkest fear had been realized. Galit had fallen out of love. She was better off without him.

Moshe had accused Avi of blaming others for his own problems, but he himself was no different. The fault lay in his own actions, all along. Far in the past. Beyond fixing.

"You're dead," Avi said. Not a threat; a diagnosis. "Now, for Galit's sake, stay dead."

Avi straightened the lapels of his jacket. He turned his back on Moshe and left the room.

Moshe stared at the cracked tiles of the floor. His breath came in short, halting wheezes. He had no right to be there. He didn't belong. He staggered through the hotel lobby, his head down, his mouth dry. He passed the gardens and the buffet. He hobbled down the steps of the slope, through the parking lot, and into the dark night.

In the distance, the trumpet played a new song.

CHAPTER 63

Moshe strolled along Hebron Road. Cars whizzed by in the night and blew exhaust fumes in his face.

He had failed in his old life. Failed at home. Failed at work. He had failed in this new life too. *A Karlin never quits*, his father had said. This Karlin had. Who said he was still a Karlin, anyway? Had he shed his heritage along with his body? The thought did not console him.

The cracks of the sidewalk pressed through the soles of his shoes. Television screens reflected off apartment windows. Stars glittered in the heavens above.

He was a single dust mote lost in an infinite cosmos. If he lived a thousand lives, would he grasp even one iota of that mystery?

An emptiness filled him. Not hunger, although he had skipped dinner. An emptiness of the soul—the desolation of a man who has nothing left to lose.

The past had always been a safe shore, a haven in stormy seas. Now the ropes had severed, and he drifted out to sea. He floated on the formless ocean. Unfathomable deep below, unreachable stars above. He might perish on that wet desert. He might sail off the edge of the world. Then again, he might discover a new horizon.

So this is how Irina felt. A clean slate, at once terrifying and liberating.

The dark hulk of the rabbi's white Subaru lay abandoned on the side of the road. Moshe laid his hand on the hood. The billowing smoke had dissipated. The metal had cooled.

The car had reached the end of the line. Salvage what you can, then move on. He left the dead chassis behind.

He placed one foot in front of the other. In his dreams, the faster he crossed the bridge, the further the grassy bank had fled. Had fate played a cruel trick on him, or had he simply been facing in the wrong direction?

By the time he reached Shimshon Street, the empty feeling had settled into an inner calm.

Irina opened the door. She wore a loose pajama T-shirt and shorts. She studied his eyes for answers to unspoken questions. He stepped into the soft lamplight of the living room. Samira and Shmuel turned hopeful glances toward him. He plopped down on the couch, and their hope subsided into disappointment.

Irina joined him on the couch. "We're sorry about your family," she whispered. The rabbi's children were probably asleep in their beds. She smelled of soap and the rabbanit's sweet deodorant. The T-shirt fell below one pale shoulder. The large fairy eyes drank him in.

"We're all family now," he said.

A loud knock on the door startled him. Who came calling at the rabbi's house at this hour? The knocking came again— *bang-bang-bang*—and threatened to wake the household. Irina gripped his arm. The specter of his former slave drivers loomed in his mind too.

Moshe approached the door, peered through the peephole, and opened.

Avi stood in the doorway, his hair a mess, his tie loose, the dress shirt creased. He shot Moshe an angry look and barged inside.

"Where is she?"

"Keep your voice down. The rabbi's kids are asleep. Where is who?"

The intruder prowled the living room, his forehead glistening. He sent fiery glances at Irina, Shmuel, and Samira on the couches, and circled back to Moshe. "Where are you hiding her?"

"Hiding who? What are you talking about?" Moshe dared not hope.

Avi seemed to age ten years in an instant. He held his head in his hands. "Galit," he muttered. "She didn't show up at the *chuppah*. Nobody knows where she is." He drew near again. "Swear to me you don't know where she is."

"I swear it."

Avi clenched his jaw. Moshe thought that his ex-friend was going to hit him again, but he just skulked out the door and into the night.

Oh. My. God. Galit had backed out of the wedding. Had she finally come around? There was only one way to find out. He made for the door.

"Moshe," Irina said. "You said you didn't know where she is."

"I don't," he said. "But I have a hunch."

CHAPTER 64

Dr. Stern launched up the stairs to the fifth floor. In another ten seconds, the Medical Genetics Institute would close for the evening.

The vague message on his phone had confirmed his suspicions: Mr. Eli Katz was no ordinary man. His genome held the secret Dr. Stern had chased for decades. Soon he would hold in his hands irrefutable proof for his suspicions.

Academic papers. Clinical trials. FDA approval. The future rolled ahead with clarity. A Nobel Prize would be nice, but he didn't care for fame or fortune. The discovery was its own reward—a milestone in human progress that would change humanity forever.

He burst through the door of the stairwell and onto the hospital corridor, collided with a cloaked nurse, and dashed toward the doors of the Institute. Lights still burned inside. He opened the door and charged toward the lab, stopping only when he reached a long, rectangular office. Computer screens, microscopes, and other specialized machinery covered the counters. He caught his breath.

A podgy technician wearing a blue sanitary shower cap folded a white lab cloak. "I was about to leave," she said.

"Dr. Stern," he said, by way of introduction. "I got your message."

"Never mind," she said. "False alarm. I should have let you know."

His heart dropped into his shoes. She had seemed so certain in her voice message. "What do you mean?"

"The protein spread was bizarre."

"Yes?"

"Unlike any known human protein. The sample was contaminated. Bacteria, probably."

"Is your equipment sterile?"

She removed the cap and reached for her bag. "Yes. Of course. The contamination must have occurred at collection. You'll have to retest the subject."

"Retest? No, that won't be possible." He did not elaborate about his complex relationship with Mr. Eli Katz. He glanced at the white strips with the waves of blue suspended by clips on the shelves. "Let me have the results. I'll double check myself."

"Sorry," she said. "I destroyed the sheet. Standard procedure for contamination."

"And the remains of the sample?"

She gave him an apologetic grin. "Destroyed too."

"Don't tell me: standard procedure."

She nodded. "I have to go fetch my daughter. Turn off the lights on your way out."

She shuffled past and left him in the empty lab.

Dr. Stern exhaled his frustration. Back to square one. The director of the Institute was an old friend. He'd have a word with him about changing procedures.

"This isn't over, Mr. Katz," he swore to the empty room. "Not even close."

CHAPTER 65

The Old City of Jerusalem looked like a shiny gold ring in a box of black satin. Moshe walked along the edge of the Haas Promenade, a bouquet of red roses on his arm. He had picked the flowers in Liberty Bell Park on his way.

Pairs of lovers, young and old, sat on the steps and benches in the soft glow of distant streetlights, enjoying the romantic night skyline. None noticed him as he passed.

On the barrier wall, toward the end of the Tayelet, a lone woman dangled her legs over the edge. She wore an elegant white dress.

Moshe sat down beside her and swung his legs over the wall.

They stared at the mighty timeless walls of the Old City, ablaze in spotlight.

"You're late," she said, a tear in her voice.

Tears of regret or joy?

"I got here as fast as I could."

He held out the flowers.

She accepted his gift and breathed in their scent.

"Did Savta Sarah get to you?" he asked.

She gave a short, sad laugh. "I was hiding in the Bridal Room," she said. "Wedding night jitters."

"Oh." She had overheard his argument with Avi. She

267

knew the truth.

"I didn't mind the late nights," she said. "Your dreams were mine. We were one person. I would have followed you to the ends of the earth." She wiped her eyes. "Until the day before your birthday party. Avi came by the house. He said he couldn't keep silent any longer. He told me about you and Sivan. I never imagined that he could have made that up. I was in shock. Then I was furious." A short, bitter laugh. "You know me. I had already invited everyone we knew. Cancelling was not an option. But afterwards, you were going to pay. It would be your farewell party and good riddance." She shuddered, as though reliving the anger and hurt of that time.

"A farewell party it was," he said, trying to lighten the mood.

She turned to him, her eyes damp. "Can you forgive me?"

"Hmm." He made a show of thinking it over, then smiled. "There's nothing to forgive. It wasn't your fault."

She gulped air and wiped her eyes again.

"Although," he added, his voice brimming with incredulity, "Avi—of all the men in the world?"

She took her time answering. "He was around when I needed him," she said. "And I knew that you never really liked him."

Moshe nodded. "Got it." She had let Avi move in to get back at her dead, cheating husband. The female heart—yet another mystery that he would never comprehend.

She gazed at the ancient golden city. "When you showed up again, I thought I was going crazy. I couldn't believe that it was really you."

Moshe chuckled. "Sometimes I'm not so sure myself."

She shot him a quick glance loaded with suspicion.

Time to put her doubts to rest. "Listen to me," he said. "It's me. And it's always been you. Only you. I don't care if we're apart for two years or two thousand years, I will always love you. And I will do anything to get back to you—so long as you still want me—even if I have to rise from the grave."

She searched his eyes for the truth. He reached out and wiped the tears from her face.

"No more crying, OK? This is a new life. A fresh start."

She leaned her head on his shoulder. Her hair rose in the breeze and caressed his cheek. He inhaled the sweet scent of jasmine. He was getting his old life back but nothing would be quite the same.

"We'll figure it out," he said, and he stroked her hair. "One day at a time."

CHAPTER 66

Two weeks later, Eli placed a crutch under his shoulder, slid off the hospital bed for the last time, and prepared to face the world.

His palms were clammy and his stomach ached. He had wanted to escape the hospital from the moment he had awoken from his coma. Now that the day had arrived, he hesitated.

The casts had come off. He hardly felt any pain. That morning, he had tied his own shoelaces for the first time. Dressing was easy—the real challenges lay outside. The world had changed since his accident. Or, more accurately, he had changed.

He took a step forward, leaning on the crutch. Then he took another.

Dr. Stern looked him over and frowned. "What's your name?" he said.

Eli laughed. "Still Eli Katz."

"Are you sure?"

"Doctor!" said Eliana, the busty, energetic nurse.

"Just asking."

"We got you a little something." Eliana presented him with a white box tied with a red ribbon.

"Thanks. You shouldn't have." Eli felt his eyes moisten.

The hospital team had become his friends—no, his family—over the past few weeks. He accepted the box clumsily, his one arm clamped over the crutch. He placed the box on the bed and undid the ribbon. A tray of Ferrero Rocher and a paperback: The Man who Mistook His Wife for a Hat. That would be from Dr. Stern.

A chain of motorcycle keys and a folded wad of black leather. Eli shook out the jacket. Long gashes marred the sleeve and bisected the flaming chariot emblem on the back. *Did I actually wear this?* No wonder they thought him insane.

He tried on the jacket.

"Thank you all. Really. You've been wonderful."

He limped forward on the crutch and shook hands with the line of well-wishers. The nurses, Liora and Nadir. His physiotherapist. Moti the Clown hugged him.

Dr. Stern handed Eli his card. "Call if you need anything."

"See you around."

"Oh, I'm sure you will."

Eli wasn't sure he liked the sound of that.

At the end of the line waited a girl in a white cloak.

"I'll carry those," Noga said. He handed her the chocolates and book.

She locked his free arm in hers and escorted him down the corridor.

After Oren's passing, Eli had studied the papers in the manila folder. According to the documents, he was a regular guy in the prime of his life, not a broken prophet on a god-forsaken planet. Life is short, Eliana had said. Oren's death had demonstrated that only too well. But he didn't have to live out his days alone. With luck, he might share them with the girl in the white cloak.

As he read and re-read the papers in the folder, he became increasingly convinced that they told the truth. For the first time in his life, he felt compassion for the sad little boy who had constructed a fantasy world from the fragments of his shattered life. When that world came crashing down, he called Noga on the phone. After a lot of convincing—and three bouquets of roses delivered to her door—she had appeared at his hospital bed, a hesitant smile on her lips.

"You take care of each other," Eliana called after them.

"We will," they answered as one.

Noga squeezed his arm and smiled. She pressed the button for the elevator.

Eli put his hand in the pocket of his jacket and his fingers brushed against a piece of paper. He unfolded the yellow square.

A telephone number and a name. *Yosef Lev.*

The name pulled him back in time. *The Mount of Olives. The bearded man by the white car.* He had called the ambulance and must have left his details with the paramedics. Eli had been on his way to meet him. *The Thin Voice. The End of Days.*

Or had he? Delusions stuck to his mind like gum to the sole of a shoe. He had scraped as best he could, but his mind was not yet spotless.

"What is it?" Noga asked.

He crumpled the note and tossed it in the waste bin.

"Nothing," he said. "Nothing at all."

CHAPTER 67

A happy thought woke Dr. Sandler from her slumber.

Today her oldest daughter, Ester, would step under the *chuppah*. When she looked at her, she still saw the bubbly toddler who had insisted on boarding the El Al flight from New Jersey to Tel Aviv on her own two feet. She had adjusted well to their new lives in the Holy Land. A week ago, the medical school of the Hebrew University had accepted her application, and she would follow in her mommy's footsteps.

She yawned and listened to the chatter of morning birds.

She had met her for coffee last night at Café Aroma on Jaffa Road—their last heart-to-heart before the big day. Ester had shared her hopes and dreams for the new chapter in her life. Her eyes grew large when she talked of her betrothed, Lior, a quiet, kind-hearted Israeli. She had chosen well. Dr. Sandler's heart warmed to see her so happy.

Her recollection darkened. A disturbance had interrupted their get-together. What was it? Oh, yes. The Arab youth at the door of the coffee shop.

Dr. Sandler treated Arab patients every day at the Emergency Unit of the Hadassah Medical Center in Ein Kerem. Over the years, she had picked up enough Arabic phrases to manage a basic conversation and help her patients feel at ease.

The Arab boy at Café Aroma was definitely not at ease. His forehead sweaty, his eyes glazed over, and the straps of a blue backpack tight over his shoulders, he struggled with the uniformed guard. She had thought to get up and intervene when...

Oh, no. No, no, no!

She opened her eyes.

Clear azure skies. She lay supine on a gravelly bed.

She clambered to her feet. A small patchy field of dirt. A low wall of rough-hewn stones. *Where am I? And where are my clothes?*

A savage migraine pounded at the back of her eyeballs. She covered her nakedness with her arms. She stumbled forward over stones and pebbles.

She had to get to the hospital. Ambulances were on their way. She needed to oversee triage and direct the interns. She had sat with Ester right at the door. She might be in one of those ambulances, or even...

She froze. Leafy trees whispered in the morning breeze. The rounded ends of Jewish tombstones poked over the wall. She panted. Her heart raced. Tears burned down her cheeks. *My Ester.* There would be no wedding today. Or ever.

The urgency of the hospital faded. Her hand moved to her head by force of habit but found no head covering. A road of black asphalt passed nearby. *Is this real?*

She staggered forward. A table stood at the side of the road, surreal and out of place, like a painting by Magritte. A white tablecloth flapped in the breeze. A gray-haired man in a tweed suit slouched on a chair. The doctor approached with as much dignity as possible under the circumstances.

"Ester," she cried. "Where is Ester?"

The man yawned. "My name is Boris," he said in Hebrew with a heavy Russian accent. He handed her a square of fabric that unfolded into a gauzy white cloak like a disposable hospital gown. Dr. Sandler turned aside and donned the gown. She accepted a disposable plastic cup of water and two white Acamol tablets.

"Thank you."

"Name?"

Dr. Sandler told him. The man filled out a form.

"Where is my daughter?"

The man said nothing.

As an observant Jewess, she believed in life after death, but in a vague and general way. Bright light. Long tunnel. A welcoming committee of dear departed souls. Pearly gates. She had never imagined the afterlife to be so, well, like life, complete with Russian bureaucrats and ballpoint pens.

"Sign here." The Russian pushed the sheet of paper toward her and held out the pen.

"What is this?"

"For your food and shelter."

Food and shelter. That didn't seem right, but she was in no position to argue.

She took hold of the pen and leaned over the table.

"No!" a distant voice yelled. A man ran toward her. "Don't sign that!"

Boris watched him without expression.

Running Man had dark hair, kind eyes, and an earnest smile. "Come with us. We'll help you, and you don't have to sign anything."

"Us?"

Running Man pointed down the road. "Around the corner. The others came out on the other side." *The others?* Hope quickened in her heart. He stuck out his hand. "I'm Moshe," he said. "Welcome to the Afterlife."

"You," Boris barked at him. "Stay out of this!"

Moshe ignored the Russian. He handed Dr. Sandler a thick white robe of soft cotton, the kind she had enjoyed at the Bellagio spa after a convention in Vegas.

Dr. Sandler chose the spa option and donned her new robe.

Moshe walked her down the road and a second table came into view, decked in blue and white, with Stars of David and matching helium balloons. A tall woman with short blond hair waved and smiled.

"I was in your shoes a month ago," Moshe said. "You probably have a lot of questions, and we'll answer them as best we can. But first, have some breakfast."

The tall blond gave her a warm smile and shook her hand, then handed her a pair of spa slippers and a paper cup of sweet mint tea.

Dr. Sandler cupped the tea in her hands and picked a *rugalah* from a platter of the chocolate pastries. Questions queued in her mind. She licked her fingers and dropped the empty cup in a small garbage bin.

"This afterlife," she asked Moshe, "will I like it?"

Moshe thought for a while. "I'm sure you will. In time. The main thing, they say, is not to be afraid." He brightened. "Irina will escort you to your ride." He pointed to a minibus taxi that idled further down the road. The driver, a balding Yemenite, waved.

Dr. Sandler turned to Moshe. She opened her mouth to ask her question but froze, afraid of the answer she might receive. Moshe seemed to have read her thoughts.

"The others boarded earlier," he said. "They'll be happy to meet you. One of them in particular." He smiled and added, "She'll be very happy indeed."

CHAPTER 68

Moshe joined in the chorus of voices. "Hi, Avner."

Galit sat beside him in the circle of a dozen chairs. He rested his hand on her knee and then retracted it. He had returned home two weeks ago, but he still slept on the couch downstairs. Galit was still adjusting to his presence. He shouldn't push his luck. Talya, on the other hand, had showered him with hugs and requests for bedtime stories, although that was probably thanks to his ready supply of her favorite candy: Elite strawberry-flavored toffee in a pink wrapper.

Avner, a gaunt young man in a black T-shirt, cleared his throat and told his story.

Night had fallen on Jaffa Street outside the window. The office space of Karlin & Son had not seen this much activity in months. At its current rate of growth, the Dry Bones Society would need to expand into the neighboring offices. Expansion required money, and that depended on tonight.

So far that evening, they had met an accountant (suicide), a Romanian construction worker (fall from scaffolding), and a doctor and her grown daughter.

Shmuel folded his arms over his chest and listened. He had still refused to discuss his own death, and it seemed he never would.

Across the circle, Rabbi Yosef smiled and nodded, encouraging the stranger who had joined their ranks.

The meeting concluded with the singing of "*HaTikva*"—the national anthem—and Rabbi Nachman's "Narrow Bridge," followed by mingling at the refreshments tables. Savta Sarah wore her apron and pushed stuffed cabbage and meatballs on her grateful clientele.

Rabbi Yosef remained in his seat. His shoulders slumped and a haze of sadness hung over him. Moshe knew what tonight meant for him. His life would never be the same.

"One moment," Moshe told Galit. He was walking over to the rabbi when Samira called for their attention. "Everyone!" she said from the edge of a cubicle. "It's starting!"

The legs of a dozen plastic chairs squeaked and Moshe retook his seat beside Galit. Irina aimed a remote at the large mounted television and switched to Channel Ten.

The stony hillside of Jerusalem panned across the screen. The camera cut to the cemetery in East Jerusalem. A man walked among the rows of tombstones. He wore a blue polo shirt.

"One summer's morning," said the voice of Eran, Shmuel's reporter friend, "Rami Alon awoke in the Mount of Olives Cemetery, naked and alone. He found his way home and made a shocking discovery: he had died three years earlier in a car crash."

On screen, Rami knocked on the door of a house and fell into the embrace of his beautiful wife and two teenage children. A close-up showed the happy family on a living room couch.

"We thought we had lost Rami forever," said the beautiful wife, holding his hand. "But God gave us a second chance."

The narrator continued. "Others have received a second chance as well, but not all were as fortunate as Rami."

The camera showed Moshe walking down Shimshon Street. The offices of Karlin & Son erupted in cheers and applause, and a smile stole onto Moshe's face. He had never appeared on television before.

"Moshe Karlin awoke two years after a fatal heart attack

and found himself on the street."

Galit gave him an apologetic pout. He had asked Eran to tone down the story for the sake of his wife and the reporter had kept his word.

The television framed Moshe as he sat at his desk. "My daughter didn't recognize me," he told the camera. "I had lost everything I held dear. I needed help."

"One man," the reporter continued, "came to Moshe's aid: Yosef Lev, the rabbi of Moshe's neighborhood synagogue." Rabbi Yosef filled the screen with his dreamy smile. More cheers from the group.

"We are witnessing the fulfillment of biblical prophecies," said the rabbi. "The Resurrection is one stage of the Final Redemption."

The real-world Rabbi Yosef watched the screen but did not smile. This was it. He had sided—on national television—with the dreaded demons of the Other Side.

"How does the Resurrection process work?" Eran the reporter asked.

"It is a great miracle," the smiling rabbi said. "Our ancient writings talk of the Dew of Resurrection, which recreates the physical body from the Luz, a small, indestructible bone in the spine."

The camera shifted to the tiered campus of the Hebrew University on Mount Scopus. "Others," the narrator said, "have provided less miraculous explanations. We spoke with Professor Yakov Malkovich of the Hebrew University."

A bespectacled man with tufts of white cotton candy hair sat behind a large desk. Certificates and awards graced the walls behind him. He was not a happy old man.

"Nonsense," he said. "Utter garbage. People do not spontaneously regenerate."

"Then how do you explain the people who have returned from the grave?"

The professor shrugged. "An elaborate hoax."

Eran the reporter appeared on the screen. He walked between rows of gravestones. "Ezekiel's Resurrection or a clever prank? One thing is for sure: the number of the self-proclaimed resurrected has grown. They come from all segments of Israeli society, and they claim to share a peculiar physical irregularity." He patted his paunch. "No belly button. Some of them have formed a non-profit to provide social and economic aid to their fellow new arrivals."

Moshe appeared again, sitting at his desk. "Rejection by family and friends. Exploitation. Bureaucratic difficulties. That is why we started the Dry Bones Society."

The shot cut to a circle of men and women sitting on plastic chairs in the office space where Moshe now sat. A balding man stood and spoke from the heart while the others listened.

Moshe's voice continued in the background. "We depend entirely on donations. If you're resurrected and have the means, or if you'd just like to help, please call our toll-free number." Then Moshe's face filled the screen. "Who knows?" he said, his expression earnest. "Your dear departed loved ones might need our help right now."

Moshe stood up in the middle of the room and clapped his hands together. "That's our cue, friends. Battle stations!"

As the toll-free number displayed on the screen, men and women—Jews and Arabs, established Israelis and new immigrants—ran to cubicles and donned headsets. Irina switched the television to the display Moshe had set up ahead of time.

The counter of incoming calls remained a large, round zero on the screen.

Moshe rested his arm on the cubicle divider. He heard the sound of his own breathing. He felt every pair of eyes on him. The office lease ended in two weeks. Their fledgling organization had burned through the little cash they had scrabbled together. The Dry Bones Society needed an urgent infusion of money. Every person in the room knew that.

A telephone rang. The incoming call counter rose by one. Shmuel raised his hand above the cubicle wall. "I got it." He clicked a button on his terminal. "Dry Bones Society," he said, as Moshe had scripted. "Shmuel speaking. How can I help you?"

Moshe heard the sound of his own heart beating. The entire room soaked up every word and inflection.

"Yes. Yes? Thank you. Thank you very much!" He put his hand over the microphone. "A hundred shekels!" A cheer and a short burst of applause. "Let me take your credit card details."

A hundred shekels. Not much but a start.

The Total Sales counter jumped from zero to one hundred. A sober silence descended on the waiting army of phone reps.

Then the phone bell rang again. And again. The incoming call counter moved from one to two to seven.

Irina punched the air. "One thousand shekels!" she cried. No cheers this time. The others were too busy fielding calls with donors.

Total Sales now covered three months' rent and change. Reporters called in, picking up the story and verifying facts. A few cynics and pranksters too.

From the corner of his eye, he saw Rabbi Yosef head for the door, his head low. "I'll call you back," Moshe told a correspondent from Israel Today. He caught the rabbi in the quiet of the corridor.

"Rabbi Yosef." The rabbi turned and managed a brief smile. "Thank you. For everything."

He left the details unspoken. The rabbi would lose his job, for sure. Moshe had realized this too late. He had overheard the rabbi talking on the phone with the rabbanit. A contingent of rabbis had visited the Lev household on Shimshon Street last week to deliver the ultimatum.

"And," Moshe continued, "I'm glad to offer you our first full-time position."

The rabbi lifted his head. "Full-time?"

"Or as full-time as you'd like. Our members need guidance and counseling. Who better to help them than you?"

The rabbi's lips parted. His back straightened, and the sparkle returned to his eyes. "I... I don't know what to say."

"Say yes. And, just between you and me, you're the only candidate. You're the only non-founder with a valid identity card."

The rabbi laughed in earnest for the first time in days.

He shook Moshe's hand and continued down the corridor, a new spring in his step.

Moshe studied the door of frosted glass. Someone had taped a white page with the words "Dry Bones Society" over "Karlin & Son."

"There you are!" Galit peered around the door. She followed his line of sight. "They'd be proud of you," she said. "Very proud."

Moshe inflated his lungs. Mending broken lives probably trumped taxi dispatch on the cosmic scales of merit. "I think so too."

"Working late tonight?" There was no hint of reproach in her voice.

Moshe visualized his checklist. He had grand plans for the Dry Bones Society: fundraising, lobbying, expansion, medical drives, and education. He didn't know where to begin.

"Nope," he said. "Strictly office hours from now on. Besides, one late night won't scratch the surface. We're only getting started."

"All right then," she said, with a mischievous glint in her eye. She took his arm in hers and led him to the elevator. "Let's go home."

An Accidental Messiah

The Dry Bones Society

Book II

DAN SOFER

CHAPTER 1

The tour guide had just welcomed his first group of the day to the Mount Herzl National Cemetery when he saw the naked man. Among the bushes at the edge of the Jerusalem Forest, the pale streaker scratched his head and stroked the stately brown beard that fell to his chest.

Despite having been trained to handle this exact situation, the tour guide choked up, and his group of Japanese tourists, with their matching yellow hats and oversized cameras, chattered among themselves and eyed their catatonic guide with concern.

He had approached the rumors with a healthy dose of skepticism at first—after all, dead people didn't spontaneously rise from their graves—until early one morning a fellow guide had discovered a man, naked and alone, among the tombstones of the military cemetery. The former soldier had saved his brothers-in-arms by diving onto a grenade during the Second Lebanon War. A camera crew had arrived to immortalize the moment of his return, and the number of visitors to the park had spiked—resurrection tourists mostly—but after a few days life on Mount Herzl had returned to normal.

Over the following weeks, however, more casualties sprouted from their graves: shell-shocked tank drivers of the

Yom Kippur War; commando fighters of the Six Day War; and then the waves of gaunt Eastern Europeans mowed down during the War of Independence.

The phenomenon, bizarre and surreal by any standard, soon became routine, and they no longer bothered to notify the media when a long-deceased Jew turned up among the hedges. They did notice one trend: as time progressed, the arrivals returned from further back in the past, and the guides placed bets on which of them—if any of them at all—would welcome back to the land of the living the personage enshrined at the heart of the national park.

Today was this guide's lucky day.

"One moment," he told the Japanese tourists in English, as he hurried over to the bushes.

The naked man looked him over with suspicion. *By God, it's him!* the guide thought. He had seen a hundred photos of the man and studied his life in detail, but today the statesman had stepped out of the pages of history—and the grave—and into the present.

The man held his head high, despite his embarrassing state of undress. "*Wo bin ich?*"

"Pardon me?" For the first time since graduating from university, the guide wished that he had studied German as a third language instead of Arabic.

The man sighed and switched to English. "Where am I?"

The guide delivered the good news with glee. "In Jerusalem, sir, the capital of Israel—the Jewish State!"

A satisfied smile curled the man's lips and a fire burned in his dark eyes. "We *did* it!" He clenched a victorious fist in the air. Then he winced and massaged his temple. "*Mein kopf!*"

Remembering his training, the guide reached into his shoulder bag and tore open the DBS First Responder Kit. He helped the man into the thick spa gown with the words Dry Bones Society sewn onto the back and then handed him the two Acamol tablets and the small bottle of mineral water.

The man popped the pills and washed them down, then blinked as cameras flashed. The Japanese had caught up and were documenting the historic event.

"Friends," the guide said to his audience. "I present to you Mr. Theodore Herzl, the Visionary of the State!"

Herzl stepped out from the bushes, bowed his head, and posed with the guide for the cameras.

Then he gazed at the sculpted gardens and stone paths. "What is this place?"

"Mount Herzl, the national cemetery named after you. Your tomb is over there, in the center." The guide pointed. "I'll show you."

Herzl slipped on the pair of spa slippers, also courtesy of the DBS, and they walked along a path of rock slabs.

"When was the State established?"

"1948."

"So late?"

"The road to nationhood was long and winding, but I think you'll be proud of the result. The land has thrived, the desert bloomed. Jews have returned from all over the world. We have an Israeli government and army, technology and culture."

"And yet you do not speak German?"

"Hebrew is the official language, along with Arabic and English. English has become the language of science and culture."

"English? How strange."

"Times have changed. You died over a hundred years ago."

"A hundred years? Incredible!"

They arrived at the large central plaza of white Jerusalem stone and approached the prominent slab of black granite in the center of a circle of grass. The name Herzl was etched into the tombstone.

Herzl sucked in a deep breath. A summer breeze ruffled his hair as he stared at his own grave. Tearing up, he turned to the guide and shook his hand. "I thank you for fulfilling my wishes and bringing my remains to the Jewish State. But how did you revive me?"

Once again, the guide leaned on his training. The instructor from the Dry Bones Society had warned the guides not to overwhelm the new arrivals with information. "You have many questions," he said, using the instructor's words. "We will answer them in time as best we can."

"A hundred years," Herzl repeated. "My children must have passed on already. Their children too. Tell me—what role did they play in the founding of the State?" A hopeful smile made his lips tremble. "Was my son the first chancellor?"

The guide swallowed hard. He had hoped to avoid that topic.

"Tell me, please," Herzl continued. "Are they buried here as well?"

The guide grasped at the shred of positivity. "Yes, they are. Over there."

Herzl gripped the guide by the shoulders. "Show me!"

This was a very bad idea but how could he refuse the Father of the Jewish State?

He led the newly resurrected visionary along another stony path. He needed to call the Dry Bones Society to arrange a pickup but stopped himself. The instructor had warned against using modern technology such as mobile phones, which might disorientate the new arrival.

He stopped before a row of three plaques. "Here they are. Paulina, Trude, and Hans."

Herzl appraised the markers in solemn silence. "The dates," he said, startled. "Paulina and Hans died in the same year—and so young!"

The guide hesitated. "Paulina suffered from depression. She overdosed on heroin. Hans shot himself on the day of her funeral."

"Depression," Herzl muttered. "The scourge of our family. And little Trude? Died 1943. Did she, at least, live a happy life? And why does she not have a gravestone?"

He was right. Behind the plaque with Trude's details, and between the two large rectangular gravestones of her siblings, lay a gaping empty space.

The guide shook his head. He had already said too much.

"Tell me!" Veins throbbed on the forehead of the resurrected statesman.

"We don't have her remains. She died in the Holocaust."

"Holocaust? What Holocaust?"

"During World War Two."

"A world war—and two of them? Please continue. I must know."

There was no holding back now. "The Germans and their collaborators systematically murdered Jews throughout Europe."

"The Germans? If you had told me the French I would have believed you, but the Germans? How many Jews died?"

"A great many."

"Tell me, boy—a thousand, ten thousand?"

"Six million."

Herzl ran his fingers through his mane of hair. "Dear God. 1943. But you said that the State was established in 1948—only five years later. Five years too late! We didn't work fast enough."

He lurched backward and the guide steadied him. He called on two of the Japanese who had followed them to support the distraught man. He should never have shown him the Herzl family plot.

"Wait here, sir. I'm going to call for help and I'll get you something to eat."

He dashed off toward the snack store and called the Dry Bones Society on his way. A team of their volunteers was on the way.

Theodore Herzl himself! The guide's skin prickled all over. The recent resurrection had raised hopes for the dawn of a new utopian era, and who better to lead the nation into a brighter future than the spiritual father of the modern Jewish State? The Visionary of the State had returned with perfect timing.

When the guide returned to the Herzl family plot with a

handful of Mars bars and a covered paper cup of sugared tea, however, Herzl had vanished.

"Where is he?"

The Japanese chattered excitedly and pointed toward the forest. The guide shielded his eyes with his hand and scanned the thick press of trees. In the distance, between the tall trunks, a bearded man in a white gown sprinted and disappeared.

CHAPTER 2

"We should set a date for our wedding," Moshe Karlin's wife said as she drove her white Kia Sportage down Emek Refaim Street early Tuesday morning.

"Right," said Moshe Karlin, who sat in the passenger seat.

Outside the window, Egged buses hissed and growled through the heart of Jerusalem's German Colony. Cars honked their horns as commuters rushed to their jobs.

Ordinarily, a man was not required to marry his wife twice, but these were not ordinary times and, technically, their first marriage had terminated with his death.

"This time," Galit continued, "I think we should try a different venue."

Moshe agreed. Three months ago, Moshe had awoken in the Mount of Olives Cemetery to discover that his best friend, Avi, had invaded his home and taken over his family business. Make that *ex*–best friend. Moshe's struggle to win back his life had culminated in a dramatic attempt to stop Avi from marrying Galit at the Ramat Rachel Hotel in South Jerusalem, the very same venue where Moshe and Galit had first tied the knot. The time had come to paint new memories on a fresh canvas.

"What do you think of Mamilla?" Galit asked.

Moshe almost choked. A ceremony at the luxury Mamilla

Hotel across the road from the Old City would be a beautiful and memorable affair. The bill, on the other hand, would empty their bank account ten times over. Their savings had run so low that, if he didn't deposit a paycheck soon, Moshe, Galit, and little Talya would have to get used to life without electricity and flowing water.

"That would be wonderful," he said, when he could draw breath.

Despite serving as the CEO of a thriving organization, Moshe was penniless. As a pre-deceased man in bureaucratic limbo, he was still unable to draw a salary. He could not vote or drive a car either. But today, all of that would change.

On the street, store owners rolled up the security gates of cafés and boutiques, while pedestrians hurried about the errands of their daily lives. At 9 AM today, finally, Moshe would join their ranks, and not a moment too soon.

"I can speak with Rabbi Yosef," Moshe said. "I'm sure he'll be happy to officiate."

The neighborhood rabbi had taken Moshe off the street and into his home despite fierce opposition from both his wife—the rabbanit—and the ultra-Orthodox rabbinate. That good deed had cost the rabbi his teaching position at Daas Torah Primary, and so Moshe had hired him as Spiritual Counselor at the Dry Bones Society.

"Sure," Galit said. "I'd like that."

"Good," Moshe said, and crossed off one expense from his mental list. The kindhearted rabbi would probably conduct the wedding pro bono.

Galit maneuvered the car into downtown Jerusalem and along the quaint back roads of Nachlaot.

Moshe felt his pockets for his cue cards. In the mad rush of preparations ahead of today's event, he had not found time to rehearse his speech.

"Nervous?" Galit asked.

He found the cards. "A little. So much is riding on today. And we'll be on national television." Butterflies had roamed his stomach that morning and killed his appetite at breakfast.

AN ACCIDENTAL MESSIAH

"You'll be great. Like last time." She was referring to the Channel Ten documentary about the Dry Bones Society, the non-profit that Moshe had founded to assist the influx of newly resurrected Israelis.

This broadcast would be different, though. This time, he was making history.

As they descended the ramp to the parking bay beneath Clal Center on Jaffa Street, the butterflies launched from his stomach into his rib cage and his breath caught in his lungs. Seeing that Moshe's first life had ended in cardiac arrest, the sudden pain in his chest did not bode well. *Not again! Today, of all days?*

"You OK?" Galit said, her face tight with concern. She had just parked in a spot marked DBS when she noticed him cramp up.

Moshe lowered his hands from his solar plexus.

"Heartburn," he said. "That's all." He managed to produce a reassuring grin. "Couldn't be better."

His heart pounded like a battle drum, but the pain had subsided. There was no need to scare her. After today's event, he'd be eligible for medical aid and he'd see a cardiologist pronto.

Reassured, Galit turned off the ignition and winked at him. "Time to conquer the world."

CHAPTER 3

The hubbub of excited human activity echoed down the central pier of Clal Center on Jaffa Street, and the decaying shopping mall seemed to quiver with anticipation.

Moshe and Galit took the small, cranky lift to the third floor, and the murmurs grew louder as they made their way down the corridor. Moshe ran his fingers over the proud silver lettering on the frosted glass of the door: The Dry Bones Society. The sign had once read, "Karlin & Son."

"There you are!" Irina hurried over to them. The tall Russian with the short blond locks and sparkling fairy eyes had been Moshe's closest friend in the darkest hours of his early afterlife.

"What do you think?" She pointed to a table dressed in blue and white at the edge of the cubicles of the call center.

Behind the table, a man in a black suit and fedora stood on a plastic chair and taped a banner to the wall above a large Israeli flag. The large black letters read, "The Ministry of the Interior and The Dry Bones Society."

"Looking good," Moshe said. "Great job, guys. Morning, Rabbi Yosef."

The rabbi stepped off the chair and shook his hand. "And well done to you, Moshe," he said. "This is all thanks to you."

Moshe picked up the single printed page that lay on the

table beside two ballpoint pens, and reviewed the copy. The Minister of the Interior's secretary had mounted the revised text on official ministry stationery and forwarded the declaration to Moshe's email yesterday. With a few strokes of a pen, Minister Dov Malkior would change the lives of all resurrected Israelis forever.

Moshe returned the sheet to the table. "All set."

A tap on the shoulder made him turn. "Moshe!" Shmuel, retired reporter and fellow founder of the Society, shook his hand. He patted the remaining strands of gray hair on his head and looked unusually formal in his blue suit. "Can you believe the day has arrived?"

"Almost," Moshe said. Another middle-aged man stood beside Shmuel, a press card clipped to his shirt pocket. "Eran, thank you for joining us."

Shmuel's former colleague shook Moshe's hand. "Thank *you*, Mr. Karlin, for another exclusive."

Men in Channel Ten T-shirts adjusted large video cameras on tripods and set up microphones.

The flat-screen television on the wall read 8:45 AM, and indicated that two callers—resurrectees in need of help or donors eager to support their cause—waited in line for the operators.

Moshe nodded greetings at the clump of volunteers and Society members who hovered beside the cubicle dividers, and he slipped his speech from his trouser pocket. The cue cards trembled in his hands. *A historic day*, he read, *for our brothers and sisters across the nation*—

"Moshe, dear," said a grandmotherly voice. "Have some breakfast. You need your strength for the big day." Savta Sarah, Galit's grandmother and the Society's in-house caterer, peered up at him, her sad eyes filling the lenses of her thick glasses, as she shoved a plate of gefilte fish at him. The sharp scent from the purple swirl of chopped horseradish cleared his sinuses at two paces.

"Thanks, Savta, but I'll eat later."

Galit came to his rescue. "Savta," she said, "I wanted to

talk to you about catering our wedding," and she herded her grandmother toward the buffet tables. Early wedding preparations had their benefits after all.

Moshe returned to his cue cards. *To you, Minister Malkior and your dedicated staff, our thanks and heartfelt appreciation.* But ten seconds of uninterrupted speech rehearsal was too much to expect.

"Moshe!" Samira, the young, olive-skinned woman in the green *hijab*, was the third resurrected Israeli they had discovered and the first Arab. "Will we receive our identity cards at the ceremony?"

"Not yet. But within a few days Minister Malkior will set up special procedures to speed up the process."

Samira smiled and wandered off.

Moshe cleared his throat and continued his rehearsal. *For allowing us to start our lives anew with dignity and with hope—*

"Mazel tov, Moshe!" This time Rafi's rasping voice had interrupted Moshe's speech. At this rate, he'd have to ad lib at the podium, which would probably make for a far shorter speech. There was a bright side to everything.

The Yemenite taxi driver gave his hand a vigorous shake. "Your father would be so proud." Moshe's father had jump-started Rafi's career decades ago, and now his replenished fleet of transport vans shuttled the newly resurrected to the Dry Bones Society's Absorption Center every morning.

Moshe found a quiet corner and studied his cue cards. *To become equal participants in society.* He pulled a pen from his pocket and tagged on the words "once more."

"You'll be fine," said a voice. Irina had sidled up to him.

Moshe sighed. "I hope I'll do us justice." He was used to speaking to a roomful of employees but he had never addressed government ministers on television.

"You already have. Today is a big deal."

A sadness had crept into her smile, and he knew what she was thinking. Three months had passed since her resurrection and still she remembered nothing of her former life, not even her real name. Having no clear identity, she could not apply for an identity card at the Ministry of the Interior.

"Your turn will come soon enough," he said. "I'm sure the minister will work something out for you."

Her eyebrows rose and fell without conviction. "I hope so."

"Moshe," called Rabbi Yosef from a nearby cubicle. He held a desk phone to his ear and covered the mouthpiece with his hand. His trademark ecstatic grin split his face.

"Donors," the rabbi said, "from the United States. They flew in this morning especially to speak with you. They're on their way to Jerusalem now. When can you meet with them?"

Foreign donors—another first. Word of the Dry Bones Society was spreading across the globe. "In an hour or so. After the ceremony."

Rabbi Yosef nodded and spoke into the receiver. "Alo," he said in heavily accented English. "Dis morning. Yes. Yes!"

Moshe fled to his corner office and returned to his speech. His change of tactic worked. He rehearsed the full text twice without interruption, then pocketed the cards and walked over to the large office windows. The ceremonial table stood at the ready. The microphones and cameras waited in position. Only one very significant detail was missing.

He pulled out his mobile phone, property of the Dry Bones Society, and read the time. 9:07 AM. He had pawned his wristwatch—the Rolex that his grandfather had handed down—to escape the slave labor camp run by Boris, a Russian mobster. Now he got by with his phone.

He stepped out of the office, glanced at the assembled reporters, volunteers, and onlookers, and gave them reassuring smiles.

Shmuel walked over, an edginess in his gait. "Is he on his way?"

"I'm sure he's just stuck in traffic."

Shmuel frowned and paced the room.

Moshe's shirt collar itched against his neck. He opened the top button and loosened his tie. Minister Malkior had been friendly and cooperative in their meetings. He had shown genuine interest in the plight of their new and unlikely demographic. He wouldn't stand them up, would he?

At 9:11 AM, Moshe dialed the minister's personal mobile number. After ringing twice, the call cut to voicemail. He dialed the office number.

"Mr. Karlin," said Tzippi, the minister's helpful young receptionist, "I was just about to call you." Her voice, usually casual and friendly, had become formal and defensive in tone.

"We're all good to go here. Is everything all right?"

She drew an audible breath. "The minister regrets that he won't be able to join you."

The floor fell out of Moshe's stomach. "I'm sorry to hear that. Would he prefer this afternoon?"

Silence on the line. "I'm afraid not," Tzippi said. "He won't be able to participate. Not today. Not ever. I'm sorry."

She ended the call.

Moshe stood there for a few moments, then slipped his phone back into his pocket, his cheeks cold, his forehead damp. A room full of anxious faces watched him in silence.

"The minister won't be joining us today," he said. "Sorry for all the trouble."

The camera crew exchanged glances and began to dismantle their equipment.

Shmuel whispered in Eran's ear, then marched over. "What happened?"

Moshe kept his voice down. "He backed out."

"What the hell?"

"Where does that leave us?" Samira asked. Fear flickered in her eyes and in the eyes of the half-dozen Society members who now gathered around Moshe.

He had given them hope, he had promised them a future—but now the iron doors of government bureaucracy blocked their path and refused to budge. They didn't deserve this. At a minimum, they deserved an explanation.

"I don't know," he said, balling his hands into fists. "But I'm going to find out."

CHAPTER 4

Moshe stormed down the corridor of the Ministry of the Interior, the letter of intent in hand and a fire in his heart. Malkior would sign the agreement today, as he had promised, press conference or not. Too many lives depended on the wave of his pen.

Shmuel and Irina followed him in a V formation. Rafi had dropped them off at the government buildings on Safra Square. Over the last few weeks, they had gotten to know those corridors well and this time they were not going to leave empty-handed.

At the sight of the charging delegation, the minister's secretary placed a hand on her desk phone. One wrong move and she'd call security.

"Tzippi," Moshe said, his voice calm and amicable. Angry words would not help them here. He glanced at the large wooden door behind her. "We just need a few moments with the minister to understand why he changed his mind. I'm sure we can work things out."

Her cheeks turned pink, and her mouth tightened. This was difficult for her. She had always spoken kindly with them. "He can't see you today. He's in meetings."

"That's OK. We'll wait."

"You'll be waiting a long time."

"We don't mind. We're right over here."

They settled on the set of four joined chairs opposite. Bureaucrats strolled the corridor, holding documents and paper cups of coffee, and glanced them over.

After all he had experienced in his second life, Moshe should be used to the floor disappearing beneath his feet.

"It doesn't make sense," he said. "More registered citizens means more taxes. More grateful voters. Elections are a month away. It's a win-win deal."

"The whole thing smells rotten," Shmuel said.

Moshe had to agree.

"But he seemed so understanding," Irina said. "He seemed to really care about us."

"All politicians do," Shmuel said. "When it serves their agenda. As a reporter, I saw that a lot."

They cooled their heels for half an hour before the door handle turned. A dozen men in black suits, hats, and gray-streaked beards left the office, chuckling and nodding. The tallest wore a silky suit and tidy bowler hat. When his eyes met Moshe's, he smiled and touched the brim of his hat.

"Oh, no," Moshe said.

"You know him?" Shmuel said.

"Rabbi Emden, Rabbi Yosef's old mentor. He introduced us to the Great Council." They had appeared before the rabbinic aristocracy within the immense Belz Synagogue in the heart of Chassidic north Jerusalem. The frenzied chant of the horde of followers still rang in his ears. *Sitra Achra! Sitra Achra!*

"The ones who claimed we're the evil Other Side?"

Moshe nodded. He had a bad feeling about this. "Let's go."

They rushed forward and slipped through the door before Tzippi could protest.

Framed photos of the Prime Minister and the President hung on the walls of a richly decorated office, the office of a man who intended to stay there a very long time. Minister of the Interior Dov Malkior looked up from his large wooden desk.

"Moshe," he said, rising from his seat as though greeting a long-lost friend. He shook his hand, then frowned at circumstances beyond his control. "I am truly, deeply sorry for having to cancel."

"Not as sorry as us," Shmuel said.

Moshe motioned for Shmuel to stand down. "Dov," he said. They had moved to first names early on. "We'd like to understand what your concerns are. I'm sure we can work something out."

Malkior returned to his seat behind the large wooden desk. "These are difficult times, Moshe. Elections are close. The coalition is in disarray. Let's speak again in a few months and we'll see what we can do."

Moshe smelled an evasive maneuver. Cab operators had used the same tactic when he approached them to sign with Karlin & Son while other dispatch agencies were courting them. "It's the rabbis, isn't it?"

Malkior blew air through his lips and threw up his hands. "What can I say? You've made some powerful enemies."

"Let me guess—if you drop the agreement with the Dry Bones Society then they'll join the new government?"

Malkior continued to smile but said nothing.

Moshe leaned his knuckles on the desk. "People are suffering, Dov. Hundreds, if not thousands, of people. Us included. We can't rent an apartment or support our families or even see a doctor. Some of us are being roped into slave labor, right now, as we were. You can help them." He placed the document on the desk. "All you have to do is sign."

Malkior leaned back in his puffy leather chair as if to distance himself from the agreement. "My hands are tied. Let's speak later, after the elections have blown over." He chuckled. "If I'm still in this office. This isn't personal, Moshe. It's just politics."

The deal was done and Malkior would not budge. Moshe turned to leave. "It is for us."

CHAPTER 5

Boris Poddobni was used to fear and panic. Usually, he elicited those responses in others, but as he waited outside a private home in the quiet suburbia of southwest Jerusalem, his pulse galloped. Depending on how his meeting went, today he might breathe his last.

In the valley below the row of houses, rose the square of the Malcha Mall and the towers of the Malcha Technology Park. Birds sang in the trees. The house betrayed few clues to the dangers that lay within. The front door of carved white wood had a silver knocker shaped like a grasping gloved hand. A security camera eyed him from a corner.

He patted his bushy gray hair and moustache and knocked twice.

Boris avoided meetings with the boss. The man was a genius, yes, and Boris had learned much from him, but he could never predict his next move. The boss had little tolerance for failure, and Boris's tidings would not make him happy.

The door opened.

"*Pree-vee-et*," Boris said. Hello. From here on, he would speak Russian. The bald man in the doorway was built like a cement truck and wore black jeans and a black T-shirt. Boris regretted having to leave his own muscleman, Igor, in the car, but not even Igor could save him in here.

The bald man looked Boris over, his face expressionless, a nasty, jagged scar down his left cheek, and indicated for him to enter with a jerk of his head.

Marble covered the entrance hall, white and shiny. The life-size statue of a young woman greeted him. A blindfold covered her eyes, but she had cocked back her head to steal a peek, and her cheeky breasts pushed through the folds of her flowing toga. In one hand, she held a square tablet, a raised lance in the other, a gesture of defiance. Or warning.

The door closed behind him.

Boris turned to the doorman. "Is The Jew here?" Boris said.

"Downstairs. And I wouldn't call him that anymore."

"No?" The nickname had commanded respect in the Russian underworld. When The Jew had moved to Israel, he had quickly swallowed up the local gangs to rule the largest network of organized crime in the country.

"He goes by Mandrake now."

"Mandrake. Like the magician? A fitting name."

The henchman glared at him.

Boris nodded. He passed the statue woman and her raised lance, glimpsed a well-furnished living room with large windows facing the mall, the technology park, and Teddy Stadium, and descended the rounded staircase to the basement.

His shoes squeaked on marble tiles as he sank deeper into the dark belly of the house, then plastic sheeting crinkled underfoot as he stepped onto the landing. A spotlight fell on an overturned wooden table at the far end of the basement. Black tape outlined the crude shape of a human form on the round red surface, like chalk marks at a crime scene.

"Boris, my friend," a sonorous voice said.

As his eyes adjusted, a bald man emerged from the gloom. He stood in the middle of the den, his back to the stairs. Muscles bulged on his shoulders beneath his black T-shirt.

The friendly tone did not comfort Boris. Cheer and sympathy could turn to violence in an instant.

The man reached into a small briefcase on a stool and withdrew a large knife. Grasping the tapered blade between two fingers, he raised the knife in the air. Then, with a movement as fast as a striking viper, he flung the knife, burying the blade between the eyes of the outline with a metallic twang.

"Business is booming, from what I hear," Mandrake said, without turning.

By "business" he meant the labor camp that Boris managed in the Talpiot industrial zone. In return for manual labor, he offered illegal aliens, ex-cons, and other unemployables board and lodging in his warehouse facility. The workers soon found themselves buried in debt for expenses hidden in the fine print of their contract.

The promise of deportation helped keep them in line, along with the threat of grievous bodily harm. Revenues had skyrocketed three months ago thanks to the sudden crop of resurrected Israelis that sprung up each morning at cemeteries around the country, providing a glut of easy prey.

Boris cleared his throat. "It was, sir, until recently. That's why I've come to see you."

Mandrake lifted another blade from the box. "Continue."

No turning back now.

Boris spoke and Mandrake listened, the blade hovering beside his ear.

"So," Mandrake said, when Boris had finished, "you collect these dead people as they wake up in the cemetery each morning?"

"Yes." Boris swallowed hard. He had not believed the tale either at first. Would Mandrake? "They are real. They've appeared on television. We picked them up by the busload until the Dry Bones Society came along."

"The Dry Bones Society?"

"A bunch of do-gooders led by Moshe Karlin, a resurrected Israeli himself. They get to the new arrivals before we can and take them in." He did not mention that Moshe Karlin had once worked for him and that Boris had let him buy his way out. Unflattering details like those would not aid Boris's chances of survival.

Mandrake held the next throwing knife in the air for a few seconds. Then his arm became a blur and the blade slammed into the wooden target, piercing the outline's heart.

The plastic sheeting crinkled beneath Boris's shifting feet and a sudden thought made him freeze. The knives. The plastic sheeting on the floor. The red paint of the target. *He's already seen the numbers!* Mandrake had been expecting him, and only one scenario required covering the floors in plastic sheeting.

Boris braced for the worst. There was no running from a man like Mandrake. Not for long. He only hoped that Mandrake had run out of throwing knives, and would opt for a quicker and cleaner death by gunshot.

Mandrake reached down and lifted a third blade from the box.

Derr'mo! Crap!

Boris closed his eyes.

"Do you believe in magic, Boris?"

Boris opened one eye. The knife still hovered at Mandrake's ear. What was the right answer? What kind of magic did his boss have in mind? Boris closed his eye again. His answer wouldn't matter. He knew the drill. Any moment, Mandrake would spin around and skewer him for his failure.

Three long seconds passed, however, and he was still breathing.

Bam!

Boris clenched up but felt no pain. He opened his eyes. The third knife quivered hilt-deep in the groin of the outline.

"I'd like to learn this magic trick," his boss said. "The leader of this Society, this Moshe...?"

"Moshe Karlin, sir."

"We should get to know him better. Find out how he operates. From the inside. And then"—he raised his hand and curled the fingers into a fist—"we will crush him."

Boris exhaled a pent-up breath. *We.* He might survive the

meeting after all.

"Sir," he said, hoping that he was not pushing his luck. "Karlin knows me and my men. I'll need fresh faces to get close."

Mandrake turned to face him, and Boris swallowed the knot of fear in his throat. Stupid, stupid, stupid! He should never have opened his mouth.

Mandrake considered him with a pair of sympathetic eyes above the largest hooked nose Boris had ever seen.

"Don't worry, my friend," he said. "I have just the man for the job."

CHAPTER 6

Eli lay in bed Tuesday morning, listening to the sounds of his new life. A girl showered in his en suite bathroom. The mattress felt warm where she had slept and her sweet scent clung to the sheets. The murmur of traffic far below seeped through the windows.

He had everything a young man could desire: an amazing girlfriend, a penthouse, his own business, and more money than he could spend.

Then why don't I have the energy to get out of bed?

Was he still adjusting? Sharing his apartment took some getting used to, as did his new identity, and the idea that he was, one day, going to die.

How did people do it? Wake up each day. Brush their teeth. Get dressed. Go to work. It seemed like a lot of effort when your life was going to end in a few years. Mortality sucked.

As Elijah the Prophet, he had had—literally—all the time in the world. The fate of humanity had depended on him. Eli Katz the man of flesh and blood, on the other hand, had numbered days and questionable purpose. But he did have one thing that even Elijah the Prophet would envy. He had Noga Shemer. Without her, he would have stepped off the window ledge a long time ago.

Noga padded into the room in her underwear and a T-shirt. She pulled on her jeans and fastened her sandals, and looked him over with a playful smile that almost hid her frustration.

"Going out today?" she asked.

He shook his head.

"Let's go for a walk when I get back. Get some fresh air."

Since his return from the hospital, Eli had spent most days on the living room couch, staring at the Jerusalem skyline.

"Change out of your pajamas, at least? Tonight we're celebrating, remember? This is my big day."

He reached for her and gave her a mischievous smile. "We can celebrate right here."

She stepped away quickly to avoid his grasp and giggled. "We celebrate here often enough. I put years of work into this. It deserves. A night. Out."

"Years of work," he repeated.

"Yes," she said, and leaned in for a parting kiss. "Out. Tonight. Understand?"

"I understand," he said. "You want to get me out of my pajamas."

She waggled a finger at him and left the room. Moments later, he heard the front door close, and she was gone.

Noga. Venus. His goddess of love. His guiding star. Today was her big day. For her, he'd make the extra effort.

He counted to ten and rolled out of bed. After a shower and a shave, he padded barefoot down the parquet of the corridor in a robe. He had done his part; he had gotten out of his pajamas. In his designer, open-plan kitchen, he poured a cup of coffee and moved to the couch of cream leather. The furry carpet tickled the soles of his feet.

He sipped his morning espresso, sunlight warming his legs. The city sprawled in the French windows. The offices of downtown Jerusalem. The fancy hotels. The ancient walls of the Old City.

He put the mug down beside the laptop on the glass coffee table and pressed a key. Lines of computer code displayed on the screen. OpenGen, the genealogy website he had founded, ticked along and paid the bills. Recording the chains of ancestry had been Elijah the Prophet's obsession and his way of tracking lineages ahead of the End of Days. He had cranked out new features and honed his marketing techniques for hours on end, and even set up a telephone support team in Bangladesh.

Eli closed the lid of the computer and slumped back on the cushioned upholstery. The next app version could wait.

He reached for the remote and turned on the television in the corner. He had not had time for television in his deluded former life, and he had a lot of catching up to do.

A bearded face filled the screen. "We are witnessing the fulfillment of prophecies in the Bible," the smiling rabbi said. "The Resurrection is one stage of the Final Redemption."

"How does the Resurrection process work?" asked an earnest, gray-haired reporter.

"It is a great miracle," the rabbi explained. "Our ancient writings talk of the Dew of Resurrection, which recreates the physical body from the Luz, a small, indestructible bone in the spine."

Eli fired the remote and the television went blank.

Prophecies. The Resurrection. His chest heaved. The remote trembled in his hand. He knew that bearded face. The man had hovered over him as Eli had lain bleeding on the ground. The rabbi from the Mount of Olives. The End of Days. He had to tell him. To complete his mission. The Thin Voice had commanded him!

He shot to his feet. "No!" he said aloud. "I'm done with that." He clutched his head in his hands and shivered. His breath came in short, fitful bursts. If he relapsed into delusion, he'd lose Noga, he'd lose the only thing of value in his life.

Calm down. He sat on the couch and sucked in air.

That isn't real. It's only in your mind. He raised the remote and pressed the button.

The screen blinked to life. A podgy man in an expensive

suit pushed through a crowd of reporters like a penguin. A penguin with bodyguards. He had a smug smile on his face. "He calls his new party Upward," the narrator said. "The breakaway has sent ripples through the political world, causing defections and havoc, with only a month until general elections, elections that Mr. Gurion initiated when he toppled the government by withdrawing his former party from the coalition."

Eli turned off the television and breathed a lungful of relief. Treacherous politicians and election fever. Reality. There was no Resurrection. No End of Days.

He had turned his back on his false memories, but now the madness had returned to tap him on the shoulder. Was that why he never left the apartment—not depression but the fear that, once again, he would lose his mind?

A new resolve launched him to his feet. He marched down the corridor and opened the one door he had not dared to touch since his discharge from the hospital. He turned on the light.

Items of various shapes and sizes lined the walls of the sanctum and the sunken den in the center, like the walls of a museum: a shaggy fur cloak, a leather shield, a sword in a leather scabbard, a rounded clay urn, an oriental rug, a clunky pistol with a rounded handle. The mementos from his imagined past were also doorways to insanity.

He rolled up the sleeves of his gown. To seal the tomb of his delusions he needed to purge every trace of his old life.

And now he knew how.

CHAPTER 7

Yosef reached out a hesitant hand, hoping to make a good impression. "Welcome," he said in his shaky English. "Welcome."

The tall, silver-haired stranger in the tailored suit gave his hand a mighty double-handed squeeze and shake. "Rabbi Lev, I presume." He spoke with an oily southern drawl.

"Yes." Yosef kept his words to a minimum to avoid accidentally insulting his guest. Moshe had yet to return from the Ministry of the Interior and so Yosef would have to entertain the honored guest in his stead.

"The name is Adams but you can call me Henry." Mr. Adams entered the Dry Bones Society with the momentum of a charging buffalo and the regal posture of an American Indian chief. A lanky suited associate followed in his wake, carrying a leather briefcase.

Adams looked around the call center, his broad, white smile and suntanned skin radiating health and confidence. He seemed to like what he saw.

"And you can, eh, call me Yosef. How was your, eh, flight?"

"As long as it needed to be, Rabbi. So this is your call center. And the volunteers?"

"In the field."

"The field?"

"At the cemeteries. For collection." Yosef had looked up English words on the Internet before the potential donor's arrival.

"Ah. Extraction teams across the country, welcoming home the returned souls."

"Yes!" Yosef could not have said it better, even in Hebrew.

"And Mr. Karlin?"

Yosef swallowed. "He had to go out," he said. "An emergency. I am, eh, very sorry."

The American frowned only for a moment. "No problem. Is there somewhere we can talk?"

Yosef ushered him to Moshe's corner office.

"We're big admirers of the work you're doing," Mr. Adams said, when they were seated. "And we want to help you however we can." He nodded at his associate, who opened the briefcase and handed Yosef a check.

Yosef inhaled sharply when he read the amount. "Ten thousand dollars?" The sum, worth about forty thousand shekels, was more money than Yosef had ever handled.

"A modest contribution to get us started."

To get us started! "Thank you, sir!"

"You'll need more of that to continue your good work."

"Yes. More supplies for the new arrivals. And, eh, more teams in more cemeteries. Yes."

"Good, good." Their benefactor seemed less interested in the operational details. "The money is yours to spend as you see fit. All we ask in return is an update now and then to see how things are progressing. I understand that the number of your Society members has been rising steadily."

"Yes. More and more each day."

"Good." Adams cleared his throat. "Now that the Resurrection is in full force, you wouldn't happen to have heard from a charismatic young man, would you?"

Yosef racked his memory. "A resurrected man?"

"Hmm. Yes, but not recently. Mid-thirties with long hair,

probably. Speaks Aramaic."

Yosef shrugged. None of the returnees spoke Aramaic.

"I see." Adams seemed disappointed. "Is it true," he continued, "that, as time goes by, the resurrected have been returning from farther back in the past?"

Surprise delayed the words in Yosef's throat. "Yes," he said. "I didn't think anyone outside knows this."

"We like to keep informed," Adams said. "How far back are we now?"

"Well, we get a lot of soldiers now. British soldiers."

Adams leaned in. "From the British mandate era?"

"Yes. Some die in the fighting. Some die from, how you say, malaria. And then some from even before! That why we start lessons."

"Lessons—you mean training courses?"

"Yes. Training. They know nothing. Nothing! No cars. No electricity. No cell phone. Need to learn everything."

Adams raised his eyebrows and exchanged a meaningful glance with his associate. "And how far back do you think this will go?"

Yosef shrugged. "God knows."

The two visitors exchanged another glance and smiled.

"We're very serious about our continued support. In fact, our organization has created a wholly owned subsidiary just to manage your funds. We'll be in touch soon about our next contribution, so please go ahead and send us the Society's bank details." Adams got up to go. His voice dropped to a whisper. "And keep an eye out for that young charismatic friend of ours. It appears that he'll be arriving when his generation returns, so I'd appreciate it if you'd call me when we reach the Roman Period."

"The *Roman Period?*" Yosef repeated. Had he heard correctly? The benefactor's words had sped by so fast and some of them had raised red flags. "Wait—what organization?"

Adams handed him a business card. The credentials read:
Rev. Henry Adams, Managing Director
The Flesh and Blood Fund

A division of the New Evangelical Church of America

Yosef almost swallowed his tongue. The words of the sages of the Great Council echoed in his ears. *Sitra Achra!* The Other Side.

Yosef had ignored their warnings, siding with his conscience, and now he was joining forces with a fundamentalist Christian organization! Had the sages been right all along? Were they falling into the grip of the unholy Other Side?

He reread the card, hoping that he had misunderstood.

"Flesh and Blood?" he said.

Adams smiled with one side of his mouth. "You're the Dry Bones, right?"

"Yes?"

"Well, we've got you covered." He chuckled, patted Yosef on the shoulder, and charged out of the room, his associate in tow.

Yosef stared at the check and the card in his hands. Drops of sweat slipped down his brow. The check would go a long way to helping people in need, but was he allowed to accept their money? For all Yosef's good intentions, his new partners might have very different motives.

He could stand the uncertainty no longer. He ran after his guests, catching up with them at the front door. "Mr. Adams," he said. "Why are you helping us?"

Adams turned and flashed his confident smile. "We've been waiting for this day a long time, Yosef," he said. "Our Daddy's coming home."

CHAPTER 8

Noga stepped onto the train on Jaffa Road and swiped her *Chofshi Chodshi* monthly pass over the sensor. For once, everything in her life was going well.

Weeks ago, she had completed the data collection phase of her thesis, the longest and least stimulating part of her research project, and submitted the batch of DNA samples for processing at a private lab. Her doctoral degree, forever in the distant future, had finally inched within grasp. Today she would return to the Shaare Zedek Medical Center to collect the results. All that remained was to analyze the raw data and make them pretty for her paper.

She found a vacant window seat and rested her laptop bag beside her. On Jaffa Street pedestrians dragged their shopping carts toward the Machaneh Yehuda market as the train pulled off.

Shaare Zedek. She smiled to herself. The hospital had provided the other new development in her life. At Shaare Zedek, she had met Eli Katz.

Within a week, Eli had swept her off her feet and she had helped him overcome his delusions. A fair exchange, in her opinion. By the time of his release from the hospital two months ago, they had become inseparable, and when the lease on her apartment had expired two weeks ago, Noga had moved in with him.

The tram veered left onto Herzl Boulevard toward the Mount Herzl military cemetery and the Yad Vashem Holocaust Remembrance Center.

She had been single and miserable for so long that she found her recent good fortune hard to believe. Eli was the love of her life, he was gorgeous, and he adored her. He also happened to be very rich. She had found the fairy-tale Happily Ever After to a bumpy early life. She only hoped that at twelve o'clock her chariot wouldn't turn into a pumpkin and her Prince Charming into a frog.

Stop worrying, girl, and enjoy your life. Those irrational fears belonged to her old life. Why shouldn't she be happy?

After two and a half months together, it was time to introduce him to her parents. Her adoptive parents. Why had she waited so long? At first, she had kept a wary eye on Eli, expecting him at any moment to explode into another impassioned rant about the End of Days or claims of immortality. Eli had done nothing of the sort. Instead, he had sunk into a sluggish routine of inactivity, and now she wasn't sure which boyfriend she preferred—the manic delusional or the depressed couch potato.

Had he grown bored with her? Noga remembered Eli's words that morning and she smiled. He still wanted her around, that much was sure. He was still adjusting to his new life. Maybe a warm extended family was the support and encouragement he needed.

The train stopped and she got off.

Inside the hospital, she passed by the Steimatzky bookstore and the flower shop. Glimpsing a glass door out the corner of her eye, she changed direction and pushed through the exit.

The secret green courtyard had not changed much. She sat on the bench, the spot where one fateful afternoon Eli had presented her with a jewelry box. She had thought that he was going to propose. Instead, he had given her the entrance code to his apartment and made his confession. He was

Elijah the Prophet, ancient and immortal, and Noga had a role to play in the End of Days. She had stormed out on him, of course, and they had never come so close to losing each other. A cold shiver crept down her spine.

That was then, this was now. Today, she wouldn't mind receiving another jewelry box from Eli Katz, and this time, a ring.

She snapped out of her memories and continued to the elevator. Her results waited for her at the Medical Genetics Institute on the fifth floor, but as the slow doors of the large metal elevator closed, she pressed the number four. She couldn't resist one more stroll down memory lane.

The linoleum corridors of the neurology ward had not changed. She waved at Nadir, who rose to greet her at the nurses' desk. Noga complimented her on her new head covering, and Nadir smiled and said, "I'll call Eliana. She won't want to miss you."

"Noga, dear," a man's voice said.

Noga stiffened. "Dr. Stern."

The department head, an older man graying at the temples and in a white medical cloak, drew near. "Lovely to see you again." His icy blue eyes scanned her. "And how is our mutual friend?"

Dr. Stern had once threatened to ship Eli off to the Kfar Shaul Mental Health Center, and his ongoing interest in his former patient triggered her defenses. She relaxed. The doctor had only been trying to protect her—and rightly so—and he had warmed to Eli in the end. "He's fine," she said. "Totally fine."

He gave her a quizzical glance, so she explained. "I've come to collect my results."

"Oh, of course. Congratulations. If you'd like an extra pair of old eyeballs to review the data, I'd be happy to oblige."

She thanked him. Then her lungs deflated as Eliana, the busty head nurse, wrapped her in a mighty hug. Noga answered the barrage of eager questions and demands. Yes, she was well. So was Eli. And, yes, she'd visit more often.

Her curiosity satisfied, Noga took the stairs to the next floor and pushed through the doors of the Medical Genetics Institute.

"Hi, Katya," she said to the Russian with the shock of blond hair and—even Noga could tell—too much mascara at the front desk. "My results are in."

"Identity card?"

Noga handed over her blue identity booklet. Katya typed a few keys and pursed her lips at the monitor. For the purposes of data security and to satisfy hospital procedures, the data was transmitted on a secure medical network from the private lab to the institute.

Katya said, "USB."

Noga opened her laptop bag and handed over her flash drive.

A sudden worry jolted her. She had worked on her doctorate for so long that she hadn't thought about the day after. She'd get a job at a pharmaceutical company, she supposed, or dream up another research project and return to the scrabble for funding. A university post didn't appeal to her much, although Hannah, her doctoral supervisor, would probably love for her to join the faculty. One challenge at a time.

Katya handed back the USB.

"Thanks!"

Noga opened her laptop on the chair in the waiting lounge and plugged in the disk.

The lab data consisted of a simple text file of comma-separated values. Each row represented a test ID and flags indicating the presence or absence of the genetic markers she had specified. In her case, the flags represented the Cohen gene sequences—known as the Cohen Modal Haplotype, a pattern of six Y-STR markers, or short tandem repeats, on the male-only Y chromosome.

She loaded the file into EPSS, the statistical analysis program she had used to simulate her expected results.

A wheel icon circled on the screen as the processor cross-referenced the test results with the demographic data she had collected and ran the merged data through the statistical engine.

The moment of truth. The culmination of two years of her life.

A few agonizing seconds later, the findings displayed on the screen in graphs and bar charts.

In her pilot experiments, the lines and bars had stood out in tidy, colorful rows, clearly supporting her hypothesis that the Cohen gene appears only in Jews of priestly descent, proving that all priestly Jews descended from a single male ancestor. For fun, she'd call him Aaron in her paper, after the biblical Aaron, son of Amram and brother of Moses.

The actual charts from her final experiments, however, made her heart skip a beat.

That's strange.

The graphs on the screen were almost identical to her pilot experiments' results. Her main thesis still held water but there was noise, a large clump of outliers that had the Cohen genetic markers, and ninety-eight percent of them belonged to one group.

That doesn't make sense.

She performed a t-test to confirm whether the outlier group had statistical significance. It did. She could not write off the noise as diagnostic errors. The rogue results were not outliers at all.

She turned the data over in her mind. Her cheeks felt cool and the roots of her hair prickled, as though she was about to faint. The data could mean only one thing.

No, she thought. That's impossible!

CHAPTER 9

"What do we do now?" Samira asked.

Good question. Moshe had perched on the edge of his desk and shared the bad news with the Dry Bones Society management. He had gone head-to-head with rivals before—both in business and in his private life—but the government was a different story. A collision with that unmoving continent would shatter their fledgling organization to smithereens. Moshe would have to change course.

"The government's doors are closed to us for now," he said. "We'll have to be patient." This was his fault. He had raised their hopes and set them up for disappointment.

"Patient?" Shmuel said. "What if those doors never open? We could all starve by then."

"No one's going to starve," Irina said.

"That's right," Moshe said. "We have money for the cafeteria and dormitories so long as donations keep flowing."

"What about health care? Private doctors don't come cheap. And there's only so long we can shack up in shared housing."

Or support our non-resurrected families, Moshe added to himself.

"You're right," he said aloud. "We need new ideas. Any suggestions?"

Samira put up her hand first. "We could ask doctors to volunteer."

"And," Irina said, "we can ask pharma companies to donate medical supplies."

"Good. Good. That will help."

Shmuel said, "I suppose we could put together a magazine, and sell advertising. It'll be tax deductible and good PR." He shook his head, obviously not thrilled about chasing after advertisers.

"Excellent. Maybe an online magazine? Or a YouTube channel. We could interview the new arrivals and share their stories. We've had some interest in our cause overseas."

Rabbi Yosef had filled him in on his meeting with their new American ally before he slipped out to cash the check. Ten thousand dollars would not last forever and he did not want to pin their survival on a single donor.

"OK, friends, let's get to work."

The team dispersed to their new tasks.

Moshe moved behind the desk and slumped over, his head in his hands.

Begging for donations. Selling advertising. Not the sexiest ways to get by, but they'd have to work with what they had.

In the call center, telephones rang as lost souls called in.

Shmuel had not been entirely wrong. Each day their expenses piled up but the donations were not keeping pace. As the dead returned from the more distant past, fewer of them had the means to contribute, and living Israelis felt less connected to them. The Society would need new revenue streams to survive the long haul.

And no matter how many donations came pouring in, Moshe was still not able to draw a salary and keep his family afloat, never mind pay for a fancy wedding. He had placed all his hopes on Minister Malkior and paid the price.

A throat cleared and he looked up. Savta Sarah stood in the doorway, her sad eyes filling her glasses. "I saved you a plate of food," she said. "Seeing that you were too busy to eat."

Moshe's mood improved the moment the scent of stuffed cabbage and meatballs reached his nostrils. "Thank you, Savta."

She placed the plate on his desk along with a set of disposable cutlery, sat down, and watched him eat.

"We moved into an abandoned apartment building after the war," she said, slipping, as she did, into the past.

She meant the War of Independence. Moshe had heard the tale before. He and Irina had visited the two-room apartment on Bostanai Street in Katamon, where Savta and her husband, of blessed memory, both penniless Holocaust survivors at the time of the war, had lived ever since.

"After a while the government notified us that we could register our apartment with the Land Registry. One of the neighbors offered to go to the ministry and fill in the forms on our behalf." She emitted a bitter laugh. "Two weeks later, Edith from the first floor came to me in tears. 'He's demanding rent!' she cried. 'Calm down,' I said. 'He can't do that— it's your apartment.' 'Not anymore,' she said. 'He registered the entire building in his own name!' She was right. The crook had registered all eighteen apartments in his own name." Savta Sarah shook her head at the man's chutzpah.

"The clerk at the ministry was no help at all. 'Sorry,' she said. 'There's nothing we can do.' *Nothing we can do?* Ha! I found out who her boss was. I went home. I got all dressed up, put on my makeup. I waited for her lunch break and then I walked right into her manager's office and sat down."

She crossed her legs, placed her hands on her knees, and spoke with her nose high in the air, reliving the moment. "'Mr. Kramer,' I said. 'You are a fine gentleman. Surely you can help our neighbors, all of them poor and honest citizens.' He said no. He said that the crook had done nothing illegal, and there was nothing more he could do. '*Mister* Kramer,' I said. 'You *can* and you *will*. I'm not leaving your office until you have corrected this injustice. And what's more, I intend to have a word with Mrs. Kramer and I'm sure she will have an opinion about what you can and cannot do.' I didn't know

Mrs. Kramer—but I would have found her. In the end, I didn't need to. Within a half hour, Mr. Kramer had set the paperwork aright. And that crook, well," she grinned, "he fled Jerusalem and never came back."

She chuckled at her own tenacity, then looked Moshe squarely in the eyes.

"If there's one thing I've learned, Moshe dear, it's that there is always something you can do. You just need the balls to do it."

With that, she got to her feet and strolled out of the office.

Moshe chewed his stuffed cabbage in silence. As always, Savta had a good point. But how did one take on the government?

He got to his feet, abandoning his meal, walked out of his office, and leaned on the divider wall of Shmuel's cubicle.

"How many members do we have?"

Shmuel looked up from his computer screen. "Several hundred. Maybe a thousand."

"That will have to do."

A sly smile curled Shmuel's mouth. "Why? What are you planning?"

"We're going to war."

"With the government? How?"

"By hitting them where it hurts most."

CHAPTER 10

Ahmed had expected rivers of honey and wine, a private palace, and a seat of honor at the Heavenly banquet. After all, he had bought a ticket to Paradise. But when he had awoken in the Mount of Olives Cemetery, a gray-haired Russian called Boris had shipped him off to Hell. The angels had made a huge mistake but today Ahmed would correct that error.

He piled gray bricks onto a wheelbarrow and wiped his brow. The damned souls around him got about their tasks. Dark skinned and light. Round eyed and squinted. He was not like them. He didn't belong here. But every day he climbed the scaffolding with them, delivering bricks and mortar. He didn't speak much. He didn't step out of line. He had seen what happened to those who did.

A tall Nigerian had argued with the foreman on Ahmed's first day in the afterlife. When the muscular African had thrown down his hard hat and strutted off the construction site, a large demon in a gray suit had followed him. The Rottweiler, as the others called him behind his back, had arms as thick as trees and a neck to match. Two minutes later, the Rottweiler had returned, dragging the Nigerian by the scruff of his neck, and dumped him on the ground in a pile of pain. The other workers had strapped a stick to his broken arm and returned to their tasks.

Ahmed did not belong in Hell. Hasan had promised him Paradise. Paradise and forgiveness. Ahmed's mother had made him share his room with his cousin from Ramallah, who had visited for a few days. *He'll be a good influence, make a man of you.* She was always saying that, ever since his father had moved out to live with his new wife five years ago.

But Hasan had discovered the copies of Penthouse inside Ahmed's mattress. A disgrace, Hasan had said, to defile himself with infidel women. A mark of shame on his family name. His father would hate him if he ever found out. There was only one way to cleanse his blemished family honor, only one way to purify his Jew-loving soul.

Ahmed had boarded bus number eighteen, his backpack stuffed with rusty screws and ball bearings dipped in rat poison, and he had pressed the detonator button. The explosion had shredded his sinful flesh and transformed him into a *shaheed*. A palace awaited him, as well as a harem of virgin brides and a seat of honor at the Heavenly feast.

Every morning, a minibus shuttled him from the bleak warehouse to the construction site. The streets through the window resembled the Jerusalem of his earthly life, the way the world of dreams mixed together memories of his waking hours, only this nightmare had lasted two months. Every night, he lay on the camping cot in his tarpaulin cubicle beneath the high tin roof of the warehouse and he prayed. He prayed that tomorrow the angels would correct this terrible mistake. Every morning, he awoke to find his prayers unanswered.

He could bear the injustice no longer. He wheeled the barrow of bricks onto the wooden plank over a clump of steps, then made for the one they called Damas, a coal-skinned demon taskmaster. Ahmed laid the wheelbarrow at his feet, brushed dirt and dust from his calloused hands, and cleared his throat.

"What?" the taskmaster said, aiming his constant scowl at Ahmed. The yellow hard hat made his skin look even darker.

"Sir," he said, in Hebrew. "There's been a mistake."

"Spit it out!"

Two Romanian workers glanced their way and Ahmed tried to ignore them. "I'm not supposed to be here," he said, speaking as softly as possible. "I was supposed to go to Paradise."

Damas glared at him for two seconds "Paradise?" he said. "Who told you that?"

Ahmed felt the press of eyeballs around him. *Let them stare. I am a* shaheed. *I am above them all.* "My cousin Hasan promised me that if I—"

"Let me guess," Damas interrupted, "that if you killed some Jews you'd get seventy virgins?" He pulled out a worn notepad from his shirt pocket and turned the pages.

Ahmed's heart did a double-flip. *Yes!* Damas, for all his scaly ways, had to answer to the angels. He'd set things right. Ahmed should have spoken up long ago.

"Let me see," Damas said, scanning the notepad. "What is your name—Ahmed?"

"Yes, I am Ahmed!"

Damas frowned. "There is no Ahmed here," he said. "But I have a Stupid. Is your name Stupid?"

The taskmaster glared at him while Ahmed tried to make sense of the question. Then the Ethiopian burst out laughing. Others laughed around him too. Hot blood rose in Ahmed's cheeks. The souls of migrants and vagabonds, lowly scum and infidels, they all laughed at the *shaheed* in their midst!

Damas recovered from his fit of laughter and clapped him on the back. "Let me tell you about promises," he said, with sudden solemnity. "When I was a little boy in Ethiopia, the wise men promised us a Jerusalem of Gold. I left the village with some older boys and we started our holy journey on foot. We walked through war and poverty, thieves and slavers. Twelve of us set out; only two survived to see the glorious State of Israel. And what did we find here? A hero's welcome? A Jerusalem piled high with gold? A life of honor and luxury?" He spat on the ground. "A Jerusalem of trash and cat piss, of street sweepers and janitors, of people who treated me like crap and told me how they had saved me from the jungle."

He scowled at the gathering crowd. "What are you all looking at? Back to work!" The men scuttled away.

"Did you see that?" he told Ahmed. "I found my promised land. I earned it the hard way." He held up his hand. Two of his fingers ended in swollen stumps. "Now I tell them what to do and nobody messes with me."

He gripped Ahmed by the shoulders. "Take it from me, Stupid. Don't believe their promises. There is no Paradise, only Hell."

CHAPTER 11

Alex Altman spotted his target at the Delek gas station on the corner of Pat and Golomb.

The thirty-something in brown chinos, a button-down shirt, and a blue crocheted *kippah* leaned against the side of the blue Ford Focus. *Fresh meat.* The car, eight years old but in good shape, matched the photo from the ad that the owner had posted on Yad2, a website for secondhand vehicles.

Let the show begin.

"David?" Alex said.

David looked up and turned a paler shade of white. People reacted that way to the ponytail, the earring, and the large biceps covered in Russian tattoos, the badges of honor Alex had acquired in multiple Soviet penitentiaries. They told law-abiding citizens not to mess with him. Alex always chose a public meeting place for his magic shows to give the target a false sense of security.

David swallowed hard. "Shalom," he said. Hello. He had a British accent, and had probably bought the car brand new using the tax break for new immigrants.

Alex circled the car. He ran his fingers over the fresh rubber feelers on the tires and the line of chipped paint on the back bumper. New treads and minor scratches. Nothing serious.

"Accidents?" he asked.

"None."

"Keys."

"Inside."

Alex climbed into the driver's seat.

"Code?"

David told him and Alex punched the numbers into the immobilizer keypad. The car started quietly. Eighty thousand kilometers on the odometer. The tachometer gauge hovered at a thousand revolutions per minute and didn't waver. No engine issues either.

Alex closed the door. "Get in."

David hurried around the car to the passenger seat and strapped on the belt.

It's showtime!

Alex stepped on the accelerator, launching the car onto Golomb toward the City Center and pressing David back in his seat. The gears changed smoothly, with no audible grinding.

Magic is five percent distraction and ninety-five percent preparation, and Alex had done his homework.

He pressed his foot to the floor, flying past the speed limit. "How much?"

David clung to the edge of his seat as the car sped down the thoroughfare. "Eighteen thousand," he said.

David had done his homework too. Eighteen thousand was the Levi Yitzchak list price for the car. A fair price, but a poor first offer. David was not much of a bargainer.

Alex weaved between cars. *Make that ten percent distraction.*

"I'll give you nine," he said.

David didn't laugh. He didn't tell Alex to stop the car and take a hike. In fact, he probably felt grateful for the offer, because, like all good magicians, Alex had pre-selected his target from the crowd.

Yesterday, within minutes of posting the ad online, David had received five phone calls. Each potential buyer had offered five thousand shekels "and not an agora more."

Compared to those offers, Alex sounded generous. Alex knew this, because all five callers–including the older man and the woman with the sexy voice—were his stage assistants.

"According to the pricelist—" David began but Alex cut him short with a laugh.

"Forget that. Nobody pays the list price."

He gunned up Gaza Road. By this point, most sellers just wanted to flee the car before Alex crashed the vehicle into a pole, but David said nothing. Brave guy.

A part of Alex pitied him. This David hadn't done him any harm. But as far as magic tricks went, David would get off lightly. Over the years, Alex had performed many feats of magic on behalf of the Organization, and some still haunted his dreams.

Alex swung a right onto Keren Hayesod. Time to close the deal, and David needed a little extra push. Alex knew what made people tick. These Anglo immigrants always felt that they were being screwed over by the locals. Nine times out of ten they were right, but things would go a lot smoother if Alex let him feel that he'd won the bargaining game.

"Nine thousand and two hundred shekels," Alex said. "Final offer."

David exhaled a deep breath. "*B'seder.*" OK.

Alex pulled up outside the post office on Emek Refaim, and extracted a wad of two-hundred-shekel notes from his pocket. David's eyes widened as Alex counted out the bills, but he didn't ask any questions. He could guess what sort of person walks around with that amount of cash.

"Registration," Alex said.

David opened the glove compartment and fished out the certificate.

Alex pulled a piece of paper from his back pocket. "Sign here." The document appointed Alex as power of attorney regarding the sale of the car. "And write down the code too. Good." He dumped the cash in David's hand. "I'll take care of the transfer of ownership. Don't let me keep you."

The Brit took the hint and almost strangled himself on the seatbelt strap in his rush to get out of the car.

Alex kept the motor running and turned up the air conditioning. He did not get out of the car or enter the post office. He glanced at his wrist watch. There was no need to rush. Yesterday he had posted an ad of his own on Yad2 and arranged to meet an eager buyer at this very spot in another ten minutes. Within the space of a half hour, Alex's street magic would have earned him ten thousand shekels, without ever having the car registered in his name. *Now you see it, now you don't.*

His phone rang.

He knew the caller's number by heart, although he wasn't careless enough to add the number to his list of contacts. That number meant trouble.

He answered but did not say hello.

"I have a job for you," said the deep voice on the phone.

A jar of acid shattered in Alex's gut. The last job Mandrake had assigned him had almost broken him.

"I already have a job, remember?"

"I know, my friend. But this job requires... your special brand of magic."

Refusal was not an option.

Alex said, "I'm on my way."

CHAPTER 12

At 6 AM on Wednesday, Moshe broke the law. From the sidewalk of Kaplan Street, the Knesset building peeked above the bushes like a broad, flat fortress, and Moshe had prepared for a long siege.

Dry Bones Society volunteers offloaded equipment from two minivans: placards, fliers, empty packing crates, folding tables, and a large supply of bottled water. Irina and Samira climbed ladders and tied a large banner to the perimeter fence, while Shmuel oversaw the construction of a makeshift platform. The banner read, "LET US LIVE!" and volunteers handed out black shirts emblazoned with the words, "I AM ALIVE TOO."

Moshe had asked Galit, Rabbi Yosef, and Rafi—anyone with a valid identity card and something to lose—to stay away. Savta Sarah had put up a fight. "An army marches on its stomach," she had said. Moshe had accepted her food but refused to put her in harm's way or to involve any of them in the illegal demonstration.

The police had given him no choice. He had filled in the Urgent Protest Application form on the Israel Police website, only to receive a call an hour later notifying him that his request had been denied because his identity number belonged to a dead man.

By the time the first vehicles arrived, the picket line had formed along the sidewalk. Their signs read, "EQUAL RIGHTS FOR ALL" and "OUR BLOOD IS ON YOUR HANDS." Shmuel led the chant on a megaphone. *Ha'am. Doresh. Zedek chevrati!* The People. Demand. Social justice!

Soon, the picket line extended around the street corner.

"How many do we have so far?" Moshe asked Irina. She was handing out fliers.

"I don't know," she said, "but we just ran out of shirts."

"How many did we print?"

"Five hundred."

Moshe whistled. The turnout was better than he had expected. By the time the television vans arrived, the line had become a throng of demonstrators that choked the sidewalk. Then the luxury cars with tinted windows finally trickled in— members of parliament getting a late start to the day. The masses of angry, disenfranchised men and women overflowed into the street and surged around the vehicles. The drivers, with dark glasses and earpieces, honked their horns and crawled toward the safety of the Knesset compound.

Shmuel handed Moshe the megaphone. "It's time," he said.

Moshe nodded and climbed the wobbly platform of packing crates, those butterflies flapping madly in his belly. A prerecorded address was one thing; speaking at an illegal demonstration before rolling cameras was quite another.

He glanced at his audience and the air fled from his lungs. "Dear God," he gasped. The roads and sidewalks were a sea of people as far as the eye could see. Thousands had answered his call—were there even that many resurrected Israelis? Their chants settled to an expectant murmur as they waited to hear his voice.

"Welcome, friends." His voice sounded deeper than usual on the megaphone and his words echoed off the crowded hills. "Thank you for joining us here today." Cheers spread across the swells of humanity. He waited for silence. "We have gathered here today not to disturb the peace, but because we have no other choice. Many of us here today have been blessed with a second chance at life. We want to be a part of society again. To work. To build. To live with dignity."

Another cheer rose in the mass of supporters. "LIVE WITH DIGNITY," they chanted. Moshe's pulse quickened but the inner butterflies fell into formation. The thrill of the crowd had an intoxicating effect that focused his attention. He was no longer nervous. When he raised his hand for silence, the crowd obeyed. It was time to get to the point.

"But the current government," he continued, "has rejected us." The people booed. "They tie our hands with red tape. Well, my friends, they can't hold us back any longer." A cheer. "We demand—"

The wail of a police siren interrupted his speech. A large black van with the police emblem—a Star of David within a laurel wreath—on the hood, waded through the crowd toward the platform and then blared its foghorn. A uniformed officer wearing a large shiny police hat stood through an opening in the roof. "Mr. Karlin," the man roared into a megaphone. "This gathering is illegal. Disperse at once."

Angry voices erupted in the crowd. A school of dark uniforms swam through the demonstrators toward him. He had a few seconds before they reached the platform.

"We will disperse," Moshe said. "Once the Minister of the Interior fulfills his promise and recognizes us as legal citizens with all the rights and—"

The siren wailed again. "Mr. Karlin, you are not above the law. Disperse your people at once."

A thousand trusting faces looked to him. They had answered his call. They had kept his terms of non-violence and zero damage to property. The least he could do was stand up for them.

"You're right," Moshe said into the megaphone. "We're not above the law. We're *below* the law. You deny us our right to demonstrate and exclude us from society, and so you have no right to silence us or—"

He did not finish the sentence. Iron hands gripped his legs. His feet slipped from beneath him and the megaphone flew from his hands. He landed hard on the asphalt. Four uniforms pinned him to the ground as he struggled.

"Let me go!"

A sweaty officer snarled over him. "Resisting arrest, are you?"

Then he slammed his baton down on Moshe's face.

CHAPTER 13

Boris waited in the parked van outside the Karlin residence on Shimshon Street and considered his future. The boss had called in an outsider to infiltrate the Dry Bones Society, a task that Boris should have handled himself. A wise man would prove his worth while he could still draw breath.

The sound of munching from the passenger seat grated on his nerves.

"Didn't your mother teach you to chew with your mouth closed?"

Igor stuffed a handful of puffed maize into his mouth from a jumbo bag of Bamba. The other men called him the Rottweiler, and now his dog breath stank of peanuts.

He grunted. "Never knew her."

That figured. The collapse of the Soviet Union had unleashed hordes of motherless ex-army thugs on the world, many of whom had found a new home in the Organization.

A white Kia Sportage pulled up outside the Karlin home and a dishy woman with dark hair got out. She unlocked the door of the house and stepped inside without even looking their way. Mrs. Karlin had returned home, and Moshe Karlin now had something to lose. Family and friends were weaknesses and Boris had taken care to accumulate neither.

Not even Igor. In the five years since the Organization

had assigned Igor to him, this was the first time Boris had inquired about his childhood. The thug had muscle for brains but caused no trouble if you kept him well supplied with Bamba to munch and bones to break. The less you knew, the less you cared; the less you cared, the longer you lived in this business, and Boris planned to live to a ripe old age.

He caught glimpses of the woman as she moved through the house. In the kitchen, she took a mug from a shelf and poured a cup of coffee.

Igor crumpled the empty bag of Bamba, tossed it out the window, and slapped peanut flakes from his hands. "Want me to get her?"

Boris shook his head. "First we watch and learn. Then, when the time is right—"

A movement on the sidewalk cut his words short. A hedge between the houses shook. Then a head appeared above the hedge and peered over the leaves. The head had a messy mop of oily hair and a face dark with stubble. The man dashed around the hedge in a rumpled shirt and dirt-stained jeans, and scuttled toward the Karlin home, his back bent in an exaggerated and failed attempt at stealth. The tramp pressed his back to the wall and stole a quick peek through the kitchen window.

"Well, well, well," Boris said. "It seems that Mrs. Karlin has a secret admirer."

CHAPTER 14

Avi Segal brushed off his jeans and sucked in a deep breath. *You can do this.* He hadn't spoken to Galit since she had stood him up under the *chuppah* two months ago.

The love of his life had left him for a zombie. That had hurt, and in a fit of rage he had sworn that he would never have anything to do with the Karlins again. But Galit had never left his thoughts. Not for a moment.

He shifted from one foot to the other on the threshold of the Karlin home. The house had been his home until Moshe had returned from the grave and stolen Galit from him a second time. This was all Moshe's fault, but now Avi would take back what was his.

He pressed the buzzer. High heels clacked in the entrance hall and the door opened.

Her welcoming smile faded when she laid eyes on him. "You have a lot of nerve, showing up here."

Avi needed to talk fast. He didn't ask for permission to enter. Inside she might throw dishes at him and her aim had improved.

"I love you, Galit. I need you. Don't tell me you don't feel the same."

"You have got to be kidding me."

"Moshe did this to us. Can't you see? He's vile. Unnatural.

He should be six feet under. How can you live under the same roof as him?"

She gave a derisive laugh. "No, Avi. You did this. With your lies." Her eyes glanced at his clothing, and derision turned into revulsion. "What's happened to you?"

Yes! Sympathy. Make her feel sorry for you.

"My parents threw me out," he said. He had slept on their living room couch through the summer, but they had turned him out when he had failed to find a job.

"Get off your lazy bum," his mother had said. "We put half our savings into that wedding, and even that went down the drain." He had run out of credit there.

"Last night," Avi told Galit, "I slept on a bench in Gan Sacher."

Pity flickered in her eyes for a moment before they hardened. "Good," she said. "You deserve worse. Is that why you're here—to leech off us again?"

The word "us" pierced his gut like a dagger, but the truth was he had nowhere left to go.

She made to close the door.

"Wait. Listen, I made mistakes, I know. Please, give me another chance."

"You're crazy. You should never have come here. I don't want to see you again. Ever."

As the door swung shut, Avi blurted, "I'll tell him!"

The door cracked open and Galit shot him a frightened look. "Tell him what?" she said but she knew only too well.

He had not meant to threaten her but she had given him no choice.

"He still doesn't remember how he died," Avi said. "I'll tell him."

Galit took a step back. "You wouldn't dare."

Avi stuck out his chest. The balance of power had shifted in his favor. "I don't want to but I will if that's what it takes. What will he think of you then?"

He had her now. A few words to Moshe, and he'd never want to see her again. Avi would do it to get her back, to save her from herself.

She lifted her nose in the air. "Then you're a liar *and* an idiot," she said, tears distorting her voice, "if you think that
threats will make me take you back."

She slammed the door.

"You're making a big mistake, Galit!" he yelled. "Galit,
please!"

Crap! He had blown it. What was he thinking? He pulled at
his hair. Now she feared him *and* hated his guts. He had lost
her for good.

This was all Moshe's fault. If not for Moshe, she wouldn't
feel this way.

Avi slunk away from the house and crossed the street. He
needed to find something to eat and a place to sleep tonight.
More than that, he needed a plan to turn his life around.

He didn't dwell on it for long. As he walked past a parked
brown van, a sliding door opened, two large hands pulled him
inside, and the door slid shut.

CHAPTER 15

Boris turned on the ceiling light of the van. Igor had cleared the interior of seats, covered the floor in plastic sheeting, and tinted the windows black, adapting the vehicle for the smuggling of goods and, presently, the interrogation of captives.

From the low bench at the back, Boris sized up the tramp. The man kicked and flailed in Igor's cement lock. Igor grunted and wrinkled his nose. Boris smelled it too. Their visitor hadn't showered in days. *Let's cut to the chase.*

"What do you want with Moshe Karlin?" he asked.

"None of your business."

Boris glanced at Igor, who straightened his arms, pressing the man's neck forward and wrenching his shoulder blades back, until the man cried out.

"I'll decide what's my business or not. Is Karlin a friend of yours?"

"No," the tramp said. "I hate his filthy guts."

"Then why are you at his house?"

"Galit," he said. "His wife. She was mine. Until Moshe came back from the dead."

Galit. Mrs. Karlin now had a name and Boris had stumbled upon a love triangle. How touching.

The tramp hung limp in the strongman's grip. "He used to be my best friend," he continued, suddenly eager to talk. "But he took everything from me."

Boris knew an opportunity when he saw one. "Tell me all you know about the Karlins," he said.

"Why should I?"

The tramp had a short memory, but Boris decided to humor him. "Do you want to destroy Moshe Karlin?"

The tramp looked up at him and his face contracted with loathing. "More than anything."

"Then," Boris said, "it seems we have something in common."

CHAPTER 16

"Hello," Moshe called through the steel bars of the holding cell. Down the corridor and out of sight, police boots clicked over the grimy square floor tiles.

An hour ago, he had woken up on the coarse blanket of a low metal cot. The only other furnishing, a metal shelf, hung from a chain on the wall. His calls for attention had received no response.

With the swing of a baton, he had lost his hard-won liberty. His possessions too. The officers had emptied his pockets of his keys, his phone, and his pocket pack of tissues. He had never felt so helpless. Even Boris's forced labor camp had provided at least the illusion of freedom. In this bleak detention cell, a man could rot.

Late afternoon light seeped through the small barred window high on the wall of the corridor. Only a few hours had passed since his brutal arrest outside the Knesset compound. Unless he had lain there unconscious for a whole day. Or days? Did Galit know of his arrest? Had she tried to reach him? She must be worried sick. He had to call her, but his jailers had not answered his cries, never mind offered him a phone call.

Footfalls echoed down the corridor and grew louder. A policewoman came into view. Finally!

"Officer," Moshe said. "Excuse me."

She waddled along and passed his cell without even glancing his way.

"Please, ma'am. I need to call my wife."

Her back disappeared down the corridor.

How long were they going to hold him? Was he going to meet with an attorney? What was the punishment for arranging an illegal public gathering? Surely he had the right to a fair trial. Or did the deceased have no civil rights? Without rights, law enforcement was just one more violent gang out to get him.

He sat down on the hard cot and tried to be patient. He massaged the tender swelling where the baton had connected with his skull. His stomach growled. They'd have to feed him eventually. They couldn't just let him starve, could they?

The demonstration had drawn the attention of the authorities, all right, just not the kind of attention he had intended. He had not expected the road to victory to be short and level, but now he thought of little Talya and her dark curls. He had read her Winnie the Pooh before bed last night. Who would read her a bedtime story tonight? Was Galit wondering why he hadn't come home? He had only just won his way back into their lives. Was he willing to lose them again?

Regulation boots clicked on the tiles again, and this time the policewoman halted outside his cell. Moshe looked up. Dinner time already? She was not holding a tray of food.

He stood up and decided to say nothing. *Stay calm. Be polite.* The change of tactic seemed to work, for the policewoman jingled a chain of keys in her hand.

"Somebody likes you," she said.

She unlocked the gate of the cell and led him down the corridor. A heavy door of thick bars clicked open as they drew near. Did he have a visitor? Would they tell him to change into a prison uniform, then lead him to a long row of booths, where Galit would stare at him through reinforced glass while he spoke to her using a telephone receiver? Moshe had seen that in a movie.

There was no orange uniform or meeting hall at the end of the long corridor, only a counter and another officer, who handed him a manila envelope that contained his keys, phone, and tissues. They were releasing him. His shoulders relaxed and he inhaled the sweet, clear scent of approaching freedom.

Galit was waiting for him in a reception hall, clutching her handbag. She ran to him, and her embrace had never felt so good.

"I came here as soon as I heard," she said. "They wouldn't tell me anything."

Moshe glanced about the room and recognized the foyer of the Talpiot police station. He had accompanied Irina there in a failed attempt to figure out her identity. The same two receptionists with dark ponytails sat behind the reception desk, but they didn't seem to notice him. Moshe didn't mind—he had enjoyed enough police attention for one day.

"Let's get out of here."

Galit had parked her Kia Sportage on the street and she drove him home.

"How much was bail?"

"Nothing," she said.

That sounded suspicious. "Aren't they going to charge me with anything?"

She shrugged. "They didn't say anything. I didn't even know you were being released."

Gears changed softly within the vehicle as other gears turned in Moshe's mind. Had his lack of a valid identity card aided in his release? Had his continued incarceration required too much paperwork? *Somebody likes you*, the policewoman had said. What did it matter? He was free.

"The others," he said. "Were they arrested too?"

"Only you, as far as I know. I saw it on TV. I saw them jump on you."

They had made the news. Excellent.

A tear trickled down her cheek. "I couldn't reach you on your phone."

"It's over now," he said. "We live in a liberal democracy.

They can't just lock people up indefinitely." Behind bars he had felt less certain of that.

"I thought I had lost you again."

"You won't. I won't let that happen."

"Promise me."

His arrest had distressed her harder than he had expected. He had gotten off lightly this time. Next time, he might not be so lucky. He'd have to make sure there would not be a next time. His career of civil disobedience would have to end.

"I promise," he said.

Back home, Moshe hugged Talya and paid the babysitter. At least his little girl knew nothing of his short incarceration. He turned on the TV and switched channels. The news broadcasts didn't mention the demonstration.

"I don't get it," he told Shmuel on the phone. "We should have gotten more coverage."

Shmuel seemed frustrated too. "I asked Eran. The editors didn't think we're newsworthy. A load of crap, if you ask me. Larger powers are at work here and they're burying our story."

"Or," Moshe added, "maybe they're right and people just don't care about us."

"Ten thousand people cared this morning."

"Ten thousand?"

"That's Eran's estimate. They can't all have been Society members. And donations at the office have tripled."

"We'll need more than money to change the system."

"What other option do we have—declare an independent state?"

The conversation stuck with Moshe during dinner. After a mass demonstration, all they could show for their efforts were a few hours of jail time and a spike in contributions. Moshe was not about to start a civil war. Without new ideas, Moshe and his fellow resurrected would remain in social limbo for the rest of their second lives.

"Moshe?" Galit called his name for the second time. He had spaced out at the dinner table. Talya sent him concerned glances and, ever since their reunion at the station, Galit had eyed him as though he was in danger of collapse.

"Sorry," he said. He forced a smile for Talya's sake. *You've worried them enough.* "Just thinking about work."

"The Dry Bones?" Talya said, and giggled.

He patted her curls. "And getting drier every day."

Moshe had set up a non-profit and the cash was flowing, but he couldn't draw a salary or apply for a marriage certificate. He couldn't lead a normal life.

It's not personal, the minister had said. *It's politics.*

The buzzer sounded.

"Don't answer that!" Galit said, her eyes wide.

"It's OK, Galit. I'm sure they won't arrest me twice in one day."

Moshe wiped his mouth on a napkin and went to the door. Unless, he added to himself, Shmuel was right and larger forces were at work. Was that how the government wore down opponents, by interrupting their dinner and dragging them back to the cells?

The man in the peephole wore, not a police uniform, but a dark suit, with dark glasses and an earpiece. Moshe's skin tingled. Had Minister Malkior sent undercover agents this time? Secret Service? Moshe's little peaceful demonstration had opened a Pandora's box of enemies.

Moshe swallowed hard, stood tall, and turned the handle.

"Moshe Karlin?" said Dark Glasses.

"Yes."

Dark Glasses walked right in, followed by two of his clones. They spread out in the hallway and scanned the interior of the home.

The leader spoke into his sleeve. "Clear."

Then a third man in an expensive suit rolled into the room like a well-preened, middle-aged penguin. A penguin with a greasy comb-over. He needed no introduction. His smug grin, familiar to Moshe from the Channel Two news and the front pages of Israel Today, belonged to the most notorious career politician in Israel.

Isaac Gurion gave Moshe's hand a meaty double-handed squeeze. "Moshe Karlin," he said. "We meet at last."

CHAPTER 17

Moshe and Isaac Gurion sat on his living room couch like old friends, while the Secret Service guards kept watch and Galit led Talya upstairs to bed.

"I sympathize with your struggle," Isaac Gurion said, his face a picture of great torment. "The difficulties you and your kind have experienced are as many as they are unbearable. This business with the Minister of the Interior is unacceptable. You deserve to live and work with honor as equal citizens."

Moshe wanted to rub his eyes and pinch his leg. This was exactly the kind of attention he had hoped for. But the savvy politician obviously had an agenda of his own.

"What do you have in mind?"

"You need friends in the right places. Friends with power. The power, for instance," and he shot Moshe a mischievous grin, "to release a friend from wrongful imprisonment."

So Gurion was behind Moshe's mysterious release, and now Moshe owed him. Every favor would require payback.

"Friends like you?"

"Exactly."

"And what do you want in return?"

Gurion seemed both surprised and insulted by the question. "Your friendship, of course." He sighed and raised his hands to the heavens, a humble man set upon by insurmountable difficulties. "Elections are in a month and we'll need all the friends we can find to ensure that our new party, Upward, can finally fix our country's problems. Judging by your event this morning, you have a lot of friends. Fifteen thousand, by the police's estimate."

Fifteen thousand! Shmuel's count had been far off.

"And," Gurion continued, "according to what I hear, you make new friends every day. How many new asylum seekers arrive each week?"

"Asylum seekers?" Had Gurion confused the Dry Bones Society with another social cause?

Gurion's eyes sparkled and he swiped his hand in the air as though reading words off an invisible campaign banner. "*Refugees from Death*. We'll need some way to refer to your Society members. So tell me, what is your growth rate?"

Moshe swallowed hard. Rabbi Yosef was closer than he to the numbers on the ground, but he would be wise not to understate the size of their unique demographic. "More each day," he said. "I don't have the exact figures, but our growth is exponential."

"*Exponential?*" Gurion licked his lips. "Well, good friends should stand together. We'll right the wrongs of society and forge a better world. Together we'll be unstoppable."

"We'll settle for identity cards," Moshe said. "We don't have any grand plans to change the world. We're not politicians."

"And you won't have to be. You won't have to sit through boring Knesset meetings either if you don't want to. We'll each stick to what we do best. You carry on with your good work and I'll sort out the red tape. What a great partnership. As I said, we'll be unstoppable."

"Unstoppable," Moshe repeated and laughed. After spending the day behind bars, that sounded too good to be true.

Gurion mistook his silence for hesitation. "Think of it, Moshe. Think of all the good you could do."

"Right now I can't even open a bank account."

"So we'll fix that. Our first order of business will be to secure full and automatic citizenship for all asylum seekers."

Moshe felt as though he had just won the lottery and wanted to jump on the couch like a lunatic. *Don't appear too eager.* "I'll need to consult with my colleagues."

"Of course, please do. But I'll need an answer by tomorrow evening," Gurion said, getting up. "Elections are around the corner."

CHAPTER 18

Ahmed returned to the Devil's warehouse that evening, his mind bubbling over with doubt. Groups of sweaty workers swarmed beneath the fluorescents of the warehouse, rushing to eat and shower before lights out.

Don't believe their promises, Damas had said. *There is no Paradise, only Hell.*

The demon taskmaster's words would not let go. Had Hasan lied to him? Had he known that Ahmed's mission would lead to eternal damnation, not unending bliss? No. That couldn't be true. Hasan had assisted many others on the path to *istishhad.* And why would he knowingly send his cousin to a world of suffering?

He pushed through the flap of his tarpaulin cubicle, retrieved his tin mug from beneath the cot, and joined the long line for dinner.

The demon had lied. Ahmed deserved this fate. He had not believed with a whole heart. Even as he pressed the detonator button, he had not truly expected to wake up in Paradise. He had wanted to save his family from shame and for his father to think kindly of him. Paradise existed but it belonged to martyrs of pure mind and clean hands.

Yet Hasan had known that his cousin was no saint. He had promised Ahmed that the mission would purge him of his sins.

The bald cook ladled thick soup into Ahmed's mug. The sludge smelled of lentils and too much pepper. Ahmed blew into the mug to cool the soup on the way back to his tent, then halted. Beside an open cubicle, a man knelt on a towel, his feet bare, his bearded face and stained turban pressed to the ground.

Do my eyes deceive me?

Ahmed drew near and waited for the righteous man to finish his prayers.

"Sir," Ahmed said. "How has a righteous man come to be here?"

The man turned tired eyes to his questioner. "What do you mean, my son?"

Ahmed drew closer and whispered, "In this Hell. I thought I was the only believer among these damned souls."

A bemused smile crept over the man's lips. "This is not the Purgatory of *Barzakh*," he said, and he stroked his beard. "Although our lot is not much better." The man's Arabic had a foreign edge, but he seemed to know what he was talking about.

"Then where are we?"

"Talpiot, Jerusalem."

"Jerusalem? We're not dead?"

The smile fled and patience leaked from the man's voice. "No, we are not dead. Not yet." He rolled up his towel and tucked it under his arm. "The lights go out soon," he muttered and trudged off. "I have no time for fools."

Ahmed froze to the spot. Sweaty laborers streamed around him. The streets had seemed familiar because they were. He had died, that much was clear. He had awoken in neither Heaven nor Hell, but in the Jerusalem of his first life.

"Lights out in ten minutes," Damas roared from the railing at the far end of the warehouse.

Ahmed snapped out of his trance and raced for his tent. He gulped down his soup and ran for the shower line.

He had just crawled beneath the rough blanket of his cot

bed when the large fluorescents clicked out. His heart thumped like a drum. He was not in Hell; he was home.

Outside the flaps of his cubicle, the footfalls died down, replaced by the creak of bedsprings and then a chorus of snores. Ahmed pulled back his blanket and got out of bed, fully dressed. He padded through the gloom of the warehouse. The corrugated door of the building slid sideways on its track, the squeaking of rusty wheels piercing the silence of the black vault like a siren. He looked over his shoulder, expecting the dark taskmaster to emerge from the shadows. He listened for the heavy steps of the Rottweiler. Seeing and hearing nothing, he stepped outside.

The stars burned overhead in the boundless canopy of heaven. A plastic bag floated in the moonlight on a gentle summer breeze. Distant cars hummed along hidden streets. Ahmed was alive and his future lay out there.

He slid the door shut behind him and slipped into the night.

CHAPTER 19

"I have a confession to make," said the young man in the black T-shirt. He had introduced himself as Ben to the circle of new members at the Absorption Center of the Dry Bones Society on Thursday morning.

Yosef stifled a yawn. He wanted to listen with empathy. Each new member of the Society had a life story in need of sharing and a soul in need of healing, but the events of the last few days had kept him awake at night. He too felt the need for confession.

Ben continued. "I'm not dead. I mean, I haven't died yet. Not physically, anyway."

He told of a childhood of delinquency and drugs, of running away from home and life on the streets.

"When I heard about your program—about starting anew each day—I thought I'd give it a try."

Yosef nodded. The confusion of his own early years was reflected in Ben's story. Over the last few days, that confusion had returned in full force.

Yosef had partnered with Rev. Adams and cashed his generous check while, at the Ministry of the Interior, Moshe had struggled against Rabbi Emden, Yosef's former mentor and guiding light. The next day, Moshe had spent the morning in jail. Yosef could ignore the cognitive dissonance no longer.

Was he still on the right side—the side of justice, of God?

The meeting concluded with the singing of "*HaTikva*"—the national anthem—and Rabbi Nachman's "Narrow Bridge," and the new arrivals dispersed to the dining hall for breakfast.

Yosef collected the song sheets and leaned against the doorjamb, staring at the empty circle of plastic chairs.

Sitrah Achrah. The Great Council's verdict rang louder in his ears each day. Had he succumbed to charms of the unholy Other Side?

A hand touched his shoulder and he jumped. "Sorry, Rabbi," Moshe said. "I didn't mean to startle you. Can you join us?"

"Of course."

The Society's informal cabinet waited in Moshe's corner office: Moshe, Shmuel, Rafi, and Irina. Savta Sarah was busy ladling porridge and frying eggs in the dining hall.

Moshe closed the door and leaned against his desk. "Isaac Gurion came to our house last night."

He told them of the politician's offer.

"That's just what we wanted," Irina said.

"More than we wanted," Moshe said. "If they do well in the elections, which seems very likely, we'll get seats in Knesset."

Shmuel folded his arms over his chest. "How many seats?"

"I don't know."

"Did he mention any ministerial portfolios?"

"No, but he seemed open to negotiation. I suppose we could push for the Ministry of Interior."

"Ha!" Irina said. "Malkior will regret double-crossing us."

"This goes beyond identity cards," Moshe said. "We could make a real difference and not just for ourselves—for the whole country."

They exchanged ecstatic glances, in disbelief at their sudden good fortune. The intoxicating scent of new possibilities wafted in the air. Perhaps Yosef had been right to throw in his lot with the Dry Bones Society after all.

"Rabbi Yosef," Moshe said. "When I first came back, you said that the Resurrection was one of many prophecies about a future world of peace and justice."

All eyes in the room turned to Yosef and the blood drained from his cheeks. "The Messianic Era," he said. "When the Messiah King, son of David, will arrive."

Shmuel guffawed. "Messiah King," he said. "The days of hereditary kings are long gone."

"You're right," Moshe said. He turned back to Yosef. "But putting the monarchy aside, what else does tradition say about that time?"

Yosef racked his memory. The midrash had made some pretty extravagant claims about the Future To Come.

"There will come a time of plenty and wonder," he said. "The knowledge of God will cover the earth as the water covers the sea. God will rebuild Jerusalem and pave her streets with diamonds and rubies. He will bring an end to death, and the righteous will feast together beneath a great canopy made from the skin of the Leviathan."

"The Leviathan?" Irina said.

Yosef swallowed. "A giant sea creature, like the fish that swallowed Jonah."

A roomful of eyes glazed over in the awkward silence.

Moshe cleared his throat. "Rabbi Yosef, are there any other opinions among the rabbis—something a bit more, ah, mundane?" Moshe had become familiar with the nature of the rabbinic thought. Few principles were free of vigorous debate.

"There's Maimonides," Yosef said. "According to him, the Messianic Era will involve neither miracles nor wonders, and only one thing will change: the nations of the world will no longer subjugate the Jews, who will be free to serve God and study His Law without distraction."

"Sounds like the Israel Defense Forces to me," said Irina. "And freedom of religion."

"Yes," Yosef said. "But Maimonides agrees that the Messiah will rebuild the Temple."

The excitement in the room cooled considerably.

"The Temple?" Irina asked.

He swallowed hard. "A great synagogue on the Temple Mount. But with, um, sacrifices."

She wrinkled her nose. "*Animal* sacrifices?"

"Um, yes," Yosef said. The idea of slaughtering bulls and sheep and sprinkling their blood on an altar made him queasy as well. Solomon's Temple had held more romantic appeal as an abstract, distant symbol. "But according to one opinion," he added quickly, "the Third Temple will involve flour offerings only."

The tension in the room eased.

"Right," Shmuel the cynic said, "all the Messiah has to do is convince the Waqf to hand over the Temple Mount and demolish the Dome of the Rock to make room for a synagogue. Piece of cake."

Moshe shrugged. "Anything else?"

"The Messiah will bring peace to the land. The lamb will lie down beside the lion.'"

The heads of those present nodded slowly, a gesture that meant either full agreement or "keep dreaming, pal."

"Well," Moshe said. "The Messiah's got his work cut out for him."

"Isaac Gurion isn't your messiah, Rabbi," Shmuel said. "Have you seen the platform of his new party?"

"I haven't been following the elections," Yosef admitted. From the looks on their faces, that went for the others too.

"His Upward party is playing the anti-religious card. Conscription for the ultra-Orthodox. No more stipends. Hard to see him building a synagogue on the Temple Mount."

Moshe said, "Then the religious parties can't steal him from us, as they did Malkior."

Irina laughed. So did Yosef, although that truth hurt as well. Partnering with evangelical Christians was bad enough; now the Dry Bones Society was joining the list of an anti-religious political party too.

"Messiah or not," Moshe concluded, "he's the only game

in town. Who's in favor?"

Despite his misgivings, Yosef raised his hand and the motion passed unanimously.

"Shmuel, we'll need another press conference. Irina, please handle the logistics. I'll call Gurion. I suppose I'll need to write another speech."

As the team scattered to their tasks, Yosef remained in his seat.

First Rev. Adams, now Moshe. Everyone was asking Yosef about the Messiah.

A messiah is born in every generation, taught the Sages of Blessed Memory. He waits anxiously for the Redemption, when he will reveal his true identity to the world. Yosef could do with his guidance right now.

He had expected the Messiah to be among the sages of the Great Council, but instead of welcoming the resurrection as the first stage of the budding redemption, the council had, quite literally, demonized the resurrected Israelis. But didn't the redeemer always arise in unexpected circumstances? Ruth, King David's ancestor, was a Moabite convert, and Perez, an even earlier forebear, was conceived thanks to the illicit pairing of Judah with Tamar, his former daughter-in-law. Perhaps Christian charities and anti-religious parties were suitable partners in the messianic enterprise after all.

"Yosef, are you OK?"

Moshe glanced at him from behind his desk, his phone at the ready.

"I wish the Messiah would reveal himself already."

Moshe smiled. "He's out there somewhere."

Yosef nodded, and made for the call center. He needed to order more chairs and bunk beds for the dormitories, and to review the new schedules that Samira had prepared for the volunteers on cemetery watch.

He glanced out the window of the call center at the foot traffic on Jaffa Street. *He's out there somewhere.* The thought gave him some comfort. Somewhere in the Holy City, the Hidden Messiah waited with formidable patience. Waited for what exactly—a phone call from Elijah?

Yosef peered at the cubicles of the call center and an idea popped into his mind. If the Messiah was truly out there, Yosef might be able to find him.

CHAPTER 20

Noga pushed through the glass doors of the Frank Sinatra cafeteria at the Hebrew University's Mount Scopus campus, and hoped that she was wrong. Terribly wrong.

In 2002, Arab terrorists detonated a bomb in the crowded cafeteria during summer examination season, killing six women and three men, and injuring a hundred. The materials in Noga's bag were explosive in a different sense, but soon they would shake up the entire Middle East.

She scanned the faces of the students who held trays while they waited in the buffet line, but she found no sign of her lunch date. No surprises there; Noga had arrived ten minutes early.

Finding a quiet spot at the end of the cafeteria, she laid her shoulder bag on the table and watched the younger students. She had come a long way since her lonely campus years. Finally, she had completed her research and found a guy. She loved her life. Contentment fluttered within reach. But the data in her bag threatened to crush that life underfoot.

The doors of the cafeteria opened and a couple of students entered. The guy with messy hair laughed as he spoke to a girl with glasses and shoulder-length curls. They collected trays and got in line.

Acid churned in Noga's stomach and she couldn't think of

food. She had hardly eaten last night during her celebratory dinner with Eli at 1868, a gourmet restaurant on King David Street. She had not told him about the anomaly in her research results. Information could be dangerous in the wrong hands and she did not want to trigger a relapse.

That's why I landed up here, in the hospital, Eli had told her in the secret garden. *To meet you!* The man who had spoken was not the Eli she loved, but the madman she had fled. He had claimed that Noga was part of God's grand plan for the End of Days. Now the data in her bag seemed to support those grandiose claims and Noga did not want to add fuel to that fire.

But how else could she explain the data? Empirical facts didn't lie. She had pored over the results, trying to find her mistake. If she could only convince herself that she was wrong, then her new, perfect life would survive another day.

A woman in a white blouse and practical brown trousers sat down beside her. "Noga, dear." Hannah dropped her satchel on the third seat and reached out her hand.

That was Hannah. Never a kiss or a hug, only the formality bred from years of competing in a male-dominated academia. No makeup either, only cold hard facts and a dab of old perfume.

"I'm starved," Hannah said. "Let's get some food."

"Go ahead. I'll pass."

Hannah shrugged and joined the line. She returned with a tray of spaghetti bolognaise, a bottle of sparkling water, and a plastic saucer of red Jell-O for dessert.

"And the winner is?" she said, and laughed. She sliced her pasta into neat parallel lines like a plowed field, and the sagging skin at her jaw trembled as she gobbled her food. "I remember the day I compiled the results of my doctoral thesis. Those days were different. No emails and attachments, just pages and pages of notes. Calculations by hand. We even did some of the testing on ourselves—don't tell a soul. A drop of this here, a sprinkle of that there. Thank the gods for the lab. And computers!" She shoveled another mouthful of spaghetti. "But I won't bore you with all that. Nu?" she prompted her student. "Does our Y-chromosomal Aaron exist?"

"On the whole, yes. But I found something else. Something unexpected."

Hannah's jowls wobbled, her fork suspended in the air. "Significant?"

She meant statistical significance. "Yes." Noga reached into her bag for the printouts and laid the sheets on the table.

Hannah glanced at the line charts and squinted at the labels. She stopped chewing. Then she put down the cutlery and studied the pages in both hands.

She gave Noga a sharp, suspicious look. "Is this some kind of prank?"

"No, of course not. I found it hard to believe too. That's why I wanted to check with you first."

Hannah stared at the sheets again. "Do you have the raw data with you?"

Noga pulled out her laptop, nudged it from hibernation, and turned the screen to face her professor. Hannah jabbed at the mouse pad and scrolled through the rows of figures.

Five torturous minutes later, Hannah pushed aside her half-eaten meal and sagged in her chair. Noga had never seen her mentor look so lost.

"Gods, Noga," she said. "Do you know what this means?"

A pent-up breath burst through Noga's lips. She had not misread the data. But if the results were accurate, they only raised more questions.

"Hannah, how can this be?"

"Beats me. But one thing's for sure—this will change our world forever."

A shiver ran down Noga's spine. *Change our world forever.* She had heard those words before. The man who spoke them had ranted about the approaching Redemption and how she, Noga, had a role to play. But that man no longer existed. Noga had seen to that.

CHAPTER 21

"Do you mean to tell me," said Fievel, the Russian with the tidy parting, greasy mustache, and old-fashioned accent, "that you speak into the little box, and your friend will hear you across the street?"

Irina stood before a dozen students and held up her cellular phone for display. "Or on the other side of the world," she said.

"Without wires?" the man said. "Astonishing!"

He used archaic Russian words and a peculiar sentence structure that Irina now associated with the late nineteenth century. Fievel had fled the pogroms that had swept over the Pale of Settlement after the assassination of Tsar Alexander II only to die of malaria in the swamps of Ottoman Palestine.

Irina taught the course every morning in a classroom at the Absorption Center down the corridor from the Dry Bones Society. The number of participants grew each session, and many of the recent new arrivals spoke the old brand of Russian. Some had yet to change out of the white spa gowns issued to them by the DBS volunteers who picked them up at the cemeteries and street corners of Jerusalem, Tiberias, and Safed. The newly resurrected were easy to spot.

Irina couldn't decide what surprised the arrivals more: their new lease on life or how drastically the world had changed. Modern technology seemed to them like black magic, and some of the poor souls had required a lot of convincing to get them to board the shuttle bus.

The educational classes at the Society included Transportation (or "how to cross the street"), a crash course on Modern Hebrew, and her current class, Technology, during which Irina displayed the wonders of mobile phones, televisions, and computers. Most had trouble wrapping their minds around the Internet, a topic that she now left for her advanced course.

"That's all for today," she declared. "Time for lunch."

They filed into the new mess hall. Savta Sarah stood beside the tables of steaming food, as the hungry students helped themselves to disposable plates and cutlery and piled on stuffed cabbage, meatballs, baked chicken, and, of course, goulash. The arrivals had no difficulty at all appreciating her cooking.

They'd be OK, all of them. With time, they would adjust to their new world. They would learn a trade and make friends. Some would find love. And soon, if the merger with Gurion's Upward party worked out, they would each receive a shiny new identity card as a graduation gift.

Irina joined the line, filled her plate, and found an empty table.

One poor soul would never graduate. Two months after Irina's return, she still remembered nothing of her former life. She had stopped studying the eyes of strangers for that flash of recognition. With no history and no name, she'd remain in the limbo of the Absorption Center forever. Her past was a sealed tomb and so she looked to the future, but forging a future with no past felt like reaching for the heavens with no solid ground beneath her feet.

Savta Sarah sat down at Irina's table. As usual she had not dished up for herself. "Nu? Any luck?"

"Nope. I'm still Irina."

Moshe Karlin's grandmother-in-law tutted. "Any boyfriends?" She had a way of getting to the point, and Irina liked her straightforward approach.

She shook her head. During her first weeks, she had grown close to Moshe and even nursed the hope that they would become more than friends. But Moshe loved his wife and Irina had stood down. She wasn't the kind to break up a family anyway; she'd have to build a life of her own. How? She had no idea. With luck, she'd find love the way that Moshe had with Galit—at first sight across a crowded room.

"I could make a few inquiries for you," Savta said. When Irina chuckled, she added, "I've made a few matches in my time. You're a pretty young woman. You'll be easy. Gita was a different story. Did I tell you how I set her up?"

"No," Irina said. She was about to find out.

"Gita had buck teeth and a lazy eye. Her sister, Bluma, however, was a rare beauty. Their mother, my cousin, passed away when they were young girls—her health never recovered after the War."

The War, Irina had learned, was how Savta referred to the Holocaust.

"Bluma would have no problem finding a man, but Gita, what would become of her? Doctor Schneider's son was a decent young man and a medical student at the Hebrew University. So I made an appointment at Doctor Schneider's visiting rooms and took along both Gita and her pretty sister. 'Doctor Schneider,' I said. 'Your son is such a fine young man. Surely he would be interested in meeting one of my lovely nieces?' I put Bluma up front. The doctor agreed to send his son over to our home the following evening. Bluma, regrettably, was not able to join us that day." Savta winked. "She had an urgent meeting far away. But two weeks later, Gita and the young doctor-to-be were engaged."

Savta chuckled at her own audacity.

"Thanks, Savta. But I'm in no rush."

Savta shrugged and looked over her shoulder. Another group of hungry students had arrived in the dining hall, and she bustled off to feed them.

Irina finished her meal and dropped the disposable plate in

a large bin at the door.

She had fifteen minutes until her next class, so she headed for the call center to contact the Ministry of the Interior and double-check the arrangements for Sunday. The press conference would be larger than the first and they still had to work out the finer details of how to determine the identities of people long dead. The paperwork would be a challenge.

As she stepped into the corridor, she noticed a man standing outside the Dry Bones Society and staring at the lettering on the door. Tattoos covered his muscular arm—a circle of Russian characters around a Star of David—and his hair fell to his back in a loose ponytail. An unexpected thrill flared in her core. Now there was an interesting story waiting to be heard.

He turned as she approached and held out her hand. *"Dabro pah-zhah-lah-vaht,"* she said. Welcome.

He turned to her and his lips parted. His eyes widened and his skin turned as white as paper.

"I'm Irina," she said, when he didn't respond. The newly resurrected often expressed shock and signs of disorientation, but she had yet to meet one with tattoos.

The introduction seemed to break the spell. He shook her hand. His grip was strong but cold.

"Are you OK?" she said.

"Have we met before?" he asked.

That thrill flared again. Not a spark of recognition—as far as she remembered, she had never met the man before—but perhaps something else? *Like an electric current,* Moshe had said of the moment he had first spotted Galit across a crowded Jerusalem nightclub. He had walked up to her and they had hit it off with an exchange of witty banter.

Irina couldn't think of anything witty to say now. The best she could come up with was, "Now we have."

CHAPTER 22

Alex washed his face in the bathroom sink. His hands trembled. He had asked for the men's room as soon as the girl led him into the Dry Bones Society. Otherwise, he would have fallen apart.

The girl lives!

Months ago he had received a call with that information but he had not believed the report. Knowing what he knew—having done what he had—how could he? The informant had not lied. But how could this be?

Mandrake had sent him to learn the magic tricks of this Dry Bones Society, and Alex had drawn the expected foregone conclusion. The dead never came back. These so-called resurrected people were collaborators in a large-scale hoax. But now the girl had turned everything he knew about the world on its head. This was no parlor trick.

Irina was no lookalike, either, or secret identical twin. Alex knew people, what they were feeling and thinking, often better than they knew themselves. He used this sixth sense to great effect for the Organization and his special talent was why Mandrake had selected him to sniff out the Society. Alex had known the girl well—perhaps too well—and this Irina tilted her head the same way, spoke with the same voice, and bore the same beauty spot on the side of her neck. No. This was no sleight of hand.

She remembers nothing. Not even her name. The informant had gotten that right as well. If she had remembered him, she would have fled the moment she had set eyes on him.

Was she planning to avenge herself? Was she holding her cards close to her chest, drawing him into a trap? After what she had experienced, he wouldn't blame her. But he dismissed the theory. Although he had almost fainted at the sight of her, the girl had seemed almost glad to meet him, and few people could control their visceral reactions so completely.

No, only one explanation remained—she truly didn't remember him. Good for her. But lost memories might resurface, and if they did...

His shoulders twitched, and he doubled over. Thankfully, he had the bathroom to himself. He splashed water on his face again and stared at the tough guy in the mirror. *Get a hold of yourself!*

He needed to go out there again, look her in the eye, and decide how much she really knew. If she remembered even a bit of her old life, he knew what Mandrake would command. Would he be able to go through that again? The first time had bent him, and driven him into semi-retirement. A second might break him for good.

He drew three deep breaths. The bathroom had two toilet stalls but he had used neither, so he flushed the one and stepped out the bathroom door.

She was waiting for him outside with a broad, friendly smile.

"Did you return this morning?" she asked.

"Return?"

"Come back to life?"

"No," he said. "I'm not one of those." To find out the truth, he'd have to play his real identity, or as close as possible. If anything was going to trigger a flashback, he wanted that to happen sooner rather than later.

She leaned in and lowered her voice. "It's OK," she said.

"We get a lot of visitors like you. Some are just curious. Others want to join the Society. You don't have to have died to want a fresh start."

He swallowed the ball of emotion that swelled in his throat. Was she hinting at their past? Was she goading him into a confrontation? He studied her large green eyes. Those eyes had haunted his dreams, but today they contained no trace of rebuke.

She looked away. "I'm sorry," she said. "That's me pushing my nose where it doesn't belong. Let me show you around. This is the call center."

She waved at the rows of cubicles manned by people with headsets. "The calls are from volunteers and donors mostly. The new arrivals usually get picked up on site."

Alex nodded his head and looked around. There was a kitchenette and a corner office with large windows.

"That's Moshe's office," she explained. "Moshe Karlin, one of the founders of the Dry Bones Society. Want to see the Absorption Center?"

He nodded.

They walked down the corridor and she showed him the classrooms, the dining hall, and the meeting room with the circle of plastic chairs that they used for their group sessions. He asked questions and she answered. She glanced at him often but without malice. If the gracious reception was an act, her performance was flawless.

"I have to give a class now," she said, and she touched her hair absently. "Funny," she said, with a bemused smile. "I still don't know your name."

"Alex," he said.

She seemed to turn the name over in her head. Any moment, he expected her to shudder and convulse with fear, to stab him with an accusatory glare.

Instead, she smiled. "Nice to meet you, Alex."

CHAPTER 23

That evening in the marble lobby of the luxury residential tower on Jaffa Road, Noga waited for the elevator and prepared to break the news to Eli.

The golden doors whooshed open and she stepped inside the mirrored box. After Hannah had confirmed the facts, she could keep the discovery a secret no longer. Would the revelation shove Eli back into the sinking sand of his old delusions?

An ephemeral black floor number projected on the golden lintel and climbed upward as the elevator rose.

Or had Eli been right from the start? She had dismissed his apocalyptic rantings out of hand, and yet now her laptop held the seeds of peace in the Middle East. Was that coincidence or Providence? Had God sent Eli to usher in the End of Days? Would Noga also play a key role in that cosmic drama? Had God caused Eli's accident, as he had claimed, in order to bring them together?

As the floor number reached P for Penthouse and the doors whooshed open, she made her decision. No, she could not hide this from her partner in life. She'd roll the dice—lay the facts before him—and hope that he'd hold it together.

She punched the code into a keypad and the lock clicked open, but when she turned the handle and pushed, the front door of the apartment stuck. Something was blocking the entrance. She peered around the edge of the door. A dozen packing boxes littered the hall.

Are we moving? Eli had said nothing about that.

She pushed harder, shifting the nearest moving box until she could slip through the crack. Each box had a white address tag taped to the top. New York, USA. Manchester, United Kingdom. Durban, South Africa. She didn't recognize any of the names. What was going on?

The trail of boxes led through the kitchen, down the corridor, and ended at the door to Eli's private sanctuary. Noga had discovered the room on her first visit to the apartment, when Eli had lain in a hospital bed at Shaare Zedek. She had avoided the room ever since. The shrine housed a collection of old weapons and personal items—mementos from Eli's imagined past and the pseudo-evidence that had fed his delusions. His presence in that room could only spell trouble.

She stood at the threshold. In the sunken den at the center of the room, Eli scribbled an address on another sealed package with a black marker, then looked up at her and smiled.

"Hey."

"Hey. What's going on?"

He hefted the oblong package in both hands and climbed the steps to the door. "Cleaning out some junk. Coming through!" He brushed past her. Nails and picture hooks marked the pale empty spaces on the walls where the artifacts had once hung.

She followed him to the kitchen. "You sold them?"

He lowered the package onto the kitchen island, beside another similar package. "People will buy anything on eBay. That's probably where I got them myself." He patted the oblong package. "This one might cause trouble in customs. A full-size claymore. A sword," he added in answer to her blank stare. "Very old, very sharp sword."

A few days ago, she would have welcomed a clearance sale of his bizarre collection. Today she wasn't so sure. "You're not keeping any of it?"

"Nope. Why would I?" His eyes narrowed. "Is everything all right? How did your meeting go?"

She placed her laptop bag on the counter beside the packaged sword and slumped onto a kitchen stool.

He moved behind her and massaged her shoulders. "Did she find a problem with the results?"

His hands felt good on her stiff muscles. "Not exactly," she said. "The main thesis still stands, but there's a glitch."

He released her shoulders and sat down beside her. "What kind of glitch?"

"The Cohen gene is real; it appears in all the Jewish participants who claimed priestly descent."

"And?"

Noga drew a deep breath. She wanted to hold onto this moment, possibly the last before her perfect life crumbled, the way it had in the secret garden at Shaare Zedek. This time she would be to blame, but there was no stopping now.

"Another group has the haplotype," she said. "In large percentages. Too large to dismiss as outliers or statistical errors. And in the same proportion as Jewish priests to Jewish laypersons."

"And the lucky group is?" he prompted.

"Arabs," she said. "Or at least those that live in Samaria and Judea. Palestinian Arabs."

Confusion crumpled his brow. "Are you sure the data is good?"

"I triple-checked. So did Hannah. There's a clear Founder Effect."

She didn't need to spell out the ramifications. If Palestinian Arabs originated from a closed group of Jewish ancestors, then she had uncovered the key to peace in the Middle East.

She gazed into his eyes, searching for the old flicker of madness and bracing for another rant about the End of Days.

But Eli didn't rant or rave; he didn't laugh at her either. Instead, he touched her arm. "I'm so sorry," he said.

"Sorry for what?"

He gave her a sympathetic smile. "That your thesis didn't

work out."

She had to laugh. "Are you kidding me? My thesis did *work out*, but along the way it proves that Palestinians Arabs are actually Jews. Don't you see? Think of what that means. This changes everything."

He frowned. "You set out to find the Cohen gene. If it shows up among Arabs, then doesn't that disprove your theory?"

She brushed his hand from her arm. "No, it doesn't!" He was being unreasonable.

He looked away. He wasn't kidding. "What's the alternative—that Palestinian Arabs just happen to be Jews? That's convenient. Now they'll hug us instead of trying to kill us? The end to the conflict? Peace in our time?"

"Yes!"

"Come on, Noga. Palestinians are Jews? How does that even make sense? The simpler explanation is that the theory is wrong. Occam's Razor says that the simplest explanation always—"

"I know what Occam's Razor is," she snapped. Now he was being mean, and his stubborn, self-assured manner was driving her insane. "You're ignoring the facts," she said, in the calmest voice she could muster. "This is shared genetic heritage, not some conspiracy theory. Genes don't lie."

He stared at her, a sadness in his eyes. "Let me tell you about facts," he said. He patted a package on the kitchen island. "This is an authentic crusader sword. A gift to me from William of Ibelin. He sang pretty well but only when he was drunk, which was often. He limped on his right leg ever since of the Battle of Hattin, where he barely escaped with his life. In the year 1187."

He pointed to another long package on the floor. "That's an oriental rug made by Yusuf of Acre, a Turk and the best carpet maker I've ever known. He traded that rug for an old mule I had, let's see, just over three hundred years ago."

With a sweep of his arm, he indicated all of the waiting packages. "These are all physical facts. Can't deny their existence. But what do they mean? To me they used to be memories collected over the course of a very long and eventful life." He grinned at her. "Did you know that Moses was a terrible dancer, or that King Ahab had dark curls and a cleft chin?" His grin faltered as he blinked back a tear. "It's all garbage. All this stuff, like the memories, they're all just strands in a thick web of lies that I told myself to give my life meaning." He turned to her and laid his hand on her arm again. "I don't want you to go through that."

She wriggled free of his grasp. "This is different," she said. "These aren't false memories propped up by random objects. This is a sound theory based on empirical evidence."

Eli gave a bitter laugh. "This time is always different."

He stared at the tangerine dusk through the French windows of the living room. "Messiahs crop up every other century. Their followers are experts at finding signs and omens. 'This time the Redemption is here for real.' The result is always the same. Disappointment. Disillusion. Often, death too. The greater the anticipation, the more destructive the devastation that follows. When will people learn? When will they stop betting everything on magical solutions and just accept the world as it is?"

He glanced at her and touched her cheek with the palm of his hand. He wasn't angry or upset, only tired. "Trust me on this," he said. "I've been there."

CHAPTER 24

Ahmed listened to the whisper of the morning breeze outside and the groan of his empty stomach within. He lay on the cold stone floor of an empty cave. Surviving the night had been the easy part; the day would be harder.

He sat up on his elbows, careful not to bang his head on the ceiling of the cave. Long ago, many hands had chiseled the crawl space into the bedrock of the hillside. The ancients had laid their loved ones to rest on the stone shelves cut into the walls, along with provisions for the afterlife. Over the years, tomb robbers and, later, archaeologists had cleared out the gifts and the bones.

As a child, a friend had dared Ahmed to sneak into one of the gaping mouths of the old tombs. He had climbed the rocky incline between his village of Silwan and the old cemetery on the Mount of Olives, more concerned about slipping on loose stones than disturbing the old spirits within. As a child adventurer, he had entered this tomb in daylight, standing tall on two feet. As an adult fugitive, he had crawled inside on all fours in the dark of night. This time, the demons lurked outside the tomb.

The old grave made a fitting home for a dead man. He had spent his first day of freedom cowering inside, the visible world shrinking to the rectangular mouth of the cave. He watched cars move between the stone houses and leafy trees of the City of David across the Kidron Valley. A woman in a hijab hung clothes on a line. Any moment he expected the mouth of the cave to darken, filling with the muscular bulk of the Rottweiler. But the day had passed without incident. He had devoured his last crusts of bread and emptied his plastic bottle of water. If he didn't leave the safety of the tomb while he still had strength, he would starve and make the tomb his home forever.

According to the old Muslim in the warehouse, this world was neither Heaven nor Hell. God had flung him from death back into the land of the living. Boris and Damas—even the Rottweiler—were men, not demons. He could not escape demons, but he might evade men. And in the real world, one place might still welcome him.

He crawled through the dust to the opening and peeked over the stony ridge. In the valley below, a white car parked next to the low square building at the Gichon spring. Satisfied that he was not being observed, he crawled outside, then rose to his full height and stretched his back. He peed into a patch of wild grass—dark yellow pee—and wiped his hands in the dirt.

Then he made for the quiet dirt road at the edge of Silwan, picking his way along the hillside and sliding down the bulge of bedrock. He strolled along the street, another dusty laborer late for work. Across the valley, a construction drill rattled. He turned this way and that, and looked over his shoulder. No one was following him in the jumble of lopsided homes and apartment buildings. The streets had no names, but he knew them by heart.

Two minutes later, he stopped before the spot where his childhood home had stood. The house looked nothing like he remembered. Tall, solid walls stood proud in a clean layer of gray paint. An impressive wooden door sealed the entrance.

Of course. His home was long gone, demolished by Israeli bulldozers, the fate shared by all the homes of suicide bombers. He had not considered that before he had boarded the bus with his bag of explosives and ball bearings. He had not told his mother about his plans for martyrdom. Some wealthy family had built over the ruins of his childhood. Perhaps they would know where he could find his mother. He clutched his stomach and leaned on the wall for support. Maybe they'd spare him a heel of bread.

The sound of scraping down the street caught his ear. A child walked toward him, dragging a stick in the dirt. He waited for the boy to pass and disappear down the street before he knocked on the door.

He was about to knock a second time when the door cracked open. An old woman in a black *niqab* peered at him with suspicion. Then her old eyes widened in the opening of the veil. She grabbed his arm, pulled him inside, and closed the door.

"Ahmed!"

She knew his name, and he knew her voice.

"Mother?"

He had not recognized her in the full head covering. His mother had always worn modest wraparounds of white and brown. She removed the *niqab* and looked him over, her braids of frizzy hair streaked with gray. The lines of her face had deepened and the skin hung looser, but the same glowing smile brightened her face.

She hugged him tight, and the first loving human touch in his new life felt so good, it pushed him to the edge of tears.

She held him out for inspection. "My little boy." Was that pride in her voice or heartbreak? He had abandoned her to become a martyr.

"I prayed for you to visit me in a dream," she said. "But I never thought I'd see you again." She shook her head and wrung her hands.

Ahmed didn't know how to explain his visit so he didn't, and changed the subject to his more pressing needs. "Mother," he said. "May I have something to eat?"

"Of course."

She sat him down at a marble table in a large, clean kitchen with every modern appliance, and soon he gorged himself on a fresh pita stuffed with his mother's homemade hummus and fried strips of lamb that she warmed in a microwave.

She watched him eat, her eyes drifting to his matted hair and filthy clothing, and concern clouded her face.

Ahmed washed the meal down with a glass of Coke. "This house," he said.

At the mention of her house, her features brightened. "When you... left, the soldiers destroyed our home." The event did not seem to upset her. "But then they built me a new house. Wonderful, isn't it?"

"Who built it for you, Mother?"

She leaned in to whisper. "A gift, Hasan said, from the governments that honor the families of our noble martyrs. Forty thousand shekels in cash too!"

"Forty thousand?" Ahmed had earned half that much in a year. He had died a martyr but his mother had received the palace. But now, he had come home.

"I missed you so, my Ahmed."

"I missed you too."

She leaned in again. "Tell me," she said, a gleam in her eye. "How are you enjoying Paradise?"

Ahmed inhaled his Coca-Cola and coughed.

"The banquet of the martyrs?" she continued. "The righteous prophets. And your wives!" She touched her palm to her cheek. "The noblest beauties in all the world, for sure!"

Ahmed cleared his throat. How could he tell his mother that, not only had he not seen Paradise, but he had passed through Hell?

"Silly me," his mother said. "So many questions. It is enough for me just to see your face again." She glanced at the front door and that troubled look returned to her face. "I'm sure you're eager to return to the afterlife. You can answer my questions next time."

"Next time? Mother, I want to stay here with you."

"Here?" A hint of annoyance had entered her voice. "That cannot be. You died a martyr, Ahmed. The people honor me.

They call me *Um-Shaheed*. They invite me to social events and public gatherings. I sit with the leaders and dignitaries. They give me money and I want for nothing." She sent another fleeting glance toward the front door, and her voice dropped to a hiss. "You're not supposed to be here. You should be enjoying your eternal reward in Paradise, not visiting your mother and looking like a starving tramp, all covered in dirt." Then she remembered herself and gave an embarrassed laugh. "You should be on your way."

She swept crumbs from the marble tabletop with her hand and took his empty plate to the sink. The street outside loomed large and terrifying.

"But Mother, I have nowhere to go."

"Nonsense!" She pulled him out of his seat and herded him toward the door. "You have your palace and your wives." She opened the door, looked up and down the street, and shoved him outside. "Enjoy your eternal reward," she said, as she closed the door and blew him a kiss, "and don't forget to visit your mother."

CHAPTER 25

Sunday morning, Moshe died and went to Heaven. Dazzling lights blinded him, not the spiritual glow at the end of an afterlife tunnel, but the glare of spotlights and the flash of press cameras in a packed auditorium at the Ministry of the Interior.

Minister Malkior sat beside him onstage while Isaac Gurion gave forth at the podium, his voice booming from speakers. He spoke of thousands of resurrected Jews and their needless suffering, of cutting bureaucratic red tape, and welcoming back long-lost family.

Moshe had a powerful friend, and there was no limit to the good they could do together.

Galit beamed at him from the front row, seated among the top brass of the Dry Bones Society, and ahead of the many rows of reporters. The idea of a career in politics had not overjoyed her at first.

"Are you sure you want all that attention?" she had asked him after Friday night dinner at home. He was asking a lot of her. Politics would shove them both into the public eye, and ever since his brief incarceration Galit had remained tense and pensive, looking over her shoulder every time they left the house.

"It's a great opportunity," he had said. "Think of all the

good we could do. Besides, I can't see any other way to get citizenship in the near future."

That argument seemed to win her over. "Promise me we'll get married right away."

"Of course. I'll book the first hall that's available."

"Forget a hall," she said. "Let's have a quiet ceremony here at home."

Moshe chuckled at her sudden eagerness. "What about your parents?" They'd need time to fly out from the USA.

"They'll get over it."

"And now," Isaac Gurion concluded at the podium, "the time has come to correct this injustice, by granting those poor lost souls recognition as citizens with all the associated rights and responsibilities."

He turned to the table where Moshe sat. "Minister Malkior, will you do the honors?"

Malkior waved his silver pen in the air like a magic wand, and signed the document on the table to the background music of flashing cameras. He gave Moshe a broad grin and shook his hand as though he hadn't double-crossed him last week. They faced the cameras, hands still engaged, for the photo op—the Minister of the Interior shaking hands with Moshe Karlin, the magnanimous Isaac Gurion standing behind them, his arms spread like sheltering wings.

Malkior picked up the microphone on the table. "I have a surprise for you, Moshe," he said.

The floor fell out of Moshe's stomach. Malkior's last surprise had involved a knife in the back.

"While we were drafting this letter of intent, our friend Mr. Gurion got busy pushing our new legislation through Knesset. This morning, the proposal passed its third reading."

Gurion shifted back to the podium. "The new law grants asylum and automatic citizenship to all new arrivals. I call it"—he paused for dramatic effect—"the Second Law of Return."

Applause broke out from the audience. Moshe glanced at the beaming faces in the front row. Shmuel clapped his hands and gave him the thumbs-up. *We've done it.* Tears welled in Moshe's eyes.

"Anticipating this," Malkior said, "I went ahead and had this made for you." He reached into the inner pocket of his suit jacket. Instead of a dagger, he withdrew a blue booklet.

Moshe opened the crisp, new covers and studied the freshly minted identity card within. *Moshe Karlin.* He had kept his old identity number. "Thank you." He shook the minister's hand and let him give him a side hug.

Gurion spoke into the microphone again. "We have another surprise for you, Moshe."

This was his cue to join his benefactor at the podium.

"I've gotten to know Moshe very well recently," he said. "He risked everything to help his brothers and sisters in need and I'm proud to count him as my friend. Our country needs more Moshe Karlins, and so I'm excited to announce that he and the worthy folks at the Dry Bones Society have agreed to join our list and run with Upward in the upcoming elections."

A commotion rippled through the audience and cameras flared again.

An aide adjusted the microphone for Moshe while he extracted his cue cards, and the hall fell silent.

"This is a truly historic occasion," he said, his voice echoing back on the speakers, deeper and more confident than he had expected. "On behalf of our resurrected brothers and sisters, I would like to thank Member of Knesset Isaac Gurion for his friendship and Minister Malkior for his quick and effective cooperation. Thanks to you both, thousands of men, women, and children are now able to lead dignified and productive lives. We at the Dry Bones Society look forward to working closely with you in future for the betterment of not only the resurrected but of all citizens."

Gurion opened the floor to questions. A multitude of hands shot into the air. Gurion picked one.

A disheveled man with reading glasses and a press card hanging at his neck stood up. "When will identity cards be issued?"

Moshe had rehearsed the expected questions with Gurion the previous night, and that one had topped the list.

Moshe leaned into the microphone. "Starting from tomorrow, the Ministry of the Interior will open special service desks to receive the resurrected. Details are on the Ministry of Interior website."

Gurion selected a female questioner. "How will the resurrected prove their identities?"

"Good question," Moshe said. His smile won a few laughs from the crowd, and he relaxed. "Those with pre-existing identity numbers will be matched with the photographs on record. There are still a few glitches to work through. The computer systems don't support multiple birth dates yet." Another round of chuckles. He was getting the hang of this. "Those without identity numbers—whose first lives predate the State—will need to provide details of their former life: dates and places of birth and death. Checks will be made—photo analysis and fingerprints—to ensure the applicants are not already in the system."

Gurion picked a third questioner. "What positions on the Upward list will the Dry Bones Society occupy?"

Gurion stepped in to answer. "Three, and then twenty through twenty-four."

The reporter raised his eyebrows. A recent poll had given Upward seventeen mandates in the upcoming election. Even with the resurrected vote, only Moshe would sit in Knesset. That didn't bother the Society much. Gurion's party had pushed through the Second Law of Return.

"I have one more surprise for Moshe," Gurion said, bringing the questions to a close.

Moshe glanced at him. Gurion had not mentioned this in their preparations.

"As you know, Moshe, we look out for our friends, so please accept this gift as a token of our appreciation." He handed Moshe a black box tied with a blue ribbon. "Go ahead, open it."

Moshe did. Inside, on a bed of soft velvet, sat a large gold watch.

"Every man of action needs a good timepiece," Gurion continued.

Moshe closed the heavy metal links over his wrist. The brand new Omega felt lighter than his grandfather's ancient Rolex. Moshe reminded himself to redeem the family heirloom from the pawn shop in Talpiot when he could afford to. The old vulture at the shop would not return the watch without a mighty negotiation. Luckily for Moshe, he had a secret weapon: Savta Sarah.

"Thank you." Tears threatened to surface again.

Gurion gripped Moshe by the shoulders and pulled him close for another photo op.

Moshe smiled for the cameras. He had nothing to worry about now; he had powerful friends.

CHAPTER 26

Noga stared at her laptop through the veil of steam from her coffee cup on the kitchen island. She had to prove Eli wrong. The data *did* support her thesis. But no matter how she arranged the charts, the conspicuous cluster of Palestinian Arabs with the gene markers of Jewish priests would not disappear. Erasing the pesky results was out of the question—she would never sacrifice her scientific integrity.

Background chatter came from the television in the living room. A Channel Two correspondent reported on early poll results. Election fever had gripped the country. Noga aimed the remote and the television screen went dark. She hated politics.

She stared at the charts and ran her fingers through her hair. The Arabs in the study were Jewish. They had to be. Hannah, her advisor, had reached the same conclusion. Noga's thesis stood strong. Her paper would appear in academic journals and, incidentally, solve the intractable Israeli-Palestinian conflict, making Noga both a world-renowned scientist and a national hero. How convenient, indeed.

Extraordinary claims, Carl Sagan had said, require extraordinary evidence, and the puzzle still lacked one critical piece—a working theory that explained how this mind-boggling reality had developed.

She exhaled a tremulous breath and her shoulders slumped.

"Thanks a lot, Eli." His devil's advocate questions had toppled her fairytale palace of cards. His counter-theory ignored the main thrust of the genetic data but still gnawed at her conscience.

Had her personal bias slanted her analysis? Was she simply not prepared to throw away two years of sweat and tears? If Eli was right, then the End of Days had arrived indeed—for her doctorate.

Was that so far-fetched? Every day, conspiracy theorists connected unrelated facts to support outlandish claims. Science had names for their logical fallacies: confirmation bias; confusing cause and effect; ignoring a common cause. Being human. Noga could easily have fallen into the same trap.

She had feared for Eli's sanity but could she be the one who had succumbed to delusion?

Her body convulsed as she laughed. She doubled over and tears seeped from the corners of her eyes. Tears of loss. Tears of relief. *You idiot!* She had been so convinced that she had stumbled onto an epic discovery! *This time is always different,* Eli had said. The list of failed messiahs proved that only too well.

She straightened on the kitchen stool and gulped her bitter coffee. So be it. *Dust yourself off and start again.*

She opened an Internet browser, typed two words into the search bar—"false messiah"—and clicked the link for Wikipedia.

"Wow," she said aloud.

Eli had not exaggerated. Messiah claimants had cropped up almost every century. Simon Bar Kokhba had led a doomed Jewish rebellion against the Roman Empire in the second century. Moses of Crete in the fifth. Most of them had met violent deaths. David Alroy, twelfth century, was murdered in his sleep. His contemporary, the Messiah of Yemen, had told his opponents to cut off his head in order to prove his claim. And on and on. Most of the names didn't ring a bell.

She *had* heard of Sabbatai Zevi. In 1666, after stirring up hope and controversy throughout Europe, Zevi arrived in Constantinople intending to conquer the globe without bloodshed and don the sultan's crown. The sultan promptly threw him in prison and gave him an ultimatum: convert to Islam or die. Zevi chose Islam and cast the Jewish world into black despair.

Some communities refused to accept his failure. A Polish Jew by the name of Jacob Frank claimed to be his successor but led his followers to Christianity. The Dönmeh sect of Turkey follow Sabbatai Zevi to this day.

Noga's heart did a double-flip. Her academic mind had discerned a pattern in the historic details, a recurring theme that united the failed messianic eras of the past but did not apply to the present day. This time really was different.

She laughed again. *Here you go again.* After only a few days of messianic mania, she still struggled to shake free. How had Eli managed to escape a lifetime of delusion? Her admiration for him grew.

At the sound of bare feet down the hallway, she switched back to EPSS, her statistical software.

Eli padded into the kitchen in pajama trunks. "Good morning." He kissed her on the cheek.

"Morning."

He fixed a cup of coffee behind her. The last few days he had been kind enough not to mention her thesis, but her vain stubborn streak had not been ready to concede defeat.

"Oh, crap," he said behind her. "I'm late." He ran back to the bedroom, returning in jeans and sneakers and pulling on a shirt as he rushed for the door.

"Late for what?"

"To pick up the bike," he said.

The bike. Eli had covered the coffee table with marketing pamphlets for Harley Davidson's latest and greatest.

"Hey," she shouted after him. "Don't forget—"

"I know," he said, preempting her. "I'll wear a helmet."

He blew her a kiss from the front door and slipped into

the elevator.

She sighed. Boys and their toys. At least his retail therapy seemed to have whetted his appetite for life.

Her phone jingled and she answered on the first ring.

"Hannah," she said. "I've been meaning to call you." She wanted to share her doubts with her advisor, but she didn't get a chance.

"Noga, dear," the professor said. She sounded unusually flustered. "I've found it."

"Found what?"

"The explanation for the results of your study."

Hannah must have figured out their mistake on her own. "Me too," she said. "I owe you an apology."

"An apology?"

"For misleading you."

"Misleading me? Not at all—you were *absolutely* right, and now I've found the key to the whole mystery."

Noga's heart fluttered. "What did you find?"

"I can't explain on the phone. You'll have to see for yourself. What are you doing tomorrow morning?"

"Nothing yet."

"Good. I'll pick you up at eight."

CHAPTER 27

Sunday evening, Alex pulled up at the Lev Talpiot Mall in his black Skoda Octavia, his heart banging against his ribs. He needed to lie to his boss—his boss and his oldest friend. Not a lie, really. An omission.

She's alive!

Once the shock had subsided, relief had set in. *She's alive!* Redemption glinted on the horizon. But soon that relief turned to dread. Mandrake must never know of her existence. If he did, Alex knew what he would command, and he couldn't go through with that again.

No. He had to close the case. To lock the door, melt the key, and never think of her again.

He parked the car in the loading zone at the side of the mall and raised the hand brake. Cops knew better than to tow cars parked in this particular loading zone. The street reeked of garbage and cat piss. A dark staircase cut into the side of the building, but no security guard manned this entrance of the mall.

As Alex reached the top of the stairs, moonlight traced an open-air corridor that ended in doors of tinted glass. The sound of toppling bowling pins met his ears as he drew near. He pushed through the doors, entering a space filled with soft light, cigarette smoke, and lounge music. To his left, a

Sephardic greaser in a leather jacket leaned over a pool table and dropped a yellow ball into a corner pocket. On his right, men in matching polo shirts rolled bowling balls down eighteen lanes to the applause of crashing pins. League night.

The Talpiot Bowling Center had belonged to an entrenched Israeli mafia clan until Mandrake had arrived in their turf and taken over their monopolies on recycling, vending machines, and protection rackets. Within a month, Jerusalem had fallen under the magician's spell.

The blonde at the front desk blew bubbles with her gum and studied her nails. Her tank top left little to the imagination. Silver trophies and special edition bowling balls crowned the low wall behind her.

"Evening, Anna," he said in Russian. "Is he in?"

She nodded. Easy on the eyes and devoid of curiosity, Anna did her job well. She even made phone calls to car sellers when required.

He went around the counter, behind Anna, and into a walk-in closet lined with shelves of bowling shoes. At the back, he glanced at the camera in the corner where the wall met the ceiling, and knocked on the door. A bolt shifted and the door opened.

Vitaly, with his bald head and scarred face, wore his trademark black jeans and T-shirt. He bolted the door behind them. "He's busy," he said, and returned to his game of solitaire at a round card table. A gun poked out the back of his jeans. Mandrake always carried a pack of playing cards and the habit had rubbed off on his foot soldier.

Alex settled on a chair in the corner, opposite the closed door of the Boss's office. Camera feeds displayed on a wall: the shoe closet; the front door; the street. Other locations of strategic interest across the city displayed on yet more screens: a dark alley; an old warehouse; a knot of loiterers with cigarettes outside a bar. From these rooms, the Boss ruled his empire.

The safest bet was to turn Mandrake's attention away from the Dry Bones Society. If he had no further need for them, he would never find out about the girl.

The office door opened and two heavyset Chinese men in business suits exited. Mandrake had extended his tendrils far and wide since the old days in the USSR. Alex didn't know half of the Organization's activities and that suited him well. He knew too much already.

Vitaly let the visitors out and bolted the door, then motioned for Alex to enter.

Alex closed the door behind him. A manager's chair of padded leather lay empty behind a bulky oak desk.

"Sit, my friend," said a voice behind him. He turned. Mandrake slouched on the leather wraparound couch. Wearing a black button-down shirt and black trousers, he puffed on a cigar.

Alex sat down on the edge of the couch.

Large, intelligent eyes studied Alex over a huge sensitive nose. The shaved head glowed beneath sunken spotlights.

"A drink?" Mandrake nodded toward a bar cabinet of polished wood. "A smoke?"

"No, thanks."

Mandrake cut to the chase. "So what have we learned about this Dry Bones Society and their magic tricks?"

Alex leaned forward on the couch. "No magic tricks," he said. "They're for real."

The intelligent eyes scanned his own. "Sasha," he said, a note of disappointment in his voice. He was the only man who called him by that name. "You surprise me. Dead men returning to life? We have been magicians too long to believe in magic *or* miracles."

Alex felt his stomach tighten. He hadn't expected the news to go over easily. "Call it what you like. It's real."

Mandrake laughed, leaned over, and tapped ash into a tray on a side table. "I did some homework too, I hope you don't mind. This Moshe Karlin threw together a demonstration last week, and got locked up for his efforts. Now he's playing politics. He's a clever trickster, but he's a trickster still." The eyes locked on Alex. "Has he tricked you as well?"

"There are signs," Alex said. "Physical signs. They have no belly button."

Mandrake dragged on the cigar, still staring.

"Like I said," Alex continued, "this is no trick. We should keep clear of them. My work is done here."

Mandrake blew a smoke ring in the air. "You're so sure of this. Why?"

Alex swallowed. There was no avoiding it. "The girl is with them," he said. "I met her. That's how I know."

The eyes didn't blink. "And how did she take to your reunion?"

"She doesn't remember a thing, not even her name. Goes by Irina now. She works at the Society."

"Could this Irina be another girl?"

Alex stared at his hands. "It's her."

Mandrake took another long drag. "If her memory comes back…"

"I doubt it. We spoke for a long time and I used my real name. They're no threat for now, unless we draw their attention."

Mandrake blew another ring and watched it disappear into thin air. "We cannot take that chance, Sasha. Take her to the Doctor."

Alex shifted on his seat. "I told you, she doesn't remember anything." His attempt at keeping her safe had backfired.

Mandrake stubbed out the cigar in the ashtray. "Take her to the Doctor, and we'll know for sure."

CHAPTER 28

Monday morning, Avi marched down Jaffa Road, propelled by indignation. The time had come to take matters into his own hands.

Pedestrians rushed along the sidewalks of downtown Jerusalem, as waiters arranged chairs and tables outside cafés.

"We can help each other," Boris had said. The Russian Mafioso had drilled him about Moshe Karlin and his plans. He had given Avi a cell phone and pocket money, and told him to pass on any new information. Together they would destroy Moshe Karlin. Five days since that promise, Moshe Karlin's star had risen only higher.

On the fuzzy television in his dingy downtown studio apartment, his old nemesis had shaken hands with politicians and fielded questions from reporters. The event gave Moshe and his undead friends new rights and influence, pushing Avi's revenge further away than ever.

With a valid identity card, nothing would stop Moshe from marrying Galit and shutting Avi out for good, and so he had sprung out of bed that morning with renewed purpose. He could wait no longer for Boris to deliver. Time was running out.

A crowd of people blocked the sidewalk, so he stepped into the road to walk around them, then froze to the spot.

What the hell? The human line stretched all the way to Queen Shlomzion Street.

He turned to a man at the edge of the crowd. "Is this the line for the Ministry of the Interior?"

"Yes," the man said, "But it's moving." He had a strange accent and wore a T-shirt that fell to his knees. He was one of *them*. The man smiled and put out his hand. "My name is Nikita. Are you also a returnee?"

"No," Avi snapped, wiping the smile off the man's face.

Avi trudged to the end of the line. *Bloody freaks.* He had set out early to avoid the crowds, planning to get inside the Ministry and cause havoc by shredding application forms and cutting computer cables. If he had to, he'd start a fire. That'd show them. The next news broadcast would have Moshe Karlin apologizing for the violent behavior of his followers.

The line inched forward.

This is ridiculous. At this rate, he'd wait an hour before he even entered the building. The undead had spawned like tadpoles. Another twenty stood in line behind him now. Their gleeful smiles made him want to retch.

Enough! He stepped into the road, abandoning his spot in the line, and marched to the head of the human python.

A mustachioed security guard raised his hand for him to wait while a young woman berated him. "What do you mean I can't go in?" she said. "I need to renew my passport."

"Ma'am," the guard said. "Today we're open only for res-urrected."

"But this is urgent. I want to talk to your superior."

"You're welcome to," he said, "but this comes all the way from the top. You'll have to come back tomorrow." He glanced past Avi at the growing line. "Or next week, by the look of it."

"This is pathetic," the girl yelled.

"Yeah," Avi joined in. "We have rights too." The girl glanced at him and smiled.

"Sorry, friends," the guard said. "Please move along."

The girl stepped aside. "The country's gone mad," she

said.

"You're right," Avi said. He gave her a wide grin. He'd like to take her out for breakfast. Judging by her fancy skirt and collared blouse, she'd pick up the tab.

She brushed a strand of hair behind her ear. "These resurrected are taking over."

"Oh, no they won't," he said. "Not if I have anything to do with it."

A light bulb flared in his head. *That's it!* All thoughts of romantic breakfasts evaporated. He walked off, leaving the girl standing there, and pulled out his phone.

"Boris," he said, when the call connected. "I know how to take down Karlin."

CHAPTER 29

Yosef snuck into the corner office at the Dry Bones Society and glanced out the large windows to make sure no one was eavesdropping. The Society headquarters had been unusually quiet the last few days, the members busy with the press conference at the Ministry of the Interior and now with the issuing of identity cards, and Yosef took advantage of the situation to work on his own private mission.

He opened his laptop on Moshe's desk and loaded the spreadsheet he had created. The first worksheet contained a list of names he had gleaned from the Talmud and Midrash. He connected to the Internet, browsed to the Bezeq Online Directory, and searched for the first name on the spreadsheet: Menachem. A blue ball traced circles on the screen while he waited.

A table of results displayed. Twenty thousand six hundred and thirteen matches. Yosef swallowed hard. He would have to narrow his search. He typed "Rabbi Menachem," hit the Search button, and the table updated. Three hundred and sixty-five matches.

Still too many. He narrowed the geographic region to Jerusalem. Thirty-six results. *Thirty-six!* The number restored his enthusiasm. Thirty-six names, like the Thirty-Six Hidden Saints of Jewish legend.

The mission might succeed sooner than he had expected.

He exported the search results, pasted them into a new worksheet, and selected the first row.

Although the Talmud discouraged Calculating the End—attempts at predicting the onset of the End of Days—many sages had succumbed to the temptation. The dates often fell only a few years hence. The Redeemer would arrive in the year 1034. No—1043 is the appointed time. Or perhaps 1111? Surely by 1204. Just a little longer, a few more years. The dates came and went, but the Messiah remained as bashful as ever. 1646—last call! The Hind of Dawn pranced forever just beyond the rise of the next hill.

Theologians speculated about his chronic tardiness. The Redeemer would appear once all of the souls in the Divine Store had incarnated, or when all sinners repented their evil ways. If all Israel kept two Sabbaths, the Messiah would arrive. If only the students of the saintly Baal Shem Tov had joined him in prayer, the Messiah would have revealed himself. If all the great sages of the generation had only met, their joint holiness would have forced the Son of David from hiding.

The Messiah would appear as a king, a leper, a lowly beggar. He would possess wondrous knowledge and insight. Hidden since the Six Days of Creation, he yearned for the Deliverance and suffered with each passing moment. The ninth day of *Av*, the day of the Temple's destruction, would be his birthday, and Menachem his name. No, Efraim. Or David. Nehorai!

Yosef dialed the first number on the phone on Moshe's desk. He had to start somewhere. The receiver trembled in his hand as the number rang. Would this call kick off the Redemption? He imagined the fateful conversation. "Reb Yosef," a sonorous voice would say. "What took you so long? The appointed time has arrived! We have much work to do."

With each ring his heart palpitated.

"Allo," said a woman's voice, high-pitched and frail.

"Is that the home of Rabbi Menachem Azulai?"

"May his name be a blessing," said the woman with not a little agitation.

"My apologies," Yosef said. "And condolences. Goodbye."

Yosef put down the phone and marked the row in the spreadsheet with an X. One Rabbi Menachem down, thirty-five to go. He dialed the next number.

A smattering of guilt marred his anticipation. There would be hundreds of Davids, though not quite as many Yannais and Nehorais. Each call nibbled at Dry Bones Society funds, and each minute on the phone was a minute stolen from his duties as the Society's first full-time salaried employee. But he had to try. The resources invested in this quest would yield dividends infinitely valuable for the Society and for humanity as a whole. The Messiah was out there somewhere, and Yosef must find him.

"Yes?" The man on the phone sounded young and energetic.

Yosef's heart skipped a beat. "Rabbi Menahem Azriel?"

"This is he." The voice turned suspicious.

"My name is Rabbi Yosef Lev of the Dry Bones Society. Have you heard of us?"

"I study full time," said the voice of Rabbi Menachem Azriel, a note of evasion sneaking into his voice. "I don't have money to spare."

Many career Torah scholars lived off government stipends. If they were caught working off the books, they were likely to lose their stipend and receive draft papers from the IDF.

"I'm not collecting donations. I just want to ask you—"

"Whatever you're selling," the voice interrupted, "I'm not interested."

"I'm not selling anything. Please, just listen. The Resurrection has started. You might have heard about us on the news."

A silent, pregnant pause. "Ahh, yes," said the voice. "I'm glad you called."

Yosef's heart threatened to stop beating. God had guided his hand, like Abraham's servant at the well of Haran, and led him to the young Redeemer on only his second attempt!

"I have a message for you," the man continued. Yosef stopped breathing too. Then the voice on the phone yelled and Yosef jumped. "Go to Azazel, you satanic bastards, and don't call me ever again!"

The line went dead.

Yosef rubbed his ear, which still rang with abuse. He marked the second row of the spreadsheet with an X and moved the cursor to the next.

The door of the office opened, and Yosef froze at the laptop, a criminal caught red-handed. "Yes?"

Samira smiled at him from the doorway, wearing a green *hijab*. Although eligible for an identity card, she had remained behind to man the call center. Members of her former family worked at the Ministry and she feared their wrath should they spot her.

"Rabbi Yosef. A man is here to see you."

Had Reverend Adams returned to check on his investment? Yosef had hoped to hand over their dealings with the Flesh and Blood Fund to Moshe. How did the reverend always know when Yosef was alone in the office?

The man who stepped up beside Samira, however, was not Reverend Adams. He wore an impeccable suit, a spotless bowler, and a well-trimmed, stately beard. "Reb Yosef," Rabbi Emden said. "Hello, my old friend." His pearly teeth sparkled. "How good it is to see you again."

CHAPTER 30

That morning, Noga feared for her life. The old, beaten-up car barreled down a bumpy, winding road at breakneck speed. Through the dusty window of the backseat, stony hills rose and fell as the vehicle snaked through Samaria, the Wild West north of Jerusalem.

A storefront with Arabic signage whizzed by, then a donkey led by a man wearing a *kaffiyeh*. A sign at a crossroads pointed right to Ramallah. Were the holes in the signpost the work of rust or bullets?

The Arab in the driver's seat had a thicket of black hair and stubble on his cheek. He had not bothered with a seat belt and drove as though he had not yet discovered the brake pedal.

Hannah sat beside her and gripped the armrest. She had picked up Noga that morning on Jaffa Road and driven north past French Hill. Passing the army checkpoint, she had pulled up on the side of the road where the old car with blue Palestinian plates waited. After Hannah introduced the Arab driver to Noga as Khalid, her "new friend," the two Israeli women had climbed into the backseat.

The car rounded another bend in the road that tied Noga's stomach in a knot.

A few years ago, three Israeli teenagers—Eyal Yifrach, Gilad Shaer, and Naftali Fraenkel—had hitchhiked home from the Etzion Bloc south of Jerusalem. The car had yellow Israeli plates, but when the driver veered from his declared destination of Ashkelon, Gilad called the police hotline on his mobile phone. The tape of the call ended with shouting in Arabic and automatic gunfire. Three weeks later, a search team located the boys' corpses in an open field north of Hebron.

Noga gripped the torn upholstery of the backseat. She hoped that Hannah knew what she was doing.

"Here," said Hannah. She handed her a piece of black cloth with a large hole at the bottom and a smaller one at the front. A hijab. She had got to be kidding.

"Put it on," she said. She had already donned her own black headdress, which covered her head and shoulders and exposed only her face. The secular academic and bra-burning feminist looked like an old beggar woman. "If anyone sees that we're Jewish," she added, "people could get killed."

Yes, Noga thought. *Us!*

She put the hijab on, which felt lighter than it looked and created a very frail sense of security.

A hilltop with the tidy red roofs of a Jewish settlement rose in the distance and then disappeared as they turned right. The car climbed a dirt road among scattered stone houses and then halted in a cloud of dust inches from a large olive tree.

Khalid got out and strolled into the Arab village, and the women followed.

A little Arab girl chased a hula hoop, barefoot in the dust. Three Arab men glared at the two women from a cement porch. A number of shanties of corrugated iron leaned between the houses. Noga's theory about the Jewish roots of Palestinian Arabs seemed even more ridiculous on the ground. Nothing seemed farther removed from the Jewish city blocks and suburbs of Jerusalem and Tel Aviv than this primitive village community. She wanted to leave the place right away.

"Hannah," she whispered. "I think I might have misread the data."

"Shh. We're there."

Khalid stood at the threshold of an old stone hovel. Hannah pushed through the door of overlapping curtains and disappeared within. Noga glanced at their Arab guide, who scanned the surrounding hills, his mouth tight. Was he guarding them against hostile Palestinians or making sure there were no witnesses to alert the authorities as to the whereabouts of two abducted Israeli women?

With no choice but to follow Hannah, she pulled the curtains apart and stepped inside. The interior looked more like a tent than a stone house. Carpets covered the floor and walls and formed a low canopy overhead. In the corner, a young Arab woman in a flowing burka tended a tin pot on a gas burner, which filled the air with the aromas of lentils and onions. Noga almost didn't notice the old man on the rickety chair. He sat very still in a thin hand-spun gown, his eyes closed, gnarled hands on his lap, a brown length of cloth wrapped around his head.

She joined Hannah on a low bench at the old man's feet. Khalid crouched beside the old man, touched his shoulder, and whispered in his ear. The old man stirred and glanced at the visitors through rheumy eyes.

"He's the patriarch of the village," Hannah whispered in Noga's ear. "That's his great-granddaughter in the corner. Khalid," she said to their guide. "Please ask him to tell us what you told me."

The Arab whispered in the old man's ear again. The old man spoke in a soft frail voice, his thin lips trembling. Noga didn't understand the man's Arabic, but she didn't need to.

"My mother," Khalid translated, "would light candles every Friday at dusk. I never knew why. One day, when I was a young man and already a leader of the clan, my grandfather became very ill. He called me to his bedside. 'Khalid,' he said. 'The time has come for you to learn the truth. Pass this secret to your grandson, as my grandfather did to me.'"

The old man's breath came in short, quick gasps as he re-lived the memory.

"He asked me to come close so he could whisper in my ear. 'Our clan,' he said. 'All of us. We are Jews!'"

CHAPTER 31

Ahmed staggered down a dirt road in Silwan. A woman in a hijab grasped the hand of her young son and crossed to the other side of the street. He must look like a monster: his hair gray with dust, his clothes rigid with dirt and dried sweat, and reeking of garbage.

Hunger had drawn him from his dry hillside tomb to the trash bins at the edge of the suburb. No longer fearful of Boris or his henchmen, he climbed into the large bins and scavenged for food. He gobbled moldy bread crusts and scraped bits of oily tuna from discarded tins. He emptied the last drops of cola and water from old bottles and cans into his parched mouth.

He felt like a monster too. Anger simmered in his belly. Nobody cared about him. His father had abandoned him years ago, and now his own mother had forsaken him for a new life of comfort and prestige.

His rage focused on neither of them, though. Only one person occupied his mind now: Hasan. His cousin, with his wavy dark hair and easy, careless gait, had pushed him to *istishhad* by threatening dishonor and promising Paradise. Hasan had arranged the mission and sent him to his death.

Ahmed pounced on a little boy on the street and grabbed him by his shirt. "Hasan Hadawi," he demanded, taking out his frustrations on the wide-eyed bystander. "Where is he?" He already knew the answer. Hasan lived in Ramallah, out of reach of penniless, filthy monsters. To his surprise, the boy pointed up the hill. "The garage," he said. Ahmed loosened his grip, and the boy slipped away and fled.

Hasan was in Silwan. Ahmed climbed the dirt road, his muscles tensing. Damas had been right: Paradise was a lie, and now Hasan was going to pay. Ahmed would clamp his hands around Hasan's neck and squeeze, and as his life's breath slipped away, he'd ask him why. Why had he deceived him, why had he destroyed Ahmed's simple, worthless life?

Music echoed off the haphazard cinderblock apartment buildings as he rounded the hill—a song with a sensual maqsoum rhythm.

As the road curved, a cement hangar came into view. The music carried, loud and clear, from the speakers of a yellow topless sports car that bathed in the afternoon sun. A bass guitar thrummed while a synthesizer climbed and fell playfully, and Dana Halabi sang.

Ahmed's mother had banned the provocative Kuwaiti diva from her household. The man who slouched in the driver's seat of the Mercedes had no such qualms. His wavy hair pressed against the headrest and his legs crossed at the ankles over the dashboard.

Ahmed padded toward the car, acid boiling in his belly, his fingers twitching.

"*Hos hos hos,*" Dana Halabi sang. Shh, shh, shh. "*Bos alaya bos.*" Look at me, look.

In the hangar, two scruffy thugs bent over a backgammon board, immersed in their game.

In the car, the man's head wobbled to the beat. An iPad lay on his lap, and on the screen, the young singer belly danced in a skimpy pink dress. She lay on a bed and sent meaningful glances at the camera. Then she posed on the deck of a yacht, gyrating her hips and hosing the vessel down, and drenching her clothes in the process. Ahmed could smell the man's cologne. He had the same wavy hair as Hasan, but longer and with strands of gray.

Shh, shh, shh. Look at me, look.

He reached out his hand and tapped him on the shoulder.

The man twisted around to glance at Ahmed and shrieked. The iPad flew into the air, landing on the passenger seat, and the music cut out. The man dived over the door of the car into the dirt, where he curled into a little ball of fear in the dust and shielded his head with his forearms.

Ahmed blinked in disbelief at the terrified man at his feet. Then he laughed.

The man peeked between his raised arms. His hair had streaks of gray and he had lines on his forehead, but the man was indeed his cousin. Hasan scuttled away, toward the two thugs who approached the commotion, then got up, straightened his loose white-collared shirt, and squinted at the dust monster. "Ahmed, is that you?"

Ahmed wiped the tears from his eyes as his laughter subsided, and nodded.

Hasan laughed too. He leaned on his knees and caught his breath. "*Halas*," he said, "you almost gave me a heart attack." He walked over and embraced his cousin. "It's OK, boys," he told the confused thugs. "This is Ahmed, my little cousin." He rubbed Ahmed's head.

The thugs shrugged and returned to their game.

Despite himself, Ahmed enjoyed the reunion with his cousin. "Were you expecting me?"

Hasan's smiled faded. "Not you in particular," he said. "But one of the martyrs was bound to turn up. The dead are rising. It's on the news."

"The dead are rising?" The words pushed all other thoughts from Ahmed's mind. He was not alone.

"More each day. They hang out at Clal Center." The dead were rising and they had a meeting place.

Hasan wrinkled his nose. "Man, you smell bad. Let's get out of here." He waved at the passenger seat. "Step into my office."

Ahmed walked around the sports car and got in. He needed to learn more about the rising dead.

Hasan pressed a button and the engine purred to life.

Cool air blew in Ahmed's face. He spotted a water bottle inside the door. "May I?"

"Go ahead."

He downed the bottle of clean cool water in one long gulp.

The Mercedes cruised down Silwan, climbed the City of David, and hugged the walls of the Old City. The road dipped down again as they passed Mount Zion.

"Nice car," Ahmed said. He had never sat in a sports car before. The leather seats cushioned his body in a soft embrace. Ahmed had blown himself up but his mother had gotten the palace, and Hasan had inherited Paradise. The anger simmered within again.

"Latest model," Hasan said with pride. "Bluetooth. GPS. The works."

"The suicide business pays well."

Hasan did not notice the bitter edge to Ahmed's voice. "It has its perks," he said. "Not as glorious as you *shaheed*s."

"If suicide is so glorious, how come you never tried it?"

"Me?" He seemed truly surprised at the question. "Nah. We each have a job. Mine is to find and dispatch guys like you. Yours is to blow up."

The engine growled like a tiger as the Merc crossed the valley of Ben Hinnom, then accelerated up Hebron Road.

Hasan seemed to relax more as they drove. Had his cousin wanted to treat him to a ride and a private chat or to remove Ahmed from his home turf? He parked at the Haas Promenade overlooking the Old City and eyed Ahmed. "You look like crap."

The questions that had crowded Ahmed's mind over the months surfaced again. "Did I kill many people?"

"Lots." Hasan clapped Ahmed on the shoulder. "Don't look so sad. You did well. Sons of pigs and monkeys, the lot of them. Killers of prophets. You showed them. You're a hero."

Ahmed didn't feel like a hero. The gastric juices bubbled in his stomach. "Aren't you going to ask me about Paradise— about my palace and wives?"

Hasan chuckled and lowered his eyes to the steering wheel.

Then Ahmed understood. "You knew all along, didn't you? It's all lies. There is no Paradise."

"Quiet," Hasan said. He looked over his shoulder. "You can't go around saying things like that. It sounds like heresy, and you know what happens to heretics around here."

"I want my life back."

"You can't. You must never go back to Silwan."

Ahmed's suspicions had been on target. "Why not?"

"You're a *shaheed*. You're a hero. You died for the faith. Your sins are forgiven. All the little boys want to be like you. The little girls too. You can't come back from Paradise and say 'I want a refund.'"

Ahmed lost his ability to speak. *He doesn't believe. He sends boys and girls to die on the streets but he doesn't believe his own promises of eternal reward.*

As a little boy Ahmed had received a plastic Kalashnikov for his birthday. A martyr's death had seemed so noble and just. Death would turn him into a superman. And now Hasan wanted him to help cover up the lie.

"How am I supposed to live?"

Hasan looked him in the eye. "I have another belt. My last one. When they built that wall we had to move to knives and vehicle attacks."

Had he heard correctly? "You want me to die again?"

"Think of it, cuz. You'll be a *shaheed* twice over. Nobody has ever done that before. You'll be the father of all *shaheeds*."

"You're crazy." Hasan had aged since their last meeting, but he had not learned anything.

Hasan gave a short laugh. "What else are you going to do?"

Ahmed had no answer to that. He opened the door and got out.

"Listen to me," Hasan called after him. "It's the only way. Hey, where are you going?"

"To a better place," Ahmed said, and he walked away.

CHAPTER 32

Yosef closed his laptop. He felt the urge to offer the padded manager's chair to his visitor. On the other side of Moshe's desk, Rabbi Emden sat ramrod straight but said nothing.

"Some coffee, Rabbi Emden?"

"No, thank you."

Why had his mentor visited him and why, of all places, at the Dry Bones Society, the society that, according to the Great Council, was in league with the unholy Other Side? Did he intend to pressure Yosef into abandoning the Dry Bones Society as he had pressured Minister Malkior?

Yosef dug his fingertips into the armrests. He believed in their cause, reverends and all.

The distinguished rabbi removed his bowler hat, lowered his eyes to the desk, and pursed his lips. He looked humble, even contrite. "I owe you an apology, my friend, for not reaching out to you since our meeting with the Great Council."

Whatever Yosef had expected, it had not been an apology. "There is nothing to forgive," he said. "You could not associate with us after their verdict. I understand that."

"Do you?" Rabbi Emden gave him a quick, penetrating look. "I failed to return your calls, even though I knew of your troubles at the school. When you needed a friend most,

I did nothing."

Yosef winced at the memory. A posse of Chassidic men had delivered the ultimatum to his house and then, the next day, the letter of dismissal from Rabbanit Schiff, the principal of Daas Torah Primary where Yosef had taught second grade. His support of the friendless resurrected had cost him his livelihood, and ostracized his family from much of the ultra-Orthodox community.

Would Rabbi Emden entice Yosef away from the Society with the offer of a new job?

"I want us to be friends again," the rabbi continued. "Can we be friends?"

"Of course!" Yosef's grip on the armrest slackened. The rabbi had checked his politics at the door and entered in his personal capacity. He had come to build bridges, not demolish them, and Yosef snatched the extended olive branch like a drowning man clamping onto a lifesaver in a stormy sea. Messianic questions weighed him down and he longed for the buoyant certainty of the rabbi's guidance.

Rabbi Emden produced a grateful smile. "Thank you."

A mad hope sprung in Yosef's heart. Had the distinguished rabbi decided to join their struggle? Had he seen the righteousness of their way? His optimism rocketed skyward. Had a messianic sixth sense alerted the rabbi to Yosef's secret phone calls? Had Rabbi Emden arrived to unmask his true identity and take over the reins of the Society as the rightful Heir of David?

"Now that we are friends again," Rabbi Emden continued, "I must confess that I am in need of your help."

Yosef's anticipation deflated like a balloon. What could the esteemed rabbi possibly need from him? "Of course," Yosef said. "Anything!"

The rabbi ran his tongue over his lips. "I understand that the Dry Bones Society has joined with Upward." The turn to party politics sank Yosef into murky confusion, which must have registered on his face, for Rabbi Emden elaborated. "Isaac Gurion's new party."

"Yes, that is true," Yosef said.

"Gurion is a godless man," Rabbi Emden said, "and a sworn enemy of religion. We cannot let his party take hold of the country."

"What are you asking, Rabbi?"

Rabbi Emden's eyes sparkled. "Join us, Yosef."

"Join who?"

"Torah True!"

Torah True, the leading ultra-Orthodox party, obeyed the Great Council. Torah True had convinced Minister Malkior to renege on his agreement with the Dry Bones Society, only to be double-crossed, in turn, when Gurion had entered the fray.

"I don't understand," Yosef said. "The Great Council called us the *Sitra Achra*. Now the Council wants to join forces with demons?"

"Not demons," Emden said, and gave a good-natured chuckle. "*Demon*-strators. The sages of the Council saw your protest before Knesset and have heard of your suffering. A host of Jewish souls such as that surely contains sparks of holiness."

"And now they have the vote." The words slipped out Yosef's mouth without passing his brain. How dare he question the Council's integrity? Shmuel's sarcasm had rubbed off on him.

Emden lowered his eyes again but didn't seem to take offense. "You are right, of course. This is politics. We cannot let the secularists rule the country. They will desecrate the holy Sabbath, and dishonor the Torah. The voting box is the only way to safeguard Tradition."

"And," Shmuel's voice said in Yosef's mind, "to keep the money flowing into the Council's coffers." The man across the desk was not truly a friend, only another politician.

Yosef studied the chipped edge of the wooden desk. He had lost his job, his unquestioning belief in the rabbinate, and now his role model. Shaking his head, he said, "Gurion got them the vote. The Society won't turn on him now."

"Then give them a reason, Yosef. You are the spiritual leader of the Dry Bones Society. Guide them to the side of holiness. You have the power—wield it. This is your religious duty. Do you want the government to fill with Torah sages or pork-*fressers*?"

Yosef stared at the desk. "I've met many resurrected people," he said. "Not all are religious. Some aren't even Jewish. God seems to like them all the same."

"Nonsense!" Emden's patience was wearing thin, but he returned to his cajoling tone. "Don't turn us down, Yosef. This is your last chance at redemption."

Yosef squeezed the armrests. "That isn't the redemption we've been waiting for."

The smile fell from Emden's face. He collected his hat and stood to his full height. "I came to speak with you as a friend," he said, placing his hat on his head. "Friends treat friends with kindness and consideration. But reject that friendship, Yosef, and the gloves will come off."

CHAPTER 33

Noga's coffee cup trembled in her hands as she sat opposite Hannah in Café Hillel on Emek Refaim. After the Samarian village, they had visited an Arab settlement in Judea where they had heard a similar confession, and long after the two Israeli women had left the West Bank, the revelations still shook them.

The discovery burned inside her, demanding that she run through the streets to share the news. So this was how Archimedes must have felt. At least she hadn't been lazing in a hot tub when the breakthrough had hit. And she still had a few questions to answer before she'd run naked through the streets of Jerusalem.

"We need to write a paper," Hannah said, infected, apparently, by the same urge. She stared into space and sipped her coffee. "The country has to know. The *world* has to know. This changes everything."

"I still don't understand how it can be," Noga said. She kept her voice low, so as not to be overheard by the couple at the next table. "Entire Arab villages, entire tribes—how can they be Jewish? It's too convenient, too easy. It doesn't make any sense."

Hannah leaned in. "There's a precedent. In the fifteenth century, Jews in Spain were given a choice: convert to Christianity or die. Thousands converted rather than leave the country where their families had lived for centuries. But many of these forced converts remained Jews in secret, and the Spanish Inquisition hounded these suspected *Marranos*, burning them at the stake."

She took another gulp of coffee. "Israel, Palestine, Judea, Samaria—call it what you like. Jews have lived here for over three thousand years. After King Solomon's death, the nation split into the Kingdom of Israel in the north and the Kingdom of Judah to the south. The Assyrians conquered the northern kingdom in 722 BCE, exiling those Ten Tribes and scattering them throughout the ancient world."

Noga thought she saw where Hannah was going. "But," she said, "if they're the Ten Lost Tribes, they should be somewhere else, not here in Israel."

"That," Hannah said and smiled, "is what most people think, and in this case most people are wrong. When we look closer at the historical record, we see a different picture. The Assyrians didn't exile entire nations, only the ruling elite—the powerful families and leaders who could coordinate rebellions and national revivals. They didn't bother with the simple folk—the farmers, villagers, and the poor."

The pit in Noga's stomach opened again.

Hannah continued. "Khalid's ancestors claim to have been here for many centuries," she said. "Before the British, the Ottomans, even the Crusaders and Muslims. When the Muslims invaded in the seventh century, they gave the native Jews the same ultimatum that the Spanish had: convert or die. Like the *conversos* in Spain, most chose to stay in their ancestral homeland and convert to the dominant faith in public, while still safeguarding their traditions behind closed doors."

She placed her coffee mug on the table. "Genes don't lie, Noga dear. They are Jews."

"The Ten Lost Tribes," Noga said, as though in a trance.

Hannah nodded. "People have been searching for the Lost Tribes across the globe when they were right here all along, under our noses."

Noga abandoned her coffee. She should feel elated. Hannah had vindicated her research. With one logical connection, they had discovered the elusive Ten Lost Tribes and traced a path toward lasting peace in their time. But this boon for the Jewish People spelled disaster for her personal life. *Why me? Why now?*

Hannah emitted a brief ironic laugh.

"What?"

"It's funny," she said. "According to an old Jewish tradition, the Ten Lost Tribes are destined to return at the End of Days, or the Messianic Era." She waved her hands in the air to express her disdain for fanciful ancient superstitions and chuckled again. "And guess who is supposed to rediscover them?"

"I know that one," Noga said, surprising her mentor. She had uncovered that factoid a few months ago, when she had researched the End of Days in order to better understand a cute but delusional patient she had met at the Shaare Zedek Medical Center. Her heart squirming, she said, "Elijah the Prophet."

CHAPTER 34

A rush of déjà vu made Moshe's skin tingle. Once again, he stood under the *chuppah* canopy on the grassy knoll between the Ramat Rachel Hotel and the event hall.

A trumpeter played the Carpenters' "We've Only Just Begun" as the sun sank behind the buildings, casting a soft golden glow over the long white carpet that ran between the rows of chairs dressed in white. The same venue, the same band, the same bride and groom. Savta Sarah's catering too. He might have traveled back in time to his first wedding eight years ago.

Only the guests were different. They trickled in from the buffet gardens and filled the rows of chairs. Not Galit's extended family like last time—her parents and brother had not been able to get on a flight from New Jersey in time—but the familiar faces of the Dry Bones Society. The unfamiliar faces belonged to the many VIPs of the Upward party list. The sheer number of guests had forced Moshe to opt for a wedding hall instead of the quiet home ceremony Galit would have preferred.

Isaac Gurion settled in the front row, cocktail in hand, beside a well-powdered Mrs. Gurion, and surrounded by an entourage of assistants and bodyguards. He nodded at Moshe and winked. The well-connected politician had twisted a few arms in the Chief Rabbinate to expedite the marriage permit.

Moshe inclined his head and smiled. Rabbi Yosef shifted on his feet under the *chuppah* and filled the wine glass on a side table. This was the first wedding ceremony he had conducted and his nerves were showing. Rafi and Shmuel, Moshe's witnesses, hovered at the edge of the wedding canopy. Rafi was doubling as his best man, the role that Avi had filled at Moshe's first wedding.

Times had changed. Only two months ago, Moshe had rushed to Ramat Rachel to stop Avi from marrying Galit on this very spot. Would Avi try to disrupt his wedding tonight?

Moshe scanned the crowd for the old thorn in his side. Spotting no intruders, he glanced at his new gold watch. The ceremony should have started five minutes ago. *Where was she?* Galit had left Avi waiting under the *chuppah*—would she stand Moshe up as well? He had lost her before without warning. Would that bolt of lightning strike him down twice?

Moshe adjusted his blue suit jacket and tie and dismissed the concern. *Don't be paranoid.*

On cue, the trumpeter played a new song, a traditional wedding ditty, and there she was. Galit stood at the end of the white carpet in her elegant white evening gown. She smiled at him through the wispy veil. Little Talya led the way in a frilly bridesmaid's dress, strewing rose petals from a miniature wicker basket. Moshe blew his daughter a kiss and she smiled from ear to ear.

Galit climbed the steps of the *chuppah*, beaming at him through the veil, and circled her groom, the train of her dress sliding over his shoes.

For all the similarities, this wedding was different. The bride and groom were older and wiser. Moshe was, literally, a new man. But the differences ran deeper than mere time passed. He had almost lost her, he had fought against all odds to win her heart again, and the effort had thickened the tendrils of love that bound them together. They were one living organism. Nothing would part them again.

Behind the rows of seated guests, Irina stood and smiled

beside her Russian friend. With his ponytail and bulging biceps, Alex had set off mental alarm bells, but when Irina had told him how her new friend had helped out at the Society and arranged for her a pro-bono appointment with a neurologist, Moshe had relaxed. Irina could take care of herself. With all his recent political activity, Moshe had had even less time to devote to her and he was glad that she had Alex's support.

Talya sat on a chair, her legs dangling, beside a teary Savta Sarah. Moshe glanced at the rows of friends and well-wishers as Galit stopped beside him and her hand found his.

Rabbi Yosef started the ceremony, and Moshe savored the moment. *This is it. This is what life is all about—moments of joy with family and friends.* Those fleeting happy times drove everything he did—not the cameras or even the salary. He had to hold onto these moments and create more of them. Which reminded him—on Wednesday he was scheduled, finally, to see that cardiologist.

A large, dark figure passed behind the crowd and a sudden dread pulled at Moshe's insides. Had he seen the hulking form of King Kong, Boris's muscular henchman, or was the vision just a trick of his mind? Had the slave master sent his crony to exact revenge for Moshe's disruption of his graveyard recruitment? Moshe should have seen this coming.

He squeezed Galit's hand but she only smiled at him. His muscles tensed, ready to rush her from the *chuppah* to safety, while he scanned the mass of wedding guests. The oversized mobster did not march down the aisle toward them, nor was he lurking among the bushes.

Moshe wiped sweat from his brow and shivered. He'd have to do something about Boris and his slave machine, and not only in order to ensure the safety of his loved ones. While Moshe celebrated his own personal happiness, many innocents languished in chains.

He'd have a word with Gurion after the election. The politician had connections at the police, and cleaning up a criminal operation would carve another glorious notch into his political belt.

The ceremony continued without mishap. Moshe sipped the wine, placed the ring on her finger, crushed the glass beneath his heel, broke bread, danced and posed for photos, but throughout the evening the dread lingered in the shadows of his mind. Let Gurion handle Boris. Moshe had kicked a sleeping tiger once and lived to tell the tale. He should avoid a second confrontation or he could lose everything.

CHAPTER 35

"Are you sure this is the right place?" Irina asked.

The three-story apartment block on Rav Berlin Street did not look like a medical clinic, and the doctor's name did not appear on the façade of grimy Jerusalem stone. A row of tall rustling trees created a reassuring sense of suburban calm.

"This is his private consultation room," Alex said. He held the gate of the yard open for her. Despite the tough-guy exterior, Alex behaved like a gentleman.

They had spent a lot of time together since their first meeting at the Society last Thursday. He had accompanied her to the press conference on Sunday, and early Monday morning, he had worked with her at the Ministry of the Interior, helping applicants fill out their forms and find the right desk. Some of them could neither read nor write Hebrew. That afternoon, during their lunch break of packed sandwiches, he had offered to take her to see the doctor.

Her memory loss fascinated Alex, but not only her memory loss. His lips trembled when he spoke with her and he moved with a self-conscious stiffness, which whispered that his interest in her went beyond mere intellectual curiosity.

She smiled to herself and walked through the open gate, down the short path of flat stones, to the door of the building. Alex pressed the buzzer for apartment number one and the door clicked open. As the building was situated on a hillside slope, they had to descend a gloomy stairwell to get to the first floor. Their footfalls echoed in the dank and cramped space.

"Are you sure I can't pay him?" she asked. She had brought a few hundred shekels and a Dry Bones Society credit card just in case. Having no identity, she couldn't apply for an identity card and thus she couldn't register for state health insurance. Luckily, she had not needed a doctor since her return. In fact, during the past few months she had been so busy trying to survive and, later, helping new arrivals at the Society that the idea of consulting a neurologist had never crossed her mind.

"He's an old friend," Alex said. "And he owes me a favor."

Alex stopped at a door on the lower floor. No name. No number. He knocked, then entered and turned on a light.

They stood in a plain rectangular room. Sunlight seeped through slatted windows on one side and fell on two simple chairs of steel and plywood. Pale rectangles on the walls remained where once pictures had hung. The small square floor tiles reeked of disinfectant. In the remains of an old kitchen at the back, gas pipes protruded from the wall. Irina clutched her handbag to her chest. This was not your typical waiting room.

A door opened and a short man in a white cloak and thick black-framed spectacles glared at them. A bald patch glistened on the top of his head. He waved them inside without a word.

A large dentist's chair dominated the center of the chamber, and a tray of medical tools sat atop a long set of drawers. *That's more like it.* But the unusual mix of medical equipment gave her pause. Did neurologists use dentist's chairs?

"Sit," the doctor said in Russian. He was not a man of words.

She made for the dentist's chair and a layer of thick plastic sheeting crinkled beneath her sandals. This was probably the most unusual doctor's room she had ever visited, although, to be fair, she remembered nothing of other medical visits.

The doctor sat on a squeaky-wheeled chair and searched among his equipment. Alex leaned against the wall and folded his arms. She was glad he had come with her.

The doctor leaned over her. "Look up," he said. He flashed a light in each of her eyes.

"Alex tells me you're a neurologist," she said, in a lame attempt at small talk.

The doctor raised his eyebrows at her, so she pointed toward the set of drawers behind her. "The dentist's drill," she said. "And the chair." She had noticed many other long, pointed tools but didn't know their names.

Alex spoke. "Dr. V has many qualifications and many talents."

The doctor gripped her wrist and glanced at his watch. "Both involve extraction," he said, a crooked smile twisting his thin, chapped lips. "As a dentist, I extract teeth. Today we will extract memories. Ready?"

Irina inhaled a deep breath. Today was the day. Her first memory. Her first glimpse at her former life. She nodded.

"Good."

There was a click and a mechanical groan. The chair shuddered as it flattened to a reclining position.

The doctor grasped a round sticker attached to a thin wire and pressed the sticker to her right temple, then attached a second sticker to her left temple. The doctor arranged her hands on the armrest and a strap tightened over one of her wrists.

"Are you sure that's——?" she began but the doctor cut her off.

"For your safety," he said.

She glanced at Alex for reassurance and he nodded. The doctor buckled a strap over her other wrist and did the same for both her ankles. She couldn't move.

She said, "Is this is really necessary?"

The doctor straightened on his seat. "Old memories can be very traumatic. This way you won't injure yourself. Breathe deeply and stay calm. OK?"

Irina drew a long, deep breath and tried to relax. She was prepared to go through almost anything to get her memory back. The doctor had dodgy rooms and unorthodox methods, but he might be able to help her.

He turned on a lamp behind her. "I will show you a few objects, and you will tell me if they look familiar. OK?"

She nodded.

He raised his arm in the air. In his hand, he held a stuffed teddy bear.

She smiled. She had almost expected a dead fish or a writhing snake. "Nothing," she said.

The bear disappeared and he held up a poster of the Eiffel Tower. "No." She shifted on the chair. This would be easier—and far more comfortable—with a computer and without the straps.

The next item made her giggle. He held a kinky bra of black lace in his hand, while he scrutinized her eyes. She shook her head and stifled another giggle. Alex studied the floor.

The next few objects helped her overcome her giggle attack. A knife with a long, thick blade. A photo of a dingy alleyway with broken trash bins and shattered windows. What strange things to show her.

"No," she said for what seemed like the hundredth time. None of the objects or photos had registered in her memory.

The doctor glanced at Alex and Alex nodded his head.

"We will try another approach," the doctor said. He leaned over her and pointed beneath his right eye. "Look here. Good." He narrowed his eyes. "Don't take your eyes from mine. Don't speak or move until I tell you."

Hypnosis, Irina realized, with mild disappointment. The first attempts had failed.

"As you follow my instructions," he continued, "nothing

in the world can prevent you from falling into a very deep and pleasant sleep."

This probably wouldn't work. Had she ever undergone hypnosis? She didn't think she was the susceptible type.

"Now, take a deep breath and fill your lungs." He lifted his hand into the air and her lungs filled. "Now exhale." He lowered his hand and her lungs emptied. He repeated the procedure twice, her breath deepening each time.

She swallowed a yawn. The doctor was good. She felt very relaxed.

"I'm going to count from five down to one. As I do, your eyelids will feel heavy, drowsy, and sleepy. By the time I reach the count of one, they will close and you will sink into a deep hypnotic slumber. Deeper than ever before."

Whatever. She'd humor him. What did she have to lose?

He raised his hand above her head and pointed into the air. "Five," he said. "Eyelids heavy, drowsy, sleepy."

He lowered his hand a notch. "Four. Those heavy lids are ready to close." His eyes filled her mind. Only his eyes existed. She blinked.

"Three. The next time you blink, that is hypnosis coming over you." The hand dropped slowly. His eyes bored right through her.

The hand fell out of sight beside her head. "Two," the voice said. "They begin closing, closing, closing, closing, closing them, close them, close them. They're closing, closing, closing. One."

Fingers closed over her elbow. A hand grasped her head at the base of the skull and shoved her head forward. "Sleep now!"

Her eyes closed.

She waited.

Hearing nothing, she waited some more.

Fingers clicked and she opened her eyes. The doctor stood over her. Over his shoulder, Alex watched her. They said nothing for a while. *It didn't work.*

"Sorry, Doctor," she said. "I don't think I'm a good candidate for hypnosis." She sniffed the air. "What's that burning smell?"

The doctor didn't answer. He leaned in and plucked a round white sticker from her temple. She had forgotten about the wires. A wisp of smoke rose from the underside of the pad, which had charred to black. He detached the other pad and removed them from sight.

Strange. She hadn't felt any burning.

"Retrograde amnesia," the doctor said to Alex. "She truly remembers nothing of her former life." He spoke as though she wasn't in the room.

"Will her memory ever return?"

The doctor shook his head. "This is caused by a lack of blood flow to the right temporal lobe, the seat of long-term memory. It is usually the result of head trauma."

Alex nodded as though that made sense.

Irina spoke up. "But I haven't hurt my head."

The doctor turned to her. "Not now," he said. "Before your death."

"Oh. Right." She had received a blow to the head toward the end of her first life. That ruled out cancer as her suspected cause of death and pushed car accident to the top of the list. Or some other violent end. She shuddered, and suddenly she wanted very much to get far away from the doctor and his dingy consultation room.

The chair groaned and shuddered toward an upright position and Alex unbuckled the leather straps, then helped her out of the chair. He escorted her up the stairwell and out of the building.

Her temples itched. When she touched them, her fingers returned with a patina of dark, crusty flakes like burnt bread. Or singed chicken.

Alex held the gate open for her. "Disappointed?"

"I suppose."

He grinned. "Don't be," he said. He seemed to be in a good mood, despite the failed attempts at recall.

The prognosis hit her. "I'll never get my memory back,

will I?"

He gave her a sympathetic frown. "Look on the bright side. You have a new life. A clean slate."

Moshe had said the same thing to console her on her first day. Irina slipped her arm in his and they walked to Alex's car together. Men were strange creatures.

CHAPTER 36

Ahmed ignored the stares as he walked up Jaffa Street. He had shaken the dirt from his soiled clothes as best he could, but some passersby made faces and blocked their noses. His own nose had grown used to the stench of trash, and he wore his stiff clothes and foul smell like armor in enemy territory.

Israeli society had not always been enemy territory. He had worked among the Jews at the Rami Levi supermarket in Talpiot without fear. He had unpacked crates, mopped floors, and laid out fresh vegetables for customers to buy. Yigal, his boss, had joked around with him in Arabic, asked after his family, and let him take Fridays off. All that had changed the moment Ahmed had stepped onto a crowded bus and pressed the detonator hidden in his sleeve.

The tired façade of Clal Center loomed over Jaffa Street: two floors of large cement squares topped by thirteen more, all stained with soot. Dark bands separated the floors, windows dotted by air conditioning units. The old building looked like a prison. Once inside, he might not be able to escape. Would they kill him on sight to avenge their murdered friends and family, or torture him first? Or would they take him in as one of their own? Ahmed the killer had died. Was there hope for the new Ahmed?

The cramp in his stomach cast the deciding vote.

He crossed the street. A handwritten sign on the door read, "Dry Bones Society. Third floor." The resurrected met at Clal Center, Hasan had said, and they had selected a fitting name.

An arrow pointed the way inside. One look at the elevator convinced him to take the stairs, but the third floor corridor was quiet. Too quiet. Had Hasan sent him into a trap? Was this Dry Bones Society a second killing field for martyrs who refused to stay dead?

He passed a door with a sign that read, "Absorption Center."

"You," said a commanding voice and Ahmed jumped. An old lady poked out the door, stared at him, then waddled over. Her eyes grew very large behind her thick glasses. "Hungry?"

He nodded.

She grinned. "Follow me."

She led him to a large room within the Absorption Center. Steam rose from a long line of silver trays on a counter. The scent of cooked meat and rice almost overpowered him. His limbs trembled. The sight was too much. He wanted to charge ahead and bury his face in the food. Had he finally reached Heaven or was this another cruel trap? The food would disappear on touch. Or he would choke, the Jews having laced the delicacies with poison.

The old lady placed a clean plate in his hands. "Go on," she said. "It's kosher. *Glatt* kosher. The classes break for lunch soon, so dish up before there's a line."

Ahmed didn't need a second invitation. He piled chicken thighs, rice, and steamed vegetables on the plate, then added the juicy cuts of meat dripping with thick gravy.

"Easy does it," she said. "You can come back for seconds."

He shoved handfuls into his mouth, then settled for a table and cutlery. So far, he had not dropped dead. If the old crone had poisoned the food, he would enjoy a very tasty final meal.

The old lady poured him a tumbler of sweet juice, and sat down opposite. "What's your name?"

He paused mid-bite. Should he lie to his generous hostess? Even if she threw him out, he would have gobbled more food in the last few seconds than he had in the past few days.

He said, "Ahmed," trying and failing to mask his Arabic accent.

The old lady nodded and pulled out a mobile phone. "Hello, dear," she said into it. "Another one just came in. Yes. In the dining hall."

Had she called security? He shoveled food into his mouth faster in case he had to dash for the exit.

"I'm Sarah," she said. "You'll want to have a shower, trust me. There's plenty of donated clothes to choose from, and I expect you'll want to stay in the dormitory."

"Dormitory?" Had she offered him a place to live?

"One floor up," she said, and pointed at the ceiling. "Nothing fancy, but it's a place to stay and close to the Absorption Center."

A tear trickled down his cheeks. The old lady was willing to accept him, alive and whole; Ahmed had found a new home in the most unlikely of places.

"That is," she added, "until you can process your identity card and make your own way in the world."

He swallowed hard. Once his old identity became known, they'd cast him out for sure. He would have to avoid that.

The old lady peered at the door behind him. "There she is."

Ahmed heard soft footfalls and turned around. The figure that stood beside their table was not a security guard, but a pretty young woman. She wore a green hijab and gave him a demure welcoming smile.

"Ahmed," the old lady said, "this is Samira. She'll take care of you."

CHAPTER 37

Is this really happening?

A number of young professionals buzzed around Moshe Wednesday evening while he waited on a comfortable armchair in the Channel Two studio. One attached a microphone bud to his shirt. Another applied a makeup brush to his cheek. Yet others adjusted spotlights wrapped in umbrellas and positioned large mounted cameras.

Beside him, Dani Tavor reviewed a sheaf of papers on the conference table while an attendant styled his wavy gray hair. Liat Arbel sat next to him and gave him a brief smile. They looked older in real life, although, to be fair, Moshe had first seen the father-and-daughter duo on the small screen fifteen years ago.

Liat brushed a strand of hair from her face. "Nervous?" she asked him.

"A little."

She smirked. "We'll try to go easy on you."

Fat chance of that. The famous duo, Dani and Liat, were known to grill their guests on the weekly television panel like plucked chickens on a rotisserie. In his previous life, Moshe had fantasized about appearing on this Israeli answer to The Oprah Winfrey Show to discuss the unrivaled successes of Karlin & Son. Moshe's current reality had surpassed even that fantasy.

Heat up the grill. Moshe didn't mind. Negative publicity was publicity too, and he represented a non-profit that aided the weakest, poorest, most miserable minority in society. How bad a picture of him could they paint?

"Five seconds," said a man with a tablet computer and a wireless earpiece.

The makeup crew fled and the famous duo sat up in their chairs. Moshe did the same.

"Welcome," Dani said into the gaping mouth of a teleprompter camera. "Unless you've been living under a rock this past week, you will have heard of the wave of new immigrants that have reached our shores. Unlike other immigrants, however, these have arrived not from another country, but from another life, or, as some would say, another world. With us in the studio is Moshe Karlin of the Dry Bones Society, the organization that he established to cater to the needs of this new demographic of resurrected men and women. Welcome to the show, Moshe."

"Thanks."

Liat took over. "You've had to face a lot of opposition and not a few setbacks over the first few months, haven't you?"

"Yes," Moshe said. He'd have to move beyond monosyllables soon, and needed to find an excuse to plug the Society's toll-free donation hotline.

Liat continued. "Many doubted the truth of the so-called Resurrection, calling it a hoax. Until recently, the State didn't recognize your people or their rights."

"That is true," Moshe said, jumping on the opportunity. "In addition to the inherent trauma of coming back to life, they aren't able to function in society—to find jobs or get medical attention. Many still have no food or shelter. We rely heavily on donations to assist newcomers. Our volunteers visit cemeteries across the—"

"But now," Dani said, cutting him off, and Moshe felt the full force of his trademark piercing look, "you've had many successes. The Second Law of Return gave you citizenship and, it seems, preferential treatment at both the Ministry of the Interior and the National Insurance Institute, which now overflow with resurrected men and women applying for identity cards and health insurance. And, of course, there's your recent foray into politics."

"Yes," Moshe said. "Thank God, we've made significant progress."

"Thank God, you say. And yet you have joined with Isaac Gurion's new political party, Upward. Isaac Gurion is running a very anti-religious campaign."

Moshe took a sip from his complimentary bottle of mineral water and placed it back on the table. He had expected comments like that. "The resurrected come from all parts of society. Religious. Secular. Jewish. Arab. We help them all and we hope that our new friends will enable us to do more good."

"Do you think," Liat asked, "that the rest of us should feel... threatened?"

Moshe had not expected that one. He hoped his mouth hadn't dropped too low. "Threatened?" he repeated. "Why should you? Our society will only gain. Lost loved ones are returning home. We've added talent and working hands to the economy, not to mention their many years of experience and insight."

"Yes," Dani said. "But each job taken by a Dry Bone—for lack of a better term—is a job lost to a First Timer. The Ministry of the Interior has been closed to them for days, and our medical services have only so much capacity. Would ordinary citizens be right to feel disenfranchised?"

Moshe's fingers reached for the buttons of his shirt. The grill had heated up. "That's a temporary spike. The load on the Ministry will ease up soon enough. The State will need to invest in infrastructure, that's true, but that will only stimulate the economy further. Most industries in Israel suffer from a lack of workers, not unemployment. We'll no longer need to import foreign workers."

Dani didn't seem to have heard him. "And now," he said, "with your new political clout, it's understandable that a few people might be concerned."

Liat said, "Not just a few. Twenty thousand. See for yourself."

The screen built into the table lit up. Hordes of people crowded Kaplan Street outside the Knesset building. At first Moshe thought this was footage of the Dry Bones Society demonstration, but these protestors wore yellow shirts with black nuclear hazard signs. The placards in their hands read "Zombies Go Home!" and "Life is for the Living!"

"This came in an hour ago," Dani explained. "Citizens in Jerusalem have taken to the streets in protest."

Moshe didn't buy the spontaneous demonstration narrative. Someone had to have printed the yellow shirts and coordinated with the police officers, whose cruisers watched from the corner. A thicket of bearded men in the black cloaks of the ultra-Orthodox held their own picket signs aloft, which read "Demons Be Gone!"

"What are they chanting?" Liat asked.

Dani said, "Sounds to me like 'Undead Stay Dead!'"

One man stood above the crowd and led the chanting. The demagogue shouted hatred into a megaphone as the camera zoomed in.

Moshe shuddered and his face drained of blood. He knew the man with the megaphone, and so he knew who had printed the shirts, arranged the crowds, and turned the country against him. Their paths had crossed before only too often. His name was Avi Segal.

CHAPTER 38

Noga led the blindfolded man from the bedroom into the corridor. He didn't reach out with his hands to feel for obstacles. Eli trusted her completely. *Good.* She would need a double dose of that trust tonight.

"Almost there," she said. She led him to the dining room and struggled to untie the scarf around his head.

"So," he said, smiling, "are you going to show me why you locked me in the room for the last hour or what?"

"Patience, Smart Ass." The knot unraveled and the scarf fell from his eyes. "There!"

He blinked at the set table and lit candles.

Noga clasped her hands together like a Queen Ester who had entered the royal court uninvited, her life depending on the king's reaction. Raise the golden scepter and she lived. Otherwise, off with her head. Noga needed a good reaction right now, especially knowing what she had lined up for later.

"Wow!" he said. He turned to her and his eyes widened further. "Wow again!"

She had used his credit card and selected a minimalist red evening dress for the occasion. Matching lipstick and half an hour with a blow-dryer and voila! A romantic dinner for two. The phone call to Oshi Oshi had provided a platter of his favorite tempura sushi.

He seated her first, then poured wine into the two glasses. "My birthday is a few months away," he said.

"I know," she said. They split their takeout chopsticks and dug in.

"What's the occasion?"

"You'll see."

He grinned and dipped his sushi in the tub of soy sauce.

"I've got a surprise for you too," he said.

"You do? What kind of surprise?" His last surprise had almost wrecked their relationship in the secret garden of Shaare Zedek.

"That depends on you," he said. "What do you prefer— the Bahamas or the Caribbean?"

"Come again?"

"There's a big and beautiful world out there," he said. "We should see it. Let's take off a few weeks and go on a cruise."

"A cruise?" A thrill ran through her body.

"Mm-hmm," he said, chewing his food. "Norwegian and Princess do both lines. Which do you prefer?"

We're going on a cruise! "Um," she said. "Both sound good. You choose."

Noga had never dreamed of going on a cruise—expensive vacations had never made it onto the menu—but Eli was going to make those dreams come true all the same.

She slammed the brakes on her enthusiasm. If the evening went according to plan, the cruise would have to wait. Was she making a huge mistake?

In the hospital, Eli had been the closet lunatic, she the voice of reason. How the tables had turned! She had double-checked her facts and rehearsed their delivery. She had shed every ounce of doubt and made her decision. Eli would hear the whole truth tonight, and to implement her decision, she needed Eli's support, not just to hold her hand, but to play an active role, the role she had dismissed months ago as a delusion.

"Everything all right?"

She put down her chopsticks and wiped her mouth on an

Oshi Oshi napkin. She had to tell him now; the stakes were too high.

"Eli," she said. "Remember that time in the hospital, in the secret garden? You gave me a rose and a jewelry box."

"How could I forget," he said.

"You asked me to listen without interrupting. To hear you out."

"Yeah," he said. "And then you threw the box at my head and stormed out."

She managed a nervous smile. "I need the same of you tonight," she said. "The 'hear me out' bit," she added quickly. "Not the storming out."

He raised his eyebrows and the smile faded from his face. He had guessed what this was about. "OK," he said. He loved her and he'd listen, just as she had.

The Jerusalem skyline darkened through the French windows in the adjoining living room. No turning back now.

"I owe you an apology," she said. His eyebrows bunched with confusion. She had hoped that the opening would pique his interest and soften the impact of her words. "I went with Hannah to Samaria yesterday," she continued. "We met with the heads of Arab clans. Their traditions back up the genetic data from my thesis. They're Jewish and they know it. And now Hannah has figured out why."

Eli stopped chewing and watched her in silence.

"They're like the *Marranos* of Spain—they chose conversion over death or expulsion—but they've been here since the First Temple. Eli, they're the Ten Lost Tribes of Israel."

Eli blinked but said nothing, so she plowed on.

"You were right about the false messiahs. There were loads of them and they caused so much damage. But they all appeared during times of turmoil and suffering. Bar Kokhba after the destruction of the Second Temple. A whole bunch of messiahs during the Crusades. Sabbatai Zevi after the Khmelnytsky pogroms that wiped out a third of European Jewry. Those messiahs arose during desperate times. These are not desperate times. We live in a democracy with supermarkets and medicine, technology and reality TV. This time really *is* different."

He drew a deep breath and exhaled. Were the facts getting through?

"Two months ago in the secret garden, you told me that you were Elijah, that the End of Days was here and that we had a special role to play together. It sounded crazy then—it still does—and I walked out on you, I know. But what if you were right?"

He gazed at her with sad, tired eyes.

"I'm sorry I doubted you, Eli. But I'm ready to make that up."

Still not a word.

"Well?"

"Are you done?"

"Yes, I'm done." His calm silence had frayed her nerves and was driving her insane.

"I'm not going to throw anything at you," he said.

A nervous gasp of air escaped her lips. The rogue was playing with her, deliberately keeping her in suspense when he was behind her all the way.

"I'm not going to storm out either." His smile faded. "But I don't want you to suffer the way I did."

"Suffer?"

"I know what it's like. The certainty. The all-consuming obsession. It wasn't easy to break free. You saw that for yourself."

Noga exploded. "Have you heard a word I've said? These are hard facts—undeniable data points—not some conspiracy theory. My thesis supervisor wants to go public and write a paper."

"And in the past," he said, in an annoying singsong, "people sold their homes to join the Son of David in the Holy Land, only to lose everything." He paused to calm down. "I heard you out, Noga. Now, please, listen to me. Delusions are delusions because they seem so real. Let her publish her papers. Her colleagues will laugh her into isolation and her career will come to a sudden and embarrassing end. Don't make the same mistake I did."

The chopstick in her hand snapped in two. She didn't realize she had been holding it. She had expected resistance, but Eli was completely ignoring the facts. He wasn't thinking rationally. Or was he right—was she the irrational one?

"I know it's hard to hear this," he said, "so don't act on it yet. Please. Cool off for a week or two. Think it over. Don't stick your neck out for some rosy chance to save humanity. That never ends well."

CHAPTER 39

It started with a single tomato. Moshe had just sat down behind his desk at the Dry Bones Society Wednesday morning when Shmuel burst in.

"Disrespectful bastards!" he said, and waved his fist in the air.

Moshe jumped to his feet, then exhaled a long, relieved breath. The spatter of red that plastered the side of Shmuel's face and trailed down his shirt was a rotten tomato, not blood. "Who did this?"

"The horde downstairs."

Moshe made for the cubicles of the call center, where a press of Society volunteers peered out the windows. Down below, a dozen picketers danced in a circle on the wide sidewalk between the tracks of the light rail and Clal Center. Three of them stood beside a vegetable crate and hurled soft tomatoes at a woman who approached the entrance of the building.

Yesterday's demonstration had not blown over as quickly as he had hoped. "Kids," he told the volunteers dismissively. "Delinquents. They'll grow tired of it soon."

They nodded and exchanged embarrassed grins, then got back to their cubicles. Avi had sparked the protest but he didn't have the staying power for a protracted campaign. The news outlets would soon lose interest and return to their coverage of the elections. He hoped the demonstration would disperse soon. He had to leave for his cardiologist appointment in a half hour.

Moshe patted Shmuel on the shoulder. "I'm sorry you had to experience that," he said. "You can't create real change without making a few enemies. We must be on the right track." Shmuel nodded and headed for the bathroom to get cleaned up.

Moshe got back behind his desk and returned to the draft of his speech for the campaign event Gurion's team had arranged. Moshe was not scheduled to speak, but he should prepare for that eventuality.

"Isaac Gurion," he typed, "has been a friend to the helpless in their time of need."

He made a correction: a *true* friend.

He had just started to polish the language of the speech when the blare of a megaphone broke his concentration.

"They've taken our jobs," said the booming voice, and the crowd answered with an angry murmur. "They've invaded our lives."

Moshe knew that voice. He got up and returned to the window overlooking the street. "Dear God."

The scattering of demonstrators had grown into a swarm that covered the sidewalk. The volunteers at the window beside him were no longer grinning.

Avi stood on a wooden crate. "They're not natural," he said. "They're zombies. Undead. They feed on the living. They call themselves the Dry Bones Society. Well, you know what we do with dry bones? We snap them!"

The rabble cheered and punched the air with their fists. "Break the dry bones!" they chanted. "Break the dry bones!"

Moshe turned as the doors of the Dry Bones Society burst open, and three girls stumbled inside. Red juice and mangled tomato flesh plastered their faces, hair, and clothing, making them look rather like Hollywood zombies. Irina and a few others dashed over to help them.

"Everybody stay calm," Moshe said, uttering the words most likely to cause panic. "I'll call the police." He turned to Shmuel and whispered, "Lock the doors. Delay the shuttles for now." Shmuel nodded and got to work.

Moshe strode to his office and closed the door. He didn't call the police. He called Isaac Gurion.

"Isaac," he said, "they're outside the building. Masses of them. They're getting violent."

"I'll call the commissioner right away."

"Thank you."

Moshe eased back in his chair and thanked God for powerful friends. He listened to the chant of the angry mob below, unable to compose his thoughts, never mind his speech. He glanced at his golden watch, then called the cardiologist's office to defer his appointment.

When he heard the bleat of a police foghorn, he raced back to the window. Two cruisers blared their horns and cut through the crowd. Three uniformed officers got out of a marked van and pushed toward the wooden crate. They raised their batons and gripped Avi by the legs, toppling him to the ground.

Moshe smiled. Avi would wake up in a prison cell like Moshe had, only Avi didn't have powerful friends like Isaac Gurion to open the door.

"It was Avi, wasn't it?" Galit said over dinner at home that evening.

He had not wanted to trouble her with the details. Avi had caused her enough suffering.

She put down her fork. "I saw him on the news. I should have warned you."

"Warned me?" Talya sat out of earshot on the living room couch and watched a cartoon.

"He came by the house last week."

Moshe stopped chewing his spaghetti. "What did he want?" He knew the answer only too well. Avi wanted to take over his life again, the life he claimed Moshe had stolen from him, the hypocrite.

"I didn't want to alarm you," she said. "He's full of lies. Promise me you'll stay away from him."

"That shouldn't be hard. The police arrested him. He won't be bothering anyone for some time."

"Promise me you won't speak with him." Tears streamed down her cheeks. The ordeal had shaken her harder than he had expected. Good thing he hadn't mentioned the rabble's promise to break the dry bones. Or had she heard that on TV as well?

"All right," he said. "I won't." That promise should be easy to keep.

There came a loud knocking at the door. Moshe and Galit locked eyes.

"Don't."

"It's not him."

Moshe walked over to the door and put his eye to the peephole. He recognized the security guards and opened the door.

"Isaac, welcome. Please, have dinner with us."

Talya jumped up when the first dark agent stepped inside. "Is that a real gun?" she said and pointed at the shoulder holster that protruded from his suit jacket.

Isaac Gurion declined the dinner invitation. He wrinkled his brow and pouted his lips. "Can we speak in private?"

Galit herded a disappointed Talya upstairs to bed and the two men settled on the living room couch.

"Thank you for your help today."

"Don't thank me yet. I have some troubling news." The politician frowned, as though loath to share the tidings. "We did some polls, as we often do. The zombie meme is spreading."

"We're not zombies."

"I know that. But, as you can imagine, the idea arouses very unpleasant reactions in voters."

The walls wavered around Moshe, the same sense of vertigo he had experienced on the phone with Dr. Malkior's secretary the morning the minster had abruptly cancelled their press conference. The ground was slipping away beneath his feet again.

"How many voters?"

"Enough. We need to cancel your appearance at the event tomorrow, to distance the party from the Dry Bones Society for now. Until the negative sentiments settle. This is a temporary measure, I assure you."

"How long?"

"As long as it takes."

Was this goodbye? Moshe was developing a healthy distrust for politicians, and his tingling doublespeak feelers indicated that Gurion wasn't telling him the full story.

"I'm sorry, Moshe. I wish things were different. This isn't personal," he added. "It's just politics."

CHAPTER 40

Thursday morning, Ahmed strolled down a narrow lane of small, round cobblestones. Potted plants lined the storefronts of Mazkeret Moshe, the labyrinth of quaint alleys behind Clal Center. Leafy trees glowed in golden sunlight while birds sang songs of hope. Beauty filled the world when a pretty girl walked at your side.

After his first meal at the Dry Bones Society on Monday, Samira had shown him the storeroom of secondhand clothes, and then his new bed—one of four simple bunks in a cramped dormitory room. He placed his box of clothes beneath his bed and enjoyed the first steaming-hot shower of his new life. Samira signed him up for carpentry classes. She checked up on him often and they shared most of their meals together. He had made his first new friend and, although their Arabic chatter drew some concerned glances in the dining hall, Ahmed finally felt comfortable in his new home.

That morning he had summoned the courage to ask Samira to go with him for a walk. They had ducked out through the parking bay beneath Clal Center to avoid the hateful demonstrators on Jaffa Street, and strolled through the maze of old stone courtyards and enclosed gardens.

A warm, fuzzy sensation buzzed in his chest as they walked. He no longer looked over his shoulder for Damas or the Rottweiler. He had left his suffering far behind, and allowed his worries to fade away until only he and Samira remained, like Adam and Eve in the Garden of Eden.

Samira tucked a strand of brown hair into her hijab. "Shall we sit here?" She pointed to a wooden bench in a courtyard.

Water flowed from the mouth of a fountain shaped like a jumping fish, and splashed into the basin at the center of the yard. Stone rabbits crouched at the edge of the flowerbeds.

"I always wanted a rabbit," she said. "When I was young we never had any pets."

"Me neither."

The air filled with the sounds of bubbling water and whispering trees.

"It's so peaceful here," she said.

"Yes," he said. "It's good to get out, to get away from them." He chuckled. He shared his room with a crazy man who ranted in Old French and three sullen and bearded Jews. Ahmed kept to himself.

"Them?"

"You know. The Jews."

Her smile faltered, and his world darkened. He would do anything to bring back that sweet smile.

"I had a baby," she said. "In my old life. A little girl. But my husband was a jealous man. He forbade me to work or even to leave the house. He spread lies that I had... that I had sinned with another man. My father," she said. "My father..." She turned to the heavens and wiped a tear from her eye.

"It's OK," Ahmed said. "We don't have to talk about it." He could guess the end of the story. Arab girls disappeared all the time. Indecent girls. Arab men as well. Collaborators, all of them. Nobody talked about the honor killings but everyone believed the rumors of their guilt. They had deserved to die. But what if, like in Samira's case, the rumor was false?

"When I woke up," she continued, "I had nowhere to go. This was before the Dry Bones Society. Only Rabbi Yosef was prepared to take me in, a dirty, homeless Arab girl." She

447

looked Ahmed over. "And Moshe Karlin saved me from slavery, even though he didn't have to."

"Slavery?" he asked.

She glanced down and rubbed the palm of her hand. "A labor camp in Talpiot. We worked odd jobs for a few days. Our task master was a cruel Ethiopian."

Ahmed's heart skipped a beat. "An Ethiopian missing two fingers?"

Her eyed widened. "You know Damas?"

"I was his slave too!" They laughed.

Ahmed inhaled quickly, almost choking on fresh air. He had kept his past bottled up so tight, it felt good to open the lid and release the pressure. "After two months in that hell," he said, "I escaped. I slept in an old tomb for a week before I came here."

"You escaped?"

"Yes, like you."

"We didn't escape. Moshe bought our freedom with a lot of money. Aren't you afraid?"

Ahmed stretched his arms over the back of the bench. "They've given up on me by now."

She nodded her head but worry still cast a shadow over her features. She cared about him, and he wished that their walk would last forever.

"What about you?" she asked.

"Me?" He gave her a questioning glance and she lowered her eyes again.

"How did your old life end?"

A ball of dread lodged in his throat. After all the Jews had done for her, the truth would horrify her. He could make something up—that he had saved a child from a speeding truck, or even that he had slipped on a banana peel at work—but he did not want to lie to her.

"I can't... I don't want to talk about it," he said.

She nodded quickly and her eyes glistened again. "I understand," she said. "We don't have to talk about it." The hint of a terrible death had awakened her sympathy for him. No, she must never find out.

"This is a new life," she added. "A fresh start."

Ahmed liked the sound of that. "Yes," he said, that warm, fuzzy feeling returning. "A fresh start."

CHAPTER 41

Moshe's dreams shattered on the morning news. The screen mounted on the wall of the Dry Bones Society showed Isaac Gurion speaking into the microphone at the offices of his Upward party.

"I am excited to announce a new partnership," he intoned in his authoritative baritone. Avi Segal stood beside him in a green suit, a self-satisfied grin threatening to split his face in two. "Mr. Segal's presence high on our list is another sign of our commitment to the hard-working middle class—the salt of the earth and the core of our society."

Moshe folded his arms. His cheeks cooled. He should have seen this coming. The winds of public opinion had shifted and Gurion's "temporary distancing" from the Dry Bones Society had become—literally overnight—the new backbone of his election campaign.

"That double-crossing bastard," Shmuel grumbled beside Moshe.

But there was more. The camera zoomed out to reveal a clump of ultra-Orthodox rabbis onstage, grinning and stroking their beards. Among them, Rabbi Emden stood erect in his satin suit and tidy bowler, and flashed his pearly whites at the press.

"And," Gurion continued, "I extend an equally warm welcome to our new friends at Torah True. Together we will guard all that our country holds dear and keep back the unnatural scourge that threatens our timeless traditions."

"Hypocritical creep," Shmuel said. "Isaac Gurion in bed with the rabbis. Who would have believed it?"

"Stranger things have happened," Moshe said. He should have seen that coming too, but the double betrayal had added insult to injury.

He glanced at the assembled Society members around him in the call center. The chant of "Death to the Dead" drifted through the window from the street below, but softer than before. The numbers of the picketing mob had dwindled. Apparently, they had more important matters to deal with now such as campaigning for the elections.

Phone operators groundhogged the cubicle dividers, concern imprinted on their faces.

"No need to worry, my friends," Moshe said, loud enough for all to hear. "Calls are still coming in. Resurrected men and women still need our help and donors are still opening their checkbooks. Let's get back to work."

Heads disappeared into cubicles and Moshe turned to his management team. "Let's talk in my office."

"Are we in trouble?" Irina asked, when the door had closed.

Moshe perched on the edge of his desk. "Time will tell."

"At least we have the identity cards," Rabbi Yosef said, finding, as usual, the silver lining. "That was the main reason we joined with Gurion."

"I suppose you're right." Moshe tried to hide his disappointment. Gurion had whetted his appetite for more than mere citizenship. *Think of all the good you can do*, he had said. *You could make the world a better place.*

"Let's not be naïve," Shmuel said. "I don't think this Segal character is going to live and let live once he's in Knesset. Rights can always be revoked. We could lose everything we've gained with another stroke of a pen."

There came a knock on the door and a new volunteer

leaned into the room. "Sorry to interrupt," he said. Ben wore a black T-shirt and a pale, worried expression as he glanced at the room's occupants. "There's a problem at the Ministry of the Interior."

Moshe's heart lurched. *Here we go.* "Have they stopped issuing identity cards?"

"No," Ben said. "But they closed the special counters. 'No more special treatment.' Things are going to take a lot longer."

Moshe swallowed his sigh of relief. "Thanks, Ben. Let us know if anything else changes."

Ben nodded and closed the door behind him.

"See what I mean?" Shmuel said. "This isn't the end."

Rafi shook his head and scowled, but Irina clenched her jaw. "Forget Gurion," she said. "We'll find another partner. There must be other parties that will work with us. What about Malkior?"

Shmuel gave a short, mirthless laugh. "Gurion promised him the vice presidency. The Ministry of the Interior is in his pocket. The rabbis too and they hated us to begin with. And with all the bad press we've had, no one else will touch us with a ten-foot pole. We're stuck."

Once again, Shmuel was right. Their situation was hopeless.

Savta Sarah leaned against the large window of the office, her arms folded over her chest, and stared at Moshe. A smile curled the edges of her lips, and for a change he knew what she was thinking. Her steely nerve had rubbed off on him. Perhaps "hopeless" was not the right word.

"We have one other option," Moshe said.

He had the room's undivided attention. His suggestion was so bold, it required an introduction and a dab of drama.

He pulled his blue identity card holder from his back pocket and turned it over. "This is nice," he said. "It helps me open a bank account and wait in line for a doctor. But in the end, it just makes me a part of the system." He dropped the card back onto his desk. "And the system stinks."

He glanced at his team. "I've had enough of crooked politicians who change their values like underwear and create new parties every other day. I'm sick and tired of having to pull strings just to get society to respect my basic rights. And I bet voters are sick of all that too."

At the back of the room, Savta Sarah's smile widened.

"They deserve better. *We* deserve better. And this is where we can make a difference. We're not just a bunch of ex–dead people. We are the past and the present. Religious and secular. Jews and Arabs. Our lives ended and we can see them for what they were, warts and all. And from this new vantage point, we can build a better future. A future with integrity and dignity, equality and harmony." He smiled at Rabbi Yosef, who swallowed, no stranger to the themes of the messianic era. "To fix the mistakes of the past."

Moshe inhaled the magical hope his words had conjured. The promise of a bright new future hung in the air and glittered in the eyes of his audience.

"That's a wonderful speech," Shmuel said, breaking the spell. "But how are we going to replace the system without powerful friends—without *protekzia*?"

Here it comes. Moshe straightened on the edge of the desk. "By becoming our own powerful friend."

Savta Sarah beamed at him from the back of the room.

"I don't understand," Shmuel said. "You want us to run in the elections—independently?"

"Why not? We have a message and a platform. We have new members joining every day."

Shmuel laughed. "An election campaign is going to require a crap load of money."

"You're right. Luckily for us, we have a new supporter with very deep pockets." He winked at Rabbi Yosef, who swallowed again. The rabbi was still not comfortable dealing with Rev. Henry Adams and his New Evangelical Church of America. He'd get used it.

"But," Shmuel said, spluttering at the lunacy of the idea. "Even if we have the money and the numbers to win a few seats, elections are less than two weeks away. How are we supposed to throw together a winning campaign in two weeks? We don't have that expertise."

Moshe had hoped that Shmuel would raise that question. "As it happens," he said, "I know someone who will be perfect for the job."

"Oh, really? And where did you find him?"

Moshe grinned. "Who said anything about 'him'?"

CHAPTER 42

The renowned sage opened his eyes. A sky of clear, dazzling blue filled his visual field, framed by the branches of leafy trees and what appeared to be a tall monument. Large arcs rose high in the air to form a lattice of metal spires. Never before had he seen such a structure—an object of great architectural beauty and no doubt the life's work of a master smith—on any of his travels or among the pointy domes of Fustat.

He brought his hands to his face and studied them, wrinkled and weathered as usual. Then he touched his beard and face, his head, chest, and thighs. His physical body was intact but without a single shred of clothing. No funerary shrouds, not even a turban for his head!

This was not the World of Souls, the immortal spiritual realm in which Active Intellects merged with the Mind of God, for there were no bodies in that world of pure thought.

This must be the Resurrection. Ha!

The deduction amused him. His detractors had accused him of denying the resurrection of the physical body, despite his inclusion of the belief in his Thirteen Principles. Even after he had elucidated his views on the matter in his letter to the Jews of Yemen, still his critics condemned him as a heretic. *A disciple of Aristotle*, they said. *A rationalist.* This'll show them!

He turned over. The hard ground beneath him was covered in identical hexagons as gray and as smooth as fresh mortar. There was nothing new under the sun, as Ecclesiastes wrote, but the artisans of This World had honed their methods since his death.

He got to his feet and took a few wobbly steps.

How long had he slept in the dust? Had the Son of David arrived?

Was his son Abraham still alive? According to his son's calculations, the Redemption would begin only a few decades hence, and, although he had warned his son against Calculating the End, now he hoped that his son's predictions had been accurate.

A dull pain throbbed in his skull. Headaches resulted from excess humors in the body. As a respected healer, he would have prescribed peppermint tea and the avoidance of dairy products, but as he glanced about the stony hillocks, he found no tea decanters, only a street of black pitch and a table.

A young man with blond hair sat at the table, which was draped in a white sheet with blue hexagrams. The man looked up from a black tablet of shiny obsidian, smiled, jumped from his seat, and rushed over.

"Welcome, Honored Rabbi," he said in Hebrew, not Arabic. How curious.

The young man helped him into a fluffy cloak as soft as fine wool and as white as snow, and tied the garment with a white sash.

"Here." The man dropped two white pellets into the palm of his hand.

"What, may I ask, are these?"

"For your headache. Swallow them." He held out a glass of water. The glass was extremely thin and transparent, and crackled in his grasp like parchment but did not shatter. Curious! He washed down the pellets and returned the paperglass cup. No, this wasn't the World of Souls and yet it was not quite the world he had known either.

He cleared his throat. "Where are we?"

"Tiberias."

"Of course." He had instructed his son to bury him in the Holy Land. Abraham had fulfilled his father's wish, although he would have preferred Jerusalem. Perhaps the sultan had not permitted a burial in the holy city.

"And how long have I...?"

The man completed his question. "Been dead? Over eight hundred years."

"Eight hundred years!" His spirits sank. His son had passed from the world long ago. Or would he meet him again in this new life? "My son, Abraham...?"

The young man seemed to know what he was asking. "I'll ask the Head Office about him."

"Head Office?"

"Yes. In Jerusalem."

"The sultan's court?"

The man chuckled. "There is no sultan here. This is the Jewish State."

"The Jewish State!" Jews had regained control of the Land of the Forefathers. The Son of David had arrived. He cleared his throat. "Are you the Son of David?"

Another chuckle and a shake of the head. He held the black tablet to his ear, then quickly pocketed the item. "You have many questions," he said. He seemed to be reciting a well-repeated saying. "We'll answer them as best we can in time. Meanwhile, have some breakfast." He pointed to a box of pastries on the table. Then he wandered off to a nearby tree, pressed the black tablet to his ear, and talked to himself. Curious indeed!

Were the denizens of the future world all insane?

He recited a blessing and gave the pastry a tentative bite. It was very sweet but quite delicious. The pain in his skull subsided. He sat on a vacant chair of thin, shiny material that bent under his weight but didn't break, and was neither wood nor stone. Fascinating!

In the Days of the Messiah the laws of nature would remain unchanged. He had reached that conclusion after a lengthy analysis of the sources with the aid of reason and philosophy. Men could discover new materials, however, and learn to bend them to their will. Of course. He knew there must be a logical explanation.

The young man returned and placed the tablet on the table. "The Head Office doesn't have a record of your son, Rabbi, but he might still be out there."

"But you said that this Head Office is in Jerusalem?"

"I spoke with them. On the phone." He looked at the small tablet.

"Phone?"

Molding new materials was one thing, but conversing across great distances—how could that be?

The young man opened his mouth to explain but a loud roar made him glance at the road of black pitch. A roaring beast sped by in a flurry of noise and smoke. Not a beast—a chariot, for he had glimpsed a woman through a window of the shiny exterior.

"What...?" he mumbled to the young man. "But where is the horse?"

"There is no horse, Rabbi. That's a car. Don't worry about it, Rabbi. They'll explain everything at the Head Office."

"But how?"

The man scratched his head. "Think of a boat. A boat has no horse but moves on the water."

"Yes, but a boat has sails. The wind pushes the boat."

"Think of this as a boat on wheels."

Metal boats on wheels. Pellets that cured headaches in minutes. Paper-glass. Tablets that carried a man's voice between cities in an instant! What would they show him next—metal boats that floated in thin air?

Ha! Some ideas insulted reason and were truly impossible. The thought gave him some consolation. This world was not so different after all. It just needed a little getting used to.

"I would like very much to meet with a philosopher," he

said, "to learn the wisdom of this New World and—"

A sudden rumble from the heavens stopped him mid-speech. The noise, which resembled thunder, grew louder but the sky above was cloudless.

Then he saw it. High overhead, an object advanced through the sky—slender and with wings and a tail. Sunlight glinted off the shiny exterior. That was no bird.

"Don't worry, Rabbi. That's just an airplane."

"An airplane?" He had a bad feeling about this.

The young man scratched his head again. "It's like a metal boat that flies through the air."

Maimonides gasped and clutched at his beard. "Oh, no," he said. "Not that too!"

CHAPTER 43

Noga had never been in a stretch limousine before but she was quickly getting used to the idea. She relaxed on the soft couch of beige leather as the vehicle glided over speed bumps with ease and the workaday world of mere mortals zipped by through tinted windows.

Eli handed her a glass of champagne and raised his in the air. "Here's to a great vacation."

The yellow-orange liquid shifted lazily below the rim of the glass as the immense car moved. She sipped the bubbly dry wine. The champagne was a first for her and, she expected, many more firsts awaited her on this trip.

Two days after her failed romantic dinner at home, the tension in the air had dissipated. She had honored his request—her laptop remained closed on the coffee table and she avoided all talk of Jewish Palestinians and the End of Days—and she had not objected when their week of "cooling off" had become a two-week cruise on the Mediterranean, the nearest departure date available.

And so Noga found herself in a limousine to Ben Gurion Airport, where they would soon board a short flight to Barcelona. Life was good when you had free time and an unlimited budget. She could get used to that too.

Noga took another sip of wine. "Are you trying to impress

me?" she said. The wine, apparently, was having its desired effect.

Eli caressed her with his dark eyes and smirked. "Always. Have I succeeded?"

Sip number three. "Getting there."

They turned off Road Number One toward Ben Gurion Airport.

Her phone tinkled, so she placed her wineglass in the sunken holder on the side table of polished wood, and fished for her phone in her handbag. A text message had arrived from Hannah. "Need any help with the paper?" Noga turned off the screen and dropped the phone back in her bag.

"Everything all right?" Eli asked.

"Yeah," she said. "Nothing urgent."

Eli's arguments had made more sense as time passed. Some Jews and Arabs shared a common ancestor. Big deal. Some local Arabs believed they had Jewish roots. So what? In the Bible, Abraham had fathered both Isaac and Ishmael, before either Jews or Muslims existed, and all humans descended from one genetic Eve. Their common ancestor might lie much further back in history, and so long as the facts had a competing explanation, she had best keep her messianic speculations to herself. She'd reply to Hannah later. The paper could wait. A deal was a deal, and Noga was on vacation.

The car slowed as they approached the airport entrance road. The windows slid down and a security guard with a machine gun peeked inside, nodded his head, and waved them in. At a traffic circle, they turned toward Terminal One. That didn't seem right.

Noga was familiar with the airport. Her old classmate from Hebrew U, Sarit, had convinced her to fly with her to Eilat one weekend in search of eligible single men. Instead, they had shared the hotel pool with loud Arab kids and aging Japanese tourists.

"I thought we were going to Barcelona."

"Mmm-hmm."

"Isn't Terminal One for domestic flights?"

"Among others." Eli smiled his rakish smile.

Her heart sank. She was pretty sure that cruise ships did not pass through the Straits of Tiran to get to Eilat. A born planner, Noga did not like being kept in suspense. "I don't understand."

"Patience, Noga. You'll see."

The limo bypassed the parking lot and proceeded to a gate with another armed guard. After a short conversation with the driver, the guard opened the gate and waved them through.

Noga sat up on the couch. "Oh my God."

The limo drove along a wide expanse of tarmac and crossed two landing strips before pulling up beside a small jet, the kind she associated with celebrities and heads of state. A uniformed pilot and flight attendant stood at attention beside a short retractable staircase.

Noga flopped back on the couch. "OK," she said. "I'm impressed."

Eli chuckled. "My dear," he said, "we're just getting started."

CHAPTER 44

Thursday evening, Avi entered his parents' apartment in Wolfson Towers to the ululations of his mother. Even his father gave him a hug. "Well done, my son. Or should I say, Member of Knesset Segal!"

Avi savored the hero's welcome, then plopped onto the living room couch, leaned back, and clasped his hands behind his head. After being screwed over so many times, finally Avi had come out on top. *So this is how it feels to be Moshe.*

His mother brought out a tray of cakes and mint tea.

The only sour face in the room belonged to Ronen, Avi's brother. "So what ministry will Gurion give you?" he asked, his pale lips quivering with spite. "Chief Garbage Collector?"

Avi grinned. Ronen was jealous. For once in his life, his snooty older brother had to share the limelight, and his obvious discomfort was the icing on Avi's cake. "Who cares?" he said. "I'll get a fat salary and a pension for life, which is more than you get at the Philharmonic."

Followed the Segal family tradition, Ronen played the violin at the Israeli Philharmonic Orchestra, and he had secured the coveted post only thanks to his father's connections. The tone-deaf Avi had been a source of chronic disappointment to his parents. Until now.

"You need to serve two terms to get a pension," Ronen

shot back, "and I bet you won't last that long."

"Enough of that, boys!" their mother chided. "Let's all be happy for Avi. This is a wonderful achievement."

"Achievement?" Ronen seemed insulted at the suggestion. "He's only aping his dead old friend. Moshe throws a demonstration, Avi throws a demonstration. Moshe joins with Gurion, Avi joins with Gurion."

Avi wanted to deck Ronen right then and there. "Moshe is out," he shouted, "and I'm in. All right?" There was no arguing with that fact.

"Calm down, Avi," his mother said.

"For now," his brother added.

"Ronen!"

Their father leaned forward on the armchair and rubbed his hands together. "Don't settle for any of those minor ministries," he said. "Go for Defense, Finance, Interior, or Foreign Affairs."

Ronen laughed. "Foreign Affairs! He can't string together two words in English."

Avi shifted on the couch. He was positioned to sit in the next government and already his parents' expectations had climbed a few rungs higher. "I'll see what's on the table after the elections. Gurion has to save the big jobs for other parties in order to create a coalition."

In truth, Avi had not discussed the matter with his party leader. He'd be grateful with Deputy Minister of the Environment if it came to that. The main thing was to be in the game. Besides, a minor position would free him to pursue his ultimate goal: Galit.

He had been stupid to threaten her and had written off his mistake to homelessness and desperation. Never mind. After the elections, she'd come to her senses and welcome him back with open arms.

Avi accepted a steaming cup of sweet tea and bit into a slice of his mother's honey cake.

The thrill of victory faded. Finally, he had outsmarted Moshe, but after standing in his shadow so long, a thread of nostalgia pulled at his heart. There was an annoying grain of truth in Ronen's words. Moshe had guided his actions and haunted his thoughts for ages. Without him, his mind was an empty shrine. If Moshe were in his shoes, what would he do next?

"There's one thing I don't understand," Ronen said. "Karlin had the Dry Bones Society to rally behind him, but you— how did you pull off that demonstration?"

Avi's face grew hot. He had not told anyone about Boris and his thugs. Although the Russian had never spelled out what he did for a living, his line of work did not involve helping old ladies cross the street. *Who cares?* Boris and his minions had served their purpose. Once Avi took office, he'd shake them off like an old coat. The thugs had befriended Avi Segal, the miserable tramp, but they wouldn't dare mess with Avi Segal, the Member of Knesset.

He washed the cake down with his mint tea. "My dear brother," he said, his voice greasy with sarcasm, "you underestimate me."

CHAPTER 45

A young woman entered the Dry Bones Society Friday morning, her high heels clicking on the floor tiles. She wore a business suit of elegant cream with a matching Louis Vuitton bag, and her blow-dried hair dusted her shoulders as she gazed about the call center.

"I missed the old place," Sivan said.

Moshe looked on with pride. The spunky girl with the faded T-shirts and torn jeans had grown up since leaving Karlin & Son. Avi had fired her after Moshe's death, having invented an affair between Moshe and his attractive employee in order to win over Galit. Moshe had learned all this only weeks into his second life, and Sivan had tried to help him set the record straight.

"Welcome home," he said.

She shook hands with Rafi, whom she knew well from her days at Karlin & Son, and Moshe introduced her to Shmuel, Rabbi Yosef, and Savta Sarah. "Sivan is the VP of Marketing at a high-tech company in Malcha."

"She's a bit young," Shmuel said, as though she wasn't in the room.

"And I'm a bit old," Savta Sarah said.

"Young for what?" Sivan asked.

Moshe had not gone into the details on the phone. "For a

new challenge," he said. "Let's talk in my office."

Moshe perched on the edge of his desk and Savta Sarah closed the door.

"I saw you on TV," Sivan said, taking a seat in the visitor's chair.

"Then you know all about the Dry Bones Society."

She nodded. "I saw the anti-zombie demonstrations too. I'd say you have a bit of a PR problem." They all smiled at the understatement. "I assume that's why you called me in—to consult."

"More than that," Moshe said. He clasped his hands together for the big revelation. "What are our chances if we were to run independently in the upcoming elections?"

Her mouth dropped open. "Independently?"

"We've been double-crossed too many times to rely on politicians. We need our own clout to make a difference. And to do that we'll need a killer campaign manager."

She laughed. "You weren't kidding about the challenge bit."

"She's not up to it," Shmuel said.

Moshe understood his resistance. Until now, Shmuel had led the Society's public relations efforts, and he was not about to hand over their fate to a pretty face in a fancy blouse. He had not seen Sivan handle tough drivers on the dispatch CB radio. The delicate exterior hid a featherweight prize fighter. But Moshe didn't have to defend her bona fides.

"The hell I'm not," she said. "I took a young start-up from zero customers to market domination."

"And which start-up was that?"

Her cheeks flushed. "Ridez."

Blood drained from Moshe's face. He had heard that name from Avi. "Some kid made an app for ordering taxis," he had said, "and our drivers jumped ship."

"Wait a minute," Rafi said. "Isn't that the company that…" He had enough tact to trail off.

"That put Karlin & Son out of business," Moshe said. "Yes."

The room fell silent. Sivan had avenged her unfair firing by joining a rival company and blowing Karlin & Son out of the water. Was that why, at first, she had not returned Moshe's calls after his return? Was that why, later, she had agreed to help him out?

Moshe continued. "That proves her abilities." Sivan gave him a repentant smile and her shoulders relaxed. "And this time," he added, "I'd prefer to have her on our side. So what do you say—what are our chances?"

Sivan inflated her lungs and stared at the wall. "There will be a lot of hurdles," she said. "But you have a clear advantage."

"Which is?"

"You're an unknown. People here never vote *for* a candidate—they vote against the other guy who disappointed them last time, and they do this by choosing someone else."

Moshe smiled. She had a point.

"And you're already well positioned," she continued. "A secular leader, a rabbi to draw in the religious vote, and Rafi for the Sephardic community. Savta Sarah takes care of both women and retirees. That means you will all need to appear high on the list."

Rafi said, "Sure."

"Of course," Savta Sarah said.

Rabbi Yosef squirmed but nodded his consent.

"Great. And you'll need to rebrand."

"Rebrand?" Shmuel said.

She nodded. "You have to appeal to the general population, not just the resurrected. You'll need to adjust your messaging."

Another good point. The Dry Bones Society had served them well, but the Society's name did limit their target market.

Sivan brushed a strand of hair behind her ear. "And, as it happens, I have the perfect name for your new party."

She told them.

"Wow," said Rabbi Yosef.

"I like it," Moshe seconded.

Savta Sarah grinned. "It's *sexy*!"

Even Shmuel couldn't hide his excitement. "It hints at hope and a clean slate, but speaks to everyone."

"So," Moshe said. "Does this mean you'll take the job?"

Sivan glowed with enthusiasm. "Hell, yeah."

CHAPTER 46

Friday night, Yosef sat at the head of his Shabbat table, staring at his bowl of chicken soup. The good news strained to burst out of him.

He had not managed to update Rocheleh before candle lighting. The planning session at the Dry Bones Society had stretched on for hours and he had returned home with minutes to spare before he had to head out to open the synagogue.

One should not plan weekday matters on the Sabbath, the Sages taught. But this wasn't really planning, was it?

"I have some good news."

At the other end of the table, Rocheleh looked up from her soup. Uriel glanced at him, but Simcha, Ari, and Yehuda continued their contented slurping.

"We're going to run in the elections."

"Who will?"

"The Dry Bones Society. Well, it's no longer the Dry Bones Society. We're rebranding. Moshe will announce the new name on Sunday."

Rocheleh returned to her soup, displaying little interest in the new branding. Over the past few months, she had softened and no longer raised her voice at him. She had made peace with their new status at the fringes of the ultra-

Orthodox community. Their boys had not been expelled from school and the sky had not fallen. He suspected that the steady income from the Dry Bones Society, along with the brand new dishwasher, the company car, and the weekly cleaner, had played a large role in their new household tranquility. Their new means had allowed her to quit her teaching job in order to become a full-time housewife.

"There's more," he added. "I'll be number two on their list."

That got her attention. "Why you?"

"For the religious vote. That's what Sivan said. She's our campaign manager. After Moshe, I'll be the next in line to sit in Knesset."

Uriel perked up at that. "You'll be in the government—like the Prime Minister?"

Simcha said, "*Aba*—does that mean you'll get your own card?"

He extracted a wad of wrinkled soccer cards from his pocket and fanned them out. A bearded rabbi stared out from the surface of each laminated rectangle.

Yosef had no idea how they selected the rabbis for their cards. "Maybe."

"Awesome!"

"Please, *Aba*," Ari said. "Can you get us some of your cards? Please! Please!"

Yosef chuckled at the excited little faces, so proud of their father.

"Settle down now," Rocheleh said, then glanced at Moshe. "Don't get their hopes up, Yosef."

She was right. Once again, gusts of optimism had carried him away. There were a lot of "ifs" in his glorious future, as well as a short and difficult campaign. Did he even belong among the country's lawmakers? The thought made him tremble.

He turned the family's attention to the weekly Torah reading and the meal continued as usual.

Later, after the boys breathed deeply in their beds and he

had loaded the dishwasher, Rocheleh led him by the hand to their bedroom.

In the dim glow of the shuttered night lamp, she pulled off her head covering and her hair fell to her shoulders. They sat on the edge of the bed, her hands clasped in his.

"You have a good heart, Yossi," she said. "You are an honorable man. Politics is no place for honorable men. They will eat you up for breakfast, without salt."

"But if the honorable men stay away, how will politics ever become honorable? How will we make the world a better place?" Moshe's idealism had infected him. He thought of Rabbi Emden's betrayal and threats. "The rabbinate is rotten," he continued. "They only care about power and money; they have forgotten their moral duty. 'In a place where there are no men,' the Sages say, 'be a man.'"

"Shh…" She placed her finger on his lips, and argued no more.

His own mind argued for her. Power corrupts. Had his comfortable new salary—a salary he had received thanks to messianic Christian donors, no less—whetted his appetite for more?

Then she pushed him back onto the bed and all thoughts of money and power fled.

CHAPTER 47

Sunday morning, Samira stood before a dozen strangers in the circle of plastic chairs. Blood pumped noisily in her ears. The Absorption Center was unusually quiet. Most members of the Society had gone to witness the historic press conference in the call center down the corridor, leaving her to receive the new arrivals.

"My name is Samira," she said, her voice quavering. She had never addressed a gathering of her peers before. In her old life, her husband had forbidden her to work outside the house, and she had grown accustomed to hiding behind walls and veils. In this new life, however, she had discovered an inner strength.

"Rabbi Yosef asked me to fill in for him," she continued. She had often assisted the rabbi with the sessions, translating his words into Arabic, but today, for the first time, she led the group. She managed a smile. In their faces, she saw fear and confusion. She knew those emotions only too well, and now she had the skills with which to guide them across that narrow bridge.

"Whatever you experienced in your previous lives," she said, in Hebrew and then Arabic, her voice finding confidence in the rabbi's words, "wherever you're from, you've left all of that behind. This is a fresh start. We are all the same now. We are family. Around this circle, every day, we tell our life stories and we listen. Share as little or as much as you like."

She broke the ice by telling her own story. Then, one by one, the men and women arose and shared theirs. When the last had spoken, she handed out song sheets for the Israeli anthem—"HaTikva"—and Rabbi Nachman of Breslov's "All the World Is a Narrow Bridge." She sang and they followed along on the printed sheets. Some used the Hebrew sheets, others the Arabic. Many preferred the transliteration in Latin letters. As the session concluded, she felt that she had crossed a long, narrow bridge of her own.

Ahmed watched her from the corner as the new arrivals handed in their song sheets and dispersed to the refreshment tables. She drew near.

"You did very well," he said.

Her cheeks warmed and she looked away. "Thank you."

"I have something for you."

In his hand he held a wooden creature with almond eyes, a rounded nose, and long ears.

"It's a rabbit," he explained. "I made it for you in carpentry class. You said you had wanted a rabbit. I'm sorry it's not better. I'm still learning."

A flutter arose in her belly along with the urge to hug her new friend. No one had ever made a gift especially for her. "It's beautiful," she said. "I love it."

After an awkward moment, they made their way to the refreshment table and he poured her a glass of orange juice. Ahmed made her feel special and understood. She could tell him anything, and over the last week she had. If all the suffering she had endured had led to Ahmed, perhaps her death had not been in vain?

She sipped her drink, gripping the pile of sheets under her arm. "You are welcome to join us next time," she said. Ahmed still avoided the group sessions.

His smile faltered. "I don't think I'm ready."

"That's OK," she said. She understood, having clung to

the shadows for months, fearful of her family, fearful of her own reflection. The hurt of a traumatic first life took time to heal. "It's not easy," she said. "I know. I keep delaying my application for an identity card. I think I'll be stuck here forever."

"That sounds good to me," he said.

"What—to be stuck here?"

"With you, yes."

She glanced away again, smiling despite herself, and adjusted the hijab over her hair. The flutter returned. He had told her that he loved her. "Yes," she said. "That would be good."

CHAPTER 48

"I have to go," Alex told the girl who called herself Irina. "I'll be back later." It was the first lie he had told her, and his last.

They stood in the corridor of Clal Center outside the Dry Bones Society. Society members streamed around them toward the call center for the big announcement.

He had struggled with his demons ever since their visit to the Doctor last week. Irina remembered nothing; she was off the hook. Alex had no cause to contact her again. That morning he made his decision and had stopped by only to see her one last time.

"It'll only take a minute." Irina feigned anger. "Don't be selfish."

He *had* been selfish but not in the way she thought. Every moment he lingered, he put her in danger, and if anything happened to her a second time, he would not be able to forgive himself.

"I have to work," he said. That much was true. He had neglected his street magic, pulling in only a third of his usual revenues for the Organization. Mandrake had said nothing yet, but eventually he would put two and two together, and then Irina would become a problem again.

"I forgot," she said. "Some of us have real lives. What is it that you do that's so important anyhow?" Until now, the topic of his employment had never come up.

"Cars," he said." Buying. Selling. Fixing." Also true, technically. He did not want to lie to her again.

"Your cars can wait, Mr. Mechanic. We're making history today." She gripped his hand and pulled. The touch of her fingers melted his last thread of resistance. She towed him into the office, and they joined the press of bodies in the call center.

TV cameras were trained on the raised podium. Moshe Karlin stood at the microphone and shuffled cue cards. Behind him, a white sheet covered a rectangular object on an easel, like a painting awaiting auction.

"There he is," Irina said. The joy in her voice stabbed Alex inside. Moshe had taken her under his wing like a little sister, and she would be forever loyal. Alex could identify with that, but her reverence for the man made him jealous, another sign that he had taken this too far. He must leave now, for her sake.

The Dry Bones chief was harmless enough. He had given Alex suspicious glances at first but accepted him as Irina's friend. Karlin was an honest man. Honest men were easy to handle. You always knew what they would do next. Mandrake didn't share that predictability, and that was why he always came out on top. If the Boss ever moved against the Society, Karlin wouldn't last long.

Which was another reason for Alex to leave. The less he knew, the better. His involvement could only cause harm.

Karlin spoke into the microphone. "Friends," he said. "Recent events have taught us that to survive in this new world we cannot rely on others, however good their intentions." A murmur of bitter agreement rose from the crowd.

"To change society for the better—for the better of all citizens, not just the resurrected—we must make a stand for our values. Stand tall, stand proud."

A man cheered at the back. "Yeah!" The mood turned from bitterness to inspired activism.

"And so," Karlin continued, "I am glad to present to you

today the new face of our organization."

He turned to an attractive young woman with salon hair and a designer business suit. She pulled at a string and the white sheet fell from the easel. A poster displayed a single short word. The bold blue letters leaned forward as though racing ahead into the future. The word was "Restart."

Hands clapped. Some whistled their approval. Irina glanced at Alex and nodded her head. "It's great, don't you think?"

He had to agree. The name was modern, punchy, and a big improvement on the Dry Bones Society.

"Our country needs a restart," Karlin declared, and cheers broke out again. "To clear out the corruption and decay of the past. To build a better tomorrow for our children and grandchildren—for all of us."

Irina cheered as well. While she stared ahead, her hand found Alex's. Emotion rippled through his body like a shock wave. Her touch pushed him back in time to a moment of happiness, the moment he thought he had lost forever. How could he walk away now?

Karlin waited for the excitement to settle. "To achieve this," he said, "I am happy to announce that Restart will run in the coming elections."

The crowd went wild. Irina jumped on the spot and then hugged Alex. A gasp escaped his mouth and he smiled like a fool. She beamed up at him, mistaking his joy for hers. He couldn't turn his back on her again. And now, he wouldn't have to.

He excused himself and made for the bathroom. Checking that the stalls were empty, he dialed a number on his phone. Moshe Karlin had given him the pretext he had needed to stay close to her a little longer.

"Check the news," he said, when his boss answered. "Karlin might be of use to us after all."

CHAPTER 49

"This is heaven," Noga said, and Eli was inclined to agree.

They stretched out on rented recliners, while gentle waves lapped at the shore of white sand. The Mediterranean sun warmed his skin and dried his swimming trunks. Only a dozen other vacationers had discovered the hidden cove, and they frolicked in the refreshing waters.

That morning their cruise liner had docked at Santorini. Whitewashed cottages and blue domes gleamed on the cliffs high above the caldera, the flooded mouth of the volcano that had sculpted the Greek Island. When they disembarked, a chartered motorboat was waiting to whisk them away to the secluded beach.

"'Heaven is a place on earth,'" he said, quoting the '80s song and making Noga laugh.

He lifted his head from the recliner and gazed at the girl beside him. Sunlight glinted in the drops of seawater on her goosefleshed skin. Her one-piece bathing suit rose and fell to the rhythm of her breathing. A gentle sea breeze caressed the locks of hair below her wicker sunhat and carried the holiday scent of coconut oil.

He basked in the awe of her beauty, pure and natural, like the sea and the sand and the sky. But that beauty ran deeper than a pretty face and slender body. He had come to rely on her honesty and razor-sharp wit. She spoke her mind even if he didn't like what she had to say, not out of spite but because she cared.

Sure, she enjoyed the luxury and pampering as much as the next girl, but he was more to her than a bank account. After all, when she had first fallen for him he had been a crazed and friendless invalid. No, Noga truly cared.

And so do I. The hairs on his arms prickled at the realization. For the first time in his real life, he cared about someone.

The large, dark lenses of her sunglasses turned to him and she smiled, bemused. "What?" He had been staring at her, a foolish grin on his face.

"Nothing," he said. "I'm just... happy."

Her lips parted as her smile widened. She shifted on the recliner and returned to her suntanning. "Let's stay here forever," she said.

"I wish we could." He wanted to seal this moment in a jar for eternity, but he couldn't. The black, clawed hand of dread closed over his heart. For the first time in his life, he had something to lose.

"Nothing lasts forever," he continued. "Not even islands. Take Santorini. People lived here for thousands of years until one day the mountain exploded and sank into the sea. A whole civilization wiped out in an instant. The ash cloud spread for hundreds of miles and hung in the air for weeks."

"How do you know all that?"

How indeed? In his mind's eye, a little boy stepped outside a mudbrick home as heavy, gray clouds crawled from the horizon and covered Goshen, shrouding the villages in gloom, and seeding stories of miraculous darkness and cities that sank into the sea. He could still taste the ash in the air.

"I read it somewhere," he said. His mind still played tricks on him, conjuring false memories of the ancient past and zombies on the streets of the present. Noga's theories about the Ten Lost Tribes had not helped him separate fact from delusion. He had to hold onto reality at all costs; reality was all that had kept Noga in his life.

He leaned back on the recliner, returning to the sun and the soft crashing of the waves on the shore. In a few hours, he and Noga would return to the boat and move on. A few hours of heaven was more than any mortal could hope for.

CHAPTER 50

Avi yanked open the sliding door of the old warehouse in Talpiot and marched inside. He wanted answers. Just when things were going his way, the eleven o'clock news had spoiled his morning.

Fluorescents suspended from the rafters illuminated the warehouse, which reeked of singed metal and stood empty except for a large glass cube the size of an elevator in the center. A lanky Ethiopian crouched beside the cube and applied the flame of a welding gun to a corner. As Avi approached, the Ethiopian stood, extinguished the flame, and lifted the welding mask from his face.

"Where's Boris?"

With a toss of his head, the Ethiopian indicated the supervisor's office in a corner two floors up.

Avi made for the metal staircase. The stairs clanked underfoot. Boris had given him the address of the warehouse for emergencies. Today was an emergency and if his so-called partner didn't fix things, there'd be hell to pay.

He marched along the narrow walkway and burst through the door of the corner office. Boris looked up from behind a cheap desk. His large Russian bodyguard stood at the wall behind him, his tree-trunk arms folded over his chest, making Avi reconsider the wisdom of his visit, but only for a moment.

"You said you'd destroy Moshe Karlin."

Boris peered at him beneath droopy eyelids, unmoved by the accusation. "I said that *we'd* bring him down together. And what of it—Gurion dropped him for you, didn't he?"

"Moshe started his own party. He's running in the elections as an independent."

The gray-haired thug grinned. "And there I thought you were upset that he married your old girlfriend."

Avi's thoughts scattered. "What? When?"

"Ramat Rachel, Monday last week." He chuckled. "You didn't know?"

Avi's throat constricted and he couldn't breathe. That scumbag Moshe had stolen his tactic and brought the wedding forward. Only this time, the ploy had worked.

Boris seemed to soften at Avi's loss for words. "Your friend is more resilient than we thought, but I wouldn't worry about his little experiment."

The Russian's dismissive attitude sparked Avi's temper. "Then start worrying—they say he could win seats in the next government all on his own. You have got to stop him."

The grin faded from the Russian's face. "I don't *got* to do anything."

"Oh, yes you do, Boris." Avi puffed out his chest. "I'm Isaac Gurion's rising star, remember. I'm going to be a member of Knesset. You clean up this mess. I can't get my hands dirty."

Boris stared at him. "What do you want me to do—kill him?"

Avi almost swallowed his tongue. He had punched Moshe in the face and threatened his life, but he had never actually intended to murder him. Boris, however, wasn't joking, and Avi had the sudden urge to pee. "Jeez, no. No, don't kill him. Just destroy his party."

"And how do you propose I do that?"

Another silence. Moshe had been the brains behind Karlin & Son. He had always had a plan. Ronen was right—Avi had only followed in Moshe's footsteps, and now Moshe was outmaneuvering him again. It wasn't fair.

"How should I know? You're the criminal mastermind. Think of something."

Avi had gone too far and he knew it. But Boris didn't set his thug on him. He didn't throw him out either. Instead, he drew a deep breath, leaned forward, and clasped his hands over the desk.

"Growing up in the Soviet Union," he said, "you learn a thing or two about power politics. When the Bolsheviks took control of the country, they didn't use physical force alone." He tapped his temple. "They invaded people's minds as well, and their memories, causing confusion and uncertainty. Soon people had difficulty predicting the past."

Invading minds. Predicting the past. What was he going on about? "What are you trying to say?"

The Russian's mustache wriggled. "It's simple," he said. "If you want to rule the future, you have to change the past."

CHAPTER 51

A week later, Noga stepped out of the golden elevator and into the dark yet familiar penthouse on Jaffa Road. Motors hummed as the blinds parted, revealing the Jerusalem skyline in orange sunset hues through the large French windows.

Eli wheeled their bags inside. "Home sweet home," he said.

Home. The cruise had surpassed her wildest dreams of the perfect romantic vacation, but she was glad to return to the place where she belonged, here with this man who made dreams come true. She wrapped her arms about his neck and he dropped the bags.

"Let's celebrate," he said, a mischievous twinkle in his eye.

She laughed. "We celebrated every day of the trip."

"Why stop now?" He scooped her up in his arms and made for the bedroom. Their bags remained in the hall all night.

Early the next morning, she fixed herself a cup of coffee and flopped on the living room couch. A muffled car horn blared from the street below. Monday morning and not a care in the world.

She aimed the remote at the TV and switched channels, settling on a rerun of Friends on the HOT Comedy Channel.

Her laptop lay shut on the coffee table. With the scant Wi-

Fi access on the trip, she hadn't bothered to check her email. She hadn't even powered on her phone, and now she dismissed all sixty-one notifications. At some point, she'd have to wrap up her doctoral paper, but she could muster little motivation to sum up her failed experiment. At least she'd get her piece of paper.

Hannah might need some convincing. Or had she stepped back from her messianic theory as well? Probably. Eli was right—no serious academic would commit career suicide over a few equivocal data points.

On the screen, Joey bet a hundred dollars that he and Chandler knew more about Rachel and Monica than the girls knew about them. Where was Phoebe?

Doctorate finally in hand, Noga would have to decide what to do with the rest of her life. She was leaning toward doing another degree. An ironic laugh escaped her lips. She was becoming like Sarit, her old friend from Hebrew U. They hadn't spoken in ages. Romance trumped girlfriends. Of all people, Sarit would understand that. Noga would call her later.

In the Friends universe, Ross pointed at a score board on a chair. The couples had tied and started a thirty-second lightning round of questions. The stakes had risen: if the girls won, the guys would get rid of their pet rooster and duck; if the guys won, the girls would switch apartments with them.

Noga's laptop beckoned to her from the coffee table. She opened the lid, nudged the screen to life, and scanned her inbox. Two hundred new messages, mostly adverts and newsletters. Hannah had emailed her three times.

Friday, the day after they had left in the limo: "How is the paper going? Call me. I have some ideas to discuss."

Monday, last week: "Send me your first draft ASAP. The university has approved a discussion paper slot for their website. The print journal closes for submissions next week. On second thought, the university journal is too small a platform for this sort of paper. We should submit to Nature Genetics."

Nature Genetics! Noga's pulse quickened. Hannah wanted to submit their paper to one of the most esteemed peer review academic journals in the world. During Noga's cooling-off period, her advisor had only heated up.

Another email, Thursday last week: "Are you OK? Can't reach you by phone. Did you get my messages?"

Noga should have at least told her she was going away. Her fear of confrontation had caused her mentor unnecessary worry.

She dashed off a reply. "Sorry for not responding earlier," she wrote. "Went overseas on short notice. Will call soon."

Eli padded down the hallway behind her. She hit send and closed the laptop.

"Hey," he said. He kissed her on the ear and moved to the kitchen. "What are you watching?"

"Friends."

"Funny name for a movie."

She turned to look at him. He wasn't joking. "How can you not know Friends?"

He shrugged. "I must have been sick that day."

Oh, right. Messianic delusions were a full-time job, and the old Eli had spared little time for petty entertainment. She relented. "It's about a group of guys and girls who share apartments near each other. This is a great episode. Joey and Chandler are playing a game of 'Who Knows Each Other Better' against Rachel and Monica. If the guys win, they switch apartments with the girls. If the girls win, the guys have to get rid of their pets."

"Their pets? That's a bit harsh."

"A rooster and a duck."

"Oh. And who's that?"

"That's Ross. He's facilitating."

"It's his apartment?"

"No, Monica's—just watch already."

Eli sat beside her and sipped his coffee.

In Monica's living room, the girls failed to answer the question "What is Chandler's job?" The boys got to keep their pets and won the better apartment. The credits rolled.

How would Noga fare if she were to play that game with Eli? Not very well.

"What *is* Chandler's job?"

"Some hi-tech thingy."

Noga switched channels. The camera panned over a sprawl of low buildings, the familiar campus of the Hebrew University.

"We return to Professor Yakov Malkovich," said the voice of the Channel Ten reporter.

A bespectacled old man hunched behind a large desk in an office plastered with certificates and awards. His bush of untamed white hair defied gravity, standing out in haphazard tufts as though he had spent hours pulling at the ends. He spoke with a wild enthusiasm and waved his hands.

"We have measured elevated levels of magnetism in the air," he said. "Perhaps the result of a recent solar flare, which appears to have had a peculiar effect on human remains, although we have yet to reproduce the regeneration in the laboratory. We are calling on volunteers from the undead community to assist with our research."

Did he say "undead"?

Eli shifted on the couch.

"Professor," the balding reporter said. A smirk pulled at the edge of his mouth. "The last time we spoke you claimed that these self-professed resurrected men and women were part of an elaborate hoax. Does this mean that you've changed your mind?"

At the word "resurrected," Noga's intestines tied in a knot.

The professor's lips trembled. "It's hard to argue with an empirical phenomenon. We just need to understand it better."

The camera switched to Clal Center on Jaffa Road, a few blocks down from their apartment complex. A mass of angry protesters covered the wide sidewalk. What were they chanting? "Death to *Zombies*"?

"Meanwhile," the reporter narrated, "other reactions to

the new demographic have been less welcoming."

Noga had noticed a crowd on the street a few days before their trip, but had found a detour to get around them. Just another political demonstration, she had thought.

The reporter held a microphone to the mouth of a young woman with long, brown hair and spectacles. She wore a yellow shirt with a black nuclear hazard sign. "They're not natural," she shouted above the roar of the crowd. "They're taking our jobs and overloading public services. The dead should stay dead. Life is for the living."

Another protester faced the mike—a man with black curls. "My neighbor died five years ago," he said. He spoke with a heavy Moroccan accent. "Scared the crap out of me when he got in the elevator with me." He shivered. "Still gives me the creeps, and now he kidnapped my cat, I swear it. She's probably dead by now, poor thing. The undead did it. They eat the brains." He nodded his head. "They're screwed up, man. It's them or us."

Eli snatched the remote from her hand and the screen went blank.

"Put it back on."

He got up. "Enough TV for one day. Let's go out."

She glared at him. He was trying to change the subject. "Did you know about this?"

He waved it away with his hand. "Election propaganda," he said. "It doesn't mean anything."

"*Doesn't mean anything?* Dead people are walking the streets." She touched her forehead, which was cold and damp, and her breath came in shallow, rapid bursts. "Eli, you heard the professor—this is real. This is the freaking end of the world!"

Eli tried to laugh. "The old guy with the crazy hair? Being on TV doesn't make him a scientist. It's all scripted, a publicity stunt for a new zombie movie."

"That was Channel Ten, Eli. It's not a joke."

He raised his hands in a conciliatory gesture. "OK. I'm sorry." He sat down beside her and took her hands in his.

"Maybe it's true; maybe it isn't. I don't know. It doesn't matter. All that matters is us."

She pulled her hands away. "What are you saying—that we should just get on with our lives, with this going on outside?"

"Why not?" Annoyance hardened his voice.

The implications rose in her mind. Hannah was right and Noga had made a big mistake. "My research," she said. "This can't be a coincidence. I have to call Hannah." She reached for her phone but he grabbed her wrist.

"Don't, Noga. Please, just don't."

"We can't just turn a blind eye."

His nostrils flared. "We can," he said, raising his voice. "And we will."

She broke free of his grip, got to her feet, and stepped away from him. "What's gotten into you?" She no longer knew the man on the couch. He had known all along. Was the cruise just a distraction to hide the truth from her?

"You can't help them," he said. "No one can."

Tears crept into her eyes and her voice cracked. "We have to."

"I'm done with humanity. Let them figure it out themselves."

Noga recognized that voice. Elijah had spoken, not Eli. But had the prophet forsaken his mission?

"You were right, Eli. I'm sorry I didn't believe you before, but we have a role to play now. Both of us. Together."

He shot her a fiery glance. "Then you're on your own. I won't have anything to do with it."

Noga's legs turned to jelly. He had moved from "us" to "you," and once again, their future teetered on the brink. But this time, the stakes were far greater than her own personal happiness.

His stubborn words sparked a blaze within her too.

"Fine," she said, and she marched to the front door. She pressed the button for the elevator, then folded her arms over her pajama shirt, waiting for him to apologize and beg her to stay. He didn't.

The doors opened, so she stepped inside. Then, spotting their bags, she pulled her suitcase into the elevator after her. *That'll show him.* But Eli just stared ahead at the view through the windows, his jaw clenched.

She pressed the button for the lobby. "You know what your problem is?" she said, as the doors closed. "You only care about yourself."

CHAPTER 52

Yosef arrived bright and early Monday morning at the call center of the Dry Bones Society—of Restart, he corrected himself. Over a week into the campaign and he still hadn't adjusted to the new name. Today, he would take a break from campaigning and return to another urgent task. With the elections only three days away, he could neglect this task no longer.

"Good morning, Rabbi," Samira said.

"Good morning, Samira."

She smiled at him and nodded at the wall. The mounted TV screen displayed his own talking head. He hadn't adjusted to that either.

His TV self wore a new suit and freshly trimmed beard. "Starting anew each day," he said, "is what Rabbi Nachman of Breslov taught and this is what Restart is about."

"How are we doing?" he asked Samira, more to change the subject than to gain information. During the mad flurry of activity in the first week of the campaign, he had starred in infomercials and interviews. The lecture circuit had taken him to synagogues around the country, and during that time he had handed over the management of the Absorption Center to Samira and Irina. They were doing a great job.

"More new arrivals every day," she said. "The fifth floor is filling up."

"I'll speak with Mr. Adams about expanding the dormitory," he said. He preferred not to use the title Reverend. "And the campaign?"

Her smile widened. "Sivan said that attendance at the rallies is much higher than expected. The polls give us twelve seats."

"Incredible," he said. Sivan had orchestrated a powerful campaign.

He headed for the corner office and closed the door behind him. The speaking tour had taken Moshe south today and freed up his office.

Yosef settled behind the desk, opened his laptop, and found the spreadsheet of telephone numbers.

So far, he had called over two hundred Menachems, Efraims, and Davids. Their responses had ranged from mild amusement to irritation. Some had shouted abuse in his ear.

But he had to continue. How could he sit in Knesset when the Son of David was out there? Yosef would gladly vacate his number two slot in the Restart list for the Lord's Anointed. Each day brought new questions that Yosef could not answer. In Knesset, that list of questions would only grow in number and importance.

Yosef scrolled down the list to where he had left off, and selected the first Nehorai. As he dialed the number, the door of the office cracked open.

Irina stood on the doorway. "Rabbi Yosef, you're on TV."

"I know. I've seen it a dozen times."

"Not this one," she said. "We didn't put this out, I'm sure of it." From the drawn look on her face, he knew that the broadcast was not good news.

He put down the phone and followed her out of the office.

His face appeared on the screen, all right, but in a photograph on the Channel Two news. The shot showed him grimacing as he got out of a car. Not the most flattering likeness.

The female news presenter gave her viewers a scandalized smile. "More bad news for Restart, the controversial new party formerly known as the Dry Bones Society."

Yosef had to laugh at the blatant attack on their new brand. These media people had no shame. As she continued to speak, however, he stopped laughing and the hairs on the back of his neck stood erect like the fur of a startled cat.

Restart was in deep trouble, and it was all his fault.

CHAPTER 53

Adrenaline pulsed through Moshe's bloodstream as he waited in the wings of Turner Stadium. In the corridor that soccer teams used on their way to the field, Sivan's amplified voice echoed from the stage outside. By now, he knew her introductory speech by heart.

Galit squeezed his hand. "Ready to conquer the world?"

"Beer Sheba will do for now," he said.

Sivan had booked the Beer Sheba Theater for his election rally a week ago. Two days ago she moved the event to the city's main stadium. The crowds had grown with each city they visited, and the unofficial capital of southern Israel had beaten all their early attendance forecasts.

Sivan's voice rose as she mentioned his name, and the cheers of countless people carried into the tunnel.

"Here we go."

Holding hands with Galit and little Talya, he marched outside, into the morning light, across the field, up a few steps, and onto the stage.

Sivan stood beside the microphone, smiling and clapping. The mass of supporters roared, filling the field and grandstands. Moshe waved at them. Restart banners hung from railings. Restart placards and flags dotted the human sea like white horses. Their goodwill surged through his body and sharpened his senses. The rush was addictive. *So this is how pop stars feel.*

He reached for the microphone and the cheers settled. Moshe no longer needed his cue cards.

"Friends," he said. "Thank you for joining us today. I know why you're here. You're here because, like us, you know we need change." On cue, the crowd murmured agreement.

"For too long," he continued, "we have endured corruption and cronyism. For too long, we have let cynical politicians divide us. Religious and secular. Rich and poor. Established and immigrant. Ashkenazi and Sephardic. And, more recently, first-timers and the resurrected. The time has come to put those divisions aside and come together as one nation. The time has come to restart our society!"

Voices cheered. Hands reached for the heavens. Flags waved. A chant rose: Re-start! Re-start! Re-start!

Moshe lifted his hands in the air like the conductor of the largest orchestra in history. He was born for this moment. A full minute later, the chant subsided and Moshe got on with his speech. He urged them to go out and vote tomorrow and make that change a reality. The crowd broke into song again and at the climax, Moshe collected his family and walked off the stage. On the way out, he leaned over the barrier fence and shook hands with supporters.

Reverend Adams waited in the wings. "Great job, Moshe," he said. He gave his hand a mighty shake and clapped him on the back. "I didn't understand a word, of course, but the crowd said it all. How are we doing?"

Moshe turned to Sivan.

"Over thirty thousand," she said in English. "Our best turnout yet. At this rate we're projecting twelve mandates."

"Mandates?" Rev. Adams was still new to the intricacies of Israeli politics.

"The one hundred twenty seats in Knesset are divided up proportionally to each party according to the number of votes received. We passed the electoral threshold easily."

The reverend's smile dropped. "Twelve is far from a majority."

"There are too many parties for that. The largest party gets to form a coalition government and divide up the ministries. At twelve seats, we're sure to be included in the coalition."

"I see." The broad, toothy smile returned.

Moshe said, "You're welcome to join us on our next stops, Reverend."

"I'm afraid I can't. I have to check up on some of our other investments. Which reminds me—Moshe, may I have a word?"

"Of course."

They stepped aside. "About our new arrivals. How far back in time are we now?"

Moshe cleared his throat. "Eighth century, last I heard. But I'll check with Rabbi Yosef."

"I see." The reverend seemed disappointed but then brightened. "I'm glad that we'll be well positioned by the time we do reach that *critical time*." He gave Moshe a meaningful glance. "You keep that seat in Knesset warm until it's needed."

"Of course."

Rev. Adams nodded and strode off, his briefcase-carrying assistant trying to keep up.

Moshe exhaled a deep breath. Rabbi Yosef would not be happy with that arrangement. They'd cross that bridge when they reached it. If Jesus did show up, he might not want to sit in Knesset, and if he did, well, he was a Jewish social activist, wasn't he? Moshe could do with all the help he could get.

"What did he want?" Galit asked.

"Just looking out for an old friend. What's our next stop? Sivan?"

Sivan held her phone to her ear and shook her head. She did not look happy.

"We have to head back right away," she said when she put down the phone.

"I thought we had a few more stops in the south."

"Not anymore," she said. "We have a problem, Moshe. A very big problem."

CHAPTER 54

Alex parked outside the Technology Park opposite the Malcha Mall and wondered what Mandrake was up to. They had never met at this address before.

He walked around the security boom at the entrance where a guard checked the trunks of cars before waving them in. As a pedestrian, Alex got a free pass.

He headed for the main set of office buildings in the center of the complex. Straight paths of paving stones crisscrossed the tidy squares of trimmed grass like electronic circuits on a silicon chip. Man-sized Hebrew letters and metallic orbs littered the grounds. He weaved between the oversized sculptures, a small, vulnerable creature inside a cold, heartless machine.

"Stay close to Karlin," his boss had instructed when Alex had informed him of Karlin's intention to run in the elections. "I want to know his every move."

And so Alex had found his excuse to stay close to Irina. She had Moshe's ear, and what she learned she shared with Alex. He had fooled himself into believing that the arrangement would last forever.

Maybe Mandrake would change tactics after the elections; maybe not. But the summons to the Technology Park the day before the elections had shattered his sense of security. Once again, he had failed to predict his old friend's next move, and his future was up in the air.

He passed the offices of the Open University, entered Tower Four, and took the mirrored lift to the eighth floor. A sign on the wall pointed the way down the clean, carpeted corridor toward the offices of Magitek.

Mandrake had probably chosen the name.

He pressed the intercom button at the glass door.

The blonde at the enamel white front desk looked up from her phone, and the door clicked open. Anna had traded her tank top for a white blouse but had kept the gum. She motioned to the side with her head. "All the way to the end. He's waiting."

Alex cut through a long, wide hall of cubicles. Young men peered at computer monitors and jabbered into their headsets excitedly in English, French, and Russian, frantic worker bees in a hive of human activity ten times the size of the call center of the Dry Bones Society.

Was this a new scam or a front for the Organization's other criminal operations? Alex had glimpsed only the tip of the iceberg of Mandrake's activities and, once again, he sensed the immense bulk that lurked beneath the surface.

At the end of the hall he found a white enamel door. A security camera eyed him from above like a sphinx. He must have answered the silent riddle correctly, for the door clicked open as he neared and he walked right through.

Mandrake stood in a plain white antechamber, a tall, bald man, the bulge of his muscles visible beneath his button-down shirt.

"Welcome to the future, Sasha," he said in his sonorous voice and smiled. "What do you think?"

Alex pointed a thumb behind him at the call center. "A new trick?"

"Binary options," Mandrake said.

"Never heard of it. Is it real?"

Mandrake's eyes glittered. "More than real—it's magic. Money disappears in one country and reappears in another.

Poof! Today, we can reach the entire world from one computer. It takes a little imagination but then again, true power has always lived here"—he tapped his forehead—"in the mind."

"And I thought revenues were down."

"Oh, no, my friend. Business has never been better. So long as people have hope for the future, they are easily parted from their money. I want to show you something."

His boss made for the far wall of the antechamber. Alex followed, and breathed at ease. Perhaps the visit had nothing to do with Karlin and the elections.

Mandrake paused at a framed mirror and combed his imaginary hair. "Mirror, mirror on the wall," he crooned.

Whoosh!

Alex took a hurried step back as the wall slid sideways to reveal a rectangular black portal.

Mandrake turned to him. "Cool, hey? Facial recognition. Only the prettiest get to go inside."

They walked through the portal. The room beyond the hole in the wall was the negative image of the call center. Black walls, dull blue light, and silence. An array of huge screens covered the walls, similar to the video feeds on the walls of the secret office at the back of the Talpiot Bowling Center, but the number of feeds had grown substantially. Computer terminals lined the walls. The swivel chairs stood empty.

"Our new headquarters," Mandrake said with a flourish of his large hands. He plopped onto a circular couch in the middle of the command room, put his hands behind his head, and admired his handiwork.

Alex joined him. "Congratulations. It's beautiful." Mandrake was sharing a milestone with a close friend. Alex was not like the other hands in Mandrake's employ. They had a special relationship. Or did Mandrake make all his captains feel that way?

Mandrake chuckled. "The bowling alley couldn't contain us much longer. Not enough cable, for one thing. Information is the key, my friend. It flows from this building to the world and back. And the world looks to us. To Jerusalem, the Eye of the Universe."

The poetry was lost on Alex, but his boss didn't explain.

"I'm proud of you, Sasha," he said. "You followed your instincts and the girl led us to Karlin's inner circle. Now I think it's time I met this Karlin."

Alex tried not to swallow. Meetings with his boss were not the kind one scheduled in an appointment book. The attendees could not refuse. Often, they did not survive. "When?"

"Tomorrow."

He couldn't be serious. "Tomorrow is election day."

"The perfect time to reap what we have sown."

Alex did not like the sound of that. "OK," he said. "I'll make the arrangements."

Let him have Karlin. Anyone who messed with the Organization had it coming. So long as the girl remained safe, Mandrake could do with Karlin as he wished.

CHAPTER 55

Irina opened the door of Moshe's office but nobody seemed to notice. The top brass of Restart—Shmuel, Sivan, Rafi, Rabbi Yosef—huddled behind Moshe and stared at the computer screen on his desk. Judging by the pensive looks on their faces, the situation was bad. Very bad.

She had walked over to the call center at lunch time looking for Alex, who hadn't returned yet from his work commitments that morning, when she had noticed the anxious team through the window of the corner office. Had the campaign rally at Beer Sheba gone awry?

"What's happened?" she asked the room at large.

No one answered, so she joined them behind the desk. The recording of a Channel Two newscast played on YouTube. A terrible photo of Rabbi Yosef was displayed beside a female presenter.

"Rabbi Yosef Lev," she said with scandalized relish, "former primary school teacher and number two on the Restart list, is an alcoholic. According to a close friend and confidant of the rabbi, he was fired recently from his teaching job, and although the school did not press formal charges, a representative confirmed that they had deemed Rabbi Lev unsuitable to work with children."

Irina shuddered. Rabbi Yosef—an alcoholic? *Unsuitable to*

work with children—the phrase implied that he was a pedophile too! *Never!* The kind rabbi stared at the screen, shaking his head and pulling at the ends of his beard.

The screen cut to a familiar angry mug. The subtitle read, "Avi Segal, Upward Party."

"These zombies are eating up the living and overrunning our country." His mouth contorted with disgust. "Now it seems that they're molesting our children too. They belong behind bars. That Restart has the nerve to run in the elections is an insult to the entire nation."

The camera cut to the news desk. The presenter's smile widened. "More scandal for the beleaguered fledgling party— as if that wasn't enough!" The photo of the rabbi became a shot of Moshe, his mouth open in mid-speech, his eyes half-shuttered. "Our investigative reporters have discovered that, shortly before his death, the leader of Restart, Moshe Karlin, had been thrown out of his home by his wife, who suspected him of cheating on her."

Sivan leaned in, clicked the mouse, and the video froze. "I know the story about Moshe is a sham. We can deny that rumor without any problems. Rabbi Yosef? Sorry, but we have to know."

The rabbi spread his hands in supplication. "I've been sober ten years."

"And the kids?"

"Heaven forbid! I taught them about the Resurrection— that's what caused the trouble with the principal. Then they fired me for working with the Society."

"Good. Then we'll fight back. We'll do a press conference right away. Shmuel, speak with Eran. Moshe and Rabbi Yosef, be ready to rehearse your messages. I think we can put a positive spin on this."

A positive spin? That sounded like a miracle.

Shmuel laughed his bitter laugh. "How will you do that?" he said, mirroring Irina's thoughts.

"Restart is all about correcting mistakes. A recovered alcoholic makes a great poster child. Moshe, we'll need Galit at your side when you make your statement."

Moshe nodded. "What's the damage so far?"

"Our telephone poll started an hour ago. Results should be in soon. Even with our denials and spin, there will be damage. This could cut our votes in half."

Moshe gave her a grim nod.

"But spin will only go so far," Sivan said. "We need to hit back and hard."

"What do you mean?"

"We need dirt on Gurion. Or Avi—he'll make an easier target. He lies and cheats in his sleep. We won't need to dig very deep. We can start with his ex-girlfriends."

Moshe wriggled on his seat. "I don't think we should go there. We're running a clean campaign. These are exactly the kind of sleazy tricks we're promising to root out."

Sivan put her hands on her hips. "Which do you prefer: a clean campaign or a winning one?"

Moshe's mobile phone rang. He gave them a meaningful glance and got to his feet. "Reverend Adams. Yes, I saw the news." He paced the room.

Don't let him cut us off, Irina prayed. *Please.*

"No, of course not," Moshe said into the phone. "A smear campaign from our rivals. We're preparing a response right now. I understand. Of course."

He put down the phone and slumped into his chair.

"Are we still afloat?" Sivan asked.

Moshe nodded. "For now. But our benefactors are uneasy about associating with adulterers and drunks. I'm sure he won't like us jumping into a mud fight either. OK, everyone, battle stations."

"How can I help?" Irina asked him, as the others filed out of the room. Poor Moshe. She knew how much he cared for Galit, how he had struggled to win her back and clear his name. The returning accusations must really hurt, and to have them aired on television? Unbearable!

Moshe managed a brave smile. "You're already helping. Thanks for holding the fort. Restart couldn't go on without you."

"And Samira," she added. "Arabic is in high demand these days. We'll get through this."

"I know. We've been through worse, right?"

Irina left his office on a wave of renewed energy. She'd spread the word. The false rumors must be circulating in the Absorption Center by now and the Society's morale would need a boost.

Opening the door of the call center, she almost collided with Alex. He must have heard the accusations on the radio, because he looked pale and tense.

"It's all a lie," she said.

His eyes widened. "What is?"

"What they're saying about Rabbi Yosef and Moshe."

"Oh, right. Yeah, I heard. It's terrible."

"I hope they pull through," she said.

He pulled her close and stroked her hair. "I hope so too."

CHAPTER 56

Ahmed steeled himself to face his worst fear.

At the opposite side of the circle of chairs, Samira listened with interest to each speaker. She sensed Ahmed's eyes on her, met his gaze and gave him that warm, encouraging smile. Basking in that smile, he could brave anything.

He fidgeted with his song sheet. The heavyset man beside him folded and unfolded his tanned arms, muttering to himself and smelling of soap.

People passed by the window in the door, fellow Society members on their way to lunch. Perhaps the session would end early and save Ahmed the torment. Would his fellow Society members guess his evil deeds? Would his guilt show on his face?

Two seats down, a bearded man with olive skin stood. "Mustafa is my name," he said. Ahmed had trouble understanding the strange Arabic dialect.

"Three young wives," Mustafa said, "ten olive groves, and a hundred head of sheep I had. Broke bread with Abd Al-Malik, the great caliph, when he visited the walled city." After bragging about his wealth and connections, however, he started to sob. "Then I awoke in this land of terrible sounds and devil-wagons. I hid in tunnels beneath the road for a week, scavenging and stealing, God forgive me. Then a young man found me in the trash bins and led me here. A thousand blessings upon you all, my daughter."

When Mustafa sat down, Soap Man stood and jabbered away in a foreign tongue.

Samira looked about the room. "Does anyone understand him?" She repeated the question in Hebrew and then in English.

"Romani!" Soap Man said. "Romani!"

Samira motioned for the distressed man to sit. "We will find someone who can speak with you, sir."

The comforting tone of her words seemed to calm him and he sat down. Samira smiled at Ahmed and her eyes glittered.

Ahmed's turn had arrived. He glanced at the door for salvation. A man passed by the window and glanced at him—the balding older man he had seen with Moshe Karlin. There was no escape now.

He rose to his feet and a dozen pairs of eyes set upon him.

"My name is Ahmed," he said. His voice sounded strange to own his ears. He wiped his clammy hands on his jeans. Samira nodded, encouraging him. In the other faces he found understanding and acceptance. "I died ten years ago. My life was not special. But my new life is. I thank God, Who led me here, for the people I have met and the experiences I have had." Samira swallowed and her eyes glittered again. He was talking about her, and she felt the same way about him. "I hope," he continued, "that in the future—"

The door flung open. The balding older man who had appeared at the window stormed into the room, and he had eyes only for Ahmed.

"Murderer!" he yelled.

Ahmed stiffened. *He knows!*

Samira turned to the source of the commotion. Others rose and shifted out of the man's path as he shoved a chair aside and cut through the circle toward Ahmed.

"Murderer!"

"Shmuel," Samira cried. "Wait!"

Shmuel clamped two beefy hands around Ahmed's neck. Ahmed fell backward, his chair slipping away. The old man landed on his chest, winding him and pinning him to the floor. The hands tightened about his neck. Ahmed couldn't breathe.

"Murderer!" the balding man cried again, raining spittle on Ahmed's face. He struggled but the man was too heavy and furious.

Then the man was yanked back, his hands slipping from Ahmed's neck. He sucked in air and scrambled to his feet.

"Let me go!" Shmuel kicked and flailed but Soap Man and the Mustafa held him back. "You killed us," Shmuel yelled at Ahmed, tears in his voice. "You blew us up. On the bus. You ruined our lives!"

Samira turned to Ahmed, her eyes wide with disbelief. "No, Ahmed. This is not true. Tell him."

Ahmed opened his mouth to lie. He wasn't a murderer. Some other boy had pushed the button, not him. He wanted to see her warm smile again, but he had lost it for good.

So he ran for the door and fled.

CHAPTER 57

That evening, Yosef slunk into the grocery store on Emek Refaim Street and kept his head down. After the exhausting hours of PR work, he never wanted to step in front of a video camera again. Daylight was fading by the time he headed home, but Rocheleh had insisted that he stop by the local grocer for odds and ends, as many stores would close tomorrow for Election Day. Fortunately, his wife had not been exposed to the slanderous reports on television.

While he selected zucchini from a tub in the vegetable section, a fat woman in a wooly shawl fondled the sweet potatoes in the next tub and gave him sharp looks. Did she recognize him from the mug shot on Channel Two? Her eyes seemed to shout, "Drunken pervert! Shame on you!"

He bagged his zucchini, selected two cartons of three percent milk, and waited in line at the till. The scanner beeped as Gavri swiped the barcodes. Yosef sank his head further into his shirt collar, a feeble attempt at avoiding conversation with the chatty store owner. He wanted to crawl into a hole and hibernate until the next millennium. The embarrassment caused by the accusations accounted for only part of the heartache.

The gloves will come off, Rabbi Emden had warned him, and off they had come. Yosef had expected a reprisal. The rabbinate had lashed out at him before—they had terminated his teaching job at Daas Torah Primary and he had felt the full force of their political maneuvers at the Ministry of the Interior.

But this time the betrayal was personal. Rabbi Emden had stood by him in his darkest moments, when Yosef had opened his heart and bared his soul. The media had not revealed the identity of their source, but only one "close friend and confidant" had heard his sacred confessions.

Yosef could absorb the financial and political blows; he could even forgive them. But now Emden had turned their years of emotional intimacy into a political weapon. Yosef had never imagined that his spiritual mentor would stoop so low, and the loss of his dearest friend and confidant hurt like a jagged tear in his soul.

Yosef stepped forward as the checkout line progressed and Gavri scanned the barcodes. *Beep. Beep.*

Having his good name dragged through the mud on television and losing his spiritual guide had seemed like enough of a beating for one day, but the afternoon had delivered the knockout punch to Yosef's peace of mind.

No matter what the world threw at him he had found comfort in the Resurrection. Over time, a pattern had emerged. Like Moshe and Samira, the growing mass of returnees had suffered tragic and untimely deaths. The Resurrection allowed them to pick up their life stories from that abrupt intermission and read all the way to the happy ending. From Hannah and her seven sons in the Hanukkah story who, rather than betray their faith, had died as martyrs at the hands of the evil Emperor Antiochus, to the victims of terror today, the Resurrection was turning those rivers of bitter tears into the sweet dew of fresh life. The returning dead not only validated ancient Biblical prophecies, they demonstrated God's justice.

Then, that afternoon, Shmuel had staggered into the call center, broken and shaking, and Yosef's rosy theology had crumbled to dust. Why would God revive a suicide bomber—an intentional mass murderer—along with his victims? What was the Resurrection if not compensation for the righteous? Or had Yosef misunderstood even that? And so, at a time when he most needed guidance, Yosef found himself lost, under attack, and utterly alone.

Yosef placed his groceries on the conveyer belt of the checkout counter.

Gavri weighed the vegetables and scanned the other items. *Beep. Beep.*

Yosef placed a fifty-shekel bill on the counter.

"Ready for the big day tomorrow, Rabbi?"

Yosef gave his questioner a suspicious glance. Was this a sarcastic hint at the rabbi's political demise or a good-natured ice-breaker? The fat woman with the evil eye waited in line behind him, and he'd prefer to avoid further public ridicule.

"It's in the voters' hands now," he said.

"Voters?" Gavri seemed to have tasted salt in his coffee. "Who cares about the elections? Tomorrow, the Messiah is coming."

Yosef's breath caught in his chest. "He is?"

"Sure. Everybody knows." Gavri waved the fifty-shekel note at him. "I think, Rabbi, that since you became a politician, you lost touch with the people." The store owner chuckled at his own joke.

Was Gavri pulling his leg? "What messiah?"

"No one knows his name or where he's from, but tomorrow morning he's going to make his big announcement."

"Where?"

"At the Kotel. Where else?"

Yosef turned to the shoppers behind him in the line. They nodded their heads. How had Yosef not heard of this? He had spent hours calling rabbis throughout the city in search of the Son of David, when the tidings of the Messiah had waited for him at the corner grocery store.

Gavri dropped the change into Yosef's hand, the tinkle of coins sounding like the rain of jackpot money at a casino. "Thank you, Gavri!"

"You're welcome, Rabbi. Next customer."

Yosef stumbled out of the store like a sleep-walker. The long-awaited Messiah would appear tomorrow at the Western Wall. Nothing else mattered.

DAN SOFER

CHAPTER 58

In a parking garage beneath Jaffa Road, Eli pulled on a black leather jacket and a pair of matching riding gloves. The winged Harley Davidson emblem gleamed in the cool fluorescent light on the matte black chassis of the Sportster Iron 883.

Once settled on the leather seat, he placed the black helmet over his head. One long stay at Shaare Zedek had sufficed, and Noga had insisted on the safety equipment. But tonight he was not going to think about Noga. Tonight he was going to forget all about her.

He squeezed the clutch, lifted the shift lever to neutral with his boot, and thumbed the starter. The V-twin engine growled to life. He clicked the remote, and the gate of the private parking bay rolled upward. Easing back on the throttle, he launched up the ramp and onto the street.

He slowed briefly at the light, then tore along King George Street. On Emek Refaim, revelers buzzed between the neon signs of Burgers Bar, Kaffit, and the Magic Carpet. The distractions he sought tonight would require a double dose of adrenaline, so he gunned down Pierre Koenig toward Talpiot.

Noga loved Eli Katz, so he had held his delusions below the waterline of his consciousness, and waited for them to drown. But just when that part of his mind had stopped struggling, Noga had changed her mind. Now she wanted Elijah back.

Did she expect him to switch his identity like clothes? She had piled on her arguments like cement bags, weighing him down again with the fate of the entire world until, last night, he had collapsed under the load. To hell with Elijah. To hell with the Redemption. He wanted out.

When she stormed out of his apartment with her suitcase that morning, he had waited for her to return. Let her cool off; she'd come crawling back soon enough. But she didn't. Fine. Her choice. Let her waste her life trying to save humanity if she liked. He was done with mankind. Good luck to her and good riddance.

On a seedy Talpiot street corner, a dozen young women in short skirts lined up at the door of a nightclub. A yellow mushroom cloud filled a poster on the wall. The sign above the door read Hangar 17, and the pulse of the dance beat within reverberated on the street. Bingo.

Eli pulled up on the sidewalk, took off his helmet, and got in line. The girls chatted, all makeup and perfume. A brunette glanced at him and smiled. He returned the smile, and followed them past the bouncer and inside.

Purple light flickered to the beat of trance music in the dark hall, illuminating figures on the dance floor and gallery like lightning. The dancers raised their arms and swung their heads. Smoke billowed at their feet and the sweet scent of alcohol wafted in the air. In a corner, a couple kissed. They had the right idea—live for the moment.

He placed his jacket and helmet on a bar stool and hit the dance floor, weaving among the couples. Some of the dancers had dressed up. One guy had an axe wedged in his hat. His partner had an arrow through her head. *Strange.* The country had celebrated Purim months ago.

At this point, he remembered that he didn't quite know how to dance. During the many years of obsessing over messiahs, apocalypses, and computers, he had not picked up that skill, so he improvised. He lifted his arms in the air and shifted his feet, closed his eyes, and moved his shoulders.

He opened his eyes to discover that a tall blonde was dancing with him. A star exploded on her black T-shirt. She had tied her hair up, the ends sticking out of her head like sunbeams. Her green eyes flashed at him. She had a very pretty smile. She leaned in to say something but her words got lost in the music, so he waved for her to join him at the bar.

"What are we drinking?" He had to shout to be heard.

"Breezer," she told the bartender. "Peach."

"Make that two." Eli had never had a Breezer before but tonight he was eager to taste something new.

When the drinks arrived, they clinked the bottles together and took their first sip. Rum. Very sweet rum. There was a time when rum was his drink of choice, in an age of sea travel and discovery—but he decided not to follow that reverie.

"What did you say on the dance floor?" he said.

"What are you dressed as?" she said.

A definite pickup line. He glanced over his black shirt and jeans. He'd have to make something up. "What's the theme?"

"The End of the World."

He laughed. "I like it." With all the zombies and weirdness lately, the theme seemed oddly appropriate. The bar managers had a sense of humor.

He said, "I'm a prophet of doom," and she gave him the thumbs-up. He took another sip. The sweetness was growing on him. "How about you?"

"I'm a supernova."

"I'll bet you are."

She held his gaze and smirked. "You don't remember me, do you?"

Oh, crap. Where had they met? "Sure I do," he said. "Remind me anyway."

"Café Aroma. On Emek Refaim. You were the big tipper who got away."

She took a long swig from her bottle and he remembered.

The waitress with the intelligent green eyes had sat down at his table and busted him for using The Magic to pour another cup of coffee from the empty milk pot.

He had brushed it off as a magic trick and offered to teach her the secret. When she rushed inside to fetch his check, he dropped a fifty on the table and disappeared. Seconds later, the Thin Voice spoke to him—he remembered that clearly—and the next day he had landed up in Shaare Zedek.

A shiver traced his spine. *That really happened, didn't it?* He took another sip. "I owe you a private lesson," he said, taken off guard by his own audacity. He glanced at the bottle in his hand. *This is great stuff.*

The green-eyed girl held his gaze. "I'm not working to-morrow. Election Day." Her cheeks dimpled as she smiled. "I've got all night."

Eli knew an invitation when he saw one. "Tell me," he said, flashing his charming smile. "Do you like motorbikes?"

CHAPTER 59

"Let me get this straight," Sarit said to Noga. "Your hot, rich boyfriend took you on an amazing cruise, and now you ditched him because... because he didn't agree with your thesis? See—that's the part I'm not getting."

Noga slouched on her friend's puffy couch. "It's more complicated than that. I'd show you the data but I left my laptop at his place."

She had not made an inventory of her belongings before storming out of his apartment. When the golden elevator had opened on the lobby, she had stayed inside, waiting for him to call the elevator back up, fully expecting him to come running after her.

Ten minutes later, she fished clothes out of her suitcase, changed out of her pajamas, and dragged her suitcase through the lobby and down Jaffa Road until she collapsed in a sobbing heap outside Sarit's apartment in Nachlaot.

On the couch, Noga told Sarit the details of her research results, Hannah's theory, and their adventures in the West Bank. "The key to peace in our time has just landed in our lap," she said. "We have to tell someone."

She still remembered the anger in Eli's eyes. *I'm done with humanity.* She felt as frightened as she had that day in the hospital when the comatose patient had grabbed her arm and spouted his deranged claims.

"OK, so you want to go public with your research and win the Nobel Peace Prize or whatever. Still, I don't understand—why did you leave him?"

"Because he didn't want to help."

Sarit laughed. "Noga, you've got to admit that your plan here does sound a little, you know." She waggled her eyebrows.

"A little what?"

"Loony? Nuts? Insane? Ah, yes—*crazy*, I believe that's the scientific term. Certifiable. Stark raving mad. Wasn't that the reason you broke up with him months ago—because he wanted to announce the End of Days?"

Noga sucked in a deep breath. "What if he was right all along? What if we *did* meet for a reason and he really *is* Elijah, and together we were meant to find the Ten Lost Tribes and announce the Messiah? Dead people are walking the streets, for Heaven's sake—is this any less believable?"

Sarit slapped the arm of the couch. "I told you he was for real!"

"You were joking. I didn't believe him either, even after I saw his apartment. You should have seen it—he had this room full of mementos from the last thousand years."

"There you go—that's your proof, isn't it?"

"Well, not anymore. He sold everything on eBay. I think he did it to please me."

"I've got it! Problem solved." For once, Sarit's indefatigable optimism seemed like a lifeline, not an annoyance. Over the years she had dragged Noga to dance classes and charity evenings and other thinly disguised singles' events. Noga had regretted all of them but now she hoped against all odds that her friend held the answer to her problems. "Here's what you do," she continued. "Go back to him. Let him think it over. In time, maybe he'll come to see it your way. *Or not.* What do you care? Either way, you get the penthouse."

"I don't care about the penthouse and I don't want to go back. He's... changed. The old Elijah may have sounded insane but at least he cared about something besides himself."

"He cares about you, doesn't he?"

"I'm not so sure anymore."

"So does that mean he's available?" Noga swatted her with a stiff cushion. "Just asking. Anyway, after dating you, I don't think I'd meet his high standards."

Sarit got up and the couch creaked. "Take it easy, girl. Watch some TV. I'll make hot chocolate and we'll be miserable together. Like the good old days."

Noga sneezed. The dusty couch was triggering her allergies. The good old days sucked.

What would Elijah the Prophet do now? According to Eli, he had possessed a holy intuition and a bag of miracles. She had neither. She needed to share her data with someone in a position of power. They'd know what to do next.

Then she'd have to find an apartment and a job. One mission impossible at a time. Sarit was right—she needed a rest. Tomorrow, she'd pick herself up; tonight she'd wallow in self-pity.

A kettle whined in the kitchenette. Noga slid the remote from the mug-stained coffee table and turned on the immense TV on the small wooden stand that looked ready to collapse.

A studio panel deliberated the elections polls. She had almost forgotten about the elections. Would she even bother to vote tomorrow? One of the new parties wasn't doing so well. A chart showed their projections drop from twelve seats to zero, despite a televised apology.

An honest-looking man in a suit threw his arm over the shoulders of a bearded rabbi. "Restart is all about starting over," the man said.

"Welcome to the club," Noga said.

He gave the rabbi an admiring glance. "Rabbi Yosef has been sober for ten years and was unfairly dismissed from his job. The other allegations made against us are also unfounded."

Sarit returned to the couch and handed over a mug of hot

chocolate.

Noga asked, "Who're they?"

Sarit performed her stunned fish impression. "Have you been living under a rock? That's Moshe Karlin of Restart, formerly the Dry Bones Society."

"The Dry Bones Society?"

"The non-profit that takes in those resurrected people. Pretty freaky, hey?"

"He's running in the elections?"

"Yeah. Handsome guy, I know, but don't bother—he's taken. Pretty wife too. Maybe he's your messiah?"

"You think he's the Messiah?"

"Yeah, why not? Although with all the scandals, he probably won't get any mandates."

Then you can do that on your own, Eli had said. A plan formed in Noga's mind and gave her new hope.

CHAPTER 60

"Oh my God," Lia said. "This place is amazing!"

The green-eyed blonde took in Eli's living room as the blinds opened and the night skyline of Jerusalem glittered through the French windows.

She had climbed onto his Sportster Iron 883 and clung to him as the bike shuddered down the bumpy Jerusalem streets. He had let her wear the helmet.

At the penthouse, he pulled two glasses from a cupboard and poured generous helpings of red wine and joined her at the window. The Old City glowed golden in the distance.

"Thanks." She took a sip. "This is good. What is it?"

"Shiraz."

She raised her glass. "Here's to new experiences." The glasses clinked and they swallowed more wine.

"You have this whole place to yourself?"

"Mm-hmm."

The penthouse had a seductive charm. How had he never taken advantage of that before? Noga, the first girl to visit his bachelor pad, had gone there alone to investigate his prophetic claims while he had lain in a hospital bed. She had broken up with him all the same.

Lia's large green eyes drank him in. "Don't you get lonely up here?"

Eli considered the question. Loneliness had never been an issue and yet he had rushed to fill the vacuum Noga had left. "I suppose I do."

"You don't have to be lonely anymore." She kicked off her sandals and dropped ten centimeters in height. Slipping her hand in his, she led him away from the window, and a knot tied in his stomach.

At the couch, she took the wine from his hand and placed both their glasses on the coffee table.

"You must be good at what you do."

Was he? Eli Katz had failed at leading a normal life, and Elijah had failed at bringing the Redemption, and neither of them had prevented Noga from walking out.

Lia's eyes twinkled in the glow of the LED lighting of the kitchen. "Success is very exciting."

She pulled a pin from the plaits above her head and blond hair spilled over her neck and shoulders.

The knot in his stomach tightened. What if Noga walked in right now? There would be no turning back. Would he ever see her again?

Lia's sweet perfume filled his head as she leaned in, her eyes closed, her lips parting.

"Wait," he said. "There's something I need to tell you."

CHAPTER 61

Yosef rushed home Tuesday morning straight after prayers. Today was the most important day of his life but he couldn't tell a soul. Not yet.

In his bedroom, he found his wedding suit in the closet and removed the plastic cover of the dry cleaners. A messiah is born into every generation and can reveal himself at any moment, and so Yosef had kept the suit at the ready for years. Two months ago, he had adjusted the trousers ahead of his fateful meeting with the Great Council of Torah Sages. Instead of greeting the Messiah, however, he and Moshe had fled the Great Synagogue of Kiryat Belz, an angry ultra-Orthodox mob at their heels.

Today would be different and that certainty warmed his bones. Gavri the grocer had shared with him the word on the street. While Yosef had wasted time cold-calling potential messiahs across the city, the true Messiah had whispered his arrival date to the city folk. Instead of attempting to force the End of Days, Yosef should have waited patiently and kept his finger on the spiritual pulse of the Nation of Israel, for, if not prophets, they were the children of prophets, and their holy intuition did not err.

Deciding to skip breakfast—who could think of food on this historic morning?—he combed his hair, grabbed his black fedora, and headed for the front door.

"It's just an election," said a voice as he marched through the living room. Rocheleh sat at the kitchen counter with her coffee and newspaper, her hair covering wrapping her head. She eyed his clothes. "There's no need to get all dressed up."

He had not shared Gavri's tidings with his wife. She would not hold the messianic promises of the local grocer in high esteem.

Yosef gave her a sheepish grin. "They might need me for a press conference later." That was true enough. Why annoy her with optimistic theories when he could delight her later with joyous facts?

She shrugged her shoulders and returned to her newspaper.

Yosef clicked the remote on his keychain to unlock the brand new Hyundai i35 on the sidewalk. The company car— the first issued by the Dry Bones Society—had replaced his broken down old Subaru, and the engine started every morning without protest.

He turned right onto Yehuda Street, cut through the German Colony, and parked outside Horev Primary School. He was third in line when the voting station opened.

"Save us from the zombie menace," said a young man at the gate. "Vote Upward." Like his friends, the young activist wore a yellow T-shirt with a black nuclear hazard sign.

Yosef just smiled and pulled his hat over his eyes. He bounced on the balls of his feet like a man in dire need of the bathroom. When his turn came, he left his blue identity book at the table of observers and dashed behind the voting booth. He placed a white paper scrap with a large Hebrew letter *Hey* for *Hat-chel*, or Restart, in his envelope, which he dropped through the slot of the voting bin.

Having fulfilled his civic duty, he got back in his car and made for the Old City, painfully aware that now he was officially shirking his professional duties. He had not told Moshe about the Messiah either. Moshe had enough on his mind on Election Day, and his absence at the Dry Bones Society would not change their inevitable defeat at the polls. And if the Messiah didn't show, Yosef would have added one more disappointment to an already depressing day.

But this morning the Messiah was going to show. He had to. The exiles were returning to the Land and the Resurrection was progressing in full force. All that remained was to rebuild the Temple and bring peace to the land—easy tasks when compared with raising the dead.

Cyndi Lauper sang "She Bop" on the car's speakers. Moshe had given him the disc of her greatest hits to replace Yosef's stretched old cassette, seeing that the new car only had a CD player. The jumpy pop song filled the sunny Jerusalem air with the thrill of adventure and discovery, although, to be honest, Yosef had no idea what the song was about.

He crossed the short bridge over the Hinnom Valley and climbed toward Mount Zion. In the jam-packed visitors' lot, he parked between two tour buses, then ran for the gates of the Old City. He passed beneath the tall arch of Zion Gate, the imposing walls around the arrow slits pockmarked with bullet holes, and jogged down the inner road that led from the Armenian Quarter.

The alleys and cobbled squares of the Jewish Quarter grew thick with tourists, seminary students, and locals. Quite a turnout for Election Day. The throng reminded Yosef of the surging crowds that formed during Passover, Shavuot, and Sukkot, the three pilgrim festivals when Jews flocked to Jerusalem from all over the world. The rumor of the Messiah had reached many more ears than he had imagined.

When he reached the stairway that descended toward the Western Wall Plaza, the pedestrian traffic came to a standstill. A quarter hour later, he had only reached the bend of the staircase.

The golden Dome of the Rock rose behind the Wailing Wall. The long massive slabs of weathered stone were all that remained of Herod's immense Temple complex.

In the Western Wall Plaza below, a tightly packed mass of people—men and women, black-hatted and bareheaded—

covered every inch of floor tile from view. Yosef had never seen the plaza so full or so quiet.

The throng of waiting Jews extended down the steps to a security inspection booth. Men with backpacks. Women with strollers. Yosef descended one step as the line inched forward and the Western Wall Plaza dropped out of view behind the barrier wall of the staircase.

Yosef glanced at his wristwatch and panic shot through him. This would take time. Far too much time. A mere hundred meters away, the Messiah was about to announce his arrival, but Yosef was stuck behind a wall, waiting in line!

CHAPTER 62

Moshe grinned at Galit over the breakfast table. "Time to conquer the world," he said.

He felt surprisingly optimistic. The PR sessions had gone well yesterday and should calm voter concerns about the moral integrity of the Restart list. Voters weren't stupid. They could smell trumped-up and politically motivated charges a mile away. And Restart only needed a few seats in Knesset to be a viable coalition partner.

Galit, on the other hand, did not share his optimism. Avi's televised accusations had hit her hard, making her toss and turn in bed. That morning, she had hardly tasted her toast and eggs.

She gave Moshe an imploring glance through puffy eyelids. "Don't go out today, Moshe," she said. "Please."

He laughed. "If we don't go out and vote, how is Restart going to win any seats? Besides, the team needs me at the office to boost morale. After yesterday's drama, the media will be watching our every move and who knows what last-minute fires we'll have to put out."

"I have a bad feeling about this, Moshe. Let's stay home. You heard their hatred on TV. People could get violent."

Violent? What had gotten into her? He got up, walked over, and hugged her. "It's an election, not a civil war. What's the worst that can happen—we don't get into Knesset?"

She stared into his eyes. "What if Avi makes up more accusations?"

"Then I'll respond right away. He's done his worst. He's out of ammunition now."

Galit did not seem convinced.

The doorbell rang. "That must be Noa," Galit said and went to open the front door. They had arranged for the teenager down the street to stay home with Talya for Election Day. Galit let her in and explained when to wake Talya, what to feed her for breakfast, and how to keep her occupied. Good luck to her with that. Their daughter packed enough energy to power a small city for a week.

Moshe freshened up in the bathroom, put on a new collared shirt, and knotted his tie. He sketched out a congratulatory speech in his head, but would pencil in the number of seats later. The official vote count would be available only late that evening.

He prepared a consolation message for his followers as well, just to be on the safe side.

Galit slipped into a green dress. "How do I look?"

"Delicious. Maybe we *should* stay home today."

Finally, he had succeeded in making her smile. Today would end well, he could feel it.

He fished his car keys from the drawer in the hall but when they stepped outside, a large black Mercedes idled on the curb.

The driver wore a dark suit and sunglasses and held the back door open. He would have passed for one of Gurion's secret service agents, except for the ponytail.

"Good morning, sir," Irina's tattooed friend said.

"Morning, Alex. What's the deal?"

"The VIP service," the Russian said and grinned. "For our upcoming Member of Knesset."

CHAPTER 63

"And then," Eli said with the manic enthusiasm of a man who had stayed awake all night, "she said that I don't care about anyone. She got in the elevator and left."

Lia, the blond bombshell, hid a yawn behind her hand. She had been very understanding. They had not kissed. They had not even cuddled. Instead, he had told her his story, and once he had gotten going he had not been able to stop. He had never experienced such an outpouring of emotion. A lifetime—a very long lifetime—of repressed guilt and failure had extinguished the fire in his soul, but these cathartic flashes had made the old coals glow again.

Her eyes became sleepy slits as she rested her head on the couch. "But you *do* care," she said. They had been through this before a number of times throughout the night, but each time the insight burned brighter. "You care about *her.*"

"You're right!" he cried. "I do!" The realization shed light on his entire life, the way the morning sun rose over Jerusalem in the French windows of his living room and bathed the couch in warm beams. He laughed with abandon, an ecstatic lover or a madman. Or both. "Now everything makes sense!"

For the first time in centuries, he truly understood God's plan. His accident, and meeting Noga. Elijah the Prophet had neglected his mission because of a serious, if understandable, personal flaw, and the Boss, in His infinite wisdom, had set him straight.

Lia stifled another yawn. "She's a lucky girl."

Did she believe his story? Was she just humoring an insane and possibly dangerous stranger? With the dead walking on every street corner, anything was possible. Either way, she had listened with empathy and put her finger on the heart of the matter.

Her eyelids closed, then opened. "You should tell her."

"You're right!" Adrenaline pumped through his arteries. "I'll call her right away."

Lia sat up on the couch and massaged the back of her neck. "And I should probably go home and get some sleep."

"Yes, of course. Thank you. Thank you so much. I'll call a cab."

He saw her to the elevator door and folded a two-hundred-shekel note into her hand for the ride home.

"See you around, Big Tipper."

"You can count on it."

When the elevator doors closed, Eli found his phone and dialed Noga's number. He would start with an apology. This was all his fault. She was right, he had made a terrible mistake, and he wanted her back—no, he *needed* her back. He'd make everything right again. There was no time to waste. They had a lot of work to do.

Then a sound made him swear under his breath. In the bedroom, Noga's phone rang.

CHAPTER 64

Sweat trickled down Yosef's neck as he waited in line under the late morning sun. He stood halfway down the staircase to the Western Wall Plaza and could see the metal detector and bag scanner at the security gate. Any moment now, he feared, he'd hear the cheer of the crowd as the Messiah delivered his good tidings, while Yosef squirmed with frustration on the wrong side of the barrier wall.

The anticipation in the air made him tipsy and created an instant camaraderie among his fellow pilgrims. Yosef's cheeks hurt from smiling. He helped a mother in a long, white headscarf lower her pram, step by step. A bearded man with a large white *kippah* grinned at him and nodded his head like a bobblehead dog on a car dashboard. After two thousand years of waiting, endless wandering and persecution, the moment of the Redemption had edged within sight. He only hoped he wouldn't miss the historic event by seconds.

Who was this mysterious messiah? Was he resurrected— had he passed right under Yosef's nose at the Dry Bones Society? The traditional texts had remained silent on this point. One thing was sure: seeing that the Resurrection had not reached the Roman period yet, this redeemer would disappoint Reverend Adams. *But enough guesswork!* The age of speculation had drawn to a close and the bright new reality would settle all questions.

Finally, he stepped through the metal detector, spread his arms for the security inspection, and joined the eager throng in the plaza. He waded through the crowd toward the men's section at the foot of the Western Wall, squeezing past Torah altars and trolleys of prayer books. Sweat glimmered on the faces of the men around him. How would he recognize God's chosen? Would he be bearded or clean-shaven, young or bent with years? What if two messiahs claimed the crown at once? Or three? Or twenty!

The sweaty faces eyed him with the same silent, bursting expectation. Yosef waded toward the towering, ancient stones.

Worst of all, what if no one emerged from the crowd? What if the Messiah had changed his mind and gone back into hiding for another two thousand years?

A gasp rose from the assembled Jewry and hands pointed to the sky. "There! Up there!"

Yosef craned his neck and shielded his eyes from the morning sun. On top of the wall and haloed in sunlight, stood a man.

White robes flapped around his thin frame in the breeze. Long locks of his hair glowed golden as they flowed from a white cotton beanie. He glanced down at them, gracing them with a loving, white smile.

Yosef trembled. Joy gurgled involuntarily in his throat, as ecstatic tears seeped from his eyes. *Yes! This is happening. In my lifetime.*

He had merited to gaze upon the Messiah. In hindsight, a shepherd's robe would have been more appropriate than his formal wedding suit, but his clothing didn't matter. Nothing mattered, except for the saintly figure overhead.

Excited whispers circled the gathering. "It's him! Thank God!" A large man in Chassidic garb beside him recited *She'hecheyanu*—Who Has Granted Us Life, the blessing for momentous occasions.

They gazed at their savior for what seemed like minutes,

when a man clambered onto a Torah altar below. His white cloak and head covering matched those of the Messiah on the Wall, only his beard was red and short. He raised his arms above his head.

"Friends and neighbors," he cried. "Behold your redeemer. Open your ears and your hearts to his message, and your eyes will behold *wonders*." He pointed to the Messiah on the Wall, then slid off the altar.

The Redeemer spread his arms over his flock, a compassionate, embracing gesture. "Friends and neighbors. The time has come. Your suffering is over. A healing sun rises upon you, and a new hope. Your eyes will behold wonders."

Friends and neighbors. Your eyes will behold wonders. The repeated phrases soothed Yosef's mind. There was a plan. The Messiah knew what he was doing.

"But first," the Redeemer continued, "let the blast of the *shofar* carry the tidings throughout the world." With a flourish, he pulled a short, twisted ram's horn from a pocket of his cloak, and then waved his arms in wild circles, like a man trying to regain his balance, while a thousand onlookers gasped.

The Messiah on the Wall found his footing again and smiled, and the crowd exhaled with relief. *Phew!* Yosef's heart returned to his rib cage. He wiped a fresh layer of sweat from his brow. *That had seemed close.* The Redeemer couldn't fall. Of course not. He just had a sense of humor.

High above, the Redeemer raised the ram's horn in the air, his body swaying ever so slightly. Yosef knew that rocking motion. He had performed that dance many times during his wasted youth, usually late at night and in dark alleys that reeked of his own vomit. Yosef dismissed the suspicion from his mind. *No, he's not drunk. It's just the breeze.*

The Redeemer pressed the shofar to his lips, drew a mighty breath, and blew hard, but for all his efforts the blast sounded like a camel passing wind.

The crowd exchanged bemused looks but hid their smiles. Another bit of humor to lighten the mood, that's all. But a dark pit opened in Yosef's stomach. *Something isn't right.*

The Redeemer tossed the horn over his shoulder. "Unbelievers will doubt us," he said. *Was he slurring his words?* The Messiah waved his finger in the air. "Do not fear them. When they ask you, 'Can he walk on water?' tell them, 'No.'" The crowd sighed with disappointment. He had promised wonders.

Then the Redeemer punched the air, as he cried, "Tell them, 'He walks on air!'"

The crowd cheered, eager to witness the miracle firsthand. Yosef's insides clenched. *No. Don't do it!* He looked about the flock, searching for another pair of concerned eyes, but all heads were turned to the heavens. Was he the only one who thought that this was a really bad idea?

Before a protest could form in his throat, the Messiah on the Wall stretched out his arms like a tightrope walker, extended one foot, and stepped onto thin air.

Yosef blinked. The walker leaned forward, resting his weight on the empty space above their heads. No glass or mirrors reflected in the sunlight. A bubble of childlike delight escaped Yosef's mouth. *He's doing it. Dear God. He's walking on air!*

"Behold the true Messiah!" Redbeard cried below, his cheeks bulging with an ecstatic smile.

A joyous cheer rippled through the masses. A voice cried out—Hallelujah!—and a dozen more followed.

Then the Messiah moved his other leg, stepping off the wall, and he fell like a stone.

CHAPTER 65

In the backseat of the Mercedes, Moshe held Galit's hand while the suburban scenery of Baka panned across the window. The driver's ponytail shifted as the luxury car negotiated the bumps.

Irina's new friend still made his skin crawl. If Rafi had wanted to treat them to a chauffeur drive, surely he would have picked them up himself? Or had Irina cooked up the surprise treat, not Rafi? If so, where was she?

Moshe chided himself for judging a man by his appearance. He'd need to learn that lesson fast if he wanted to survive in government.

The phone rang in his jacket pocket.

"Where are you?" Sivan asked.

"We're on our way to the voting station," Moshe said. "We'll head to the office right after."

"Good. Remember, you're registered for the International Convention Center. Yaron has a camera team at the voting box."

"Anything else?"

"Yes. The telephone poll came in."

"Great. Galit's here, I'll put you on speaker." Time to find out where Restart stood.

Sivan said, "Now remember, the poll went out just as the

story broke and before we could answer the rumors."

Moshe and Galit exchanged anxious glances. Sivan was trying to soften the blow, so the results must have been terrible. "Go ahead. We understand."

The car rose and fell over another speed bump.

At the end of the line, Sivan drew a long, audible breath. "Nothing."

"Nothing?"

"We don't get any mandates, according to the poll. We don't pass the electoral threshold."

Moshe felt the blood drain from his face. "But that's only three percent."

"Three point two five percent. Out of tens of thousands of participants, only a handful said they were definitely voting Restart."

Galit squeezed his hand. He pictured the sea of supporters in Beer Sheba and a dozen other cities. Had they all abandoned him so quickly?

"As I said," Sivan added, "that was before your response hit the media."

He masked his heartbreak with sarcasm. "I'm sure Channel Two gave that the widest possible exposure."

"We have to work with what we've got."

He thanked her for the update and tucked the phone into his pocket. Avi's false accusations had erased weeks of intense campaigning. They would be lucky to win a single seat in Knesset.

A Karlin never quits, his father had always said. When the Arabs forced Jews out of the Old City in 'forty-eight, Moshe's grandfather lost his business, but he started over from scratch. His own father had created a successful dispatch company from nothing. But how could Moshe undo the damage as voters already made their way to the ballot boxes?

A sharp pain flared inside his rib cage.

"Are you OK?" Galit turned to him with large, frightened eyes. He was clutching his chest.

The pain faded. "Yeah, I think so. It's been a stressful

couple of weeks." Had he rescheduled that cardiologist appointment? He had been reckless with his health, his eyes always on the future. If he ignored his health any longer, he might not have a future.

Galit slumped back on the seat and gave him a wan smile. "Maybe it's for the best, Moshe. If we're no longer a threat to Avi, maybe he'll finally leave us alone."

Avi, Avi, Avi. His ex–best friend had become the proverbial thorn in Moshe's side. He had stolen Moshe's wife in the past and now he had torpedoed his chances in the election. Judging by his recent behavior, Avi wouldn't be content to live and let live when in power. The new career in politics and the dirty campaign were just stepping stones to Avi's ultimate goal—Galit—and to get her, he'd have to do more than beat Moshe in the elections.

Out the window, the Great Synagogue towered over King George Street. They were traveling in the wrong direction.

"Alex, we're expected at the International Convention Center. We should have made a left onto Ramban."

The ponytail bobbed. "My mistake," Alex said in that lethargic Russian accent. "I'll double back as soon as I can."

Traffic slowed, then stopped. The line of cars ran on and on toward a distant red light. They had dived headlong into peak traffic.

Far behind them, a motorcycle horn bleated. His fellow citizens had set out to vote early so that they could enjoy the rest of the day at parks and beaches. Moshe wouldn't mind joining them. Instead, he would have to watch helplessly as his campaign imploded.

The light was still red. The growl of a motorcycle engine grew louder.

Moshe leaned forward to peek at the side mirror. The biker sped toward them in the emergency lane. The rider wore a full white helmet, thick jacket, and gloves, like an off-road racer.

The growl became a roar as the biker whizzed by their window. Then his brakes screeched and the rear wheel arced, spinning the bike ninety degrees and into the line of cars, where it halted in front of the hood of their Mercedes, blocking their path with the length of the bike.

The biker pulled out a large handgun and pointed it at their windshield.

"Oh my God!" Galit cried.

Without a word, Alex raised his hands in surrender.

"What the hell...?" Moshe blurted, although he knew exactly what the hell was going on.

They were going to die.

CHAPTER 66

Voices gasped as the messiah plummeted, and the men in his trajectory pressed backward to avoid the impact, squeezing the breath out of Yosef in the compacting crowd.

There was a sickening *crack*. The masses held their breath, waiting for their messiah to jump up with a smile and an "I'm OK!"

Instead, someone at the front puked.

Oh no!

The press of bodies eased as the crowd dispersed in a hurry.

Yosef stood frozen to the spot, a rock in a stream of panicked men. "Paramedics!" he cried, but none of them were listening. He turned around and stood on tiptoe to shout above the crowd. "Call the paramedics!"

The fleeing men flowed toward the turnstiles at the exit, but one of them ran for the Red Star of David van positioned beside the security checkpoint.

Yosef waded against the current, toward the towering wall until he reached the clearing that had formed at ground zero, like a crime scene cordoned off by yellow tape. Multitudes had flocked to greet the Messiah; fewer were willing to scrape him off the tiles.

In the center of the clearing, the former messiah lay in a

heap of twisted limbs, his white robes spattered with blood. The stench of half-digested food rose from a fresh puddle of vomit.

For the second time that summer, Yosef wished that he had learned first aid. He turned to the white-faced bystanders. "Is there a doctor here?"

A gray-haired and bewildered man detached from the edge of the clearing. "I'm an anesthesiologist."

"That'll do."

The man crouched over the mangled messiah, laid a trembling hand on the messiah's neck, then looked up at Yosef. "I think he's dead."

Yosef turned around. "Stand back!" he shouted. "Let them pass!" as the medics, carrying a folded stretcher, negotiated a path through the human obstacle course.

A paramedic pulled open the blood-stained robes and attached the pads of a defibrillator to the injured man's chest, while his colleague pumped his heart. They stood clear and the messiah's chest rose from the ground as an electric charge passed between the pads. The paramedics examined the still body again, then lifted him onto the stretcher and rushed him away on their shoulders. He might live yet.

Yosef wiped his brow on the back of his hand. He had observed paramedics at the scene of an accident two months ago. The leather-jacketed biker at the Mount of Olives Cemetery had rocketed up an access road and slammed into a truck.

That rider had survived too. Yosef had handed the paramedics a note with his own contact details, but had heard nothing since. He didn't even know the biker's name.

Yosef didn't know the name of the fallen messiah either, but he had believed in him all the same. *You old fool. When will you learn?*

He stood among the clump of dazed witnesses, who stared into space like lost children.

A finger tapped his shoulder. "You're Rabbi Lev, aren't you?" It was Redbeard, who had introduced the former messiah. "Rabbi Lev," he repeated, "of the Dry Bones Socie-ty?"

Yosef nodded. He couldn't imagine how the man must feel. "I'm so sorry," Yosef mumbled. "So very sorry."

The man gave Yosef's hand an eager shake, his cheeks bulging as he smiled, his eyes large and radiant. "I'm Tom. Tom Levi. We need to work together," he added, "you and I."

"Work together? I don't understand."

It was Tom's turn to look surprised. "Why, to spread the good tidings of course." He laughed. "What else?"

"You can't be serious." Yosef pointed at the blood-stained floor. "Didn't you see what happened? He's badly hurt. He might die."

Tom lifted his hand, palm up, like an ascending elevator. "Then he'll just have to rise from the ashes. Everything that happens is part of God's plan." He became very serious. "We should talk about the Temple."

"The Temple?"

Tom nodded in the direction of the Western Wall. "The Third Temple. We need to get rid of that golden monstrosity and then—"

Yosef held up his hand. "I have to go now. I'm sorry." He hurried toward the exit and away from the madman without looking back.

"Nice to finally meet you, Rabbi Lev," the man called after him. "We'll speak again real soon."

CHAPTER 67

Ahmed woke up that morning with a start. A ceiling of stone hovered inches from his nose, and the chill of bedrock seeped through his clothes, through the flesh of his back, and into his bones. His mouth tasted of dust. Outside, a valley breeze whistled.

Where am I?

Memories of the previous day rose in his mind: the balding older man kicking aside a chair as he charged toward him, shouting accusations; the pressure of his fingers on Ahmed's throat; the look on Samira's face before he turned and fled.

He had dashed down the streets of downtown Jerusalem, running blind, trying to escape the anguish in his head, until he found himself back in Silwan. He scrambled up the stony hillside, clambered into the old burial cave, and stretched out on a rough-hewn shelf. Like the previous occupants of the tomb, he was trapped.

When he closed his eyes, he saw her face, the disbelief, the disappointment, and the fear. He had lost her beautiful smile forever, and he wished he no longer existed. How long would it take for him to starve to death?

His stomach rumbled. Against his better judgment, his body wanted to live.

Why had he pushed that stupid button and stained his soul

543

for eternity? But had he not died, would he have met Samira? Was this God's punishment for evil men—to offer them Heaven on a silver platter, only to yank the platter away? None of the fires of Hell came close to that torment.

He lay there, suspended between death and life, and shuddered as he sobbed.

Damas was right—he was a fool. A fool to have believed Hasan's lies. An even bigger fool to believe that he could start over. No, he was worse than a fool. He was a monster. He did not deserve to live.

He would lie there until his body withered. The rats would find him first. The thought made him sit up and he bumped his head on the rocky ceiling. *Serves you right.* A coward even in death.

He slid off the shelf and crouched on the cave floor. The mouth of the tomb was a rectangle of blue sky. A hammer sounded in the distance, and cars rumbled on hidden streets. Arabs and Jews got about their daily business.

He crawled to the opening, and two small birds fled from a grassy outcrop as he poked his head out of the tomb.

The Kidron Valley sprawled below, the dry riverbed and the Gichon spring, beneath the City of David. But not a single soul in sight.

He staggered out into the open and stretched. Dirt and dry sweat plastered his body. His hair was thick with dust. He scratched a spider bite on his ankle. Above the tomb rose the Mount of Olives, the mass of grave markers like scales on the back of a sleeping dragon. How many sandaled feet had trampled that hillside over the centuries, building and burying, toiling and murdering—and for what?

He peed, dousing a clump of weeds in dark yellow fluid, then hobbled down the steep hill to the dusty streets of Silwan. He trudged along, dragging his feet in the dust like a zombie. Only one path remained to him.

He passed by the streets of his childhood and his mother's new house, and he climbed the unpaved incline.

The yellow Mercedes was parked outside the cement

hangar. Hasan's two thugs sat on crates and stared at their backgammon board. Another seductive melody blared from the speakers of the car to a maqsoum beat. *"Ma Tegi Hena?"* Why don't you come here?

Ahmed approached the luxury vehicle from behind. Hasan slouched in his usual position. On the iPad, Nancy Ajram danced in a fruit market. She wore a skintight red dress and ran her hands through her long curly locks. She gyrated her hips and sent suggestive glances at the camera as she carved watermelons with a butcher's knife.

A cold, cruel idea froze Ahmed's breath in his lungs. Lunging forward, he could seize Hasan's head in both hands and, with one mighty twist, break his cousin's neck with a satisfying crunch before his henchmen knew he was there. They would kill Ahmed but he didn't care. His life was no longer worth living.

Five cowardly seconds passed, but Ahmed did nothing. Instead, he touched his cousin on the shoulder.

Hasan flipped on the seat like an omelet in a frying pan. "You crazy bastard, Ahmed. You've got to stop sneaking up on me like that." He shook his head, laughed, and paused the music. "So, cousin, have you considered my offer?"

Ahmed stood over him and nodded. He said, "I'm ready."

CHAPTER 68

In the middle of the city center and in broad daylight, a biker pointed his long-barreled gun at the windshield of their car.

Time stood still and Moshe's senses sharpened. His heart pounded in his ears. His lungs inflated with his final breath.

He had watched enough Jason Bourne movies to know what would happen next: the *thump-thump* of shots fired through a silencer; the bullet holes in the windshield; the death dance of the trapped victims. Bourne would dodge the bullets and escape in the nick of time, but this was no movie and Moshe was no Jason Bourne, so he froze on his seat, squeezed Galit's hand, and braced for the worst.

The gunman didn't fire his weapon. Instead, tires screeched as a large brown van pulled up beside them in the lane for oncoming traffic.

It happened very fast. Thugs in ski masks poured out of the van. Galit's door opened and a masked man leaned inside, pressed the release for her seatbelt, and pulled her, kicking and screaming, from her seat. Her hand slipped from Moshe's. He lunged forward to grasp her waist but his seatbelt held him back. He disengaged the belt when his door opened and powerful arms locked around his neck and shoulders, yanking him out of the car and lifting him in the air.

He flailed his legs, trying to find traction or to wriggle free of the steel grip. The immense thug carried him off with ease as though Moshe was a baby and Moshe thought of King Kong, the Russian henchman from the slave labor camp.

Then Moshe floated in the air and landed hard on a metal floor. A sliding door banged shut, casting him into darkness.

Moshe scrambled to his feet, but the floor moved and he fell onto one knee. Outside, a motorbike engine growled. A light bulb ignited on the ceiling of the van, making him blink. Two thugs pinned Galit to the floor and wrapped her wrists in duct tape. Moshe dashed at her but something heavy collided with his arm and again he slammed into the metal floor. Pain seared through his shoulder.

A ski-masked giant crouched over him, his head blocking the glowing bulb. He pulled the mask from his head and the ugly mug of King Kong grinned down at him.

"Miss me?" the Russian asked, and he slammed a boulder-sized fist into Moshe's face.

CHAPTER 69

Eli woke up face down on his bed, still fully dressed, his brain pounding inside his skull. He was starting to regret last night and not just the drinking.

His phone read 12:04 PM. There were no missed calls on his phone, and the only missed call on Noga's was from himself. He plugged her phone into a charger. Even if she had decided to leave for good, she'd probably come back for her phone and laptop.

He trudged to the bathroom, his head exploding, his mouth tasting like glue. He popped two Acamol tablets, stripped, and stepped under a hot shower.

That morning he had passed out on a high, having rediscovered his true identity. Finally, he understood God's plan, and the revelation empowered him to both win back Noga and redeem the world. Wonderful.

Nothing dampened the human spirit like a hangover. He had surrendered his identity once before to find favor in her eyes. Was he ready to do that again? And if, this time, he was right, where was the Thin Voice? And where were his legendary miraculous powers?

He turned off the water, wrapped a towel around his waist, and sat on the edge of his bed. The pair of mobile phones lay motionless on the bedside table. Elijah the Prophet had summoned fire from Heaven and revived the dead. If he really was the famous prophet, surely some of those abilities remained?

He stared at Noga's phone, then closed his eyes. He imagined the Samsung Galaxy floating in the air, as weightless as a feather in a gentle updraft. He flexed the muscle in the center of his brain. In his mind's eye, the black tablet rose a centimeter above the table.

He opened his eyes. The phone remained grounded. His shoulders slumped. Then the phone rang.

He glanced at the display. Who was Hannah? The name sounded vaguely familiar. Was Noga calling from a friend's phone in order to locate her own? Or did she want to speak with him, to mend their bridges and come back home?

He answered.

"Noga?" said the voice of an older woman.

"This is her phone."

"May I speak with her?" The voice had the tone of restrained annoyance.

"Who's calling?"

"This is Professor Hannah Rechter, her doctoral supervisor. And who, may I ask, are you?"

"A friend," he said. He did not say "boyfriend." Their relationship status still hung in the air and the fewer details he shared, the fewer questions he would have to answer. "She left her phone here by accident," he added. "I'll tell her to call you as soon as she can."

The professor exhaled her frustrations into the receiver. "Please do. I've been trying to contact her for weeks!"

"She's been... distracted lately." The distraction had answered her phone. "But she'll be back on track soon."

"I hope so. If we don't submit soon, we'll have to wait months."

Eli put the phone down, the professor's urgency reigniting his own. He had to find Noga and not just to deliver the professor's message. Not even to patch up their relationship.

If Noga was right, he had a job to do, and his job was...

what exactly? Elijah had always known the where, the how, the why—the Thin Voice had whispered the details directly into his brain. Eli Katz, however, was lost. Clueless. But together, he and Noga might just figure things out.

He pulled on some clothes, gulped down a glass of milk, and collected his riding jacket and helmet. He pocketed an apple as well. This might take some time.

As he waited at the front door for the elevator, he bowed his head. *Boss, if ever there was a time for a hand up, it's now. Where is she?* He waited for the soft whisper, the sudden flash of clarity.

The doors opened on the golden elevator but he made no move to get in. What was he going to do—drive around the city hoping to spot her on the street?

The elevator doors closed. He dumped the helmet on the kitchen island, returned to the bedroom, and picked up Noga's phone. The screen wasn't locked. Ignoring the pinch of guilt for invading her privacy, he scrolled down her call history and found another vaguely familiar name.

CHAPTER 70

Yosef had hoped to sneak into the office unnoticed, but the call center of Restart, formerly the Dry Bones Society, had never looked so crowded. Or festive. Balloons and streamers in blue and white hung from the ceiling and windows. On the mounted TV, political commentators dissected the mounting exit polls. Party members and reporters chatted and glanced him over as he entered. Some members wore party hats.

"Where have you been?" their eyes seemed to ask. Was his guilt written on his face? The answer was as embarrassing as it was predictable: Yosef had believed. He had followed a false messiah, basing his blind faith entirely on the rock-solid authority of—wait for it—his local greengrocer. Thank God that he had not shared his messianic convictions with Moshe or with his own wife. Rocheleh was right; Yosef the gullible fool had no place in public politics. Was he even worthy of guiding a charitable organization?

"Hi, Rabbi!" Irina said. She knelt beside a large packing box at the entrance and stared up at the rabbi, who flinched preemptively at the expected interrogation.

Her cheerful countenance faltered. "Are you OK? You look pale."

"I'll be fine." He gave her a quick, feeble grin to back up his claim and made for the secure isolation of Moshe's office.

"Rabbi Yosef," called another female voice, and he stopped in his tracks. Sivan had spotted him from across the call center and strode toward him. He braced for the worst. *Here it comes.*

"I'm glad you're here," she said, breathless, and she looked over her shoulder at the sea of reporters. Her painted-on smile failed to hide her anxiety. "Where's Moshe?"

The question caught him off guard and he glanced around for their party leader. "I haven't seen him yet. Is something the matter?"

Yosef had a bad feeling about this. It wasn't like Moshe to abandon his team in times of trouble.

Before Sivan could answer, Irina joined them, the cardboard box in her arms. "Here's the confetti we ordered. Where do you want it?"

"In Moshe's office for now," the campaign manager said.

"How are we doing?" Yosef asked softly.

"Not good," Sivan said, still smiling at the packed room. "We should have hit back harder. That's what you get for running a clean campaign."

Yosef swallowed. This was his fault. His failings had crippled Restart. Rabbi Nachman of Breslov taught that one can start life anew each day, but a new today didn't erase a shameful yesterday.

"Pray for a miracle," she whispered and walked off.

Perhaps Restart would fare better without his prayers. He should resign and let them be. Not now, of course, like a rat abandoning a sinking ship, but after the elections. His presence drew calamity the way magnets drew iron filings.

"Let me give you a hand," he said to Irina, and reached for the box. At least he could help out with the manual labor without causing more damage.

"I almost forgot," she said. "There's someone here to see you."

"To see me? Who—Mr. Adams?" Yosef was in no state to host their Christian benefactor.

"No, a woman. She wanted to speak with you or Moshe.

She said it's important."

Had a messenger of the failed messianic cult beat him to the office? "Was she wearing a white cloak?"

Irina's eyes narrowed and she gave him a bemused smile. "A white cloak? No. Are you sure you're OK?"

"Yes. Of course. Never mind." His cheeks warmed. "I'll see her in Moshe's office."

Yosef placed the box of confetti in a corner of the office and settled behind the desk. The countless calls he had made at that desk to potential messiahs had achieved nothing. He would never find the Messiah—if he existed at all.

Yosef shuddered at his heretical thought. What if the Messiah was a myth—a futile exercise in communal wishful thinking, an imaginary fairy godmother for centuries of miserable Diaspora Jews?

For starters, Yosef should stop wasting time in trying to find him. In fact, he should stop accepting everything he read or heard. If he didn't grow up soon, he'd bring more disgrace to himself and those around him.

Irina opened the door for a pretty young woman with tied-up dark hair, and moved on to her other tasks. The woman approached the desk, her eyes large and expectant, her mouth drawn, and she put out her hand. After a moment's hesitation, Yosef shook her hand and beckoned for her to sit. Despite his numerous interviews with female reporters, physical contact with a woman other than his wife still made him uncomfortable.

What did this pretty young woman want with him? Had Avi Segal sent her to generate more scandalous rumors?

Two reporters glanced at them through the large windows of the office. He had better send the woman on her way as soon as possible.

"How can I help you, Miss…?"

"Shemer. Noga Shemer. I'm a doctoral student at the Hebrew University. My research—"

"Then I must refer you to Professor Yakov Malkovich," Yosef said, cutting her off. "He's already heading up a study of volunteers from our Society at your university. I think he'll be happy to discuss your research."

Miss Shemer glanced at the desk, and seemed taken aback at the interruption and abrupt dismissal. "My research is different and, in my opinion, of great interest to you."

Yosef felt ashamed at his curt behavior. He had no choice but to hear her out. "I'm sorry. Please go on."

"My study aimed to find a genetic link between Jews of priestly descent—the Cohen Gene."

"And did you find this link?" He still didn't see how this was relevant to the Dry Bones Society.

"Yes. But I discovered something else, something unexpected. I won't bore you with the technical details but the bottom line is this: I think I've found the Ten Lost Tribes of Israel."

Yosef considered her words. According to Rabbinic sources, Elijah the Prophet would reveal the Ten Lost Tribes at the End of Days. Now this pretty young student claimed to have discovered them in a test tube.

"The Ten Lost Tribes?" he repeated, and he tried to conceal his smile beneath his moustache. He folded his lips into his mouth to stop them from trembling. After his experiences that morning, her statement was just too much.

She studied his reaction in tense silence.

Trying to keep his voice level, he said, "And where are these lost Israelites?" Had she spotted them between the chromosomes in her lab, or perhaps the lost Jews had colonized the moon?

"They're right here, Rabbi Lev." She lowered her glance to the table again. "Among us. Palestinian Arabs are the Lost Tribes."

His body shook with pent-up laughter. He did not want to embarrass the girl but—Palestinian Arabs! A sobering thought helped curb his sense of humor. First, the weirdo messianic cult; now a pretty young pseudo-scientist. He should hang a sign on the door: "Fools Anonymous. We buy anything. All manner of crackpot theories welcome. Leave reason at the door." *This is what you've become, Yosef: a magnet, not for calamity, but for lunatics.*

He drew a deep breath, stared at the ceiling, blinked back a tear, and counted to ten. Composed, he retrieved a yellow square from a pile of notepads. "As you can see outside, we're a bit swamped with the elections today. But please leave your name and number and we'll try get back to you later."

The girl stared at the sheet, then scribbled down her contact details and stood. "Thank you for your time," she said, her voice soft and defeated, and she left the room. She had read between the lines.

Try to get back to you, he had said; he had made no promises.

CHAPTER 71

A pain at the back of his neck roused Moshe to consciousness. He was slumped over on a hard chair in a dark place. Daylight seeped through the filthy slats of windows high on corrugated walls. The floor stank of old motor oil.

He wanted to massage his neck but he couldn't move his arms. Thick duct tape secured his wrists and ankles to the metal frame of the chair. He made to speak but his lips were taped shut, and he breathed heavily through his nose. The skin over his cheekbone felt raw and tender.

He turned at the sound of a whimper at his side. Galit sat strapped to another chair, a line of silver tape over her mouth, and fear glittering in her eyes.

Moshe had never intended to put her in harm's way, but he should have seen this coming. Boris had done this. King Kong had pulled him from the car and King Kong did Boris's bidding. Moshe may have bought back his own freedom with hard cash, but his Dry Bones Society had ensured that none of the newly resurrected landed up in the crime lord's slave labor machine. Fewer slaves meant less money. The backlash had been slow to arrive but inevitable, and now Boris would settle the debt.

Where was Alex? Their driver had raised his hands in the air when the biker had trained his gun on their car. Had he tried to resist when the thugs had pulled Galit and Moshe from the back seat? Moshe didn't recall hearing gunshots, but the abduction had happened so fast and King Kong had knocked him out.

The future rolled out in front of him. Boris could have had them killed in the car if he had wanted. No, he had something else in mind. Torture. Threats. A lesson Moshe would never forget. Would Boris hurt Galit or was she there only to remind Moshe of what he had to lose? No, he wouldn't hurt her, would he?

A pitiful snort of fear and remorse escaped Moshe's nose. He should have kept his head down and been thankful for his freedom. Instead, he had rushed headlong to save the world, and in doing so he had drawn a bull's-eye over his loved ones. Poor little Talya was probably wondering why they hadn't come home. But how could he have done nothing while Boris led other new arrivals into slavery?

Don't panic, Moshe. Stay focused. His first priority was to get out of there alive and in one piece. He'd tell Boris whatever he wanted to hear. Afterwards, in safety, he could figure out how to help others without jeopardizing his family.

Moshe looked around. He heard no movement. They seemed to be alone in the abandoned warehouse. A third chair stood empty beside a large circular table that had been toppled onto its side, the round surface painted red like a single bloodshot eye. Beyond the table, a thin line of daylight framed a door in the corrugated wall.

He pulled at his bonds, rocking the rickety chair on its metal feet. If he could dislodge the wooden surfaces, he might be able to free his hands and then—

A door creaked open behind them and fluorescent strip lights flickered to life overhead. Heavy footfalls drew nearer.

A tall bald man in black walked around the chairs and stopped before them. He turned his immense nose and large sensitive eyes to them, his arms folded behind his waist like a restaurant host eager to serve his guests.

"Welcome, Mr. Karlin," he said, with a distinctly Russian

accent. "Mrs. Karlin." He inclined his head. "We meet at last. Thank you for joining me on such short notice. I must apologize for leaving you alone for so long. You know how things are."

Moshe did not know how things were, but from the conciliatory tone he inferred that he might be released sooner than he had thought.

"I'm so very proud of you, Moshe," the man continued. "You don't mind if I call you Moshe, do you? Look how far you've come! From practically a slave to a contender in today's elections. Although," he wrinkled his nose, "the exit polls have not been very kind, have they?"

This comrade of Boris knew far too much about Moshe for his liking, and his tone of exaggerated friendliness did not put Moshe at ease.

The man seemed to read Moshe's discomfort on his face, for he slapped a large hand to his forehead. "I have such bad manners. My name is Mandrake." He bowed, then snapped his fingers. "Vitaly, if you will."

Another man stepped into view. Like Mandrake, Vitaly wore black and had shaved his scalp, but he was built like a tank and a long, jagged scar bisected his left cheek. When the henchman leaned over him, Moshe flinched, expecting another blow to the face, but the man peeled the tape from Moshe's mouth.

"That's better, isn't it?"

Moshe's lips stung from the hastily removed tape. "What do you want from us?"

Mandrake looked insulted. "You misunderstand me. *I* am here to serve *you*. I prepared this show especially for you."

Moshe was about to ask "What show?" when the door behind Mandrake rattled.

"Excuse me," Mandrake said, "but I think our other guests have arrived."

The door of the warehouse swung open, and three men walked toward them in a momentary nimbus of bright light. Moshe knew them all by sight: Gray-haired Boris in his usual

tweed jacket; King Kong trudging beside him.
The third visitor made Moshe's blood boil.

CHAPTER 72

"Sit," Hasan said and Ahmed obeyed, settling on the simple school chair. Plaster flaked from the walls of the room, which stank of damp rot. No one lived there. This was no place for the living.

"Take off your shirt."

Again, he obeyed.

Hasan had led him to the empty apartment in Silwan, two streets down from the garage hangout, to prepare for his mission. Before his first mission, his skin had tingled and he had worried about being captured by the Israeli authorities. This time, he felt numb. He would do whatever Hasan commanded. Soon it would all be over.

Hasan pulled a pair of thick gloves over his hands and draped a stained sheet over Ahmed's shoulders. With the handle of a worn toothbrush, he stirred the mixture inside a plastic tub and applied the thick yellow paste to his cousin's hair. The chemical broth smelled of rotting fish, like the crates of offal Ahmed had lugged to the trash enclosure outside the Rami Levi supermarket in Talpiot.

Ahmed closed his eyes and focused on the gloved hands that pulled at his hair and worked the dye into his scalp, the last human touch he would experience in this life.

"No one has done this before," Hasan said. "A double

martyr. You will be a hero. No, more than that—a legend."

Ahmed opened his eyes. He would be neither. He no longer believed the lies. The mission would line Hasan's pockets but Ahmed would find neither glory nor Paradise. He sought neither of those now, only the black emptiness of nothingness.

Hasan placed the tub on the floor and plugged a blow dryer into a cracked wall socket. The machine whined and blew hot air over Ahmed's sticky head, then fell silent. The stench of singed hair hung thick in the air.

"What now?"

"We wait."

"Is this really necessary?"

"The Jews have wised up over the years. No one does buses anymore. Their wall has made moving explosives difficult, and the bus stations are full of soldiers. You can't walk around looking like a sad Arab kid."

Ahmed nodded. He waited in silence while Hasan leaned against the wall, smoked Peter Stuyvesants, and toyed with his fancy mobile phone. After a few minutes, he glanced at his shiny watch and stubbed out his cigarette. He dried Ahmed's hair with a towel and plugged another machine into the wall. The clippers groaned and vibrated over Ahmed's head as severed blond locks piled in his lap.

Hasan turned off the clippers, pulled off the sheet, and threw him a new black T-shirt. "Stand."

Hasan placed a harness over Ahmed's shoulders and tightened the straps about his chest. Bulging packs of explosives pressed into his ribs, covered in plastic bags stuffed with metal screws and ball bearings. Last time, Ahmed had hefted the payload in a shoulder bag; today his body was the bomb. Maybe this time he would stay dead.

Hasan helped him into a thin black jacket and threaded the detonator cable through the sleeve.

"Remember how it's done?"

Ahmed nodded. "Where do you want it to happen?"

His cousin shrugged. "Find a crowd during rush hour."

He glanced at his wristwatch. "You have enough time to get into position." He held up a mirror for Ahmed. "What do you think?"

Ahmed stared into the frameless, chipped square in his cousin's hands. A boy with a blond Mohawk stared back. The boy wasn't him; Ahmed was already dead.

CHAPTER 73

Tuesday afternoon, Eli stood outside a large blue door on Shilo Street and prepared to bare his heart. He pressed the buzzer. Pulling off a riding glove with his teeth, he combed his hair with his free hand. The other hand held a fresh bouquet of roses and the delicate aroma of new beginnings.

He had changed and Noga would forgive him—of course she would!

A gutter ran down the center of the narrow cobbled lane. Short metal poles of red and white guarded the grubby stone façades from passing vehicles. Nachlaot, a labyrinth of courtyards and stony alleys, had sprouted in the late nineteenth century, when Jews settled the hills outside the Old City walls in order to escape the cramped conditions within. Mishkenot Yisrael, Mazkeret Moshe, and Knesset Yisrael had followed. A century later, as the city expanded further, the hive of arched windows and haphazard balconies had fallen into decay until recent gentrification projects had revived the quaint neighborhood and sent property prices soaring.

Eli had not researched the neighborhood's history on the Internet; he had witnessed the evolution firsthand. His memories were real, not the creaking of an unhinging mind. Noga's research proved that.

A giddy sense of release flowed through him. No longer

did he have to repress his memories or deny his identity. He was Elijah of Tishbe, priest, prophet, and messianic harbinger. Granted, his prophetic intuition had fled along with his miraculous powers. He lacked the tools to fulfill that destiny and the sheer magnitude of the task scared him to his core. But despite all that, his all-night catharsis had unearthed an empowering insight along with a hidden vial of optimism for the fate of mankind. And so, he had never been both so ill prepared and yet at the same time highly motivated to complete his historic mission. The irony was not lost on him.

Behind the gate, feet thumped down steps, but the footfalls were too heavy to belong to Noga.

When the gate swung inward, a large woman blocked the path to the apartment building. Her small eyes moved from the flowers to his face, and the mouth on the pudgy face smiled, revealing a large set of buckteeth. The image of a chipmunk rose in his mind, a chipmunk ogling a mound of tasty acorns.

"You must be Sarit," he said. "I'm Eli."

"I know all about you," she said, and smirked.

Eli swallowed, hoping that at least some of what she had heard about him had been flattering. "Is she here?"

She leaned a flabby arm on the edge of the gate. "How did you find me?" The playful lilt in her voice implied that she had waited all day for his arrival. Her smile widened and Eli feared she might start gnawing at his head.

"With this," he said, and he retrieved Noga's phone from his pocket. "And the Internet."

She held out her hand, palm up, and he handed over the phone.

"Come on up," she said, and she sauntered toward the apartment block, rolling her hips.

He followed her up a flight of stairs, his heart thumping in his chest, and he rehearsed the speech he had prepared on the way. The words had a lot in common with his previous revelatory speech, the one he had delivered to Noga in the secret garden courtyard at the Shaare Zedek Medical Center. That speech had ended in disaster, but a lot had changed since then. He only hoped that this time she'd be more forgiving.

Sarit unlocked an apartment door and stepped into a small but homey living room. Well-thumbed novels crammed an IKEA bookshelf. In a small fishbowl, a guppy circled a water plant. A patterned rug led to a sagging couch, but no sign of Noga.

His hostess slipped into the kitchen, returned with a vase, and relieved him of the flowers. "Have a seat."

Eli settled on the edge of the couch, expecting Noga to emerge from the corridor any moment.

Sarit sat down beside him. "So," she said, brushing a lock of mousy hair behind her ear, "you're the one with the private jet?"

How much had Noga shared with her? "A charter," he said, and avoided her hungry chipmunk eyes. "I don't travel often."

Her head bobbed up and down. "Can I get you a cup of coffee?"

"No thanks."

"Something stronger?" Her voice had dropped to a knowing purr. Was she stalling?

"Is she here?"

"No," Sarit said, still grinning at him.

"Where is she?"

Sarit laughed as though he had asked her to dance on the ceiling. "I can't tell you that."

"Why not?"

"Because then you'll try to stop her."

"Stop her?" he repeated. "Stop her from what?"

CHAPTER 74

In Avi Segal's fantasies, he drove Moshe Karlin's car, owned his home, and lived with his wife. Moshe himself had not featured in these fantasies. In fact, the defining characteristic of Avi's romanticized victory was the complete and utter absence of his ex–best friend and, lately, political adversary.

But now, as he stood over the cowed figure tied to a chair in a dank warehouse, surrounded by Boris's henchmen, he couldn't resist rubbing Moshe's nose in his defeat.

"Moshe, Moshe, Moshe," he said. "I told you to stay away from her."

In the offices of Upward earlier that day, Avi had been busy sipping wine and high-fiving Gurion's campaign and media teams while the exit polls rolled in, when Boris had appeared in the doorway.

"We're busy here," Avi had hissed at him. "What do you want?" He could not be seen with the thug, who seemed intent on spoiling his moment of glory.

"I have a surprise for you," was all the Russian would say, and Avi had grudgingly followed him out of the building.

A surprise was an understatement! Tying Moshe to the chair seemed a bit too dramatic, but the message was clear: I win, you lose. For once, Moshe had run out of witty comebacks. *That'll teach him.*

He turned to tell Boris to let the runt go—Avi had places to go—when a whimper drew his attention to a second seated figure, bound and gagged, who peered at him with a mixture of fear and pleading in her eyes.

"Boris," he said. "What the hell is the matter with you? Let her go right now!"

Boris said nothing and made no move to release Galit.

"Aren't you happy with our little gift?" said a bald man in black. He had an enormous nose.

"Who the hell are you?" Avi was having none of this. He had powerful friends. As number nine on the Upward list, he would soon be a member of Knesset himself.

"My apologies," Big Nose said. "We have not been formally introduced. Mandrake." He gave a slight bow. "I make dreams come true."

What was this Mandrake smoking? Avi turned to Boris, who stared at the floor in meek silence. It was apparent that Mandrake called the shots in here, so Avi opened his mouth to tell him to free Galit, when Mandrake said, "Vitaly, will you do the honors?"

Another bald thug in black stepped toward Moshe and placed a long-barreled handgun to his temple.

"Wait!" Avi cried, his voice echoing off the corrugated walls. All eyes turned to him. "Don't... don't shoot him."

Mandrake peered at him with surprise. "I don't understand. Moshe Karlin is your enemy. Surely you want to be rid of him?"

Moshe blinked at Avi, his chest heaving. Galit stared, her eyes wide.

"I don't want to *kill* him!" This Mandrake was a real wacko. How had he gotten mixed up with these people?

"Oh, I see. Very well." Mandrake waved his hand and Vitaly stood down, the gun disappearing into his clothes.

Then Mandrake gave his head a slight nod, and thick arms grabbed Avi under the armpits, lifting him into the air, pushing his neck forward and his shoulder blades back, and he cried out in pain. Avi had experienced these sensations before, and so he knew that Boris's giant held him in a steely vise.

"Put me down, you idiot!" He had powerful friends. A seat in the government. They couldn't hurt him, could they?

Mandrake scratched his head. "You've put me in a tricky situation, Avi. You see, I have two horses in this race—you and our friend Mr. Karlin here. No point competing against myself. Your numbers are looking more favorable at the moment, so I had thought to keep you, but I suppose now you've given me no choice. Vitaly, if you will?"

Vitaly stepped forward, drew his gun, and aimed at Avi's head.

"No!" Avi cried, losing all sense of entitlement. "Please, no!"

CHAPTER 75

By the afternoon, the crowd at the Dry Bones Society had thinned as reporters left to cover parties that might actually win a seat in Knesset. Society members also slunk off one by one, each remembering that they had urgent things to do somewhere else.

Irina collected empty paper cups off the refreshment tables and the floor of the call center and tried to stay out of Sivan's way. The campaign manager stood in the middle of the room, her arms folded, and stared at the screen where a pair of political commentators analyzed the results. At first they had joked about Restart's lack of support; now they didn't bother mentioning the once-hopeful party at all.

"I don't believe it," Sivan muttered. "We'll demand a recount."

"Let them finish counting first," Shmuel said. "Not that it'll help any." He leaned against the window of Moshe's office beside Rafi, who stared at his feet. The rabbi hadn't left Moshe's office since he had arrived. Irina didn't blame him.

"Where is he?" Sivan had asked the same question all morning. It wasn't like Moshe to hide from defeat, but Irina didn't blame him either. He had bet everything on winning seats in the election, and without friends in the new government, their hard-earned gains would disappear overnight.

"Meatballs?" Savta Sarah said. She peered up at Irina, her eyes filling her glasses, disposable bowls of steaming food on the tray in her hands. "Stuffed cabbage?"

"No thanks, Savta."

"Cheer up, girl. While there is life, there is hope."

A caustic laugh escaped Sivan's mouth but she stayed glued to the big screen.

"Where is your boyfriend?" Savta continued.

Irina sucked in a deep breath. Another good question. Aloud she said, "He went to pick up Moshe this morning, but they haven't arrived yet. They're not answering their phones either."

Savta seemed taken aback. "That's not like Moshe—not to show up for work. Have you called the police?"

"They're probably sharing a beer in a bar somewhere," Shmuel said. "Which is not such a bad idea." The poor results had sharpened his cynicism.

"Savta's right," Irina said. "Maybe something happened to them."

Knuckles rapped on the door of the call center. A man stood on the threshold. He wore a black leather jacket and held a large bouquet of roses. Irina walked over to greet the stranger, who had obviously lost his way.

"Hi," he said. "I'm looking for Noga Shemer."

Irina shrugged and shook her head. The name didn't ring a bell.

The man frowned. Stubble peppered his manly jaw and thick locks of jet-black hair fell over his forehead. This Noga Shemer was a lucky gal.

"She was on her way here this morning," he said, "to meet a Moshe Karlin. She's about twenty-eight. Average height. Intelligent. Beautiful. Stubborn, at times." He smiled.

Irina remembered. "Oh, her! She waited all morning for Moshe, but he wasn't in so she spoke with the rabbi. She really is quite pretty." *You're rambling, Irina. Stop that.* "She left about an hour ago."

"Oh." His expression darkened. Broken stems stuck out

where some of the flowers had fallen off. He had obviously been searching for her a long time. Hope flickered in his dark eyes. "Did she say where she was going?"

"No."

He nodded, thanked her, and left.

She turned around to find that the others—Shmuel, Rafi, and Savta Sarah—had joined Sivan, and together they watched the screen with open mouths.

Enough was enough. "Guys," she said, "maybe it's time we turned that off."

"Shh!" they said as one.

Irina drew near. A bar chart was displayed on the television while the commentators jabbered in the background. Of the dozen colored bars, three rose above the others and one of them towered even higher. "What's happening?"

"We're in the lead," Sivan said without turning from the screen.

Rabbi Yosef emerged from the office and joined them.

"I don't understand," Irina continued. "I thought we had no votes."

"Those were the exit polls," Shmuel explained, his lower lip trembling. "These are the real results."

"What did we get?"

"Two seats so far," Sivan said. She turned to stare at the others and a maniacal smile broke over her face. "We're in!" she cried. They shouted. They jumped up and down and hugged like soccer teammates after a deciding goal.

"We're in! We're in!"

They were so busy celebrating the turn of events that they didn't hear the door open again. Sivan saw him first and gasped. A man leaned against the doorpost. Dirt stains marred his T-shirt, a fresh bruise his cheekbone. He staggered inside and Irina launched forward to help him. "Alex!"

CHAPTER 76

Moshe gulped air, his chest heaving. Moments ago, the hard, cool barrel of a gun had pressed against the side of his head. *Game over*, he had thought, as a dagger of pain pierced his heart and slashed his left arm. At least the bullet would end his life quickly.

Then Avi had cried out. Years ago, in a cold army position in the Judean Hills, Avi had thrown Moshe to the ground, saving him from a terrorist's automatic gunfire. Today, against all Moshe's expectations, Avi had saved his life again.

But now Mandrake had turned the tables.

King Kong held Avi in a neck lock, lifting him in the air like a rag doll, while Vitaly walked over and put his gun to Avi's head.

"No!" Moshe cried. "Don't!"

Mandrake's shoulders slumped like a frustrated teenager. "Moshe," he chided. "This is your moment. We're doing this for you. Your old friend here betrayed you and deceived you. He's done everything in his power to destroy both you and all that you've worked so hard to create."

Mandrake sighed. "I know what you're thinking. 'He just saved my life, so now I should return the favor.' Awkward, isn't it?" He gave an embarrassed chuckle. "Personally, I think he did it for the girl—your wife. She'd never forgive him if he let you die. But let me tell you a secret." His voice dropped to a whisper, but loud enough for all to hear. "I wasn't really going to kill you. You're far too valuable to me. You're a natural leader. Avi here, on the other hand, well"— he turned to Avi—"no offense, Avi, but you're an idiot. Nobody believes in you. Nobody is going to follow you into battle."

Mandrake paced before them, as though lost in thought. "Tell you what, Moshe, let me do you this favor, and then I'll let you and your wife go. Little Talya is waiting for you. I'm sure that young babysitter of yours must be very anxious by now. Just say the word. Vitaly will put Avi out of his misery and we can all go home. What do you say?"

Moshe looked at Avi. As much as Moshe detested him, he had no desire to watch his head explode. And Moshe didn't believe Mandrake's promises either. None of the captives would leave the warehouse alive. The psychopath was toying with them.

"Please, Moshe," Avi pleaded, misinterpreting Moshe's long silence. "I'm sorry." He convulsed with tears. "I never meant to hurt you. I'll give up politics. I'll leave the country. I'll do anything, just please don't kill me!"

"Say the word," Mandrake crooned, "and all your troubles will be over. You don't have to pull the trigger. You don't even have to say the words. Just nod your head. Nod your head and we'll understand."

Galit sobbed beside him. Whatever he answered, the result would be the same. So Moshe said nothing, and kept his head as still as humanly possible.

What did Mandrake really want? If Moshe could find that out, he could make a deal. But nothing the man did made any sense. How did you bargain with a psychopath?

"Moshe," Avi pleaded. He was bawling now. "I never wanted to kill you. I just wanted to be like you. That's all. Can't you see?"

Moshe could remain silent no longer. "Don't hurt him," he said. His voice sounded weak and foreign to his own ears.

His mouth had dried up. "Leave him alone." Then he closed his eyes and braced for the worst. Who would they shoot first?

A chair leg scraped on the cement floor and Moshe opened his eyes. King Kong was tying Avi to the third steel-framed chair.

Mandrake padded toward Moshe. "I'm disappointed in you, Moshe. You could have ended it all." He towered over him like a large bird of prey and smiled. "But between me and you, secretly I was hoping you'd do this."

He danced back a few steps and spun around on one foot. "Ladies and gentlemen," he cried like a circus ringmaster. "A warm round of applause for our brave volunteer, Moshe Karlin." With a wild flourish of his arms, Mandrake indicated the overturned tabletop. "The show must go on!"

CHAPTER 77

Alex stumbled into the call center of the Dry Bones Society. Irina gripped his arm and the rabbi wheeled over an office chair, and they eased him onto the seat. A half-dozen worried faces huddled over him and stared at his face with pained expressions. They had fallen for his act.

The black eye was real. After the street show on King George Street, he had stopped by his apartment in downtown Jerusalem, munched a tuna sandwich, and slammed his bed-room door into his face. The injury added an element of realism that nipped any doubts in the bud.

"What happened?" Shmuel and Rafi said at once.

"Where is Moshe?" Sivan said.

"We were ambushed," he said. "On King George Street. They took Moshe and Galit."

Irina gasped. Sivan swore.

"Who did?" Shmuel again.

"Men with guns. They wore masks." That much was true. "They shoved them into a van and sped off. One of them got away on a motorbike."

Shmuel and Irina exchanged meaningful glances. Did they doubt his story? Or had they run into these goons before?

"This is Avi's work," Sivan said. "Gurion wouldn't do any-thing as stupid as this."

"No," Shmuel said. "It's Boris." Sivan didn't know the name, so Shmuel explained. "We were practically his slaves in his labor camp until Moshe bought our freedom. After that, the Society saved new arrivals from falling into his hands."

"Organized crime?" Sivan put a hand to her forehead as though she had a fever. "You went up against organized crime? Perfect!" She turned to Alex. "What do they want—ransom money?"

Alex raised his hands in a gesture of helpless ignorance. Irina swept strands of hair out of his face and dabbed a damp tissue over his wounds. He *had* to deceive her; it was the only way to keep her safe.

"Thank God the press has gone," Sivan said, "but they'll be back soon."

"They will?" Alex said. The show was to proceed on the quiet, without public attention.

Sivan waved at the screen. "We're back in the game. Just when our numbers go up, this has to happen."

Alex glanced at the bar chart on the television screen, which showed Restart ahead of Upward and the other parties. He had to tell Mandrake. Surely this would change his plan for Moshe and Galit.

Rafi said, "We should call the police."

"Are you crazy?" Sivan said. "No one can know this. People are still voting out there. We have to get him"—she pointed at Alex—"out of sight. We'll go public once the voting ends."

"No!" The single word dazed them into silence. Rabbi Yosef had spoken for the first time. His forceful utterance seemed to have surprised him as much as them. "We can't just wait here and do nothing. We have to help Moshe. He'd do the same for us."

Irina and Shmuel nodded.

"What can we do?" Rafi said.

The rabbi blinked. "Try and find him? At least we'll know where to point the police. Alex, what color was the van?"

"Brown. A brown GMC."

Shmuel said, "So what are we going to do—drive around the city and hope we bump into them?"

"We don't have to." This time Rafi had spoken up. "Most cabbies still have CB radios. I'll put the word out to look for a brown GMC."

Sivan said, "And I'll speak with my friends at Ridez. They can broadcast messages inside the app. It's worth a shot."

"I'll take my cab out now," Rafi said. He mopped his dark, balding forehead. "Alex, which way were they heading?"

"Toward Talpiot," he said. He knew exactly where they were heading. He moved to get up. "I'll come with." If they were going to play the hero, he had better keep tabs on them.

"But you're hurt," Irina said.

"I can drive. And two cars are better than one."

"Three cars," the rabbi said. "I'll head out too."

"Oh, no you don't," Sivan said. "You're number two, remember. We need you to hold the fort and speak with the press. This place is going to explode soon. It's what Moshe would want."

The rabbi relented.

"I'll go with you," Irina told Alex.

Alex considered refusing. She might see things she wasn't supposed to, and he had to keep her out of harm's way. But how could he persuade her without raising questions that he couldn't answer?

"OK. Call if anything comes up," he told the others. "Wish us luck."

CHAPTER 78

Eli parked his Harley Davidson in the private garage beneath Jaffa Road and ran for the elevator. Wind and turbulence had decapitated most of the roses in the bouquet, and now he was running out of both flowers and options.

Noga had been at Sarit's apartment and the Dry Bones Society, but Eli remained two steps behind. He had called some numbers from her phone, but neither Hannah nor her adoptive parents had heard from her, and now she had disappeared from the face of the planet.

A new anxiety gnawed at his heart. Something had happened to her—something sudden and terrible. His stubborn refusal to help her had pushed her into the ever-waiting jaws of tragedy, and he had lost her forever.

The Thin Voice had not told him this; the whisper of Divine providence remained as silent as ever. Instead, his fears fed off a vague and very human premonition. But the premonitions of Elijah the Prophet meant business.

As the elevator climbed toward his penthouse apartment, his heart clung to one final possibility: that while he had sped along the streets of Jerusalem in search of her, Noga had returned home. To her *real* home, with him. Whether she had come back to make peace or to claim her stuff didn't matter; he didn't mind if she hated him, as long as she was alive and well.

Never delay, Oren had warned. His late former roommate in the neurology ward of the Shaare Zedek Medical Center had shared far more wisdom than, apparently, Eli had accumulated in centuries. But Eli had not taken that advice to heart in time. Happiness had fluttered into his life and he, with the carelessness of a jaded immortal, had left the window wide open.

The floor numbers incremented on the digital panel inside the elevator. She would be waiting for him when the door opened, and she'd greet him with conciliatory smiles and hugs—or a well-deserved slap across the face—either way, preemptive tears of joy welled in his eyes.

But when he punched in the code and the door clicked open, he found the apartment dark and empty. The blinds slid on their tracks and spotlights faded in as the Jerusalem skyline basked in late afternoon light. He placed the surviving roses on the kitchen island. Her laptop lay closed on the coffee table. He made a quick search of the penthouse, checking the bedrooms and bathrooms—even his den, the walls naked and forlorn. Selling his mementos had been a rash move, and he would never see them again. Would he see Noga again?

He dashed back to the elevator and pressed the button for the lobby, his feet twitching as he waited, like an edgy racehorse at the starting gate. As the doors opened, he rushed to the front desk.

"Tomer," he said, reading the watchman's name on the identity card clipped to his shirt pocket. Eli had never bothered to find out his name, a factoid he added to the growing evidence against his former callous personality. "Has Noga come by—today or last night?"

Over the past few months he must have seen her come and go, although in his line of work it was wiser not to ask too many questions about a tenant's casual visitors.

Tomer looked up from his book and raised his eyebrows, so Eli added some identifying details. "Long dark hair. Pretty.

About twenty-eight—and don't tell her I told you her age."

Tomer smiled but shook his head. "Not today, but Evgeni might have seen her last night. I can call him, if you like, but he's on his way here for the night shift."

Evening already? The late summer sunlight was misleading.

Eli swallowed his disappointment and his fear. "Thanks."

Had she snuck in undetected? Even watchmen took bathroom breaks.

He dialed Sarit on his phone. "Anything?"

"No," she said. "I called her folks again. Her professor too. Now they're worried as well."

The dark cloud of foreboding returned. Noga was in danger. More than ever, she needed him. But where could she have gone? "Are you sure she didn't mention any other places or people?"

"Nothing. She borrowed my disc on key, though."

"Your disc on key?"

"You know, a USB thumb drive. She didn't say why."

A theory kindled in his mind, a final desperate spark. *You stubborn girl.* "I'm heading out again," he said. "I think I know where she's gone."

CHAPTER 79

As the henchmen fastened leather straps over his wrists and ankles, Moshe realized his mistake. The round, upended table was no table at all, but an oversized archery target.

King Kong and Vitaly stepped back and admired their work. They had strapped Moshe, his limbs extended like the Vitruvian Man, to the target, the tender flesh of his belly over the bull's-eye.

A lever thumped and a spotlight in the rafters beamed a brilliant circle of white over the target, making Moshe blink and avert his eyes.

"Ladies and gentlemen," Mandrake cried in his stage voice, "another round of applause for our brave volunteer!"

Galit and Avi stared at Moshe in horrified silence, unable to comply, gagged and bound as they were to their chairs. Moshe's suit jacket hung limply on the empty third chair.

Mandrake turned to the two seated figures and palmed his forehead. "Silly me! Your hands are tied. But cheer him on. He'll need your moral support before the show is over. Go on!"

Galit and Avi made muffled noises through the duct tape.

"That's better." He clapped his hands twice. "To work, boys. We can't keep our audience waiting."

King Kong inflated red balloons with large gulps of air

and handed them to Vitaly, who tore lengths of adhesive tape with his teeth and stuck the balloons to the target. He positioned the first balloon below Moshe's left armpit, beside his palpitating heart, and the second balloon beside his left ear. Moshe had seen enough magic acts to know what would come next. They were just trying to scare him. They wouldn't really throw knives at him, would they?

"I apologize for my vulgar assistants," Mandrake said, like an old friend striking up conversation. "But the pretty young women were unavailable on such short notice."

The two assistants completed their preparations. King Kong scuttled aside, veins bulging on his forehead from the effort of inflating the balloons. Amplified sound rung in Moshe's ears from the plastic orbs on either side his head, and he felt the pressure of those under each armpit. Vitaly placed the final red balloon between Moshe's legs and uncomfortably close to his crotch.

"Hold it tight," Vitaly said. Moshe pressed his knees together, gripping the balloon between his thighs as tightly as his bound ankles would allow.

Satisfied, Vitaly hurried away and set a leather case on a low stool before his boss, then returned to the shadows.

"I don't like guns," Mandrake said. "So cold and impersonal. If you're going to kill a man, you ought to get to know him up close and personal, don't you agree?"

Kill—did he say kill?

Mandrake opened the case and extracted a long, sharp throwing knife. Galit moaned and shifted on her chair. Moshe glanced at her and put on a brave face. Mandrake wouldn't risk impaling him, would he? Moshe was his prized race horse. He planned to pressure Moshe for favors once he was in office. But Restart had dropped in the polls. Moshe would never set foot in Knesset and Mandrake must know that already. Was he expendable? Would his painful death be an example to Avi?

Mandrake held the blade horizontal, placed a single finger under the edge of the hilt, and balanced the knife in the air. "I know what you're thinking. 'I hope this guy can throw straight!'" He laughed at his own joke. "Rest assured, Moshe Karlin. I practice often, and I hardly ever miss." His eyes twinkled, and he laughed again, enjoying himself.

Moshe's legs began to shake against his will. The balloon slipped from between his thighs and bounced on the stained cement floor.

"Aw, did I upset you? Vitaly, please help our friend. This time, Moshe, hold tight." Vitaly emerged from the shadows and lifted the balloon into position again. Moshe clamped his legs together, the awkward position demanding a lot of effort, but when he glanced at the knife held so casually in Mandrake's hand, the tremors returned to his legs.

"Not so brave, after all, are we? Vitaly..."

Vitaly returned to the circle of light and taped the balloon in place.

"Don't be ashamed, Moshe. I understand how you feel. You're afraid the knife might cut you... over there. Of course! How thoughtless of me. Vitaly, see what you can do."

Vitaly disappeared behind the target and emerged holding a silver cooking pot, which he positioned over Moshe's nether region.

"Very good. But Vitaly, this is Moshe Karlin we're dealing with. Can't you find something a bit more... suitable?"

Vitaly made a show of scratching his head, then slipped behind the target again. This time he returned with a silver tea strainer and tested it on Moshe for size. The tiny strainer barely covered the button of his trousers.

"Much better!" Mandrake laughed again. His henchmen chuckled as well, while Vitaly attached the handle of the strainer to the belt of Moshe's jeans with a large safety pin. They had planned the routine ahead of time and were enjoying every moment. This was a joke. A prank. After they'd had their fun, they'd unstrap him and let him go. They would all go free.

Mandrake flipped the knife in the air and caught it by its sharp, silver tip. Vitaly scampered out of the way. White spotlight danced off the blade.

"Are you ready, Moshe? To be honest, I'm a bit nervous myself. I'm not used to performing in front of a crowd."

Sweat trickled into Moshe's eyes. He tried to weave a plan in his mind, but his thoughts scattered.

Mandrake raised the knife in the air, and Moshe's muscles tensed, the straps biting into his wrists.

Mandrake lowered the blade. "You're right," he said, his face contorted with sudden doubt. "This is scary. Too scary. Vitaly, please. A blindfold."

The henchman reappeared at Moshe's side and tied a red bandana over his eyes. The world went dark.

"That's better," Mandrake's voice said.

Vitaly's feet shuffled away. Moshe moved his head, trying to find an angle that allowed him to peek through. The sound of his own breath—quick and shallow— filled his ears, along with the pounding of his heart. He was afraid to move, afraid to speak.

"Ready?" Mandrake called, his voice loud and distorted through the balloons at Moshe's ears.

Ready for what—to die?

His muscles squirmed. *No. He won't do it.*

"Three!" Mandrake counted out loud.

He can't. Galit squealed and the feet of a chair scraped the floor.

"Two!"

He's just trying to scare me. More shifting noises and grunts of protest. Even Avi's growl had joined the commotion.

"One!"

Moshe froze. He didn't dare breathe.

Crack! Thunder exploded an inch from his left ear, the deafening sound of metal slicing through a balloon and plunging into wood.

CHAPTER 80

From the sidewalk opposite Clal Center, Ahmed scanned the windows of the third floor. Some of the faces he recognized from his stay at the Dry Bones Society. Most he did not. And none wore a green hijab.

People had stared as he walked past the Old City. At Jaffa Gate, a young woman in a green Border Police uniform had looked him over, her machine gun slung at her waist. Could she sense the explosives beneath his light jacket? Would she tell him to stop for inspection? He walked on without incident.

It was his hair. The mane of peroxide blond had made them stare. "Another weirdo kid," they must have thought. Hasan knew his job well.

Ahmed walked on and on until he reached the light rail shelter opposite Clal Center. Television vans pulled up at the corner and camera crews entered the building.

Election Day. A day of rejoicing for the Society. Their leaders were expected to enter the new government. Would Samira join the celebrations? Had she forgotten him already? Surely she despised him. How could she do otherwise?

And yet, here he stood, a lone outsider once again, hoping to steal a glimpse of the girl with the warm smile. Had he expected her to sit at the window, waiting for his return? To rush across the street in order to speak with him one last time?

He had tasted Heaven in this new life for one brief moment, and he deserved not even that. She was right to hate him. His evil actions had stained his soul forever. There was no redemption for him, only death.

Ahmed was running his thumb over the detonation button, when an old man bumped against him and almost set off the explosives.

"Pardon me," the old man said.

A group of commuters grew around him at the shelter. *Sons of pigs and monkeys. Killers of prophets.*

No. Hasan was wrong. Rabbi Yosef had taken Samira in, and Moshe Karlin had bought her freedom. Did they deserve to die?

With one flick of his finger, the fires would ignite. The screws and ball bearings would shred his flesh and shatter his bones, and the projectiles would mow down all those around him.

He shuddered at the memory of his first death. The shifting of the bus underfoot. The pain, momentary but excruciating. Then he had woken up an instant later, naked and alone on the Mount of Olives. Would Boris be waiting for him a second time?

No. This time, he would not come back, he was sure of it. He would not enter Paradise either. The promises of Heaven and eternal pleasure were fictions created by cruel men to get fools like him to do their bidding.

This time he would end his life but not for the promise of pleasure or to erase his shame. He glanced at the third-floor window of Clal Center one last time. *For you, Samira.* This time he would die to set her free of him forever.

CHAPTER 81

After her meeting with Rabbi Lev, Noga trudged down Jaffa Road in a daze, feeling numb and hollow. The rabbi had tried not to laugh in her face, but he had not been able to conceal the effort. She wanted to crawl under a rock and shut out the world. Eli had warned her that no one would listen. *So this is how he felt all those years.*

She hadn't eaten all day, so she stopped at a shawarma store and bit into a pita stuffed with slivers of steaming turkey. *Galgalatz* Radio played on speakers in the corners of the pokey fast-food joint, and the news broadcast summed up the exit polls. For a change, Noga followed the election results with interest. Restart had received no mandates. *Strange.* Their promise to sweep clean the political establishment was supposed to have won a lot of popular support. Were Moshe Karlin and Rabbi Lev the wrong partners for her after all?

The meal revived her spirits. No wonder the rabbi had dismissed her as a lunatic. She had rushed over to Restart without any hard evidence in hand. In his shoes, she would have done the same. The evidence lay on her laptop in Eli's apartment, and she was not going back there.

Although he hadn't quite lied to her, Eli had hidden the truth. Worse yet, he had let her walk out the door. He hadn't run after her to bring her back. She was a pudgy teenager again, the plain girl none of the boys had given a second glance.

He didn't want her? Fine. She didn't need him either. Let him keep her laptop and her phone. She'd replace them, just as she'd replace him. Let him rot in his penthouse with his money. She'd push on without him. The world needed to know, and she would tell all.

She poured *tehina* from a ketchup bottle onto her half-eaten shawarma. No matter which political influencer she turned to in the end, she would need her data. If she hurried, she might take care of that today.

She bunched up the shawarma wrapper, emptied her can of Diet Coke, and prepared to move on, when the news reader interrupted with another election update. The real vote counts were rolling in, and this time, Restart emerged with an early lead.

Noga laughed. The obituaries in the media had arrived prematurely; the party of resurrected Israelis refused to stay dead.

She tossed the empty wrapper into the trash bin and hit the street. Boarding the Red Line at City Hall, she found a seat at the back of the train.

Her hand found Sarit's flash drive among the change in her pocket, the remains of the money her friend had lent her. She'd obtain another copy of her research data from the hospital, transfer it to the USB, install her software on Sarit's laptop, write up her paper, and publish the discovery with Hannah.

The train slowed at the Davidka station outside Clal Center.

Soon, Rabbi Lev, you'll believe me. You'll have no choice.

A fresh group of passengers made their way down the carriage and found their seats. The punk with the blond Mohawk caught her eye.

Haven't seen one of those in years.

The strip of peroxide blond clashed with the olive scalp of his shaved head. Sweat glistened on his forehead as he moved down the aisle, his arms folded over his chest in his thin black jacket, his eyes roving, self-conscious.

She averted her eyes. *Poor kid*, she thought.

CHAPTER 82

Moshe felt the vibrations through the wooden tabletop as the knife shuddered in the target.

I'm OK! He hit the balloon!

In his dark, sightless world, relief turned to horror. *Oh my God—he threw it! He actually threw the knife!*

Mandrake laughed. "Ha-ha! That was close, Moshe. My hand is shaking. I wish you could see it. One down, four more to go."

Four more?! His body convulsed.

"No," he cried. *Think, Moshe, think! What will make this madman stop?* "Please let us go."

"We're just getting started, Moshe. Which one should I do next? Never mind—it'll be a surprise. Three!"

Galit and Avi bleated, trying to cry out despite the rags in their mouths.

"Two!"

Oh God, save me, please!

"One!"

Crack-thrung-ung-ung! The balloon at his right ear burst, the knife vibrating from the force of the impact.

"Two in a row! We're on a roll, Moshe. Whoo-hoo!"

Nnn-gggrhh-mmm!

Galit's groans turned to sobs. This was too much. He had

to make it stop. Did their torturer want to feel power over his victims? Moshe would give him what he wanted.

"Please, Mandrake, sir! Let them go. You can have me, but please, just let them go."

"What a man," Mandrake said, with awe. "Even in his final moments, he's thinking of others. Which reminds me, Moshe. Seeing that this might be our last opportunity to chat," he chuckled, "in this lifetime, I want to pick your brain. Tell me, one magician to another, how did you do it?"

He'd just thrown two knives at Moshe and now he wanted to chat? "Do what?"

"You know, that trick where you die and come back to life?"

Was he serious? "That's not a trick," he mumbled, knowing that his captor would not like his answer. "It just happens."

"I'm disappointed, Moshe. I thought we were friends. You'll have to learn to trust me. Luckily, I can help with that. Three!"

"No, please."

"Two!"

A familiar sharp pain seared inside his chest.

"One!"

Cr-rack! Thrung-g-g-g!

The knife buried into the wood between his legs, catching the edge of his trousers.

"Three in a row! I never get three in a row. Moshe, you're my lucky charm."

Moshe's stomach churned. His fingers felt cold, the blindfold wet with perspiration. The pain in his chest subsided, and he gulped air. How much more could he take?

"I know, I know. This doesn't seem fair, but think of Boris. You know Boris. Poor old Boris. He had a thriving business until you decided to play the hero."

Helping the new arrivals had involved a risk, Moshe had known that from the start, but he couldn't stand idly by as Boris roped thousands of unsuspecting men and women into slavery. Had he really thought that he could get away with it?

"Tell you what," Mandrake's voice said. "I'm a reasonable man. I'll give you one more chance."

"Oh, thank you. Yes. Please. I'll do anything you want."

Galit no longer whimpered. Had she passed out?

"Here it is. You can either die here in front of your lovely wife, or you can let us kill your old traitorous friend here, Avi Segal. A life for a life. What do you say?"

Moshe said nothing. He had been willing to do anything—to shut down Restart and the Dry Bones Society, to stay out of public life. To hand over his worldly possessions. But this—this was murder. To fight in self-defense was one thing, but to kill someone else to save his own skin?

"A quick death, I promise. Over in a second. You won't have to pull the trigger. Then you and Galit go home to sweet Talya."

Mandrake seemed intent on turning Moshe into a killer. Was that some evil rite of passage or just another deception? Would he carry out the order? Nothing was certain with this man.

Moshe hung his head.

"OK," Mandrake said. "It's your funeral. No hard feelings. I wanted to break my record anyway. Four in a row would be awesome. Just thinking of it makes my hands shake. Here goes."

Moshe braced his body for impact, sucking in air with feverish gulps like a woman in labor, his limbs shaking.

"Three!"

Moshe's head swam in the blackness. His mother glanced down at him and patted his hair. His father handed him a heavy silver watch. *This is yours now.* He rested his hands on young Moshe's shoulders as they smiled at the cameras outside the brand new offices of Karlin & Son. *A Karlin never quits...*

"Two!"

Galit met his eyes across the dance floor of Hangar 17. "You're late," he said to her. She smiled. "I got here as fast as

I could." Then her face crumpled with effort and she squeezed his hand. She lay on the hospital bed in the Shaare Zedek labor ward, perspiring with the effort, and he felt a rush of joy as Talya burst into the world.

"One!"

CHAPTER 83

Daylight faded over the Talpiot industrial zone as the black Mercedes cruised down Pierre Koenig. Alex had not had time to clean out the rental car before Irina had settled onto the passenger seat. Any moment now, she might blow his cover.

A loaded Glock lay in the glove compartment above her legs, and the trunk contained reams of plastic sheeting, a bundle of rope, and a pack of cable ties. He'd have trouble explaining away the equipment, which he had packed in case the abduction of Moshe and his wife veered from the script.

Irina dialed a number on her phone and thumbed on the speaker. "Any luck?"

"No," Rafi's voice said. "Nothing yet. I'll let you know as soon as we do." CB radio static roared on the other side of the line. Across the city, friends of the Yemenite driver, in cabs and shuttles, scanned the streets of Jerusalem for a brown GMC.

Alex had given an accurate description of the vehicle used by Mandrake's extraction team. Eyewitness accounts would surface later anyway.

Irina pointed to a side road of old, derelict buildings. "Let's look over there," she said.

He turned the wheel.

"That's it," she said. "Stop here."

They idled outside a nondescript warehouse of corrugated fiberglass.

"You know this place?"

"I wish I didn't. We lived here for a few days—Moshe, Samira, and I—after we left the rabbi's home. Our first job, or so we thought. We had a roof, two square meals, and a contract that made us their slaves. The place is a trap for refugees and illegals, anyone without the right papers. That's where we met Shmuel. Moshe got us out."

Alex grunted in sympathy and stared at the decrepit warehouse, yet another tentacle in Mandrake's ever-growing empire. He knew what Irina was thinking: Moshe had crossed the slave drivers before, so maybe they had returned to collect their dues. She was right, of course, but she had no idea just how long and grasping those tentacles had grown. Neither did Alex.

"No brown vans here," he said.

"Let's try the streets nearby."

They did. There was no harm in humoring her. Mandrake was holding Moshe and Galit far away, but Alex couldn't take her there. Not until Mandrake was done with them, and by then it would be too late.

Irina slapped the armrest in frustration.

It pained Alex to see her suffer. She cared for Moshe, her friend and guide in difficult times, and Alex was grateful for that.

Had Irina and Moshe been more than friends? Unlikely. Moshe was too clean and by-the-book. Again, he felt that stab of jealousy. One thing was sure: he did not envy Moshe Karlin now. Alex had advised restraint, but there was no guessing how far Mandrake would go. He had learned that lesson early on and a world away, in Korosten.

The linoleum floor and whitewashed walls of the People's Primary had reminded the young Alex of the hospital where his father had died. On his first night after lights out, the other boys had wasted little time in welcoming the newcomer.

"That's a nice suitcase," said the leader of the pack, a

stocky blond kid with crooked teeth. The night light, a naked
bulb above the door, cast a ghostly glow over the long row of
cot beds in the dormitory.

Alex hugged the case to his chest. "My father gave it to
me."

The boy smirked and cast a glance at the thugs behind
him. "And now you're going to give it to me, Jew-boy."

Alex had closed his eyes and tensed for the worst. He
didn't remember the boy's name, but he'd never forget the
expression of disbelief on his face when, three seconds later,
his tormentor was sprawled on the shiny floor, touching a
trembling finger to his tender, bloody lip.

A stranger stood over the pack, the cruel boys crumpled at
his feet in varying states of pain. "That's no way to welcome
our new friend," the stranger said, his bare hands pressed
together in a polite gesture that was at once adult and ominous. The wolves scattered.

The savior remained at the side of his bed and grinned.

"How did you do that?"

The boy put a finger to his lips and winked. "It's a kind of
magic."

Alex stayed close to him from that day on. They shared
their meals and exercised together in the training yard. His
name was Gennady but behind his back the other boys called
him The Jew. Strangely, he seemed to like his nickname.
Nobody messed with The Jew. Only later did Alex learn
about knuckle busters and the virtues of lead piping hidden
up a sleeve.

A year later, as Chernobyl burned and the authorities
evacuated Korosten, the two Jewish boys set out on their
own, leaving behind the world of cold institutions and hateful
rules. They were thirteen years old.

As Gennady honed his repertoire of street magic, the two
friends found early successes and had a few close brushes
with the law. When the Soviet Union collapsed, opportunities
for energetic men with the right skillset sprouted from the
ruins. The local criminal networks, however, guarded their

turf with iron fists and limited their expansion.

The Middle East beckoned, drawing them with the sweet scent of lawlessness, and the free one-way tickets offered by the Jewish State, an oriental fruit, ripe for the picking. They learned the new turf and language, and quietly set the stage for a new, improved show. In Israel, no one called them Jew-boys.

Irina's phone rang.

"Any luck?" Rabbi Yosef asked on the speaker. The hubbub of voices in the background made his voice hard to hear.

"Nothing yet," she answered. "How are we doing over there?"

"It's a miracle!"

She glanced at Alex, an excited twinkle in her eye. "More mandates?"

"We're twenty seats ahead of Upward."

Twenty seats!

Irina's mouth dropped open.

"Everyone's asking for Moshe," Yosef said. "I can't hold them off much longer."

Irina ended the call. "This is amazing," she said, but then her enthusiasm turned to worry. "We have to find Moshe."

"You're right," Alex said. Had Mandrake seen the results? Would that change his plan? With Irina sitting beside him, Alex had no way of contacting his boss.

Irina's phone rang again. "Anything?"

"Yes," Rafi's voice said. "A driver saw a similar van heading west on Golomb, toward the city outskirts."

"We're on it." She ended the call. "Do you think they left the city?"

"Anything's possible." Alex doubled back onto Pierre Koenig and headed west. "It's worth a shot."

Ready or not, he thought, *here we come.*

CHAPTER 84

Eli dashed out of the large steel elevator and onto the fourth floor of the Shaare Zedek Medical Center. Memories flooded his mind at every step. Racing down the linoleum corridor in his wheelchair, Noga calling after him to slow down. At the water cooler in the kitchenette, eavesdropping while Moti, the therapeutic clown, had dissected Eli's psyche for the entertainment of a young nurse.

Nut case, the carrot-haired clown had said of Eli. *Trapped.* They had pitied him, and he had absorbed their worldview. Now Eli had come full circle.

He reached the neurology ward, half expecting to bump into Noga in her white cloak.

Eliana, the large Russian head nurse, stood at the information desk and looked over the shoulder of Nadir, the Arab nurse with the white hijab. They both looked up.

"Eli," Eliana said, smiling. "Welcome home." She glanced at the battered bouquet of roses in his hand—only three of the flowers remained intact—and gave him a bemused smile. "Is everything all right?" If Noga had spoken with her, she had not mentioned their recent split.

"Did Noga come by today?"

"No. Was she supposed to?"

The premonition reared its horrible head again. Noga was

in danger. He had to find her right away.

"I think so. She left her phone at our place, and I haven't been able to reach her. Can you call me if you see her?"

Bemusement turned into concern, and he knew what she must be thinking: surely Noga could call him if she wanted?

"We had a fight," he confessed. "And I owe her an apology."

Eliana handed him a notepad and he jotted down his number. "I'll call if I see her."

"Thanks."

Eli walked over to room 419C, his old room. Oren's bed lay bare and empty. *Don't delay*, he had said, urging Eli to make amends with Noga. His words were all the more relevant today.

Eli walked past the plastic divider curtain. A young girl lay in his old bed by the window, eating her hospital dinner on a wheeled tray, a white sanitary bandage wrapping her forehead. She looked up at him and paused mid-chew.

"Hi there," he said.

"Hello."

"This used to be my bed."

She blinked at him, probably wondering what the stranger with the black leather jacket and fistful of abused roses wanted. He pointed at the window with the steamed glass. "Have the crows come to visit yet?"

She shook her head. Of course not. The cruel birds had carried a message for him, a message that now, two months later, he finally understood. "If they do," he said, and he winked, "say hi for me."

Nadir sat alone behind the nurses' desk when he returned. He leaned against the desk. *Where to now?* Noga had borrowed Sarit's flash drive. She must have wanted to get a fresh copy of her research results in order to move forward with her mission without him. But the nurses hadn't seen her.

He cleared his throat. "Nadir, Noga came here a few weeks ago, right?"

"Yes. She came to collect her data."

"Did you help her with that?"

"Oh, no. She just stopped by on her way to the Medical Genetics Institute. All the data goes through there."

Bingo! "And where is that?"

She pointed upward. "Fifth floor."

Eli raced down the corridor to the elevators and pressed the button. After five frustrating seconds, he pushed through the door to the stairwell. He took the stairs two at a time, losing another rose in the process, and burst onto the fifth-floor corridor, gulping air like a drowning fish.

Following the signs, he rounded a corner and marched down a passageway of glass walls. The desks and counters within sat motionless in the gloom. When, finally, he reached the entrance of the Medical Genetics Institute, the glass doors held fast. A handwritten note taped to the door explained that the Institute had closed early for Election Day.

If Noga had been there, he had missed her. But why hadn't she returned to Sarit's apartment, and why hadn't she called?

Outside, a siren sounded—the all too familiar wail of an ambulance. The noise grew louder. A second wail joined the first, then a third.

The remaining flowers dropped to the linoleum floor.

Oh, God, no! Not Noga!

CHAPTER 85

"Four in a row!" Mandrake's voice cried, as another knife twanged in the wooden board, inches from the tender skin of Moshe's right armpit. He had flinched on impact, but less than before. The unrelenting tension had drained his adrenaline and numbed his reflexes.

The pain in his chest had become a constant pressure at his core. A warmth spread over his crotch, ran down his legs, and trickled onto the floor.

Let it be over. Kill me already.

"Vitaly," Mandrake said. "Let him have a look."

Feet shuffled, then fingers lifted the blindfold from Moshe's head.

Moshe blinked against the spotlight. Mandrake smiled at him. His bald head glistened under the fluorescents. "Look, Moshe." Moshe obliged. The black handles of large daggers protruded from the target on either side his head, under his right armpit, and between his legs. The last balloon hovered to his left, by his heart.

Galit sagged forward on her chair, her head hanging limp—had she passed out? Avi looked away, the twisted cloth digging into his mouth.

"We make a great team, Moshe, you and I, don't you agree? Think of what we can accomplish together, if only you'd let me help you."

Mandrake's glance dropped to Moshe's feet and he wrinkled his nose. Moshe glanced at the cement floor. A reeking puddle spread beneath him.

"Aw, Moshe. Did you pee your pants? It's OK. I won't tell anyone. This will be our little secret. Soon, it won't matter." He lifted another knife in the air. "One more to go, Moshe. What do you say—should we risk it? Is five in a row too much to hope for? Are we pushing our luck too far? What the hell." All concern emptied from his voice. "You're mine, Moshe, do you understand? Your life belongs to me." He wiped his brow on his sleeve, and smiled again. "Feel the tension—huh?"

Moshe closed his eyes. *Let it be over. Start the countdown.*

But Mandrake wanted to chat. "I can't lie to you, Moshe. I'm nervous. Look at my hand. Open your eyes." Moshe did as he was told. Mandrake held up his hand. The fingers shook. "This is scary. Too scary. I can't bear to watch it either." He rested the knife on the leather case, pulled a red kerchief from his pocket, and tied it over his eyes. "There, that's better." He felt around for the knife, found it, and raised it in the air by the tip. He faced a point off to Moshe's left.

A sudden gust of optimism lifted Moshe's spirits. He might survive this throw after all.

"Boss," Vitaly said.

Mandrake lifted his blindfold. "Ha! Silly me. Thanks, Vitaly." He corrected his position, lifted the knife, then rolled the blindfold back into position. "Help our friend with his blindfold again, won't you?"

The thug pulled the blindfold over Moshe's eyes, and the world went dark again.

This is it. He's done toying with me. It's all over now.

"Three!"

Moshe swirled wine in a glass at his fortieth birthday party. Among the buffet tables in the Italian restaurant at the Botanical Gardens, he searched for Galit. He wanted to raise a toast to her. He stepped outside onto the terrace overlooking the pond, and in the still night air, he heard her voice.

"Two!"

Walking down a dirt path through the trees and bushes, he saw them. The man leaned against a tree, his back to Moshe. A high-heeled foot ran up against the man's leg, exposing a woman's leg as it pressed against his thigh.

His wineglass cracked on the stony ground, and the couple broke apart like a flock of startled birds.

"Galit!" His voice was distant, incredulous. Galit stepped away from Avi and straightened her dress, a mixture of surprise and defiance in her large, pretty eyes.

"One!"

No! Pain exploded in his ribcage, and he clutched at his chest. As the cheating couple gaped, he collapsed to the ground, and the world faded to black.

CHAPTER 86

Eli rushed out the doors of the Emergency Department and onto the street. Hospital staff in luminous yellow vests pulled stretchers from the ambulances and wheeled them inside. Eli glanced at the bloodied civilians as they passed: an old man; a little girl; a young woman with brown hair. Noga was not among them.

"Out of the way!" a paramedic shouted and Eli stepped back, trying to identify the wounded at a distance.

"What happened?" he asked, but received no answers from the busy medical staff. His premonitions had given him little to work with. *Thin Voice, I need you now!* But the psychic silence continued.

The third ambulance emptied. Had they already wheeled Noga inside? Or did her absence mean the worst—that she was beyond help, her remains collected for interment by the bearded volunteers of Zaka?

He passed the security check to reenter the building and pushed through the double doors of the Emergency Room.

"You're not allowed in here," a nurse said.

"I'm looking for my girlfriend, Noga Shemer. Mid-twenties, dark hair."

The nurse shook her head. "You'll have to wait outside."

Eli retreated. He paced the corridor while medical staff

bustled around him.

He pulled at his hair. *You fool. After all the warnings and hints the Boss sent you, you let her slip through your fingers, and now it's too late!*

A familiar face exited ER, severe-looking and graying at the temples.

Eli ran to him. "Dr. Stern!"

The head of neurology turned at the mention of his name, and his eyebrows rose. "Mr. Eli Katz. You got here fast."

The doctor had treated Eli after his accident, and he knew Noga well. He would have recognized her among the injured. Eli tried to divine her fate from his pale blue eyes.

"Did you see Noga?"

Dr. Stern's eyes narrowed with confusion. "I told her today that I wanted to speak with you, although I didn't think you'd visit so soon. To be honest, I wasn't sure you'd respond at all."

The doctor had taken a very close interest in Eli's case, especially his speedy recovery and delusions, and now was probably not the time to mention his recent relapse. But the doctor had spoken with Noga.

"Is she OK?"

"Yes, of course." Dr. Stern followed Eli's glance to the double doors of the Emergency Room. "Chain accident on Road One," he said. "Horrible mess. A bus and seven cars, I believe, but there's no work for me there."

Noga didn't drive. Had she tried to leave the city by bus? The scenario didn't fit.

"She's not in there?"

"No. She stopped working here a month ago, as you know."

"When did you see her?"

"An hour ago, at the Genetics Institute."

Noga had arrived at the hospital in one piece. Thank God for that. She had bypassed the neurology ward and headed straight to the Medical Genetics Institute. But where was she now?

"She was upset," Dr. Stern continued. "The Institute had deleted her data, and she had to resubmit her request." He brightened. "Shall we talk in my office?"

"Another time, Doctor," Eli said.

He ran down the linoleum corridor, weaving between nurses and anxious civilians. Noga had been at the hospital very recently—and she might still be there. There was one place he hadn't checked.

CHAPTER 87

Noga slumped on the bench in the gloomy twilight of the secret garden, and shook her head at the ironies of life. Two months ago, she had met with Eli in the grassy courtyard of the hospital, expecting a declaration of love. Instead, she had received a deranged proclamation from Elijah the Prophet.

While he ranted and raved about the End of Days—and the special role he and Noga were to play in the imminent apocalypse—a part of her had died inside. She had fallen for a madman. Feeling stupid and naïve, she had stormed out, determined to prove him wrong.

And she had succeeded. The mountain of evidence she had gathered for the Eli Katz of flesh and blood had buried the immortal prophet in the depths of Eli's subconscious. In return, she got her dream boyfriend, a life of luxury, and a carefree future. There was only one small problem: she had been wrong.

If the Jewish Arabs outed by her research data had failed to convince her, the zombies on the streets left no doubt. The world she knew was ending, and now that she actually needed Elijah, he was nowhere to be found; she had killed him.

If she had accepted his story that day in the secret garden, she might have saved everyone a lot of trouble, and maybe

Eli wouldn't have turned into the selfish jerk who cared about nothing, not even her.

Noga sucked in air and her body trembled. She couldn't do this alone. Rabbi Lev had laughed her down, and soon, if she submitted the paper Hannah wanted her to write, the academic world would do the same. But she wouldn't crawl back to Eli either. To him she was a pretty face, a shiny trophy on his mantelpiece. He cared about her in a self-interested way—seeing her as an extension of himself—and not enough to make him change course. Not again.

The handle of the door squeaked. Noga sat up and wiped the tears from her cheeks. She didn't want the pity of strangers. But the intruder was no stranger.

Eli stood there, rectangles of amber light from the hospital rooms above projecting over his leather jacket. Her body tensed. Had he come to drag her back to his mantelpiece? In his hand he held a single, bent rose.

He drew near, sat down beside her on the bench, and looked up at the stars.

"You were right," he said. "I should have told you about the Resurrection. At first, I thought I was hallucinating. Then, I was afraid. If I was Elijah without my powers, I was useless."

Was this the truth, or was he telling her what he thought she wanted to hear? She said, "I'm not going to change my mind."

"I know."

"I'm not going to back down."

"That's OK," he said. "I'll help you."

She studied his eyes. "I thought you didn't care about humanity."

He stared ahead at the flowerbed. "I did, at first. But the centuries passed, and the world didn't move any closer to redemption. There were hopeful eras, sure, but they always ended badly. Little by little, I dried up inside. Humanity would never be worthy, so why bother? To hell with them all. It wasn't my fault. But you taught me something."

"Oh, did I?"

He gave her his charming, boyish smile. "As a matter of fact, you did." He read his thoughts off the still night air. "I wasn't just afraid of failure. I was afraid of losing you." He gave her a quick, self-conscious grin, then looked away again. "Humanity is just a word. Humanity doesn't exist; people do. I don't have to care about humanity. But if I care about one real person, maybe that's enough, maybe that makes the world worth saving. And by loving that one real person, maybe I'll learn to love the rest." He held out the dilapidated rose.

The emotion that had swirled within her bubbled over and she couldn't hold back. She leaned in and he wrapped his arms around her. He was back. Eli, or Elijah—it didn't matter. The rest was details.

He cleared his throat. "I was talking about myself, obviously. 'Learning to love yourself is the greatest love of all.' Hey! No tickling."

They sat there for a while together, then Eli pulled away. "We should get home. We've got preparations to make."

"We do?"

"Oh, yeah. And a messiah to anoint."

CHAPTER 88

Moshe came to, the sound of a woman's sobbing in his ears. His shoulders burned, as did his wrists, and the stench of pee assaulted his nostrils. The pain in his chest had subsided to a dull throb.

He opened his eyes—he could see! The red bandana hung at his neck, damp and limp. He was still tied to the round wooden target.

A fifth knife stuck in the wood, inches from his heart. Five in a row—Mandrake had broken his record, but there was no sign of the mad magician or his thugs. They must have turned off the spotlight on their way out. The show was over.

Bound and gagged, Galit and Avi sat on their chairs under the ghostly fluorescent light of the derelict warehouse, their heads hanging low.

When Galit looked up, her sobs became muffled cries of teary relief, and her shoulders shuddered. Avi glanced up at him with wide, wild eyes. Had they thought that he had died?

"Are they gone?" he whispered. His throat felt rough and parched.

The two seated prisoners looked about them and nodded. Had Mandrake left them to rot, or would he return any moment for his fancy throwing knives?

They had to free themselves and flee the place while they

could.

Moshe strained against his bonds, curling inward like a spider, but the straps on his wrists and ankles were leather belts threaded in brass buckles, and they held fast.

He pressed his thighs against the handle of the throwing knife between his legs. If he could just get hold of a blade...

No. His legs were too far apart, so he tried a new tactic. He shifted his weight from side to side, pushing against the flat edge of the blade with the inside of each thigh. After a dozen swings, the knife shifted out an inch and lurched downward. Now, to press the blade between his thighs...

The knife clattered to the cement floor. He had hoped to launch the dislodged blade closer to the other two captives, but this would have to do.

"Avi," he said. His ex-friend and nemesis looked up at him, sweeping the greasy fringe out of his eyes with a flick of his head. Or was that "former" nemesis? They had spared each other's lives, after all.

Moshe sent a meaningful glance toward the knife on the floor. "Shift closer," he said. "Topple over near enough and you'll get to the knife."

Understanding glimmered in Avi's eyes. He rocked on the chair, the legs lifting off the floor and edging toward Moshe.

"That's it. Keep going."

Avi rocked harder, inching faster toward the circular target, his nostrils flaring over the knotted cloth in his mouth.

"Easy does it."

The warning came too late. Avi lost balance and fell sideways, groaning as his bodyweight crushed his forearm between the metal frame of the chair and the hard floor. He writhed and wriggled, shifting the chair in useless circles, until he gave up, moaning and sweating.

So much for that.

Moshe glanced at Galit. She nodded, made a valiant effort to shift the chair with the tips of her toes, but made no progress.

I guess it's up to me.

Avi's failed attempt gave Moshe an idea. He leaned forward, then threw his weight back against the wood. It barely moved. *That won't work.*

He shifted to the side and soon he wished that he had not. The wooden circle rolled on its edge like a wheel, grating against the rough floor and turning him upside down before it slowed to a stop. Blood drained to his head, a dizzying sensation that made him want to puke. The fallen knife lay on the floor—now the ceiling—far off to the side.

He shifted in the opposite direction and the wheel rolled back, coming to rest two feet behind where he had started. His plan had not worked out, but at least he was right side up. The knife glinted on the floor.

One option remained. The new plan might just bring the knife within grasp. On the other hand, it might impale or crush him. Either result beat waiting for Mandrake to return.

He lunged forward, straining against the straps. The target tilted forward, then slumped back. Galit shook her head and groaned in protest. She didn't seem to think that toppling the heavy wooden tabletop onto his body was a good idea and she was probably right. But with only one path left to freedom, he had to take that chance.

He lunged forward again, a Samson straining at the pillars. This time, he leaned back on the rebound, adding momentum to the next forward swing and, for two fateful seconds, the table teetered on a fragile equilibrium before succumbing to gravity.

Oh, crap!

Galit shrieked. Moshe cried out as well, closed his eyes, and clenched every muscle in his body as the unforgiving floor of hard cement rushed up toward him.

The crash echoed against the warehouse walls.

Moshe opened his eyes. He lay, face down, in the newly formed crawl space between the overturned target and the floor, supported by the knives that their mad captor had lodged into the wooden target.

He laughed, a tense, happy-to-be-alive, teary laugh. "I'm

OK," he said. The knives had saved his life, and his spread legs had ensured that the base of the target had not crushed his feet.

But the sound of the falling target would not go unnoticed. He waited ten seconds, catching his breath, listening for the return of heavy footfalls. None came.

Although alive, Moshe lay suspended from the toppled target like a turtle under an oversized shell, unable to move.

He craned his neck. The loose knife lay directly below his shackled right wrist, but twenty centimeters of air still separated his grasping fingers from the key to freedom.

He threw his weight to the left, the target tilting like an unsteady table, then rocking to the right, the heavy wooden surface now pressing against the side of the knife legs, threatening to loosen the blades from the base and crush Moshe. His fingers had just brushed the knife handle, when pain flared in his right foot, which was now pinned beneath the edge of the table and the floor, and he cried out again.

Working fast, his fingers jabbed at the knife, at first rotating it out of reach—*no, please no!*—then caught the blade as it rotated back. *Yes!*

He shifted to his left again, pushing the floor with his right knee. The target rose off his foot and settled back onto the knife legs.

His fingers managed to hold the blade—barely—but they couldn't slice the straps from that angle.

Now what?

He ran the blade along his fingers and grasped the handle. He couldn't saw through the strap, so instead he inserted the point into the buckle and between the straps, pushing down on the handle, using the lower strap for leverage, teasing the tongue of leather out of the brass buckle.

Encouraged by his success, he inserted the point inside the buckle a second time, slipping the strap over the brass prong, and his wrist fell free to the floor. After some stretching and painful contortion, he unstrapped his right ankle, heaved the table upward, and tended to the remaining restraints. The turtle had slithered out of his shell.

He limped over to Galit and Avi, his limbs trembling. "You OK?" He pulled the gags from their mouths.

"Thank God!" Galit said. "I thought you were dead."

"They were messing with you all along," Avi said, from his painful position on the floor.

"What do you mean?"

"He didn't really throw the knives."

"But he did. I heard them. The balloons..."

"Vitaly stuck them in by hand. When you passed out, they did CPR, then split. They weren't trying to kill you, just scare you."

"Well, they succeeded." All of this, just to freak him out. Gagged and bound, Galit and Avi had no way of telling him that it was all a show. Mandrake was one seriously deranged criminal.

Moshe faltered on his feet. This was too much. If they managed to escape tonight, he would withdraw from public life. He had stood out from the crowd once and become a target for dark forces. For all his good intentions and honest desire to fix the country, few things were worth losing his life, and nothing was worth losing his family.

As he stood over the bound couple, knife in hand, a memory triggered in his mind, a dark moment that he had buried deep in his subconscious.

"We should get out of here," Avi said. "Before they come back."

"He's right," Galit added. Then, "What's the matter?"

The girl had pressed her high-heeled foot to the man's thigh, her dress rising up her leg.

"You were there," Moshe said. "Both of you. In the garden."

"What garden?" Galit said.

Avi hissed, "Moshe, we need to go. Now!"

"At the Botanical Gardens."

Galit and Avi exchanged glances and fell silent.

"Against the tree," Moshe continued. "He had his hand on

your waist, your leg over his."

Moshe's brain added one strange fact to another. The morning of his return, Galit had screamed and climbed the walls. She had not been surprised, but terrified.

Avi had given a nervous laugh at the offices of Karlin & Son. "Why did you come back?" he'd asked. "To haunt me?" Then, "You don't remember, do you?" *Remember what?* "Dying."

Galit had sat on the wall of the Tayelet overlooking the Old City. "Can you forgive me?" she'd asked. *There's nothing to forgive.*

Moshe towered over the chained couple in the abandoned warehouse. "You cheated on me," he said, choking on disbelief. "Before I died."

Galit teared up and Moshe felt as though he had died all over again.

"That's what killed me—that's what brought on the heart attack. And you both just stood there and watched me die."

Galit began to bawl and could hardly get the words out between sobs. "I'm so sorry, Moshe. I thought you had cheated on me!"

Moshe shook his head and squeezed the handle of the knife. He should have let Mandrake kill Avi—kill them both, for what they had done.

"She's right," Avi said. "It was my fault. I screwed everything up."

Moshe remembered Avi's earlier confession. "You just wanted to be like me?" His words dripped sarcasm like venom.

"I'll make it up to you, Moshe, I swear to God, if it's the last thing I do."

"You ended my life, Avi. And now you've ruined it." Galit's tears continued to flow, but he kept on going. "How are you going to make that up to me?"

Avi swallowed. "You're right. I can't. Do what you want with me—whatever it is, I deserve worse." He hung his head. What did he deserve? A knife in the heart, right here, right now? Moshe wanted that. Mandrake had wanted that too.

"But," Avi added, "don't take it out on her. I practically forced myself on her. It wasn't her fault."

Moshe stood there and the urge for violent retribution subsided. She had thought he had cheated on her. She had felt the way he did now. He drew three deep breaths, then got to work, cutting the tape that bound their wrists and ankles.

Galit stepped up to him and threw her arms around his chest, clinging to him, her body trembling. She looked up at him, a plea in her eyes. He put his arm around her and touched her shoulder, a reflex, mechanical gesture, unsure what he felt. He would not figure it out here.

A car engine growled outside and yellow light flashed in the gap between the warehouse doors.

"Quick, get a knife," he hissed to Avi.

Avi hurried to the overturned target, while Moshe pulled Galit by the hand and ran to the doors of the warehouse. Bringing knives to a gunfight, they'd stand no chance against Mandrake and his thugs, but if they hid behind the opening doors, they might escape into the night.

Or they'd surprise them and fight for all they were worth. He gripped the handle of the throwing knife.

Outside, car doors opened and closed. Avi joined them at the corrugated wall, a knife in each hand. Moshe put his finger to his lips for silence. He peeked through the crack of the doorjamb. A black car idled beside a dormant brown van. A man and a woman crossed the beams of the headlights. They peered into the windows of the dark van, then walked around it. The man wore a ponytail; the girl had the leafy blond hair of a fairy.

Alex and Irina! Were they walking into a trap? "Wait here," he whispered to the others.

"Don't go," Galit said, but he pushed the doors open.

"Moshe!" Irina cried and ran to him. "Thank God we found you. Are you OK?"

He blinked back the bright lights of the car and shielded his eyes with his arm.

"I think so. For now."

Alex joined her. A large bruise around his eye shone in the headlights. "The whole country has been looking for you."

"I doubt it."

"They have," Irina said. "We won the elections."

His heart thumped in his chest. Had he heard her right? "We got a seat?" That was amazing. Unbelievable. He had lost hope of Restart ever making an impact.

"More than one, Moshe. Far more. And there's something else you should know."

She told him.

"What?" Moshe said, trying in vain to wrap his brain around the words. His recent trauma had taken its toll.

She told him again and, for the second time that day, Moshe passed out.

CHAPTER 89

Eli punched in the code for the front door of his apartment, nausea spreading through his gut. On the bike ride home, he had not expected the Thin Voice to speak inside his head. The Divine whisper had remained adamantly silent for months; why would that change?

But now, as the door clicked open and Noga followed him into the penthouse with the calm confidence of a trusting disciple, he realized that, in a secret corner of his heart, he had hoarded a desperate hope of hearing that guiding voice in the nick of time. In other words, he still had no idea what to do next.

Noga found her laptop on the coffee table and tucked the device under her arm.

"OK," she said, primed for action. "What now?"

"We anoint the Messiah."

"And where do we find him?"

"Or her," Eli said, and gave an awkward laugh. She glanced at him, expectant. He swallowed. He licked his lips and opened his mouth, then closed it.

"You don't know, do you?"

He shook his head.

"But if you don't, who does?"

He plopped on the couch. "The Thin Voice usually tells

me what to do."

She sat down beside him. "The Thin Voice?"

"Only I can hear it, like my brain is tuned into God's will."

She nodded, but her mouth became a short, tense line. Apparently, she had not factored obstinate Divine voices into her new life's mission.

"I haven't heard the voice in months," he continued. "Not since the accident."

She shrugged. "Then we'll figure it out ourselves."

"It's not that simple. Even if we think we've figured it out, how will we know we're right? With the Thin Voice, there were no doubts. All my intuitions since then have been wrong."

She considered his words. "What was the last thing the voice said?"

"I was to anoint the Messiah on the Mount of Olives. But as I got there, I slammed into a truck."

"You didn't meet the Messiah?"

Eli searched his memory of that fateful morning. "There was a white car and two men. The one with the beard called the paramedics." Another memory surfaced. He hobbled out of the neurology ward, one arm supported by a crutch, the other in Noga's. His fingers brushed against a folded note.

"What?" Noga said.

"He must have left that note in my jacket pocket. It had his name and number."

"Do you have it?"

He shook his head again. He had crumpled the yellow note and tossed it into a trash can at the hospital elevator. "The name was Yossi. No, Yosef." He strained his powers of recollection. "I don't remember his last name."

"There are a lot of Yosefs out there."

"There was a girl too," he said. "She had short hair. Blond, almost white."

Noga perked up. "I met a girl like that at Restart, when I spoke with the rabbi. Rabbi Lev. Wait a minute." She opened her laptop on the coffee table and ran a search.

The website of a political party loaded and displayed the picture of a rabbi. Streaks of gray ran through his neat brown beard.

"That's him!" Eli read the name in the title. "Rabbi Yosef Lev." He laughed. That was quick. "Restart—that new party?" Eli never bothered with politics or elections. Only God selected potential messiahs and He whispered their names in Eli's third ear. But the messianic task called for a charismatic and popular leader, and Noga's theory was showing promise.

"Yeah," she said. "The exit polls weren't optimistic, but last I heard, they were bouncing back."

She grabbed the remote control and thumbed on the TV in the corner. A woman sat at a studio discussion table. "It was inevitable, if you think about it," Liat Arbel said to her father and co-host, Dani Tavor. "For years, voters have felt disenfranchised, so they turned against the Establishment."

"But the exit polls painted a different picture," countered the gray-haired analyst. "How do you explain that?"

The woman shrugged. "With all the party's recent bad publicity, nobody wanted to admit that they were voting Restart."

"So they lied to the pollsters."

"Sure."

A chart of election results displayed on the screen. "Wow," Noga said. "I don't believe it. Restart took the elections."

"Whatever the explanation," Dani said, "this is the first time an unknown party with an inexperienced leader has trumped all the other candidates in the elections. Who knows what's in store for our country? So far, the Prime Minister-elect is keeping us in suspense, shying away from the cameras all day. This evening, however, he has promised to deliver a message to the country from his home in Jerusalem."

A photo of a clean-shaven man filled the screen.

"That's him," Eli said. "The new prime minister—he's the other guy from the Mount of Olives."

"Are you sure?"

"Yes."

"One thing is certain," Dani continued on the screen. "Prime Minister–elect Moshe Karlin has his work cut out for him."

CHAPTER 90

That night, Ahmed strolled in the shadows, while the towering walls of the Old City bathed in spotlight.

The explosives chafed his ribs. On the train, as his thumb hovered over the smooth detonator button, he had wanted to escape into the black hole of death. But when he gazed into the eyes of his fellow travelers, he hesitated.

True, he was a monster. He was not worthy of life. Yet God had brought him back from the grave. Why? To torture him—to rub his nose in the suffering he had caused? Ahmed had tasted that purgatory. God might as well turn him back to dust. Or was God not done with him yet?

In any event, did he really think that his journey would end if he were to repeat his mistakes? There was no escape in this universe. His deeds today would greet him tomorrow. He knew that now. Promises of Paradise had not saved him from his actions and neither would his desire for oblivion.

"Hey, kid," the conductor called to him, breaking his trance. "Time to get off."

The train had reached the end of the line and the last passengers had alighted.

Time to get off. To Ahmed's ears, the words had emanated from Heaven.

He stepped off the train and into a new world. The old

Ahmed had committed terrible crimes and swallowed lies; he had not been worthy of Samira's smile. That Ahmed had died.

He left the Old City walls behind, passed through the City of David, and descended into the Kidron Valley. Silwan rose above him in the night, lights glimmering in the windows of the chaotic apartment blocks and houses.

He climbed the rocky hillside and crawled into the cool emptiness of the old tomb. Turning on a plastic flashlight, he extracted his arms from the straps and placed the explosive belt on the vacant shelf.

Then he left the cave and made for the trash heap at the edge of Silwan. Picking a trail through the fresh refuse, he chewed a crust of stale pita bread and spotted a discarded pizza box. When a tin can tinkled nearby, he turned and pointed his flashlight. The light revealed neither Damas nor the Rottweiler, but a young man in ragged clothes.

He shielded his eyes with a grimy forearm. "I don't want any trouble," he said in Arabic. The man sounded about Ahmed's age. "I'm just hungry."

Ahmed lowered the flashlight to the man's torn jeans, just another wretched soul scavenging for food. At least he wasn't alone.

"I'm Dara," the man said, his voice hungry for conversation too. "What's your name?"

Ahmed considered the question. "You can start life anew every day," the rabbi at the Dry Bones Society had taught. Now was as good a time as any.

"Walid," he said. The word meant newborn. "My name is Walid."

CHAPTER 91

As the light turned green, Eli pulled back on the throttle, and the Harley Davidson surged forward. Once again, he was back in the saddle and racing to anoint a messiah, but this time everything was different.

He made sure to wear his helmet, for starters, and traffic lights no longer gave him preferential treatment. Doubts plagued him, both about the target and the success of his mission. Without the Thin Voice, he was flying blind.

Strangely, none of this troubled him. On the contrary, the uncertainty exhilarated him. His sudden optimism had something to do with the pretty young scientist who clung to his waist. He might be flying blind, but he was not flying alone. He and Noga would figure it out.

They had to—the fate of billions depended on them, and humanity was worth saving.

He pulled up outside a minimarket on Emek Refaim, and purchased a rectangular bottle of Yad Mordechai virgin olive oil. The Machaneh Yehuda market closed at nightfall and his home olive press would take too long. This time he would not stand on protocol. Maybe this time, he'd finally get it right.

Anointing oil checked off the list, they zipped up their riding jackets, put on their helmets, and sped off into the night.

Eli had looked up the address on the Internet. He made a left into Yehuda Street before diving into suburban Baka.

When he turned into Shimshon Street, however, he squeezed the brakes. Black SUVs with tinted windows blocked the street and straddled the sidewalks. Men in black suits with close-cropped hair, earpieces, and hi-tech machine guns cast suspicious looks at the clump of curious neighbors and camera crews that gawked from a safe distance.

Eli parked on the sidewalk and stowed his helmet on the bike. Noga did the same. Then, hand in hand, holding a laptop and a bottle of oil, they walked down the street.

A black suit stared them down. "This area is off limits," he said, his tone not allowing for negotiation.

"We need to speak with Mr. Moshe Karlin," Eli said. "It's urgent."

The agent asked for their identity cards and told them to stand back while he radioed in their details.

Noga met Eli's glance. He knew what she was thinking: What were the chances that the Prime Minister–elect would let them in? Their names still meant nothing to him.

Eli drew a long, deep breath and closed his eyes. He focused on the muscle at the center of his brain. *Flex.* Let us through. *Flex.* Moshe Karlin will understand. *Flex!*

The guard handed back their cards. "You're not on the list. On your way."

Eli's attempt at Jedi mind control had failed.

"But we have an urgent message for him," Noga said.

The agent nodded toward the crowd of onlookers. "So do they. Now move along." He tightened his grip on the handle of his gun.

Eli touched her shoulder and she relented. They turned back toward the bike. *So close and yet so far.*

"What do we do now?" she said.

He understood how she felt. Frustration had been his staple meal for centuries. But this time would be different. This time the Redemption would arrive. It had to. God alone knew for sure, and He was keeping His cards close to His chest.

"Simple," Eli said, pumping his voice with a confidence he did not feel, at least not yet. "We'll have to get on that list."

CHAPTER 92

A week later, Moshe found himself on a cream armchair in an office lined with bookshelves and jammed with reporters and clicking cameras.

The President of the State of Israel, a red-faced, white-haired man, filled the other armchair. Through thick reading glasses, he squinted at the fancy document set on blue velvet in his hand, and recited the formal declaration with some hesitation and intonations of disbelief.

Moshe shared his sentiments. On his first visit to the President's Residence on Ha'Nasi Street, the president was appointing him to form the next government of the State of Israel.

In another life, the achievement would have overjoyed him. Today, Moshe would have preferred to avoid the limelight. Reaching for the stars seemed like a good idea until you got burned. But now he had no choice.

The president signed at the bottom of the declaration, they shook hands, and they smiled for the cameras. The president leaned in. "Good luck," he said and smirked. "You're going to need it."

"Not luck," Moshe whispered back. "I need a miracle."

They chuckled and patted each other on the shoulder.

Galit, looking fantastic in a new white evening dress, waited in the entrance hall among the Members of Knesset and reporters—a delectable lamb among the wolves. She smiled up at him, her lipstick glistening, and brushed a speck of dust from his suit jacket, which she had helped pick out along with the silk tie in stately blue.

He had recovered from their ordeal on Election Day and no longer flinched at her touch. The memory of his death had hurt him to the core, and he supposed their relationship would never quite be the same, but he couldn't blame her. Avi had deceived her—he had testified to that himself—and, for a change, his old friend had brought Moshe and Galit closer.

The time had come for healing. Healing and forgiveness. To accept the past and look to the future.

"Ready to conquer the world?" she asked.

He took her arm in his. "One small country is more than enough."

They made for the garden and passed a rotund man with a bad comb-over, who made a conspicuous point of turning his back to them.

Moshe tapped him on the shoulder. "No hard feelings?"

Isaac Gurion swiveled, his bloodshot eyes flashing like angry daggers. Recovering quickly, the older politician shook Moshe's hand but bared his teeth as he smiled. "None at all." He seemed to be trying to crush Moshe's hand in his meaty grip.

"Remember," Moshe added, "it isn't personal; it's just politics." And he left the career politician snarling on the carpet.

A podium with microphones waited for Moshe at the edge of the garden, as did a healthy crowd of dignitaries and members of the press.

Moshe extracted cue cards from the inner pocket of his jacket, while an aide adjusted the microphone.

"Feeling grateful and humbled," Moshe said, "I accepted the president's appointment today. My heartfelt thanks go to those who made this moment possible: our team at Restart, my wonderful wife and daughter, and of course, you—the people of our beloved state. I will do everything in my power to serve as prime minister for all citizens, even those who opposed me. Thank you."

He opened the floor to questions.

The aide selected one of the raised hands, and a weasel of a reporter stood. "Seeing that you have no political experience, Mr. Prime Minister–elect, were you surprised by the president's appointment to form the government?"

Moshe had expected snide questions, but he did not reply in kind, resolving to behave with the dignity worthy of his new role. "Not really," he said. "Restart received the majority of the seats in Knesset. The president didn't have much of a choice." His remark won a few laughs from the crowd.

From among the faces in the packed garden, Reverend Adams gave him the thumbs-up and winked. Moshe responded with a subtle nod. One day, his wealthy backer would call in his favors.

And not only him. Moshe scanned the crowd for a bald head and hooked nose, and prayed that Mandrake's thugs had not slipped past the security detail. *You're mine*, Mandrake had said. *Your life belongs to me!* The mafia boss had revived Moshe and let him slip away. From their encounter Moshe had drawn two conclusions: resurrected people can die; and, sooner or later, Mandrake would return with his own demands of the new prime minister.

Another reporter stood. "With sixty-one seats in Knesset, are you going to form—for the first time in our history—a single-party government?"

"No, that's not my intention. We need to work together to meet the challenges ahead. I call upon the leaders of all parties to join our unity government and work with us to build a brighter future for all. Thank you very much."

He took Galit by the hand and followed Alon, the head of his security detail, to the waiting cavalcade, where another secret service agent held the door of a black SUV.

They climbed inside.

"That went smoothly," Galit said, as the car pulled off and

the world passed by their window.

"Yes it did. Let's hope that's a sign for the future. Where to now?"

"Dr. Klein."

"Right." Dr. Klein. The cardiologist. One advantage to being prime minister–elect, Moshe discovered, was the ease with which specialists became available on short notice.

The SUV, one of five identical vehicles in the cavalcade, pulled off.

Another advantage was the security detail that stood between his family and organized crime. Moshe had better make sure he stayed in office.

People lined the streets, hoping to catch a glimpse of their new prime minister. Some waved Israeli flags and streamers; others hefted signs of protest. One placard read, "Undead Stay Dead." Among the crowds stood a vaguely familiar man with a long stately beard and what appeared to be a white DBS spa gown.

Moshe's invitation to the party leaders was sincere, and not just because he needed their political experience. As the shock waves of the Resurrection rippled through the country, tensions grew. Never mind forming a government, he'd be lucky to avoid civil war.

"Look," Galit said. She pointed to a large clump of demonstrators in white robes and headdresses. The large banner over their heads displayed an abstract portrait of Moshe and the words, "Welcome, King Messiah!"

Moshe swallowed hard. "Talk about high expectations," he said.

Moshe wasn't the Messiah. At least, he didn't think he was. He would have known if he was. Did he even believe in a messiah? Until recently, he hadn't believed in a resurrection either.

Galit squeezed his hand. "Piece of cake," she said.

Moshe laughed and shook his head. He didn't know about that.

Messiah or not, the time had come to get to work.

A Premature Apocalypse

The Dry Bones Society

Book III

DAN SOFER

CHAPTER 1

"What was that?" Fahid said. The sudden noise in the dark tunnel behind him made the hair on the back of his neck bristle. Was somebody else there—or some*thing*?

Hisham slowed to a stop. "What?"

Fahid put his finger to his lips and listened. He could have sworn he'd heard the shuffle of feet, but now his ears only detected the distant drip of water. Was his mind playing tricks on him?

Hisham aimed the beam of his flashlight, tracing the electric cables that ran down the cement ceiling and casting long, eerie shadows along the endless gray walls.

He bared his teeth. "Scared of ghosts?"

"I'm not scared," Fahid lied. He still slept with a nightlight in the room he shared with his two older brothers, but he would never admit that to his friend.

"We're under the Enemy's feet now," he added. "What if they've found the tunnel?"

For months the two boys had shoveled dirt, mixed cement, and plastered the tunnel walls. In return, they received a hamper of Hershey's chocolate bars every other week. The tunnel started in a storage room beneath the UNRWA Hospital in Gaza City and wormed its way beneath houses and apartment buildings, crossing the immense border wall, and ending in an empty field at the outskirts of two Israeli farming villages.

Their work was not without danger. Fahid had lost two school friends to collapsing ceilings. Another had drowned when the Egyptians pumped sea water into a tunnel near the Rafah Border Crossing. Their own tunnel had surfaced in enemy territory two days ago, and now the threat of detonation by the Israel Defense Forces haunted their every step. If enemy soldiers had slipped into the tunnel behind them, they would cut off the boys from escape.

"They haven't found it," Hisham said. "C'mon. Let's finish up and go home."

They had to complete their survey by dawn so that tonight, the Arab fighters with their heavy packs would not trip on loose stones or slip in puddles. Such mishaps might detonate their bombs or trigger machine gun fire, killing their comrades underground and alerting the Enemy.

Faster, the boys pressed onward.

Uuungggh...

A low moan issued from the darkness behind them, the sound of an injured animal. A wolf?

The boys halted, and Fahid gripped Hisham by the elbow. This time, Hisham didn't mock him for being scared. His eyes were large and white; he had heard it too.

Hisham grabbed him by the shirt. "Is this a trick? Are you messing with me?"

"No. I swear it! Turn on the lights."

"We're not allowed to, remember? The current makes the tunnel easier to find."

The groan rose behind them again. A second voice joined the first; then a third. Not a lone wolf but a pack of suffering creatures. The voices sounded almost human—humans unlike any Fahid had ever encountered.

"What if it's *them*?" Fahid hissed.

"Who?" Hisham knew exactly what Fahid meant. Everyone had heard the stories even if they refused to talk about them.

Fahid swallowed his pride. "The Dead Jews."

"Those are lies," his friend said. "Lies told by the Enemy to plant fear in our hearts. The dead do not rise, certainly not dead Jews."

"But they do. They sprout from the ground, and now they rule the Zionist Enemy!"

"Nonsense!" Hisham said, but his arm trembled.

Mnnnnngggrrrrhhhh....

Hisham clutched Fahid's arm too. The groaning came louder now, closer. There was a scraping sound as well, the shuffling of a hundred feet over the rough tunnel floor toward them.

Hisham swore and waved the beam of the flashlight behind them. Fifty meters back, the tunnel turned a corner and disappeared.

"Come on," he said, and he pushed forward.

Fahid kept up with him, glancing back every few steps at the darkness.

The moaning continued. The boys quickened their pace, then broke into a desperate sprint. They ran and ran until they met the solid stone wall at the end of the tunnel. They turned around and pressed their backs against the wall. The flashlight beam faded into the dark. The unseen creatures were worse than any night monster Fahid had ever imagined.

Unnngggrrrhhh...

The voices grew louder, ghoulish voices from the murky realms beyond This World. Hisham aimed his beam, which cut the black void like a laser but didn't extend far enough. He swore again and hit the switch at the end of the electric cable. Their eyes shuttered as fluorescent strips sizzled to life and white light flooded the tunnel.

Silence. Empty, blessed silence. No groans. No footfalls. Hisham exhaled a deep breath. Fahid did the same. They chuckled. But not for long.

Unnngggrrrhhh!

The shuffling started again, faster and more urgent. The bright light had not dispelled the terrors beneath the ground.

Fahid's hand found Hisham's, which was cold and wet. Hisham did not shake him off.

"The ladder," Fahid muttered. They had hammered steel rungs into the rock wall of the shaft above them. Breaching the surface would expose the tunnel to the Israeli enemy, but anything was better than facing the monsters at their heels.

Hisham stared ahead but said nothing. Moments later, Fahid saw why and he wished his friend had not turned on the lights.

The first figure to round the corner of the tunnel had long gray hair, matted with dirt. The dead man's head lolled from side to side, his eyeballs rolling in deep sockets. His naked body was wrinkled and grimy, and his arms swung as unnatural forces dragged his feet forward.

Hisham squeezed Fahid's hand so hard it hurt. A second ghoul trudged behind the first. Then a third followed, a woman. A dozen more marched behind them. The army of the dead grew so thick, Fahid could no longer tell them apart. Young and old. Men and women. The mass of lumbering limbs closed in on them, slow but determined and unstoppable. Their groans echoed off the plastered walls, becoming a deafening roar of otherworldly misery. Deep below the ground, the boys shuddered, trapped between a horde of Dead Jews and the Zionist Enemy.

When the monsters stepped within reach, Hisham snapped out of their petrifying spell.

"Up!" he cried. "Now!" He gripped the first of the steel rungs and scrambled upward into the tall shaft.

Fahid followed, his dusty sneakers slipping on the smooth rungs as he climbed upward away from the groping hands of the undead. Then he collided with Hisham's legs and his ascent halted.

"Keep going!"

"I can't. The hatch is locked!"

Below Fahid, the Gray Ghoul ogled the first rung with glazed eyes. They were unnatural, mindless monsters; they couldn't climb a ladder, could they? As if in answer to Fahid's unspoken question, the ghoul gripped the steel, gave the rung a tentative pull, and heaved his body upward. Behind him, more Dead Jews followed.

"They're climbing the ladder!"

"What am I supposed to do?"

"Break it open!"

Hisham banged the base of his flashlight against the handle of the hatch. Nothing happened. He banged again and again, and yet again, until finally there came a metallic *crack*. A draft of cool air ruffled Fahid's hair, and Hisham launched upward.

Fahid raced after, clambering into the night and rolling onto the dirt and patchy grass. The full moon bathed them in pale light.

Hisham slammed the hatch shut. "C'mon!" He pulled Fahid to his feet. "Over there." He pointed to a clump of yellow lights a few hundred meters away.

"That's the Enemy!" Fahid protested. Moments ago, the Israeli village, with its schools and kindergartens, greenhouses and factories, had been their target.

"Rather them than those things down there!" Hisham dragged him forward and Fahid relented.

They sprinted in the night, crossing half the distance to the village before slowing. Crickets chirped in the night as they panted. Fahid's legs burned, the chill air searing his throat and lungs. They paused to catch their breath and smiled at each other in the dull light. They had escaped the monsters.

Then the hatch swung open, and the boys spun around. The Gray Ghoul climbed out of the tunnel and lumbered after them.

Letting out a cry, the boys dashed toward the yellow lights of the nearest village. The groans rose behind them, piercing the night like icy daggers.

Fahid sprinted for all he was worth. Then he crashed into Hisham, and they tumbled to the ground. Fahid got to his elbows and saw why his friend had stopped. A half-dozen bushes formed a semicircle around them. Their camouflaged legs ended in heavy black boots. Beneath their leaves, the barrels of machine guns glinted in the moonlight.

"Stop or I'll shoot," said one bush, in Arabic.

They had run straight into a trap. The boys stared at the commandos, their muscles twitching, the groans behind them growing louder, as did the shuffling feet.

Fahid cringed and clamped his eyes shut. Any moment, the cold claws of the Dead would dig into his shoulders, their sharp teeth into his neck. Or bullets would rip through his body, shredding his flesh and shattering his bones.

But five terrifying seconds later, Fahid still lay there, alive and whole. The groaning had settled; the footfalls ceased. An early morning breeze blew on his damp, sweaty clothes, and an unearthly silence reigned. He opened one eye, then another. The gunmen were no longer looking at him and Hashim, but beyond, their mouths open.

He exchanged a fearful glance with Hisham, and, very slowly, they turned around.

Instead of otherworldly ghouls, men and women shivered in the breaking dawn, pressing their arms over their naked bodies. Their backs had straightened, and they looked about with surprise and confusion, as though they had woken up in an unfamiliar place.

The Gray Ghoul blinked at them and cleared his throat. "Excuse me," he said, in Hebrew. "Are we in Heaven?"

CHAPTER 2

Wednesday morning, Prime Minister Moshe Karlin prepared to do what no person in his position would ever do. Well, no *sane* person.

He strode down a hallway inside the Knesset building, the seat of the Israeli Parliament, his two trusted advisors in tow. When he reached the designated conference room his hand hesitated on the handle. The group of oily politicians behind the door hungered to see him fail, and his proposition would weaken his new government. Was he making a mistake?

"Are you sure about this?" said Shmuel. The balding former reporter and current Minister of Foreign Affairs had come to know him very well over the past months.

Was he sure? Moshe had not even wanted this job. And he'd made mistakes before.

He'd been a workaholic in his first life. In his drive to expand his family business, he had neglected his wife, Galit, and his daughter, Talya, and almost lost them both.

Since waking up in the Mount of Olives Cemetery five months ago, he had learned his lesson but then discovered a new obsession. With his newfound popular support, he'd fix society. Goodbye cronyism and corruption; hello justice and equality. Utopia was one election away. This time, his ambition had sent him into the clutches of organized crime and almost cost him his life.

But just when he'd foresworn political activism, another miracle occurred. Moshe found himself at the helm of the Jewish State and in an unprecedented position to make good on his campaign promises. But he knew he'd better tread carefully. The establishment played dirty and would not surrender power without a fight. If his plan worked, he wouldn't have to worry about that.

Moshe winked at Shmuel. "Keep your friends close," he said, "your enemies closer?"

Shmuel frowned. "Not close enough to stab you in the back."

"I warned him," said Sivan, the other advisor. "They're our enemies." Her good looks and Louis Vuitton suit hid the featherweight prizefighter who had managed their winning election campaign and now served as Director General of the Prime Minister's Office.

Moshe gave his friends a brave grin. "Isn't it time we turned them into allies?"

Shmuel gave a short, humorless laugh. "That's asking for another miracle."

"Not a miracle. An offer they can't refuse."

He opened the door and made for the head of the conference table.

"Well, well, well," Isaac Gurion said. "If it isn't God Almighty, descending from on high to mingle with the mortals."

Moshe ignored the gibe from his former patron. The portly seasoned politician had turned sour ever since the elections. With only twelve seats in Knesset, his newly minted Upward party had more bark than bite, but Moshe needed the Opposition Leader's cooperation for his plan to work.

On the chair beside Gurion sat Avi Segal, Moshe's ex–best friend and Gurion's current protégé. Avi stared at the polished wood of the conference table, a somber expression on the face beneath the greasy fringe. During their last encounter, with mafia guns pointed at their heads, Avi and Moshe had spared each other's lives. In an unexpected show of maturity, Avi had taken responsibility for tearing Galit and Moshe apart, and his confession had helped mend their marriage. Yet here he sat on the Opposition bench, and Moshe would place no bets on where his loyalties lay.

"Gentlemen," Moshe said. He nodded at Rabbi Yosef, the neighborhood rabbi who now served as Vice Prime Minister, Minister of Education, and Minister of Religious Affairs. "Ladies." He nodded at Savta Sarah. Galit's grandmother filled the roles of both Minister of Finance and Minister of Justice while knitting a scarf. With so few trusted friends on the Restart list, they had to wear many hats.

Only Rafi, the Yemenite taxi driver turned Minister of Transport and Minister of Defense, was absent. Something must have come up. *No matter.* Moshe had already run the proposal by his cabinet before arranging the meeting.

The remaining members of the Opposition snarled at him, but he turned to all present.

"The time has come," he said, "to beat our swords into plowshares and work together to make our nation great. Sivan?"

On cue, Sivan opened her briefcase and distributed copies of the proposal to the seated politicians.

Gurion scanned the document and licked his lips, then frowned and patted his comb-over. "So now you're dishing out ministries? Is this another little ploy?"

"Show some gratitude, son," Savta Sarah said. "Moshe doesn't owe you a thing. He's doing this from the kindness of his heart."

Gurion rolled his eyes. "Thanks for the lecture, granny."

"That's Minister of Finance to you," Moshe said. "And Minister of Justice. You'll note that Savta Sarah has agreed to offer both ministries to your party."

That shut Gurion up.

"And she's right," Moshe continued. "We're running the tightest government in our country's history—with few ministers and low expenses to the taxpayer. Adding ministers won't make us look better."

Truth be told, Moshe needed their help. The tiny cabinet could juggle only so many ministries.

And Gurion's political feelers had not failed him—Moshe had an ulterior motive. Only a strong, broad government could pass the reforms needed to fix the country's problems. In short, Moshe needed Gurion onboard.

Gurion consulted the document again and raised his eyebrows. "You want us to do the work and give you all the credit?"

"The credit will be yours. Far more than you'll get for twiddling your thumbs on the opposition bench."

Moshe eyed Rabbi Emden, in his silk black suit and tidy bowler hat, and said, "Torah True will get Religious Affairs *and* Education. Rabbi Yosef will forgo them both in the interest of a national unity government."

Rabbi Emden stared at the table and nodded. The rabbi had remained reticent throughout the meeting and did not even meet Rabbi Yosef's gaze across the table. Moshe filed that away for later. Right now, he had a coalition to cement.

Gurion dropped the document on the table. "This isn't enough. We should get the premiership."

Moshe had to laugh. The man had chutzpah. By "we" he meant "me."

"Restart has a majority in Knesset. The nation didn't choose you as their leader."

"Rotation, then. We'll take turns at playing Prime Minister, switching every year. We'll even let you go first."

Moshe shook his head.

Gurion folded his arms. "We won't settle for anything less than the vice premiership."

Moshe sighed. Placing Gurion a heartbeat away from the premiership would not bode well for Moshe's personal well-being, but he didn't say that.

Instead, he said, "Restart won the election by promising a clean sweep of the establishment. If we put you in a top spot, we'd lose credibility. This government will do great things; you can be a part of that. The country can use your experience and skills. We need more unity, not more division. Why rot on the sidelines when you can make an impact?"

He let the words linger in the air like fairy dust. The members of the Opposition eyed the documents on the table and tried not to drool.

"How long do we have to decide?"

Moshe stifled a grin. The negotiations had proceeded faster than expected. During his days at the helm of Karlin & Son, his father's taxi dispatch business, Moshe had used deadlines to great effect in clinching deals; now would be no different.

"The agreements are ready for signing," he said. Sivan withdrew a second wad of documents from her briefcase and slid them down the table. "I've arranged for a press conference ten minutes from now. They're setting up in the next room."

Cries of protest erupted around the table. "Ten minutes? That's preposterous! We need more time!"

"We've wasted enough time," Moshe said. "Let's work together."

The assembled politicians pored over the agreements, and Sivan handed out pens. They would sign, Moshe could feel it. He would have his unity government and push through the new legislation with far less friction.

Justice. Equality. Those elusive values would become an everyday reality. But the coalition was the first hurdle; more lay ahead. Good thing Dr. Klein, his cardiologist, had implanted those stents in Moshe's clogged arteries. He'd need a strong heart to survive the rest of the way.

The door opened, and Rafi poked his head inside. "Mr. Prime Minister, a word?"

There you are. From the balding Yemenite's pinched expression and his unexplained absence, Moshe knew the matter was urgent.

He joined Rafi in the corridor outside where a team of uniformed military personnel waited. "What's going on, Rafi?"

"You need to see something," Rafi said. He looked over his shoulder to make sure no one was eavesdropping. "Your helicopter is ready to leave."

Helicopter? Moshe sent a longing glance toward the conference room. "But they're about to sign. And there's the press conference in ten minutes. Can't this wait a few hours?"

"No," Rafi said. "It can't."

CHAPTER 3

The IDF chopper headed west toward the Mediterranean coastline, then banked south toward the Gaza Strip. Moshe peered out the back-seat window and swore under his breath.

Perfect. Just what he needed—a war during his first month in office. Instead of making meaningful political change, he'd have to mobilize reserve forces and manage a military crisis. But if the Gazan border had flared up again, surely Rafi wouldn't risk a helicopter ride so close to the Strip?

"Over there," Rafi said, his voice a crackle in the headset over the roar of the rotors. He pointed.

Far below, a dozen streams emerged from empty fields on the Israeli side of the border wall and flowed toward the villages. The tributaries converged and pooled beside a clump of large brown military tents.

The chopper dived toward the encampment, and Moshe's stomach churned.

He squinted at the streams, which before his eyes, became long columns of moving human beings. Hundreds of them— no thousands—and they were all naked.

Dear Lord!

For months, volunteers at the Dry Bones Society had collected the newly resurrected from cemeteries across the country. The new arrivals arrived each morning, naked and confused, in dribs and drabs. Moshe had never witnessed such a large influx of resurrected people and never in the middle of nowhere.

The chopper landed at a makeshift helipad at the edge of the campsite. Moshe, Rafi, and Sivan disembarked, keeping their heads low to avoid the whining rotors.

A soldier stood at attention. "Prime Minister Karlin," he said. A badge depicting a sword crossed with a leafy branch perched on his shoulder. "I'm Brigadier General Levi. The Chief is expecting you."

He escorted them along the edge of the enclosure formed by lengths of plastic tape between metal stakes. On the other side, men, women, and children with rough blankets draped over their shoulders gaped at the people who had just stepped out of the giant metal bird.

The First Responder Guidelines, which Moshe had written for the Dry Bones Society, advised volunteers not to disorient the new arrivals with displays of modern technology. But the guidelines did not prepare the volunteers for such a wave of new members.

The Prime Minister and his entourage climbed into the back seat of a waiting Humvee and sped off. The driver rounded the tents, hurried past a stream of returning humanity, and then stopped beside a second Humvee.

Chief of Staff Eitan stood in green military fatigues, arms akimbo, as he observed the steady march through dark sunglasses.

"Seen nothing like it," he said, after greeting the visitors. A team of soldiers handed out blankets and directed the pale-skinned arrivals to the enclosure.

Moshe had trouble believing his eyes too. What could account for this mass of resurrected people?

"Is there a cemetery nearby? Mass grave?"

"Beats me."

"An old burial site or battlefield?"

"Unlikely. Our officers interviewed a bunch of them. They're from all over history. But they're sure making our regular jobs easy—they're surfacing from terror tunnels based in Gaza."

"Gaza?" Rafi said. "They don't look like Arabs."

"No sir, they do not. They speak English, mostly, although we're getting a lot of French and Spanish too."

Moshe rubbed his forehead. Europeans in Gaza—that made no sense at all.

Sivan said, "What's that noise?"

Moshe heard it too—a low moaning from further down the line.

"Oh, that," Eitan said. "Follow me. And try not to freak out."

He marched a few feet toward the eerie sounds, then stopped.

"Notice anything... different?"

The men and women lumbered forward like sleepwalkers, their heads hanging loosely at the shoulders, their mouths open, and their unseeing eyes glazed over.

"Dear Lord!" Rafi said.

"Oh my God!" Sivan gripped Moshe's arm. "They're like... like..."

"Zombies," Eitan said, and he cleared his throat.

A shiver ran down Moshe's spine. During the elections, Avi Segal had branded the resurrected as the unnatural undead and stirred up fears about a zombie invasion.

"That's how they emerge from the tunnels. After a few steps, they come to. Good luck falling asleep tonight, folks."

A vague memory roused Moshe from shock. "Resurrection Tunnels," he said, and won blank stares from his companions. "Rabbi Yosef mentioned those once. It's an ancient tradition. During the Resurrection, righteous people buried abroad will roll through the tunnels to get back to the Holy Land."

"Strange as this sounds," Eitan said, "that might explain it. Some tunnels merge with natural subterranean caves. The network of caves could run beneath the sea floor."

Moshe shook his head in wonder. "Another ancient prediction checked off the list. Rabbi Yosef will be glad to hear that. We must call in the Dry Bones Society."

"No way," Sivan said.

"You're right—this job is too big for the DBS. We'll need to allocate funds in the new government budget."

"I mean," Sivan said, "we can't tell anyone. This has to stay here."

Her refusal to help caught Moshe off guard. "But they'll need food and clothing and accommodation."

"Nobody can know about this. Not until the coalition is signed and sealed. Do you know what a media circus this will become if anyone finds out? Imagine this"—she framed the scene of lurching naked people with her fingers—"on prime time TV. An army of zombies is all the Opposition needs to make our lives a misery. We'll need time to spin this in a positive light."

She had a point. "OK, let's keep this top secret for now. Rafi, what can we do in the short term without causing a fuss?"

"We have emergency stores in case of war and disaster."

"Excellent. Release those."

"And fast," Eitan said. "We're running out of blankets and food."

Moshe asked, "What about shelter?"

"We're setting up campsites. But we'll need a long-term solution soon, especially if this keeps up." He glanced at the zombies and swallowed hard. "Winter is coming."

CHAPTER 4

Wednesday morning, Yosef tried not to retch.

"Minister Lev!" gushed Rabbi Mendel of the Torah True party. He gripped Yosef's hand over the large oak desk of Yosef's chamber within the Prime Minister's Office building. "Pardon me. I meant to say, *Vice Prime Minister* Lev!" He plopped onto one of the leather visitor's seats and took in the room. "I *love* what you've done with the place."

Yosef glanced around his new spacious room. The only thing he had changed since taking office was the framed photo of the Prime Minister, which now displayed Moshe Karlin in a stately blue suit and tie. Yosef still didn't feel like he belonged behind the heavy desk. If he was a fraud, he was now in very good company.

A few weeks ago, Rabbi Mendel's puppeteers at the Great Council of Torah Sages had branded Yosef an agent of the *Sitrah Achrah*, the evil Other Side. They had fired him from his teaching job at Daas Torah Primary. During the election campaign, Mendel's political allies had libeled Yosef on national television as an alcoholic pedophile. But now that Yosef had attained a position of power, Rabbi Mendel pretended that none of that had happened.

Yosef suppressed his gag reflex and held his tongue for the same reason he had not redecorated his office. Soon he would vacate the room along with his ministerial positions as part of Moshe's coalition agreement.

Yosef didn't mind.

"You're a good man," his wife, Rocheleh, had said. She had meant "gullible." A little less gullible now, after all he had experienced, but still she was right: he did not belong in politics. As a regular Member of Knesset, he'd be able to help Moshe pass laws in Knesset and still have time to counsel new arrivals at the Dry Bones Society.

He drew a deep breath. "How can I help you, Member of Knesset Mendel?" The greedy politician did not deserve the title "Rabbi." True rabbis had a working moral compass.

"About the coalition agreement," Mendel said. "As you surely know, the gravity and demands of the Department of Religious Affairs require a number of deputy minister positions that appear to be missing from the list."

Yosef guessed where this was going. "And you were wondering whether I'd have a word with the Prime Minister about adding a few jobs?"

Mendel winced at the word "jobs" but didn't let the veiled condemnation derail his greed. "Five positions, to be specific."

"I see." Five extra ministerial positions with the associated salaries and benefits. Moshe wanted to reduce government expenses, but for the sake of the coalition, he would compromise.

Now that he had Mendel's attention, Yosef wanted to scratch an itch of his own. "I'm curious—why you? Member of Parliament Emden has known me for years. Surely he'd be the one to approach me?"

Spite boiled within him and Yosef flushed with shame. He knew perfectly well why Emden hadn't shown his face. His former mentor and confidant had turned their years of friendship into a political weapon when he had exposed Yosef's secrets in the smear campaign. The memory was a knife twisting in Yosef's back.

Mendel touched his nose. "Rabbi Emden went home early. He wasn't feeling well."

Yosef gave a short and mirthless laugh. Did Emden regret the betrayal, or did he fear that his presence would hamper Yosef's willingness to cooperate?

"A speedy recovery to him," Yosef said. "I'll speak with the Prime Minister and see what he can do."

He dismissed Mendel, along with the poison in his own heart. The Torah forbade bearing a grudge. Soon, he'd be able to wave it all goodbye and leave the politics to the politicians.

The phone buzzed on his desk. "Yes, Ram?"

Of the many ministerial perks, the personal assistant had taken the most getting used to. The Knesset bureaucrats had tried to pair him with a pretty young girl. Although Yosef had not doubted her secretarial credentials, he had requested a male replacement. One smear campaign was more than enough, and Yosef did not want to feed the rumormongers.

Ram had not disappointed him, although his effeminate lisp created the nagging suspicion that the bureaucrats had played their little joke on him all the same.

"Tom Levi is on the line for you."

"Tom Levi?" The name sounded familiar.

"He says he represents the Temple Faithful."

Yosef remembered.

"The Messiah is coming," Gavri the grocer had told him, and so, early on the morning of Election Day, Yosef had rushed to the Old City. Dressed in white shepherd's robes and a matching cotton beanie, the bearded and drunken messiah had stood atop the Western Wall and attempted to walk on air. Then reality hit in the form of the hard-stone floor of the plaza, and the paramedics rushed his broken body away on a stretcher.

While the stunning failure of the Messiah on the Wall had brought Yosef face-to-face with his own naivety, the catastrophe had not discouraged the messiah's followers in the slightest. Then and there, his red-bearded spokesman had tried to rope Yosef into a scheme to demolish the Islamic

Dome of the Rock on the Temple Mount and to rebuild the Jewish Temple in its place. "I'm Tom," the lunatic had said. "Tom Levi." Yosef, the lunatic magnet, had fled the scene.

"Shall I transfer the call?" Ram asked.

"No."

"Schedule an appointment?"

"No! Tell him I'm unavailable."

"Yes, sir."

"Thank you."

Yosef exhaled, long and slow. A secretary provided definite advantages. Tom Levi would no doubt try again, but by then Yosef would have relinquished his ministerial position, and the lunatic would be somebody else's problem. *Good luck with that, Mendel. Ha!*

The phone buzzed again.

"Yes, Ram?"

"Reverend Adams is here to see you."

Yosef's pulse quickened. "Please send him in."

He stood and wiped his palms on his trousers as the broad-chested American burst into the room like a force of nature in an expensive suit. The silver-haired Christian gave Yosef's hand a mighty double-handed squeeze that threatened to dislocate the rabbi's shoulder. "Vice President Lev, my congratulations," he said in his Texas drawl. "What an honor to meet with you again." His ivory teeth glinted as he smiled.

"Vice *Prime Minister*," Yosef corrected.

"Right, yes, of course!"

Adams was not a stickler for details. He took a seat, and his spindly, briefcase-toting assistant followed suit.

Yosef's heart palpitated faster, and not just because he had to deploy his minimal English skills. He knew which question his benefactor had dropped by to ask, and Yosef's answer would break his heart.

The New Evangelical Church of America had created a wholly owned subsidiary, The Flesh and Blood Fund, to bankroll the Dry Bones Society. He had also given the nascent Restart party the infusion of funds needed to jumpstart their winning election campaign. Would he turn off the tap when he realized that his church's key motivation for supporting those enterprises had not borne fruit?

Adams got straight to business. "You're a busy man, so I won't hog your time. Tell me, Rabbi," a smile sparkled in his eyes, "have we reached the Roman Period?" He sent a gleeful glance at his associate, who smiled and blinked at Yosef with expectation.

Each morning, the dead returned from further back in history. Casualties of the Israeli wars had preceded resistance fighters of the British Mandate period. The hapless dead of the Ottoman Empire, and Islamic and Crusader eras, had followed.

"Yes, we have," Yosef said. "The Roman Period and *earlier*. We find professors to speak with the new arrivals. Latin. Ancient Greek. Aramaic. And, how you say, Phoenician? Or Proto-Canaanite? I forget." Yosef chuckled, but his delay tactics failed.

Adams leaned forward. "Excellent. So, has *He* stopped by yet to visit his colleagues?"

"He?" Yosef clasped his trembling fingers on his lap.

"Yes. *He*. With a capital H. Our charismatic friend. The Aramaic speaker."

"M-many new arrivals speak A-Aramaic. And some are very... charismatic?"

Adams's smile froze. It thawed. Then it evaporated. He flopped against the backrest, and all that good cheer left him like air escaping a balloon. He glanced at his concerned assistant, then at the wall behind Yosef. "I... I don't understand. Surely by now..."

He shook his head, and his eyes glistened. The reverend had predicted that his Savior would descend from Heaven to rejoin the resurrected of His generation. Although this Second Coming would have created very awkward theological issues for the rabbi, Yosef felt a stab of empathy.

Yosef had tasted bitter disillusion too. The Resurrection

rewarded the world's victims with a second chance at life. But then Shmuel had unmasked a suicide bomber among the members of the Dry Bones Society, and that understanding had come crashing down. Did a cold-blooded mass murderer deserve a second chance?

And so, ironically, just as Yosef reached the pinnacle of success and power, he had lost his naïve faith both in the rabbinate and in cosmic justice.

Yosef searched for words to comfort both his fellow believer and himself. "Perhaps this resurrection is not what we thought."

CHAPTER 5

Eli Katz glanced at the whiteboard on the easel that Noga had set up in the living room of his penthouse on Jaffa Road. He had not felt this hopeful in, literally, a thousand years.

"I like it," he said. "It's a great plan."

"Honest?"

"Definitely."

Noga jumped on him and kissed him long and hard.

Eli came up for air. "And it's looking better by the minute."

"You're not just saying that because I kissed you, are you?"

"Nope, although that did help. Hey!" He evaded her jabbing fingers. "Here's why I like it," he added, to avoid death by tickling. He cleared his throat and read the three-step plan out loud. "'Publish paper. Contact media. Meet Prime Minister.' It's short, simple, and doable. Once *Nature Genetics* gives us our academic creds, the newspapers will carry the story. Once the story spreads, Moshe Karlin will come calling."

Moshe Karlin was their leading candidate for the role of Messiah in the cosmic drama. The resurrected man had stormed the political scene overnight, winning over the country with a clean campaign that promised to end corruption and cronyism. He was also the man that God had told Eli to anoint. At least, so Eli thought.

Five months ago, the Thin Voice had sent Eli, also known as Elijah the Prophet, to anoint the Messiah at the Mount of Olives Cemetery. Eli had spotted three people at the rendez-vous point. Later, he would identify them as Moshe Karlin, Rabbi Yosef Lev, and a mysterious blond Russian woman who worked at the Dry Bones Society.

Unfortunately for humanity, before Eli could anoint the Messiah, he crashed his Harley into a truck and woke up in the Shaare Zedek Medical Center. The Thin Voice had fallen silent ever since. In the hospital, Eli met Noga. She stole his heart, rekindled his faith in humanity, and saved him from the head of neurology, Dr. Stern, who had developed an un-healthy interest in Eli's speedy recovery.

In hindsight, Eli's motorcycle accident was yet another step in the Divine Plan. God had led him to Noga, but not merely to jump-start an ancient prophet's rusty motivation. Noga's doctoral research project identified Palestinian Arabs as the Ten Lost Tribes of Israel, a demographic that Elijah the Prophet was to uncover during the Messianic Era. To reunite the Twelve Tribes of Israel in the Holy Land was high on the to-do list of the long-overdue Messiah. Without the Lost Tribes, the moment of Redemption might slip away yet again.

As for Moshe Karlin, a charismatic new leader of the Jew-ish State made sense as the Messiah. His layers of Secret Service security, however, made bumping into him on the street impossible. "Hey, Moshe. How you doing? And by the way, you're the Messiah. Good luck!"

But the publication of Noga's findings in one of the world's most esteemed peer-reviewed academic journals would open the path to Moshe Karlin. Noga had submitted her paper last week, and they used the wait to hone the rest of their plan.

Eli frowned. "We're forgetting one critical thing."

Noga's face became a battleground of fear and uncertain-ty. "What?"

"Breakfast."

Eli fixed shakshouka in a frying pan—heavy on the tomato, light on the chili—and popped a few slices of bread in the toaster. Sitting at the island of his designer kitchen, they munched away while the sun warmed the Jerusalem skyline through the French windows.

"Things were easier in the past," he said. "If I wanted to give King Ahab an earful, I'd just wait in the woods for his chariot to pass by."

"You should speak with archaeologists," Noga said. "They'd learn so much."

Memories from his earlier life used to freak Noga out. After she located the Ten Lost Tribes and discovered that dead people were rising from their graves throughout the country, her boyfriend's longevity no longer seemed so far-fetched.

"Nah," Eli said. "Even if they believed me, it's anecdotal evidence."

"Right." Her eyes narrowed as she thought. "How did you know where to wait?"

"For Ahab? The Thin Voice."

"Figures. Everything's easier with a direct line to God's Mind."

"Yeah." He sighed.

Without the Thin Voice, he'd never know for sure whether Moshe was the Lord's Anointed. He was flying blind. But maybe that was the point. After centuries of false messiahs, maybe this time really was different. Maybe this time the Final Redemption would arrive.

Noga's phone rang. She washed down a mouthful of shakshouka. "It's Hannah." She answered. "Hi, Hannah. How are you?"

Noga listened, her brow tense. They hadn't expected to hear from her doctoral supervisor for weeks. Academic journals took their time to analyze and reproduce results before including a paper in their next edition.

"Aha," Noga said. She stared into space, and her expression slackened. Something was wrong. "I see."

She put down the phone. "They're not going to publish the paper."

"Did we miss the deadline?" A delay would set back their plans by months.

"No," she said. "We submitted in time, but they still won't publish it. Not now. Not ever."

CHAPTER 6

"Are you sure it's safe?" Ahmed asked Dara. He did not ask, "Is it legal?"

They stood on the edge of a dirt road on the outskirts of Jerusalem, the surrounding hills strewn with stones and wild grass. His new friend handed him a large rock from a large mound. Ahmed hefted the stone in one hand, wondering how far he could throw it.

"Yeah, sure. I've done it many times. And if you get shot, they pay more."

Ahmed hesitated. As much as he hated eating from dumpsters, he did not like the idea of getting shot. But he needed money. A roof over his head would be nice too, instead of that old tomb at the edge of the Mount of Olives. His friend's promise of employment had sounded too good to be true. And when something sounds too good to be true, you run for your life. He had learned that the hard way.

Still, he had to start somewhere. And if he had a job, maybe Samira would want to see him again.

"Murderer!" the older Israeli man had roared. In the group session room at the Dry Bones Society, he had tried to throttle Ahmed. He had recognized Ahmed from the bus, the day Ahmed had pressed the detonator button threaded through his sleeve and thrown the commuters into a fiery hell.

Keep dreaming, you fool. Samira knew what he had done; she'd never want to look on him again.

"What if we get arrested?" Ahmed asked.

He feared capture more than injury. If the authorities found out who he was, they would imprison him for sure. And they weren't the only ones who wanted to put his head on a spike. In his nightmares, Boris the slave driver found him, and his henchmen dragged Ahmed back to the life of hard labor he had fled.

His cousin Hasan would be next in line. "A double martyr," he had told Ahmed. "You will be a hero. No, more than that—a legend." Ahmed had accepted the second explosive belt but then aborted his mission. How would the suicide bomber pimp receive him now? Probably not with hugs and kisses.

"You worry too much," Dara said. "Here." He pulled a white-and-black-checkered *kaffiyeh* from a plastic bin and handed it to Ahmed. "Put that over your face and you'll be invisible. OK?"

Ahmed glanced at the clump of young Arab men in rough clothes, loitering across the road. What other options did he have? "OK."

An unmarked bus barreled down the road, kicking up dust, and stopped beside the mound of stones. The two friends got on, along with the other desperate young men. Instead of buying a ticket, they scribbled their names on a lined sheet of paper using a pen attached by a string. *Walid*, Ahmed wrote. The word meant newborn. His new life was not progressing as he had hoped.

"Where does the money come from?" Ahmed asked when they had found a pair of seats at a dusty window.

"Europe," Dara said. "Germany, mostly."

"What do Germans want here?"

"To help the Palestinians."

Ahmed chuckled. "You're kidding, right?" He got that too-good-to-be-true sensation again.

"Their money is no joke. Their non-governmental organizations spend millions of dollars here."

"Wow." A million dollars was an unimaginable amount of money. Where did those millions go?

When they got off the bus, he found out. Ten other buses offloaded similarly wretched Arabs at the meeting point. A few dozen more arrived with the same cargo as they waited. Some were kids; the youngest looked seven years old.

An army of Europeans in flak jackets and sunglasses smoked cigarettes and joked around in foreign tongues. Most of them held microphones or shouldered television cameras.

"We're starting," cried an Arab man, who seemed to be in charge. "This way."

Two hundred Arabs pulled *kaffiyehs* over their faces and marched down the dirt road, the cameramen flanking them. The crowd stopped twenty meters from what looked like an oversized call box surrounded by cement blocks where two Israeli soldiers watched cars passing on a paved road. The soldiers wore helmets, bulky equipment jackets with high lapels, and machine guns across their chests.

"Wait for it!" the Arab leader yelled. The cameramen were still setting up their tripods.

One soldier talked to the other and pointed toward the waiting crowd. Inside the call box, another soldier spoke into a telephone handset.

"Now!" the leader cried.

"Let the show begin," Dara said.

The first rock hit a soldier on the head. The man collapsed behind the cement barrier, and two of his colleagues dragged him into the call box. To Ahmed's surprise, none of the soldiers returned fire.

Ahmed turned to see whether the reporters had caught that, but they had their cameras trained on the Arab rioters.

Rocks bounced off the cement barriers and cracked the windows of the call box.

"Why aren't they firing?" Ahmed asked.

Dara laughed. "They're too scared. If they kill any of us by mistake, they'll go to prison. C'mon, throw something."

Ahmed looked at the rock in his hand.

"C'mon, give it to those sons of pigs! Killers of prophets!"

In his first life, Ahmed had worked at the Rami Levi supermarket in Talpiot. His boss, Yigal, had joked around with him in Arabic, asked after his family, and let him take Fridays off. And when Ahmed's own mother had turned him out on the street, the Dry Bones Society had given him food and shelter. Moshe Karlin and Rabbi Yosef had saved Samira from Boris and his henchmen. What if these soldiers were their brothers and sisters?

Dara glared at him. "No stones, no money."

Ahmed lunged forward and threw the rock with all his might. It bounced into a clump of grass at the side of the road.

"Man!" Dara said. "You have the worst aim ever." He chuckled.

While Ahmed threw wide, the others had no inhibitions. Rocks rained on the call box, then targeted the passing cars. A windshield smashed, and the car veered off the road, almost colliding with oncoming traffic, then returned to its lane and sped off.

After that, the soldiers stepped out of their shelter and aimed their rifles in the air.

Some rioters fled to the back of the crowd.

"Go! Go!" the ringleader said, and a group of Arab kids advanced on the soldiers, hurling curses and stones.

Camera shutters clicked as they captured the scene: Israeli soldiers firing over the heads of seven-year-olds.

Ahmed swore. He had seen a lot of messed up things in his life, but the choreographed riot with its pint-sized human shields left him speechless. Where were their parents? And how much would they earn for an injured child?

He had been one of those boys once. And so, the wheel turned.

A military van pulled up outside the call box, and soldiers poured out the back. Weapons fired, and Ahmed ducked out of the way. A cloud of white smoke billowed nearby. The gas burned his eyes and seared his throat.

"Fall back," Dara shouted. They ran away from the tear gas and back to the meeting point where the buses idled.

The show was over.

CHAPTER 7

Beneath the tall dome of the empty hall in the Knesset building, Avi reread the coalition agreement for the tenth time. The document was the answer to his prayers.

The Plenum Hall of the Knesset stood three floors high, the rows of seats arranged before the Speaker's dais in the shape of a candelabrum. As a member of the Opposition, Avi sat at the back.

Within a month, he had gone from sleeping on benches in Sacher Park to dozing off on the comfy chairs in Knesset. Who would have believed it?

His new fortune in life had placed him in a bind. He had landed his spot on the Upward party list by stirring up popular discontent for the Dry Bones Society and their "undead zombies." Boris the gangster was his patron, Isaac Gurion his mentor, Moshe Karlin his sworn enemy, and Galit his rightful girl. But on Election Day, his worldview had flipped one hundred and eighty degrees. Nothing makes a man see the error of his ways like a gun pointed at his head.

Mandrake, Boris's sadistic and psycho boss, had tied up Avi and Moshe and urged them to blow each other's brains out—right in front of Galit. When it came to the crunch, Avi couldn't do it. He had never wanted to kill Moshe, he realized; he had wanted *to be* Moshe. His rash entry into politics had almost killed the two people he cared about most. No longer could he blame Moshe for his own failings.

The revelations had not faded after his narrow escape from death, not even after Moshe's resounding victory in the elections. And so Avi found himself in Knesset, on the Opposition bench, while secretly he was rooting for Moshe.

For two weeks, he had haunted the corridors of Knesset, trying to be invisible. He avoided his party leader, Isaac Gurion, who radiated pent-up rage and frustration and often vented both on his subordinates. Avi had skipped as many Knesset sessions as possible, preferring to creep into the Plenum Hall when vacant, like now.

But Moshe's generous coalition agreement would set the world aright. He and Moshe would be on the same team again. They'd be buddies like in the good old days at Karlin & Son before Avi's mad jealousy had led him to betray Moshe and ruin everything.

The memory of Karlin & Son gave Avi an idea. He rushed out of the empty hall and sped down a corridor.

He found Gurion lounging in a committee room in the Kedma wing and chuckling with Rabbi Mendel of Torah True.

Gurion looked up at his flushed minion. "Hello, Avi. Getting some exercise?"

He's in a good mood. Great. Avi gave a quick smile. "About the coalition—I was wondering: is the Deputy Minister of Transportation position available?"

"Why, are you interested in *going places*?"

Gurion and Rabbi Mendel chortled again. Why were they so happy?

"I think I can contribute there. Before I entered politics, I worked in the, ah, public transportation industry, and—"

"You mean at Karlin & Son?"

The mention of that detail unsettled Avi. Gurion had done his homework. But would he wonder where Avi's loyalties lay now? "Well, yes," he said, "but—"

Another chuckle cut him short. Again, Avi was out of the

loop and two steps behind; he hated that.

"What if you were to *head* that ministry—wouldn't you do even more good?"

Him—Minster of Transportation? "Yeah, sure. But I'm not high enough on our list, and with the amount of positions Karlin is offering..." More chuckles. They were driving him crazy. "What?"

Gurion motioned for Avi to sit next to him and placed an arm around his shoulders. "We're not going to join the coalition, Avi."

"We aren't? But then how will we get any ministries?"

"By taking them. We're going to bring down Karlin's government."

The floor of Avi's stomach fell away. "Bring down the government—but how?"

"That's easy," Gurion said. "Together."

CHAPTER 8

"Mr. Prime Minister!" said a voice in the corridor behind him. Moshe had hurried from the chopper pad into the Prime Minister's Office building, hoping to slip into his room unnoticed, when the man called his name. Of all people, he had hoped to avoid the Government Secretary.

Moshe turned as the eager little man ran over. "Yes, Rubi. How can I help you?"

"The question is 'How can *I* help *you*?'" He gave a nervous chuckle. With his square glasses and rounded features, Rubi reminded him of an owl. "I hear there was a meeting this morning with Opposition MPs. My department's job is to coordinate between you and Knesset. If I'd only known in advance—"

Moshe held up his hand, cutting him short. "I know, you would have taken care of everything."

Since Moshe's first day in office, Rubi had pressured him to avail himself of his teams of bureaucrats. Moshe had selected an employee from the pool of secretaries but drawn the line at more sensitive roles. Like the intelligence agencies, the Government Secretariat was part of the entrenched establishment. Over the years, they had nurtured relationships with career politicians such as Gurion, and they resented Moshe's new upstart party that had stormed the halls of power. They probably feared that he aimed to terminate their comfy ten-ured jobs; on that point, they happened to be right. Could he trust them not to leak top secret information to their old pals? Considering that morning's events on the Gazan bor-der, Moshe's decision seemed wise.

"It's not just the logistics," Rubi continued. "We have speech writers and spokespeople. A prime minister who wants to get things done can't do everything on his own."

"I appreciate your concern," Moshe said. "But I prefer to write my own speeches, and Sivan is managing our press relations. I'll be sure to contact you when the need arises."

He continued down the corridor, but the bureaucrat wasn't giving up. "At least let us help next time, I'm sure you'll see our added value. Will you be making any an-nouncements soon?"

Moshe halted outside his office and studied the eager owl's face. Was he interested in proving his worth, or was he fish-ing for information? He must have heard of Moshe's sudden helicopter excursion. What else did he know?

"Mr. Prime Minister," said Ettie. Moshe's elderly secretary peered at him over half-moon spectacles from her desk out-side his office. "The American Ambassador is waiting for you inside."

Interesting. "Is this a scheduled appointment?" He didn't re-call any diplomatic meetings on his calendar today.

"No, sir. But he says it's very urgent."

Were the Americans going to pressure him into yet anoth-er Peace Process already, or had some new crisis arisen? Either way, he'd found the perfect excuse to brush off the Government Secretary. "If you'll excuse me…"

"Of course," Rubi said, and trudged away.

"Ambassador Smith," Moshe said in English, closing the door of his office behind him. He shook the burly American's hand and took his seat behind the Prime Minister's desk. "To what do I owe this pleasant surprise?"

The ambassador had presented his credentials to the new prime minister during Moshe's first week in office. Smith had been cool and dismissive, but today the ambassador greeted him with a broad, eager smile, his cheeks flushed with ingratiation.

"I am happy to bring Your Excellency an urgent message from the President of the United States."

"Wonderful," Moshe said and swallowed hard. *Here it comes.*

Smith's smile threatened to split his face in two. "The President would like to remind you of the special bond between our great nations. As the only liberal democracy in the Middle East, Israel shares with the United States not only political interests but a cultural and moral heritage."

Moshe shifted on his padded seat. Such an introduction implied a very large ask. What could the President of the United States want from the Jewish State?

"The President would also like to remind Your Excellency of the United States' long history of friendship with and support for the State of Israel, both financial and political. From sharing intelligence and generous military funding to vetoing hostile resolutions at the United Nations."

Moshe fought the urge to interrupt. That "friendship and support" had often fluctuated with changing American administrations, and always came with a catch. Their demands for action—and inaction—often endangered Israeli lives.

"Above all," Smith continued, "the American People have always felt a deep connection with the Nation of Israel and concern for its fate."

Moshe was learning the complex dance of political statesmanship. The steps included demands cloaked in compliments and accusations dressed as gratitude. Translated into plain English, the president's message meant, "You owe us big time and it's time to pay up."

Fortunately, Moshe could dance too.

"On behalf of the State of Israel," he replied, "I thank the President for his kind reminder. Please let him know that we are very grateful and deeply appreciate his nation's friendship and *ongoing* support."

He emphasized the word "ongoing." Translation: what's in it for us?

Ambassador Smith drew a deep breath and gritted his teeth. Beneath the veneer of cordiality, the career diplomat resented having to dance with Moshe Karlin, the former unwashed civilian. But orders from the President were orders.

"The President would like to formalize our special relationship by offering the State of Israel full membership in the federal republic."

Moshe must have misunderstood. "The federal republic?"

Smith pursed his lips. "In short, he's inviting the State of Israel to become a part of the United States of America."

"The fifty-first state?"

"Exactly."

"Wow." That was an unstatesmanlike thing to say, but Moshe couldn't control himself. "But... we're in the Middle East."

Smith shrugged. "Hawaii is in the middle of the Pacific Ocean. Alaska is on the other side of Canada."

"Forgive me for asking, Mr. Ambassador, but why?"

"The benefits are many. Any attack on Israel would be a declaration of war against the United States. The full force of the United States Army would stand behind you. Israel would no longer have to impose high taxes to fund its defense needs. Uncle Sam would take care of you. Your country would benefit from our international ties and credit rating. Israeli citizens would no longer require visas to visit or work in the United States."

"I understand," Moshe said. "But what I meant was, what would the United States stand to gain?"

Smith cleared his throat. "Of course, Israel would have to adhere to federal law. Israel would have to adopt the US currency and controls. Your Excellency would become the Governor of the State of Israel, and your government would integrate with the Senate and House of Representatives. We will make provisions to retain the unique character of the Jewish State as the homeland of the Jewish People."

Smith's eyes darted to the table. The ambassador was dancing around the topic, and they both knew it.

"But surely the United States doesn't need another state? Israel has been targeted for extermination by Muslim countries. Wouldn't this invite conflict?"

Ambassador Smith pouted as he mulled his next words. "The President feels that this is the right thing to do. In addition, the United States would gain access to Israel's resources."

A short laugh escaped Moshe's lips. "We have no oil or precious minerals, and little natural gas. Our main assets are technology and human resources."

"Precisely," Smith said, his mouth twisting into a knowing sneer. "In the Information Age, it's those resources that count."

Moshe wasn't buying it. The US already had access to the technology of Israel's start-ups and military. This sudden desire to adopt the Jewish State must somehow be related to the Resurrection. Did the American government, like Reverend Adams and his Evangelical Christians, believe that the world was approaching the End of Days? Were they hedging their bets ahead of Armageddon?

Smith seemed to have read Moshe's thoughts. "The times are changing," he said. "We expect that the State of Israel will be at the epicenter of that change. And, Your Excellency, we intend to be right there at your side."

Moshe had seen the posters with his portrait on the streets of Israel. "Welcome, King Messiah!" they read. Moshe hadn't let that go to his head. He wasn't the messiah; surely he would know if he was? With his rise to prominence, news of the Resurrection had spread across the world. Had the Americans contracted the same messianic fever?

Moshe swallowed again. He would have to tread carefully.

"Please thank the President for his very generous offer. Obviously, I'll have to discuss this with my cabinet. The coalition agreement we hope to sign soon will make the President's proposal much easier to implement. Please thank the President for his patience."

"Very well," Ambassador Smith said. He rose to leave. "One more thing. The President would appreciate it if you'd keep this offer secret. We wouldn't want other interested parties to create any obstacles."

"Of course."

Moshe shook his hand, escorted him to the door, and paced his office.

The fifty-first state! The proposition would be a hard sell to the Israeli public. But was accession to the United States in Israel's long-term interests? Moshe had hung his personal hopes on powerful friends before and paid the price; he did not want to repeat that mistake on a national scale.

There was a knock on the door before it opened, and Sivan entered.

"I've rescheduled both the coalition signing and the press conference for tomorrow."

"Excellent."

"And I think I've found the right spin for the developments in the south."

"The miracles never cease. What's the angle?"

She sucked in a deep breath. "The Sixth Aliyah."

As usual, Sivan's marketing genius had nailed the solution. Since the late nineteenth century, Jews had arrived in the Holy Land in waves, each known as an *aliyah*—an ascension or immigration. Some immigrants came to lay the foundations for a future Jewish State, others to escape persecution in Europe, the Middle East, and Asia.

By naming the recent influx of resurrected as the Sixth Aliyah, Sivan framed the phenomenon as the natural continuation of the first five mass immigrations. And why not?

Besides, anything was better than Zombie Invasion, the phrase that Gurion's Opposition would use if they ever got wind of these new arrivals.

"I like it!"

"Thought you would. Great, that's settled then. Now we just need to keep a lid on things until the coalition agreement is signed."

The intercom buzzed, and Moshe thumbed the speaker-phone.

"Yes, Ettie?"

"The Russian Ambassador is here to see you, sir."

First the Americans; now the Russians? "I don't suppose he made an appointment either, did he?"

"No, sir. But he says it's very urgent."

CHAPTER 9

"You know what this place needs?" Irina said, over breakfast. She glanced at the peeling wallpaper of Alex's kitchen.

Alex looked up from his cornflakes, his ponytail switching behind him. "A bulldozer?"

She laughed. His second-floor apartment in downtown Jerusalem had seen better decades, that was clear, but wasn't ready for the wrecking ball yet. The three-room rental with the chunky plaster and noisy plumbing had an Old World charm. It was an apartment they would remember fondly after moving to the suburbs.

"Flowers," she said. "Some color."

Over the past weeks, Irina had spent more evenings at Alex's apartment than her Dry Bones Society dormitory room; she'd come to think of the bachelor pad as home.

"Good idea," he said. He seemed relieved. Had he thought she'd planned to go through his wardrobe and discard his old T-shirts? Irina made a mental note to do just that later.

She and Alex had grown close since their random meeting at the Dry Bones Society. Beneath the bulging muscles, she'd discovered a gentleman and a kind soul. There was still so much for her to learn about the new man in her life. The Russian tattoos hinted at a difficult past. She had yet to meet his friends and family. A thrilling thought struck her—had he met hers?

Moshe Karlin and Rabbi Yosef had discovered her among the tombstones of the Mount of Olives Cemetery. Five months later, she still recalled nothing of her former life, and not for want of trying.

Alex had enlisted his neurologist friend to crack the mystery of Irina's sealed past. Despite the doctor's unorthodox methods, which had involved a dentist's chair, electrodes, and hypnosis, her former life remained a locked vault. "A lack of blood flow to the right temporal lobe, the seat of long-term memory," Dr. V had explained. "Usually the result of head trauma."

Traffic accident, she assumed. She shivered at the idea of her violent first death and pushed thoughts of her demise from her mind. The possibilities in her new life were far more interesting.

Alex finished his bowl of cereal. "Want me to drop you at the office?"

He meant the Dry Bones Society. With Moshe's move to the Prime Minister's Office, Irina had inherited the reins of the charitable organization. She and Samira, the Arab girl she had met early in her new life, had taken over his corner office in the DBS call center. Moshe didn't mind; running the country kept him more than occupied.

"Not today," she said. "I'm going south."

Alex raised his eyebrows. "South?"

"Special mission. Hush-hush. I'm scouting out development cities with basic infrastructure."

"More new arrivals than usual?"

"That's the strange thing. The numbers have leveled out since we hit BCE. Something's going on, but the details are still under wraps."

Alex looked at his wristwatch and downed the rest of his coffee. He grabbed his keys, kissed her goodbye, and stepped out.

Irina put the milk back in the fifty-year-old fridge and washed the bowls in the ancient enamel sink. Out the window, buses hissed and growled along Shamai Street.

A development town! Where would the returnees come from?

Although she enjoyed her work at the Society, the outing would provide a welcome break in the routine of day-to-day logistics and troubleshooting. She missed teaching the training classes, a task she now delegated to other volunteers to clear her schedule for her new responsibilities. At their rate of growth, soon she'd need to delegate even more. She also missed having Moshe and Rabbi Yosef around the office. They still maintained a keen interest in the Society's functioning, and the expansion into development towns might give them an excuse to get together.

Irina changed into the fresh clothes from the shoulder bag she had brought along last night. She still had a half hour before she was to meet Samira at the Central Bus Station, so she turned her logistical talents to Alex's wardrobe.

Among the stacks of jeans and T-shirts, surprisingly few called for the trash bin. His winter shirts collected dust beside two sweaters on an upper shelf. Alex did not hoard clothing and he hardly used the hanging space. She pushed the jacket and pairs of corduroy trousers aside, clearing plenty of space for her own clothes. Moving in with him made sense, seeing how much time she spent at his place. She'd raise the topic tonight, make him think it was his idea.

The floor of the closet might pose a problem. His pairs of sneakers, beach sandals, and a scuffed pair of leather boots took up most of the floor space. She'd need a separate closet for her own footwear, which, like the Dry Bones Society, displayed exponential growth.

A crack between the boots drew her eye. Shoving the footwear aside, she touched the floorboard and a square panel shifted inward. *Hello.* A secret compartment? The panel lifted easily in her hands to reveal a white shoebox. Was this where he hid photos of his ex-girlfriends?

Exactly how many young women had his bad boy looks reeled in? Judging from the weight of the box, quite a few.

Fighting a pang of guilt for invading his privacy, she removed the lid, and the mischievous smile fled from her lips. Inside the box, a large black handgun glinted in the dull light.

CHAPTER 10

"Ambassador Gurevitch," Moshe said in English. He shook the hulking Russian's hand and took his seat behind the Prime Minister's desk. "To what do I owe this pleasant surprise?"

Sparks of déjà vu tingled down his spine. Back-to-back surprise meetings with the world's superpowers were not the work of pure coincidence.

Gurevitch removed his military visor hat and took his seat slowly as though performing a squat. A dozen medals covered his heart, pinned to his tight brown uniform blazer. He sized up Moshe without smiling, drops of sweat massing on his bulbous forehead.

"Your Excellency has an urgent message from the President of the Russian Federation." The ambassador dabbed at his brow with an embroidered handkerchief.

"Wonderful," Moshe said. The sparks of déjà vu exploded like fireworks.

"The President would like to strengthen the ties between our great nations and invite the State of Israel to join the Russian Federation."

"Wow," Moshe said, breaking protocol for the second time that day. What was going on here? "Forgive me for speaking frankly, Ambassador Gurevitch, but Russia has not exactly been a friend of the Jewish State. Russia has armed and funded our mortal enemies and stood against us in international forums."

The ambassador overcame his befuddlement. "Yes, but imagine how the map would look with us on your side!"

"You'd abandon the Arab states?"

"Absolutely!"

The truth was well known: if Israel were to lay down her weapons, there'd be no more Israel; if the Arabs were to do the same, there'd be no more war. Peace in the Middle East—wouldn't that be an achievement for Moshe's first month in office! Peace in the Land was also an objective that Rabbi Yosef had assigned to the Messiah of David. Moshe swept the thought from his mind.

But the ambassador's offer raised questions. Was Russia willing to erase decades of power politics to bring Israel under her wing? And why were the world superpowers suddenly so desperate to adopt the Jewish State? This time he was going to get some answers.

"Level with me," he said. "This is connected to the Resurrection, isn't it?"

Gurevitch ran a tongue over his teeth, seeming to sense that the talk was not going his way. "We have known of this Resurrection for some time, Your Excellency. And our recent analysis indicates that you are now weaponizing the undead."

Weaponizing the undead? Moshe didn't even know what that meant, and he said as much.

Gurevitch's face whitened. "Soldiers that cannot be killed."

What was he going on about? "That's ridiculous. We have no such weapons."

"Please, Your Excellency, do not insult our intelligence. Our satellites have spotted your recent military activities on the Gazan border."

"But the resurrected are not immortal." Moshe had discovered this firsthand. He had suffered a second heart attack while in Mandrake's custody, and the thugs had revived him with CPR. Moshe reminded himself to deal with the local Russian mafia while he could.

Gurevitch rolled his eyes. "We waste time with these denials, Your Excellency. If these weapons of mass destruction should fall into the wrong hands, the resulting catastrophe could destroy the planet."

By "wrong hands" he meant the Americans, and now Moshe gazed on the full picture in all its crazy glory. The United States had satellites too, and they were not above spying on their allies. Noticing the military camps surrounding the streams of naked dead, their analysts must have reached the same outlandish conclusions.

So much for "shared cultural and moral heritage." The Americans wanted to adopt the Jewish State to obtain the new shiny toy in the Weapons of Mass Destruction store. Did all espionage think tanks employ wacko conspiracy theorists?

Moshe bit his lip. How could he allay the ambassador's fears without leaking news of the Sixth Aliyah—and without endangering his coalition agreement? So far, the Russian had seemed impervious to Moshe's attempts at denying the claims.

Or could that work in his favor?

Moshe folded his arms on the desk. "I cannot comment on any of that." Gurevitch leaned back in his seat, a self-satisfied smile creeping over his mouth. "Please thank your President for his generous offer. I will have to discuss this with my cabinet once we've solidified the new coalition."

"Of course." The Russian got to his feet and strutted to the door. "And Your Excellency?"

"I know," Moshe said. "This will be our little secret."

With another self-satisfied smile, the ambassador closed the door behind him.

Weaponizing the undead. Moshe would never have thought of such an abomination. *They think we're monsters.* For centuries, haters had accused Jews of the worst crimes imaginable: poisoning wells, murdering Christian children to bake their blood into matzo bread. Never mind that the Jews drank from the same wells and that Jewish law forbade the eating of blood. Haters project onto their victims the evil in their own hearts.

A knot formed in Moshe's innards. He was a poodle caught between two snarling Rottweilers. How long could he hold them off?

CHAPTER 11

Avi followed Moshe Karlin into the men's washroom and prepared to burn his bridges. Again.

"Psst, Moshe!" he hissed.

Moshe spun around. In his eyes, surprise turned to suspicion. He leaned against the counter of wash basins.

"What can I do for you, Avi?"

Avi checked under the doors of the toilet stalls. They were alone. He had spent the entire morning walking past Moshe's office and avoiding eye contact with his secretary. He didn't want his meeting with Moshe to appear in the visitors' log. So, he had floated in the corridors, watching the bureaucrats of the Prime Minister's Office come and go, until finally, he managed to steal a moment alone with Moshe. Thankfully, the Secret Service didn't shadow Moshe in the men's room.

"I've come to warn you," he said, keeping his voice low. His eyes darted to the entrance door, which could open any moment and destroy the opportunity. "Gurion is going to double-cross you."

Moshe folded his arms. "How so?"

"I don't know the details, but he's going to make sure the coalition fails."

"Before or after he joins?"

"All I know is that he's setting a trap. He said he's going to bring down the government."

Moshe glanced at his shoes. "And in return you want...?"

Avi shrugged. "Nothing."

"A seat on the Restart list? My eternal gratitude?"

The thought of switching to Moshe's camp had crossed Avi's mind. But Moshe had a majority in Knesset. He had no use for a turncoat MP. No, Avi was more valuable to Moshe behind enemy lines. He said, "I just want to help."

Moshe laughed. "Forgive me if I find that hard to believe."

The implied accusation stung. "I don't blame you for thinking that." He didn't need to list his offenses: deception; turning Galit against him; dragging Moshe's name through the sewers. "But, honest to God, I've changed. I'm risking everything by speaking with you now."

"Unless Gurion sent you. If I withdraw the agreement, then I'm the bad guy, and the Opposition finally has a fact to use against me."

"Gurion doesn't know I'm here. He'd fire me if he did."

Moshe frowned and shook his head. He wasn't angry, just sad. "Thanks, Avi," he said. "But I'll take my chances."

CHAPTER 12

"Where to, sir?" said Baruch from the driver's seat.

"Home," Yosef said. He ran his fingers over the leather upholstery of the backseat for possibly the last time.

Of all the perks due to a minister, Yosef would miss his personal chauffeur the most. Baruch, with his flannel fedora and perfectly groomed pencil mustache, seemed to have stepped out of an era when shoe polishing was an art and trouser length an exact science. He kept the black Audi in pristine condition, the air within redolent of lavender.

"Very good, sir," Baruch said.

The car pulled off, leaving the government precinct in Givat Ram and gliding toward the German Colony. As the light faded over Jerusalem, the world beyond the spotless windows floated by, quiet and peaceful.

"Cyndi?" Baruch asked.

"As always."

The driver's eyes smiled in the rearview mirror, as he pressed a button to play Yosef's favorite CD, Cyndi Lauper's Greatest Hits.

Yosef would miss Baruch. With the signing of the coalition, his driver and car would fall to the new minister. Yosef would have to make do with the pool of ministerial cars and drivers, or simply drive himself to work. To think that only months ago he had been content with his old white Subaru, which had run on hopes and prayers in addition to gasoline. How quickly one adjusted to the comforts of life.

Shedding his governmental responsibilities would provide another major advantage—the peace of mind to focus on his own spiritual growth. The Jewish High Holidays approached: Rosh Hashanah, the awesome Day of Judgment; Yom Kippur, the hallowed Day of Atonement; and Sukkot, the joyous Festival of Booths, when the righteous celebrated their favorable Divine verdict. Between political campaigning and the interminable chores of government, Yosef had little attention left over for the things that really mattered.

After months of obsessing about messiahs, resurrections, and politics, he longed for the simplicity of his personal religious regimen. Say your prayers, keep the Sabbath, and watch what you eat; God will take care of the rest. The world had ticked along well enough before fate had thrust Yosef into Knesset; it would continue once again without him. "The righteous," the Sages said, "have their mundane affairs handled by others."

Safely ensconced in the four cubits of his religious inner world, he wouldn't have to face the cracks in the mirror of external reality. He wouldn't have to wrestle with Divine justice and the other ogres of incongruous theology. Once more, he'd walk the Earth wrapped in God's invisible armor.

"*Aba! Aba!*" Simcha and Ari cried, as Yosef walked through the door of his single-story home on Shimshon Street. They jumped up and down in the living room, their earlocks flying, and their skullcaps of black velvet slipping from their heads.

Yosef didn't merit that hearty welcome every day, but today was no ordinary day. He planted a kiss on each little forehead, opened his briefcase on the dinner table of scratched wood, and handed each boy a sealed pack of laminated trading cards. Instead of soccer heroes, each card displayed the portrait and name of a famous rabbi.

"Thanks, Aba!"

Thank Ram, Yosef thought. His new secretary had gotten hold of the new editions on behalf of the Vice Prime Minister.

The boys tore open the nylon packaging and riffled through the cards with glee.

"Aba," Ari said, pouting with disappointment. "Where's your card?"

"Apparently, I'm not that important." Yosef didn't know who printed the cards, but they fell under the umbrella of the Great Council's influence.

"But Aba, you're the boss of the whole country!"

Yosef chuckled. "Democracy doesn't work that way. You don't get to tell everyone what to do. Being in government just means that everybody hates you."

He made the rounds, distributing kisses. Uriel did his homework at the dinner table, and little Yehuda, in pajamas, tested the flight capabilities of his favorite toy car.

"Yossi," said Rocheleh. Her head wrapped in a new flower print head covering, she pored over a thick brochure from Semel Kitchens on the counter. "What looks better—granite or Corian?"

Upon receiving his first ministerial salary, Yosef had signed a hefty twenty-year mortgage and purchased a larger property down the road. For the first time in their lives, the boys would sleep in separate bedrooms. Rocheleh had selected the seven-room house and was designing her new kitchen, which, Yosef suspected, would require a second mortgage.

Yosef glanced at the brochure. The kitchen counters looked identical to him. "Whatever you prefer," he said.

Rocheleh groaned. "You're no help at all!" But she smiled and gave him a delicate hug.

Their marriage had changed beyond recognition. Gone were the dismissive comments and accusatory stares. What a difference a comfortable salary made to *shalom bayit,* household peace! And how good it felt to say yes not only to their material needs but quite a few of their wants.

Whatever coalition agreement Moshe struck, at least Yosef

would keep his ministerial income.

A knock at the door snapped him out of his pleasant reverie. He peered through the peephole, and a very different emotion bubbled in his gut. Yosef opened the door, a hot flash of anger surging through his body.

Emden stood on the dark threshold, his shoulders hunched and his trademark bowler hat missing from his head.

"Call my office if you want to speak," Yosef said, skipping the usual friendly formalities. After all he had done, how dare he bother Yosef at home?

Emden gave Yosef a quick, guilty look. His eyes were red and sunken as though he hadn't slept in days. There was something both pitiful and disturbing to see the once proud and regal rabbi in this disheveled state. He looked sad. No, not sad. Frightened.

"This is a personal call," he said, his voice shaky, defeated. "May I come in?"

Yosef seethed. Emden had threatened him before in the guise of friendship. "If this is about the coalition, it can wait until tomorrow."

Emden flinched at the implicit rebuke. "No, Yosef. It's not that. I've resigned from Knesset."

The news caught Yosef off guard. Emden had held his eminent position at Torah True for years. Why would he resign?

"I've come to warn you, my friend," he continued. "Your life is in danger."

CHAPTER 13

Moshe followed his security detail into the Talpiot Police Station. How the tables had turned! During his previous visit, he had languished for hours behind the bars of a holding cell. Today he would call the shots.

The two receptionists stood at attention. Perky and Bored, as he had labeled them, sported identical blue uniforms and dark ponytails. This time they displayed broad toothy grins as well.

"The Commissioner is waiting for you," said Perky—or was it Bored?—and pointed at a long corridor of office doors.

Moshe nodded and smiled. This time he did not have to present his identity card.

As he passed the doors of offices, his presence of mind faltered. Prime Minister or not, the tables could always turn again. He had learned that lesson well. While Moshe was tied up in a dark abandoned warehouse, Mandrake had put a gun to his head and threatened to turn him into either a murderer or a corpse. Moshe's next move would place him in direct opposition to the sadistic mafia boss.

He knocked on the door at the end of the corridor, stepped inside, glanced at the Commissioner, and did a double-take. The large policeman with olive skin and barrel chest got up from behind the desk to greet him. "Mr. Prime Minister."

"Commissioner Golan, congratulations on your promotion." The name *had* sounded familiar. Months ago, Golan, then a homicide detective, had assisted Irina and Moshe in their attempt to discover her identity. They had failed, but Officer Golan had offered his calling card and sympathy.

His grip was warm and firm. "Thank you, sir. Any luck with our mutual friend? Irina, wasn't it?"

"Irina, yes. Still no leads and no memories."

"That's a shame."

"Yes, it is. But she's doing good work at the Dry Bones Society."

After the exchange of pleasantries, Moshe asked his security guards to close the door of the office, and he took a seat.

Again, he weighed the wisdom of prodding the sleeping bear. Only this bear was no longer sleeping.

"What can you tell me about a man known as Mandrake?"

Golan's Adam's apple jumped. "Russian mafia. Moved in a few years ago. Displaced the local cartels in Jerusalem and the rest of the country. Real nutcase. We've been itching to lock him up, but so far, we have nothing solid on him. Why do you ask?"

"What would it take to reel him in and dismantle his network?"

A smile spread across his face. "Organized crime? We'd need a new undercover program and better equipment. A lot of our resources are deployed to prevent suicide bombs and knife attacks."

"That's what I thought," Moshe said. "So I made a special provision in the new budget earmarked for fighting organized crime. It's time we made that a priority."

"Thank you, Mr. Prime Minister. We'd like that very much." His eyes lingered on Moshe. "You've met this Mandrake, haven't you?"

Moshe's fingers trembled at the thought of the warehouse, and he wasn't sure how much information he should share.

"I've heard enough to know we can't ignore him."

Golan nodded. "I'll take care of it."

"Good. Let me know if you need anything."

Moshe had set the wheels of justice in motion; now he could only wait.

He turned to leave, then paused at the door. "One of his operations runs in a warehouse off Pierre Koenig Street. They rope illegals into forced labor. The manager's name is Boris. Start there."

CHAPTER 14

In a dark chamber deep within the Malcha Technology Park, a red notification light flared. Mandrake placed his deck of playing cards on the glass table and turned to face his laptop. The cards helped him think. He'd done that a lot these past few weeks. Thinking and waiting. Now, it seemed, the time for waiting had ended.

A large, red letter A filled the screen as an encrypted call connected.

"Mandrake," said an electronic voice, the human qualities of the speaker garbled beyond recognition by distortion software.

"Yes, my lord," he said. The voice commanded respect. The voice had given, and the voice could take away.

"We have encountered some unforeseen developments," said the voice. "Proceed with Plan B."

A thrill shot through Mandrake's body, and his shoulder twitched. Plan B. He had hoped for this result.

"I understand."

The electronic voice spoke again. "Name your target."

Mandrake said the name out loud.

The voice repeated the name, seeming to savor each syllable despite the electronic garbling. "How appropriate."

"Preparations are already underway," Mandrake said. His

foresight had paid off, and now was the time to ask for a favor. "One request, my lord, if you will?"

"He's yours," the voice said, reading his mind. "When the End Time arrives, he's all yours."

"Thank you."

The screen faded to black as the call disconnected, and the red notification light bled out.

Mandrake smiled with anticipation. He'd had the pleasure of the target's company once before, and he had enjoyed bending him out of shape. This time, he'd break him.

"You're mine," he said in the dark. "Moshe Karlin, you're all mine."

CHAPTER 15

Eli offered the older woman a box of Kleenex.

"Thank you," Hannah said, and she blew her nose.

Noga's doctoral advisor sat on Eli's living room couch, wearing sensible slacks and smelling of a gender-neutral perfume. She had dropped by the penthouse with the letter she had received from *Nature Genetics*. There was something heartrending about watching the professor cry.

Noga said, "Did they explain why?"

Self-doubt flickered in his girlfriend's eyes. Noga had triple-checked her data and searched her conclusions for weaknesses. "Extraordinary claims require extraordinary evidence," Noga had said, quoting Carl Sagan. Eli had doubted the theory too, at first. Are Palestinian Arabs the Ten Lost Tribes? The results of her genetic research strained the limits of credulity.

Hannah blinked her eyes clear. "They didn't bother. They just called the idea 'ludicrous, sensational, and unworthy of serious consideration.'"

"Didn't they review the data?"

Hannah's short laugh sounded like a cough. "They probably didn't even read the whole paper."

"So much for academic neutrality," Eli said, but his attempt at humor failed to lighten the mood. Eli knew how they were feeling. He had been on the other end of incredulity. *Crazy. Delusional.* The condemnations hit harder than sledgehammers. He had succumbed to those pressures too, giving up his identity to win Noga's love. Would Noga give up on her convictions too? Right now, she needed his support.

"We can submit to other journals, can't we?"

"Academia is a closed, tight group," Hannah said. "Word has spread by now. We're the talk of the town. No self-respecting journal will touch our paper after that resounding rejection. My name is a joke. Appealing their decision will only make matters worse. I could lose my post at Hebrew U."

Guilt stabbed Eli's conscience. He had warned Noga of the scorn and derision she could expect for sharing her theory with the academic world. Then Hannah had supported her analysis and even found corroboration in the oral traditions of Arab tribes in the West Bank. Eli had hoped that the growing mountain of evidence would force skeptics to take them seriously. He had been wrong.

"What do we do now?" he asked.

Hannah shook her head. "Nothing. The Israeli-Palestinian conflict is too charged a topic. The same goes for anything that might appear to support Biblical prophecies. You can't reason with emotion. We can only wait, let things quiet down, and hope that someone might reevaluate the paper without prejudice."

Noga sat beside him like a wilted flower. If the first step of their plan had failed, there was no way they were going to share their discovery with the Prime Minister. The Ten Tribes would remain secret, the Messianic potential unrealized, and the Final Redemption out of reach. How long would the cosmic window of opportunity stay open this time? Waiting was not an option.

Eli had not spent his years fostering contacts in politics or academia. He had spent the last decade developing skills that were much more mundane. Could that too be part of the Divine Plan?

"What if we tried a different approach?"

Noga perked up at his words, and Hannah glanced at him with interest for the first time. Did the boyfriend have something useful to contribute? Noga and Eli had decided not to tell her supervisor about his identity. They already had one extraordinary claim to prove; adding to the list might tempt the scientist to flee for the hills.

"We've been aiming for a top-down solution. Convince the academics in their ivory towers and the information will drip down to the masses. But what if we started at the bottom?"

Hannah laughed again, scornful. "Science by press release?"

"No, not the media. Not at first. That's just another set of gatekeepers we'd need to pass. No tabloids either. We don't want people to group us with alien abductions and conspiracy theories. We want credibility, but of a different kind."

"What is he going on about?" Hannah said to Noga. The prospect of losing her job had shortened her fuse. His idea would not help her with that either, but they were beyond worrying about academia. Their goals aimed far higher.

Understanding blossomed in Noga's eyes, and she smiled. "I think I know where you're going with this," she said. "It's worth a shot."

CHAPTER 16

Yosef faced his former mentor across the dinner table, his shoulders tensed. Rocheleh had cleared the living room and herded the boys off to bed.

Emden sat there, his eyes lowered to the table, his hair unkempt beneath the black skullcap. By all appearances, he was a broken man, and pity muddied the hurt in Yosef's heart. Pity and fear.

Your life is in danger. The warning had gotten Emden through the door, and it had better not be another cynical ploy.

"I owe you an apology," Emden said.

"You've apologized before." The olive branch Emden had extended during the elections had been a political stick disguised as a carrot.

"You're right. I've made many mistakes over the past months. First and foremost, I was wrong to betray you. That is my deep and everlasting shame." He let the words float in the air, disarming Yosef. "I don't expect you to forgive me, but I hope at least to make it up to you in some small way. You see, I made another mistake, and in this, I joined the entire rabbinical leadership. We did not believe that the Final Redemption was upon us. We explained away the resurrected, so comfortable we were and set in our ways."

Yosef shifted in his seat. The resurrection on the street did not meet all the expectations of Jewish tradition, he would admit that. The flaws bothered him too. But what was Emden driving at?

"But since yesterday," Emden continued, "there can be no doubt."

Now Emden had surprised him. "The coalition?" he said. Had Moshe's offer changed the religious establishment's worldview?

"No, not that." Emden raised his gaze for the first time and studied Yosef. "Moshe hasn't told you? He must have his reasons. You'll find out soon enough."

"Find out what?" Was Moshe keeping secrets from him? Or was this Torah True's way of pitting Yosef against his dear friend and partner to create a rift in the Restart party? *Divide and conquer.* Yosef's shoulders tensed again.

Emden explained. "The teachings of the Final Redemption fall into three categories, Yosef. Restorative traditions predict a return to times of yore: The scion of David will rule again, reinstate the Temple sacrifices in Jerusalem, and ingather the Lost Tribes.

"Utopian traditions take this a step further: The Messianic Era will raise society to unprecedented levels. Food will be aplenty. Precious stones will cover the streets of Jerusalem. The Third Temple of Fire will descend from the Heavens. The nations of the world will grasp the tassels of our clothes in their thirst to learn our Torah, and the righteous will feast. In the end, we shall defeat even Death."

Emden swallowed hard. "But there is a third set of traditions, Yosef—the Apocalyptic. These traditions are the reason that the sages, even though they yearned for the Redemption, prayed that the birth pangs of the Messiah would not appear in their lifetime. A terrible war will rage, and the mighty armies of Gog and Magog will amass in Jerusalem. Natural disasters will rend the Holy City asunder. The monstrous Leviathan will roam the ocean depths, and the evil Armilus will attack the Messiah. Many will die; many more will wish they were dead. And the Lord Almighty will judge them all."

Yosef shuddered. He had heard many of the claims about the Messianic Era, but they had sounded far away and exaggerated. Coming from the usually calm and collected Emden, the predictions sent shivers through his every bone.

"Two messiahs appear in our ancient writings. The Messiah of David, the rightful King of Israel. But a second messiah will stand at his right hand. His life will be difficult, his sufferings many. He will die in that perilous time, so that the Messiah of David may live. It is because of the Second Messiah I seek you out now, my friend."

Yosef had seen the posters on the streets. "Welcome, King Messiah!" The banners carried the portrait of Moshe Karlin, the Prime Minister of Israel. But, after his recent embarrassing experiences with popular belief, Yosef had not taken the posters seriously.

"Wait a minute. Are you telling me that Moshe Karlin is the Messiah of David?"

"Look around you, Yosef. The dead are rising. The Jews are returning. And, only months after his resurrection, a political unknown controls the government and promises social justice?"

Yosef had searched long and hard for the Messiah. He had hoped to find him among the sages of the Great Council. Once upon a time, he had even considered Emden as a candidate. Yosef had cold-called hundreds of potential messiahs in the Bezeq Online Directory. He had rushed to the Old City's Western Wall to greet a self-proclaimed Messiah only to watch him plummet to the ground and leave on a stretcher. Yosef had exhausted all possibilities until he had toyed with the inevitable heretical conclusion that the Messiah was a comforting fiction invented by generations of miserable Diaspora Jews.

Had the True Messiah stood right in front of him all along? But if Moshe was the Messiah of David, who stood at his right hand if not the Vice Prime Minister? Yosef felt sick to his stomach.

"Please, my friend, listen to me. You must flee!"

"Flee where?"

"As far away as possible. Here." Emden withdrew a stack of airplane tickets from his pocket. "I'm leaving tonight with my family. I urge you to do the same before it's too late!"

Yosef read the destination on the tickets. "Hawaii?" This was insane. Emden had lost his mind. "You can't be serious!"

Emden held his gaze. "I quit the government and left Torah True. I have never been more serious."

"But why me? Even if I'm the Vice Prime Minister, surely the Second Messiah could be anyone?"

"Because, my friend, the Second Messiah has a name. He is also known as the Messiah of Yosef!"

CHAPTER 17

"Is everything OK?" Alex asked over breakfast, Thursday morning.

Irina forced a smile. "Yes," she lied.

Early in her second life, she had gone undercover, sneaking into a Zumba class to meet Galit Karlin. Adopting another persona had come so easily to her that she'd wondered whether she'd been a spy in her forgotten first life. The idea of living a lie seemed less exhilarating now.

Last night, she had slipped into bed early and pretended to be asleep when Alex came home. She had not wanted him to touch her before she discovered the truth about him, and today she would do just that.

Alex chewed his cornflakes and considered her. He did not seem convinced by her answer, and for once she wished the tough guy exterior had not come with an extra dose of emotional intelligence. "How was your trip to the south—did you find what you were looking for?"

"Far more than I expected," she said. While she and Samira had traveled by bus to Ofakim and Mizpeh Ramon, dusty development towns on the edge of the Negev desert, the large black gun had filled her mind. Why did a car salesman hide a scary handgun in his closet? And boxes full of bullets? Many people carried guns in Israel but in the open and on their person, in case of terrorist attacks.

Who was Alex Altman? She hadn't met his friends or family. Suddenly, the ponytail, biceps, and tattoos seemed to be hiding more than a sensitive soul. Sometimes appearances did not deceive. In her desperation to find love and belonging, had she overlooked the obvious?

Alex took his bowl to the sink and found his car keys. "Can I give you a ride?"

"I'll go in later. I have to run an errand or two." That was true enough.

"OK." He kissed her on her forehead, seeming to sense that more than that would not be welcome. "Have a good day."

"You too."

The moment the door closed behind him, she shot to her feet, returned the milk carton to the fridge, and grabbed her handbag. She listened at the door, waiting for Alex's footfalls to fade in the stairwell before she eased the handle down and slipped outside.

The engine of his car turned as she left the apartment building. She walked away from the sound, turned a corner, flagged down a white taxi cab, and got in the back seat.

"Follow that car," she said.

"The black Hyundai?"

"Yes. But don't get too close." *Always stay two cars behind.* She had learned that from a movie.

The driver chuckled, and they pulled off down Shamai Street. The cabbie wore a black leather jacket, and his hair gel smelled of fish. His eyes crinkled in the rearview mirror. "Checking up on your husband?"

She groaned within. A chatty driver was the last thing she needed but shutting him up would not improve her chances of success. "He's not my husband."

"Boyfriend?"

"Yes."

"You should dump him."

"Yeah?"

"If he hasn't married you by now, then he's stupid. I'd marry you right away."

"Oh, really?"

Irina had to smile. The black car turned again, flowing through downtown Jerusalem. They climbed Agron, passing Independence Park, then crossed the busy intersection at King George, descending into the tree-lined streets of Rechavia.

Most car dealerships had shops in Talpiot to the south, but Alex was heading west. Where was he going?

"So, what's this about—another girl?"

"No. It's... complicated."

Irina felt a pinch of guilt for following Alex. She'd never suspected him of cheating on her. He truly cared for her. Then why was she tailing him in a taxi? *Silly girl.* His morning detour was nothing diabolical. Alex ran errands too. She'd probably catch him red-handed at Home Depot buying plastic flowers for their apartment, to please her. Shame on you for doubting him.

The black Hyundai barreled down Herzog Boulevard, then slowed as traffic thickened, waiting in line to turn left toward the Malcha Mall.

Malcha Mall had a Home Depot. Her cheeks warmed with shame. But the mall didn't open until ten o'clock. Was he moonlighting at a department store?

The Hyundai slipped across the intersection just as the light turned red, leaving the taxi stuck in the line of cars.

"Don't worry," the driver said. "We'll find him. I have a sixth sense for finding people."

Irina rolled her eyes. She considered calling off the search and heading for the DBS when the light changed, and they rolled over the intersection and into the Malcha valley.

The square mall loomed to their right, no black cars in sight. The parking section had multiple floors, and, although the bays were still mostly empty, they'd waste a lot of time searching them all.

"Never mind," she said. "I think we lost him."

"Just a minute." The cabbie overtook an Egged bus, passing the entrance to the parking bay, and rounded the traffic circle.

He made a left instead of a U-turn and said, "Voila!"

A black Hyundai had parked on the side of the road opposite the Technology Park.

"What did I tell you—I have a sixth sense. There's your man."

He pointed. Across the street, Alex walked through the gate toward the tall main tower of the office buildings.

Alex, at the Technology Park? The sight reignited her curiosity. "Can you wait a few minutes?"

"I'm right here." The cabbie turned off the meter. "This one's on me. Anything for a damsel in distress."

Irina didn't have time to argue. If the slick cabbie thought he would get her number in return for his efforts, he was dreaming.

She crossed the street and headed for the gates, keeping the glass building of the guard station between her and Alex, in case he glanced behind him. The security guards checked the trunks of cars but paid no attention to the lone woman with the handbag.

Slipping through the gates, she made for a tree and peeked around the trunk. Alex was following the path that cut through the well-trimmed lawns and manicured hedges.

What was he doing here? Did he pick up cars from customers at their workplace?

Man-sized sculptures of Hebrew letters in reflective metal dotted the lawns. Irina followed, darting from an oversized Dalet to an arch-shaped Chet. If the engineers in the buildings peered out the windows at the gardens they'd think a crazy woman had broken into their Technology Park.

Alex walked full steam ahead, his gait rigid, without turning around once. If he had spotted her behind him, he gave no sign of it. He walked through the glass doors at the base of the main tower. Signs in the windows read The Open University and the names of a dozen other technology companies.

She waited in the cover of a large Vav and was about to dash toward the entrance when the doors opened, and a man stepped out. Irina's breath caught in her throat. She knew him.

His tweed jacket looked out of place in the Technology Park, as did the gray hair and mustache. He belonged in an abandoned warehouse in seedy Talpiot where the hopeless traded their freedom for a roof and two meager meals.

Irina had found herself among those lost souls until Moshe had risked his life to set her free. The man who had ruled the slave labor camp now shuffled down the path of the Technology Park with a smug expression on his face. His name was Boris.

CHAPTER 18

Ahmed broke into a sweat when he saw the line of dusty men. The unpaved street in the heart of Silwan was the last place on earth he wanted to hang out. Here in his old hometown, people would recognize him. His mother, or worse yet, Hasan.

"C'mon," Dara said.

"Can't you go for me?"

"You have to collect in person. Those are the rules. C'mon, it won't take long."

Against his better judgment, Ahmed stepped forward. The line led into the doorway of a low building. The men exiting the next door smiled and patted their pockets.

A dozen other men stood in line behind Ahmed and Dara. They met his stare, then looked away. Just another rioter collecting his wages. They didn't recognize him.

His mother's house lay two roads down. Would she acknowledge him if she saw him on the street? She had refused to let him stay. "You have your palace and your wives," she had said, as she'd shoved him out the door. "Enjoy your eternal reward." His visit had upset her picture of the world and threatened her newfound prestige as an *Um-Shaheed*.

Hasan had parked his yellow Mercedes sports car by the prefab hangar at the top of Silwan. Any moment now he

705

might pass by and identify his traitorous cousin.

The line inched forward. Inside, he saw no Germans. The gruff man behind the table had a thick mustache and barked questions—"Name? How many stones? Any injuries?"—and handed out crumpled fifty-shekel bills. The Arab's manner had something of Boris, the Russian slaver, despite the Arabic and the rough worker's hands. Both men lined their pockets with the lives of desperate men.

Behind the money man, a younger, muscular Arab stood and ogled the advancing line of men. A large gun stuck out of his belt.

Ahmed lowered his eyes. *This was a mistake.* He would not let Dara talk him into doing this again. But who would employ a former suicide bomber with no identity card? The doors of the Dry Bones Society had closed to him. Never again would he bask in Samira's warm smile. A new name wouldn't change that.

"Hey, kid," Gruff Mustache said. "I said, 'Name?'"

"Walid."

He checked the name off a list. "How many?"

"Um, five."

"May as well have been none," Dara said, laughing. "His aim is crap."

Ahmed gave him a "what the hell are you doing?" glare, and Dara covered his mouth with his hand.

Gruff Mustache didn't seem to care. "Injuries?"

"Only his pride." Ahmed would beat Dara well and good when this was over.

The Arab held out a fifty-shekel note, and Ahmed snatched the money.

"Next!"

"You," said the gunman at the back. One hand touched his ear, the other rested on the handle of his gun. "Come here."

Ahmed's heart skipped a beat. The gunman was staring right at him. "Me?"

"I was just kidding," Dara said, the smile an old memory.

"About the stones. He threw them, I saw it."

The gunman pointed at Dara. "You stay."

Ahmed stepped forward, his limbs stiff, as though walking in a dream. Did the man know him? *What does he want with me?*

"This way." The gunman walked up a set of stairs at the back.

Ahmed followed, his limbs trembling. He climbed the steps, sweat slipping from his brow and down his cheeks. His senses intensified. Each passing second seemed like an eternity. The spiral cord of an earpiece sprouted from Gunman's left ear. The gun shifted in his belt as he moved, the back of his shirt damp with perspiration.

Ahmed was back on bus number eighteen, his backpack heavy with rusty screws and ball bearings dipped in rat poison. Any moment, the explosives would roast his sinful flesh in a ball of fire. Only this time, the end would arrive in the form of a bullet to the head.

The steps ended in a cement shell of a room. The only furnishing was a wooden desk. A man lounged in a chair, his legs and boots crossed over the desk. His hands rested on his head of wavy dark hair spiked with gray, his elbows pointing to the sides.

"Hello, cousin," Hasan said. "What a lovely surprise."

CHAPTER 19

Thursday morning, Galit Karlin reached into a brown packing box and withdrew a pink stuffed animal. Moshe had bought the teddy bear for the newborn Talya. If only she could reach back in time to that day and make things the way they were.

In many ways their lives had improved beyond their wildest dreams; in others, they felt broken.

"We need to close that, yes?" the mover guy said, in shaky Hebrew.

"I'm sorry." She dropped the bear back into the box. The team of strong Russians in dungarees worked fast and in silence. When they spoke, their Hebrew was stilted and accented beyond recognition.

Galit stood in the center of the living room. Empty of furniture, their home on Shimshon Street felt like an empty shell. Like her life. And it was all her fault.

Galit had believed Avi's lies, believed that Moshe had cheated on her. Her stupidity had led directly to Moshe's death. When he returned from the grave, she had fallen for other lies: Moshe was a ghost. No, he had faked his death and spent two years living it up with other women.

Moshe had not given up on her. But after tearing down the web of deceptions, he had discovered her own shameful secret: her affair with Avi.

She could blame Avi all she liked—and he had confessed his role in the drama to Moshe—but the damage was done. And she felt the difference. Although they shared a home and a bed, Moshe didn't look at her the same way. Each day he buried his head deeper in his work. Did he still love her?

So, she did the same. The move to Beit Aghion, the Prime Minister's Residence on Smolenskin Street, had kept her occupied for a week. She called movers to pack up and store most of their old furniture. The renters were arriving next week, and they had been particular about finding the house "clean and empty." Which reminded her, she needed to call the cleaning service to confirm their appointment.

"Mrs. Karlin?" one of the Russians called to her from the kitchen. "The other dishes are where?"

He held up Exhibit A, one of the few remaining dinner dishes of the set they had received for their wedding. The missing dishes had exploded against the walls of the kitchen and living room. She had thrown them, first at Moshe, then at Avi. Her cheeks burned with shame.

"Those are all we have left," she said. "On second thought, put them in the trash." Their new home had its own set of crockery and her days of Frisbeeing dishes were over. For one thing, the security guards outside the fortified Prime Minister's Residence would come running with machine guns. And Henri, the in-house chef, would use one of his carving knives on her if she dared to harm his precious kitchen.

The thought made her laugh. She'd have to be on her best behavior from now on.

The sound of knocking on the front door made Galit jump. After her experience in Mandrake's torture warehouse, loud noises startled her. A Secret Service guy peeked in the front door, and she breathed a sigh of relief. So long as Moshe stayed in office, their security detail would keep them safe.

"Mrs. Karlin? Some people are here to see you."

Had the renters arrived early? She did not want them to

see the house in its current state of disarray.

She strode to the doorway, and her jaw dropped.

A smiling middle-aged couple stood on the steps, trailing four large suitcases. A bald patch glimmered on the top of the man's head and the woman clenched her mouth tight, her eyes ready to stream. Behind them waited another family with three teenage children.

"Mom, Dad," she said. "What a surprise!"

CHAPTER 20

Ahmed froze to the spot. Hasan stared at him from behind the desk, his eyes filled with anger or disgust, Ahmed couldn't tell which.

A window stood open behind Hasan. Ahmed could dash across the room, dive through the window, and hope to break his fall on the heads of the waiting rioters. Sprawled across the chair and desk, Hasan would not be able to react in time, but the gunman at Ahmed's back would.

"Walid, is it?" Hasan said, a smirk spreading across his lips. "I like it. A fresh start. What do you think of my new digs?"

Ahmed released the breath he had been holding. Hasan had not used his real name or outed him for his failed mission. Was he not the grudge-holding type, or was the small talk a distraction, a playful moment of torture before his execution, the way cats toyed with mice?

Having no choice but to play along, he glanced at the walls of rough cement. "Could use some paint."

Hasan laughed, swept his legs from the table, and sat up. "I agree. Doesn't look like much but looks can be deceiving. I've been expanding. Diversifying." He got to his feet, stepped around the desk, and leaned against it. With a nod of his head, he dismissed the gunman, and Ahmed felt the tension ease out of his body.

"You had me worried, little cousin."

"Worried that I wasn't dead?"

Hasan laughed. "There is that. I wondered what had happened to you, disappearing off the face of the planet."

"You're not upset with me?"

"It's for the best. As it so happens, I have another opportunity for you."

"Another chance to kill myself?" The fear dissipated, and his anger at his cousin returned. Hasan had goaded him into killing himself. He was responsible for the pain Ahmed had endured and the impossible situation in which he found himself, and now he wanted to use Ahmed all over again.

"No, Ahmed. I'm done with that."

"For the Germans?"

He seemed surprised at Ahmed's inside information. "For the Shepherds of our nation." He meant the Imams, the spiritual guides of their community. Was this Ahmed's ticket back into the fold?

"What's the catch?"

"There is no catch, Ahmed. This time you will not die." Hasan winked. "You'll get filthy rich."

CHAPTER 21

With his many flight hours at the podium, Moshe had thought he'd get over his public speaking jitters. As he entered the auditorium in the Knesset's Negba Wing, he realized that he'd been wrong.

Reporters and photographers packed the three hundred seats and every inch of standing room. In the front rows, Knesset members waited with folded arms and crossed legs. The event would not be easy for any of them. Restart ministers were surrendering their hard-won positions, and members of the Opposition would have to swallow their pride.

Moshe had been ambitious. Too ambitious, according to Shmuel. Today, as he applied the final touches to his tower of cards, he only hoped that the whole thing wouldn't come crashing down.

Sivan met him halfway to the podium.

"They signed?"

She nodded and glanced at the piles of folders on a low table beside the podium. "You've done it. I can't believe it."

"*We've* done it," he said. "And to be honest, I can't believe it either." The tension of the last few weeks eased like steam from a pressure cooker. *We've done it.*

He drew a deep breath and marched to the podium. Camera shutters clicked as he surveyed the assembled politicians and news people. In the front row, Isaac Gurion patted his oily comb-over and frowned. Moshe would have to get used to that frown at cabinet meetings. But at least he'd be on Moshe's side of the table when the government passed the new legislation that the state so desperately needed.

In the next seat, Avi Segal mimicked his boss's expression. His last-ditch attempt to torpedo the coalition had failed. After all they had gone through together, he'd thought Avi would have had the decency to keep quiet and stop his machinations. Some people never changed.

Rabbi Yosef, Shmuel, Savta Sarah—the rest of the cabinet and all one hundred and twenty members of Knesset waited with bated breath for his announcement.

Keep it short; keep it simple.

"My fellow Ministers," he said, "Members of Knesset and the press. Thank you for joining us on this historic occasion. Despite Restart's dominance in Knesset, we have worked hard to form a new unity government, a broad coalition that includes all major parties, new and old." He paused to let the gravitas of this moment sink in.

"This was no small accomplishment. We've all had to put aside our personal agendas and grievances to come together as one for the sake of our beloved country. I have full confidence that together we will work hard to make life better for all our citizens."

A frenzy of clicking cameras set in during his final dramatic pause. "I call upon Isaac Gurion, formerly Head of the Opposition, and now a minister in our new unity government, to say a few words."

Gurion got to his feet and shuffled to the podium. As he gave Moshe a meaty double-handed shake, they posed for the cameras, and Moshe stepped aside.

"I would like to thank Prime Minister Karlin for his generous offer," Gurion said, following the scripted speech they had agreed upon. Then he lifted a folder from the pile of signed coalition agreements and opened it on the podium.

Sivan sent Moshe a concerned look. This had not been in the script.

Moshe gave his head a slight shake. *Not to worry.* Gurion wouldn't do anything stupid; he had too much to gain.

"He offered us power and money," Gurion continued.

Nauseating vertigo gripped Moshe, the "oh crap" moment of the cartoon coyote who has just stepped off a cliff. Gurion had abandoned the script altogether. *Oh, no.*

Gurion extracted the stapled pages of the agreement and raised them in the air. *What is he doing?* But Moshe already knew, and he was powerless to stop him.

"However," Gurion continued, "our conscience won't allow us to be a fig leaf for his corrupt government!"

A hush swept over the auditorium as Gurion turned to glance at Moshe, and, with a smile like a snarl, he tore the agreement to shreds.

Gurion let the scraps float to the floor along with the metaphorical cards of Moshe's meticulously constructed tower.

"Karlin spoke of a better life for all citizens, but he lied." Gurion jabbed a finger at Moshe. "He lied to us all. This very moment he's assembling an army of undead in the heart of our land. He's preparing a zombie invasion that will take our jobs, our homes, and, if he has his way, our very way of life!"

No, no, no! Moshe's face moistened. Cameras clicked. Reporters grinned like sharks smelling blood in the water. What a scoop!

Oh God, make him stop!

But Gurion didn't. "We will continue to fight for the common people against this unnatural—"

Sivan came to her senses first. She dashed to the podium, shouldered Gurion out of the way, and grabbed the microphone. "That's all for today," she said. "We'll take questions at another time, and provide details for the Sixth Aliyah, the new wave of returning Jews who are bolstering our country."

She disconnected and pocketed the microphone, and gathered up the remaining agreements, whatever good that would do. The coalition was dead.

Sivan motioned for Moshe to follow her out of the room, but Gurion's sneer transfixed him.

"You just made a terrible mistake," Moshe said. "It doesn't have to end this way."

"Oh, this isn't the end," Gurion said, his face contorted with hate. "This is just the beginning."

CHAPTER 22

Alex drew a deep breath and pushed through the glass double doors of the Technology Park tower. A man didn't often enter a lion's den voluntarily, but Alex had made his decision. Would he walk away unscathed?

Down a short passageway, elevator doors opened, and Alex collided with a middle-aged man with a tweed coat and fluffy gray mustache. The man grunted an apology in Russian and made for the exit. He did not fit the hi-tech yuppie stereotype. Then again, neither did Alex. But despite his tattoos and ponytail, the techies wouldn't give him a second glance. They'd write him off as a delivery man, not a criminal. Since meeting Irina, he no longer felt like a criminal either.

The elevator doors opened again, and he followed the signs for Magitek.

Irina remembered nothing of their shared past. That trick of fate had granted him that rarest of gifts, a second chance. The Girl had died, but Irina lived, and with her, he could build a future. But for that future to survive, Alex needed a miracle.

He pressed the intercom button at a thin glass door.

A redhead sat at the front desk of enamel white and studied her nails. *Where's Anna?* The gum-chewing blonde had manned the gates of Mandrake's headquarters for years. Had the boss moved again? Unpredictability was the crime lord's signature. Alex should have called ahead and made an appointment.

The receptionist blew a bubble, glanced up, and Alex realized his mistake. The door clicked open.

"Love the new hair," Alex said, in Russian.

"Thank you," she said, as though each word pained her like a tooth extraction.

"Don't blondes have more fun?"

"What?"

"Never mind." He walked toward the room at the end of the corridor. If things went well, he'd never have to speak with her again. If things went badly, he'd never see her again either.

He walked through the hive of cubicles, where hundreds of young men jabbered into headsets, then he stared at the security camera above a white door.

When the door clicked open, Mandrake was waiting for him with a broad smile.

"Sasha, what a surprise." His boss wore black jeans and a turtleneck. He placed a strong hand on the small of Alex's back and guided him to the framed mirror on the opposite wall of the antechamber.

"Were you expecting me?"

"I'm always hopeful."

Closed-circuit television cameras. Of course.

This time, the whoosh of the hidden panel didn't startle him as the wall slid sideways, and they stepped through the black portal. Unlike last time, they were not alone in the darkened command room. Men in black uniforms manned the terminals, and the soft plastic patter of their keystrokes filled the air.

Mandrake strode through the control room and opened another door. Inside, dim purple ambient light filled the office. His boss flopped on a low backless couch in the center, beside a low table with a laptop and a deck of cards. Mandrake's office; the lion's den.

He patted the spot beside him on the couch. Alex preferred to stand, but he obeyed.

"A drink?"

"No, thank you."

"Smoke?"

Alex shook his head. *Where to begin?* How could he phrase his request so that his old comrade-in-arms would not take it the wrong way? Was there a right way?

Mandrake lit up a cigar and blew a smoke ring. "You want out?"

Alex blinked at him. *How does he know?*

"How long have we known each other, Sasha?"

"Since Korosten."

Mandrake's smile widened. "Ah, the People's Primary."

Alex choked up at the memory of the Soviet orphanage. "You saved my ass, that first night. Those stupid kids didn't know what hit them."

They chuckled, two orphan boys standing up to a cruel, cold world. The Jew and his sidekick.

"We've come a long way from Korosten, haven't we?"

For a moment, he wasn't Mandrake, but Gennady, the tough kid with the hooked nose and love for all things magical.

"We sure have." Alex no longer knew the full extent of his friend's dealings, nor did he want to. Since the Girl's death, something had snapped within, and the old friends had drifted apart like continental plates, slow but inexorable.

Mandrake frowned. "Your timing is terrible. New opportunities are sprouting up every day. You could run an entire division of the Organization."

Alex stared into the purple gloom and said nothing.

"It's the Girl, isn't it?"

The mention of her made Alex flinch. "No," he said. "Not only that. It's been a long time coming."

Mandrake took a long drag on the cigar and exhaled. Two perfect gray rings floated in the air, and the smaller sped through the larger. "I understand."

"You do?"

"We had a good run together. All things come to an end. No hard feelings."

Once again, his friend had shredded Alex's expectations. "Thank you."

"Cigar?"

"Sure." Alex had walked through the lion's den and emerged without a scratch.

Mandrake lit the cigar from the glowing embers of his own and handed it over.

"I just need one last favor."

Alex coughed, from both the cigar fumes and the condition. He had counted his blessings too soon.

"What kind of favor?"

"A simple one. And the perfect way to wrap up your career."

Alex had a bad feeling about this. "Who's the target?"

Mandrake blew another perfect ring. "Our good friend Moshe Karlin."

CHAPTER 23

Thursday afternoon, Yosef planted his elbows on his desk and held his head in his hands. *Calm down, Yosef!* He closed his eyes and sucked in deep, long breaths. If Rabbi Emden's visit last night had unsettled him, today's two newsflashes had slammed into him like speeding freight trains.

Lying in bed last night, Yosef had mulled over Emden's tidings. Two messiahs? Yosef could not see the need. And the title "Messiah of Yosef" probably meant "a descendant of Yosef," the Biblical Joseph, as with "Messiah of David."

This Armilus character sounded like the Devil, and Judaism had rejected such dualism. God reigned alone and supreme; no creation could oppose His Divine will. Add to that the world wars, the Leviathan—the legendary sea monster destined to be slain in the Messianic Era, its hide used to form a banquet tent for the righteous—and precious stones in the streets of Jerusalem, and the whole story moved beyond belief. The Messianic Era would not overturn the Laws of Nature, Maimonides had written, and Emden's predictions of preternatural mayhem stretched even Yosef's credulity.

Besides, this resurrection, suicide-bombers and all, was probably not *the* Resurrection, and the Final Redemption lay far ahead in the future.

Having poked holes in the prophecies of doom, Yosef had

drifted off to sleep.

Today, however, Yosef had learned of the so-called Sixth Aliyah. The floodgates had burst, and waves of newly resurrected foreigners washed over the country. Yosef had nothing against the second-timers—he had sheltered them in his own home—nor did he fear that the State of Israel could not absorb them. He wasn't even troubled by the zombie-like behavior of the new immigrants before they awoke in the Holy Land. It was the theological implications of the phenomenon that had triggered his panic attack.

Jewish traditions had whispered of Resurrection Tunnels. Righteous individuals who had not merited burial in the Holy Land would walk upright through these subterranean pathways to the Promised Land. The Sixth Aliyah meant that yet another ancient prediction had materialized. Perhaps this resurrection was indeed *the* Resurrection, and the Final Redemption was at hand. And if so, could Yosef indeed be the ill-fated Second Messiah, the right-hand man who must die so that the Messiah of David may live? Yosef had yearned for the Redemption, but was he willing to sacrifice his life—to widow his dear Rocheleh and orphan his precious sons?

No! That made no sense. Yosef was just a simple neighborhood rabbi. He didn't belong on the stage of history just as he didn't belong in the office of the Vice Prime Minister. *Never mind.* Soon Yosef would relinquish his ministerial posts, including the Vice Premiership. He would be safe.

Then Yosef had learned of the second news item. The spectacular implosion of Moshe's coalition agreement meant that Yosef would remain Vice Prime Minister for the foreseeable future. As Vice Prime Minister, Yosef remained Moshe's right-hand man and next in line. *The Second Messiah has a name,* Emden had said. *The Messiah of Yosef!*

Yosef shuddered again. Emden had urged him to flee like Biblical Jonah, but Yosef knew how that story had ended. He could resign from the government, but the timing could never be worse. "Vice PM Resigns Amid Claims of Prime Minister Corruption," the headlines would read. "Prime

Minister's Inner Circle Flees Zombie Invasion." How could he betray Moshe at this time?

No, there must be another way. Emden was wrong. Yosef grasped at the facts that disproved his theory. Moshe had not discovered the Ten Lost Tribes; neither had he rebuilt the Third Temple. And where were the other signs of the Messianic Era—the war of Gog and Magog, the evil Armilus, the natural disasters, the devastation?

Yosef nudged the laptop on his desk to life and searched the Internet. According to Wikipedia, the Jewish Second Messiah would lead the Ten Lost Tribes of Israel and reunite them with the tribe of Judah. This warrior Messiah would wage war against Armilus and die in the battle.

Hah! Yosef had not located the Ten Lost Tribes, and he was no warrior. He scanned the references at the bottom of the article. They included ancient Jewish writings that the Jewish Biblical canon had rejected. *Enough!*

The intercom buzzed.

"Yes, Ram?"

"Rabbi Levi of Torah True is here to see you."

Rabbi Levi? Yosef didn't recognize the name. Was Torah True keen to join the government even without Gurion? The visitor might provide the escape hatch from public office that Yosef craved.

"Show him in!"

Yosef patted his hair and straightened the lapels of his suit jacket. This time he would be more receptive to the rabbis' demands. Let them be the Messiah of Yosef.

He stood as the door opened, and Ram showed the young rabbi in.

Rabbi Levi shook Yosef's hand but kept his head down, only the ends of his red beard peeking beneath his black hat.

When the door closed behind him, the young rabbi raised his head and fixed Yosef with a pair of radiant blue eyes.

Yosef's shoulders sagged. "You're not here for Torah True, are you?"

Tom Levi, the messianic cult spokesman, grinned like a

naughty little boy caught with his hand in the cookie jar. He sat down. "I'm glad you found time to meet with me, Rabbi Lev."

Yosef ignored the veiled recrimination. He could call security, but that might push the lunatic to more desperate measures yet. Perhaps all the little boy needed was some fatherly attention. "How can I help you?"

"You should take your job more seriously."

"As Vice Prime Minister?"

"No, your *real* calling. Vice Messiah."

Yosef almost swallowed his tongue.

"We've got work to do," Tom continued. He leaned back in the seat as though he lived there and glared at Yosef.

"Like rebuilding the Temple?"

"Among other things. Such as reinstating the priestly sacrifices."

"And how do you propose we do that?" Yosef didn't even want to debate whether sacrifices in the twenty-first century were a good idea.

Tom leaned forward and smiled his blissful, crazy smile. "The Temple Institute has already prepared the sacred vessels, and they've figured out the incense recipe too."

"And the Temple Mount?" Yosef asked. "Do you expect the Waqf to just hand over the Dome of the Rock so you can rebuild the Jewish Temple? They don't even allow Jews to pray at the site."

"Screw the Waqf and his golden dome. We'll bulldoze that monstrosity whether he likes it or not."

"The last time an Israeli Prime Minister visited the Temple Mount, the Arabs rioted."

"That's why the Prime Minister must come out, and soon."

"Come out?"

Tom rolled his eyes as if the answer was obvious. "Announce that he's the Messiah. Then he can get on with business, and nobody will dare stand in his way."

Yosef bunched his eyebrows and tilted his head. "I don't

understand. Wasn't your friend supposed to be the Messiah?"

"Who?"

"The Messiah on the Wall. The man you introduced at the Kotel."

"Oh, him. He died."

His matter-of-fact delivery of the tragic news shocked Yosef, and he couldn't resist a jab.

"Isn't he going to 'rise from the ashes'?" He raised his hand in the air, palm up—repeating the words and gestures Tom had used moments after the paramedics had carried away his former leader on a stretcher.

Tom shrugged. Talk of his dead friend seemed to bore him. "Whatever. That didn't work out. But our Moshe Karlin, he's the man!"

Yosef thought of the mangled body on the stone tiles of the Western Wall Plaza, of the giddy hope and expectation he had nursed in his breast that morning. This messiah idea was a dangerous business. He needed to cool Tom off before he did more damage.

"We all want the Messiah," he said, keeping his tone calm and devoid of sarcasm. "But we have to be very careful. Nobody can force the Redemption. We need patience. It's too early to jump to conclusions. We need time to think this through."

Tom ground his molars, staring absently at the wall behind Yosef. He shrugged again and got to his feet. "You do your thinking, but don't take too long," he said. "We've waited two thousand years. That's long enough."

CHAPTER 24

Maimonides riffled through the glossy magazine he had found on the side table of the waiting room. The lifelike paintings on the pages displayed a wide variety of animals and breathtaking vistas that he'd never glimpsed before. There was so much to learn—so much to see! Today he was taking the first step in his own voyage.

He glanced up at the secretary behind the desk, a young woman of about fifty years of age, who peered at him over her glasses, then returned to her reading. She had not forgotten him.

With difficulty, he read the cover title of the magazine. *National Geographic.* He had no idea what the words meant. English was the key to knowledge in this World to Come. Although the Dry Bones Society had provided an introductory course, he would need to master the language if he was to advance his studies.

Telephones. Mechanical carriages. Flying metal ships! The wisdom that humanity had accumulated over the past thousand years boggled the mind and burst the limits of the imagination. After his initial shock and disorientation, the thirst for knowledge overpowered him. He must study with diligence and discard his prior assumptions. Mankind had uncovered the secrets of Creation, and come what may, he would learn them too!

He turned the page and yet another picture took his breath away. Planet Earth in all her glory, a blue dot in the black vastness of space. The image astounded him each time. The Earth revolved around the sun, of course, not vice versa. This was so embarrassingly obvious when you thought about it. Men had landed their flying ships on the surface of the moon and returned home to tell the tale!

Questions multiplied in his brain; his ignorance was unbearable.

"Rabbi Maimon," the secretary said. "The President will see you now."

"Oh, thank God!" Maimonides jumped to his feet with the energy of a much younger man and strode toward the white door.

The President's office was neither very large nor ornate. Framed certificates and photos with various dignitaries lined the walls. A thin clean-shaven man smiled at him from behind his desk and got up to greet his visitor.

"Good morning, Rabbi Maimon," he said, in Hebrew. "It is an honor to meet you."

"The honor is all mine."

Maimonides sat in the vacant chair. The President had white hair. Good. The task ahead required a man who had devoted his life to studying.

They smiled at each other.

"Would you like a tour of the campus?"

"Maybe later."

"OK." The man cleared his throat. "How can I help you, then?"

Where to begin?

"I want you to teach me."

The man gave a good-natured chuckle. *Good.* A sense of humor. He would need patience, too. Lots of it.

"What would you like to learn?"

"Everything!"

Another good-natured laugh. "Could you narrow that

down for me?"

"Sir, in my first life I began my studies at a very young age. I learned Aristotle by heart and became expert in all branches of knowledge: Mathematics, Astronomy, Philosophy, and Medicine. I served as physician to Sultan Saladin and his royal family. And, of course, I wrote extensively on Jewish law and philosophy. I expect that my religious treatises supplied the final word on those topics. The modern sciences, by contrast, have advanced greatly since then. In short, Mr. President, I want very much for you to be my mentor and master, to teach me the knowledge of the New World."

The President of the Hebrew University blinked. This time he did not chuckle. Had he gone too far? Did the list of his achievements sound like the boastings of a braggart, one unworthy of the master's time?

The kindly man cleared his throat. "Rabbi Maimon, I don't think that is possible."

The words stung like a slap in the face. "Pardon me for asking, sir, but why not?" His fingers dug into the padded armrests of the chair.

"You see, Rabbi, the amount of knowledge we teach at the university is immense. Take the Faculty of Science. One can devote an entire lifetime to the study of one sub-branch of one sub-specialty and still not know all there is in that field, never mind an entire branch. You could devote many lifetimes to study and still only scratch the surface. And by then what you learned would already be out of date. You see the problem?"

"But surely a few intellectual giants have mastered all fields?"

The man just shrugged. "Impossible. The best you can hope for is a shallow knowledge of a handful of sub-specialties."

Many lifetimes. He had started a new life, but the Resurrection was a one-off event. He could bank on, at most, another seventy years.

"But if no one man can understand everything, how do

you make critical decisions?"

"We don't. We rely on experts. And they, in turn, rely on other experts. Together, we can get a fuzzy picture of what's going on. The human brain just can't process all that information."

Maimonides' hands trembled on the armrests. So much knowledge, and all beyond his reach!

The President leaned over the desk and touched him on the shoulder. "Don't worry about it." When he sat down again, his eyes brightened. "I have an idea." He turned the computer screen toward his guest and typed away at the keyboard. "Let me introduce you to someone. Your new best friend."

Ten minutes later, Maimonides strolled along the stony paths of the campus grounds and sighed. Knowledge used to be the great leveler. Not everyone was born a king or priest, but the Crown of Torah lay waiting to be claimed by all who made the effort. But the days of mastering all the world's knowledge were gone.

Still, there was hope. He stared at the name scribbled on the square of yellow paper the President had given him. Even if he couldn't know it all, he could at least learn something about everything, and all thanks to his new best friend. This friend was always available and would never get tired of answering questions. His name was Google.

"Your Excellency!"

He turned to the source of the greeting. A plump man in a suit waddled toward him, trailed by serious young fellows in black jackets.

"Your Excellency!" The man stopped to catch his breath, mopped his forehead with a square of cloth, and brushed long strands of oily hair over his bald spot. "I'm so glad I found you."

"You've been looking for me?"

"Yes, yes! Our great sage and teacher, Rabbi Moses son of Maimon."

Maimonides straightened and found his smile again. At

least his works of Jewish law remained timeless. They would not go "out of date" to make way for some new discovery.

He cleared his throat. "How may I help you, my son?"

The plump young man turned serious. "A great sage such as yourself—isn't it time you took up your true calling?"

"Well, I'd be honored to join an academy for Torah study."

"Torah study?" The man laughed. "A sage of your eminence deserves far more than a mere teaching job. Do you know what they say about you? 'From Moses to Moses, none compares with Moses.' In other words, since the time of the Moses in Egypt, none has arisen like Moses son of Maimon. That's right! And the first Moses wasn't just a teacher; he was a leader."

"Oh." *A leader.* "I suppose I did guide the Jewish community of Fustat in spiritual matters. And I answered questions on Jewish law and practice from the entire Jewish world."

"Don't think small," the man said. "Think big! Men like you belong at the very top—at the head of the Jewish State!"

The head of the Jewish State. That did sound appealing.

"And who are you?"

The man gripped his hand and gave him a feisty, double-handed shake. "Isaac Gurion, at your service."

CHAPTER 25

Thursday evening after dark, Moshe slunk home to the Prime Minister's Residence on Smolenskin Street. He needed a hot bath and an early night; he'd get neither.

Constructed in the 1930s by a wealthy Jewish merchant, the mansion known as Beit Aghion had at various times housed a Yugoslavian king and Jewish fighters wounded in the War of Independence. As Moshe trudged through the arched doorways, he felt like a battered soldier, not royalty.

Galit stood in the hallway, a forced smile on her lips and a group of visitors at her back. Moshe's hopes for that hot bath and early night died on the spot.

"Miki!" Moshe said, extending his hand to his father-in-law. He hugged his mother-in-law too. "Ita!" Behind them stood another couple with three bored teenagers. "Dudu and Orit!" More handshakes and hugs for the brother-in-law and family. "What a surprise!"

Moshe hoped he hadn't overdone his display of excitement.

"Yes, it is," Galit said with a plastic smile. She hadn't known about the visit either.

"Join us for dinner?"

Henri, in his chef's white formal jacket and hat, served up platters of roast meat at the dining room table of polished oak, usually reserved for entertaining foreign dignitaries. He'd done a phenomenal job on such short notice.

"Miki, how long is your stay?" Moshe said, and sipped his red wine.

With his balding head and roving eyes, Moshe's father-in-law resembled a large rodent.

"Now that you're Prime Minister," Miki said, a knowing sparkle in his eyes, "we're back for good."

Moshe almost sprayed red wine over the embroidered tablecloth. He didn't dislike his father-in-law. They got along very well at a healthy distance—in their case, a ten-hour intercontinental flight. Galit's parents had not wanted their daughter to remarry her dead husband, and their sudden invasion of Moshe's home raised red flags.

"So, Israel's not going to be wiped off the map anymore?"

From across the table, Galit fixed Moshe with a chiding glare. After the Six Day War, Miki's brother had moved to New Jersey, convinced that the Arabs would make good on their promise to "drive the Jews into the sea." Soon after Galit and Moshe got married, Miki had joined his brother.

Miki dismissed the comment with a chuckle. "Not with you in charge."

Was that a compliment? Moshe's suspicions multiplied. "Where are you staying?"

Galit answered for her father. "They were going to stay at our old house, but seeing that we've rented it out, I invited them to stay here with us."

Moshe almost choked on a chunk of roast meat.

"Just for now," Ita said. "Until we find something long term."

"Wonderful," Moshe said. Just what he needed; a battle on the home front too.

After dinner, the men retired to the library for a drink. Moshe poured Glenmorangie into three tumblers and collapsed into an armchair.

"Everyone in the US is talking about the Resurrection," Miki said. "You can't imagine the excitement."

"Yeah?"

"It's all over the news. And you—they just love you."

At least somebody does. Moshe decided not to burden his father-in-law with his recent governmental failings. Things always looked better from the outside.

Ice cubes floated in the honey-colored sea in the glass, like icebergs waiting for the Titanic. *This is only the beginning,* Gurion had said. The bulk of that iceberg lay beneath the surface. Moshe would have to steer clear and chart a course into calm blue oceans.

"You look tired," Miki said.

"Running the country is tiring work."

Miki opened a box of cigars on a side table and lit up. Moshe, the non-smoker, declined his offer to join him.

"Take it easy," Miki said. "You'll wear yourself out if you keep on like this."

"I suppose I could do with a vacation."

"Vacations don't last forever. All that weight on your shoulders. You need to delegate if you're going to last a full term."

Finally, Moshe understood where the conversation was going. "You mean, by hiring helpers."

"Exactly."

"Like you?"

His father-in-law smiled. "You can always trust family."

"It's not that simple, Miki. Restart promised to get rid of cronyism, and the Opposition is already crying corruption. I can't just hand out jobs to my in-laws."

"Sure you can. You're the Prime Minister—you can do what the hell you like."

Moshe chuckled but shook his head. If only that were so.

But as the heady vapors of single malt whisky numbed his mind, his father-in-law's advice sounded less crazy. *Do what the hell you like.* Maybe he was right.

CHAPTER 26

Conflicting emotions crashed inside Alex as he parked his car between the gloomy stilts of his apartment building Thursday evening. Soon, he would be free. Against all expectations, Mandrake was cutting him loose. Alex would start life anew.

The path would not be easy. He'd have to find a new career. A legitimate career. His days of swindling were over. Nothing in his life had prepared him for this.

In a way, he had become like Irina. The thought comforted him. They would reinvent themselves together. Despite the difficulties, the sight of freedom on the horizon calmed him. Any struggle was worth that second chance.

He turned off the ignition.

Only one hurdle lay between him and that new life, and that final magic trick put everything at risk.

He got out of the car, locked the doors with the remote, pushed through the door of the apartment building, and climbed the stairs.

He'd find work in sales or start his own company with the money he'd stashed away over the years. Irina deserved a better home than the dingy two-room apartment in downtown Jerusalem.

He knocked and turned the key in the door of his apartment.

Irina sat at the kitchen table, her shoulders tense and her face drawn. She looked up as he entered, her eyes damp and bloodshot. A bad day at the Dry Bones Society? She had seemed edgy that morning.

A sudden suspicion wrenched his guts. Had memories of her past returned? No, that was impossible. "Retrograde amnesia," Dr. V had said. "Caused by a lack of blood flow to the right temporal lobe, the seat of long-term memory." The horrors of that first life had been sealed away forever. Or had they? He searched her eyes for clues.

"Hey," he said and placed his shoulder bag on the shelf by the telephone. She didn't reply. "You OK?"

Her voice strained and accusatory, she said, "What's this?" She raised her hands from her lap. In them, the Glock looked large and menacing.

Alex exhaled his relief. She had found his spare gun, that's all. "That's for self-defense." That was no lie. In his line of work, that need arose very often.

"Hidden in your closet with boxes of bullets?"

Alex sat down opposite her and smiled. He could handle this. "Many people have guns," he said. "This is the Middle East."

His words were not having the desired effect. What was really on her mind?

"Shouldn't this be in a safe?"

Alex laughed. She was overreacting, that's all. "This is a rented apartment. I'm not going to invest thousands in a safe, and the landlord won't either, believe me."

His words had no effect.

"What do you do, Alex?"

The change of topic unsettled him. "I told you, I work with cars. Buying and selling."

She looked him in the eyes. "At the Malcha Technology Park?"

Oh, crap. The gun had stirred her suspicions, and she had followed him. "No," he said. "That's our head office. I meant to tell you about that. Today I quit my job."

Her eyes teared up, and she shook her head. "Stop lying to me!"

The hurt and fear in her voice startled him. He'd do anything to save her from pain. That's why he had risked everything this morning. "It's true, I spoke with my boss, and—"

"With Boris?"

"Who?"

"Boris."

"Who's Boris?"

Irina gave him a brief sarcastic smile. "Gray hair. Mustache. Tweed jacket."

Alex remembered. The Russian guy with the self-satisfied smile had jostled him on his way out of the elevator.

"He runs the slave labor camp in Talpiot," she continued. "Shmuel, Samira, and I would still be trapped there if Moshe hadn't saved us."

Double crap. The older Russian had seemed out of place in the hi-tech park. Alex had almost collided with another of Mandrake's foot soldiers, and the coincidence had made him guilty by association.

Lies lined up in Alex's mind. He didn't know what she was talking about, and he had nothing to do with this Boris. Feigning insult, he could turn the conversation against her. She was paranoid or taking out her work frustrations on him.

The tactic would work. She'd feel bad, and he'd get off scot-free. But he couldn't do it. He'd told her enough lies, and it had to stop. This morning, he'd taken the first and hardest step, and if they were ever going to live happily ever after, he'd have to come clean. Well, not completely clean. If she knew the whole truth, she'd never want to look at him again. It was a thin rope to walk, but he had to try.

"You're right," he said. She shifted back, away from him, so he added, "But not the way you think." His words seemed to have calmed her, or at least prevented her from fleeing out the door. She still believed in him; otherwise, she would have left before he came home and avoided the confrontation.

He took a long, slow breath. *Here goes.* "I do work with cars, or at least I did until this morning. The work wasn't completely honest. For years I've worked for a criminal organization. The boss is my oldest childhood friend. We met in an orphanage in the Ukraine. I don't know Boris, but I suspect he works for the same organization."

She frowned, and a tear slipped down her cheek.

"I haven't been fully honest with you, I know, but I'm changing that. That's why I quit today. I'm done with all that." He reached over and grasped her hands in his. "I want a new start, to build an honest, new life together, the two of us."

Irina stared into his eyes, still suspicious, but she did not withdraw her hands. "And your friend is just going to let you go, no hard feelings?"

A laugh escaped Alex's lips. *No hard feelings.* Mandrake had used the exact same words. "It wasn't easy," he said, "but he knows I've been uncomfortable for a long time. And there's a small catch."

"What catch?"

"He's given me one last job." Alex swallowed hard. "And to get it done, I need your help."

CHAPTER 27

Sunday morning, Avi's dress shoes squelched in a muddy patch of grass beside the Menachem Begin Expressway. "A treasure hunt," Gurion had said, before dispatching him to the highway that cut through Jerusalem from north to south. *More like a wild goose chase.*

Was this a joke—or payback? Gurion knew everything about everyone. Had the Opposition leader learned of Avi's attempt to warn Moshe Karlin of the planned betrayal?

A lot of good that had done. Moshe had not listened. Why should he have? He'd dismissed Avi's risky gesture as a clumsy ploy to bury the coalition before it was born. Despite Avi's best efforts, his dream of joining with Moshe had died with the coalition, and he was stuck doing Gurion's bidding.

Avi glanced behind a bush beside the fence of Gazelle Valley, the urban wildlife park. Nothing.

Beyond the fence, a baby gazelle eyed him and chewed grass.

"Yeah, I know," Avi said aloud. "This is stupid." He made for the next turnpike and groaned as mud seeped into his socks.

Maybe Moshe would listen to him next time. If there was a next time. Gurion kept his cards close to his chest, telling Avi only what he needed to know. This time he had only told him where to go and what to say. Even if he found his target, what did Gurion hope to gain? If anything, the move would push him further from the seat of power.

Moshe would know what Gurion was up to. But would he believe Avi if he told him what Gurion had instructed him to do?

Avi halted. In the shadow of the turnpike, a figure crouched.

Avi drew closer, picking his way through the twigs and autumn leaves. The man huddled over a small campfire. The letters DBS appeared on the back of the grimy bathrobe that had once been white. A thick mane of dark hair hung low over his back.

At the crackle of a leaf under Avi's shoe, the man turned. He had a long, thick beard and large, dark eyes. Smoke and the sweet scent of roasting meat wafted from the stick in his hand, which ended in a skinned rabbit.

Well, what do you know? Gurion had been right.

"Good morning, sir," Avi said. He was to be polite and persuasive. "Sorry to disturb you."

The man stared at the intruder. "Five years," he mumbled. "Five years!"

Whatever. The hobo met the description but appeared to be out of his mind.

Avi kept to the script. "A great statesman such as yourself should take up his true calling."

The man cocked his head to one side like a chicken. Had the words gotten through to him?

"Five years!" Theodore Herzl cried. "Five years too late!"

CHAPTER 28

"There's a leak," Sivan told the ministers at the round conference table. "I know it."

"Don't look at us," Shmuel said.

Moshe interceded. "Nobody's making accusations."

He had called the urgent cabinet meeting in the Government Room of the Knesset building Sunday morning to discuss their new plan when Sivan had aired her suspicions.

"Somebody talked," she said. "How else did Gurion find out about the tunnels?"

"Any of those soldiers could have told family and friends," Shmuel said.

"Unlikely. The IDF blocked cellular communications for the entire area and canceled all home visits. The Chief of Staff or the intelligence chiefs are to blame. They owe their positions to the previous administration. We should replace them all!"

Moshe sighed. "It might not be their fault. A rogue staff member could have leaked. We'll weed out the bad guys in time, but for now, we need damage control. Sivan?"

She said, "As you know, we're calling it the Sixth Aliyah."

"Nice!" Savta Sarah said. She turned to Moshe. "She's good!"

"Indeed. Sivan will present the details to the public this afternoon and try to calm things down. The Dry Bones Society has stepped in to help and located absorption towns for the new arrivals. But that's not why I called you together. I wanted to discuss our new way forward." He glanced around the table. "Where's the Minister of Defense?"

The assembled ministers shrugged. Rafi's unscheduled absence was never a good sign, but Moshe had to push on. He'd update him later.

"Our coalition efforts failed. Fine. We'll drag them into the future, kicking and screaming."

Calls of agreement rose around the table. *Do what the hell you like.*

"We don't need their votes. It's time we got down to business and drafted our new legislation. This is our chance to fix the State, and it might be our only chance, so let's make it count. Minister of Finance?"

Savta Sarah cleared her throat and shuffled a stack of papers. "Our team did the research you requested, Moshe. The situation is appalling. Our deficit is at an all-time high and growing. Half the country lives in overdraft, and ninety percent of the wealth belongs to ten tycoons. It's shameful!"

"As we suspected," Moshe said. "What can we do about it?"

"We can use common sense. Money doesn't grow on trees. Spend less than you earn and pay off your debts. We studied other economies, as you asked, and the data backs this up. In addition, we need to open the market, encourage competition, and incentivize small businesses."

"Excellent. Move on to a proposal. Talking of opening the market, Minister of Foreign Affairs?"

Shmuel said, "We need to strengthen our economic ties with other countries. Asia and Africa are hungry for our technology. Our back-channels indicate that Saudi Arabia, Qatar, and Yemen want to normalize diplomatic relations too."

"Wonderful!"

Sivan said, "It must be the Resurrection. There's nothing

like a monopoly on life after death to win new friends."

"But that goodwill won't last forever," Moshe countered. "Shmuel, move forward with those trade agreements. We'll need to schedule diplomatic visits to solidify our new friendships and—"

The door opened, and Rafi entered, breathless. "Sorry I'm late."

He stepped up to Moshe and whispered in his ear. *Oh, no.* Moshe had been expecting something like that, but not so soon.

"What's the matter?" Sivan asked.

Moshe let Rafi share the tidings.

"We've sighted an American aircraft carrier in the Mediterranean, ten miles off the Haifa coast."

"No harm in that," Shmuel said. "They're an ally."

"At the same time," Rafi continued, "a Russian aircraft carrier has moved into the Gulf of Aqaba and is heading for Eilat."

Moshe sighed. There was no way around it now.

"There's something you should know." He told them about his urgent meetings with the ambassadors, their offers and their unshakable belief that the Jewish State had turned the resurrected dead into weapons of mass destruction.

"But we've done no such thing, have we?" Sivan said.

"Of course not. But nothing will convince them otherwise. Each side wants to get their hands on our imaginary weapons before the other superpower does."

"Should we be worried?" Rabbi Yosef asked.

"Things don't turn out well when superpowers think you're hoarding weapons of mass destruction. Just ask Saddam Hussein." Around the table, the ministers shifted in their seats. "We'll keep stalling and hope they come to their senses. Meanwhile, we've got work to do. Where were we? Minister of Interior, what can we do to cut bureaucratic red tape?"

Rabbi Yosef opened his mouth to speak when knuckles rapped on the door and two uniformed police officers entered the room.

"Excuse me, Mr. Prime Minister," one officer, a young man, said, his cheeks red with obvious discomfort. He must have drawn the short straw.

"We're in the middle of a confidential meeting." Where were the Knesset security officers when you needed them?

"I understand that, sir. But I'm afraid you'll have to come with us."

"What?"

The officer handed Moshe a document printed on official stationery. "This warrant comes straight from the Attorney General. We need you to come with us for questioning."

"Right now? That's ridiculous!" Surely the Prime Minister had rights too. "On what charges?"

The officer's lips trembled. "There's a list."

CHAPTER 29

Ahmed watched in awed silence from his seat of honor at the main table on stage. Men gawked at him from the packed rows of the event hall in Bethlehem. He wore a new suit beneath a white robe and a *kaffiyeh* of distinction on his head. Beside him, Imam Basel sang his praises into a microphone. Had the martyr promises finally come true?

No! He had committed a vile and cowardly crime and cut short innocent lives. The hell he had crawled through in his second life wouldn't atone for a fraction of his guilt. This event was a show, a charade. Hasan had told him nothing of his new job, only freshened him up, changed his clothes, and deposited him at the hall. Once again, he was a tool in cruel hands. He was sure of it.

And yet... this felt so good.

"A hero," the Imam declared, "and a warrior. Our son returned to us at this critical time to fulfill his destiny. He is a sign from Above of comfort and consolation. Of redemption!"

In the crowd, men smiled, and their eyes sparkled with hope. Because of Ahmed. After months of suffering, the lost sheep had returned to the warm embrace of the fold.

The speech ended. Imam Basel hugged him. Well-wishers lined up to shake his hand, then drifted to the tables laden with food and drink. Ahmed's cheeks hurt from smiling, his elbow from countless handshakes.

When the line ended, a short, rotund woman in a black burka drew near, the corners of her eyes wrinkling through the slit. The only woman at the gathering, she had sat at the edge of the table of honor, and now she pounced on him and squeezed the breath from his lungs.

"My Ahmed!"

"Mother?" He choked on the knot of emotion in his throat. At the end of their last meeting, when he was friendless and alone, she had turned him out onto the street.

"I knew you would return, my boy," she said. "Forgive me for not letting you stay. How was I to know that you are the One?"

The knot of emotion dropped to the pit of his stomach. "The One? Mother, what do you mean?"

She gave his chest a playful tap. "Always so humble. I must hurry off. See you soon!"

"Mother!"

But Dara had taken her place. "Ahmed, is it?" he said. He was still wearing his filthy street clothes. "So, you hid your real name and the fact that you're a *Shaheed*. A resurrected *Shaheed!* Sorry, I didn't know. Otherwise, I would have bowed and kissed your hand."

"Knock it off." His mother's words had broken the spell. "This whole situation stinks." He glanced around for Hasan.

"What do you mean? You're a hero. You're the man!"

Ahmed spotted his cousin, who wore a fancy suit and handed one of the organizers an envelope.

Ahmed stormed over to him. "What's going on?"

Hasan smiled and clapped him on the shoulder. "Great job, cuz!"

"Cut the crap! I'm the One—what does that mean?"

Hasan herded Ahmed aside, the smile still painted on his face. "Calm down. This is a good thing for you, and it comes from the very top."

"Imam Basel?"

"Higher. From the Shepherd himself."

"The Great Imam?"

Hasan nodded. The spiritual leader of the Palestinians had gone into hiding years ago. The Great Imam had said that he, Ahmed, was the One!

"What does that mean?"

"You, my cousin, are the long-awaited Mahdi."

"Who?"

Hasan lowered his voice. "You know, the Guided One."

Ahmed still understood nothing.

"The Redeemer who appears at the Resurrection and destroys evil. Got it?"

What had Hasan been smoking? "You're crazy. I'm not a redeemer."

"Don't look at me. This comes from Above."

Ahmed wasn't buying it. He wasn't special, and Hasan had lied to him before. "Give me my money, and I'll be on my way."

Hasan gave him a charming smile. "You'll get your money. There'll be so much, you won't be able to carry it all. You'll wipe your ass with hundred-shekel notes. But what's your hurry?" He slung his arm around Ahmed's shoulder. "Stick around. Trust me, you do not want to miss the after-party."

CHAPTER 30

Late that afternoon, the tycoon exited her private gym on the twentieth floor. Radiating heat and soaked to the bone, she marched toward the elevator. She'd told Itai, her personal assistant, to have her helicopter ready in an hour, and so she did not have time for the balding man in the tacky suit who waddled toward her.

"Shirley, my darling!" Isaac Gurion crooned, his smile wide enough to swallow her whole.

She glared at Itai, who threw up his hands in a mime of defeat, and mouthed the words, "He wouldn't leave."

Gurion leaned in for a kiss.

"Don't touch me," she said, without breaking her stride, "I'm sweaty." Thank goodness for small mercies.

Gurion jogged beside her to keep up. "Now I know that you're very busy," he said, and he made her laugh. Busy, indeed; the slimy politician had no idea.

That morning she'd met with her lawyers to sign the contract for an apartment complex on prime Tel Aviv property. The luxury tower project—her third that year—had posed zoning challenges, and she'd deployed an extra set of incentives and kickbacks to get the mayor on board.

In the afternoon, a museum opening had moved her to tears, dedicated as it was to the memory of a dear friend. That left an hour for TRX with her personal trainer before the gala dinner that evening.

She wasn't sure why the Whatever Organization was honoring her with the Whatever Prize, but awards always meant that said organization required more donations.

"But," Gurion continued, "this matter is both urgent and of great interest to you."

"What do you want?"

"That's what I love about you," the politician gushed. "Always to the point."

"You were saying?" The elevator doors were only a few meters away. Gurion had her ear for ten seconds, tops.

"A new joint venture," he said.

The little man sure had a nerve! "As I recall, our last joint venture flushed a truckload of money down the toilet."

"Karlin stole that election!" he cried, red in the face.

She pressed the button for the elevator and chuckled. "Tut-tut, Isaac. It's not like you to lose your cool. He beat you fair and square."

A spiteful fire burned in the silly man's eyes. "And now he's set his sights on you!"

Her smile dropped. "What do you mean?"

"He wants to open the markets and increase competition. Level the playing field."

Level the playing field. Demagogues had been threatening to make life difficult for decades. Once in power, they always came around to her way of thinking. But Moshe Karlin was not your garden-variety politician, and he didn't come from money either. He'd be a problem.

"How can you be so sure?"

"I have eyes and ears everywhere."

She swore under her breath. Even fat little silly men had their purpose in the grand scheme of things. "How much do you need?"

Gurion smiled, and the image of a penguin in an oil slick rose in her mind. "I knew you'd understand."

CHAPTER 31

Ahmed could not believe his eyes. Platters of fish and meat covered the tables in the garden of the mansion, along with a dizzying variety of cold drinks, cakes, and fruit. Steam rose from the swimming pool and into the crisp night air. On the deck and lawns, young, beautiful people smiled and danced, their bodies swaying to the enchanting beat of the sensual music. Had he finally entered Paradise?

A luxury car had carried Ahmed to the mansion in Bethlehem, and for the first five seconds, he had stood at the edge of the garden and gaped. The revelers did not appear to be martyrs or saints. Especially not the girls. Clad in frilly underwear that barely contained their curves and high-heeled sandals that drew his eye to the shapely contours of their bare legs, they gyrated to the rhythm, raising their arms and kicking back their heads. There were so many of them!

A hand draped his shoulder and snapped him out of his trance. "Welcome to Paradise, cuz!" Hasan said. He had taken off his suit jacket and swirls of chest hair peeked through his unbuttoned shirt. "How do you like your new home?"

"I can stay here?"

"For as long as you want. Look at those girls." He leaned in to whisper in Ahmed's ear. "A little secret—they're not virgins." He laughed as Ahmed's cheeks burned. "Trust me, cuz, it's better that way. Here, have a few of these." He held out a bowl of yellow M&Ms, and Ahmed scooped a handful. "Easy! Just one or two. Knock 'em back."

"What are they?"

"They'll help you relax, enjoy yourself."

"Drugs?" Hot anger rose within him again. He knew this was too good to be true! This was a trap.

"Chill out, Ahmed." Then he raised his voice. "Hey, everyone! The Mahdi is in the house!"

The revelers turned to them and cheered. Some raised beer bottles and wine glasses in the air. "Drugs," Ahmed hissed, "*and* alcohol?!" Islam outlawed all intoxicants.

"You worry too much, cuz."

"Hey!" Dara came up behind them, smelling good and dressed well. Hasan had sent him upstairs for a shower and change of clothes. "What did I miss?"

Hasan ignored him and waved to a tall young woman, who smiled and sashayed over to them. "This is Fatima," he said to Ahmed. "She'll take care of you."

Fatima bowed her head. "It is an honor to meet you, Mahdi." Her voice was soft and sensual.

Ahmed was about to say that he was not the Mahdi, but she drank him in with those deep, dark eyes and his tongue forgot how to form words. Instead, he swallowed the pills in his hand.

"Be gentle," Hasan said, a smile in his voice. "It's his first time."

"Then we'll make it memorable."

We? Ahmed's legs turned to jelly. He used all his willpower to stop his eyes from stealing a glance at the rest of her.

"Go on," she whispered. "Don't be shy. Feast your eyes. But we won't stop there."

Ahmed obeyed and glanced down the length of her. The porous clothing left little to the imagination. His breath came fast and shallow. The small part of his brain that could still think made an observation. She had said it again, hadn't she? *We.*

Fatima glanced to the side with a smile, and two more divine beauties strode up beside her. Taking his hand in hers, she led him into the house.

"Hey, what about me?" Dara called, but nobody was listening.

Fatima led them up a set of stairs. The other two girls fell in beside him and rested their hands on his waist.

Ahmed's heart thumped in his ears. The music swirled around his head and grew softer as they reached the upper level. He floated on air.

Soft red light filled a bedroom. The girls pushed him back onto a bed of soft linen.

Fatima smiled down at him, while the two girls climbed onto the bed.

"I've never served a Mahdi before," said one. Her voice was flowing honey. Her fingers caressed his chest, sending goose bumps over his flesh.

"We're so lucky," said the other. Her hands loosened the buttons of his shirt.

Ahmed was the Mahdi. Everyone was saying it. And why not? He had died a Shaheed and awoken from death. *I am the Mahdi.*

Their fingers traced a path from his torso to his trousers.

He inhaled sharply and closed his eyes. In his mind's eye, a different girl stood over him. Her smile was warm and welcoming.

Samira.

The demure girl at the Dry Bones Society had snuck back into his thoughts, the way she had stolen into his heart. She must hate him now, knowing what he had done. The moment she had discovered his crime, heartbreak had glazed over her kind eyes, and Ahmed had fled from her sight.

But the girls on the bed didn't hate him. They adored him. In their eyes, he wasn't a murderer, but a redeemer.

I am the Mahdi. One day, Samira would see that too.

Ahmed's clothes melted away. The mattress shifted and

fabric ruffled as the girls undressed.

Their soft hands were on him again, exploring and soothing. He pretended they were Samira's hands.

Yes. Samira would understand now. She'd give him a second chance.

CHAPTER 32

"Is this a joke?"

The middle-aged woman pulled her shopping cart up Jaffa Road on Monday morning, no doubt on her way to the Machaneh Yehuda open-air market. She had paused when Eli had walked up to her, flashed his charming smile, and handed her a flyer.

How times had changed. Eli had spent centuries avoiding direct human contact, interacting only enough to keep his ear to the ground for changes in culture and language. Relationships would only blow his cover and compromise his Divine mission. Today, however, he mingled with the common people.

"Not at all," he said. "This is based on a scientific genetic study."

"Oh."

She glanced again at the flyer's title, "Have We Found the Ten Lost Tribes?" After hooking the reader's attention, the flyer pushed the reader down a slippery slide. "New scientific research has discovered the Ten Lost Tribes of Israel in the most unexpected of places."

Eli said, "Be sure to visit our website, and see for yourself." He pointed to the URL in large letters at the bottom of the flyer: TheTenLostTribes.org.

Her eyes brightened. "I'll ask my grandson to find that for me. He's a wizard on the computer. Thank you!"

"You're welcome."

He moved on to the next passerby.

Web design. Copywriting. Internet marketing. By creating the OpenGen website, Eli had inadvertently acquired the exact skillset he would need for his grassroots campaign to spread the word of the Ten Lost Tribes. Perhaps he had lost the Thin Voice because he no longer needed it? The Boss sure worked in mysterious ways.

Noga approached at a brisk walk.

"How's it going?" he asked.

"Great. I need more flyers."

Eli reached into his shoulder pack for a fresh pile of color leaflets.

"The website really adds a lot," she said.

"Authority building," he said. "Just like the photos." They had selected stock images of white-coated scientists and the familiar double-helix of DNA. The website created the impression that established research institutes backed the study.

"How are the ads doing?"

Eli consulted the Facebook Ads app on his iPhone. "Picking up. So far we're popular with millennial men and middle-aged women."

Noga laughed. "I can't believe this is actually working."

"Neither will Hannah," he said, and Noga laughed again. The idea of distributing leaflets to the masses had appalled her doctoral supervisor.

It was so good to see Noga happy again. He said, "The world has never been smaller. Soon everyone will know."

"And then the media will come calling?"

"If we can't go to the Prime Minister..." He trailed off.

"Then he'll have to come to us!"

She looked at the handful of flyers. "I'll need more of these. It's crazy down there." She pointed toward the side street that led to the pedestrian mall on Ben Yehuda Street.

"Have they come here to learn about the Ten Tribes?"

She laughed again. "I wish. There's an event."

His interest piqued, Eli escorted her back through the alley. She had not been kidding. A river of humanity, tourists and locals, pooled from the side street tributaries and flowed down Ben Yehuda toward Zion Square.

Above the heads of the crowd on the small square rose a platform. A podium with a microphone stood empty on one side of the dais, a dressed table on the other, beneath a banner that read, in large golden letters: "Welcome, Kings of Israel!"

Behind the table sat a royal panel of three men with serious beards and large golden crowns on their heads.

"What the hell?"

CHAPTER 33

Avi jogged down Ben Yehuda Street toward Zion Square. He was late and empty-handed. Gurion did not react well to the failures of his underlings, and if he suspected that Avi was collaborating with Moshe, this failure would only confirm his suspicions.

He waded through the thick audience toward the stage in the middle of the square. Spectators covered the sidewalks and overflowed into the streets, and police officers redirected traffic.

Gurion must have serious connections and money to pull off the event. For Avi's own anti-zombie demonstration a while back, he had leaned on Boris and his murky underworld ties and still received a smaller turnout.

He spotted the politician beside the dais and called to him from the barrier of yellow police tape. Gurion waved to an officer to let him through.

Gurion smiled as he considered the crowd, in a good mood. "Where's Theodore?"

"He wouldn't come."

"My instructions were clear—"

"He's cracked. Barely understood what I was saying. Kept going on about 'five years' or something. Trust me, you wouldn't want him here, anyway."

"Doesn't matter," Gurion said. "I found something better."

He nodded toward the stage where three bearded guys sat at a dressed table. They wore flowing purple robes and golden crowns. The name tags on the table read "King David," "King Saul," and "King Solomon." "You found them—the actual kings of Israel?"

Avi had heard of historical personages returning among the resurrected—Herzl had been one of them—but he was sure major biblical characters would have made the evening news.

Gurion sneered through his teeth. "No, you idiot. I wouldn't bring actual kings here. We need famous names that will win popular support but won't turn around and elbow us out of the way later. Maimonides didn't take the bait—he prefers his books—so I had to improvise. I took three drunks off the street, cleaned and dressed them up, and promised them a crate of wine for their trouble. They look pretty convincing if I do say so myself."

Avi swallowed. Gurion's mad plan was starting to make sense. He'd use the kings of yore to breed discontent with the current government, then step into the vacuum when Moshe stepped down.

Avi had to warn Moshe. Had he heard of the gathering already? A Channel Two news van straddled the curb on Jaffa Road. Moshe would know how to counter Gurion's deception. He glanced around but saw no sign of the Prime Minister or his cabinet members. Avi had to stall the event, to buy Moshe some time.

"What about Karlin?" Gurion gave Avi a quick, searching glance, so he added, "What if he shows up and interferes?"

"I wouldn't worry about your old friend." Gurion grinned with renewed enthusiasm. "Right now, his hands are very, very full."

CHAPTER 34

Monday morning, Galit rolled over in bed to find Moshe's side empty and cold. He had left early and without saying goodbye. Last night, he had come home late and hardly said a word to her.

Her stomach cramped. Her worst fears were materializing. *He hates me.*

She lay in bed for a while. Being First Lady had its advantages and sleeping in was her favorite. The housekeeper made sure Talya was awake and fed before the Secret Service dropped her off at kindergarten. Now that she had cleared out and cleaned up their home on Shimshon Street, she had to deal with her visiting family.

Galit climbed out of bed and freshened up in the adjoining bathroom. She had eaten breakfast in her pajamas in her old home—her own home. In the Prime Minister's Residence, she had to dress up.

In the kitchen, the chef whipped batter in a baking tub.

"Morning, Henri," she said.

"Good-a-morning, Mrs. First Lady. Pancakes?"

"What's the occasion?"

"Our *new* guests, of course," he said. From the subtle sneer with which he said the word "new," he made known his disapproval of the interlopers. "They have quite an appetite.

This is their third batch."

A lump of embarrassment formed in her throat, and she gave the chef an apologetic smile.

Her nephews were in the games room, judging from the sound of ping-pong balls. Her father lay across the living room couch, his stomach rising and falling through his wife beater undershirt while he stared at infomercials on the big screen.

"Morning, Dad."

"Morning." He didn't look up.

She picked up the dirty plate he had left on the polished side table.

Greta, the housekeeper who reminded her of a German governess from old movies, had asked her to be extra careful not to scratch the antique furniture, and Galit lived in continual fear of her stern looks.

"Dad, what did we say about cleaning up?"

"Thanks, dear." He popped a cigar in his mouth and reached for a lighter.

Something snapped inside her. Galit snatched the cigar from his mouth.

"Hey, what was that about?"

"It's time you got dressed, don't you think?"

"What?" He stared at her as though she had spoken Chinese.

"You know—get a job, find a place to stay. You're eating us out of house and home!"

"I think the State of Israel can afford it."

"No, we can't!" she said, louder than she had intended.

Fear and frustration surged through her, as she sobbed. Her father stared at her, his eyes wide and confused.

"What's going on?" Galit's mother had arrived in a bathrobe, curlers in her hair. She threw an accusatory glance at her husband. "What did you say?"

"Nothing!"

She hugged Galit and walked her to the bathroom.

"He hates me!"

"Your father?"

"No. Moshe. We never talk."

"Well, dear, he's been pretty busy. He is the Prime Minister, after all."

"It's not just that." Galit weighed telling her mother the truth of her complex history with Moshe and Avi, then thought better of it. "It's complicated," she said.

"Hush now. Every relationship has its ups and downs. How often do you think I've wanted to throw your father out onto the street, hey? Sometimes, I wish I had." She searched Galit's eyes for a sign of comfort.

How could Galit make her understand? She alone was to blame. Moshe had done nothing wrong.

She said, "It's like there's a wall between us, and I'll never break through."

Her mother thought awhile. "Be patient, dear. In time, all walls crumble, and he'll bounce back when he's ready. Just make sure you're there for him when he does."

CHAPTER 35

"I demand to see the Commissioner!" Moshe said. He was losing his patience and fast.

Yesterday evening, the police officers had dragged him to the Talpiot Police Station for questioning regarding undisclosed charges. He'd been very polite and cooperative. This was all a big misunderstanding. They'd sort it out. The new Police Commissioner was his partner in fighting organized crime. And his efforts seemed to be working—they had released him on condition that he return to the station first thing in the morning.

This morning, however, they had kept him waiting a full hour, along with his lawyer and security detail, in a small interview room. Now he wanted answers too.

The young officer at the interrogation table shook in his boots. "The Commissioner is unavailable at present."

The kid was just doing his job, but enough was enough. "Then he'd better become available. I have a country to run. I can't wait here all morning."

"I'm sorry for the delay, Mr. Prime Minister. I'm sure—" But he didn't finish. A door clicked open behind Moshe, and the officer sighed with relief. "Oh, thank God."

Commissioner Golan swaggered into the room. "Mr. Prime Minister. Apologies for the delay." He dismissed the officer, sat down, and dropped a thick manila folder onto the interview table.

He leaned back, stretched his shoulders, clicked his neck, and opened the folder. Gone was the eager and easy manner of their first meeting, and no flicker of recognition registered in his dark eyes. "We want to question you about some criminal charges that have come to the attention of the Attorney General."

Criminal charges! Moshe had hardly had enough time in office to do anything illegal.

"What are the charges?"

"We'll get to those shortly." He glanced down at a list on the top page. "Do you have your attorney present?"

"Yes."

"Do you realize that anything you say can and will be used against you in court?"

"Yes. Mr. Commissioner, let's skip the formalities and cut to the chase. We've both got a lot to do." He did not say "like fighting organized crime," but he hoped his eyes conveyed the message. "What are the charges?"

"Corruption."

Moshe wanted to roll his eyes. Like his foot soldiers, the Commissioner was stretching out the interview far longer than necessary. "Can you be more specific?"

Commissioner Golan inhaled and glanced at the second sheet. "Child labor."

"What?!" That was preposterous.

"Says here that, for the past two years, you have employed a minor to do menial labor in your home on Shimshon Street."

"That's news to me. Who was the alleged worker?"

"A Miss Carmel Schneider."

It took a few seconds for Moshe to make the connection. "The babysitter? Since when is hiring a babysitter considered corruption?"

"The babysitter," he repeated. "Are you sure?"

"Yes."

"And that was all she did?"

"Yes."

"And Mrs. Karlin will corroborate that version of the story?"

"Yes. There is no story here, so there's not much to corroborate."

"Good."

"Can I go now?"

"There's more." He leafed through the pages of the file. "Is it true that your in-laws have moved into the Prime Minister's Residence?"

Moshe shifted on the hard seat. How on earth did he know that already?

"They're visiting; they haven't *moved in*."

"So, they're paying the government for their food and lodging?"

"Do you have in-laws, Commissioner?"

"Please answer the question."

"No, of course not. They're our guests."

"I see. It seems that the residence received a delivery of cigars. Very expensive cigars. Were these for diplomatic consumption or for your guests?"

Oh, crap. Moshe pictured Miki lighting up in the library. He had assumed that his father-in-law had owned the cigars, but now it seemed that Miki had turned his stay into an all-inclusive vacation. "I'll have to look into that," he said. "I don't keep track of every item ordered at the residence."

Commissioner Golan grunted, stared at the papers, but said nothing.

"C'mon, Commissioner. What's going on here? We're both just trying to do our jobs. Last week I increased your budget for organized crime—"

Golan looked up, and Moshe regretted his words instantly. "Are you trying to bribe me?"

"No. Of course, not. I'm just reminding you that we're on the same side. Now, are we done?"

Golan glanced at his wristwatch. "We'll be done in five

minutes."

Five minutes? Then it hit him. Isaac Gurion was behind the charges, and the Opposition Leader knew Moshe's every move. Sivan had suspected a leak; Moshe had discovered an open fire hose.

Moshe would deal with Gurion later. First, he had to end this interrogation—this diversion—and get back to governing. Golan was in Gurion's pocket. Corruption existed, all right, and its roots ran deeper than Moshe had thought. If Gurion could buy the Commissioner, others could too. And Moshe had entrusted him with the war on organized crime!

"That's enough." Moshe straightened his suit jacket and got to his feet. "This meeting is over. Tell your men to open the door and let us go."

Golan held his gaze. The command had wounded his pride. "Or else what?"

Indignation boiled within Moshe. A dozen juicy threats came to mind, but Golan would turn them all against Moshe as an attempt to obstruct justice.

But Moshe didn't need to make threats. The door shuddered in its frame. The table shifted on its legs, inching toward the wide-eyed Commissioner as though it had come alive. And then the ground shook beneath their feet.

CHAPTER 36

"Are you sure this is the right place?" his friend asked.

Ahmed nodded and pressed onward, entering Clal Center on Jaffa Street. Dara peered at the tired floor tiles and blackened windows of the decaying shopping mall with doubt. Ahmed hid his own hesitation.

An arrow pointed the way to the Dry Bones Society. The last time he had set foot in the Society, he had come under attack. The balding man had recognized him from bus number eighteen and pounced on him with the fury of a much younger man. *Murderer!* Samira had looked on, her eyes clouding over with disbelief, then disappointment, and Ahmed, unable to lie to her, had fled.

"I hope this girl is worth it," Dara said.

"She is."

Hasan had warned them not to leave the mansion in Bethlehem, their new home. For his own protection. As word spread, many would seek out the Redeemer, and Satan's followers might wish him harm.

"Better than the girls last night?" Dara chuckled. "That's hard to imagine."

Ahmed's shaved cheeks warmed again at the memory. He had brought his new friend along to increase his status in her eyes—a witness to support his claims—but perhaps that had been a mistake.

"She's different," was all he said.

Would she recognize him today? Hasan had filled his closet with white satin robes and shiny suits. New clothes for a new man. No longer did they call him Ahmed, or even Walid, only Mahdi. Believers bowed their heads at the sight of him; they muttered praise and whispered prayers. Samira should be proud. She should welcome him with joy. Once again, he would bask in the warmth of her smile.

The quiet unnerved him. The bustle from the Absorption Center on the fourth floor had always echoed down the central pier of the Center. Had the Dry Bones Society moved? The offices of the Call Center would hold the answer. Wherever she was, he would find her.

Avoiding the rickety elevator, he led Dara to the stairs. The third-floor corridor brought a fresh wave of memories: Savta Sarah calling to him, leading him to his first warm meal in his second life; Samira stepping up to their table, that demure smile on her lips. "She'll take care of you," the old lady had said. Longing surged in his chest, an intense, painful yearning for that lost moment. The time had come to reclaim what was his.

He marched down the corridor, passing the Absorption Center, to the main offices and the doors with the words "The Dry Bones Society" emblazoned on the frosted window. Ahmed inhaled, puffed out his chest, and knocked twice.

At that moment, his courage fled. What if the old man answered? Surely others would recognize him. Would they cry murder and pounce on him again to finish what the old man had started? Dara's presence would make them think twice. He had been wise to bring his friend, but was the entire visit a mistake?

As he made to retrace his steps, the handle turned, and a young woman with olive skin and a green hijab stood in the doorway. The sight of her sent a bolt of lightning through his heart. Samira radiated calm and welcome, and his concerns evaporated. He had come home.

"Ahmed?" The welcoming smile faded. She looked over her shoulder, then down the corridor. "What are you doing here?"

She did not curse him or chase him away, although concern wrinkled her beautiful features.

"Can we talk?"

She glanced at the watch on her wrist. "I have to go in five minutes."

"Five minutes is fine!" His soul soared. He'd trade a year in Boris's purgatory for five minutes in her presence!

She relented. Inside, she led them past the cubicles and buzz of the Call Center to the manager's corner office with the large windows. At the door, Ahmed turned to Dara. "Give us a moment?"

"Sure."

He closed the door behind him. Samira leaned against the desk. Something had changed in her. She stood taller and held his gaze longer.

"Is this your office now?" The office had belonged to the founder, Moshe Karlin.

Samira smiled. "In part. Irina and I run the Society, now that Moshe and Rabbi Yosef are in government."

Government. There had been an election the day Ahmed had failed to blow up. The day Ahmed had become Walid. Restart had launched Moshe and the Rabbi into Knesset.

"We've been so busy," Samira continued. "You cannot imagine. Waves of new arrivals. New Absorption Centers in other cities, mostly in the south. I was about to head over there when you arrived."

Her excitement infected him. "Do you still lead the welcoming sessions?"

She laughed. "There's no time for that anymore, and too many sessions. Teams of volunteers and society members handle that."

"I pity the new arrivals," he said. "You were so good at that."

Her cheeks flushed, and she glanced at her feet, her mouth forming the demure smile he had missed so much. "I still keep an eye on their training," she said, "to make sure they're doing a good job."

They smiled at each other, the recent past a long-forgotten nightmare. Five minutes was not enough.

Her eyes took in his clothes, and she got serious again. "Why are you here, Ahmed?"

The question made his eyes moisten. He didn't belong here with her. "To see you," he said. "I too have changed. You'll hear about me soon. They call me Mahdi. The Guided One," he added when she shook her head. "The Redeemer. I'll be addressing a gathering at Al-Quds University tomorrow. The word is spreading. Samira, this is my true destiny!"

Samira didn't lower her head. She did not mutter praise or whisper a prayer. "You're a Redeemer?"

The skeptical note in her voice spiked resentment in his chest and tried his patience. Other girls, far more desirable in their makeup and high heels, had felt honored to keep him company, to satisfy his every desire, but this outcast girl doubted him?

"*The* Redeemer," he said, keeping his temper in check. "This is the reason I returned. The Shepherd has decreed that I am the One."

"The Shepherd?"

"The Great Imam."

"You met him?"

"No, but he has spoken."

She lowered her eyes again. Had she finally understood?

"Ahmed," she said, her voice soft and calm, pleading. "Do not make the same mistake twice."

The same mistake? "There is no mistake—"

"Please, Ahmed. Listen to me. The shepherd tends the flock, and the sheep believe he is their friend. But the shepherd is not truly their friend. They realize this when they enter the slaughterhouse, but by then, it is too late."

Ahmed's anger flared again. Why couldn't she be happy

for him? Why did she have to invent flaws in his newfound fame and fortune?

He opened his mouth to chide her, to refute her words, and humble her, but he didn't get the chance, for at that moment the windows shuddered in their frames and the building shook.

CHAPTER 37

Clutching a small handbag, Irina stepped into the airy ante-chamber of the Prime Minister's Office on Kaplan Street in Jerusalem's Givat Ram neighborhood. She stepped up to the guard desk and flashed her visitor's pass. Although Moshe had granted her free access to the buildings of the government precinct, today she felt like an infiltrator and a traitor.

You're not doing anything wrong.

Alex had come clean. He had confessed his criminal past, the past he was leaving behind to start a new life with her. And she believed him. One last task stood between them and that new life, a job as simple as it was seemingly harmless. If all went according to plan, she'd settle the matter today.

The heels of her pumps clacked over the stone tiles as she made for a corridor. Moshe had given Irina and other members of the Dry Bones Society management a tour of the Knesset and Prime Minister's buildings during his first week in office. Although she often thought of Moshe and they discussed Society matters on the phone, she hadn't seen him in over two weeks.

Moshe's secretary munched a sandwich at her desk outside the Prime Minister's office.

"Morning, Ettie."

Ettie looked up from her newspaper and swallowed her

mouthful.

"Irina, welcome back."

With graying hair and half-moon spectacles on the edge of her nose, Ettie would not give Moshe's wife any cause for jealousy, no doubt one of the reasons that Moshe had selected her from the list of State secretaries.

"Is the Prime Minister in?"

Confusion passed over the secretary's face for a moment—or was that concern? "Not yet."

"Oh." Moshe's absence would compromise her plan. She should have made an appointment, but she didn't want to leave a trail.

Knock it off, Irina. You're not doing anything wrong. No matter how often she repeated her mantra, the very fact that she was acting on the orders of the criminal underworld made her feel dirty.

"When will he get back?"

That concerned look again. "I can't say. Soon, I hope."

"I see." Was something the matter? Prime ministers were busy people. He was probably stuck in meetings or attending to any number of crises in the Jewish State. All in a day's work.

She settled on the waiting bench and straightened her skirt.

Alex had worked for the underworld. The thought still made her shudder. The same organization as Boris, although Alex hadn't had any direct dealings with the slave driver. Thank goodness for that.

Moshe had sacrificed all he had to extract her from Boris's slave trade. By comparison, Alex's path to freedom sounded too easy. Was there a catch hidden somewhere, a consequence that she hadn't anticipated?

She cared for Moshe. At one point, she had loved him. She'd never knowingly hurt his career, never mind put him in danger. Would she regret this? Criminal elements had tried to harm Moshe before. They had abducted him and his wife on Election Day, and, although Moshe had not gone into the details, their battered and bruised state indicated that the experience had not involved polite talk and cups of tea.

Irina crossed her legs on the bench.

No, there was no harm in this. She wouldn't be proposing anything new. People already shouted it from the street corners. The move would boost his popularity and strengthen his standing. She'd just be giving Moshe a little nudge in the right direction.

She glanced at her wristwatch. Fifteen minutes had passed. Today wasn't the best day for this. She positioned her legs to stand when a familiar bearded man walked up to the secretary's desk.

After a short, hushed exchange, the secretary turned toward Irina, and the rabbi followed her glance.

"Irina, good to see you." Rabbi Yosef smiled and made for her.

She stood. "Good to see you too." The rabbi had gained a few more worry lines on his face and strands of gray in his beard. Government work had taken its toll.

The worry lines deepened. "Is everything all right at the DBS?"

"Busier than ever, but good. Is Moshe around?"

"I hope so." There it was again. The people in government were doing a lot of hoping. The premonition returned. "Let's talk in my office."

He closed the door of his room when they were inside, and Irina settled in the visitor's chair before the desk. Moshe smiled at them from the framed photo on the wall, an Israeli flag behind him.

Rabbi Yosef took his seat. "Moshe's still with the police."

"The police? Is he OK?" Had Moshe been in an accident?

"They took him in for questioning yesterday. Some sort of corruption probe."

"But he's only just taken office. He hadn't held a public position before."

"Exactly. It's probably nothing, trumped-up charges from the Opposition."

Irina sagged in the chair. Isaac Gurion and Avi Segal had bombarded Moshe and Rabbi Yosef with smear campaigns during the election. She'd have thought they'd stop dragging his name through the mud once he ruled the country. Apparently, she had been wrong.

"Poor Moshe," she said. "After all he's been through."

The rabbi raised his eyebrows, a gesture both of empathy for Moshe and pessimism for any cessation of hostilities. "This all has to stay between us."

"Of course."

"Maybe I can help you—while Moshe is out?"

The rabbi was right. He could help her. In fact, he'd make the job much easier for her. "Rabbi Yosef, I have a question about the Messianic Era."

"Sure, go ahead." At the mention of religious doctrine, the rabbi seemed to relax. This was his area of expertise. Moshe had questioned him about the Messianic Era before proposing that they run as an independent party in the elections.

"The Messiah is supposed to rule the Holy Land and bring justice to the Land?"

"Among other things," he said, and his eyes narrowed. "Why do you ask?"

"I was just thinking. You've seen the posters around the city. People have been talking. Could Moshe be the Messiah?"

There—she had said it. She had done her part, and now the rabbi would do the rest.

Rabbi Yosef laughed, not in surprise or delight, but irony. His eyes hardened.

"What?" she asked, and her brow moistened. Did he suspect she was acting on behalf of others? Would he ask who had sent her?

"Nothing. Just... you're not the first person to ask me that."

Irina breathed again. She was not the first. Others had made the same suggestion. The mission had a greater chance of success, and she shared the burden of guilt with others. *What burden of guilt? Knock it off!*

"I understand," the rabbi continued, "why people would think that. Moshe came out of nowhere and shot to the top. He's trying to fix the system. But the Messiah is supposed to do many other things as well: rebuild the Temple in Jerusalem; bring back the dispersed tribes of Israel. It's hard to see those things happening soon."

Irina couldn't believe her ears. A month in Knesset had worn down the rabbi's indomitable optimism. "What about the Resurrection—isn't that one of the signs?"

He shrugged. "A great miracle, nobody can deny that. And another sign of the End Days. But is it *the* Resurrection? Many of the details do not match traditional expectations. And there are so many other signs that have not come to pass."

Irina stared at the man behind the desk. Was this the Rabbi Yosef who had physically bounced with excitement at her return, who had gushed about the approaching Redemption with unshakeable confidence? The man before her doubted the miracles that surrounded him. He would not aid her mission; he'd stand in her way.

"Signs?" she asked. "What other signs could we need?"

He stared at the desk, and his lips trembled. "Wars," he muttered. "Disasters. For example—" But he didn't complete the sentence.

A teaspoon tinkled. They stared at the coffee mug on his desk, which shifted over the polished wood. And then the walls shuddered.

CHAPTER 38

"Are they for real?" Noga said.

Among the masses around Zion Square, Eli gaped at the kings on the dais. The scene was wrong. Very wrong.

How could this be? Had the Boss raised the former kings from their tombs and crowned them anew without him? A deep pit opened in the floor of his stomach. Had the Thin Voice abandoned him, not because his mission no longer required Divine intervention, but because the Boss had replaced him with another prophet?

A rotund man in a suit bounded onto the platform and took the podium. He gave the crowd a sincere stare and patted his sweaty comb-over.

"My fellow citizens," he intoned, and his voice reverberated between the buildings and stores of downtown Jerusalem. "This is a historic day. Behold the return of your kings of old, the mighty kings of Israel!"

Whispers circled among the crowd, fermented excited chatter, and erupted in cheers.

The man pointed with his arm. "I give you King Saul, the first King of Israel; King David, the Sweet Singer of Israel; and the mighty King Solomon, the Wisest Man on Earth."

At the mention of their names, the kings rose from their seats and bowed for the crowd. A chant rose among the

masses. *David, King of Israel. Alive, alive and well!* Men in white
knitted skullcaps danced and waved their arms. An old lady
broke into sobs. Little boys climbed onto their fathers' shoulders to get a better view of their royalty.

Then the realization hit.

"That's not them," Eli said.

"Who?"

"The kings. They're imposters."

"Are you sure? It's been a long time."

"Three thousand years," he said. "I kept to the north mostly. I only saw David a few times and at a distance. But he wasn't a redhead, and he had a much smaller nose. The real Saul would rather fall on his sword than sit next to him, End of the World or not. As for Solomon, he wasn't *that* fat."

The sweaty man on the dais raised his hands for silence. "Alas, my friends. Our rightful kings will not rule again."

A stunned silence descended on his audience.

"'Why?' you ask. Because one brazen man has usurped their God-given rights and stolen the crown for himself and himself alone!"

Boos resounded from every direction, then the crowd fell quiet to hear more about Public Enemy Number One.

"You know who I'm talking about—the wicked villain, Moshe Karlin!"

Eli and Noga exchanged a look of shock. Was he really accusing the current Prime Minister of being the anti-Messiah?

"That's right!" the man roared into the microphone. "King Karlin sits on their throne and lords over us. But he hasn't stopped there. His hunger for power knows no bounds. Thirsting for your blood, he has opened the gates wide for a zombie invasion. And while you struggle to keep your homes and your very lives, he feasts on the fat of the land, filling his pockets with our beloved country's wealth."

"This is crazy," Noga said.

"Not crazy," Eli said. "Evil. Who's the prophet?"

"Not a prophet," she said. "A politician. Isaac Gurion, head of the Opposition."

"That explains it." Eli glanced around. The mob was growing angrier by the minute. In a different generation, Eli would have marched over to the raised platform. He would have challenged the imposters and rained fire from Heaven. But the Magic had fled, along with the Thin Voice.

He grabbed her hand. "Let's get out of here."

"Why?" Her eyes widened.

He nodded toward Gurion on the stage. "I have experience with false prophets. They never end well."

They pushed through the crowd, cutting a path back toward the pedestrian mall on Ben Yehuda.

Gurion's voice boomed behind them. "At this very moment, the police are questioning *King* Karlin regarding multiple counts of the darkest corruption. We, your faithful servants, will not rest until we have removed the usurper from our midst. Down with King Karlin!"

"Down with the king!" the people chanted, their faces twisted with rage. "Down with the king!"

Noga squeezed his hand. "Wait—did you feel that?"

He had—a tremor along the cobblestones. The mob stamped their feet in time to their chant. Could a thousand feet cause the ground to shudder?

The earth shook again. Voices cried out around them, this time not in anger but surprise. A bulky man in a checkered shirt bumped into Eli. "Sorry!"

Eli turned around. People held onto each other to keep their balance, bracing for another jolt. Fear filled their eyes. On the dais, the kings gripped the table, like a raft in a raging sea, while the false prophet jumped down the stairs and disappeared into the crowd, a rat abandoning ship. But was that ship sinking or merely buffeted by a large swell?

The answer came in the form of an eardrum-tearing *crack*. Before their eyes, the dais shifted to the side, then plummeted like a rollercoaster car, and the entire platform, along with the podium, the table, and the "kings," dropped out of sight.

Women shrieked. People pushed and shoved each other, as the ground split and shattered beneath their feet. The earth parted, the buildings falling away on either side, as jagged fissures raced from Zion Square and snaked up the cobbled streets.

"Get back!"

Eli pulled Noga away from the widening crevasse, pressing into the packed walls of humanity as, around them, people slipped and fell, screaming and flailing, into the chasm. Great chunks of the torn road rose into the air as though God Himself had taken a chainsaw to the planet's crust.

Patches of cobblestone crumbled into the void. Eli cried out as he forced his way forward, away from the fissure, pulling Noga after him. Another crack sounded and Noga cried out. Her hand slipped from his.

He turned, dropped to his knees, and peered over the edge. She hung by her fingertips from a rock ledge a few feet below the surface. "Eli!" The dark chasm yawned beneath her.

"Hold on! I'm here." He pulled at a chunk of sidewalk, testing that it held, then reached down with his other hand. "Take my hand!"

His fingers brushed hers, half an inch from the rock ledge. No, not a rock; rather, a large translucent stone that refracted daylight into his eyes. *What is that?*

"I can't let go," Noga said. "I'll fall!"

"No, you won't. Just reach out with one hand."

Another shudder knocked the fleeing masses to the ground, and Noga shrieked.

Eli reached further, willing his body to stretch, to grab her wrist and pull her to safety. Noga's eyes projected terror and disbelief.

"You can do it."

She reached for him, and he gripped her fingers for all he was worth. He couldn't hold her much longer. "Good. Now grab the next ledge." He eyed another handhold, another shiny outcrop further up. She did it. He heaved upward. Her boot found traction on the wall of the fissure, and she inched toward the surface.

A smile flashed across her face for the first time since the ground had opened. She was going to make it. Soon, they'd roll back onto solid earth.

Then, with another loud *crack*, the ground gave way beneath him, and they fell.

CHAPTER 39

"What's the damage?" Moshe asked the ministers around the conference table. He had called an emergency cabinet meeting in the Government Room as soon as he got back to Knesset.

Sivan glanced at the data sheet she had compiled. "The earthquake hit a magnitude of seven point two on the Richter scale and tore downtown Jerusalem to shreds. Buildings within a ten-kilometer radius show damage. There's concern about aftershocks."

"Casualties?"

"Dozens dead, a hundred missing. But the main danger is the aftermath. Electricity and water services are down across the city. Three gas installations exploded. A dozen roads are unusable. In short, the capital's a mess. And the cellular networks are down—overloaded by people trying to contact their loved ones."

Moshe sank into his chair. With zombies on the march and his coalition in ruins, he faced trumped-up corruption charges, while superpowers flexed their muscles at the borders. As if that wasn't enough, now he had to deal with a major natural disaster—and all in his first month!

"Gurion's going to go to town with this."

Sivan shook her head. "Unlikely. He led an antigovernment protest this morning at Zion Square. Something about replacing you with the Kings of Old. The earthquake hit during the middle of his speech. Eyewitnesses say the ground opened, swallowing the stage and everyone on it. Gurion hasn't been seen since."

Silence reigned in the Government Room.

"Dear Lord." Moshe had aimed to outmaneuver Gurion, his virulent critic and rival, but he'd never intended him any physical harm. The timing of the earthquake was uncanny. To the casual observer, God had taken Moshe's side. Moshe glanced at Rabbi Yosef, who seemed to sink deeper into his chair.

"I wouldn't get complacent," Sivan said. "The Opposition is already spinning this against you."

She pulled out her phone and played a video clip. Rabbi Mendel of Torah True spoke into a Channel Two microphone, the sirens and strobe lights of emergency vehicles in the background. "This is the work of Moshe Karlin," he said, "He's plunged the nation into turmoil to distract our attention from his corruption charges."

"He has got to be kidding!"

Shmuel said, "So much for 'acts of God.'"

"There's been looting too," Sivan continued.

Moshe never understood how people could take advantage of a national tragedy to steal. "The police won't be enough. We'll need to call in the army to protect businesses until we can get a handle on the situation."

"It's not just the businesses that need protection. The rift exposed diamond deposits in the ground."

Had he heard her right? "Diamonds?"

"And other precious stones. People have been hacking away at the disaster site with hammers and picks, and many have fallen into the fissures."

Moshe didn't know what to say. He'd run out of exclamations. The situation became more bizarre and surreal each passing moment. He turned again to Rabbi Yosef—was this another sign of the Messianic Era?—but the rabbi kept his eyes on the table.

"Moshe," Rafi said, snapping him back to practical concerns. "The army is already stretched thin with the Sixth Aliyah. We don't have the manpower for this."

Moshe considered all the pieces on the board. *Why the heck not?* "We don't, but others might. Shmuel, let's meet right after and put things in motion."

Sivan glanced from Moshe to Shmuel, and back. "What's the plan?"

Moshe glanced at the walls. Gurion had learned about the Sixth Aliyah, and the Police Commissioner knew the goings-on at the Prime Minister's Residence. The Knesset Government Room might be no different.

"I'll tell you all soon. Sivan, we need to address the public and calm everyone down. Meanwhile, those not involved with disaster management, push ahead with the new legislation."

He adjourned the meeting, and the ministers rushed to their tasks.

Sivan caught him at the door. "What's with the secrecy?"

He threw another glance at the walls. "You were right about the leak," he whispered. "It's worse than we thought. Gurion's people know everything we say and do. At Knesset and at home."

Sivan's lips parted as the realization hit. "They've bugged us?"

Moshe nodded.

"I'll have the Secret Service do a sweep."

"Our offices too."

"I'm on it."

Moshe met Shmuel in the hallway. "Let's walk and talk. It's time to call in favors."

CHAPTER 40

Monday afternoon, Yosef wandered through Ground Zero in a daze. Large stretches of street and sidewalk had broken away and pointed heavenward. Jets of steam spouted from the immense dark chasm. The air smelled of burnt wood, gas, and rotten eggs. He hazarded a glance over the edge. Precious stones glittered along the walls of the rift. *This can't be.*

As both Vice Prime Minister and Minister of the Interior, he needed to see the situation on the ground in person. Leaving his security detail at the military cordon, he strolled down what remained of the Ben Yehuda pedestrian mall. Buildings on either side leaned away from the fissure like so many towers of Pisa. A steaming hole was all that remained of Zion Square. It was as though he had stepped onto the Hollywood set of a disaster movie.

A man crouched at the precarious edge of the crater. Soldiers walked over and grabbed him by the shoulders. Diamonds, large and encrusted in dirt, trickled from his pockets as they dragged him to safety.

Natural disasters will rend the Holy City asunder, Rabbi Emden had said. *Precious stones will fill the streets.*

Had the Messianic Era truly arrived? Was his life in danger?

But the list was not complete. Elijah had not returned, nor

had the Third Temple of Fire descended from the Heavens. Leviathans did not swarm the oceans. And, as far as he was aware, human life still ended in death.

Did this disaster even qualify? Earthquakes were a natural phenomenon. The timing was remarkable, but Israel did lie along the Dead Sea Transform, a well-known fault system. Tremors shook the Holy Land every couple of decades. The Galilee earthquake of 1837 had almost leveled the cities of Safed and Tiberius. This was just the worst tectonic event in recent history.

A golden crown lay amid the rubble. Yosef picked it up, the thin plastic crown of a child's Purim costume. *The Kings of Old*, Sivan had said.

"Mr. Vice Prime Minister!" said a voice in English. The soldier who approached him had the same southern drawl as Reverend Adams, his uniform the patchy earth colors of digital camouflage. "We've secured the site."

"Excuse me!" said a soldier with a thick Russian accent. He wore a different patchwork uniform and a green beret. "He means that *we* secured the site!"

Moshe had called in both the Americans and the Russians. Both armies had aircraft carriers stationed off Israeli waters and had airlifted the commandos to Jerusalem within an hour.

Now Yosef stood between the fighters of rival superpowers in the heart of a torn and bleeding Jerusalem. Rabbi Emden's voice whispered in his ears again. *The mighty armies of Gog and Magog will amass in Jerusalem.*

"Both of you," Yosef said. "Together!"

The soldiers scowled at each other, then backed down. For the moment, Yosef had averted World War Three. His small country had enough troubles.

Yosef continued his survey. A fleet of ambulances with the Red Star of David insignia carried off the remaining injured, and extraction teams rappelled into the crevasse to search for the missing.

"Rabbi!" A soldier ran over to him. An American. What new disaster had the day brought?

The soldier dropped to his knees at his feet. "This is the End, isn't it?" The soldier grabbed the string tassels that stuck out from Yosef's belt. "Teach me, Rabbi!" Tears flooded his eyes. "Teach us your Torah. Save us!"

Yosef moved his mouth but failed to find the right words in English or any other language. *The nations of the world will grasp the tassels of our clothes in their thirst to learn our Torah.*

While Yosef blinked in amazement, two of the soldier's compatriots walked over, patted the teary soldier on the back, and hauled him away.

Another sign. Another portent. Yosef's fateful death drew one step nearer.

The ground shook again. Yosef crouched down, steadying himself with his hands on the broken cobblestones. Metal groaned as a street lamp collapsed and shattered.

When the tremor subsided Yosef got to his feet. An eerie sound made him turn around. A throaty groan, not quite human. The jungle nightmare whimper of suffering. The noise had emanated from the steaming chasm.

Yosef inched closer to the broken edge. Then a large, grimy hand clamped onto the lip of the crevasse, and Yosef jumped. A second hand joined the first.

A survivor! A survivor with thick, rough fingers. Yosef took another step forward when a large shaggy head poked above the surface. Large unseeing eyes stared right through him and curdled his blood.

Yosef stumbled backward. He had seen no one like him. The survivor's brow ridge protruded over his eyes. He had a broad, projecting nose and a small chin. Was this an earthquake survivor, or something very different?

With a grunt of effort, the man leaped over the edge and stood erect on solid ground. Well, almost erect. Thick swirls of hair coated his body, but not one scrap of clothing.

A second manlike creature climbed out behind him. And a third. Within seconds, two dozen hairy hominids—the females only slightly less hairy—stooped over the trembling rabbi, who had just noticed another key detail. Hairy or not, none of them had navels!

The creatures shook their heads like wet dogs, blinked their eyes, and took in the street scene with visible curiosity.

The leader of the pack considered Yosef, cocked his head to one side, and said, "Ook?"

CHAPTER 41

Isaac Gurion staggered down Shamai Street, his suit trousers torn and flapping at his shins. His ribs hurt, the side of his head was damp and sticky, his ears rang, and dust coated his entire body. He didn't care about any of that, only the anger that raged within. *He tried to kill me. The bastard tried to kill me!*

He pulled his iPhone from his breast pocket of his jacket. The screen was a web of shattered glass. He tossed the lifeless device into the gutter, pushed through the doors of the Dublin Irish Pub, and climbed onto a stool at the bar.

He tossed a crumpled fifty onto the grimy wood.

"Whisky," he said, his voice like a croak.

The bartender delivered a glass tumbler with two fingers of golden liquid. Gurion knocked it back, and the alcohol stung the bite marks on his tongue. The ground still shook beneath his feet, but the liquids in the bottles behind the bar didn't.

"More!"

The bartender complied.

The ringing in his ears subsided to a low hum, and the chatter of a television screen made him turn. A newscaster babbled away, and a photo of Moshe Karlin appeared on the screen.

"In the wake of today's catastrophe and despite recent

corruption charges, Prime Minister Karlin's approval ratings are higher than ever."

"You'll pay for this!" Isaac growled at the screen. The couple at the corner table eyed him. "What are you looking at?" he yelled. They turned away. Bloody cowards.

He dropped another crumpled note on the counter. "Turn that crap off."

Again, the bartender complied.

Gurion sipped his drink and closed his eyes. In his mind's eye, the dais lurched sideways. He dived off the platform, and seconds later, the ground swallowed it up.

Demons, Avi Segal had called them. Unnatural and undead. Hyperbole, Gurion had thought. Election propaganda. Now he understood. Karlin wielded supernatural forces. He raised the dead and conjured earthquakes to smite his rivals. He had no limits and zero inhibitions. How could a mortal man, as powerful or rich as he may be, contend with an enemy like that?

He slurped his drink and savored the pain of his open wounds. He'd find a way. If he had to sell his soul to the Devil, he'd take Karlin down.

"Unfair, isn't it," said a sonorous voice beside him.

On the next stool sat a black trench coat. A bald head rose above the lapels.

"Who the hell are you?"

"Your protest was going so well. Even I wanted to believe in the Kings of Old. You could almost smell the desire and the fear."

Irritation smoldered inside. The stranger knew more than he should, and Gurion did not enjoy being on the uninformed side of a conversation.

"What do you want?"

"To help a friend in need."

The trench coat turned, and Gurion came face-to-face with an immense beak nose and large, sensitive eyes. The man smiled. His poise and measured speech spoke of patient plans and an iron will. A man with no limits and zero inhibitions.

Gurion patted his comb-over, located the greasy strings of hair at his ear, and pasted them into position.

"What do you have in mind?"

"You deserve better, Mr. Gurion. Much better. Pick a card."

A deck of cards fanned out in the man's hands, face down. Gurion had no patience for parlor tricks, but he humored him and selected a card.

"Hello, King of Diamonds," the man said.

Gurion turned the card over. He was right.

His new friend gave him a toothy smile. "One king alone may sit the throne. Don't you agree?"

CHAPTER 42

Eli woke up with a start. Bright light shuttered his eyes. He made to cover his face with his hands, but his arms wouldn't budge. Thick straps held them at the wrists. His ankles too. He tried to sit up, and another hard restraint pressed into his neck. He writhed on the hard, flat surface at his back to the hum of fluorescent lights. The place smelled of formaldehyde. *Where am I?*

He craned his neck to turn his face away from the harsh light. The ceiling sagged and curved inward, the inside of a tent. A metal trolley stood beside the hard metal bed and contained medical implements: scalpels, hypodermic syringes, and sterile cotton swabs.

Then it came to him—the earthquake at Zion Square. Noga reaching for his hand. Him clutching her fingers, heaving upward. They were safe, on solid ground. Then they fell.

A hospital. Of course. A field hospital! That would explain the tent, if not the silence. But what kind of hospital kept patients strapped to metal tables?

The light swung away and a man in a blue surgical mask and cap stood over him. Blue penetrating eyes evaluated him through rimless spectacles.

"Welcome, Mr. Eli Katz." The mask muffled the voice, but Eli still made the connection.

"Dr. Stern?" Eli's muscles relaxed, and he fell limp against the cold metal slab. He was back at the neurology ward of the Shaare Zedek Medical Center. But the hospital had looked very different. "Thank God it's you. Can you help me with the straps? Where are we?"

"Somewhere safe. You were lucky I found you. The hospitals are very crowded."

Eli's muscles tensed again. They were not at the hospital.

"Where's Noga?"

"Don't worry about her. For now, you just need to relax. You'll need your strength."

"Have you seen her? We were together when... when..."

"Hush now." The doctor made no move to undo the straps. Instead, he stabbed a large syringe through the lid of a sealed vial and pulled back on the plunger.

"What is that?"

"This will help you relax."

"I don't want to relax. I have to find Noga." Dr. Stern extracted the syringe, pushed the plunger, and a jet of liquid sprayed into the air. "No, Doctor, please." This wasn't real, this was a nightmare. "Help!" he shouted. "Somebody, help me! Help!"

The doctor maintained an eerie calm. "Save your strength. Nobody can hear you here. And besides, the city is in chaos. You're just one more missing person." He swabbed Eli's shoulder with an alcohol pad.

"You can't do this. Let me go!"

The doctor's cold blue eyes locked on his. "You were right, you know."

The needle pricked Eli's skin. "Ouch! Right about what?"

"When you emerged from your coma at Shaare Zedek, you claimed to be Elijah the Prophet and over three thousand years old. You said you had to fulfill your destiny and anoint the Messiah. I didn't believe you then, but I do now." The doctor lowered the surgical mask and smiled. "But you got one thing wrong."

The doctor's face swam in circles. "Oh, yeah? And what

was that?"

"Your destiny wasn't to anoint the Messiah." His words echoed as the room spun and faded. "Oh no. Your destiny was to meet me."

CHAPTER 43

Ahmed stepped up to the podium, his fingers trembling on his cue cards. Below the stage, three hundred faces stared at him in silence. Cold sweat trickled down his temple. His lips quivered. The audience this morning was much larger than that of the event hall in Bethlehem—and an impressive display of popular support for the Mahdi, considering the havoc of yesterday's earthquake. But the size of the turnout had not caused his nerves.

Black flags lined the expansive courtyard between the faculty buildings of Al-Quds University in East Jerusalem. The flags honored Hamas and Islamic Jihad, and although the terrorist organizations would have applauded Ahmed the suicide bomber, they would not like the words he had decided to say today.

A man cleared his throat. And another. *Why was the Mahdi silent?* From the front row, Hasan gave him a plastic smile, his eyes widening with a silent demand: *Get on with it!* Sitting there among the dignitaries in his fancy clothes, his cousin had forgotten their argument earlier that morning. The sight of him hardened Ahmed's resolve.

He leaned into the microphone. "Yesterday's earthquake was a sign," he said, his voice loud, echoing off the facades of white Jerusalem stone. Not *his* voice; the Mahdi's.

"A sign of a new era ahead," he continued. "A time when we will stop talking about struggle, because victory will already be ours. The End Times."

Heads nodded in the crowd, like so many sheep. They bleated their agreement.

The shepherd is not their friend, Samira had said.

Ahmed turned to the next cue card. The words spoke of God smiting the Jews in downtown Jerusalem. They called for a Final Intifada, in which the entire Arab world would unite to wipe the Jewish Stain from the Middle East.

He looked up, away from the cards, at the blue heavens.

"A time," he continued, in his own words, "of forgiveness and reconciliation. An end to the hatred in our hearts and the lies in our ears."

Murmurs of confusion circulated among the herd, unaccustomed to a message of peace from their leaders.

He skipped to the final card. "Tomorrow," he said, raising his voice to counter the rising hubbub, "meet me at Al Aqsa. Bring your sons and fathers, daughters and mothers. Each has a part to play in the final chapter of our story. Only together, as one, our hearts filled with unwavering belief, will we succeed where others have failed."

He turned from the podium and hurried to the stairs, ready to flee. A tight throng of men blocked his path to the base of the platform. Not masked men in black with knives and Kalashnikovs, but elders with kaffiyehs and ingratiating smiles, each eager to shake hands with the promised Mahdi. He shook their hands. In their eyes, he found not anger but gratitude.

"*Shukran!*" Hassan shouted. Thank you! He pushed between the well-wishers and their Mahdi. "So much to plan! So much to do!" He grabbed Ahmed by the arm and marched him away.

"What the hell do you think you were doing there?" he hissed when they reached the cover of an arched passageway. "Your instructions were very specific. Are you trying to get us both killed?"

Ahmed clenched his jaw. His gamble had worked, and he would not throw away his winnings. "I want to see the Shepherd."

Samira's words had loomed in his mind ever since their short reunion. She was right—he had no idea who was behind Hasan's actions. If Ahmed was being led to another slaughterhouse, he had better find out soon, and the only way to know for sure was to hear it from the Shepherd himself.

Hasan ran his hands through his hair. "I told you, that's impossible."

"Then get ready for more surprises. Next time, at Al Aqsa." Hasan had paraded Ahmed before the world as the Mahdi; he couldn't touch him. And he knew it.

Hasan punched the air and cried out, "Fine! I'll take you to the Shepherd. But from now on you do exactly as I say."

Ahmed tried not to smile like an idiot. For once, he had outsmarted his cousin; he would meet the Great Imam himself.

"Promise me!"

"OK, I promise. I'll do exactly what you say." Once he had met the Shepherd, why shouldn't he?

"Good. You'll see your precious Shepherd. But trust me, you'll regret it."

CHAPTER 44

Irina burst out of her corner office at the Dry Bones Society. With their recent activity in the south, thanks to the Sixth Aliyah, the Jerusalem office had grown quiet. Deceptively quiet. Then, yesterday, all hell had broken loose. She was going out of her mind.

Manic hominids ran around the Call Center, grunting and whooping, while frantic society members tried to catch up.

"Get down from there!" she cried.

One of the new arrivals had climbed out of the third-floor window of the Call Center and strolled along the outer ledge above Jaffa Street.

"Get back in here, right now!"

Like most of the new arrivals, the hairy imbecile could not wrap his head around the idea of clothing, and now he pressed against the window, giving her an uncomfortable close-up of his nether regions. She groaned.

"Do something!" she yelled, her gaze falling on the nearest bystander, Ben, a lean twenty-something and one of the non-resurrected volunteers.

"They don't listen," he said, throwing his hands in the air. "They don't even understand what we're saying."

He was right, of course. The cave dwellers also had no clue about private property or personal hygiene, and the dormitory upstairs smelled like a zoo.

"Where's the professor?" Irina said over the ruckus. "Professor!"

Professor Grommet shuddered at the sound of his name, as he nursed a paper cup of coffee to calm his nerves. The academic had doctorates in linguistics and anthropology and had helped them communicate with resurrected men and women in Assyrian, Babylonian, and even Sumerian.

Irina raced in his direction, dodging a pair of thick-browed children as they played catch with the swivel chairs.

"Help us!"

"It's no use," the professor said. "Their language is too primitive—mere grunts and gestures. We could try sign language."

"Sign language—are you kidding me?"

"Chimps can learn sign language, and these, ah, *members*, are far more advanced. Neanderthals, I assume, or Homo erectus."

Irina didn't know what he was talking about, and she didn't care. She had hundreds of semi-humans in her care, and the kitchen had run out of bananas. And today she'd seen more of their "members" than she could stomach.

She made for the front door. Samira needed backup in the Absorption Center. She had worked overnight to get the generator running, and the water had returned that morning, but the new residents were not making life easy. If she didn't make progress soon, she had half a mind to call pest control.

At the door, she collided with Alex. His eyes wandered to the charging hominids. "Not a good time?"

"Nothing gets past you."

"We need to talk. It can't wait."

In the mad panic at the Society, Irina had forgotten her own personal troubles.

They stepped into the corridor, and she closed the door.

"Will he do it?"

Irina looked over her shoulder by reflex. Her mission to the Prime Minister's Office on behalf of Alex's criminal handlers still made her feel like a traitor. "No. I didn't get to speak with him, and Rabbi Yosef didn't like the idea. I don't think Moshe will either. With all that's going on, he doesn't have time to think about it."

Alex gripped her shoulders. "Then we have to leave. Now!"

"But we're in the middle of a crisis, Alex. When things settle, I'll try him again."

"It doesn't work that way. The people I work for, they don't accept excuses. We must disappear now while the whole country is in chaos. This might be our only chance."

Irina glanced down the corridor. The muffled noise of pandemonium continued unabated behind closed doors.

How could she abandon Samira at a time like this? The Society needed her.

"I saved some money," Alex continued. "We can get new identities. New lives."

A new life. Since Moshe and Rabbi Yosef had discovered her among the gravestones on the Mount of Olives, that was all Irina had ever wanted—a new life with a man she loved.

"Tomorrow?" she said. The word was a plea.

Alex scrunched his lips, and his chest heaved. After a moment that seemed to last an eternity, he nodded. "Tomorrow."

A PREMATURE APOCALYPSE

CHAPTER 45

"Horrendous!" the Texan said. "Preposterous!"

Reverend Henry Adams gripped the armrests of the seat before Yosef's desk with large, manicured hands, his face red.

"Yes, yes," Yosef said, in English. What had so upset his benefactor? "You mean the earthquake?"

"No, no. That was a sign from the Lord Above and a blow to Moshe's detractors."

Yosef swallowed hard. "You mean the... monkey-men?"

The early hominids had amazed Yosef too but not shaken his worldview. *How* God had created humanity didn't really bother the rabbi. But representatives of the earlier stages in human evolution might disturb those who clung to a more literal reading of Genesis.

The reverend's brow wrinkled. "Monkey-men?"

"Never mind. Ah! You mean the accusations against Moshe. Of, eh, corruption?"

"No, of course not! I won't dignify those with any attention."

Yosef scratched his beard. Which of the many recent troubling events had infuriated the reverend so?

"Did you receive our email, Rabbi?"

Yosef nudged his laptop to life. Coordinating emergency activities throughout the country had left him no time to

799

check his Inbox. He turned the screen to allow the reverend a better view. The message from that morning contained a single link, and Yosef clicked it.

YouTube played a news broadcast from Al Jazeera. "High hopes are spreading across the Arab world that the End Time has arrived," said the clean-shaven Arab presenter. "In the wake of a major earthquake that wreaked havoc and destruction on Jerusalem, a Mahdi-claimant has arisen in the Holy City and won hearts and minds across the Muslim world."

The clip cut to a grainy handheld video of a young Arab in a smart suit, white cloak, and headdress, who spoke into a microphone at a podium. He looked vaguely familiar.

"Known only as Ahmed, the former suicide bomber rose from the ashes to lead the faithful to a new era of victory."

The Arab kid from the DBS! *The suicide bomber!* Yosef said nothing. If the boy had aroused Adams's ire, Yosef had better not tell him that the Dry Bones Society had fed and housed the boy on his dollar.

The camera cut to the tree-lined grounds of the Temple Mount. Opposite the towering golden Dome of the Rock, a group of workers in blue overalls shouldered building materials and constructed a raised platform.

The narrator continued. "Preparations are underway for the largest ever gathering at Al Aqsa tomorrow when the Mahdi will deliver his message."

Something in the images caught Yosef's eye, but then the clip ended, and Reverend Adams gave Yosef a stern, expectant look.

"What is this Mahdi?" Yosef asked.

"The Messiah."

"Ha!" So the Muslims believed in a Messiah too. "And this is a problem?"

"Rabbi Yosef." The reverend sounded disappointed. "Our Daddy running late is one thing, but an *Islamic messiah*—unacceptable!"

"I don't understand."

"Nature detests a vacuum; left alone, the empty space fills

with evil." He made a sucking noise to illustrate his point.

"And this messiah has filled the vacuum?"

"Exactly. He will lead people astray in the hope that he's the real messiah. If he's the only contender, that is."

Adams straightened on the chair and cleared his throat. "Now I know what I'm about to say is unexpected. Believe you me, we don't take this lightly. But after long and careful discussion, our board feels that there is no alternative."

Yosef got lost in the long words, and the reverend seemed to notice. "In short," he concluded, "we want Moshe to know that the New Evangelical Church of America stands behind him."

Adams seemed to be waiting for a response.

"And?" Yosef said.

"And we will back Moshe when he claims his rightful title."

The meaning hit Yosef like a raging buffalo. "You want Moshe to say he's the Messiah?"

Dear God, what was wrong with everyone? First Emden, then Irina, and now—of all people—Reverend Adams himself. Did they all want Yosef dead too?

"But he's Jewish!"

Adams winked. "So was Jesus." He became serious again. "I know this may seem surprising and counterintuitive. Believe me, this Resurrection of yours has created enough theological issues for us."

"It has?"

"Of course. If this is the afterlife, this reunion of sinful body and pure soul, then—excuse me for saying so—what a letdown! People have endured all kinds of suffering in the hope of entering the pearly gates of Heaven, only to get thrown back right where they started—in this cesspool of sin and folly! Is this the eternal bliss we yearned for?"

Yosef didn't understand the reverend's poetic language, but he got the gist. Was this the World to Come—Heaven on Earth?

"Never mind the theology," Adams continued. "We'll

work that out later—Moshe will be a son of Jesus, or an incarnation, or what have you. To be clear, he'll have to step down when Christ does appear. But, for now, a Moshe is far preferable than an *Ahmed*."

"But Moshe never claimed that he's the Messiah."

"What's stopping him? The move is bound to win popular support. The people are already screaming it from the rooftops. In his time, we've seen miracles and wonders, and first and foremost is the way he won that election!"

Yosef stared his imminent death in the eyes. If Moshe Karlin was the First Messiah, did that make Yosef the Second?

"Moshe Karlin is the Messiah," Adams said, and he gave the desk an authoritative thump. "Get the word out now, before it's too late. C'mon, Rabbi. What have you got to lose?"

CHAPTER 46

In downtown Jerusalem, Moshe smiled for the cameras, his arms on the shoulders of the Israeli relief workers at his side. He took care not to accept photo ops with the American or Russian soldiers. There was no need to inflame superpower rivalries.

The camera operators gave the thumbs-up and Moshe headed for his cavalcade, flanked by his security detail. The torn streets and lurching apartment buildings smelled of dust and disaster, but, all things considered, the catastrophe could have turned out far worse.

In the back seat of the ministerial SUV, he hit a speed dial button on the phone, and Sivan's face appeared on the display. "What's our status?"

"Power and water are back up, and so are key access roads. The light rail will take longer. Only a handful of citizens are still missing, and we've relocated residents in unsafe buildings to temporary housing."

"How temporary?"

"We'll have to bulldoze much of the city center to rebuild it. The Ministry of Tourism is talking of designating ground zero as a national monument and museum. The projected tourism revenues will more than cover new housing projects. And then there are the diamond and mineral reserves the earthquake uncovered. We've listed a public tender for the mining rights. Those will add tremendous revenues to State coffers."

"Great job."

"And you were right about the bugs. The sweep found monitoring devices in almost every office. The committee rooms too."

Moshe's hunch had paid off. "Gurion's work?"

"Probably, but we don't have a direct link to him yet."

"Pity he's gone. We'd press charges of our own."

A message flashed on the screen.

"About that," Sivan said, but Moshe cut her off.

"The American Ambassador is on the line. Let's catch up in my office." He touched the display, and Ambassador Smith's face filled the screen. His eyes were red and puffy.

"Mr. Ambassador," Moshe said, ready to apply a thick layer of heartfelt appreciation.

"How dare you!" The ambassador's mouth twisted with rage. "After all we've done for you." So much for "Your Excellency."

Moshe threw up his hands. "Hold on a minute. What are you talking about?"

The ambassador didn't seem to hear him. "The Russians—you picked the Russians? You're messing with the wrong administration. We'll bomb you into the stone age before we let the Ruskies get their paws on your undead army!"

"We've done no such thing, Mr. Ambassador! Believe me, you're our closest ally. Always have been."

"Oh, yeah? Then you better clear that up real soon, Mr. Prime Minister. Or else!"

Another message flashed on the screen. The Russian ambassador. *Crap!* He'd done nothing to indicate he'd sided with the Russians, and he'd only told his cabinet of the offers in broad terms. Who in Moshe's camp would have done something so stupid?

"I will," he said, "right away." His stomach juices swirled

as the vehicle took a corner. Another touch of the display and the Russian Ambassador's face filled the screen.

"You little worm!" Gurevitch snarled as he spoke and emitted drops of spittle. "We will squish you underfoot!"

"What? Why?"

"Don't play stupid with me, Mr. Prime Minister. The whole world knows you've handed your technology to the Americans. You take our kindness but spit in our face. You will pay the price."

"Mr. Ambassador, there's been a mistake!"

"You can say that again. See you in hell!"

"But we haven't—!" The call cut out.

What in God's name was going on? How could they both think he'd betrayed them and partnered with the other superpower? A third message flashed on the screen. Sivan was already calling him back.

"Put on Channel Two," she said. "They've been playing it in a loop."

"Get the cabinet together. I'm on my way."

Moshe fumbled with the controls, found Channel Two on the television feed.

Well, what do you know? Isaac Gurion stood at a podium, back from the dead. The slimy politician raged into a microphone. "He tried to kill me in broad daylight. In the process, he destroyed our capital and murdered innocents."

Moshe shivered. Did people believe that?

Gurion spoke with visible glee, a crazed smile on his face.

"But mass murder isn't enough for our dear Prime Minister, oh no," Gurion continued. "Yes, blood couldn't satisfy his lust for power and personal gain. Foreign soldiers fill our streets. He's sold our nation to a superpower. A mass murderer and a traitor! And now his undead soldiers are on the march and will not stop until they have conquered the entire world!"

"Dear Lord." Moshe had preferred Gurion when he was dead. His claims were contradictory and absurd. If Moshe craved power and had a personal zombie army, why would he bow to a superpower? But devastation and loss had racked the nation, and fear and suspicion didn't always respond to reason.

Besides, Gurion's target audience was not the average Joe but the superpowers. Gurion had confirmed their worst suspicions: the undead army was real and Karlin had partnered with their archenemy.

In his bid for power, Gurion had jeopardized the existence of the Jewish State. This wasn't another diplomatic crisis; this was Armageddon.

As they neared the Knesset compound, the cavalcade slowed. Protestors massed in the streets. Not long ago, Moshe had stood outside, chanting slogans at ministerial vehicles. The crowds appeared more menacing from behind the tinted windows.

The placards called to "End the Occupation" and to send the "Traitors to Jail." They were talking about him! A man with wild hair pressed his pudgy face to the glass. "You killed our friends and family!" he said, the window muffling his angry cry. "You'll hang for this!"

Moshe doubted that. Israeli law didn't hold with capital punishment. Besides, he had murdered no one. Gurion and his cronies had chosen the wrong time and place for their libelous campaign. An act of God had struck them down, literally, and the people still blamed Moshe!

The car lurched forward, and the protestor stumbled away. Soon the security gates closed behind them.

Moshe opened the door before the vehicle came to a complete stop, and he ran for the entrance. In a corridor, halfway to the Government Room, Shmuel called to him.

"Moshe, a package arrived for you."

"It'll have to wait. I've called an urgent cabinet meeting."

Shmuel shook his head. "Moshe, you need to see this."

CHAPTER 47

Eli came to, confused and groggy. His tongue lolled in his mouth like a slug and tasted of burned rubber. The tent flaps floated above him. He lay on the same metal table, his limbs restrained by thick straps. How long had he been out cold? He had to get out of there pronto, and not only to find Noga.

Dr. Stern had gone insane. He had kidnapped Eli from Shaare Zedek and tied him to a dissection table. The doctor had rambled on about immortality and destiny. Eli had preferred the skeptical Dr. Stern who had threatened to send him to the Kfar Shaul Mental Health Center. Now the tables had turned. What experiments did the mad neurologist want to run on him? He had better not stick around to find out.

He listened for movement but heard only the beep of a heart monitor. No sign of Dr. Stern or anyone else. He pulled at the restraints. The effort drained his strength, and he stifled his groans.

The Magic. Elijah the Prophet had rained fire from heaven. He had caused drought, created bottomless pitchers of oil and flour, and he had revived the dead. Dealing with a few leather straps should be child's play.

He willed his breathing to calm, his heart rate to slow. Closing his eyes, he found that invisible muscle at the center of his brain.

Flex. Turn the straps to dust. *Flex.* Make them disappear! *Flex!*

He moved his arm, but the bonds held fast. Eli swore under his breath. He wanted to cry out. *There's no magic*, Noga had told him months ago. *No miracles.* She had doubted his claims then. Now she believed him, but it made no difference. He was useless. During the earthquake, he had failed to protect her. She might be dead, and he wouldn't know.

Tears burned his eyes.

No! She had to be OK. There was a chance she had survived, and she might need his help. He wasn't going to give up on her.

He turned his head to the side, blinking back the tears. The metal trolley still stood inches away from the table. If the bed had wheels, he might just be able to reach it.

With every ounce of strength, he rolled to his right, until the leather straps cut into his skin. The table shifted. *Yes!* He relaxed, drew a deep breath, and repeated the action.

The table clicked against the trolley. He stretched his hand through the restraint as far as possible, gripping the edge of the trolley and pulling it flush with the bed. He dug his nails into the gauze sheet beneath the medical instruments, dragging them closer, and his quivering fingers touched the thin, rounded handle of a scalpel.

Shoes clicked on the floor behind him, and he retracted his hand.

He closed his eyes and feigned sleep, but the accelerated beep of the heart monitor betrayed his anxiety.

"Good morning, Mr. Katz."

There was no point in pretending. Eli opened his eyes. "How long have I been under?"

"A day. You should be proud of yourself. We've been very successful."

A horrifying thought made Eli break out in a cold sweat. Had Dr. Stern operated on him while he was unconscious? He didn't feel the pain of stitches or the pull of bandages on his skin. "What did you do to me?"

The doctor walked around the bed and into view. "Don't worry, Mr. Katz. I drew blood, that's all. I'm not a monster."

Right, Eli thought. You just keep your patients tied up against their will in your private laboratory. *Keep him talking. Distract him from the trolley parked alongside the bed.*

"What progress have we made?"

The doctor grinned. "Do you know how long turtles live, Eli?"

The turn of conversation did nothing to calm his concerns, but the doctor had called him by his first name.

"I don't know. Twenty years."

Another parental grin. "Try again."

"Fifty?"

Dr. Stern moved closer and shifted the trolley away to sit on the edge of the bed. The scalpels rolled out of reach.

"The correct answer," Dr. Stern said, "is forever. They never die."

"What do you mean?" Eli would have heard of a thousand-year-old turtle if one had existed.

"They age. But at a certain point that stops. Their metabolism levels off, their cellular activity stabilizes. The phenomenon is called negligible senescence. Most people think that aging is just a fact of life, and the body must inevitably wear down, but turtles prove otherwise. If it wasn't for predators, disease, and road accidents, turtles would truly live forever."

"Oh." Now that sounded familiar.

"Unfortunately, studies of turtles have done nothing for mankind. Their biochemistry is too different. Believe me, I know."

"You have a thing for turtles?"

Dr. Stern didn't rise to the challenge of a witty response. Instead, he sat on the edge of the bed and stared at his hands.

"Five years ago, my granddaughter was born with Hutchinson–Gilford syndrome, a form of progeria. People with the syndrome age at ten times the usual rate. They don't live past their thirteenth birthday. That's how my interest in turtles began."

The doctor seemed to age right before Eli's eyes, and he felt a pinch of empathy for the man, despite his own current predicament.

Dr. Stern removed his glasses and wiped them with a lint cloth. "Genetics wasn't my specialty. I had much to learn, and I spent a lot of money to set up this lab. But I was getting nowhere. The gap between turtles and humans was unbridgeable. And then you came along."

"Me?"

"Scientific research tends to focus on the norm and to ignore outliers. But the outliers teach us the most. Your recovery from that accident—I'd seen nothing like it. Your cells regenerated beyond the ability of normal human cells, and they did not appear to age. You were an outlier. At last, I'd found my human turtle. The applications were endless: healing progeria; treating cancer; regenerating severed limbs; and the holy grail of human ambition, immortality."

Dr. Stern replaced his glasses. "And that's why you should feel proud. Yesterday, I hit a brick wall. No matter how I analyzed your DNA, the algorithms found nothing unusual. Just another male human genome. But then I turned my investigation to epigenetics and the non-coding RNA sequences that determine which genes to activate and which to suppress. Now there was something very interesting! The secret to immortality had been sitting there for millennia, locked away in our dormant DNA; and now we have found the key to open it."

"Then let me go," Eli said. "You've got my blood, my DNA, and RNA. You don't need me anymore."

"It's not that simple. The theory needs testing, and I might need you on hand for some time. You slipped away before; I won't make that mistake again."

Eli wanted to shout and hurl threats, but he kept his mouth shut. The doctor would only sedate him again.

Dr. Stern stood. "I'm sorry," he said. "But it's for the greater good." He patted Eli on the shoulder and left the tent.

Eli lay there in silence and focused on his breathing. When he had counted to fifty, he lifted his right hand from over the scalpel he had snatched from the trolley. *Sorry, Dr. Stern, but Noga needs me. The greater good will have to wait.*

CHAPTER 48

"Sir, we're being followed."

The captain of the USS Ohio swiveled on his bucket seat in the dim red light of the control room. When you were a nuclear-powered submarine on a stealth mission in foreign waters, a tail was not good news. They sped through the Mediterranean toward the coast of Tel Aviv, all fourteen thermonuclear warheads ready for launch. He could slice the tension in the air with a Ka-Bar knife.

"Followed by what?"

The junior officer at the sonar station squinted at the display. Johnson was a NUB, or newbie, with a shaved head and an eager expression, but he'd performed well so far.

"I don't know, sir," he said. "The sound signature is not in the system. Whatever it is, it's big."

"A boomer?"

The nuclear subs of other nations snooped around the oceans too. Friendlies operated at pre-allocated depths to avoid collisions. Non-friendlies were the problem. Something was cooking in the hallways of power, but Command had sent no warnings of potential underwater confrontations.

"Too big, sir."

"Whales?" They'd sighted a sperm whale off Malta last week.

"Negative. The target is way bigger than us."

The captain swore and ran a hand through his hair. A foreign sub would have lurked in the baffles, the sonar blind spot directly behind them. Unless they hadn't noticed the USS Ohio yet. That would explain why they were making enough noise to register on the passive sonar.

"Drop another hundred feet," he told the navigation officer. Then he grabbed the 1MC handset and pressed the broadcast button. The crew fell silent for the duration of the message. "Rig for ultra-quiet," he said, his voice echoing among the chambers of the pressurized tube. "All non-essential personnel, move to your racks at once."

He lurched forward as the accelerator disengaged and the sub lost speed.

"Toby," he said to his executive officer and second in command. "Make sure they shut off the water heater and reactor cooling pumps."

Toby nodded and hurried off, his boots clanking on the steel floor.

The captain held his breath while they floated one thousand feet below the surface. Over his ten years in the Silent Service, he'd seen a lot of crazy stuff, but a vessel that large appearing out of nowhere was a first. If they lay still, the threat might pass them by unnoticed.

"Still there?"

"Yes, sir," Johnson said.

The unidentified submergible had not spotted them. Otherwise, it would have slipped behind them and disappeared, or clamped down in full stealth mode, as they had. Unless... unless the craft didn't consider them to be a threat.

Terror gripped his heart as he remembered a science fiction film he had seen as a teenager. An alien spacecraft parked at the bottom of an oceanic abyss had gobbled human subs and drilling platforms. Was an extraterrestrial vessel, with technology and firepower far superior to their own, hunting them?

"Sir, they're closing in on us. Fast."

Crap!

"Battle Stations Torpedo!" the captain cried. "Ahead Flank Cavitate!"

The order meant "get the hell out of here and make a splash if you have to!"

The crew sprang into action, pushing buttons and pulling levers. Their sub's forward acceleration pressed the captain against the hard back of the seat. The XO returned to the control room, holding onto shelves and piping to keep his balance.

The sub could reach twenty knots, twenty-five at full throttle and in perfect conditions. That might be enough to outrun the foreign craft, but not its torpedoes.

"Any fish in the water?" Torpedoes, he meant.

"Negative, but they've picked up speed. They're gaining on us!"

If the foreign craft's goal was to freak them out, it had succeeded.

"Join the Navy," they had said. "Subs haven't seen combat since the Second World War, and nuclear warfare isn't a real threat." He should have gone for a desk job on solid ground.

"Any change?"

"They're almost on us, sir. No sign of slowing."

"Dear God!" They would ram them—a suicide mission one thousand feet beneath the deep. But no government had such a large submergible, never mind terrorist organizations.

The captain squeezed the 1MC handset. "Inbound! Brace for impact!" He had drilled the emergency procedures for many unlikely scenarios but never a high-speed intentional collision. He dropped to the floor and wrapped his arms around his seat.

Three tense seconds passed.

"Johnson?"

Johnson shook his head, failing to believe his eyes. "She's on top of us, sir. Now to starboard. Wait, no. Port. It's as if she's... swallowed us."

The captain shuddered. Heads turned to him, eyes wide.

"Outside pressure?"

Another engineer said, "Unchanged sir. We're still one thousand feet."

"She hasn't swallowed us," the captain said. "She's swimming circles around us." Time to test his theory. "Slow us down, nice and easy."

The hum of the engines fell.

"Johnson?"

"No change, sir."

Whatever was toying with them had perfect maneuverability in the ocean.

"Turn on the sonar speaker."

Johnson flipped a switch.

Two seconds passed in silence. Then a loud baritone gurgle made him jump. Biologics, for sure, but this wasn't the chatter of dolphins or the drone of whale-song. The sound was unlike anything he had heard before.

"Let's breach, nice and slow."

Metal groaned from the ballast tanks as air rushed in and expelled seawater.

The ascent took three long minutes.

"We've breached, sir."

The captain could tell. The vessel's rounded hull, optimized for underwater performance, pitched from side to side, the sickening rolls they experienced during surface transits.

"XO," he said. "You have the Deck and Conn."

"Sir!"

"Open the hatch."

Without explaining, he made for the stairwell. He had to see this with his own two eyes.

The wheel turned and the hatch lifted outward on its hinges. A few rungs further and he stepped into the blue sky. A crisp sea breeze ruffled his hair. The deep blue of the Mediterranean lapped at the immense, sleek bulk of the sub, and stretched to every horizon.

He twisted around at the waist. Behind him, the black sail of the sub towered above, a crown of sensory masts jutting into the sky.

They were alone. No sign of their mysterious escort. Had she shied away from the surface, preferring the cool, dark depths?

The captain was about to return to Command and Control when the waterfall sound of crashing water sounded behind him—the unmistakable roar of a breaching sub.

He turned slowly. A large black mass rose above the waves. The smooth slippery mountain rose and rose, its shadow eclipsing the sub.

That was no sub.

Barnacles speckled the slick blubbery hide. But this was no whale either. A flipper breached the water, like the wing of a Boeing 747. He followed the line of the elongated neck, which stretched on and on, passing over the tall sail of the sub and falling toward him.

The captain twisted around and came face-to-face with the creature. The head, tiny in proportion to its body, was taller than the captain. A wet warmth spread through his trunks and trickled down his leg. His muscles turned to stone.

Large reptilian eyes considered him with interest and blinked. Then the scaly lips parted, revealing rows of long, sharp teeth, and the sea monster smiled.

CHAPTER 49

"Don't go!" Galit ran after her father as he dragged his suitcase out the door of the Prime Minister's Residence. "Please, *Aba.*"

Her family's arrival had overwhelmed her and heightened the tensions between her and Moshe, but the sight of her father storming out of her home clawed at her conscience.

"No jobs," he said. "No cigars. Searching through our stuff like we're common thieves!"

"But Aba, I told you. They were searching for bugs."

"Bugs, shmugs! We can tell when we're not wanted."

Galit's mother rolled her eyes at his histrionics but followed him.

"Mom, do something!"

"It's no use, dear. I'll call you when we land. Good thing we didn't sell the house."

Outside, her father handed the suitcase to a Secret Service agent, who hefted it into the trunk of a ministerial SUV. Her brother, sister-in-law, and their kids waited in the ample back seat of another SUV.

"Bye-bye, Granny and Grandpa!" Talya said.

Galit's mom leaned down to kiss her granddaughter. Her dad mussed Talya's head of dark curls.

Then he cursed. "Look at that crowd."

Galit did. Outside the gates, a throng of protesters blocked the street. When they caught sight of her, they hurled abuse.

"Murderers!" said one, an old lady in a green shawl.

"Traitors!" cried another.

"Run along inside," Galit told Talya.

The country had gone crazy. On Channel Two, citizens fought in the streets and peaceful rallies turned bloody as the cameras rolled. Now the barbarians were at the gates.

Galit stepped up to the open window of the SUV. "Are you sure it's safe to leave?" Did the storm clouds of anarchy have a silver lining?

"We'll sure as hell drive out of here!"

The car doors slammed, windows closed, and the SUVs advanced toward the gate. Galit didn't watch them go; her presence would only agitate the angry mob.

Back indoors, she threw herself onto the living room couch and burst into tears. A month after becoming the First Lady, her life had fallen apart. The entire country had followed suit. Earthquakes. Riots. Police interrogations.

A lifetime ago, when Moshe had told her about Gurion's proposal, she had known that politics would shove them into the public spotlight, but she hadn't expected the attention to be so cruel or unbearable. She missed the old days. Moshe and her against the world. Now they seemed separated by a chasm wider than that caused by the earthquake.

There came a loud knocking on the door. Galit wiped her tears and rose to answer.

Her father marched inside when she opened the door, his head cowed, but still seething.

"We're back!" her mother said, singing the words. Her brother and his family followed her in.

"Couldn't get out?"

"Your security people know how to handle them. But our flight was canceled."

"When's the next one?" Flights to the US left Israel many times a day.

"All flights to the United States have been canceled until

further notice. An executive order from the President himself."

"Your husband," her father growled, pacing the entrance hall, his hands balled in his pockets, "has wrecked our relations with our main ally. If only he'd listened to my advice. To any advice!"

Her mother shook her head and walked off to the guest rooms. "Time to unpack," she said. "Again. Have those lovely Secret Service men bring the bags up."

Galit blinked. Her conscience quieted. Beware what you wish for. Now she had to put up with her family—indefinitely!

More knocking at the door. This time, two uniformed police officers stood in the doorway, a string bean and a sweet potato, both with serious looks.

"Let me guess. More questioning?"

"Yes, ma'am," said String Bean.

"Moshe's still at the office. The Prime Minister has things to do besides talking with you."

The officers exchanged a look. "We're not here for the Prime Minister," String Bean said. "We've come for you."

CHAPTER 50

Tuesday afternoon, the cabinet members stared at the object on the conference room table—a large golden envelope with Moshe Karlin's name embossed in the center.

"When did it arrive?" Moshe asked.

"This morning," Ettie said. She had transported the letter to Knesset from the Prime Minister's Office building. Her manner had soured since the earthquake. Did his secretary believe the corruption charges or did she also hold him responsible for the earthquake?

"Security checked it?"

She gave him a look of reproach over her half-moon spectacles. "Of course. They said it's clean. No traces of anthrax. Or fingerprints. What's surprising is how it got here with no one noticing. Besides for the contents, of course."

Moshe picked up the envelope. Everybody else seemed to know what lay within and it was time he caught up.

"Thank you, Ettie."

Taking the hint, she left the room and closed the door behind her.

The card within, like the envelope, was gold. The thick paper had a satin sheen. He read the message aloud: "The Messiah Coronation. Wednesday, 12 PM. The Sultan's Pool, Jerusalem. Dress: Formal."

Moshe glanced about for the hidden camera. "Is this a prank?"

Shmuel said, "Someone went to a lot of trouble to pull it off."

Sivan said, "And somebody seems to think you're the Messiah."

"The mob outside would disagree. According to them, I'm a murderer and a traitor. Besides, the invitation doesn't say *I'm* the Messiah of this coronation."

"It could be a good PR move," she said.

"What could?"

"Crowning you as the Messiah. Things have gotten pretty weird lately: the Sixth Aliyah; earthquakes. People could use the crutch."

"Yeah, but what happens when they find out I'm not the Messiah?" The room fell silent. "Come on, you don't really think...?" He turned to Rabbi Yosef—he'd set them straight—but the rabbi wasn't there. "Where's Rabbi Yosef?"

"With Reverend Adams," Sivan said. "Last I heard."

"Ah." He'd have to argue this one alone. "I think I'd know if I was the Messiah. And I hope he'd do a better job. Who's behind this 'Messiah Coronation' anyway?"

"Nobody seems to know," Shmuel said. "A stage is under construction at the Sultan's Pool. The sign outside mentions the Jerusalem Cinematheque, but their office knew nothing about it."

Moshe pushed the letter aside.

"This is another of Gurion's diversions. We have bigger problems to deal with." He waved at the seats, collapsed onto a chair, and surveyed the ministers who had made it to the meeting. Once again, Rafi was missing. He sincerely hoped that this time he'd return bearing good tidings. "Sivan, can we speak freely?"

She nodded. "This room is clean of bugs."

"Bugs?" Shmuel said.

Moshe spelled it out. "Gurion's been eavesdropping on our every word since day one, and he's used that information well. On my way here, the ambassadors of both the US and Russia called. Each is convinced that we've made a secret pact with the other and that we're going to use our new weapon of mass destruction, the Zombie Army."

Savta Sarah said, "What Zombie Army? Those new arrivals can barely tie their own shoelaces."

"You're right, but the ambassadors won't listen. Gurion's got them both threatening war. We need to calm things down before matters really get out of hand. Sivan, we need to make another announcement. Shmuel, get both Presidents on the line. Not at the same time," he added.

On cue, the door opened and Rafi entered, breathless. "We have an emergency," he said.

"Take a number and get in line."

"This can't wait. We've sighted nuclear submarines off the Tel Aviv coast."

"US or Russian?"

"US. The Russian subs have entered the Gulf of Aqaba, on course for Eilat. They're all carrying multiple thermonuclear warheads. The aircraft carriers have ordered their troops to return."

Sivan said, "If they've made them visible, it's a warning."

"More than a warning," Rafi said. "Both sides are using their influence to isolate us. Foreign airlines have withdrawn from Israeli airspace. Other countries have canceled incoming El Al flights and grounded Israeli planes in their territory. They're preparing for war."

"Shmuel," Moshe said.

"I'm right on it." Shmuel left the room at a trot.

"OK, what's next? Rafi, when can we replace the foreign troops with our soldiers?"

"Right away. The Sixth Aliyah is slowing. If the Dry Bones Society and social services take over the relief efforts, we can redeploy the reserve units to the city."

"Excellent." The situation had seemed so fragile, but one by one, their problems had solutions. Divide and conquer.

Glass shattered behind him and he cringed. Alon, the ever-present head of Moshe's security detail, drew his handgun and moved to the edge of the window. Then he spoke into his sleeve. "Four agents to the gardens."

A rock wobbled onto the carpet at Moshe's feet on a bed of glass shards.

On the other side of the smashed window, two men hiked across the lawns, pickets waving in their hands. At the perimeter fence of the Knesset compound, demonstrators gripped the steel posts and pulled their bodies upward. Like their stone-throwing comrades, they were not content to exercise their freedom of speech.

Within seconds, four agents in black suits waded through the flower beds toward the intruders. When their quarry turned to flee they fired shots in the air. Ten seconds later, two ruffians lay face-down in the manure, hands cuffed, as they awaited justice.

"That's not a demonstration," Sivan said. "That's a lynch mob."

Her phone rang, and she answered. "What?" she said, clearly surprised at the news. She ended the call. "It's Galit," she said.

Moshe envisioned a similar mob outside the Prime Minister's Residence, and his pulse quickened. "Is she OK?" He should have returned her missed calls.

"The police have taken her in for questioning."

"On what charges?"

"They haven't said yet."

"Gurion, that bastard. Now he's coming after my family too?"

"And pushing the entire country toward nuclear war," Sivan reminded him.

Earthquakes. Civil unrest. Nuclear war. And now Galit in police custody. Not since his abduction by Mandrake's goons had Moshe felt so vulnerable. If only he *could* conjure natural disasters and take out his enemies. Gurion more than deserved it.

"He's gone too far," Moshe said. "This has to stop."

"He's hitting us from every side," Sivan said. "But we're stronger. We'll get through it."

"I hope so."

The door opened, and Shmuel rushed back in. *That was quick.* The Foreign Minister did not look happy. "We have a problem," he said.

"We know. Many."

"No. A new problem."

Moshe threw up his hands. "Bring it on. Things can't get any worse."

Shmuel's jaw wobbled. "Actually, they can. Much worse."

CHAPTER 51

Eli sawed at the strap on his right arm, trying to make as little noise as possible. If Dr. Stern walked in now, his escape gambit would fail.

His wrist ached from the awkward movement, and his neck hurt from lifting his head from the metal cot and straining to see what he was doing. Gripping the scalpel backward between his fingers, he jerked his hand inward, slicing the hardened leather strap with the surgical blade.

As the knife ate away at his restraints, he slowed his pace. The scalpel blade hovered an inch above the tender skin of his inner forearm. If he wasn't careful, he'd cut right through the strap and slit his wrist.

As he worked, the doctor's words bounced around his brain. Over three millennia, Eli had survived numerous life-threatening injuries. His longevity had been a miracle, the hallmark of his special Divine Intervention, and a necessary tool for his eschatological mission. But if Dr. Stern was right, God had not guided Eli's every step; he had merely tinkered with his DNA.

No longer was the Almighty a fairy godmother who popped out from behind the curtain of existence to save the day. He was a grandmaster who set plans in motion billions of years before the game began and watched from afar as the moves played out. Having discovered the natural mechanism behind his longevity, Eli felt less indestructible.

The scalpel blade lurched toward his wrist as the strap gave way, missing his skin by millimeters. *Phew!* He stretched his free arm, and then ran his fingers over the strap at his neck, searching for the buckle.

"The holy grail of human ambition," Dr. Stern had said. "Immortality." The words recalled other, much older declarations. "He will swallow Death forever," Isaiah had prophesied of the End Times. "The Lord will wipe the tears from every face."

Was the doctor right—was this his true calling, to safeguard the genetic key to immortality until the Messianic Era?

And what of the Thin Voice—did those Divine Whisperings have a mundane explanation as well? Was he both remarkable and delusional? The Thin Voice had led him to the Mount of Olives and to Moshe Karlin. Was Moshe truly the Messiah or was their abortive meeting the random side effect of a runaway imagination?

He unbuckled the second strap. Eli sat up, reached over, and made short work of the remaining restraints.

Right now, he had only one mission—to find Noga. She needed his help. And if anything had happened to her... *No! Don't even think it.*

He turned off the ECG and ripped the electrode stickers from his chest. Shifting his legs over the edge of the bed, he eased his bare feet onto the cold cement floor. His legs supported his weight. This time he had broken no bones. The thin hospital gown flapped at his thighs. He needed clothes. The tent had no storage cabinets. Where had Dr. Stern stashed his things?

After taking a step forward, something pulled at his groin, holding him back. A catheter tube. *Oh, gross.* He detached the drainage pouch, and the loose tube dangled to his feet. *Freedom first; catheter later.*

He limped to the doorway of the tent, a set of overlapping flaps, parted them slowly, and stepped through. He found himself in another tent, another makeshift hospital room. A heart monitor beeped on a stand, and a respirator wheezed.

A sudden premonition tied his insides in a knot. He tip-toed toward the cot and the still form of the woman beneath the sheets. An oxygen mask covered her mouth and nose. As he drew closer, the knot in his gut tightened. *Oh, no!*

He touched her arm. "Noga, wake up!"

She didn't open her eyes; didn't move at all.

"Noga, we have to get out of here."

"I would advise against that," said a voice behind him.

Dr. Stern stood at the tent flap, his hands in the pockets of his lab coat.

"What have you done to her?"

"Saved her life. For now." His words were not a threat, only a sad diagnosis.

"What's wrong with her?"

The doctor stepped up to the gurney and gazed at Noga. "She was comatose when she arrived at Shaare Zedek. That level of brain trauma is irreparable."

Brain trauma. Irreparable. No! It couldn't be.

"Usually," Dr. Stern continued, "I'd advise the next of kin to pull the plug." He looked Eli squarely in the eyes. "You're her only hope."

CHAPTER 52

In the passenger seat of Hasan's yellow Mercedes, Ahmed's heart bounded like a terrified rabbit. The sports car zoomed along the dirt roads of Samaria north of Jerusalem, kicking up dust and cutting corners, as Hasan blared the horn at donkeys and their drivers. Hasan's reckless driving was not the only cause for Ahmed's adrenaline rush.

Little old Ahmed was going to meet the Shepherd—the Great Imam himself! No, not Ahmed; the Mahdi. Only a select few in a generation merited this honor. Ahmed had chosen the finest suit from the closet in his room and now racked his brain for clever questions. The Mahdi should prove himself worthy.

Hasan leaned his arm on the door and said nothing, a scowl on his face. The meeting must have cost him a lot of favors. At first, Ahmed had doubted whether his cousin had access to the Leader of the Generation, or whether the Shepherd even existed. The Great Imam had avoided the public eye for years and lived in great secrecy and austerity.

His money was real enough. Ahmed had grown used to his new life: the hot showers and clean clothes; the soft bed and fresh linen; the fridge and cupboards full of every imaginable delight.

But those material benefits had not impressed Samira. She

would not approve of the harem of beautiful young women that had served him so eagerly that first night either. Ahmed blushed at the memory. He'd better keep those details to himself.

Hasan turned right at a signpost pointing to Ramallah, his hometown.

Ahmed returned to the question of what to say. He'd start off with lavish thanks. Ahmed was not worthy of the title and mission that the Great Imam had bestowed upon him. He'd beg forgiveness for his ignorance, but inquire about the end goal of his mission, and ask the Shepherd's advice on how best to fulfill that destiny.

Ramallah panned by in the passenger window. Ahmed had never ventured into the city, notorious for its seething refugee camps and terrorist training grounds. The houses and apart-ment buildings on the outskirts had resembled the dilapidated housing of Silwan.

The inner belly, however, painted a different picture of life in the West Bank. Luxury hotels and technology centers stood tall with fresh marble and rounded edges that gleamed with tinted windows. Modern mansions stood in spotless Jerusalem stone, with paved driveways, manicured gardens, and fountains—the opulence reserved for the well-connected.

Some of the flock had grown filthy rich while others blew themselves up. *Why do we raise our little boys and girls to love death?* He didn't have the guts to ask the Great Imam that. Maybe one day he'd find the answer, after Al Aqsa, when his fame had spread throughout the land—throughout the world! Then, even Samira would kiss his feet.

The car pulled up beside a vacant lot beyond the luxury suburbs.

Hasan got out, leaned against the car, and lit a cigarette. Ahmed climbed out of the passenger seat and brushed off his suit.

"Is this the meeting point?"

Had the Imam's security guards selected a random spot for their face-to-face, to avoid capture?

"Go on, say hello." Hasan waved his hand at the empty lot. "Greet your Shepherd."

Ahmed scanned the vacant lot but found no Imams or security personnel, only a dented, burned out metal barrel. "I don't understand."

Hasan swaggered over to him and pointed at the battered bin. "There he is. Speak your mind. Talk all you like."

Was his cousin making fun of him? "The Shepherd is an old barrel?"

"You wanted the truth. Here's the truth—nobody's seen the Shepherd in years."

That made no sense. "The money," Ahmed said. "The speech. How do you know what he wants?"

"He drops off his instructions in that bin. Every week, every month. Whenever the Shepherd feels like it. The money too." Hasan dropped the cigarette in the dirt and ground the stub under his shoe. "This stays between me and you, OK? You can't tell anyone about this place. Understand?"

"No!" Hot anger boiled in his chest. Hasan was lying to him. Again. "You said I'd meet the Shepherd and ask all my questions."

"Go ahead. He's listening. Just don't expect any answers." He chuckled.

"This isn't funny, Hasan. You're calling meetings, telling people I'm the Mahdi when you've never even seen the Shepherd, never heard his voice."

"Keep your voice down, cousin. That's the way things are here. The leaders keep their heads down or they lose them. They still call the shots and pay the bills."

"Oh, yeah? And what does he say right now?"

Hasan rolled his shoulders. "Why don't we find out?"

He strutted to the bin, lifted the jagged metal lid, and reached his arm inside. When he withdrew his arm, he held a dusty burlap sack. He opened the mouth and peered inside.

Ahmed walked over. This was another trick. Hasan would whip out a dead rat and laugh when Ahmed jumped. But there was no rat, no trick.

"Here," Hasan said, his face blank and glistening with sweat. From the sack, he extracted a large golden envelope. "It's addressed to you."

CHAPTER 53

Boris strutted into the Magitek offices Tuesday afternoon, feeling on top of the world. The secretary at the white front desk looked up and popped her bubble of gum.

"Afternoon, Anna."

He had always sensed that the buxom Russian gave him *that* look. Others might have interpreted her deadpan as boredom, but Boris knew better. She was warming to him, and as he climbed the rungs of the Organization, she was turning red hot.

"He's waiting for you."

Boris nodded and continued his swagger down the corridor, through the busy cubicles of the Call Center. Not long ago, the thought of a face-to-face with the Boss had made him tremble. The revenues of his branch of the Organization had dipped, thanks to the nosy intervention of Moshe Karlin, his former slave, and Mandrake had called in a third party to get close to Karlin. Boris had feared that the Boss would terminate him.

Since then, Boris's luck had improved. He had redeemed his career—and extended his life expectancy—by running a special operation to infiltrate Israeli politics. The mission had culminated with the capture and subjugation of Moshe Karlin himself, bringing their interactions full circle and with a sweet dose of poetic justice.

Now Mandrake had entrusted him with a new task, one that would drive the final nail into Karlin's coffin. The preparations were right on schedule. Unlike that earlier meeting with the Boss, this time Boris did not fear losing his head.

He looked up at the camera at the end of the corridor, and the white door clicked open. Once inside the antechamber, he walked up to the mirror at the far wall, and a panel shifted sideways. Boris walked through the dimly lit control room, ignoring the technicians at their data terminals, and knocked on the door of Mandrake's office.

The door clicked open.

Mandrake waited for him on the low backless couch in the center of the chamber, draped in purple ambient light. He looked up from the laptop on the coffee table.

"Enter, my friend. Have a seat."

Boris obeyed. He settled on the couch beside his boss, close but not too close. He glimpsed a large letter A on the screen before Mandrake shut the laptop.

The gesture upset Boris's confidence. Mandrake didn't trust him. Had Boris misunderstood the purpose of the meeting? Instead of a pat on the back, had his boss summoned him to deliver something far less pleasant? With Mandrake, he never knew what to expect.

"Are we ready for tomorrow?"

"Yes, sir. We're all set."

"I'm pulling you off the project."

Boris's heart dropped into his trousers. He had been looking forward to watching Karlin meet his end. Had Boris messed up? Had someone libeled him to his boss behind his back? Or perhaps he'd done nothing wrong, but Mandrake would kill him to keep the secret safe. These might be his final moments; he'd better use them well.

"The stage is set," he said, in his defense. "All the pieces are in place. As you instructed."

"I know, my friend. But I have another task for you." He considered Boris, his large intelligent eyes bridged by a beak nose, like a raptor considering its next meal. "Do you believe in the Devil?"

Boris swallowed. These questions were better left unanswered. His boss had a thing for stage magic and the theatrical, but the sudden turn to the supernatural worried him? Had Mandrake lost his mind?

"Should I?"

"Of course not. But it is a useful idea. As the story goes, the Devil was once God's favorite angel. Until he rebelled. But even then, I suppose, God couldn't bear to destroy him." Mandrake fixed him with those large, intelligent eyes. "There's a devil in our midst, Boris, a traitor who requires elimination. It's very sad, really. A dear, old friend. I don't have the heart to do it myself."

Boris highly doubted that. Beneath the amicable facade, cold blood ran through veins of steel. Had Mandrake just compared himself to God? *Whatever.* Boris knew what was expected of him.

"Let me do it for you."

Mandrake gave him a warm, appreciative smile. "I'll tell you the story in full, my friend. I think you'll enjoy this task. It involves an old friend of yours too."

Mandrake slid two photographs on the table toward Boris. He didn't recognize the first photo. The devil, he assumed. The second, he recognized only too well.

Well, well, well. Full circle, indeed.

CHAPTER 54

Yosef pored over the holy books on his desk in the Vice Prime Minister's Office, Reverend Adams's words ringing in his ears. *Moshe Karlin is the Messiah.*

But how could Yosef know for sure? He needed more information. In the past, he had turned to Rabbi Emden and the Great Council. Who was left to guide him now?

The task was impossible. There were too many variables, too many contradictory traditions. This wasn't even his job. Elijah the Prophet should make these decisions. But where was he?

He must not get this wrong. The stakes were too high: the world's Redemption; and Yosef's life.

If he was going to make any progress, he had to reexamine his assumptions, and not just about the Messiah.

"Is this the eternal bliss we've been hoping for?" Adams had said. Yosef felt the stab of disappointment too.

For centuries, the dispute had raged among the sages. Did the Future Reward require the reunion of body and soul in This World, or did that eternal bliss belong to the World of Souls alone?

When Moshe had awoken in his second life, he had remembered nothing of the World of Souls. What was the soul, anyway? Did the soul even exist? If the body was all we

835

had—all we were—then what of eternal reward? The axioms of life, the very ground beneath his feet, wavered over a dark abyss.

He closed the heavy tomes of Talmud.

Body and soul. God and Satan. Dualism appeared in many guises. But there was only one God. No devil encroached on His dominion. Was the body-soul divide an illusion? The six hundred thirteen commandments sanctified life in this world. But if we have no incorporeal existence, then the Resurrection made sense. Without the Resurrection, there could be no afterlife. The World to Come was the here and now, just later.

Yosef's phone vibrated. The text message from an unknown number contained a single word: BOOM.

Yosef's guts clenched. He made an educated guess as to the identity of the sender. How had he obtained Yosef's personal mobile number? The same way he had sneaked into his office under false pretenses. Had the sender graduated from persuasion to bomb threats?

A sudden apprehension made Yosef nudge his laptop from slumber.

The YouTube clip from the reverend's email still displayed on the screen. Yosef clicked play and skipped to the end. A jarring detail in the video had gnawed on the edges of his consciousness, but he couldn't put a finger on it. On the Temple Mount, men in blue overalls constructed a dais opposite the golden Dome of the Rock ahead of tomorrow's mass gathering.

Yosef played the section again. One worker had caught his eye. The man kept his head low as he carried a package on his shoulder. The shot was distant and pixelated, but Yosef knew the red beard and sparkling eyes beneath the flat cap.

Oh, no. Yosef guessed what he was up to and had to stop him.

Yosef grabbed his desk phone.

"Ram, get the Police Commissioner on the line. It's urgent!"

CHAPTER 55

Avi heard the voice of a ghost when he stumbled into the offices of Upward on Keren Hayesod Street. The ghost was cackling.

Avi halted, then winced as his arm in the plaster cast swung forward. The last time he had met a ghost, Moshe Karlin had returned from the dead and wrecked his life. Was this happening all over again?

He peered around the corner and blinked his eyes. *This cannot be!* He had seen Gurion on the platform, giving forth at the microphone, when the ground had collapsed.

Avi had danced sideways, as cracks tore through Zion Square, and he fled for his life. Looking over his shoulder, he saw the entire platform disappear into a gaping hole as if swallowed by Godzilla.

Then the earth flipped Avi like a burger, his arm slamming into an iron street pole. He had known pain before, but never like this. Bright lights sparked before his eyes as the mob surged ahead, tripping over his legs and trampling his injured arm until the world faded to white.

He awoke in Shaare Zedek hospital, a fresh cast on his arm. After an overnight stay for observation, the nurses released him. Only when he'd left did he realize his luck. The hospital had generators and water reserves. Outside, the situation was bleak.

He called his parents—the screen protector of his phone had shattered in his back pocket—and walked to their apartment in Wolfson Center. They'd never been so happy to see him. Gurion's stage had descended into the belly of the earth, and they had assumed that Avi had followed close behind.

He lay on the couch, munched his mother's honey cakes, and sipped sweet tea boiled over a gas burner. With Gurion gone, Upward would disintegrate, and when his term in Knesset ended Avi would need a new job. That gave him time. Few administrations lasted a full four years, but something told him that Moshe might break that rule.

Moshe. Avi had tried to warn him. He'd even tried to spy for him behind enemy lines. Now the Opposition was in disarray. With Gurion as his champion, Avi hadn't bothered to invest in warm relations with the other party members. If he was to be of use to Moshe, he'd need to butter up the next in line, or his days in politics were numbered.

The emergency services had done a great job. Within a day, they had reinstated critical services, and life had gone back to near normal. Soldiers filled the streets and kept downtown under wraps. They had to—according to the rumors, the fault line was encrusted with diamonds!

And so, Tuesday afternoon, Avi made his way to Keren Hayesod Street to figure out which way the political winds were blowing.

At the door, he heard Gurion's voice, and he was laughing. Was that a recording? Gurion was gone. Had he survived, he would have nothing to laugh about either. But when Avi stepped inside, sure enough, there he was—Isaac Gurion in the flesh, alive and well—if a bit scratched up—and chuckling.

"Isaac—you're alive!"

Gurion glanced at him but continued cutting a newspaper with a pair of scissors.

"Were you resurrected?"

Gurion glared at him. "Don't be ridiculous. I'm not one of

them. Oh, no." He hummed to himself as he cut along the edges.

Avi looked to the others in the room. A group of aides and Upward members of Knesset stood to the side and watched their leader from a safe distance, fear in their eyes. Avi wasn't the only one to have noticed the change.

He drew near. Gurion cut around the frame of a photo in the newspaper, a photo of Moshe Karlin. The headline read, "PM Karlin: Israeli Sovereignty Unshakable."

"Are you OK?"

"Never been better." Gurion cackled. Discarding the newspaper, he kissed the photo of Moshe and pinned the cutting to the corkboard on the wall. He stepped back to consider his handiwork.

"Long live the king," he muttered, and he giggled again.

That's it. Gurion had escaped the earthquake with his life but lost his mind. But his sudden adulation for Moshe Karlin gave Avi hope.

"Is this the new plan?"

"What?"

"Is there a new plan to defeat Karlin?"

Or, Avi thought, *will we join him at last?* He must have said something hilarious because Gurion crumpled into a fit of teary laughter. Avi looked at the bystanders, who were not laughing, but cringing.

Gurion recovered and stared at Avi as though seeing something beautiful for the first time. "We're not going to defeat Karlin," he said, his old venom returning.

Then his arm was a blur and with a loud snap, the scissors lodged into the corkboard, the blades planted smack in the middle of Moshe's face. "Oh, no. We're going to kill him."

CHAPTER 56

"You should have told me," Eli said. He sat beside the hospital gurney. Noga lay beneath the sheets, unmoving, her breathing shallow.

Dr. Stern stood beside him. "You were in a bad state and needed rest. Besides, we could have lost her any moment. I feared that you'd despair and slip away. I couldn't risk losing you again."

Eli stroked Noga's hair. For the hundredth time, he called her name.

Irreparable. This couldn't be the end. They had set her plan in motion. Soon the entire country would know the truth about the Lost Tribes. They were so close to their goal. Noga had to be there to see it.

"I'll do it," he said. "Whatever you need to heal her."

"We must move quickly; her vitals are falling. The good news is that we don't have to manipulate her DNA. That would require equipment far more advanced than I've cobbled together here. But this treatment is obviously very experimental. Normally we would perform lengthy testing and clinical trials."

"But that could take months," Eli said.

The doctor nodded. "More like years. I think I've identified the epigenetic activators associated with your healing abilities, as well as the aging inhibitors. But to generate those in the lab will take more time and equipment. Our only option is to harvest the activators from you directly."

Harvest. That sounded painful. "Whatever you need. And you can skip the theory. Just tell me what to do."

"We need your blood."

"My blood?" At the mention of the b-word, Eli felt lightheaded.

"We're in luck. You're Type O Negative, the universal donor."

Eli swallowed hard and held out his arm. "How much do we need?"

Dr. Stern gave him an apologetic frown. "A lot. A transfusion is the only option. Bring in the gurney."

Eli nodded. He rushed through the tent flaps, wheeled in the metal bed, and positioned it alongside Noga, while the doctor arranged the blood equipment. At the sight of the needles, Eli's head spun so he climbed onto the gurney and lay down. He turned his head away and stared at Noga.

Once upon a time, people had thought that bloodletting was healthy. Eli had never bought into that. "Ouch," he said, as the needle punctured his skin.

"Sorry about that," the doctor said. "The nurses do the blood work at the hospital."

"Yeah, I can tell."

The tube warmed against his skin as his lifeblood flowed. A metallic taste filled his mouth, and a white frost accumulated at the edges of his vision.

Think of something else, something good.

When this was over, he'd take Noga out for a juicy steak dinner. They'd clink their wine glasses together and watch their website traffic climb.

An electronic alarm sounded from the ECG. The beep of Noga's heart had slowed and the numbers on the display shifted.

Dr. Stern walked over and disabled the alarm.

"What's happening?"

"She's losing blood pressure. Her systems are failing."

"Then do something!"

"I am!"

Eli's chest shook as fear ripped through him. Noga lay right beside him, her life seeping away, and he was powerless to save her. He reached out and held her hand in his. *This can't be happening. You can't let this happen, God!* Noga had reignited his will to live; she had renewed his faith in humanity. Without her, he might as well give up.

"There," the doctor said, his voice soft and far away. "She's connected. Now we wait."

Tears dripped from Eli's eyes onto the metal gurney, and the world frosted over.

CHAPTER 57

Numbness spread over Moshe's body as the stranger delivered the news. The scientist's lips moved but Moshe no longer understood the jargon. The tidings had frozen his brain. This was the end of the road. And not just for Moshe. For everyone. Humanity's plans and schemes, hopes and dreams—everything anyone had ever done—all amounted to nothing. This was, literally, the end of the world.

Moshe held up his hand to interrupt. "Let's start over," he said. "Where did you get that?"

He pointed to the image on Professor Stein's tablet computer: a blurry white speck on a backdrop of inky black.

"The Hubble Space Telescope," he said. "NASA forwarded us the images an hour ago." The professor, a slight man with tidy gray hair and lined cheeks, headed the Israeli Space Agency, a division of the Ministry of Science and Technology.

"And we're looking at an asteroid?"

"Correct. That's a large body of rock. This asteroid, PK-7, originated in the Asteroid Belt between Mars and Jupiter." He talked slower than before and used simpler words.

"And this asteroid is heading for earth?"

"Yes."

"Are you sure of that?"

"PK-7 will hit Jerusalem tomorrow at twelve oh-three

PM."

Moshe couldn't argue with that level of specificity. During a nighttime hike in the desert hills outside Eilat, he had admired the shooting stars. Meteor—and asteroid—showers happened all the time, didn't they?

"Has this sort of thing happened before?"

"An asteroid of this magnitude? A bunch of times."

Moshe relaxed his death grip on the armrest of his chair. This had happened before. How bad could it be?

Professor Stein continued. "The last one hit sixty-five million years ago and wiped out the dinosaurs."

"Oh." That sounded less positive. "And what can we expect from this PK-7?"

"The main impact will obliterate everything within a twenty-mile radius and leave a deep crater."

"I see." Israel would lose her capital along with her important religious and archaeological sites. The loss would injure tourism revenues, but the country would survive. Jerusalemites could evacuate the city within a day. But the professor wasn't done.

"Of course, the region lies near a major fault line, so the impact event will trigger severe earthquakes across Israel."

"Worse than Sunday's earthquake?"

"Far worse."

Moshe felt the blood drain from his face. He'd have to beg the foreign troops to return. Major population centers would need to evacuate, perhaps across the border.

"Shmuel, get the ambassadors of the USA and Russia on the phones. We need to resolve that diplomatic crisis and beg them to allow flights to leave the country and save as many people as possible!"

"Sorry, sir," Professor Stein said. "But I wouldn't bother." The professor was a real downer. Moshe would not be inviting him to official cocktail parties. "The aftermath of the asteroid strike will be much worse than the initial damage. The impact will eject large amounts of dust and ash into the atmosphere. This dust cloud will spread over the planet, blotting out the sun. Photosynthesis will cease. Within weeks ninety-nine percent of life on Earth will perish."

A short, incredulous laugh escaped Moshe's lips. "But humanity will survive, right? We have technology and science..."

Professor Stein shook his head. "Even the deepest nuclear-powered bunkers will eventually run out of supplies. We're talking total annihilation. They call it Planet Killer Seven for a reason."

Moshe stared at the faces of the cabinet members around the conference table, the last cabinet of the State of Israel.

"How did we not know about this earlier?"

The professor cleared his throat. "The asteroid was in a secure orbit and not on any astronomical watch lists. It appears that the unusual solar flare a few months ago tugged the asteroid just enough to send it our way. Until today, Mars had blocked the asteroid's trajectory from Earth's line of sight."

Silence reigned in the room. Scientists had attributed the Resurrection to the effects of an unusual solar flare. The solar flare had given, now it was taking away.

"On the bright side," Professor Stein said, and all eyes clung to him for a shred of optimism, "CO_2 levels will decrease markedly after a few hundred years, and the planet will cool. Climate change will no longer be an issue."

The assembled ministers gaped at him. If humanity was extinct, nobody would be left to worry about climate change.

Moshe's father's voice whispered in his ears. *A Karlin never quits.* A final spark of resistance flared within.

Moshe slammed his fist on the desk. "Then we have to prevent it. At all costs. We'll shoot it down or land astronauts on the surface and nuke it to pieces."

Professor Stein coughed. "Hollywood physics do not apply. All the nukes in the world would be unlikely to change the outcome."

"There's no hope of escape?"

The professor frowned. "Bomb shelters will crumble. Tidal waves and fires will follow. The few to survive the impact will die of hunger and disease."

"So, this is the end—there's nothing we can do about it?"

"That sums it up pretty well."

"Thank you, Professor."

"You're welcome." He reached out and shook Moshe's hand. "It's been a pleasure to meet you, Mr. Prime Minister. Our team at the Space Agency wanted you to know that we're very proud and think you could have really fixed the country. Best of luck to you all."

The professor left the conference room.

The cabinet members pondered the situation in stunned silence. Failed coalitions and corruption charges—even earthquakes and imminent world wars—no longer seemed important. Nothing mattered. Tomorrow, they were all going to die.

"Has the news hit the press yet?" Moshe said.

"That's the strange thing," Sivan said. "Nobody's mentioned it. Not in Israel, not the international media either."

"Then I suppose we'll need to tell the nation ourselves."

"Bad idea," Shmuel said. "People will panic. Our last minutes will be pandemonium."

"He's right," Sivan said and wiped a tear from her face. She had agreed with Shmuel; the world really was ending. "It's too late to do anything, and nothing we do will make a difference."

Moshe got to his feet, and the world shifted and swirled around him. He was a rudderless ship on a choppy ocean in the dead of night. He'd faced the fearsome waves before, but this time no safe shore beckoned on the horizon.

"We owe our citizens the truth," he said. "The news will leak soon enough; at least they'll hear it from the government first. I'll prepare a final statement."

He took one last look at his cabinet, his loyal supporters through the highs and lows of the last stormy months of human history. They looked to him for guidance and inspiration, but what hope could he offer? This time they would all go down with the ship.

"Thank you," he said. "For your service and your friendship."

CHAPTER 58

Late that afternoon, Yosef paced the foyer of the Talpiot Police Station and glanced at his wristwatch. He'd been waiting an hour—an hour too long. If his suspicions were right, something terrible was about to happen.

He approached the front desk. "Officers," he said. The two young women at the desk might have been identical twins. Both sported dark ponytails, and both had told him to wait. "This is a matter of life and death—when will the Commissioner see me?"

"Sorry, Mr. Vice Prime Minister," said the one. "But the Commissioner is very busy. You'd best try him again tomorrow."

She got up and swung a handbag strap over her shoulder. "Can you give me a ride?" she asked the other. Their resemblance was uncanny, and Yosef wondered how their coworkers told them apart.

"Sure," the other replied. She stood and swung an identical bag over her shoulder.

"You're leaving?" Night had fallen an hour ago, but Yosef had assumed that law enforcement didn't keep strict business hours.

"You're welcome to call the Police Hotline. They're open twenty-four/seven."

And with that, they were off.

In what twisted world did the Vice Prime Minister have to wait hours for the Police Commissioner to discuss a matter of *piku'ach nefesh*, life and death?

Yosef's business couldn't wait any longer. He looked over his shoulder. A telephone rang down a corridor, but no officers were in sight. For the first time, Yosef regretted forgoing the security detail usually assigned to the Vice Prime Minister. He could do with some backup now.

He walked around the reception desk and down a long corridor, scanning the signs on the doors of the offices. The Commissioner's room was at the far end.

Yosef knocked once then turned the handle.

Commissioner Golan looked up at his unannounced visitor, annoyance passing over his face for a moment.

"Mr. Vice Prime Minister," he said, without rising from his seat. "What an unexpected honor." He sounded anything but honored.

"Pardon me for intruding, but this is a matter of life and death."

Golan leaned back in his chair and indicated for Yosef to sit in the visitor's chair. He did.

"I have reason to believe there will be a terrorist attack on the Temple Mount tomorrow."

Golan said nothing, so Yosef plowed on. "During the speech of the, ah, Mahdi."

"The Arab Messiah?"

Yosef swallowed. "Yes."

Golan smiled. "Afraid he'll beat the Prime Minister to the punch?"

"The Prime Minister has never professed to be the Messiah."

Golan snorted. "Not yet. But that would be convenient, wouldn't it?"

Yosef had expected the Commissioner to send Special Forces to sweep the Temple Mount for explosives. Instead, he had accused Yosef of political schemes.

Focus on the facts. "A news clip from yesterday shows workers preparing the Temple Mount for the Mahdi's speech. One of the workers is Tom Levi. His cult aims to destroy the Dome of the Rock and rebuild the Jewish Temple. He told me that himself. I think this Mahdi has pushed him to act now. Today, he sent me this."

Yosef displayed the text message on his phone.

Golan said, "You think he'll blow up the Temple Mount along with the Mahdi's followers?"

"Yes!" Finally, Yosef had gotten through to him. "An attack on the Temple Mount would cause interfaith tensions to explode."

Golan nodded. Surely, he would do everything possible to prevent that.

"Mr. Vice Prime Minister," he said. "Let's be frank. This is about the corruption charges, isn't it?"

"What? No!"

"Another cynical attempt to direct our attention away from the Prime Minister's crimes. His wife's crimes too."

"No! Please listen to what I'm saying. People will die if we don't act."

Golan just smiled. "Let me guess, you want the police to cancel the Mahdi's speech, for their own safety, creating a media storm and removing the other messiah from the scene all in one stroke. Brilliant, I must admit. But I'm not falling for it."

Yosef couldn't believe his ears. Had the Commissioner heard a word he'd said? "The earthquake was not a cynical trick and neither is this."

"I wasn't talking about the earthquake." Golan glared at him. "Haven't you heard the news? According to your boss, terrorist plots are the least of our worries tomorrow. You people really should get your stories straight."

"What news?" What was he going on about?

Golan turned his laptop to face Yosef. "See for yourself. Straight from the Prime Minister's Office."

The front-page article on Ynet displayed a grainy photo of

a bright object in a black sky. A star? "Breaking news," read the headline.

Yosef read the first paragraph and fell off the chair.

CHAPTER 59

Dani Tavor wheeled his Samsonite carry-on bag into the international departures terminal at Ben Gurion airport and almost had a heart attack. As a celebrity, he was not used to waiting in line, but now he stood at the end of the mother of all lines.

Every Israeli and his sister had shown up at the airport with bulging suitcases and sharpened elbows. The few travelers not arguing at the top of their voices with the airport staff looked about with glum, doomsday faces. A few of the glazed glances stirred with momentary recognition at the sight of him.

Dani was having nothing of it. He whipped out his iPhone and dialed his daughter Liat's number, but got that annoying "out of service, try again later" message. He swore under his breath. Liat, her husband, and the grandkids had set out a half hour before him, but he couldn't spot them in the crowds. He hoped they had boarded a plane and would leave this Godforsaken country in time. Had they reserved him a seat?

With a final huff, he gripped the handle of his carry-on bag and marched on, flanking the unruly line, and made for the El Al Business Class reception desk. Into the bag he'd stuffed a change of clothes, a wad of hundred-dollar notes from his safe, and his Lifetime Achievement Award from the

Tel Aviv House of Journalists.

He rounded the corner and halted. The Business Class counters stood empty. He swore again.

In recent years, he'd arranged charters for his travels but as of today, all planes had fled the Middle East. Not for the first time, he wished he could afford a private plane. Fame in Israel came with all the annoyances but few of the perks. Today, however, his talk show career might just save his life.

He returned to the long line of Economy Class check-in desks. Flashing his fetching smile at the woman at the front, he cut in.

"Excuse me," he said. "Just a question."

The woman turned on him, ready to offload her frustrations and fears on the cheeky older man when that flash of recognition sparkled in her eyes. "Oh. Hi!" She ran her hand through her hair and smiled. "Honey, it's Dani Tavor!" She nudged her geeky husband in the ribs, who looked up from his phone. Their three kids gawked at him from behind the suitcase trolley.

"Thank you!" Dani gave them a free sample of his trademark penetrating stare, then turned to the clerk behind the desk. "My daughter reserved a seat for me earlier. I've no luggage to check in."

The clerk had exhausted her quota of smiles for the day. "Dani Tavor," she said, as she typed at her keyboard. "Nope, sorry. Nothing here. Where are you flying?"

"Anywhere."

"I'm sorry, you'll have to buy a ticket like everyone else."

Like everyone else—the nerve!

A finger tapped him on the back. "Hey," the husband said. "We were here first. Get in line."

Dani ignored him. "I'll take whatever you have," he told the clerk. "The further away, the better."

She glanced at the screen. "The only seats left are to Timbuktu."

"I'll take it!"

"Do you have a visa for Mali?"

"I'll use my foreign passport."

The clerk reached out, so he handed over his mint condition German passport. His mother had barely escaped the Holocaust, and her former nationality had allowed Dani to apply for German citizenship. As with many Israelis, he had procured the second passport "just in case." His forward thinking had paid off!

"That'll be fifty thousand."

He almost choked. "Fifty thousand shekels—for Timbuktu?"

The clerk wasn't joking. "No," she said. "Fifty thousand *US dollars*. When the exchanges open tomorrow, the shekel will be worthless."

The airlines had no shame—to take advantage of refugees, fleeing for their lives! He'd do a special exposé on airline extortion when he got back. But he wouldn't be back. Tomorrow an asteroid would obliterate the country. But still, fifty thousand US dollars!

"Move along," the clerk said.

"I'll take it." He held out his Visa Platinum Card. "Here, take my fifty thousand dollars."

She did. Good thing he'd removed the limit on his card. He glanced over his shoulder at the lines of desperate fellow travelers. How many of them could swipe fifty grand on their cards? There weren't enough seats for them all anyway, poor things.

In his lengthy career, he'd covered tragedy and sorrow, but he'd never looked the victims in the eyes hours before disaster struck. Oh, well.

The clerk printed the ticket and wished him a pleasant flight.

On the way to passport control, newsrooms displayed on muted television screens. "Breaking news," flashed the ticker in red. But for a change, the talking heads were smiling. Why were they still in the studio?

A familiar self-satisfied face filled the screen. Dani drew near. Isaac Gurion, that old devil, had survived the earthquake. What mischief could he possibly be stirring up during the final hours of the Jewish State?

"Asteroid Hoax," read the ticker.

What? He moved close enough to hear Gurion speak.

"Do not be fooled," Gurion said, looking calm, a beatific smile on his lips. "And do not be frightened. The apocalypse Moshe Karlin has promised is yet another lie. Fear not. Tomorrow, your true Redeemer will arrive."

Dani stared at the fifty-thousand-dollar airline ticket in his hand and he swore again.

CHAPTER 60

Galit stared at her husband's face on the television screen. This couldn't be real. She'd had Henri whip up a dinner of Moshe's favorite foods to comfort him and make up for the trouble she'd caused.

She'd spent the morning at the Talpiot Police Department, answering questions about the new First Lady's spending habits and use of state funds. The investigation was another travesty, she knew, but she still felt responsible. She had become another front in the political war against Moshe.

That, and the return of her family to the Prime Minister's Residence. They would be staying much longer than anticipated. A fancy dinner would not solve that problem either but would give comfort in these trying times.

"He'll bounce back when he's ready," her mom had said. "Just make sure you're there for him when he does."

She watched her husband deliver his recorded statement from the Prime Minister's Office, the Israeli flag behind him, and her petty concerns faded to nothing. In a matter of hours, a speeding chunk of cosmic rock would succeed where armies and haters had failed for decades—to annihilate the Jewish State. The screen switched from Moshe's serious face to an image of the asteroid.

The diplomatic dinner table, set to perfection by the kitchen staff, would go to waste. Who could eat at a time like this?

The door opened, and she ran to the entrance hall. Galit overheard Moshe speaking with his security detail. He used the words with which he had concluded his televised address. "Head home and spend time with your loved ones." Alon nodded and left.

Moshe turned around and met her eyes. Giving her a brave grin, he walked up to her and held her face in his hands. "I guess we won't be conquering the world after all."

"I never wanted the world," she said. "Just you."

He gave her that sad grin again and kissed her on the forehead. He wasn't angry with her. Moshe had always weathered her moods and outbursts with patience. Another trumped-up charge from the Opposition wouldn't make him turn on her. She should have known that.

"Dinner's ready," she said, a tear in her voice, hoping to find something positive in their last hours. "We'll have one hell of a final meal."

Moshe forced another smile, then trudged down the corridor to their bedroom.

Her father had sidled up beside her. "What's for dinner?"

Some people always had an appetite, end of the world or not. "Didn't you see his address?"

"Oh, yeah. Sneaky move."

"Sneaky?"

"That'll keep everyone busy for a while and deflect attention from the scandals. It's better than faking a war and easier to clear up after. Phew! The astronomers got it wrong. Sorry for the scare. Maybe I underestimated him. It's brilliant."

"You think Moshe made that up?"

"Don't look at me. That's the analysis on Channel Two. The timing is too convenient." Her father cleared his throat. "Shall we serve ourselves?"

"Go ahead." Galit made for their bedroom. She knew Moshe. He wouldn't make up something like that.

She knocked on their door. Hearing no response, she turned the handle. The room was dark, the lights off, and curtains drawn against the street lights. "Moshe?"

A soft grunt came from their bed. She walked in and sat on the edge of the bed. His head poked out from the bed-spread.

"You coming to eat?"

"I failed you," he said. "We're all going to die, and I can do nothing about it."

"It's not your fault. You don't have to carry the world on your shoulders."

"We had the superpowers on their knees yesterday. Now they all want to see us die. If I'd just chosen one..."

Galit didn't know what he was talking about. He didn't share details of the government's inner workings with her, and she accepted that. But she didn't need to know the de-tails. She knew her husband, and he always did the right thing.

"It'll be OK."

"No, Galit. This time it won't." He gave an ironic laugh. "They all think I'm a messiah, but they're wrong. I'm done."

She shushed him and stroked his hair. He was always the one calming her down over some silly, inconsequential noth-ing that had set her off; she'd never seen him so devastated and drained of life. Moshe had returned from the dead. He had faced off criminals, shaken up an unfeeling bureaucracy, and beaten the political establishment at its own game. He'd beat this too. She knew it. But not like this. "C'mon Moshe. You're not done yet."

"I am," he said, his voice louder, harder.

He pulled the covers over his head, knocking her hand away. Hurt flashed in her mind. *We've only got a few hours left on this Earth and he wants to be alone?*

She left the room, slamming the door behind her, and leaned against the wall. The hurt boiled away, leaving a silt of gloom. *We're all going to die.* She'd never taken that possibility seriously. Moshe always swept in to save the day. He was her personal Superman. But with Moshe in this state, she ran out of hope.

Hearing a knock at the front door, she ran to answer. She opened without thinking, forgetting the mass of demonstrators outside the gates. But no angry protesters waited on the threshold as the door swung open, only one man.

A series of emotions swept over her: revulsion and rage, and then pity. He hung his head, the face beneath the oily fringe for once devoid of guile and cocky self-assurance. The plaster cast on his left arm hung in a sling. When he looked up, fear flashed in his eyes.

On the welcome mat stood Avi Segal.

CHAPTER 61

"What are you doing here?" she demanded.

On the threshold of the Prime Minister's Residence, Avi avoided Galit's glare. After his deceptions and betrayals, he had no right to be there, but now he forced himself to look her in the eye. "Is Moshe home?"

Home. Moshe belonged here, not him, but Avi had to get inside at all costs. Moshe's life depended on it.

"Shouldn't you be with your pal, Isaac Gurion?"

"I left Upward. I quit politics."

Her short, dismissive laugh told him that she didn't believe a word. He didn't blame her, although, after their experiences in Mandrake's warehouse a month ago, he had hoped that she would have softened.

They had sat side by side, bound to their chairs and gagged. Avi had refused to let their mad tormentor kill Moshe. Later, when memories of Moshe's first death came flooding back, Avi had risen to her defense, and shouldered the blame for their unfaithfulness. He had deceived and betrayed them both.

The traitor in Avi had died, but earning back their trust would take time. Now time was running out. For what it was worth, he had to try.

"I need to speak to Moshe."

"About what?"

"His life is in danger."

She shook her head. Not the response Avi had hoped for, but the words seemed to have worked. She stepped aside and let him enter.

The hall of the Prime Minister's Residence had the high ceilings and fancy paintings of a museum. A glimmer of pride for his friend warmed his heart. *Look how far you've come, my bro.*

Galit closed the door behind them. "I guess you didn't get the memo. We're all going to die."

"I mean immediate danger. Gurion's gone crazy. He's not interested in defeating Moshe; he wants him dead. I tried to warn Moshe before, but he wouldn't listen to me. You must tell him. What?"

She shook her head again and considered him with a sadness that bordered on pity. "When I said 'we're all going to die' I wasn't being philosophical. 'All men must die.' I mean, we're all going to die tomorrow—every person in the State of Israel. The rest of the planet too, probably. We're expecting an asteroid strike at noon."

"What?"

She shrugged. "Check the news if you don't believe me."

We're all going to die. Did Gurion know? Would that make any difference?

"Then why are you still here? You should get as far away as possible."

"There's an international embargo. Most countries have pulled their planes and taken our aircraft hostage. Our neighbors have closed their borders, and tsunamis are expected in our waters."

"Dear Lord. What's Moshe going to do?"

Galit glanced down a corridor. "He's... not in a good state. I couldn't get through to him. I've never seen him so depressed."

"But he always has a plan. He always knows what to do."

"Not this time."

"Mommy," said a youthful voice. Talya padded toward them in her pajamas, rubbing her eyes with the back of her hands. She saw him, and her eyes widened. "Uncle Avi!"

She ran to him, and he lifted her into his arms. He gave her a great big hug and breathed in her little girl scent. She had called him *Aba* in the past when Avi had tried to erase every trace of Moshe and take his place. How he had missed her.

"Can't sleep, sweetie?"

"I had a nightmare," she said. She opened her eyes wide. "There was a witch."

"There are no witches," he told her. "Everything will be OK."

Her eyes brightened. "Will you put me to bed?"

Avi looked at Galit, and she nodded.

"Yay!"

Avi lowered her to the floor. "Lead the way."

He tucked her in and waited outside the door until her breathing came slow and regular.

He found Galit at the table of a large kitchen in cream paneling, a glass of red wine before her.

"Want a drink?"

"Yes, ma'am."

She poured a second glass and placed it before him. The dry red had a bitter aftertaste. The second sip was easier on the palate.

"I'm sorry," Avi said, apropos nothing. "I really screwed everything up."

"Not everything," she said. "Despite your best efforts."

Avi didn't mind the humor at his expense.

"For what it's worth," she said. "I forgive you." She took another swig of wine.

"You do?"

"Sure. We wouldn't want to die angry at each other, would we?"

"Do you think Moshe will forgive me too?"

"I think he has it in his heart, but I can't speak for him.

You'll have to ask him yourself, and good luck with that."

Avi gulped his wine. Moshe, depressed and stuck in bed—
he never thought he'd live to see that. "I think I'll pass. If you
couldn't get through to him, then I have no chance."

He topped up his glass from the bottle. They'd need more
of those. At least he hadn't caused *this* catastrophe. Hanging
out with the Karlins in the Prime Minister's Residence—he
couldn't think of a better way to spend his last hours.

He put down the bottle and opened his mouth to share
that thought with Galit, but he didn't. Instead, he stared at
Galit. She held the glass to her lips, frozen, staring into space.

"You OK?"

"We can't get through to him," she said.

"OK."

"But someone else might."

Avi smiled. He knew who she had in mind. It was worth a
shot.

CHAPTER 62

Moshe Karlin emerged from a deep sleep with a premonition of impending doom. The dawn chorus of birds reached his ears, distant and muffled through the window pane. He lingered in the warm embrace of the soft mattress and silky sheets.

In his dream, he had risen from the dead to become prime minister. He'd create justice and equality—alone if he had to and without the treacherous bureaucracy. Despite his meticulous plans, he suffered defeat and betrayal. None of it mattered. A rogue asteroid sped through outer space to pulverize the State of Israel and snuff out life on Earth.

That was just a dream. What a relief!

Unlike his other nightmares—the rickety bridge over the dark chasm, his father and grandfather on the grassy bank moving further away with his every step forward—this dream had seemed so realistic!

Soon, he'd roll out of bed, have breakfast with Galit, and drop Talya at kindergarten on his way to work. He had big plans. Karlin & Son would expand to Tel Aviv, then north and south, completing the vision of his late father, David Karlin, of blessed memory.

But as the features of the room emerged from the dark, the gloomy premonition returned. This wasn't his house on

Shimshon Street, but the Prime Minister's Residence on Smolenskin.

His nightmare was a reality, his struggles for naught. He could have spent his time better lazing at home with Galit and Talya. They were the reason he had wanted to make the world a better place.

He should reach out to them now, to hug and console them, but his body had turned to lead. What consolation could he offer? Everything would *not* be OK. Everything would cease to be. He had failed them. He had failed his father, his grandfather's legacy, and his nation.

The mound of impossible obstacles cast a dark shadow over him. Had he really thought he could play prime minister? He was completely out of his league.

A Karlin never quits. Moshe hadn't quit; the cosmos had quit on him. Time had run out; history was ending.

He released a long, defeated breath and discovered that he wasn't alone in the early morning gloom. On a chair beside the bed sat an old lady.

"Good morning, Moshe," she said, her eyes large and sad through the thick lenses.

"Savta. Where's Galit?"

"Outside. She's worried about you."

His conscience twinged. While he wallowed in self-pity, Savta Sarah was holding things together, and she had suffered far worse ordeals than him.

"She wants to talk to you but has forgotten how. So she brought me here to speak for her."

Another sting of guilt. Lately, he'd returned home from work sapped of strength and with little energy for family life. Since their trauma in Mandrake's warehouse, Galit had lurked in the shadows, and he had not pulled her near. Was he still angry at her? Would they die without working through their complicated history?

"Nobody thought they'd live," Savta Sarah said, slipping, as she did, into the past. "At first we did. But after a few weeks, we learned the truth—the only way out of the camp was through the chimneys." She stared at the ghosts in the dim light of the bedroom.

Moshe knew Savta's stories by heart. The SS men who took her father. The cattle train to Auschwitz. Her ballsy survival antics in the nascent Jewish State. But she had never spoken of life inside the death camp. Until now.

"Some lost their will to live. Others became animals, stealing crusts of bread and snitching to the guards—anything to survive another day. But some people chose the third option. They helped others, if only with a kind word. They held prayer groups in secret even though discovery would mean certain death."

She shook her head. "They didn't do those things so that God would save them. We heard no news of the war. Nobody left that place alive, and as far as we knew, no one ever would. They did those things because, in their final moments, they wanted to live well."

The twinge of guilt became a stab of shame, and he turned away.

"We all die," she continued. "We can't control that. The only thing we can control is how we live."

CHAPTER 63

The click of a closing door woke Avi. Early morning sunlight seeped through blinds on the kitchen windows. He leaned over the kitchen table, three empty wine bottles at his head. His chin ached from the pressure of the tabletop, his forehead from leaning on his plaster cast.

He had fallen into a drunken slumber. Heels clicked over the corridor tiles as Savta Sarah approached the kitchen. She'd entered Moshe's room hours ago, and Avi tried to divine the success of her visit from her expression.

Galit stirred on the living room couch. "What did he say?"

"Nothing."

"That took a long time," Avi said.

Last night, Galit had tried to call Savta, but the cellular networks were still down. Despite Gurion's misinformation, millions of Israelis were trying to finagle a way off the sinking ship. Moshe had dispersed the staff of the Prime Minister's Residence, each returning home, so Galit had found a bunch of car keys and placed them in Avi's hand.

After failing to locate Savta Sarah at the Knesset, the Prime Minister's Office, and the Dry Bones Society, he visited her small apartment in Katamon. Savta had answered the door wearing an apron. The world might be ending, but Savta was cooking.

Galit and Avi had waited outside the bedroom door. After fifteen minutes, they had retired to the kitchen. Another fifteen minutes later, they'd opened the second bottle of wine.

Savta shrugged. "I let him sleep. He needed his rest, and he'll need all his strength today."

"Does he have a plan?" Avi asked.

"Time will tell."

Avi jumped as a door burst open, and Moshe strode down the corridor, wearing a suit and knotting his tie. "Morning," he said.

Galit launched from the couch and converged with Moshe at the kitchen. He pecked her on the cheek. "Coffee?"

"Sure. I'm making." She put on the kettle.

Moshe whipped his phone from a pocket and dialed.

"Sivan," he said. "Yes, I'm at the Residence."

The networks were up again. Either the panic had subsided or most people had already left.

"Yes," Moshe continued. "Get the ambassadors on the phone. Both of them. No, not the ambassadors—get the presidents! And bring in Professor Stein. Whatever it takes. I'm on my way." He ended the call.

Galit handed him a coffee mug, and he took a sip. "Excellent." He drew her near, and she gasped as he gave her a long, hard kiss. "Thank you," he said. "You're a lifesaver. I'm nothing without you." She blushed, and tears streaked down her smiling cheeks.

He turned to her grandmother. "Savta, what do you say we pass some legislation?"

"Great idea."

Avi wanted to ask what was going on. An asteroid was about to blast them to smithereens and Moshe wanted to sign new laws?

Moshe's eyes turned to Avi. "What's he doing here?"

"He found Savta," Galit said. "And helped put Talya to bed."

The Prime Minister looked Avi over as if for the first time

and nodded. "Thanks, buddy."

"Moshe," Avi blurted. "Gurion's gone mad. He wants to kill you."

"Then tell him to get in line. We've got a planet to save."

Yes! Avi was back at Karlin & Son, at Moshe's side. They were a team again, working together to meet a common goal.

"How can I help? I can drive you."

"No."

The word nipped Avi's enthusiasm in the bud. *He doesn't trust you.* Why should he?

Moshe stepped forward and tapped him on the shoulder. "I need you to hold the fort." He leaned in to whisper. "Take care of Galit and Talya, in case anything should happen to me. Can you do that?"

"Yes, sir."

"Great." He took another gulp of coffee, put down the mug, and pulled Galit in for another kiss.

She teared up in his arms again. "Ready to conquer the world?"

"Ready or not, here we come."

She straightened his tie, stepped back, glanced at the floor, and didn't seem to know where to put her hands. "Be careful," she said. "Come back to me."

"I'll do my best."

With a final wave goodbye, he and Savta Sarah walked out the front door.

"He'll come back," Avi said. The words were designed to comfort Galit, but he clung to them too. "He always does."

DAN SOFER

CHAPTER 64

Moshe sat upright in the command chair of the Knesset's War Room and prepared for the negotiation of his life. The results would determine the length of that life, the lives of his citizens, and all life on the planet. *No pressure.*

"OK," he said. "Put them on."

The world came into sharp focus. The scent of destiny wafted in the air, and Moshe's body tingled. Every experience since the day of his birth had been preparing him for this moment. Every deal he had sealed, every challenge he had overcome, even his failures. Everything rode on these next few minutes.

In the gloomy depression of his bed that morning, he had gained an insight. He'd been doing things wrong. Alone, he'd never achieve justice and equality, never mind save the world. He needed help. Lots of it.

He glanced around the polished table, looking each friend and cabinet member in the eye, sending silent messages of faith and gratitude. Only Rabbi Yosef was missing. Efforts at contacting him had failed and they could delay the call no longer.

Many great men and women had sat around this table and other tables throughout history. Many had given their lives for this two-thousand-year-old hope. Moshe had reached this

870

day thanks to them, and he would honor their memory. He would not let them down. And if he failed, he'd go fighting.

"Here we go," Sivan said, as the conference call connected.

Two rectangles displayed on the large mounted television screen. A grandfatherly statesman in a blue suit and red power tie grinned at them on the left. A bald eagle spread its wings over the circular seal of the President of the United States of America on the wall behind him. On the right, a stony face frowned at the camera. A double-headed eagle struck a symmetrical pose on the Russian Federation coat of arms. The Russian wore a similar suit of blue and red. The leaders of the world's two superpowers seemed to employ the same fashion stylist.

"Mr. President," Moshe said. "Finally, we speak face-to-face."

"Mr. Prime Minister." The American's head wobbled in a gesture of mocking self-satisfaction. "Or should I say, the last Prime Minister of Israel. You should have accepted our offer while you could."

The Russian's visage reddened with rage. "How dare you! A joint conference call—and without warning!"

"My apologies to you both, but I could see no better way to prove my point."

"This had better be good!"

Moshe turned to the Russian. "As you must have noticed, Mr. President, we have no agreement with the United States. And," he turned to the American, "from your counterpart's reaction, as well as the lack of Russian assistance in this time of desperate need, you can see that we've made no pact with them either."

The Russian leaned in and growled. "Do you think I'm an idiot? The two of you could have staged this."

"And why would we do that?"

"Because you are liars! The Americans are embarrassed by their inability to save you, their new fifty-first state, and now you need our help."

Reading between the lines, Moshe glimpsed confirmation of what Professor Stein had explained only minutes ago—that, in an ideal world, there *was* something they could do to avert the demise of the Jewish State.

He'd have to appeal to the best within the heart of each leader.

"You're right," he said. "I need your help. Seven million Jews, Muslims, Christians, and others need your help. With prompt action, you can save us. History will remember you as heroes. Do nothing, however, and our blood will be on your hands."

The American wobbled his head again. "I'd say your blood is on God's hands. We didn't send that asteroid your way. Who are we to second-guess the Almighty or sabotage His plans?"

Both presidents chuckled. *And they think we're the monsters.*

"As you know," Moshe said, "the asteroid will not destroy Israel alone. The dust cloud will suffocate all life on Earth. By helping us, you're helping yourselves and saving millions of your own people."

The Russian shrugged. "We'll take our chances. Your tiny country will absorb the main thrust of the impact, but our mighty nations will survive."

"I'm inclined to agree with my Russian counterpart," the American said. "Besides, thanks to all those zombie apocalypse movies, half our citizens already have bunkers and stockpiles—you name it! Many will perish, but the American people will endure. Considering the threat of your new weapons of mass destruction, we call that an acceptable loss. Oh, and don't bother appealing to the sympathy of our citizens. We've blocked news of the asteroid from the media. Consider NASA's notification of your space agency a personal courtesy."

In Moshe's periphery vision, the cabinet members shifted in their seats. The superpowers had partnered up against the Jewish State. Moshe's appeals to virtue and self-interest had fallen flat, and it was time for Plan C. When desire fails, use fear.

"You're right," he said. The change in tone subdued the laughter. "I lied to you." Now he had their attention. Suspicion flashed in their eyes, the concern that they had miscalculated and fallen into a trap.

"I told you that we had not weaponized the undead. The truth is, we have. Zombie super-soldiers. Unkillable. Unstoppable."

The Russian slammed his hand onto his desk. "I knew it!"

Moshe continued, "We've been amassing our zombie armies for months. I expected you to reject our plea for help, so I've already unleashed the undead on the world."

"You're bluffing," the American president said. "Our satellite footage shows that the troop buildup on the Gazan border has dissipated, not increased."

"That's because we've deployed them in subterranean tunnels. Until now we used the tunnels to hide the buildup of undead warriors, but this morning I gave them their marching orders. Tens of thousands of zombie soldiers are on their way to you as we speak. They only respond to my command, and unless I call them back, they'll be arriving at your capitals two days from now."

"Dear Mother of God," the American President said. He slapped his palm to his forehead. "What have we done?"

The Russian's skin turned paper white. "Turn them back at once!"

Moshe plowed on. "Dust clouds won't interfere with these weapons. They don't need food or sleep. By our projections, within a month, only one superpower will remain." Moshe paused for dramatic effect. "The Dead."

The presidents of the world powers shouted together, their pleas and promises forming an unintelligible ruckus.

Moshe raised his hands for silence, and the leaders obeyed. "Here's what we're going to do."

CHAPTER 65

That morning, Yosef opened and closed his mouth like a stunned fish. His wife had asked a simple question, but he had no idea how to respond. It was all so confusing.

Last night, Moshe had addressed the nation on TV. An asteroid would hit Jerusalem at noon. Then the news channel had switched to Isaac Gurion, who explained with an angelic calm that there was no need to worry, the world was not ending, and the Prime Minister's fear tactics would not distract anyone from his corruption charges.

Having no television, Yosef's children knew nothing of this, and their blissful ignorance made his decision only harder.

"Yosef," Rocheleh repeated, "is there school today or not?"

He had shared the news with his wife. "I don't know."

She placed her hands on her hips. "Well, if the Minister of Education doesn't know, who does?"

Yesterday evening, Yosef had tried to reach Moshe on the phone, or Sivan or anyone on the cabinet. Every time, he received a "network unavailable" message. This morning, the networks had resumed service, but his calls went straight to voicemail. On Emek Refaim Street, stores opened, buses zoomed, and commuters rushed to work as usual. What was going on?

"I don't know," he repeated. He had not issued an order to close the schools today.

"Well, if they're not going to school, *you* keep them occupied."

That settled it. "OK," he said. "Take them. Just check that the teachers are there too."

Rocheleh shook her head at his dillydallying and made for the front door. "Come on, boys. Let's go."

Yosef kissed them goodbye and wished them a fun day. He hoped he'd see them again.

He tried Moshe's number for the twentieth time. Voicemail.

Where was everyone, and why was Yosef out of the loop? Moshe wouldn't have invented an asteroid threat. But if it was real, how could the country carry on, business as usual?

He dialed another number. "When choosing between an uncertain outcome and a certain one," the Sages of the Talmud instructed, "prefer the certain one." Following their advice, Yosef focused his energy on another imminent catastrophe.

"Thank you for calling the Israel Police Service," the now familiar recorded female voice said. "Our operators are busy with other calls. Please wait or dial nine to leave a message."

Yosef exhaled a puff of frustration. Did the operators expect citizens caught in the middle of a terror attack to hold the line as well?

As usual, Yosef waited. He needed answers. Certainty. Elijah the Prophet. But Elijah was last seen disappearing into the heavens in a fiery chariot. The prophet dropped by Passover meals and circumcision ceremonies around the globe yet remained invisible. He was not the sort of person Yosef could call on the phone. At the right time, Elijah would appear out of nowhere in a cloud of smoke.

But now time was running out.

Elijah, where are you?

CHAPTER 66

Eli blinked his eyes open. He lay on a metal gurney in a tent. His bones were sore, and a tube yanked at the crook of his arm. Last he remembered before passing out, Noga's blood pressure had dropped as her body's systems collapsed. Had she survived?

He turned his head away from her, afraid of what he might see. A long plastic line ran from a suspended pouch to Eli's other arm. An infusion. He had lost a lot of liquid.

Beyond the transparent pouch, the doctor hunched over a desk. Eli tried to divine Noga's fate from the doctor's posture.

Then the chair swiveled, and the doctor hurried over to him, a steaming paper cup in hand.

"Have some tea," he said. "And there's a six-pack of mineral water in the corner."

"Is she...?" Eli began.

Dr. Stern smiled. "Her vitals are back to normal. I disconnected the transfusion a half hour ago."

Oh, thank God!

Eli rolled over, and there she was. Her chest rose as she breathed, but the eyes above the oxygen mask remained closed. "Did she wake up?"

"Not yet. We need to be patient."

Eli followed the doctor's orders. He drank his sugared tea and guzzled water. Noga's improving health gave him strength. Her body was recovering. But what of her mind? *We need to be patient.*

Eli flopped on the chair beside the gurney.

"Is there another laptop? Internet?"

Dr. Stern glanced at the jumble of medical apparatus on the desk. "Here, use this." He handed Eli an iPad.

Eli logged into the analytics portal for TheTenLostTribes.org. Visitor statistics had climbed yesterday morning, a sign that the Facebook campaign was working, but then, in the afternoon, the hits dropped off.

The earthquake. A natural disaster of that size must have caused havoc. Researching the Ten Lost Tribes would no longer appear on the average citizen's list of priorities.

He searched for news of the earthquake in Jerusalem and clicked through to an article on the Ynet news site. The front page covered the aftermath of the earthquake: electricity and water outages, gas explosions. Downtown Jerusalem looked like a war zone, with soldiers on every street corner holding up their hands to turn away reporters. Were those Russian uniforms?

A more recent editorial called for the Prime Minister's immediate resignation and ranted against his cynical use of natural disasters for political ends, such as the earthquake and the... the *asteroid scare?*

The earthquake had been real enough—Eli could vouch for that—but was Karlin stupid enough to invent an asteroid strike out of whole cloth?

He tapped back to the front page and the breaking news ticker. The headline sent cold shivers down his spine.

"What the hell?"

A man in a suit spoke into a bouquet of press microphones. Eli recognized him. He had first sighted the oily politician at Zion Square on a stage beside three imposter kings. The Earth had devoured the stage, but the ringleader had survived to make another speech.

Eli read the quotation and shook with righteous indignation. The lying creep was trying to usurp Eli's destiny.

"Oh, no you don't," he said, his voice a growl.

"What's that?" Dr. Stern asked, without looking up from his laptop.

"The news. This Isaac Gurion thinks he's Elijah the Prophet."

Dr. Stern smirked. "I thought that job was taken. He must be delusional."

Eli's fingers tightened over the iPad. "I know his kind. I've hunted them all my life. He's not delusional; he's a false prophet."

CHAPTER 67

Yosef dashed into the Talpiot Police Station to find the reception desk empty. He had arrived before the secretaries. After a few seconds of frustration, he realized this might work to his advantage.

He charged down the corridor to the sounds of ringing phones and muffled conversations, expecting at any moment to hear authoritative voices challenge his right to wander around the station.

Yosef would demand immediate action from the Commissioner. He was an elected minister of the State of Israel. That counted for something, didn't it? Yosef had never made a threat in his life, but if it came to that, he would. A governmental committee appointed police commissioners. Yosef could use his sway to put the fear of the Lord into the civil servant and galvanize him to avert the imminent tragedy. And if Yosef's intuition proved wrong, he'd live with it.

The corridor ended, and he reached his destination without objection. Yosef knocked twice on the Commissioner's door, then tried the handle. The door was locked. The Commissioner was getting a late start as well.

Yosef returned to the reception area. He perched on the edge of the hard, plastic seat, then got up and paced the room. Last night he had become familiar with every floor tile, every crack.

He halted. Had the police changed their minds about Moshe's announcement? Had they gone home to spend their last hours with their families? The murmurs of telephone chatter disproved that theory. He followed the sounds, determined to ask the first officer he encountered when the doors opened, when the twin receptionists strolled into the station.

Yawning and bleary-eyed, they dropped their handbags behind the desk. Yosef approached the counter. "I need to see the Commissioner. When will he be in?"

The women glanced at him, and without a word, they turned their backs on him and disappeared around a corner. Yosef drummed his fingers on the counter. He heard their idle chatter and the whistle of an electric kettle. Another long minute passed before the women returned, each nursing a mug of coffee. They took their time sitting down and arranging their desk equipment before one of them registered his presence.

"How may I help you?"

"Same as yesterday. I need to speak with the Commissioner."

"Do you have an appointment?"

"No, but we spoke last night. He knows what this is about."

That seemed to satisfy her. She put a phone receiver to her ear and sipped her coffee.

She put down the phone. "He's not in yet. Please wait."

Yosef wanted to pull out his hair. "When will he be in?"

The secretary shrugged.

He forced a smile and returned to his seat.

Over the next fifteen minutes, another four officers arrived, greeted the twins, and moseyed along the corridor to their offices. So far, no commissioner.

The relaxed atmosphere at the police station indicated that Moshe was losing the PR battle. Was the asteroid a hoax? Sivan had used many creative ploys to herd public opinion in the desired direction, but the end-of-world scenario sounded extreme even for her.

After millennia of human suffering and struggle, of hopeful waiting, would God destroy his Chosen People in one fell swoop? What of the Messianic Era? Even the prophecies of doom ended with the eternal rule of Heaven. The story of humanity had to have a happy ending.

Yosef approached the reception desk again and received the same answer, topped up with a "Please be patient." Yosef returned to his seat, and the receptionists returned to their nail polish.

Be patient.

Yosef *had* been patient. The Jewish People had been extremely patient. While they waited for their Messiah and the shofar blast of Elijah the Prophet, they had endured persecution and genocide. When would the waiting end?

Yosef wrung his hands. Right now, hundreds of men and women gathered on the Temple Mount, unaware of the danger.

This was Yosef's fault, in part. He had brushed Tom Levi off. But Tom Levi was no idiot and he had stopped waiting.

Yosef blinked. When madmen acted, how can the rest of humanity sit and wait?

A sudden gust of determination lifted him to his feet, and he charged at the reception desk.

"This can wait no longer," he said. "Where is the Commissioner? You must have a way of reaching him." Both twins opened their mouths to object, but Yosef cut them off. "Try his home number and his mobile. This is a matter of life and death!"

The raised eyebrows told him that the women seriously doubted his claims, but the one on the left raised the phone again. This time, she spoke to someone.

After a short conversation of monosyllables, she put the phone back down. "The Commissioner has taken the day off. Please come back tomorrow."

Yosef snapped. "You have got to be kidding me! Then get

me somebody else. There will be an attack on the Temple Mount today! A bomb!" The women stared at him as though he was insane. "I'm the freaking Vice Prime Minister! Do something!"

More plastic smiles.

"I'm sorry," Lefty said. "You'll have to speak with the Commissioner. Tomorrow."

He huffed and puffed and stormed off. What a colossal waste of time!

Baruch, with his flannel fedora and perfect pencil mustache, leaned against the black Audi on the curb. He swung the back door open for Yosef, then hurried around to the driver's seat.

"Where to, sir?"

"The Old City," Yosef said. He had stopped waiting.

CHAPTER 68

Moshe rounded up his broadcast and glanced at the camera in the Prime Minister's press office for the last time.

"And so," he said, "my fellow citizens, our plan is in motion—our only hope to save our nation from destruction. I urge you all to gather your loved ones, go home, and wait in your reinforced rooms. Those without such rooms must move to the nearest public bomb shelter. Within the next hour, we'll learn our fate. May God be with us. *Um Israel chai!*" Long live the People of Israel!

The red dot above the camera blinked out, and the operator gave the thumbs-up. An assistant removed the microphone from Moshe's lapel and shook his hand. "It's been an honor," she said.

"Here too. I hope we meet again. Now go home."

He drew a deep breath and exhaled. Things were out of his hands now.

Sivan met him at the door. They speed-walked down the corridor toward their waiting cars. "The broadcast went out?"

Sivan tapped at the screen of her phone. "Yes, and posted on all government sites and social media accounts. There's a breaking news bulletin starting soon on Channel Ten. Radio too."

"Great. Join us at the Prime Minister's Residence. We've

got a bunker and the best popcorn in town." He had invited his cabinet to join him too.

"I'll take you up on that," she said. "But first I have to pick up Cleopatra."

Moshe gave her a quizzical glance. He hadn't heard of any ancient Egyptian queens turning up at the Dry Bones Society.

"From the cat parlor."

"Oh, right. She's welcome too."

"Thanks!" At the ping of a notification, she looked at her phone. "Oh, crap!"

She stopped in her tracks, and Moshe glanced at her phone too. The Channel Two news displayed the face of Isaac Gurion. This would not be good.

Sivan turned up the volume. Gurion smiled at the camera, his face radiating calm. "Do not let the asteroid scare deceive you. Join us now one and all at the Sultan's Pool and behold your Redeemer! Prime Minister Karlin himself will be in attendance."

"What?" Moshe said. "Avi was right. He's gone insane."

The newsreader said, "Thousands have gathered around the Messiah Coronation Center at the Sultan's Pool outside Jerusalem's Old City." On the screen, a bird's-eye view of the narrow valley was displayed. Thick crowds of people flowed toward an immense black rectangular structure in a grassy knoll below a short bridge. "Unnamed sources claim that the Messiah may already be inside the building."

Sivan said, "The bastard is going to crown himself the Messiah."

Moshe looked at the thousands of innocent bystanders. Even Professor Stein's most favorable projections predicted widespread damage and destruction in Jerusalem.

He said, "And all those people are going to die."

CHAPTER 69

"More tape!" Irina yelled.

She had spent all night putting a lid on the pandemonium of their simian ancestors, when this morning, a video clip had appeared on the official Facebook page of the Prime Minister's Office, and the Dry Bones Society once again exploded with activity.

Volunteers stuck cardboard and plastic bags over the windows to prevent shattering. They toppled desks to create reinforced crawl spaces. Not designed as a residential complex, the meager bomb shelter beneath Clal Center could not house the entire dormitory of the Dry Bones Society. They had to improvise.

"Here!" Samira called from across the Call Center, and she tossed Irina another roll of duct tape. They had an hour to secure the site, and Irina had to fit in secret plans of her own. The asteroid was real. Moshe had dispelled the confusion and given them the instructions they needed to survive. All the cardboard and overturned desks in the world would not protect them from a direct hit, but Moshe's ballsy plan gave them hope for survival.

A handful of volunteers ran for the front door, little backpacks on their shoulders. "Hey, where are you going?"

Ben gave her a guilty look, then continued out the door.

"Where are they going?"

"The Sultan's Pool," Samira said. "The Messiah Coronation."

"The what?" Moshe had not mentioned that in his address and he had warned against staying outdoors.

"It's Gurion's work," Samira said. "Let them go."

How people could believe a word that slimy politician excreted, Irina could not understand.

She completed blocking her current window, then paused. Alex stood at the front door.

"We're out of time," he whispered when she came near. "We have to go now."

"But the whole country is in chaos. The asteroid—"

"We can worry about that later. If we don't disappear now, we're dead anyway."

Irina cast one last glance at the Call Center. Samira kneeled on the floor and sliced cardboard sheets into window-sized squares with a box cutter. Others shifted desks and boarded windows. There was no way to explain her sudden need to leave without exposing her friends to the criminal world.

"OK," she said.

Alex took her hand in his and led her outside and down the corridor. They passed the Absorption Center, her job. The Dry Bones Society had been a temporary home. Now she must build her own home, with her man.

Alex had parked his car on the pavement behind Clal Center.

"Did you bring my bag?" Irina said.

"Which bag?"

"The things I left at your place." Irina's bag contained clothes and toiletries to get her through their first week on the run.

"I haven't been back since yesterday. It's too risky. They might be watching."

"Where did you sleep?"

"In the car." He grinned.

That seemed a bit paranoid to Irina, but Alex knew what

they were up against. "Then I'll go." His lips tightened, so she added, "I'll be quick—I promise. In and out."

"OK," he said. "But I'll wait a few blocks away."

"No problem."

Shamai Street was only a few turns away through downtown Jerusalem. The car crossed over King George, and Alex stopped at a back street on the edge of Independence Park.

"Be back quick?" he said.

"In and out," she promised, and, leaving him with a hurried kiss, she jumped out.

The streets of downtown Jerusalem seemed empty for a Wednesday morning. The few people she encountered rushed off and didn't seem to notice her. A hurtling asteroid and messianic frenzy had created the ideal conditions for two lovers to escape into thin air. The thought thrilled her. They were embarking on an adventure into the unknown, just the two of them.

She paused at the corner to scan Shamai Street from a safe distance. Finding no unfamiliar cars in the parking bay and no suspicious men hiding behind newspapers, she walked beneath the stilts of Alex's building and punched the code for the front door. She skipped up the two flights of stairs, glancing up in case a thug had arrived ahead of her. Then, her heart pounding in her chest, from both the climb and the tension, she slid her key into the hole and walked inside.

Her bag lay on the kitchen table. Closing the distance in two strides, she grabbed the bag, slipped the strap over her shoulder, and turned to leave. She gasped. A man stood between her and the door. He wore a tweed coat and pointed a large black gun in her direction.

His gray mustache shifted as he smiled. "Nice to see you again, Irina," Boris said. "It's been too long."

CHAPTER 70

Ahmed stood in the wings behind the stage. This was his first visit to Al Aqsa and his last.

The murmur of the waiting crowds beyond the partition buzzed like the hum of twenty thousand bees. He checked the order of his cue cards with shaky fingers. The golden envelope could mean only one thing—he was nearing the slaughterhouse.

Hasan stepped in front of him, straightened the turban on Ahmed's head, and adjusted the collar of the white robe. Ahmed's cousin looked pale and his forehead glistened, but not because of the late morning sun. The drop-off bin in Ramallah meant that Hasan was also in the dark. For years he had danced for unseen puppeteers, blindly accepting their money without ever understanding their true intentions. Did he also sense that the end was drawing near—for them both?

"You look perfect, Mahdi," Hasan said. "Remember our agreement and keep to the script this time."

Ahmed nodded. Although Hasan had not fulfilled his promise to introduce him to the Shepherd, he had done his best. Was he not a victim too?

"Because if you don't, this time I'll blow your brains out myself."

His empathy for Hasan evaporated.

Hasan gave him a final clap on the shoulder. "Good luck." Then he rushed away to his seat of honor among the other dignitaries in the front row.

Alone at last, Ahmed turned to his last urgent task before stepping before the crowds to meet his fate. This task he could not fulfill in person.

"Dara!" he hissed. "Dara!"

With a whish of fabric, his friend appeared, all smiles and pride. "Here I am, O Mahdi. Your faithful servant is ready for your commands."

"Enough of that, you idiot. I have an important mission for you."

"Anything for my Mahdi."

"This is serious." He withdrew the sealed white envelope from the folds of his robe. "I need you to take this to Clal Center. Give it to the girl, Samira."

Dara accepted the letter and sniffed it. "A love letter—can I have a peek?"

"This is serious, Dara. And urgent. Take it to her right away, and only to her."

"What, now? And miss your historic speech? First, you disappear on me this morning, and now you chase me away?"

"Yes, now. Please, my friend. This means more to me than any speech."

Dara's shoulders sagged. "OK, my friend. But try to drag out your words, I don't want to miss the after-party." He winked and hurried off.

Good. The favor would also keep his friend far from the slaughterhouse that awaited.

Ahmed sucked in air, filling his lungs. He had been preparing for this day a long time. Everything he had experienced in his second life had led here. Today, he would meet the Shepherd, and he would prove that he had learned his lesson. This time, he would face his fate with honor.

He forced his legs to carry him around the partition and onto the stage. The excited murmurs rose as his sandaled feet trod over the white carpet that led to the white podium.

Placing his cue cards on the podium, he glanced beyond the microphones.

Beneath the clear blue canopy of heaven and crowned by the towering golden Dome of the Rock, Arab men of faith covered every inch of the Temple Mount plaza. Dignitaries in kaffiyehs and turbans filled the first five rows. Guards of the Islamic Waqf in dark trousers and white collared shirts lined the aisles. Beyond them stood the endless mass of pilgrims. The common folk wore their finest clothing and waited for their Redeemer.

This time nobody spoke ahead of Ahmed. The good tidings had spread, and the Mahdi needed no introduction. Besides, Hasan had said, rival imams and political figures had lobbied so fiercely to stand at his side that choosing any of them might spark a conflict that would engulf them in flames for decades.

From the front row, Hasan nodded at Ahmed to begin.

"My friends," Ahmed began, reading from the cards, his voice bursting from immense speakers around the expansive plaza like the voice of God. "You have seen the signs. Today we begin a new era. A time when we no longer talk of struggle, because victory is already ours. The End Times."

Cheers erupted throughout the crowd. The ecstatic hope of the crowd surged through him like a drug, and a smile spread across his face without bidding. *Yes! An end to their struggles.*

From his vantage point, the pilgrims at the back were dots of color, shapeless sheep in the herd, their murmurs of relief, contented bleating, secure in their trust of the Shepherd.

If only he could channel that power for good. The struggle should end, not because one side has defeated the other, but because the struggle was an illusion, a deception created by cruel shepherds to satisfy their own base desires.

But by telling them, he would break his promise to Hasan and risk the wrath of the Shepherd.

Would the people listen? In Bethlehem, the audience had not stoned him for heresy; they had warmed to him and gripped his hand. No doubt his words had surprised them, but they had longed to hear that message of peace.

He glanced at the next card. It spoke of the sons of pigs and killers of prophets, of yet another *intifada* and days of rage, of martyrs and streets flowing with infidel blood. And of his coronation later that day when he would strike the first blow that would start the Mother of All Wars.

The excited murmurs settled, and an expectant hush washed over the sea of eager faces. In the pregnant silence, fifty thousand men held their breath. How would the Mahdi bring The End? How would he snatch that final victory from the jaws of struggle and stagnation?

The courage Ahmed had nurtured behind the partition fled. How could he take on the Shepherd? How could he overturn centuries of hatred? He should turn and run. Run and hide. Hasan's assassins would catch him one day, but at least Ahmed would not stain his soul again with innocent blood.

His sweaty palms slid over the sides of the podium. His lips trembled, and his tongue dried up in his mouth.

A ripple in the sea of spectators drew his eye. An inlet had formed at the side of the crowd. The inlet widened as people pressed against each other and struggled to move away from the disturbance. In the center of the clearing stood a man.

Then the man shouted at the top of his voice. Another murmur spread over the waters, as the lone madman parted the sea, crying out and waving his arms.

Fingers of cold terror closed over Ahmed's heart as the man ranted and raved. Ahmed knew the madman, who now directed his words at him!

CHAPTER 71

Moshe dialed a number on a landline in his office, ready to concede defeat. He'd plead and beg—whatever necessary to save lives.

"You don't have to do this," Shmuel said, sitting beside him. "Chances are, we're goners anyway."

Most other cabinet members had left for the Prime Minister's Residence, where they'd follow the operation from the relative safety of the bunker.

Moshe gave him a brave smile. "I'm an optimist." Then he covered the mouthpiece with his hand. "It's ringing."

Shmuel lifted the other receiver to his ear and covered the mouthpiece.

Moshe's pulse thumped in his ears. Although they had traded threats and blows via press releases, he hadn't spoken with his adversary directly since the coalition had imploded. Now Moshe came crawling on his knees. *Pick up, Gurion. I know you're waiting for my call.*

Why else had the politician done this? His so-called Messiah Coronation was an exercise in brinkmanship. For Moshe, it was a catch-22. If he accepted the invitation, his presence would be proof of his haughty, overbearing rule. King Karlin, Gurion had labeled him, a corrupt dictator who holds himself above the law. If he didn't show, Gurion might claim that golden crown for himself, riding the wave of messianic fever to the crest of public opinion. And while Moshe deliberated, thousands of citizens waited in the open, putting their lives in graver danger with every passing minute.

It was a game he couldn't win and so he wouldn't play.

The line continued to ring.

Had Moshe misunderstood—was Gurion intentionally trying to increase the death toll so that, even if Moshe averted total annihilation, he'd still shoulder the blame for thousands of casualties? Or had Gurion's hatred blinded him to the dangers of the asteroid?

The call connected.

"Well, well, well," said the familiar, greasy voice. "If it isn't King Karlin himself."

"Hello, Isaac."

"We're waiting for you. The table is set. All that's missing is our Savior."

Moshe scanned his options one last time, but no way out presented itself. All good things came to an end.

"You win," he said. "Call off this coronation of yours and send those people home. I'll stand down. I'll resign as Prime Minister, dissolve the government, and appoint you as my interim replacement. I'll dismantle Restart too and leave politics forever."

"Moshe, Moshe," Gurion said, sounding injured. "What do you take me for?"

"Don't take my word for it. I'll sign a declaration or whatever you want. Just send those people to their bomb shelters." Moshe eyed Shmuel, who nodded. He had to reveal their plan; at this point, there was no harm in doing so. "We've set a process in motion. There's a chance we'll beat the asteroid, but even in the best-case scenario, there will still be widespread destruction. The crowds outside the Messiah Coronation Center will die if they stay out in the open…"

He trailed off. Gurion was laughing.

"Sorry," Gurion said, recovering. "I couldn't hold back."

"It's real, Isaac. Check with NASA. Check with any astronomical organization—they'll all say the same thing. The asteroid is—."

"I know, I know." Gurion's voice quavered with residual humor. "I never doubted you, King Karlin."

Avi was right—Gurion had lost his mind, and in his insanity, he would slaughter innocents. "Think of the people you've gathered outside, Isaac. Their families, their children."

"I don't want you to resign, Moshe. Oh, no. I want much more than that. You tried to kill me. Now come here and face me like a man." His voice became gruff with pent-up fury. "This isn't politics, Moshe; this is personal."

The call cut out.

"He's gone mad," Shmuel said. "He wants to get at you, even if it means killing thousands."

Moshe got to his feet. "You should head for the Residence now."

Shmuel gaped at him. "You can't be serious."

Gurion had cornered him. "I need you to oversee the operation while I'm gone."

"Don't go there. That's exactly what he wants."

"I need to warn those people. They're there because of me. I should have denied the rumors that I was the Messiah while I could. Now they'll only listen to me."

"But he'll murder you. He practically said so himself."

Moshe gave him another brave smile. "I hope it won't come to that."

CHAPTER 72

Yosef had never entered the Muslim Quarter of the Old City alone and for good reason. Most attacks against Jews occurred there. But today Yosef walked past the knot of Border Guard soldiers at Jaffa Gate, and into the unfamiliar labyrinth.

Every second counted. He hurried along narrow alleys that squeezed between high walls of white stone. Decades of sun and rain had worn the cobblestones smooth. As he delved deeper, the metal street names on the walls no longer bothered with Hebrew or English, only Arabic.

An Arab man, rough and unshaven, glared at Yosef. A woman, covered from head to toe in a flowing burka, averted her eyes. With his velvet skullcap and fringes flying from his belt, Yosef dared not ask for directions. A lone Jew in the Muslim Quarter was vulnerable; a lost Jew was asking for trouble. For the second time that day, he regretted forgoing his security detail.

The trickle of pedestrians became a steady flow, and Yosef knew he was moving in the right direction. As he bustled along, he searched for a solution to an imminent problem. Of the eleven gates to the Temple Mount, non-Muslims could only enter through one, Mughrabi Gate, via a ramp next to the Western Wall Plaza. Tourists had to schedule their excursions in small groups and during limited visiting hours. Yosef had not scheduled a tour for today, and he approached from the north. How on earth would he get past the Temple Mount guards?

As the foot traffic thickened, the number of robes and kaffiyehs increased. Yosef flowed with them, until, turning a corner, he glimpsed the tall arch of the Gate of the Tribes.

An immense leafy tree cast a shadow over the arched gateway. The crowd meandered between metal dividers, bolted to the ground. A battery of men in dark uniforms eyed the worshipers, assault rifles slung over their shoulders, as the visitors passed beyond black crowd-control barriers emblazoned with the word Police.

Once through the gate, Arab men massed on the green expanse, exchanging smiles and pointing to something to the south and out of sight.

A month ago, Yosef had waited in line outside of the Western Wall Plaza to greet a different messiah. He had tasted the ecstatic rush that now reflected in the eyes of the Arabs. This time, he hoped the gathering would not end in mass tragedy.

The line advanced. A young bearded officer with olive skin and mirror glasses raised his hand at the sight of Yosef. "You can't go in there." His voice had the harsh guttural inflection of an Arabic speaker.

"I need your help," Yosef said. "There will be an attack on the Temple Mount by Jewish extremists."

"Whoa, slow down, Rabbi." The officer motioned for his colleague to stand in for him as he led Yosef to the side.

He raised his sunglasses onto his forehead. "What attack?" he said, his voice hushed.

"Have you seen a man with a beard—a redhead?"

The officer shrugged. "Buddy, most people here have beards."

"This one is Jewish. I saw him on the Temple Mount. It was on the news. He must have planted explosives."

The officer did not look impressed. "What makes you

think that?"

"His cult wants to destroy the Dome of the Rock to build the Jewish Temple in its place. By any means. He told me so. We need to evacuate the area."

The officer looked over his shoulder at the thousands of worshippers on the Temple Mount. "That won't be possible. And you are?"

The officer clearly didn't recognize him. Yosef had hidden from the cameras ever since the election campaign. "I'm the Vice Prime Minister of the State of Israel."

The officer didn't stifle his laugh. "And I'm the Genie of the Lamp."

"This isn't funny. I'll hold you personally responsible for whatever happens."

"Run along, Rabbi. Don't make me arrest you."

Yosef had feared this scenario. *Don't panic. Be firm.* "I've spoken with Commissioner Golan!"

At the mention of the Commissioner, the officer's smile disappeared. The Commissioner hadn't heeded Yosef's warning either, but saving lives justified the half-truth.

"Last I heard, it's business as usual."

"Then you're not up to date."

"One moment." The officer pulled out a walkie-talkie and spoke in Arabic.

Oh, great. Had Yosef expected the guard to take his word? The Commissioner's office would expose Yosef's deception. If he wound up in a holding cell, he'd have no chance of averting the tragedy.

On loudspeakers beyond the wall, a voice boomed in Arabic, and a cheer rose from the audience like the crashing of waves on the seashore. The gathering had begun, the Mahdi addressed his unsuspecting crowd, and Yosef stood on the wrong side of the wall.

Starry-eyed worshippers poured through the gates and into harm's way. How could he stand idly by as they rushed to their death? The ruins of the Jerusalem Temple, the most sacred spot on earth, chosen by God to bring peace unto the world, would soon become the scene of a terrible crime that would sow suffering and conflict for generations.

Stop waiting, Yosef. Do something!

With a sudden jolt of wild desperation, Yosef stepped up to the nearest worshipper.

"Don't go in there," he said. "Something terrible is about to happen!"

The elderly Arab sneered at him from beneath his kaffiyeh and hurried along.

Yosef accosted the next in line, grabbing him by the arm. "Go home—you are in danger!"

"Hey!" the officer called behind him. "Stop that!"

Heavy boots clapped on the stone courtyard behind him.

"All of you—leave this place! Run for your lives!"

A hand gripped his shoulder, but Yosef ducked and dived sideways, evading the officer's grasp. He cut back and sprinted for the open gate.

As the gate grew larger, Halachic qualms flashed in his mind. Jewish law prohibited Jews from treading on the holy ground of the former Temple but permitted almost anything to save even a single human life. How many men, women, and children would perish if Tom Levi executed his cruel plan?

His legs carried him forward. Crossing the threshold, he almost slammed into the burgeoning crowd of Arab worshippers. The Temple complex was much larger than he had imagined. And so green! People flowed over the lawns and around the towering golden dome, its octagonal base tiled in blue, yellow, and green. The white stage stood before the Al Aqsa Mosque to the south.

Yosef had expected the guards to apprehend him by now. Glancing over his shoulder, he discovered why they had not. The black-clad police officers glared at him from the threshold. The officer with the sunglasses spoke into his walkie-talkie, his forehead glistening with sweat.

Ha! The Israel Police entered the Temple Mount only to escort tourists and catch terrorists, delegating the management of the holy site to the Jerusalem Islamic Waqf. Mass gatherings such as today were especially sensitive, and a charging group of armed Israeli officers in the middle of the speech would create a diplomatic incident of international proportions. Yosef had a few seconds before the officers got permission to grab him.

He scanned the worshippers for a red beard. None paid him any attention, their eyes fixed on the white-robed figure on the stage. The Mahdi's voice roared from the many loud-speakers.

Tom Levi would stay far away for the detonation. Yosef had better search for the explosives. Where had he placed them? What did explosives look like? And if he found them, what could he do to prevent them from detonating?

Nothing. Time was running out. He had to clear the place, and if the police would not help, he'd do it alone.

"Hey!" he cried at the top of his voice.

Two men at the edge of the crowd scowled at him, then returned to the spectacle on the stage.

Yosef ran south along the flank of the standing audience.

"Hey! All of you! Shoo! Get out of here. You are in danger. The Temple Mount is about to explode. Leave now!"

The speech continued unabated. Yosef's ranting had won only short-lived glares of irritation and shushing. What was this Jew doing here, interrupting their Messiah's speech?

He glanced back. The officers were running toward him now. His time was up. If only they had believed him.

He charged at the crowd, waving his arms and roaring like a raging bull.

That did it. The worshipers in his path lurched away from the raging Jew, clearing an opening in the mass of bodies.

"Your lives are in danger!" he declared. "Leave this place! Leave now!" He walked on, the horrified robed men edging away from the ranting madman, their eyes bulging.

Yosef pressed on, walking deeper into the crowd, repeating his mantra at the top of his voice and waving his hands. On and on he charged as the mass parted like the Red Sea.

The Arabs stared at him from an arm's length away. Did they understand a word he was saying?

He spun around, pleading with them, imploring them to flee, and discovered that the opening had closed behind him. The path had become a small air pocket within an ocean of Muslims. The police officers peered at him from the sidelines, their rage replaced with fear and concern for the trapped Israeli civilian.

Then the Messiah on the stage fell silent. The susurrus of a thousand whispers circled the crowd like a host of murmuring spirits. The worshippers blinked at Yosef, their surprise turning to annoyance and edging toward outrage. In their eyes, he read their thoughts. *An infidel in our midst! An intruder at our holy site!*

When the Messiah spoke again, his tone had changed. Yosef didn't understand a word, but he guessed the meaning as the clearing shrank and the crowd closed in on him. Not all the worshipers were old and frail. A dozen rough hands clamped onto his arms and prodded him forward. He fell over but didn't hit the ground. More hands gripped his legs, lifting him overhead, stretching his limbs in every direction.

He glimpsed blue skies above, and pain shot through his joints. Closing his eyes, he braced for the worst. His life was at the mercy of the mob now. He muttered a final prayer—*Shema Yisrael!* Hear O Israel!—when another voice echoed in his mind.

Your life is in danger!

CHAPTER 73

Eli sat at Noga's bedside, stroking her hair and willing her to wake up. Her vital signs had returned to normal hours ago, but she remained unconscious. Misinformation was tearing the world apart at the seams—on the one hand, fear of extinction by rogue asteroid; on the other, hope in a false messiah. Eli needed to go out there and fulfill his destiny before time ran out, but how could he leave her in this state?

"How much longer will it take?" he asked.

Dr. Stern looked up from his desk in the private field hospital. "I don't know. Judging by the speed with which her body recovered, I thought her mind would follow soon, but—"

"How long?" Eli had not meant to shout.

Dr. Stern lowered his eyes, looking old and haggard. "A few minutes. A few years. Never. Nobody's tried this treatment before, and she was out for so long. Maybe too long."

An anguished gasp escaped Eli's mouth. This was why he had avoided entanglements with mortals. Love might last forever, but humans didn't. Only Eli. Dr. Stern had located the Fountain of Youth in Eli's epigenetic makeup, but the discovery had come too late for the only girl who mattered.

Dr. Stern returned to the comfort of his computer screen.

"Don't do this to me," Eli whispered, addressing Noga or

God—he couldn't tell.

Had Noga served her purpose in the cosmic drama and become expendable? Did the same apply to Eli as well?

Months ago, lying in his hospital bed and mourning the loss of his powers, Eli had suspected that God had abandoned him. Perhaps he had lost the Magic because there would be no Redemption. Had God finally given up on humankind? That same depressing scenario rose in his mind now. In the time of Noah, God had promised never to send another flood. But there were other ways to wipe out humanity.

According to Moshe Karlin, at noon today, an asteroid would slam into the country, pulverizing the Jewish State. The impact would inject the atmosphere with enough dust and ash to create a year-long winter that would extinguish ninety percent of the planet's living creatures. Had humanity become expendable too?

He grasped Noga's hand. Was she better off asleep? That way, she wouldn't see her dream die and her world blasted into oblivion.

Her fingers twitched in his hand, and Eli bolted upright. "Noga?"

The eyelids fluttered.

He stroked her hair. "Noga, can you hear me?"

She opened her eyes and stared into his. "Eli?"

Her voice was soft and weak, but she was looking at him and she knew who he was. Eli couldn't hold back. A tense halting laughter jerked his body, and he bawled into her hand.

A chair shifted as Dr. Stern rushed to her bedside.

"Why are you crying?" she said. "Aren't you happy to see me?"

Eli wiped the tears from his cheeks, while Dr. Stern stood over them, his eyes glistening.

"Never been happier," Eli said.

Her eyes shifted back to him. "How long have I been gone? Does Karlin know about the Ten Tribes?"

Eli shushed her. He wanted to tell her that everything

would be fine, that she should rest and take it easy. There would be time to talk about everything. But that wasn't true. "It doesn't matter," he said. "You're OK. That's enough."

"No," she said. "We have a job to do." She struggled to sit up.

He placed a hand on her shoulder, holding her back. "Don't worry about it. You need to rest."

"Then you must do it," she said. "Go on without me. Promise me."

He looked at Dr. Stern, whose brow furrowed with unspoken questions. *Karlin? The Ten Tribes?*

"The thing is," Eli said, "it's too late."

"It can't be!"

There was no way around it now. "I'm so sorry," he said, "but it is. An asteroid is heading for Jerusalem. Karlin said so on the news. We have an hour left. I'd rather spend that hour with you."

"No," she said, shaking her head.

"I didn't want to have to tell you, but it's the truth. It's over, Noga. I'm sorry."

"No," she said. "It's only over when we stop trying."

Dr. Stern cleared his throat. "The asteroid scare might be a hoax."

"Then we have to try!"

"It doesn't matter. Isaac Gurion, that false prophet, has set up his own Messiah Coronation. It's underway right now."

"Who's he going to crown?"

"That's unclear. He claims that Karlin will attend the ceremony, but he hasn't said who his messiah will be."

"Then this is our chance. Maybe our final chance to get through to Karlin."

She might be right. "But... I don't want to leave you."

"Do it for me, Eli. We've come so far, you've waited so long."

He had waited long, but now that the moment had arrived, he faltered. Was this really about Noga, or, without the Magic and the Thin Voice, had he lost his nerve?

903

Dr. Stern jerked his head to the side, and Eli joined him a few steps away for a hushed consultation.

"Humor her," he said. "It might raise her spirits and aid her recovery."

Eli grasped around for more excuses. "What if you need me for another transfusion? Or your granddaughter? She needs treatment too."

As unpleasant as the transfusion had been, Eli would go through it a hundred times to spend his last hour with Noga.

The doctor's face slackened at the mention of his granddaughter. "That won't be necessary. She died two months ago." Dr. Stern seemed to crumble as he spoke the words.

Two months ago. During his stay at Shaare Zedek, Eli had evaded Dr. Stern's probing about his speedy recovery, desperate to conceal his identity. If he hadn't, the doctor's granddaughter might have lived.

"But," the doctor added, "it's not too late for Noga, or for this other little project of yours."

Another memory from Shaare Zedek rose in Eli's mind. *Never delay*, Oren, his roommate had said, shortly before his untimely death. *Or you will lose her.*

Eli stepped back to the bed. "OK," he said. "I'll do it." The smile on her face made his decision worthwhile. "But I want you feeling much better when I return."

"Deal!"

He kissed her, long and hard, then turned to Dr. Stern. "I need clothes."

CHAPTER 74

"If you don't mind me saying," Moshe's security chief said from the driver's seat later that morning, "this is a bad idea."

Alon might be right. Outside the windows of the SUV, people poured into the road beside the Mount Zion Hotel and the Jerusalem Cinematheque, thick as bees in a hive. In sweaters and ski caps, the common folk had hit the streets to greet their Messiah.

Moshe had set out for the Sultan's Pool with a single guard and without his usual cavalcade. The rest of his security detail he had sent home to their families. Yesterday, protestors had jumped the Knesset perimeter fence and hurled rocks at his window; would this gathering turn violent too?

The citizens didn't seem angry. Sighting the SUV, pedestrians jumped out of the way and let them pass. Many waved at the tinted windows or gave the thumbs-up.

As they rolled onto the bridge over the Hinnom Valley, Moshe learned why. A sequence of large images was displayed on a two-story billboard: a golden crown, Moshe's own likeness, and a turbaned young Arab.

What was Gurion up to? Spinning lies like webs, he had lured Moshe to the Messiah Coronation. Once caught in his sticky trap, would Moshe be able to wriggle free?

Let Gurion spin his webs. Moshe had his own mission to

complete, and then he'd hightail it to the Prime Minister's Residence.

"Stop here," he said.

"Sir, I recommend that you stay inside the vehicle."

"I'll stay close."

The SUV idling on the curb of the bridge, Moshe swung the door outward.

"There he is!" a man said.

More excited voices spoke. "That's him. That's Moshe Karlin!"

Moshe cringed, expecting a rotten tomato or a hook to the jaw. Instead, he found hopeful smiles.

He smiled back, crossed the road, and stepped up to the railing.

The Hinnom Valley squeezed between Mount Zion and the rise of modern West Jerusalem. The corner where the mountains converged had served the Ottomans as a reservoir. Today, the so-called the Sultan's Pool functioned as a stadium for open-air concerts.

Moshe leaned over the low stone wall of the bridge and peered through a gap in the Plexiglas barrier. This concert had sold out.

People blanketed the tidy rows of seats on the valley floor. Vendors moved between the rows, selling drinks and snacks. A red carpet ran along the main aisle and ended in a huge, black, boxlike structure, at least several stories tall, that dominated the stage. This Messiah Coronation had involved some serious preparations.

Alon joined him at the wall. He faced the street and unbuttoned his jacket, allowing free access to the holster at his side.

Moshe lifted the bullhorn he had packed for the ride and placed it between the Plexiglas dividers. Then he climbed onto the low wall and held down the press-to-talk button of the handset.

"Friends," he said, broadcasting his voice into the valley. Heads turned heavenward at the sound of the voice from above. "Fellow citizens. I know why you're here."

Voices cheered below; hands clapped. Bystanders filmed him on their mobile phones.

"You've heard unbelievable things in the media and from the Prime Minister's Office. Some are easier to swallow than others. We don't want to believe that our lives are in danger, or that the world we know is ending. It's much easier to hope that things will be OK."

The morning breeze played with his hair and caused feedback on the megaphone. He released the button. Every head turned to him. In the tense silence below, a man coughed. He had their undivided attention now.

He pressed the button again. "People exploit our desires and fears to get what they want and with little consideration for others. So, I've come here to tell you the ugly truth. The asteroid is real. We are all in great danger. The government is working to minimize the damage, but you must go home now, collect your loved ones, and take cover in the nearest bomb shelter."

Somebody cried out below. "You'll save us!"

Cheers erupted, then the voices chanted. *Kar-lin! Kar-lin! Kar-lin!*

Moshe enjoyed hearing his name as much as the next guy, but his supporters would remember Moshe Karlin in a very different light after their country got pulverized and they lost their loved ones.

"I should have said this a long time ago," he said into the handset, and the chant died down. "There are no magic wands. I cannot perform miracles or conjure natural disasters. I'm just a human being like you. And I am not the Messiah."

There, he had said it. Had they finally gotten the message? Voices echoed below. They were laughing. What was so funny?

The loudmouth cried out again, "That's what they said you'd say!"

The chant rose again. *Kar-lin! Kar-lin! Kar-lin!*

Moshe glanced at Alon, who shrugged. Once Gurion had

planted the seed of hope, how could he prove that he wasn't the Messiah? He glanced at his golden wristwatch, the piece Gurion had given him a lifetime ago for running with Upward in the elections. Under thirty minutes to impact. He needed a new tactic and fast.

"OK," he said. "If I say I'm the Messiah, will you go home?"

Cheers and applause.

What did it matter? He squeezed the talk button again. "Fine. Your Messiah commands you to go home and take cover. You have less than thirty minutes to reach safety. Go!"

More cheers below. His audience stood, but the crowds didn't run for the exits. Instead, they clapped. Another chant emerged. "Show us! Show us! Show us!"

Moshe released the button and swore under his breath. There was no winning with these people.

They wanted a show. Fine, he'd oblige. If he couldn't get through to them, he'd find someone who could.

"Isaac Gurion," he said into the loudspeaker. "Show yourself. You wanted to meet face-to-face. Time to show yours."

All eyes turned to the black box on the stage. The dark, foreboding structure recalled the warehouse where Mandrake had held Moshe captive. Whatever he did, Moshe should not go down there.

"Come on out, Isaac. Stop hiding."

As if in answer to the taunt, a loud *clank* issued from the box. A door-shaped rectangle fell away from the front of the box and crashed to the ground. All present waited with bated breath, but not a soul emerged from the box.

A new chant rose from the crowd. "Mo-she! Mo-she! Mo-she!"

The dark opening beckoned.

Gurion was running this show. Moshe wasn't the Messiah, and the people needed to hear it from Gurion.

"Mo-she! Mo-she! Mo-she!"

Fine!

Moshe climbed off the stone wall and returned to the

sidewalk. Abandoning the megaphone, he descended the ramp into the Hinnom Valley and the Sultan's Pool. The chant grew louder with his every step.

Let Gurion have his way. Let him hurl insults and accusations. If that was the fastest way to send his believers home, Moshe could handle it.

Moshe stepped into the arena. People rose from their seats and clapped their hands as he passed. He waved and pressed on, Alon at his heels.

The box rose five stories above him. Would the walls fall away as the door had, to reveal a dazzling stage to the delight of the audience?

He stood opposite the open doorway and peered inside, but the dark passageway faded into shadow.

C'mon, Isaac. Where are you?

The gaping hole called to him.

Moshe glanced at his wristwatch. Time was running out for the citizens in the arena. He'd have to end this charade quickly. He turned to Alon. "Wait here."

"But sir—!"

"It's OK. Gurion won't harm me in public, and I can't exactly walk onto the stage with an armed escort."

He stepped forward, and the crowd cheered. Another few steps and he was inside the box. The inner walls were of painted wood. Three meters in, the passage turned left.

Hinges creaked behind him, and he turned back. The door rose from the floor with a whoosh, snuffing out daylight, clicking shut, and entombing Moshe in darkness.

Oh, crap!

What a colossal mistake. Avi had warned him that Gurion wanted to kill him. But Moshe had not listened and now he had walked right into a trap.

Calm down. He won't kill you. Gurion wanted a public confrontation. He wanted to flaunt his power and hand Moshe a resounding defeat. He wouldn't resort to murder, would he?

Moshe had to get out of the box right away. He felt his way forward, retracing his steps to the door. His hands searched for a handle. He pushed outward, but the door wouldn't budge. He threw his weight at the wall, ramming with his shoulder and all his strength.

Then something hard slammed into the back of his skull, and he slumped to the floor.

CHAPTER 75

Ahmed watched as the rabbi's body floated over the crowd toward him.

"That's it," he said into the microphone. "Gently now."

The sight of the rabbi in the clearing, one bearded Jew in a sea of Muslims, had slapped Ahmed back to his senses and decided his internal conflict. He could not let this dear man die before his eyes. The rabbi had lost his mind, or he had a very urgent and important reason for risking his life. Either way, Ahmed would shelter him as the rabbi had done for him.

The body reached the end of the standing masses. "Now, place him on his feet." The befuddled men obeyed their Mahdi.

The rabbi stood, his shoulders hunched, every muscle in his body tensed for sudden flight. He looked up at him.

Ahmed beckoned with his hand. "Come here," he said in Hebrew. "Don't be afraid."

Many heads turned in the crowd and mouths tutted. Most of the crowd had not known the identity of the strange man they had supported over their heads, and the Mahdi's use of Hebrew now confirmed their suspicions.

The rabbi, clad in a black suit and skullcap, a brown beard streaked with white, and the white tassels of religious garb pouring from his belt, climbed the steps of the stage and inched toward the podium, his eyes filled with apprehension and focused on Ahmed.

Questions floated in the whispers of the multitude. What was a Jew doing here—and onstage with the Holy Mahdi?

In the corner of Ahmed's eye, Hasan writhed on his seat, his fists balled. This was not in the script. The Shepherd would exact a price for the failure. His cousin was probably weighing the benefits of rushing onto the stage to execute him on the spot, against the alternative of fleeing for his life. For now, he remained seated.

Ahmed had made his decision. The rabbi had forced his hand, and he was glad of it.

He laid a hand on Yosef's shoulder, and the rabbi flinched. "Welcome, Rabbi Yosef," he whispered. "Be not afraid."

The rabbi swallowed, not entirely at ease yet. He said, "We're in danger..."

Ahmed cut him short. "Nobody will harm you while you're with me."

The agitated murmuring of the masses below grew with each passing second. He had to calm them while he could.

"This man," Ahmed continued, speaking into the microphone in Arabic, "saved my life, and the lives of other Arabs. He took them into his home when they had nowhere else to go. Fed them. Clothed them. In return, he asked for nothing."

The whispers had settled, and in the many eyes, he saw anger turn to surprise and curiosity. As in Bethlehem, he sensed the thirst for a new message and a budding joy akin to relief.

"This man is not your enemy. Our enemies are lies and fear." At the edge of his vision, in the front row, Hasan twitched and buried his face in his hands.

Ahmed would pay for this later, and pay dearly, but for now, he rejoiced. This would not undo his terrible crimes, but for once he would spread light instead of darkness. He thought of Savta Sarah and Moshe Karlin. Most of all, he thought of Samira. By the time she heard of his speech today, it would be too late for Ahmed, but she would remember him with pride.

"We will only triumph," he continued, the words pouring from his soul, "when we realize that the true foe is not this nation or that, this belief or that, but the hatred we sow in our hearts."

He felt a tug on his arm. "Ahmed," Rabbi Yosef said. "There are explosives on the Temple Mount. We must ask everyone to leave at once."

The warm euphoric feeling fizzled in an instant.

"What explosives?"

"There are terrorists who want to destroy the Temple Mount, along with everyone here. A man with a red beard. He must have planted explosives all over."

Ahmed felt the blood drain from his cheeks. It was one thing to deliver a new message of hope, but to follow it with the threat of violent death?

The rabbi was not lying. At once, Ahmed understood why he had burst onto the mount and endangered his life.

While the two men on the stage conferred, the whispers resumed.

Ahmed cleared his throat. "This man saved my life. Today, he has saved us all. Now, listen carefully," he added, "and please, do not panic."

CHAPTER 76

Savta Sarah glanced at the next paper on the Speaker's podium.

"Item twenty-four," she read into the microphone. "The Tax Reform Law. I trust you all are familiar with it."

By "you all" she referred to the three Restart members of Knesset who had joined her in the Plenum Hall. They nodded their heads.

"All in favor, raise your hands."

Three hands rose in the air.

"Very well. Mrs. Secretary, please note that the law has passed."

The previous twenty-three laws had passed without incident and in record time. Today would go down in history as the most productive day the legislature had ever known.

"Mrs. Speaker," a man in a black suit called from the back row. "I must object again!"

Well, almost without incident.

Rabbi Mendel of Torah True had turned up and objected to every word that came out of her mouth. The nerve!

"Yes, Member of Knesset Mendel?"

"You cannot pass laws with such a low level of attendance!"

"We've been through this before, Mr. Mendel. This legislation requires no minimal quorum, and—"

In true Knesset tradition, Mendel didn't let her finish the sentence. "And," he spluttered, "you cannot pass laws with a single reading."

She rolled her eyes. "Again, Mr. Mendel, the first law we passed lifted those requirements for the legislation proposed today."

"But... but..."

She ignored the thorn in her side, turned the page, and ran out of pages. "Mrs. Secretary, have we reviewed all the items on our schedule?"

The Secretary, Mrs. Weinreb, a delightful young woman in her sixties, had tended to the red tape with a rush of taps on her keyboard. Working with professionals was such a pleasure.

Mrs. Weinreb read from her screen. "Let's see. We passed the Tycoon Law, the Law of Limited Government, the Tenure Abolition Law, the Anti-Cronyism Law, Land Registration Law, the six Transparency Laws, and the Law of Free Negotiation...."

That had been Savta's own modest contribution. Store owners could no longer complain when she asked for a discount. By law, she had the right to ask.

Mrs. Weinreb finished going through the list. "I think that covers everything."

"Excellent. Then it's time to go home."

Savta Sarah left the papers on the podium and made for the exit where Rafi waited. She put her arm in his, and they made for the car park. The Minister of Defense had stayed behind to make sure she left the building and got to safety in time. Moshe had seen to that, lovely boy.

"How did it go?" he asked as they strolled through the Knesset corridors.

"Very well. It's about time the country ran freely and fairly."

"Yes, indeed. I hope we get to see that in practice."

"Me too."

Outside, he held the door of the car open for her. "To the Prime Minister's Residence?"

Moshe had invited her to watch the operation from the safety of the Prime Minister's bunker. "Not today," she said. "Take me home. I defrosted all that meat; it'll go bad if I don't get to work soon."

"You're cooking—today of all days?"

"Rafi, dear, if we survive this, there will be celebrations. And celebrations need food."

CHAPTER 77

From the driver's seat, Alex reached over and opened the glove compartment. He grabbed his Glock and checked the cartridge before lodging the gun between his legs. Something wasn't right.

His black Hyundai idled a short walk from Shamai Street. Irina had left to collect her things fifteen minutes ago. She should have been back by now.

He had spent so long under Mandrake's wing that he'd never imagined how it felt to be on the wrong side of him. By now the crime lord had realized that Alex would not deliver on his final mission.

Nobody left the Organization. After all he and Mandrake had been through together, Alex had believed that he'd be different. He'd been kidding himself. In hindsight, he should have disappeared without a word. Instead, Alex had opened his big mouth and triggered the fulfillment of his worst fears.

Had Mandrake even expected him to follow through or had he assigned him an impossible mission, one he would surely fail? His twisted mind enjoyed creating that semblance of justification. Mandrake didn't crave the moral high ground; he had strangled whatever conscience nature had endowed him long ago. But the moralizing seemed to give him a sadistic pleasure, to torture a man with the idea that he had brought Mandrake's cruelty down on his own head.

A hundred terrifying scenarios flashed through his mind: Irina slumped over, a tidy round hole in her forehead; Irina strapped to Mandrake's man-sized red dartboard, pleading for her life.

He should never have allowed her to return to his apartment. Now she had fallen into Mandrake's hands, and only one more decision remained: was Alex going to follow her?

He swore and thumped the steering wheel with his fists. Why had she popped back into his life and turned everything upside down? Not that he'd been happy before; her death had torn him apart. But at least he had been alive. Now, Mandrake saw him as a traitor, and in this line of work, traitors didn't live long.

You idiot! Alex had deluded himself that he could redeem his past, that he and Irina could live happily ever after and leave the terrors of the past behind. Now he had lost everything: his love, his oldest friend, and the only career he'd ever known.

Only his life remained. For how long, he didn't know. If he wanted to keep breathing, he'd better shift the stick into Drive and never look back.

A blond woman appeared around the corner of the building and his heart jumped in his chest. The woman spoke into her phone, a handbag tucked under her arm, and marched on. She wasn't Irina.

Alex punched the wheel again. Then, leaving the motor running, he opened the door and got out. He shoved the handgun into the back of his jeans and beneath his jacket.

He couldn't do it. Not again. Alex had given her up once before, and the trauma had ripped his soul.

He walked around the back of his apartment building, scanned the street for Mandrake's thugs, and continued to the entrance. This second chance wouldn't come again. He'd already decided. A dozen times, he could have walked away, out of her life. Each time, he had returned. If he abandoned her again, his soul wouldn't tear; it would shrivel and die.

What point would there be in breathing?

Shoving fear and indecision out of his mind, he focused on the task at hand. This was a job, like any other, but this time, he was working for himself. For Irina.

He punched the code into the keypad and pushed through the door. Taking the steps two at a time, he landed on the balls of his feet and glanced up the pier, gun in hand, searching for killers lying in ambush.

He reached the door of his apartment without incident and touched the handle. Had the fear all been in his head? Had she taken a bathroom break?

Unlocked, the door swiveled inward. He checked the corridor, then stepped into the kitchen.

Irina stood by the counter, facing him, her arms hugging her chest. He exhaled a pent breath. She was alive! But her fearful eyes flitted to the side where a man slouched in a kitchen chair—the gray-haired man in the tweed coat from the elevator. The man stared at Alex, the revolver in his hand trained on Irina, while a smile spread beneath his bushy mustache.

Alex could slug him, but not before the man fired his gun at Irina, and, at this range, he wouldn't miss.

Before Alex could decide what to do, the question became moot. Thick arms slipped under his armpits, lifting him off the floor and spreading his arms wide like useless wings, while tough hands shoved his head downward. His gun clattered to the square tiles of the old kitchen.

"Finally," Boris said. "The man of the moment has arrived."

CHAPTER 78

Yosef stared at the crowd of Arabs below the stage. Moments ago, they had seemed ready to rip him limb from limb; now, they were helping him catch a terrorist.

"A redhead," he whispered to Ahmed, "with a beard. Not an Arab." The former suicide bomber translated his words into Arabic and spoke them into the microphone.

Headdresses shifted from side to side as worshipers conferred with each other and glanced around the Temple Mount.

"They should spread out and leave the Temple Mount in an orderly fashion using the nearest exits." Ahmed nodded and translated. The masses dispersed, exposing the neat lawns and cobbled pathways of the wide enclosure, and clustered at the exits.

Yosef's heart thumped in his ears. Any moment, the stones and trees could burst into flame as the charges detonated around them.

A clean-shaven Arab from the front row approached the stage and yelled at them. Yosef didn't understand the angry words, and he was glad for it. Ahmed stared the man down but said nothing. Then the Arab stalked off.

The lines at the gates shrank as the Temple Mount emptied. Had Yosef sounded a false alarm? Had Tom planned merely to disrupt the gathering? Yosef could live with that.

A commotion broke out, and voices shouted. A half-dozen white-robed Arabs burst back into the Temple Mount, pushing and shoving another man. Their quarry stumbled forward and fell to the ground. The *kaffiyeh* fell from his head, revealing a head of red hair.

"Get away from me!" he cried in Hebrew, and even at the distance, Yosef recognized Tom Levi's voice.

"What do we do with him?" Ahmed asked.

One of the Arabs kicked Tom, and Yosef shuddered. He had wanted to prevent bloodshed, but now he had turned a scared and angry mob against a lone, defenseless Jew.

"The police," Yosef said. "Hand him over to the police."

Ahmed spoke into the microphone again. The robed Arabs stood down as black-clad officers rushed to the beleaguered man and dragged him away.

"Thank you," Yosef said. Together, they had averted a catastrophe.

"No," Ahmed replied. "Thank you." A sadness clouded his features. "Now I must go. I fear we shall never meet again."

The gloomy words surprised him. "What do you mean?"

But Ahmed didn't explain. "Tell Moshe Karlin to stay away from the coronation."

"What coronation?"

"The Messiah Coronation. At the Sultan's Pool. I must go. It is my fate. But Moshe is a good man; he must stay away. This will not end well."

Questions vied for attention in Yosef's mind, but he held them back. Moshe was in danger; Yosef had to warn him. "I haven't been able to reach him since yesterday. I was busy with, well, with this." He gestured at the Temple Mount around them.

Ahmed walked to the ramp at the side of the stage. "Find him," he said.

Arabs in kaffiyehs and turbans greeted him and escorted him as he walked.

Find him. Yosef felt his empty trouser pockets. His cell phone must have slipped out when the crowd had carried him overhead and shattered beneath a thousand pairs of trampling feet.

This "Messiah Coronation" did not sound like good news. In Yosef's experience, such events never were.

Ahmed and his believers grew smaller as they moved through the grounds of the Temple Mount. Somewhere beneath the lawns and pathways, the Great Temple had once stood. Yosef must have trodden on that holy site tonight, transgressing a handful of Biblical prohibitions. Now that he had averted the bombing, was he permitted to cross that hallowed ground again?

The Talmud allowed Jews to travel on the Sabbath to redeem Jewish hostages. The law also allowed them to return home, desecrating the holy day a second time. Otherwise, they might not have embarked on the sacred mission. Did the same apply to Yosef today? If Ahmed was right, another life depended on his mobility—the Prime Minister of Israel.

Yosef raced after the receding entourage. "Hold on," he cried. "Wait for me!"

CHAPTER 79

Eli descended the ramp to the Sultan's Pool that morning, a bottle of oil in his hand and a fire in his heart. *How dare Gurion!*

Eli detested false prophets. Fame motivated some, fortune others. Some were simply off their rocker. All three factors seemed to apply to Isaac Gurion. Eli Katz was the last true prophet, and Gurion would pay for his brazen lies.

A thrill of déjà vu made him shiver. This was Mount Carmel all over again. The result would probably be the same. The common folk enjoyed a good show. Rain fire and brimstone, and they'd fall to their knees. Tomorrow, they'd return to their old idolatrous ways.

That didn't absolve Eli of his task, and this time should be easier. At Mount Carmel, he had stood alone against two hundred prophets of Baal. Today, he'd face only one opponent. If only Noga could see it.

He had left her in the doctor's care after borrowing an ill-fitting set of clothes and a wad of cash and set out to meet his destiny. At a corner store on Hebron Road, he'd picked up the rectangular bottle of Yad Mordechai virgin olive oil. After confronting the false prophet, he'd anoint the true Messiah. He'd work out the details on the way.

The common folk had packed the stadium in the small

valley to capacity. They didn't seem concerned about the asteroid threat, and he understood why. Trust in the news outlets had eroded in recent years as conflicting editorials muddied the waters of truth.

Today, the People of Israel would find clarity. He felt it in his bones. Not the certainty of the Thin Voice, but a very human sensation in his gut. The Boss had a plan. Eli had learned his lessons. The world was worth saving, and the End of Death was within grasp. The Grandmaster had positioned the pieces for the final checkmate, and Eli stepped onto the board, ready to play his part. This time *would* be different. It had to be. Maybe this time, when the smoke cleared, the people would learn their lesson too.

Spectators overflowed from the seats and perched on the rocky slopes of the Hinnom Valley. Thousands of years ago, the valley had glowed red with the pyres of human sacrifice. Humanity had progressed since then, but today the valley would burn once more.

Eli halted in the main aisle between the rows of crowded seats. A black square monolith dominated the stage, rising fifty feet into the air like an alien spaceship. No sign of Gurion, or Karlin for that matter. He scanned the sea of spectators. They watched the stage and chatted among themselves.

The path ahead was clear: confront the prophet, anoint the Messiah. But where were they?

"Hey!" said a voice, and a hand waved at him a few rows back.

The man with brown curls had a rounded, pudgy face. Eli didn't know him. Was he another player in the Divine game? Eli drew near.

The man held out a fifty-shekel note. "We'll have two Maccabees," he said. "And make it snappy; the show's about to start."

"Two what?"

Did he say "Maccabees"? During the Hellenistic Era, Eli had avoided the guerrilla warriors. Look at them the wrong way and they'd accuse you of being an Antiochus sympathizer and relieve you of your head.

This pudgy man, however, seemed uninterested in ancient Jewish rebellions. He gave Eli an "are you deaf or just stupid?" look, and said, "Beers. Two of them. And a large popcorn too."

Eli glanced at the bottle of oil in his hand and understood what had happened. "I'm not selling anything." The man frowned and looked around for another vendor. "Tell me," Eli added, turning the interaction to his own benefit, "have you seen Isaac Gurion?"

"Not since we got here. Only the Prime Minister."

"Moshe Karlin?"

The question won him another "yes, stupid" look. "The one and only. He walked into the black box. Haven't seen him since. Pretty lame teaser, if you ask me." He glanced at the stage and chuckled. "Looks like his security guard didn't get the memo."

Eli turned to look at the large black structure. Sure enough, a military type in a dark suit jacket walked around the black box, testing the walls for a way in, and scratching his head.

Eli's gut writhed. The false prophet had stood him up, and a large black box had just devoured his only Messiah candidate.

Then voices murmured, and arms pointed toward the ramp. Two men entered the valley, their entourage of white kaffiyehs following at a respectful distance. One of the vanguards wore a white flowing robe; the other sported a black suit and familiar brown beard. Rabbi Yosef Lev!

Hands clapped, and people stood to get a better view of the Vice Prime Minister and his Arab companions.

"Finally," the pudgy man said. Then he swore. A woman screamed, and a dozen hands pointed at the sky.

Eli looked up. In the blue dome above burned a star, bright and large. The celestial light waxed larger every second, and a short tail stuck out behind, as though the star was heading right for them.

Not a star. An asteroid!

More voices joined the cry. Men and women launched from their seats, pushing and elbowing as they charged for the exits. Eli stepped aside and dodged the trampling herd.

He lost sight of Rabbi Yosef in the pandemonium, but as the spectators surged up the ramp and hurried out of the valley, the field cleared. Among the abandoned seats, strewn with popcorn boxes, spilled drinks, dropped shoes and scarves, three men remained at the base of the black box.

Eli joined them.

The rabbi turned at the sound of his footfalls, and his eyes widened.

"You," he said. "The biker." A short burst of joy escaped his lips. "You survived."

Eli raised the bottle of oil. "My jar of quality stuff didn't, so this will have to do."

The rabbi looked from Eli to the bottle of olive oil, and his eyes widened further.

"Are you a part of the coronation?" asked the security guard.

"I'm not with Isaac Gurion if that's what you mean, but his phony event has pushed up our schedule. We haven't been formally introduced." He put out his hand to Yosef. "Elijah of Anatot."

Rabbi Yosef released another gasp. He accepted Eli's hand, his fingers cold and thin. "I thought you'd never arrive."

"Same here."

The rabbi's lips moved as he pieced the information together. "That day at the Mount of Olives—you were there for Moshe?"

Eli gave the rabbi what he hoped looked like a wise and mysterious grin. He still was not one hundred percent sure of anything.

"I've been through a lot since then, as have we all." He looked up at the asteroid burning overhead. "And we're running out of time."

The rabbi shook his head as if waking from a trance. "This is Ahmed."

The Arab shook his hand, his expression distant, sad. "We must warn Moshe not to come here," he said. "The coronation is not what he thinks."

"Too late. He's already inside."

Ahmed turned back to the sealed black box. "Inside—but how?"

As if in answer, a panel at the front of the box fell outward like a drawbridge and slammed onto the floor of the stage with a heavy wooden *thunk*.

They stared at the black hole. Although not exactly inviting, the passageway had placed only one option on the table.

Eli had waited two thousand years for this moment, the reason for his existence. The box held the future Messiah and, probably, the last false prophet. What other surprises waited within?

The way ahead would be dangerous. His weapons included a bottle of oil and centuries of experience. But the situation was unfit for mortals.

"You three go home and take cover. I'll take this from here."

"Try to stop me," said the security agent. "The Prime Minister just disappeared on my watch."

Rabbi Yosef straightened. "Moshe might need my help. He'd do the same for me."

"No," Ahmed said. "None of you belong in there." He pulled a golden envelope from a fold of his robe. "The Shepherd invited me, not you. I have blood on my hands, but you don't. Save yourselves."

Eli sighed. "OK then." He turned toward the black doorway. "After me."

CHAPTER 80

Samira raced a wheeled trolley down the corridor of the DBS fourth-floor dormitory, peering in the doorways and distributing extra blankets. She had ten minutes to finish her rounds and take cover before the asteroid hit.

The DBS had heeded Moshe's warning and made preparations, while the rest of the country dashed for cover in panic.

A volunteer named Nir ran toward her. "There's chaos in room 439," he said, pointing down the corridor. "The monkey-men are tearing bags off the windows!"

"Here." Samira reached into her canvas shoulder bag and dumped a pack of crayons. "Let them draw on the walls. They love it!"

"Great idea!" Nir sprinted off.

"Irina's," Samira said. "Works like a charm."

Thanks to Irina's stroke of genius, a hundred prehistoric humans scrawled animals and stick-figure hunters on the dormitory walls instead of causing their usual havoc.

She hadn't seen her friend and partner since early that morning. Samira hoped she had taken cover already. They had drawn up a set of instructions for DBS Absorption Centers around the country. Now they could only wait and hope that Moshe pulled off another miracle.

Moshe had saved them from physical slavery, redeemed

them from bureaucratic limbo, and catapulted their cause to the pinnacle of power. He had also coordinated an astounding recovery from an earthquake of unprecedented devastation. If anyone could deal with a speeding asteroid, he was the man.

Out of blankets, she dumped the trolley in a corner and took the stairs to the third floor. She'd make one final round of the Call Center to check for stragglers, then crawl under the cot bed in her own room, arms over her head, and brace for impact. The asteroid would hit Jerusalem, Moshe had said, but there was no time or resources to transfer the many DBS residents to other cities.

In the Call Center, she checked the cubicles and peered through the glass window of the corner office. All clear. As she made to leave, a man blocked the doorway of the Call Center. The Arab wore white robes and a *kaffiyeh,* and for a moment fear nailed her to the spot. Had her father discovered that she was alive? Had he hunted her down to restore his tainted family honor?

She recognized the face. The man was neither her father nor a relative, but Ahmed's new friend, Dara. Now other emotions struggled in her heart.

In Ahmed, she had found a friend and true confidant. Violence had snuffed out their short first lives, and they had endured the same trauma of exploitation in their second. He had treated her with warmth and concern and given her gifts. She had imagined a future together, an escape from the terrors of her past. Together they would build a new family for their new lives. That dream had exploded into a thousand shards the moment Shmuel had identified him and pummeled him on the floor of the DBS. Her Ahmed, a murderer? That couldn't be! But Ahmed had not denied the accusation; instead, he had run away. From his crimes. From her.

She had thought of him often. Her Ahmed was no cold-blooded murderer. And yet, every day, ordinary men and women committed unimaginable violence. Who knew that better than she did? Had Ahmed fallen prey to the death machine that lurked in the shadows?

She had wondered what had become of him. Had he found a new home? Had the slave driver, Boris, and his frightening musclemen found him and hurt him? Was he dead already?

The answers had turned up on the doorstep of the DBS a few days ago. Ahmed was alive! He had new friends and a new name but had he learned nothing. She had seen through the money and the fancy new clothes and found the same death machine.

Now, Dara had turned up again, alone. She studied Dara's eyes for clues. Had the machine sucked Ahmed into the grinder again?

"Is he alive?" she said.

Ahmed's friend seemed surprised at the question. "Yeah, he's alive. Today is his coronation." He rolled his shoulders, a gesture of arrogant self-assurance, the fool. "He wanted me to give you this." Dara held out a letter.

A prickle of hurt registered inside. "Is he too important to speak to me in person?"

"Take it," Dara said. "Please. This is very important to him. If he could deliver it in person, he would have. He made me swear to hand this to you and only you."

Samira sighed. She had no time for games.

"Whatever," she said. She took the letter and shoved it into her canvas shoulder bag. "Now if you'll excuse me, I have to go."

CHAPTER 81

Alex saw his own death before his eyes. He writhed in the thug's iron embrace, kicking his legs in the air, while Boris smiled and trained the barrel of the gun at his chest. If he fired, the bullet might pass through him and hurt his hench-man, and for the moment that had worked to his advantage.

The muscleman pressed his hands forward, shoving Alex's head downward and pulling his arms back. Bolts of searing pain pierced his neck and shoulders like electric shocks. He stopped struggling, and the pressure eased. Resistance was futile.

A month ago, Alex had sat in the front seat of a black Mercedes on King George Street. A motorcyclist had aimed a handgun at the windshield while a brown van had screeched to a halt in the opposite lane. In the rearview mirror, a masked thug had pulled Moshe Karlin from the backseat like a baby from a crib, then walked behind the car, holding his captive in the same immobilizing grip.

These were Mandrake's men. They would act without hesitation or mercy. He had seconds to turn the situation around.

He'd bargain with the gunman, beg him to let Irina go—Alex was the one Mandrake wanted, not her—and he'd use the diversion to surprise them. Alex opened his mouth to speak, but Boris beat him to the punch.

"I'm glad to meet you," he said. "My name is Boris." The gun relaxed in his hand, the barrel resting on his leg. "We share an employer."

Alex didn't fall for the friendly words. Boris had borrowed a page from Mandrake's playbook. Alex should expect the worst, but for now, he'd play along.

"Is this how you greet all your coworkers?"

The mustache shifted again as he smiled. "My apologies. Igor, please."

The muscleman released his grip, easing Alex to the floor, and he slid the gun from the floor.

How much had Mandrake told him? And how much of that had Boris told Irina? Had she had learned the truth? He feared that more than Boris's bullets.

His eyes flitted to Irina. She was breathing heavily, her lips pressed together, terror reflected in her eyes.

He could rush Boris. With luck, he'd overpower him before he could fire his weapon, but that hulking Igor would be close behind. Alex could handle himself in a fight, but alone and unarmed, the odds were against him. And Igor would make short work of Irina. If she was lucky.

"I've come for the girl," Boris said. "She didn't deliver the goods so she's outlived her utility. Which is where I come in. I have a little debt to settle here too. Irina and I go way back. But," he added, "not as far back as you two."

Irina's brow wrinkled as her eyes searched his. "What is he talking about?" they asked.

"Oh, yes," Boris continued, his mustache askew over his smile. "I only met Irina in her second life. But you two go back even further, don't you?"

CHAPTER 82

Moshe hovered in the dark like a hummingbird. Or an angel.

His arms were wrapping his body, and his legs had fused. An appendage pulled at his back between his shoulder blades. Did he have wings?

Was this the Spirit World that Rabbi Yosef had mentioned—the immaterial dimension between lives?

The back of his head stung. He had stumbled in the dark of the black box when something had struck him. Was this real pain or the memory of his physical body, the itch of an amputated limb?

A switch clicked, and a spotlight blinded him. Heavy footsteps approached. This was not the Spirit World; this was Gurion's web.

Moshe prepared to negotiate with his nemesis. He would offer him the world. He would beg and plead. Whatever it took, he'd get Gurion to send the civilians outside to safety.

The footsteps halted in front of him. But when Moshe hazarded a peek through his shuttered eyelids, his heart sank. His field of vision filled with a beak nose and large, sensitive eyes. This was not Isaac Gurion; this was his worst nightmare.

"Welcome back, Moshe," Mandrake intoned in his Russian accented baritone. This time, his bald abductor sported a thick handlebar mustache and a tuxedo, complete with frilly dress shirt and bowtie. The madman looked both ridiculous and terrifying. He grinned. "Did you miss me? I missed you." He stalked off into the shadows of what appeared to be a stage.

Moshe had to escape and fast. He used the respite to take in his surroundings. A white straitjacket pinned his arms to his chest. Heavy, bulky pads wrapped his legs together. The long, taut rope that suspended him from his back disappeared into the darkness above.

"Get ready for the show of a lifetime," Mandrake continued from the shadows. He chuckled. "Well, *your* lifetime."

Mandrake returned to the spotlight. A cape of black satin fell over his back, and a top hat sat at a rakish angle on his head. He adjusted the mustache beneath his nose and rapped the wooden floor twice with a silver-pommeled walking cane.

"I've waited a long time for this day. So many preparations. Things never turn out quite as one plans, do they? We'd hoped for a larger turnout, but we'll make do with this small private audience."

With a flourish of the cane, he indicated the gloom behind him. Beyond the black wooden planks of the stage, a row of three shadowy figures shifted in the darkness. Tied to their seats and gagged sat Alon, a stranger with thick hair, and... was that Rabbi Yosef? What was he doing here?

"Unfortunately," Mandrake said, "due to time constraints, we've had to trim the program down. Shall we skip to the grand finale?"

He gave the cane a sharp switch to the side, and the bottom flew off to reveal a long thin blade.

In a dark warehouse on Election Day, Mandrake had blindfolded Moshe and pretended to throw knives. This time, his tormentor would not limit his act to scare tactics.

Mandrake laughed. "Oh, Moshe. No, this isn't for you. It's for him." He pointed the blade to the left.

An upright, mirrored box sat on the stage. From large holes protruded two arms and a head with a flowing white *kaffiyeh*—the Arab boy from the billboard. Smaller holes covered the mirrors at his chest—slots for the insertion of long, thin blades. The boy stared ahead, his eyes glazed over.

"For you, Moshe," Mandrake continued, "I've prepared something special. Vitaly!" he cried. "Positions."

Footsteps thumped on the stage behind him, and wheels turned in pulleys. The rope at Moshe's back jerked upward, lifting him ten feet in the air and out of the sword's reach. His relief was short-lived.

Mandrake's bald assistant in black tied off the rope to a steel clasp on the stage floor, then pushed a large glass container the size of an elevator into view. Water sloshed in the brimming open roof as Vitaly positioned the container beneath Moshe's feet.

Oh, God, no! Moshe inhaled shallow, panicked breaths.

"Ta-dah!" Mandrake cried. He spun around, and his cape billowed behind him. "How sweet. Our two Messiahs, together for the first time. And the last."

Two messiahs? Mandrake too thought that Moshe was the Messiah, along with the poor Arab kid. But would he murder them both in front of three witnesses? With chaos and destruction about to descend on the country, he'd get away with it.

Moshe's body writhed. Soon, the entire country would burn, but his survival instinct chose "sudden pulverization later" over "slow drowning now."

"Now, for the magic," Mandrake said. "I'm old school. I don't hold with smoke and mirrors. Our audience deserves the real thing—real blood and real guts."

Moshe wriggled and strained against his bonds. His life couldn't end this way. He had to escape. Despite his efforts, he still jiggled over the watery deathtrap.

He had to create a diversion, to delay a little longer. "While there is life, there is hope," Rabbi Yosef had said. Any minute, the asteroid would hit, bringing either instant death or a lifesaving miracle.

"Aw," Mandrake said, his voice dripping with false empathy. "I know, I know. This sucks. You'll die a slow, miserable death, and I'll walk away. You think I'm a bad person, don't you? Well, step into my shoes for a moment. This isn't what I wanted. I just wanted to be loved." He leaned in and hissed. "The *goyim* made me who I am. Everywhere I went I was 'the Jew.' I mean, look at me." He tapped his beak nose. "I couldn't escape it. One look at me and they saw a cheat, a thug, a murderer. One day I stopped running. I embraced it. I became the monster. And you know what? It worked. Everybody feared 'the Jew.'"

The madman's words crowded Moshe's adrenaline-charged brain. He wasn't buying the sympathy ploy, but there was a thread of truth in the criminal overlord's story. But whereas Moshe had leveraged the same malignant projections to save lives, Mandrake used them to justify his reign of terror.

Mandrake grinned. "Thanks for listening, Moshe. I appreciate it. But now it's time to say goodbye."

He stepped up to the steel clasp on the floor and rested the sword on the rope. *No!* Moshe scrabbled for diversions to draw out the inevitable. *Think, Moshe! Keep him talking.*

"I'm not the Messiah," he said, his voice a croak in his parched throat.

Mandrake cocked his head to the side and put a finger to his lips. "Do you hear that?"

Moshe did. The distant rumble outside grew louder, the familiar patter of rotors. A helicopter circled above. Were IDF commandos about to rescue their Prime Minister? Moshe grasped at the straws of hope. *Oh, God, please!*

The chopper did not seem to bother Mandrake.

"Speak of the Devil," he said, and he chuckled. "Ladies and gentlemen, you are in luck. This is a rare honor. A rare honor, indeed!"

Moshe had that sinking feeling. Mandrake had been expecting the helicopter, just not now. The aircraft was his escape route ahead of the asteroid strike. But what was this dubious "rare honor"?

He didn't guess for long. The chopper landed on the roof of the rectangular structure with two heavy thumps. Light poured in from above as a trap door opened and closed, and shoes clanked on metal steps.

"Ladies and gentlemen," Mandrake boomed. "Prepare to meet your Maker!"

CHAPTER 83

A knocking on the cabin door disturbed the captain of the USS Ohio during the climax of his favorite movie, The Hunt for Red October. He paused the player on his iPad, pulled off his earphones, and prepared to unload his annoyance on the visitor. *What now?* The crew knew better than to disturb him on his off time. A month of latrine duty should teach the NUB a lesson.

But when he swung the steel door open, his executive officer stood in the passageway, apprehension painted over his face. His annoyance evaporated, replaced by the same nausea he had experienced only yesterday.

"Is the sea monster back?" he whispered.

"No, sir."

The captain exhaled a pent-up breath, and his nausea returned. They were on their way home and nearing for the Strait of Gibraltar. "Well, what is it?"

"Orders just came in." The XO handed him a printout of a decrypted message.

The captain read the orders, and the sinking feeling returned. After ten years in the Silent Service, he'd thought he'd seen it all, but within the space of two days, he'd been blindsided twice.

"This must be a mistake."

"I asked for confirmation, sir. Confirmation received and double-checked."

The captain swore under his breath and grabbed his captain's hat. Without a word, the officers hurried down the narrow, rounded corridor to the Command Room.

"Did you check with the other subs?"

"Yes, sir. They all received identical orders."

Dear Lord. The orders were clear and so were the ramifications. World war. Mutual assured destruction. The end of civilization.

A dozen pairs of nervous eyes greeted the officers as they burst into Command and Control and took their positions.

"Officers, open the launch tubes."

"How many, sir?"

"All of them. XO, relay the target coordinates."

"Done, sir."

The captain moved from his seat to peer over the shoulder of the launch engineer. He had launched dozens of missiles in training simulations but had never encountered coordinates like these. "What's with that extra figure, officer?"

The officer looked up. "Altitude, sir."

The captain took a few seconds to process the information. "The target is airborne?"

"Yes, sir. Well, to be more precise, in orbit."

The hotshots in the Oval Office were taking out satellites. The Trident missile had an internal guidance computer with precision correction provided by its star sighting navigation system. But hitting a satellite required accuracy beyond the missile's capabilities.

And what satellite justified that much firepower? Each missile contained twelve warheads, each with a yield of one hundred kilotons—six times more destructive force than the nuke that flattened Hiroshima. Yesterday, sea monsters; today, attacks on UFOs?

He returned to his seat. At the end of the day, he was a soldier and he'd execute his orders. He just hoped the President knew what he was doing.

"Officers," he said. "Wait for my mark. Launch commences in five minutes and counting."

CHAPTER 84

Moshe dangled over the water chamber as their visitor stepped off the metal staircase and walked to center stage. Moshe's mouth dropped open. *Prepare to meet your Maker*, Mandrake had said. In many ways, the man was just that. He was also the last person Moshe had expected to see here today.

"Hello again," the man said, in English and with his usual Texas drawl.

Moshe gawked at the silver-haired, suited juggernaut that was Reverend Henry Adams. Words eluded him. Had the reverend flown in to save him? Or had he also fallen into Mandrake's trap? The American stood beside the rabid magician, two old friends surveying their handiwork.

Adams looked over his shoulder at the three bound men. "Rabbi Yosef," he said, by way of greeting, then turned back to Moshe. "I'm sorry our arrangement has to end this way. You were doing so well. Far better than we had anticipated."

Moshe found his tongue. "Did Isaac Gurion put you up to this? Don't believe a word he says. He's a liar!"

Adams chuckled. "Oh, I know. Not a pleasant man, either. He had a way of getting ahead of himself. But this time his head got away from him." He smiled at his own joke. "He won't be bothering you again. Or anyone else. Not unless he returns from the dead as you did."

The words stunned Moshe back into silence. Gurion was dead. Adams had seen to that. But why?

"If it's any consolation, you make a much better messiah."

"But I'm not the Messiah!"

"What you are doesn't matter, only what people *think* you are."

Moshe thought he understood. "Your messiah didn't show, so you want the other messiahs dead?"

Adams sent Mandrake a bemused look. "Moshe," he said, his voice patronizing and disappointed. "We never wanted a messiah. The New Evangelical Church of America is a front, a helpful tool to part fools and their money. Our organization is larger than any one religious institution. And far, far older. Its tendrils stretch around the world, and yet each branch knows little of the others."

Adams drew near and stared up at him. "The last few centuries have been very good to us. We made tidy profits off wars and drugs. Now we've gone hi-tech. Anything can become a weapon in the right hands: airplanes, medicines, words. The most powerful by far is hope.

"Take Paradise, for example. The hope for a spiritual reward in the hereafter allows good people to endure suffering and ignore injustice in the here-and-now. And why not? This world is just a passageway. God will repay their injured souls a thousand-fold in Heaven. So, they busy themselves with their prayers and their rituals. Fixing the world isn't their job, anyway. That task belongs to the Messiah.

"And so, while believers yearn for paradise and the redeemers of tomorrow, our organization spreads its roots today."

He pointed at Moshe and snarled. "Then you came along with your resurrection. The afterlife is here. People would ask questions. 'Is this our ultimate reward?' 'Is this is the only world?' 'Should we stop praying and start paying attention?' All we needed was a messiah to come along and declare the end of history. But history must go on. Hope must go on.

Our business model depends on it. And so, the Messiahs must die."

Now Moshe did understand. "You kept the Dry Bones Society close, waiting for the Second Coming, so you could nip the Messiah in the bud. When that didn't materialize, you created your own messiah. I was a natural candidate. But when I refused to claim the title, you set up this coronation and got Gurion to lure me here."

Adams bowed his head, then circled back to Mandrake.

"It won't work," Moshe said, desperate to keep the conversation going. "I'm just one man. Others will rise up after me and complete the work I've begun."

Adams seemed amused. "Will they? Messiahs have cropped up over the ages. They all failed. Many met unpleasant deaths, and my predecessors were glad to help out with that." He winked. "But guess what happened right after the messiahs' spectacular failures. Did their believers give up or change their tactics? Oh, no. Their faith increased. They had misread the signs or miscalculated the dates. The Messiah would be back and even sooner than they thought."

The reverend—no, the Anti-Messiah—glanced at his wristwatch. "And now, history repeats itself once again. And where better than Jerusalem, the Eye of the Universe, to which all believers turn in hope. Your plan to save the planet might just work, Moshe. We appreciate your efforts on our behalf. Once the dust settles, the survivors will discover that, alas, their Messiahs have perished. The hope will go on. And we'll be there to reap the profits."

Adams turned to Mandrake. "The stage is yours." Then, to the room at large he added, "Please forgive my theatrical colleague over here, but I find that, now and then, it's best to indulge his flair for the dramatic. Enjoy the show."

Mandrake raised his sword.

"Wait!" Moshe cried.

But Mandrake didn't. He swung the blade with all his might at the rope.

CHAPTER 85

Irina stared at Alex, the gun in Boris's hand forgotten. Was it true? Had Alex known about her former life and not told her? What role had he played in that life?

"Oh, yes," Boris said. "You go way back. Isn't that so, Alex? But you didn't tell her. I understand why."

She searched Alex's eyes for the truth. His face turned pale, but he said nothing. His silence said it all. Alex was not the man she thought she knew.

Boris turned to her. "Our boss entrusted Alex with a whole new department. He placed advertisements in Lithuanian newspapers, offering secretarial work overseas for a few lucky young women. The job required no prior experience, only a photograph. The approval process was very selective. But when the lucky applicants, all pretty girls from unfortunate backgrounds, arrived in Israel, they learned that the work expected of them required neither typing nor organizational skills. Instead of the stylish business suits in the adverts, their dress code was—how shall I put it?—minimal. The office conditions were cramped, the work hours grueling. The customers many and demanding. Not the gentle sort, either. They cared little for the girls' personal safety, and they always got their money's worth."

Boris chuckled. "No, this was not their Promised Land.

But what's a poor girl to do? Their employers had taken their travel documents. They were illegal aliens employed in forbidden work in a foreign country. And they were in debt. Their handlers demanded recompense for their travel expenses. They didn't speak the language. And their shame was great. So, they shut their eyes and held their noses, resolving to endure their two years of hard labor and return home."

Irina's limbs stiffened. Often, she had fantasized about her first life. As a wealthy heiress—a modern-day princess—she flitted across the globe to exotic getaways and dodged the advances of celebrities and moguls. Then she fell into the powerful embrace of her tall husband and doted on her brood of laughing children. Had the truth been far darker?

Alex stared at the floor and swallowed hard. Had he deceived her into a hellish life of the worst human slavery? Her head shook from side to side. *No, it couldn't be.*

"One girl stood out from the others," Boris continued. "She made the most of her situation. A born organizer, she took charge of the other girls and kept them in line. She learned the language. Soon, her hard work paid off. Alex gave her more responsibility and improved conditions. A special bond formed between them, the pimp and his star performer. He fell in love. Then tragedy struck." Boris adopted a tone of fake sympathy. "His lady love used her new freedoms to escape. She alerted the authorities, and Alex's world came tumbling down. Only it didn't. Fortunately for Alex, the policeman the girl had turned to belonged to the Organization."

Tremors shuddered through Irina's body. She could guess what followed. Her former life had ended in violence, the violence that had damaged her brain and obliterated her memory. To hear Boris spell it out was almost too much for her to bear, but she needed to know, to bring closure to months of uncertainty.

Boris tutted. "Alex's boss wasn't happy. He made sure she suffered for her crimes and never escaped again. Then he let Alex clean up the mess. And what a mess it was. Alex was never the same again. But the boss had a soft spot for him."

Alex stood there, his head hung low. Irina digested the information. She had thought that once she learned the truth of her first life, the memories would come gushing back. But although the words shocked her, the tale seemed strange and foreign. That wasn't her. Those terrible things had happened to some other poor girl. For once, her amnesia was a blessing and not a debilitating curse.

The gray-haired slave driver turned to Alex. "But this fairy tale has a happy ending. Years later, Alex gets a new mission—to infiltrate the Dry Bones Society. And who does he meet right out of the gates, but his old sweetheart, back from the dead. Only, she doesn't remember him; she remembers none of it. Good old Alex thinks he's hit the jackpot. They can continue their romance where they had left off, only this time without all that unpleasant baggage. And this time, it's Alex who tries to escape."

Alex made eye contact with her. His eyes begged her to believe. He was sincere. Despite his past deeds and despite the ugly circumstances of their first meeting, he was prepared to leave it all behind. For her.

Boris sighed, his face a mask of pity. "Of course, his boss finds out, and he sends me here. But don't be sad. We're getting to that happy ending. The girl had a second chance at life, and so Alex's boss gives him a second chance, too." Boris got up, placed his gun on the kitchen table, and flopped back on the armchair. "But this time Alex has to silence the girl himself."

Every cell in Irina's body tensed. *No, he won't do it!* Alex loved her. He wouldn't kill her. But did she know him anymore? He had made her disappear before. Was he willing to die for her? She held his gaze, waiting for his signal, waiting for him to refuse.

Alex's eyes lost focus. He glanced at the gun on the table. Taking one large step forward, he picked it up and raised his arm, and the man she loved aimed a gun at her head.

CHAPTER 86

Duct tape binding him to a chair, Yosef stared at the horrific scene on the black stage above. Moshe dangled over a glass deathtrap filled with water. A magician's sawing box entombed Ahmed, who minutes ago had saved Yosef's life. This was wrong—so very wrong!—and in more ways than one.

When the Arab mob had closed in on him that morning, Yosef had accepted the inevitable conclusion. Rabbi Emden was right; Yosef was the Second Messiah.

He had resisted the idea at first. Yosef didn't want to die. And why should he? He was a simple neighborhood rabbi with a pitiful past. A recovering alcoholic didn't belong in the hallways of Knesset, never mind at the vanguard of the cosmic drama. But when hundreds of innocent lives had hung in the balance, he could not stand down.

"In a place where there are no honorable men," the Sages of the Talmud said, "be an honorable man." The police commissioner had ignored his warnings, and so Yosef had stepped up. The act might cost his life, but perhaps this was his fate. And if his destiny was to depart this world early, he'd rather perish while saving lives than cowering under his bed.

And God had blessed his path. Not only had he prevented the catastrophe, but—thanks to Ahmed of all people!—he had survived the Arab lynch mob. Then, Elijah the Prophet had sprung from the pages of the Bible. The Divine guidance he craved had arrived at last. His every cell trembled with joy. Everything would be all right. The Redemption was here!

And then everything went terribly wrong. After following Ahmed, Elijah, and Alon into the black mouth of the box-shaped structure at the Sultan's Pool, the trapdoor had snapped shut and plunged them into darkness. He heard a scuffle, felt a sharp blow to the back of his skull, and woke up bound and gagged at the foot of the black stage.

Mandrake, the crazed magician, strutted across the stage in his tuxedo. The villain had abducted Moshe on Election Day. Now he would murder Moshe before their eyes. And Yosef was helpless to stop him.

This can't be happening! Yosef belonged on that stage, not Moshe. Yosef was the Second Messiah; he must die so that the Moshe could usher in the World to Come.

Yosef struggled against his bonds to no avail. He cried out—"I'm the one you want! Take me!"—but only muffled groans reached his ears.

Just when he thought he'd reached the peak of anguish, a new character had descended the metal staircase and proved him wrong—Reverend Henry Adams!

As Yosef stared in disbelief, the reverend joined Mandrake on the stage and took charge. A sudden, desperate hope sang in Yosef's breast—Adams had swept in to rescue them from the murderous madman. Then Adams spoke, and the song fell silent.

From the start, Yosef had felt uncomfortable dealing with the clergyman. *Sitrah Achrah*, the sages of the Great Assembly had said of the resurrected Israelis—the evil Other Side. Yosef had ignored their warning and accepted hefty checks from the Evangelical Christians. But the reverend's money had helped the Society, and Yosef had made peace with the situation.

Yosef's instincts had not deceived him after all. But he had misunderstood—and far underestimated—the threat. Adams was no man of God; quite the opposite. And Yosef knew his real name.

Armilus!

Rabbi Emden had whispered the name as though the word's mere mention might attract misfortune. Yosef had not taken the myth seriously. Judaism rejected dualism. God reigned supreme. No archangel could challenge His authority.

But Adams was no demon. Who needs supernatural devils when we have human beings? This particular human being embodied all the evil and suffering in this world, and he had won.

"The stage is yours," Adams said to Mandrake. Then he turned to the captives and apologized for his colleague's theatrical flair.

Mandrake raised his sword.

Alon and Elijah shuffled and moaned on their chairs beside him. The three men—the Second Messiah, the head of Moshe's security detail, and Elijah the Prophet himself— would watch helplessly as these human monsters killed the Lord's anointed.

No, not anointed, for Elijah had missed Moshe by minutes. Yosef had spent months searching for the Messiah. All along, the Scion of David had sat right in front of his nose. He had slept in Yosef's home. They had toiled side-by-side at the Dry Bones Society, and later, mere meters had separated their ministerial offices.

Yosef should have focused his efforts on finding Elijah the Prophet, the man who had sought him out on the Mount of Olives on the second day of Moshe's new life.

Today, as with that failed first meeting, tragedy had struck at the critical moment. This time, instead of shipping Elijah off to the hospital, they would both watch, their hands tied, as murderers snuffed out all hope of redemption.

"Wait!" Moshe cried from his vulnerable perch.

But Mandrake swung the blade, severing the rope his assistant had tied to the stage floor.

Moshe's body dropped into the water and sank to the bottom. He struggled in the straitjacket, bubbles of precious air escaping his mouth. Adams and Mandrake stepped up to the glass to watch his final moments.

You can do it! Yosef willed Moshe's bonds to open, for him to slip free and rise to the surface. The escape wouldn't put him out of danger, but the reprieve would give them all another chance. *While there is life, there is hope.* Yosef had said that much to Moshe in the dark depression of his first day. Yosef had believed that then, and he clung to those words now.

CHAPTER 87

Irina stared down the barrel of the gun in Alex's hand. He wouldn't shoot her, would he? She knew him. They loved each other. He was serious about leaving his criminal past. He had pushed her to leave sooner. She should have listened to him. But now, regardless of what he wanted, did he have a choice?

She tried to divine her fate from his eyes, but she found no twinge of indecision or hesitation. He had made up his mind.

His eyes shifted sideways, a secret instruction for her to jump out of the way, then he turned the gun on the thug in the armchair.

A loud click echoed in the silence.

A smug smile spread over Boris's face. "Traitor," he jeered. "I knew it!"

Then Boris reached for his belt, and Irina knew he had another weapon.

"Run!" Alex cried. She stared at him. "Get out of here!" He lunged at Boris, slamming his fist into the seated slave driver's face and knocking the second gun out of his hand. This gun would not be empty.

With a deep roar, Igor lumbered toward the two men and pulled Alex off his boss by the shoulders.

Her first instinct had been to rush to Alex, to help him fight off the goons, but she had no delusions about her ability to tackle two hardened killers. She slipped behind the giant, rounded the kitchen wall, and ran for the front door.

As she pulled the handle toward her, an arm in a tweed coat slammed against the door, shutting the only exit. Boris snarled at her, his face uncomfortably close and murder in his eyes. Blood from his nose and upper lip had drenched his mustache, painting it red.

Irina fell backward into the entryway, then scrambled to her feet and finally, she followed Alex's advice. She ran.

Behind her, Alex gasped and grunted as he wrestled with the hulking thug. She fought back tears. No man stood a chance against that mass of muscle. A scrape of metal on the tiles told her that Boris had retrieved his gun, and his footsteps followed her.

"Go on," he said, "run." He was taunting her, taking his time. "There's nowhere to hide."

Irina wasn't sure about that. She dived into Alex's bedroom and locked the door.

She slid open the window. The cracked pavement stared back, two flights down. If it didn't kill her, the drop would break her legs, and she'd abandon Alex to fight off both henchmen alone.

No! It can't end this way! They had snuffed out her first life; she would not let that happen again. She dashed toward the closet and opened the doors. He'd discover her in a second.

A loud crash made her turn around. Boris stood in the doorway, panting. The doorframe splintered where the bolt tore through the wood. He had kicked the door in, and now he raised his arm and aimed the gun at her head.

His nose rumpling with malice, he said, "Time to die. Again."

CHAPTER 88

"Where is Prime Minister Karlin?" the President of the United States demanded.

Good question, Shmuel thought.

After setting his plan in motion, Moshe had run off to confront Isaac Gurion, while the rest of his cabinet followed the operation from the safety of the Prime Minister's Residence.

In the bunker below the Residence, Shmuel sat at the conference table of lacquered wood and put on a brave face for the camera, while world leaders stared him down from the mounted television screen.

"He had to attend to an urgent matter of life and death," he said. "He'll be back as soon as possible."

The gruff Russian President chimed in. "We're about to launch every nuclear warhead on the planet. What could be a more urgent matter of life and death?"

He had a good point. "Saving a bunch of doubting, ungrateful citizens" was not the answer they wanted to hear.

"Exactly," the American President said, agreeing for once with his Russian counterpart. "This is his show. Either he leads, or the deal is off!"

Shmuel knew what they feared. If Moshe had disappeared, who would stop the Zombie Armies? But he would not let them slip out of their commitments that easily. "Moshe's instructions are clear. He told us to continue without him, and we all know how to proceed. Remember," he added, and tried to maintain his poker face, "our Zombie Armies are already halfway to their targets."

The world leaders shifted in their seats. "Now, now," the American President said, suddenly ingratiating. "There's no need for threats. We're here to help however we can."

"Yes!" the Russian said. "Yes! And we've pulled every string to make this happen."

"You have." Shmuel exhaled a silent breath of relief. In his career as a journalist, he'd interviewed many important public figures, but he'd never had to face off the leaders of the world's superpowers together. *Moshe, where are you?*

He glanced at the countdown timer on the screen. The Time to Impact counter had dropped below five minutes.

"Professor, at your mark."

Shmuel shifted over to allow Professor Stein to face the conference camera. The bunker, added as an afterthought to the older structure of the Prime Minister's Residence, could barely contain the table, and sitting room was limited. Designed to withstand the primitive missiles of Palestinian terrorists, the bunker would not afford much protection from an asteroid strike.

The Knesset had only recently approved the construction of a new billion-shekel government compound beside the Supreme Court in Givat Ram. The command center would include a huge underground bunker to be used by the Prime Minister in times of national emergency. Little good that did them now.

And so Shmuel, Professor Stein, Sivan, Chief of Staff Eitan, and a few military technicians had squeezed into the bomb shelter along with Galit and Talya Karlin and their extended family. Avi Segal too. At the end of the world, political divisions no longer mattered.

The professor pored over the calculations on his laptop. At Moshe's request, he had devised the strategy for averting the imminent disaster, and the planet's future lay in his hands.

The professor looked up at the world leaders on the screen. "You all received my targeting instructions?"

A chorus of affirmations resounded from the leaders in the smaller squares on the screen. Each square displayed the war room of a nuclear power: The United Kingdom; France; China; India. Even Pakistan and North Korea had joined the world initiative under dire threats from their mentor super-powers.

"Good," the professor said. "Timing is critical if we're to change the asteroid's trajectory. The joint blast force might not be enough to do the job, and a mistake might shift that trajectory onto any of your home states."

There was a commotion of whispered consultations in the war rooms and expressions of surprise and dismay from the lesser leaders. Apparently, this potential side effect had not dawned on them, and the benefits of their full cooperation became crystal clear.

Professor Stein read out the list of countries and their se-quence of launch times and missile locations. The checklist checked, the professor sat back in the padded-leather chair.

"Switch to orbit view," he said.

A military technician tapped at a tablet. The pictures of command centers around the world shrank to the bottom of the display. Two other feeds took their place: a live video of the speeding asteroid and a schematic of the revolving Planet Earth. A small red dot to the left indicated the approaching asteroid.

"The game is in play," the professor said. "All we can do now is wait and pray."

Shmuel glanced around for the Vice Prime Minister. They had not managed to contact Rabbi Yosef all morning. Shmuel hoped that both he and Moshe had found a safe place to weather the storm.

"God help us all," Shmuel said, and every person present answered Amen.

A cluster of small white dots rose from the schematic

Planet Earth, like shotgun pellets. Dotted lines traced their trajectories toward the larger red dot.

"China has launched," Klein said.

More white pellets left the turning planet.

"India. Pakistan." Then clusters of missiles launched from land and sea around the globe. All converged ahead of the red dot, at the point where the asteroid would pass in a few seconds.

"All armaments are in the air."

The professor gripped the armrests of his chair and sweat soaked his face. Even the slightest miscalculation would cause the warheads to miss their mark.

Shmuel glanced around the room. All eyes turned to the screen. Galit Karlin held her daughter close, her eyes watery. Avi placed a hand on her shoulder. Galit met Shmuel's eyes, and they both smiled. *He'll be fine*, their eyes said. *Moshe always is.*

CHAPTER 89

Moshe gulped air as he hit the cold water and went under. The weights on his legs dragged him down and clanked against the glass floor of the aquarium.

He struggled against the straitjacket, but it was no use. Harry Houdini might free his hands and legs and break the surface, but Moshe was no escape artist.

He needed to think outside the box. Pun intended! Gallows humor wouldn't help him now. His lungs screamed for air, but the situation was hopeless. With his legs bound to the anchor, he couldn't kick or shoulder the glass.

Precious bubbles of air fled his mouth with the effort. How had he gotten into this mess? He had only tried to make the world a better place.

A Karlin never quits.

Since he could remember, he'd struggled. Build Karlin & Son. Escape Boris's labor camp. Found the Dry Bones Society. Launch Restart.

Every now and then, he'd had an epiphany. Work fewer hours, spend more time with his loved ones. But soon enough he found another cause and off he went, trying to save the world again.

Why did he push so hard?

"Not for them," Avi had told him in a moment of anger

when Moshe had tried to stop him from marrying Galit. "You did it to prove yourself, to please those old photos on the wall."

There was truth to Avi's accusation. The tales of his fore-bears' former glory had lodged in his brain and driven him onward.

But he was tired of struggling. Let someone else step in and save the day. People thought he was the Messiah, but right now he needed a savior as much as anyone.

He forced his eyes open in the water. Two murky figures watched him through the glass: Mandrake, his sadistic tor-mentor, and Henry Adams. If that was his name. Moshe had known his debtors would come calling, but he hadn't realized that they were one and the same.

A painful ball of injustice burst in his heart. Adams, his benefactor and ally, had manipulated Moshe for his own evil ends.

His murderers would not face justice. They would fly off in a helicopter whether his plan beat the asteroid or not.

His lungs burned. Every cell of his body cried out for oxygen.

Savta Sarah was right. In the end, Death wins. No matter who you are or what you've done. Moshe had done his best. He had helped others and risen high, against the odds. His father and grandfather would be proud; he'd have to find comfort in that.

His lungs couldn't take any more. He surrendered to his breathing reflex. His final breath escaped, and chilly water rushed into his lungs.

Little Talya popped into his head. He'd never meet the young woman she'd become. He spotted Galit for the first time across the dance floor in Hangar 17 and he walked right up. "You're late," he said, the first two words he'd ever spo-ken to her. She hadn't batted an eyelid. "I got here as fast as I could."

These past few weeks, they'd hardly talked. He had left so much unsaid. He'd tell her... he'd say...

But his thoughts unraveled in the depths, and the world faded to black.

CHAPTER 90

The giant plucked Alex off Boris and flung him against the wall of the apartment. Alex slumped to the floor and stayed down. He waited for the thug to move closer so he could draw the final ace up his sleeve. Boris had disappeared from the couch, evening the odds but piling on the tension. The slave driver had chased Irina down the corridor, so Alex had better play that winning card soon.

The giant lumbered forward and leaned over him. Alex sprang upward and buried his fist into the thug's ample solar plexus. The larger man doubled over, expelling a breath that stank of peanuts, his eyes bulging with pain and surprise.

The blow would not have disabled Igor had Alex not slipped his fingers into a set of knuckle busters. The steel rings around his knuckles focused the impact, while the rounded grip in his palm spread the opposing force away from his own fingers.

After a lifetime at Mandrake's side, Alex had learned a thing or two.

He followed the blow with another, this time a jab to the face. The giant groaned and shifted sideways, but still didn't fall. So Alex slammed both fists onto the cowed man's spine, and he hit the tiles with a satisfying *splat*.

One down, one to go. The gray-haired bureaucrat should

make an easier opponent. Alex took one step toward the corridor when he heard a shot ring out, followed by the unmistakable *flop* of a body hitting the floor.

In the deafening silence, Alex froze.

No! Not Irina!

CHAPTER 91

Shmuel held his breath as the clusters of white dots converged on the larger red one. The live feed of the glowing asteroid went blank.

A military engineer stared at his laptop. "We've registered multiple direct hits."

The denizens of the cramped bunker glanced at each other and at the tense faces on the smaller squares on the mounted screen. The white dots had disappeared from the schematic, but the red dot remained. The missiles had found their mark, but was the full force of the planet's combined nuclear arsenals enough to divert the asteroid from its path?

Shmuel's fists whitened at the knuckles. All eyes turned to Professor Stein, who tapped at his own laptop, bobbing his head as he consulted charts and calculations.

Professor Stein looked up from his screen. "The trajectory has changed. The asteroid will miss Earth by a few miles. We did it!"

The people in the command centers jumped in the air and hugged their neighbors.

Shmuel released a pent-up breath and mopped his forehead with a handful of tissue paper. If only Moshe could have seen that! Shmuel had to let him know that the danger had passed. Citizens could leave their homes.

He reached for the desk phone and dialed Moshe's mobile number from memory. The call cut to voicemail. Was Moshe all right?

Then he glanced at the live feed and tugged Professor Stein's arm. "What is that?" He pointed at the big screen.

The bright light had faded, and the asteroid was visible again. Only now the large glowing rock had two smaller siblings, which veered away from their big brother.

Professor Stein gasped. "The blast split the asteroid into chunks." The room fell silent again, and the giddy smiles vanished. "The main bulk will miss us, but the others…" He trailed off and punched at his laptop again.

"The others?" Shmuel asked.

Professor Stein looked up from his calculations, and his face turned white. "They're heading for the Middle East. Right for us!"

CHAPTER 92

In his long life, Eli had seen empires rise and fall, cities burn and sprout from the ashes, languages transform, and accepted wisdom overturn. He'd seen kindness and joy, tragedy and suffering. He'd even experienced love. But he'd seen nothing as heartrending as what his eyes beheld now.

On the black stage, Moshe Karlin—his only messiah candidate—writhed and twisted in the watery glass chamber.

This is your fault. Eli had twiddled his thumbs at Noga's bedside. After waiting millennia for the True Messiah and receiving countless hints from the Boss, he had still not acted in time.

In his defense, this was not from lack of trying. Failing to contact the new Prime Minister, he had assisted with Noga's plan to build a grassroots awareness of the Ten Lost Tribes. The plan might have worked, had a premature apocalypse not ripped through Jerusalem. Eli's timing sucked.

But identifying the Lost Tribes was only part of his job. God sent prophets to anoint His chosen kings. Despite rushing across the city to fulfill this part of his mission, he had missed his crucial meeting by minutes.

In hindsight, he should have approached Moshe Karlin before the elections, when he was more accessible. But by then Eli had lost his way, determined to become Eli Katz, the young Internet entrepreneur, while suppressing Elijah the Prophet in the depths of his psyche. And why had he done this? To win the affections of a mortal woman.

But had there been any other way? The Elijah that Noga had met in the hospital had abandoned hope for humankind. He had despaired of redemption, inclined to let the Boss scrap humanity and start over. He had done so before.

Noga had not only messed with his mind, she had recalibrated his moral compass. The world was worth saving. But by the time he'd recovered his will to fulfill his destiny, he'd missed the boat.

It wasn't fair. It wasn't right. In the past few months, he'd discovered the secrets of the Ten Lost Tribes and the End of Death. Why would the Boss hit the reset button now? Why would He render Eli useless, his body taped to a chair of plywood and steel, while the Messiah drowned before his eyes?

Two Messiahs, as it happened. In yet another twist of cosmic irony, the details fell into place only now. Moshe, son of David Karlin, represented the tribe of Judah. The Arab kid in the magician's box stood for the Ten Tribes of Israel. Noga's research had found proof of that. But why would God kill them both?

Unless Eli had screwed up. *Was* Moshe Karlin the Messiah?

On the stage, Moshe Karlin's body twitched twice, then fell still. The show over, the magician and the suited visitor lost interest in him and moved on to their second victim.

"What's that?" said Suit, in English and with his Texas drawl. "What's he saying?"

The magician nodded to his assistant, the black-clad thug with the scar down his cheek, who walked up to the Arab boy. "It's Arabic," he said. Another Russian, by his accent.

"Kid," he said, in Hebrew. "Speak Hebrew if you have any last words." He chuckled.

Eli couldn't hear the Arab's words, but the assistant translated them into English. "He wants to ask you a question," he told the suit.

The magician and the suit exchanged glances. The magician shrugged, hefted his long thin sword, and the two men drew closer.

"He asks if you are the... Shepherd?"

The magician seemed confused, but the suit laughed and puffed out his broad chest.

"I am. Nothing like a golden ticket to make a man feel the greed." He chuckled again. "I know that you were eager to meet me, and now I've granted your wish."

The boy spoke again, longer this time.

"He says you've hurt many people, that you've turned others into killers." The henchman smiled. "He says he won't let you do that again."

The three villains had a good laugh. The boy's empty threats wouldn't save him.

Adams recovered from his fit of laughter. "You've got guts, kid. I admire that. But our time is up, and we have a flight to catch."

The magician raised his sword, positioning the sharp point at the mouth of the slat over the center of the Arab's chest. One Messiah floated, motionless, in a watery grave; the other had a sharp blade aimed at his heart. Eli couldn't bear to watch, so he closed his eyes.

On Mount Carmel, he had faced off the prophets of Baal. Despite their prayer and dance and self-flagellation, the false god had failed to answer their offering with fire. Elijah had scorned them. He dug a deep trench around his own altar and filled it with water. He turned his eyes heavenward, and the Boss answered his call. Lightning had struck his altar, igniting the wood, engulfing his sacrifice in flames, which lapped up the water too. The people had fallen to their knees and bowed. "The Lord alone is God!" they had chanted. "The Lord alone is God!"

And now, from his front row seat at the foot of the stage, Eli understood. He had a role to play. A single, final act to surpass all the miracles and wonders he had wrought over the centuries. Had the Boss led him here for this reason? Was this act the ultimate purpose of his life? He'd never know for sure. But a purpose it was, a purpose he now chose.

Elijah turned his heart heavenward. The Magic had fled, the Thin Voice fallen silent. But like Samson, defeated, blinded, and chained to the pillars of a Philistine palace, he prayed. He envisioned fire and brimstone, an explosion of heat and flame to engulf the men who sowed death and destruction. To engulf them all.

Goodbye, Noga.

His final tears streamed down his cheeks.

Please, Lord. Answer me one last time.

He found the invisible muscle at the core of his brain. *Flex! Flex! Flex!*

Nothing happened. More nothing happened. No heat, no flame. No explosion. His prayers had gone unanswered.

Eli opened his moist eyes. The three evil men, anti-Messiahs and murderers, stood over the Arab, as the magician, grinning, leaned into the hilt of the sword. The Arab boy did not cry out. Instead, he muttered a few soft words.

"What was that?" the suit said. "What did he say?"

"I don't know, sir," the henchman said. "It's Arabic. Something about *Samira*. I think that's a name."

Then, with a glint of victory in his dark eyes, the Arab smiled and balled his hand into a fist.

The world turned yellow. A fireball expanded with a whoosh, swallowing the stage, singeing Eli's eyebrows, drying his tears, and throwing him back. The chair toppled, his head hit the floor, and everything went dark.

CHAPTER 93

Irina was dead. The reality hit Alex harder than any physical blow.

In the living room of his apartment, he stood frozen to the spot beside the toppled giant. His reason to live had died with her.

You idiot! He should have taken Boris first. How had he let the thug go after her? Had he thought he'd make short work of his henchman? Now Boris had his gun. Any moment now he'd appear in the corridor to finish what he'd begun.

The ground disappeared beneath his feet, and Alex collapsed to the ground. The giant had swept his legs from under him, and his back hit the floor hard. Before he could react, the giant rolled on top of him, pinning him beneath his immense weight.

Alex swung at the bloodied face, but a large hand caught his fist and squeezed. Alex gasped as the steel grip dug into his palm. The giant grinned with pleasure, inches from his nose. Alex got in a left hook, but the giant lunged forward with both arms, pressing meaty forearms over Alex's upper arms, and the huge hands closed over his head.

The thick fingers tightened around his skull like iron clamps, the pressure increasing.

"Now this ends!" Igor roared, and his thumbs closed over

Alex's eyes, pressing them into their sockets.

Flashes of bright light exploded in Alex's head, the last sight he'd ever see. He cried out as the pressure on his cranium mounted, threatening to implode his head.

Bang!

Another shot had rung out. At once, the pressure subsided, the thumbs slipped from his eye sockets, and the bloody face dropped onto his chest. A large chunk was missing from the side of the giant's head.

Alex crawled backward from beneath the dead thug. Irina stood over him. Her arms were rigid, her face rippled with fear. A wisp of smoke rose from the barrel of the gun she held in two hands—the spare loaded Glock he had kept hidden in his cupboard.

She trained the gun on him as if considering whether to shoot him too. He'd lied to her. In a former life, he had let her die. Now that she knew the truth, the whole truth, could she forgive him? He'd turned his back on that old life, but he hadn't turned his back on her. He had risked everything to save her and start a new life together.

After three long seconds, Irina lowered the weapon. She held out her hand and helped him to his feet. Then she hugged him for all she was worth.

CHAPTER 94

Moshe retched his guts out. He knelt in a puddle of water and vomit. Shards of glass littered the floor and glinted like diamonds. Hazy light poured from the heavens like angelic rays.

The moist air smelled of roast chicken and singed hair. He had drowned in a glass elevator filled with chilly water. But now the straitjacket hung from his frame in long white scraps and only partially restrained his left arm.

He paused to fill his raw chest with air. Breathing—what a sweet, glorious sensation!

He extracted his body from the jacket, and the scraps of material that fell to the floor were stained red. *Blood?* He ran his hands over his side and back. His fingers traced a dozen shallow cuts. A small, hard object stuck to his skin. He winced as the foreign body came away in his fingers, a small silver screw. What the hell had happened?

He glanced around. A metal frame remained where the glass elevator had stood. Torn wooden boards creaked around the rough hole in the ceiling. The place looked like ground zero after a terror attack. Adams, Mandrake, and their henchman had disappeared. Moshe would not wait for them to return.

He struggled with the weights around his feet, his fingers numb and clumsy. Staggering to his feet, he took a step, and his soaked shoes kicked against chunks of blackened meat on the stage floor. Grilled chicken had rained from the sky. The paint of the stage had peeled away to reveal naked wooden panels. Smoke rose from the black patches, which grew thicker and darker toward....

Dear Lord! The magician's box had disappeared, leaving only the charred remains of the base. High above, a smoldering white bundle dangled from the lighting scaffold. The Arab boy's white kaffiyeh. Moshe felt the urge to vomit again, but he had already emptied his gut.

Oh my God. A powerful charge had detonated right where the Arab boy had sat. The explosion destroyed the glass elevator and vaporized the water, releasing Moshe from certain death.

A black top hat sat on the stage floor. Moshe leaned over and picked it up. *Ouch!* The hat singed his fingers and fell to the floor, landing right side up. Then it burst into flame.

A groan drew his attention beyond the stage. Picking up a shard of melted glass for defense, he hobbled to the edge.

Three men lay on their backs, their legs in the air, their limbs still taped to chairs. Moshe descended the stairs and got to work, slicing the bonds with the sharp glass. Alon, Rabbi Yosef, and the stranger got to their feet and rubbed their bruised arms.

"Moshe!" The rabbi wrapped him in a bear hug.

"Easy there. My back feels like a sieve."

Rabbi Yosef apologized. So did Alon.

"It's not your fault, Alon. You tried to warn me."

He gave the stranger a questioning glance. A bystander, in the wrong place at the wrong time? The man put out his hand. "Elijah," he said.

Moshe shook the hand. He'd never met an Elijah.

A loud bang overhead made them cringe. The sound came from outside, the sound-barrier crack of a hundred fighter jets.

They reached a unanimous agreement. "Let's get the hell out of here!"

They made for a bright tear in the side of the box and poured into the empty arena of the Sultan's Pool. Shielding their eyes from the searing daylight, they glanced at the skies. There was no need to point. High above them, a large fireball streaked earthward.

Oh, no! Moshe's plan had failed. The asteroid had entered the atmosphere and tore through the skies overhead, toward the rise of Mount Zion.

They ran.

CHAPTER 95

With much huffing and puffing, the tourist reached the pinnacle of the Rock of Gibraltar when he heard the boom. A thought worried him. Had his wife been right?

Too nervous to take the cable car, she had remained at the visitors' center. Her hip ruled out a hike on foot, and so she had let him "risk his neck" alone.

And risk his neck he had. The line for the cable car had been short, as had the ride, and when he'd stepped outside—oh, what a view! The Mediterranean Sea stretched out as far as the eye could see.

He'd held onto the railing, taking a moment to catch his breath, and nodded a greeting to a bushy-haired Barbary macaque that had perched on the metal fence and seemed more interested in people-watching than in the awe-inspiring vista.

The salty sea breeze filled his nostrils and refreshed his lungs. Far below, the lines of ocean swells crept over the deep blue like the slow, calming motion of distant clouds. A colorful, multi-decked cruise ship made for the Port of Gibraltar below.

Then the deep rumble had sounded, and even the monkey had jumped.

Had the cable snapped, the car's passengers plummeting

to a miserable and violent death? But the boom had come from above.

There it was! A large rounded object passed overhead, its fiery tail tracing its slow but inexorable path toward the blue horizon. The object was too large and rough for an aircraft or even a UFO. *Dear God!* That had to be the largest shooting star he'd ever seen.

Was he hallucinating? His family doctor had changed his blood pressure pills two weeks ago. No. Other visitors stood transfixed, their mouths open, their eyes and hands following the descent of the meteor. Some held phones in the air, recording the cataclysm for posterity.

Just his luck. He'd spent forty years in retail, saving up for retirement. Two months ago, he'd signed away his grocery store on the West End. The week in Gibraltar was the first trip he and his wife had embarked on, and they had planned much more: a week in the Greek isles, a weekend in Venice, and a two-week stint at a villa in Tuscany. Couldn't the end of the world wait another few months?

The flaming meteor scuttled across the heavens and disappeared into the horizon, the smoking tail still hanging in the sky. He waited for another boom. None followed. Perhaps the meteor was only passing by or had crashed in a distant land, poor buggers. By the looks of it, somewhere in the Middle East. That'll put an end to their wars—ha!

The other visitors started to talk among themselves, processing what they'd witnessed. He'd better get back to his wife. She'd regret not taking that cable car. He'd stood at the right place at the right time for the best possible view of what was surely a once-in-a-lifetime historic moment, and he had bragging rights.

As he turned to face the cable car station, however, the tone of the ambient chatter changed. Excitement had turned to concern. A young Japanese woman gasped. They were pointing again, so he turned around and made for the railing.

At the distant horizon, a white pillar rose from the sea, like a cloud. More hands pointed, this time at the waters far below. The waves retreated from the shore, sucking the cruise ship back, away from the port and out to sea. This was not a good time to be on the water.

The meteor had hit the sea. Although he was no expert in these matters, he'd seen enough Hollywood blockbusters to know what would happen next. The waters would surge back. Tidal waves. Mass hysteria.

His fellow tourists must have shared his thoughts, for they streamed toward the cable car station. He joined them. He must get off the Rock and head for high ground. As he passed the turnstile, his arms trembling and his heart rate soaring, a more practical thought crossed his mind.

He'd paid in advance for the hotel in Crete. Was it too late for a refund?

CHAPTER 96

Tom Levi couldn't believe his luck. In the holding cell at the Talpiot Police Station, he'd perched on the edge of the cot and wrung his hands. His rump hurt from the stiff, thin mattress. He'd better get used to that. According to the rough officers who had arrested him, he'd be in a cell for the rest of his life. Why had the Lord abandoned him? Then the plump woman in the blue Israeli police uniform appeared at the bars. The bunch of heavy keys jangled in her hands as she hurried to unlock the cell door.

"You're free to go," she said and bustled down the long corridor.

He followed her, joining the flow of officers and offenders. The doors of the other cells stood open, as did the gate at the end of the corridor.

"What's happening?" he asked a uniform.

"An asteroid is about to hit the city. The station isn't equipped to protect you, so you're being released."

Tom laughed out loud. God had heard his voice and seen his affliction, and now the Almighty had arranged world events to further His servant's goal.

He'd heard about the asteroid. The media had dismissed the doomsday predictions as fake news, political ploys designed to draw the public's attention away from the Prime

Minister's failings.

The midday sun smiled overhead as convicts and uniforms flooded the sidewalks of Talpiot. Tom turned his feet toward Hebron Road and the Old City. This time he wouldn't fail.

He'd been so close to his goal that morning. After infiltrating the Temple Mount maintenance team and planting his explosives, he had watched the grounds fill with Islamic usurpers. If they weren't terrorists, they were enablers who provided financial and moral support. They had no right to trample the holy grounds of the Jewish Temple; they deserved to die.

And their deaths would spark the Redemption. Vice Prime Minister Lev didn't have the guts to act, so Tom would force his hand. He had waited outside the Gate of the Tribes, remote detonator in his pocket. But just as the Temple Mount reached full capacity, the Vice Prime Minister himself had stormed the grounds.

Tom had half a mind to blow him up along with his Arab friends, but then Israeli security guards had followed Rabbi Lev inside. No Jews were to die that day; the goyim had spilled enough Jewish blood. He'd wait for the guards to leave with the misguided rabbi. Then he'd push the button.

But the first men out of the gate were Arabs. They fled to the alleys of the Arab Quarter. His quarry was escaping! He reached into his pocket when hands grabbed his arms, lifted him off the ground, and dragged him onto the Temple Mount.

To insinuate himself into the maintenance team, he had pretended to be a mute, but now he cried out. The detonator slipped from his pocket onto the large stone tiles and disappeared among the rushing feet of the crowd. Rabbi Yosef Lev had botched his plans again.

As the squad car drove him to the station, the irony hit him—the Israeli security guards were Arabs too!

The Old City walls rose over Jaffa Road. The streets stood empty. The city had taken the asteroid threat to heart. With nobody to get in his way, his job would be easy. He'd locate the detonator and complete his mission. The Temple Mount would return to rubble today, empty or not, along with that hateful golden dome.

He picked up his pace, hitching up the hem of his robe and crossing the short bridge over the Hinnom Valley. Billboards announced a coronation ceremony and displayed images of Moshe Karlin and the Mahdi. What an abomination! To display the true Messiah along with that Arab imposter. With the Temple Mount razed to the ground, rebuilding the Temple would be easy. Karlin would thank Tom and reserve for him a seat of honor at the Great Feast under the Leviathan-skin canopy.

A deafening boom overhead drew his eye beyond the billboard. The sun burned in the sky. The glowing orb seemed smaller than usual and had grown a short tail. Before his eyes, the orb waxed larger. That wasn't the sun.

Tom raced up Mount Zion. He sprinted through Zion Gate, bounded along the silent cobbled alleys of the Old City, and zeroed in on the Temple Mount.

His sandals slid over the rounded stones as he took a corner and spilled into the courtyards before the Gate of the Tribes. He searched the smooth stone tiles for the detonator.

There it is! He launched toward the small gray rectangle when a shadow passed over the courtyard and blotted out the sun. A fierce hot wind knocked him off his feet and hurled him back.

His body slammed against the far wall of the courtyard and slipped to the ground. Chips of rock and dirt pelted him like rain. Clouds of dust billowed, then dispersed. A slow groan came from his throat as he exhaled. His shoulder and hip burned. Smoke rose from his singed robes. The Gate of the Tribes and Golden Dome were no more. In their stead, fallen stones crumbled and fires raged. The flames licked at the heavens like the pillars of an immense building, a temple not of wood and stone but of fire that had descended from on high.

With a superhuman effort, he got to his feet and hobbled

forward. A fit of ecstatic laughter overcame him, and his slight frame shuddered both with great joy and bone-grinding pain.

Then water fell from the sky, wet and hard, and doused the fires. The flash shower lasted two seconds, as though God had emptied a heavenly bucket. *Strange.* The afternoon had been cloudless. The downpour soaked his tattered robes and matted his hair—and tasted of salt! As he doubted his sanity, a high-pitched whistle sounded, the terrifying whine of a Nazi V2 bomb descending on London.

He looked up, then jumped. *Splat!* Two steps away, a large fish gawked at him through dead eyes. The stone floor tile had cracked beneath the unfortunate creature. Another whistle and another squelch. This time, a tuna. Two more whistles. Three. Dozens. Tom limped to the shadow of a stone wall as fish, sharks, and a large octopus pelted the ground.

The whistles ceased. Tom hazarded a halting stroll among the piled-up wares of the unlikely fishery. He had skipped breakfast that day and lunch. Hungry as he was, he had lost his appetite for seafood of any kind.

There it came again—another whistle, but much deeper. A shadow fell over him, so he looked up. Another object fell from the heavens, but he had trouble identifying this one. It was large. Very large. He glimpsed a long, tapered neck and long lateral fins, spread like the wings of a very large bird or a passenger jet.

His last thought before that final squelch was, "I should probably get out of the way."

DAN SOFER

CHAPTER 97

A month later, Yosef jumped out of bed early in the morning, his heart racing. Today was the day.

He freshened up and hurried to the Yael Street synagogue for morning prayers. The air was redolent of palm branches and citrus fruit—the scent of the Succoth festival and new beginnings—and the leafy canopies of Sukkah booths peeked over the walls on Shimshon Street.

Returning home, he opened his bedroom cupboard to dress a second time. His wedding suit hung on the rack, immaculate within its nylon cover, dry-cleaned and tailored to his current dimensions.

Yosef had imagined that the Messiah's arrival would be sudden and unexpected, a bugle call to arms from out of the blue. But, as always, reality had surprised. As Vice Prime Minister, he had played a key role in the meticulous planning of the ceremony, along with the Prime Minister and Elijah the Prophet. But knowing every step of the way ahead today did not diminish the immense joy that filled his heart to bursting.

Dressed in his designated suit and new black fedora, he stepped into the living room and gasped.

"What?" Rocheleh asked. She ran a self-conscious hand through her flowing jet-black locks. For the historic event—one might say the *final* event of history—she had splurged on a new wig.

"You're beautiful," he said.

She blushed. Truth be told, he almost hadn't recognized her, but he kept that confession to himself; he wasn't married yesterday.

Beside her, their four boys stood at attention in identical suits and smiled from ear to ear.

"*Aba!*" Ari and Simcha cried as one. "We got you!"

They held out their new trading cards, and Yosef examined them. *Well, what do you know?* The laminated cards displayed Yosef's own visage, with a healthy dose of Photoshop.

"You've got me indeed." Yosef had his very own rabbi card. The world was ending for sure. "Shall we go?"

Outside, Baruch held the door of the limo open, and they piled into the ample back seats. The car pulled off.

"Cyndi?" Baruch asked, his eyes smiling in the rearview mirror.

"As always."

The driver pressed a button and, on the limo's speakers, Cyndi Lauper sang "True Colors."

The streets of Baka had emptied for the public holiday, the shutters of stores drawn, tables and chairs stacked behind the darkened windows of coffee shops. Even Hebron Road was desolate of traffic, like a Sabbath day in the middle of the week, and a fitting start to the Day of Complete Sabbath. The Messianic Age.

Most citizens and a swath of foreign dignitaries had already claimed their seats at the ceremony. The rest of the world would watch via live video feeds.

He who prepares on the Sabbath eve will eat on the Sabbath, the Sages said. The preparations lay in the past now. Some had been thousands of years in the making. Now humanity could sit back and enjoy the show. He only hoped that for once in the history of humankind, things would go according to plan.

There had been some thorny theological issues to iron out as well. Yosef had consulted with ancient texts and commentaries. Occasionally, he had conferred with the resurrected authors of those texts and commentaries. They had reached two conclusions.

The first insight had come from an unlikely source— the *Sitrah Achrah*. The evil Other Side. The Anti-Messiah. Armilus. Henry Adams had identified the hidden message of the Resurrection. The message reinforced everything Yosef had learned about life, the universe, and everything, and became the cornerstone of their official view of the Redemption.

Human beings only find true expression as unified wholes—thus the need to reunite bodies and souls. But physical reality has its limits. As such, the world and humanity are imperfect, incomplete. This was by design. God entrusts humans with the task of completing the world and perfecting themselves, and in doing so, they become partners in Creation.

Secondly, Maimonides was right—the Messianic Era did not break a single Law of Nature. The time for magical thinking had passed. Instead, the epoch relied on miracles of science.

The Aging Vaccination, created by Dr. Yariv Stern of the Shaare Zedek Medical Center, was a prime example. People who opted for the treatment—developed in collaboration with a Mr. Eli Katz—would, quite literally, live forever. As Isaiah had foretold, "He will swallow Death forever." The only side effect to be noted over the next few years would be a phobia for extreme sports and motorized vehicles.

The walls of the Old City towered on the horizon as the limo crossed the Hinnom Valley and joined the line of diplomatic limousines and SUVs that wrapped around Mount Zion. Traffic police manned the sidewalks and kept the approach roads to the Mount of Olives Cemetery open to VIP traffic only.

Security agents in dark suits and glasses waited for Yosef, his wife, and children outside the limo and ushered them toward the large platform at the top of the cemetery.

For the Messianic Era Induction Ceremony, the State of Israel had constructed the platform, complete with podium and microphones, beneath a protective canopy of—what else?—a Sukkah booth. But this was no ordinary booth. The sides were lined with the hide of a very large aquatic creature, previously thought extinct and roused recently from the watery depths by the same solar flare that had triggered the Resurrection and dislodged Planet Killer Seven from the Asteroid Belt. The sea monster had landed with deathly force in the Old City after the asteroid had vaporized the Mediterranean Sea. Yosef had arranged to rename the creature Leviathanosaurus.

As they climbed the path to the platform, the foothills of the Old City sprawled before them.

"Wow," the boys said as one.

Long lines of seats ran between the rows of gravestones, and the hills beyond bristled with spectators as far as the eye could see.

The murmur of the waiting masses was the susurrus of a surging ocean, excitement in their whispers and tears of joy in their laughter. This time the Messiah would not disappoint.

But who was the Messiah—or Messiahs? Yosef had discussed the matter at length with Moshe and Elijah. Surprisingly, Elijah had no idea. The prophet had lost the frequency of Divine revelation along with his miraculous powers. And although Moshe's achievements seemed to qualify him for the role, he had balked at making messianic claims of any sort. In Yosef's mind, paradoxically, Moshe's refusal to reach for that crown proved that he *was* indeed the Messiah!

After days of doubt, a solution presented itself. Their approach was simple—even trite—but seemed to be the one least likely to cause mass hysteria and pandemonium. The concept explained Elijah's failing powers too. Yosef had even found a supporting source among the ancient texts. *Yes.* The more he thought about it, the more he liked the idea. The answer had been there all along. But only after millennia of failed messiahs was the world ready to hear it.

Was their answer *the* answer—*the* solution? Who knew? Yosef craved certainty, but in the end, he'd found none. He'd learn to live without. Tom Levi had been certain of his apocalyptic plans. Perhaps a little self-doubt was a good thing after all.

The security guards deposited his family among the front rows at the foot of the platform and continued with Yosef onto the stage.

In the distance, the Old City gleamed, unrecognizable. In one fiery instant, the asteroid had vaporized the sacred grounds of the Temple Mount, obliterating the mosques, the domes, and the Western Wall, and uprooting centuries of buried history and smoldering conflict.

The flat slab of bedrock that remained solved two contentious issues. With no vestige of the hallowed Temple Mount, technically there was no way to build a third Temple. And with no Temple, the topic of sacrifices became moot. Sorry.

The clean, open space stretched from the former Western Wall Plaza to the outer edge of the Temple Mount, with no indication of where synagogue ended and mosque began. Thanks to Noga Shemer's findings regarding the Ten Lost Tribes, there was no need.

Instead, the State had earmarked the grounds for a new non-denominational structure, a memorial to centuries of bloodshed. The display would include a huge holographic model of the Jewish Temple. A Temple of Fire, indeed!

On the platform, Yosef took his seat beside the young dashing man in the black leather jacket. Yosef had suggested a more "appropriate" choice of clothing—a flowing robe, perhaps, and a pointy hat, but the prophet would have none of it. "I'm not a wizard," he had said. "Or a Greek." He didn't seem to like the ancient Greeks much.

Yosef nodded a greeting.

Elijah folded his arms. "He's late."

Yosef gazed at the endless crowds, at the hats and kaffiyehs, the skullcaps and the healthy bare heads of hair. From the first rows of seats, Rabbi Emden tipped his hat at him. Beside him sat all seven sages of the Great Council. Tears seeped unbidden into Yosef's eyes.

"Better late than never," he said. "Better late than never."

CHAPTER 98

That morning, Moshe Karlin made a detour on his way to the Mount of Olives. He had an important errand to run. The Prime Minister's cavalcade stopped outside a dusty store on the seedier side of Pierre Koenig Street in Talpiot. His mission was close to impossible. Luckily for him, he'd brought along a secret weapon.

A bell chimed as he pushed the glass door open and they walked inside. Knickknacks crowded the shelves and floor: embroidered chairs with carved armrests of polished oak, a selection of wall clocks, and, beneath the glass countertop, an array of wedding bands and diamond-encrusted rings.

The old man behind the counter looked up from his coffee and newspaper, as he had the first time Moshe had entered the pawn shop. But today a glint of suspicion sparkled in the vulture eyes beneath the wisp of cotton candy hair, and his shoulders tensed.

Moshe placed his hands on the counter. "I've come to reclaim my watch."

If the old vulture had recognized his Prime Minister, he made no sign of it. "It's not for sale." The declaration was an opening bargaining position if ever Moshe had heard one.

Moshe didn't argue. He didn't have to.

Moshe's secret weapon let out a derisive harrumph. "You

should be ashamed of yourself, young man," Savta Sarah said. By the looks of him, the storekeeper had not been addressed as a "young man" in over seventy years. "Moshe's grandfather bought that watch and passed it on to Moshe's father after him. It is a family heirloom of great *sentimental* value." Her implication: sentimental but not monetary value.

The vulture behind the counter licked his lips. Finally, he had met a worthy opponent, and he savored the challenge. He slid Moshe's old watch from beneath the glass display. He caressed the leather strap and pointed to the brand name that glittered in gold leaf.

"This, madam, I'll have you know, is a Rolex Bubbleback, 1948 Limited Edition. Few have survived to this day and none are in such pristine condition. This collector's timepiece is worth at least eighty thousand shekels."

Moshe had asked for half that amount when he'd pawned the watch to buy his freedom from Boris. In his desperation, he had settled for ten thousand.

"*Eighty thousand shekels?*" Savta Sarah gasped. "I could buy this entire store for eighty thousand shekels, including its owner."

Moshe stifled a chuckle, stepped back, and enjoyed the show. The old man gave Savta a run for her money, but even he was no match for that indomitable force of nature. In the end, Moshe had to cut the negotiation short and handed over twenty thousand shekels in crisp two-hundred-shekel notes. The wily pawnbroker had made a tidy profit. Moshe didn't mind. There was no need to create rumors that the Prime Minister was stingy. Besides, he felt sorry for him. While haggling, the old vulture had pulled out most of his remaining hair, and alarming blue veins had bulged on his forehead.

Moshe removed his golden Omega, the gift from Isaac Gurion during the honeymoon days of Moshe's early foray into politics, and he strapped on his grandfather's Rolex. The watch was heavier, the strap a little tighter, but it felt right. The timepiece was the last purchase his grandfather had made before the war had taken everything. He had sworn never to sell the watch. It was a reminder of the life he had wanted to regain. "A Karlin never quits," his father had always said. It was the motto that had kept Moshe going in his darkest hours.

Secret Service agents held the door as Moshe and Savta climbed back inside the ministerial SUV.

"Twenty thousand shekels," she said, shaking her head. "I could have got him down further if you'd let me."

"That's all right, Savta. You did very well. And we can't spend the whole day bargaining. We have another important appointment today, remember?"

CHAPTER 99

A cool morning breeze greeted Moshe at the top of the Mount of Olives when he stepped out of the SUV.

This was where it had all begun. Six months ago, he'd woken up in the ancient cemetery, naked and alone. He had lost everything. The muezzin call to prayers on the loudspeaker had sent a thrill of fear through his mind. This morning, he had arrived in a cavalcade, wearing his finest suit. The voices on the loudspeaker spoke in Hebrew, Arabic, and English, and they called every man, woman, and child to join their gathering.

Secret Service agents lined the path to the raised platform which faced the Old City below.

Galit waited on the curb, her hands clasped, looking as radiant as that first moment he had glimpsed her. She kissed Savta Sarah on the cheek, then turned to her husband.

"You're late," she said, a playful smile curling her lips.

"I got here as fast as I could."

"Daddy!"

Talya jumped up and down and hugged his waist. Moshe picked her up and mussed her thicket of dark curls.

The first two weeks after the asteroid strike had kept them both very busy. He had a country to patch up, foreign relations to mend, and international relief efforts to coordinate.

The fact that they had survived the impact at all had required some explaining, and Professor Stein was happy to oblige. As it happened, PK-7 was not an asteroid but a comet, a ball of rock *and ice*, and so the nukes had not only bumped the threat off course but broken it apart. Comets hang out in the Asteroid Belt too. Who knew?

The larger of the comet's two remaining chunks had landed in the Mediterranean Sea, which had softened the blow but still sent tsunamis racing toward every shore.

Galit had faced her own tsunami challenge—getting her parents to move out of the Prime Minister's Residence—and Moshe had not envied her. With hard work and a lot of collaboration, they completed both missions successfully.

Then Moshe did something unexpected—he took off an entire week. Instead of flying to exotic islands or hiking up north, Moshe, Galit, and Talya stayed home. No phones or emails, no Internet, only quality time together. They slept in, ate ice cream, watched movies, and played board games. Most of all, they had talked. The results were spectacular.

At the Mount of Olives Cemetery, Galit linked her arm in his, and they walked along the line of security agents.

"Ready to conquer the world?" she said.

"I'm not sure 'conquer' is the right word."

"You did save us all."

"Well," he said, noncommittally. "That still sounds a little grandiose. I suppose we did avert a global extinction event. And achieve worldwide nuclear disarmament. Within twenty-four hours and by means of a few conference calls. We can be proud of that."

"Not 'we,'" Galit corrected him. "*You.* You did all that."

As much as the idea tickled Moshe's ego, he couldn't abide the lie. "If there's one thing I've learned," he said, "it's that no one man can fix a country, never mind the world. I had a lot of help. And I'll need more yet."

Galit, Talya, and Savta made for their seats in the front row, and Moshe continued onward.

Rubi, the owlish Government Secretary, waited for him at

the ramp of the raised platform.

"Is everything in order, Rubi?" Moshe had finally yielded to his eager helper's requests, entrusting him with the logistics of the day's event.

"Yes, sir! Thank you for the honor, Mr. Prime Minister!"

"No, Rubi. Thank *you*. You've done an excellent job. And I'm sure I'll have many more projects for you in future."

Rubi swallowed hard. "Thank you, sir. I'll convey your message to the team."

Careful what you wish for, Moshe thought. He patted the man on the shoulder and continued on his way.

As he climbed the ramp to the raised platform, Jerusalem opened up like a flower in bloom. Sections of the ancient Old City walls peeled back like petals, and in the open heart of what was once the golden dome and Temple Mount, the tiny figures of innumerable people stood in white, black, and the full spectrum of colors. The hills flowed with humanity as far as the eye could see, right up to the rows of seated dignitaries among the tombstones.

At Moshe's entrance, hands clapped and voices cheered, the sound of rolling waves rushing to greet the seashore.

Two figures sat at the table of honor beside the podium, Rabbi Yosef and Elijah.

"Thank you for your patience."

"After two thousand years," Elijah said, "what's a few more minutes?"

Moshe smiled.

If anyone had asked Moshe to picture Elijah the Prophet, he would have gone for flowing robes and white beards, not jet-black hair and leather jackets. Reality never ceased to amaze.

"Is she here?" Moshe asked.

Eli smiled, touched that Moshe had remembered. "Front row," he said. He pointed to a girl with long dark hair. Noga, Eli's injured girlfriend and the discoverer of the Ten Lost Tribes, waved up at them. She and Dr. Stern sat among the dignitaries and world leaders who had turned out for the occasion.

Noga had figured out the hardest part of the Messianic equation—how to resolve the Israeli-Palestinian conflict—and for that, he was eternally grateful. If not for that, and the biker's earlier unfortunate attempt to meet Moshe and Rabbi Yosef at this very spot, Moshe might have doubted Elijah's credentials.

Moshe nodded at Irina and Alex in the second row. The day of the asteroid strike—or Day One, as people were calling it—the Russian couple had faced off another branch of Adams's criminal organization. During the confrontation, Boris and King Kong had met their end.

Moshe nodded at the new Police Commissioner in the second row. Alex's testimony had put the former Commissioner, Golan, behind bars for his collaboration with organized crime. Rooting out the Organization's tendrils would take time, but the process had begun, and Interpol would do the heavy lifting.

With the rustle of fluttering wings, a black crow alighted on the table before Elijah, cawed once, and flew off.

"What was that about?"

"An old friend," Elijah said. "He said it's time we got started."

"Right." Moshe approached the podium, cleared his throat, and the cheers rose again across the Holy City. His face appeared on projector screens along the hillsides to give even the most distant spectators a good view of the ceremony. *What to say?*

Moshe, Rabbi Yosef, and Elijah had met several times to discuss the way forward. Three things became clear. A new era had begun. They had saved the planet from extinction, brought peace to their corner of the Middle East, crippled a global consortium for organized crime, and defeated death. Secondly, they needed to mark this fact to give the people closure and guidance. Thirdly, none of the three men had a clue what they were doing.

So they'd worked with what they had.

Moshe waited for the hubbub of the murmuring crowd to settle. He had written up his thoughts earlier but decided against cue cards. From here on he'd improvise.

"My friends and fellow citizens," he said into the microphone. His amplified voice bounced off the Jerusalem hills under the warm sun of a clear autumn day. "For millennia, we have waited for the End Times. We have hoped for the end to our suffering and striving, for a brighter future of truth, peace, and justice. Some have taken advantage of that hope, cynically manipulating our beliefs to further their own greedy agendas. Today, the wait ends."

Cheers and wolf whistles rose from the masses of rapt humanity.

Moshe raised his hand for silence. "Today we mark the end of history." The ominous ring of those words ushered in total silence. "Not because time is ending. On the contrary, life is starting anew. For those who choose it, eternal life. But the story that began with two kids in God's garden has concluded, the script in which we hang our hopes and dreams on Divine intervention. *His* story has ended. *Our* story has begun."

The breeze ruffled Moshe's hair and whistled in the branches of the olive trees.

"Some have claimed that I am the Messiah." Another roar from the crowds on the hills. Moshe waited for silence. "Many have pressured me to reach for that crown myself. But I must disappoint you. No one human being can fix society. No individual can beat crime, end suffering, or fight injustice."

He drew two deep breaths and used the dramatic pause to recall the exact wording he had drafted with Rabbi Yosef and Elijah.

"I am not your Messiah. God alone is our Redeemer, and He created us all in His image. Our job is to learn from His example and to complete the process that He started. In short, to fix the world together."

Hands clapped, and the hills echoed with applause. A

chant carried on myriad voices. "Fix the World! Fix the World!"

The chant had a certain appeal. It sure beat "Undead Stay Dead!" or "Break the Dry Bones!"

Moshe smiled as the voices rose and fell. After a full three minutes, the chant subsided.

"Before we conclude the proceedings, please join me in remembering those who are no longer with us."

Moshe spoke of friends and family who had passed away during those tumultuous few months, and those who had not yet returned from death.

Moshe found Samira in the second row, and their eyes met. She smiled as tears traced shimmering trails down her face. They were both thinking of one lost friend in particular—Ahmed.

While she waited for the asteroid strike, cowering beneath her bed at the Dry Bones Society, Samira had read Ahmed's letter. He wrote of his love for her and his decision to heed her advice and not repeat the mistakes of his first life. The Messiah Coronation would bring him face-to-face with the Shepherd, he was sure of it. He promised to confront the Shepherd and end his rule of terror. Samira had not known what he had meant, but the truth soon came to light.

Forensics experts at the Sultan's Pool confirmed that Ahmed had saved Moshe's life. He had detonated a suicide vest beneath his robes, incinerating Adams, Mandrake, and their henchman. His act of self-emollition had decapitated the Hydra of organized crime, freed Moshe from his watery grave, and spared the lives of the three men the criminals had bound and gagged below the stage.

More than that, his brave words of reconciliation at the Temple Mount had set the table on which Moshe had served the tidings of the Ten Lost Tribes and helped a suffering population digest that vital dish.

Could noble actions erase a suicide bomber's past? Did saving one group of innocent lives make up for the snuffing out of another? Shmuel would say no. Moshe for one hoped, wherever the universe had blown Ahmed's soul, that this time he would find peace.

"We will remember their sacrifices forever," Moshe concluded.

He stepped back as Elijah and Rabbi Yosef took the podium. The rabbi held the long, twisted shofar—a hollowed-out deer horn—while Elijah applied his lips to the pointy end and puffed out his cheeks. The blast came deep and smooth. The single note was long and sad but determined, and as the sound waves echoed off hills and fields and homes, Moshe thought he heard the eternal city answer with hope.

Then Elijah raised a large rectangular bottle of virgin olive oil and pumped the lever of the spray nozzle. Clouds of oil wafted downwind, anointing every man, woman, and child with tiny drops of the sacred liquid. Moshe had thought this unnecessary, but Elijah was a stickler for protocol. "If they're all messiahs," Elijah had contended, "I must anoint them all." Moshe had relented. The prophet's Divine intuition and miraculous powers had disappeared for good, and Rabbi Yosef had chalked that up to this new era of human intervention. Moshe didn't have the heart to deny the prophet his anointing role too.

The proceedings concluded with the singing of the Israeli anthem, *Hatikva*. The Hope.

Od lo avda tikvatenu / Our hope is not yet lost

Hatikva bat shnot alpayim / The hope of two thousand years

Lihyot am chofshi be'artzenu / To be a free nation in our land.

The ceremony complete, Moshe led the way down the ramp, rejoined Galit and Talya, and walked the path back to the street.

"Masterful speech!" the American President said. "Well done, sir!"

"Agreed!" chimed in the Russian President. "You brought tears to my eyes."

The two world leaders had jetted in for the ceremony and become great pals. Their camaraderie had made the nuclear non-proliferation agreements easier to sign. It also helped that neither side had any nuclear arsenal to speak of. Both presidents had afforded the Israeli Prime Minister every form of aid over the past month in the relief efforts across the Mediterranean. In return, Moshe never mentioned the zombie armies.

"Have you seen our proposal? For the IGO…"

"Oh, right!" Moshe has seen the email, but not read the details. "I'll have a look as soon as possible." He hurried along the path, leaving them in his wake.

"The IGO?" Galit asked.

"International Governmental Organization. Apparently, they want me to head a unified world government."

"Wow!"

"I know. Talk about conquering the world."

"Are you going to accept?"

"I don't know. I stand by what I said—one small country is more than enough."

She chuckled, and he sensed that she wasn't disappointed. He'd spent enough time away from home and swimming against the stream. From here on, Moshe's new motto would be "delegate everything."

"Irina!" Moshe hugged his friend and her boyfriend.

She held up her hand, and a diamond twinkled on her finger. Make that fiancé. She deserved a happy ending.

Moshe teared up. "Congratulations, Irina! I mean Valentina." He kept forgetting to use her real name.

"That's OK," she said. "I'm sticking with Irina. A fresh start."

Moshe understood. "I hope you'll invite us to the wedding."

"Of course! Rabbi Yosef, perhaps you can officiate?"

The rabbi gaped for a moment. *Oops.* She had unintentionally put the rabbi in a spot. Irina wasn't Jewish. Could he marry her to Alex?

"Um," Rabbi Yosef said. "I'll look into it."

Irina jumped for joy.

Moshe thumped the rabbi on the shoulder and moved on.

He'd leave the conundrums of Jewish Law to him. That was why God had created rabbis.

A few steps down the line, a Secret Service agent held back an older Arab man.

"Hold on a moment."

"Mr. Prime Minister!" the man pleaded, then, spotting Rabbi Yosef, "Mr. Vice Prime Minister!"

"It's OK," Moshe told Alon, and he let the man draw closer.

"My son," he said, in shaky Hebrew. "You knew my son?" In his hand, he held a crumpled poster of an Arab kid wearing a black bandana and a suicide vest.

"Ahmed?"

"Yes!" He pointed to the picture. "Ahmed. My son. I am Yousef."

Yousef. Why did that sound familiar?

Moshe turned to Rabbi Yosef, whose eyes widened, and Moshe remembered what the rabbi had explained. Tradition had talked of two Messiahs. Rabbi Emden had thought that Rabbi Yosef was the doomed Messiah of Yosef, the leader of the Ten Tribes.

A shudder tingled down Moshe's spine. In Arabic, *Yosef* became *Yousef.*

"Your son saved our lives," Moshe said.

"Yes! My son." Then tears came, and the man hugged his Prime Minister and wept on his shoulder for the son he had lost. By the shaking of the man's body, it seemed he had lost his son a long time ago.

Moshe whispered to Alon to follow up with the man and see what assistance he needed. Then he moved on. He shook hands with well-wishers.

With each step, he thought of the thousands of men and women who had come before him. Through untold hardships and hopelessness, they had longed for this day, for the end of the seemingly endless road of history. Each step he took, he took for them.

At the end of the path waited a bearded man in a shiny

dark suit and top hat. He stuck out his chest, and the tails of his coat brushed the pebbly floor of the car park.

Moshe knew the man, but only in black and white, not in the full color of real life.

"Grandfather?"

The man blinked and smiled. "I thought that might be you," said the grandfather Moshe had never met. He had a thick Eastern European accent. "How many Moshe Karlins can there be?"

"Galit, this is my grandfather, Moshe Karlin!"

Moshe Karlin Senior doffed his hat and bowed. "At your service, Mrs. Prime Minister." He bent over and peered at little Talya. "And who might you be, young lady?"

Talya hid behind Moshe's leg. "Say hello to your great-grandfather, Talya."

This was too much to take in at once. "Please," Moshe said, "join us."

His grandfather obliged, and they tumbled into the back of the SUV.

"I'm proud of you, Moshe," said his grandfather. "Very proud."

"It's all thanks to you. Look." Moshe removed the Rolex from his wrist and held it out for display. "This was your watch. My father drummed that lesson in deep. 'A Karlin never quits.'"

His grandfather seemed confused. "What is this 'Karlin never quits'?"

Had his memory faded, even in the afterlife? "Your saying. The family motto. This is the watch you handed down to your son, David Karlin—my father. The last thing you bought before you lost the business in the war. And the house."

His grandfather swatted the words away with his hand. "That trinket? I won that cheap imitation shooting tins at a town fair."

"But," Moshe continued, "you refused to sell the watch. It was a reminder of the life you wanted to regain. 'A Karlin never quits,' you always said. That motto kept you going through your darkest hours."

Moshe Karlin Senior shook his head with irritation. "I didn't lose the business—my nephew, your father's cousin, took it over. Your father and his pipe dreams! He never had the head for business, always wanting to break out on his own, always arguing. He caused so much trouble that I disinherited him. The rest of the family wanted nothing to do with him either."

Moshe stared at the Rolex, the watch he'd redeemed for twenty thousand shekels. He turned to Galit, and she shrugged.

"But it's a good story," his grandfather said, jovial again.

"It is, isn't it?"

"*A Karlin never quits.* Ha! I like it. And it got you this far, didn't it?"

Moshe stared out the window as the world moved by. A better world. A world he had helped create. Did it matter that his father had been blessed with an active imagination? The lessons within his tales had stood the test of time.

He strapped the Rolex back onto his wrist. "Yes," he said. "I suppose it did."

CHAPTER 100

The attendant at the Academon Bookstore on the Mount Scopus campus of the Hebrew University of Jerusalem thought she had seen it all. Until, that is, the man with the broad gray beard and flat cap stepped up to the counter.

A bit old to be a student, isn't he? The man waited while she reviewed his list of supplies.

And what a list that was! The textbooks included first-year tomes on a wide variety of subjects ranging from astrophysics and advanced mathematics to anatomy and computer theory to anthropology and sociology. He seemed to have copied the book list for the entire Faculty of Science.

"Sir," she said, "are you sure you need all these?"

The man peered over at the list, then nodded.

"What program are you registered for?"

"I'm on the PhD track."

"For which field?"

"All of them."

"All of them?"

He nodded again, profusely, and flashed her the grin of a kid in a candy store with Mommy's credit card.

Whatever. It's his money. She made a tour of the store, sliding hardbacks from the shelves and checking off items from the list. After ten minutes, four stacks of textbooks rose from the counter and reached her nose.

She scanned each volume and rang up the total. Could he afford these on a pensioner's budget?

"How do you want to pay?"

He handed her another piece of paper. The letter, signed by the president of the university, indicated that the bearer, Rabbi Moses Ben Maimon, had been awarded a full scholarship for his studies and that she should charge his expenses to the Dry Bones Society Scholarship Program.

She checked the man's identity card, then processed the payment.

"Would you like these delivered?"

"Yes, please." He jotted down a Jerusalem address on a note, then selected three tomes with unabashed relish, looking at the crisp new books as though he intended to gobble them for lunch. He placed the books under his arm, thanked her, and turned to leave.

"Sir," she said. "If you don't mind me asking. A single PhD takes eight years on average. How are you going to finish them all?"

Maimonides smiled that boyish smile again, and he rubbed his shoulder as though massaging a vaccination wound. "I have a lot of free time, my daughter," he said. "All the time in the world."

ALSO BY DAN SOFER

Revenge of the Elders of Zion

A Love and Beyond
(Gold Medal Winner, American Book Fest 2016)

ABOUT THE AUTHOR

DAN SOFER writes tales of romantic misadventure and magical realism, many of which take place in Jerusalem. His multi-layered stories mix emotion and action, humor and pathos, myth and legend—entertainment for the heart and soul. Dan lives in Israel with his family.

Visit **dansofer.com/list-dbs3** for free bonus material and updates on new releases.